I0590247

# The Witch of Toledo

## Elanor Landrie

Samples & Jernigan Press

Included text from *Amadis of Gaul* is gratefully quoted from the public domain eBook provided by Project Gutenberg. All included scripture is gratefully quoted from the Catholic Public Domain Version (CPDV) of the Bible. Many thanks to all involved for graciously offering these resources to the public.

CONTENT WARNINGS:

This novel contains mature material. It also deals with difficult themes, including: animal death, sexual assault, torture, oppression, persecution, and ideologically motivated violence. Though I have handled these themes with as much sensitivity as possible, some sequences or passages may be upsetting to some readers.

Printed in the United States of America.

First Printing, 2025.

ISBN: 979-8-9987451-0-2

Samples & Jernigan Press

Book Cover by Damonza

# Contents

# Chapter One

# THE COURSE IS SET

Fray Ignacio marked me for abduction the first time he tortured me in the name of his god. The year was 1513, and I was barely ten.

The night before that final day of my childhood, Father Manuel, my guardian, had abandoned the tiny rectory we shared and traveled into the heart of Toledo, leaving me with our teenaged housekeeper. Antonia had stayed the night, and I'd woken when she'd begun to stir just after dawn. I hadn't been able to go back to sleep, so I'd sat at the table near the fireplace that heated the single-room house, halfheartedly peeling a pile of onions she'd placed before me to keep my hands occupied.

Around seven or eight in the morning, a knock sounded at the door. When Antonia opened it, Fray Ignacio stood at the threshold, his black-and-white robes ruffling in the gentle breeze. He pushed Antonia aside, entered without so much as a word of greeting, and told me there was something happening in the city he wished me to see.

"What is it?" I asked.

He smiled down at me. "It's a surprise, but it's in the Plaza de Zocodover."

"Alright!" I leapt from my seat.

Though he'd never been my favorite friend of Father Manuel's, a trip to the plaza with the bullfights and the festivals and the carts full of honeyed sweets was well worth a morning spent in Fray Ignacio's company.

"Hold on," Antonia objected. "Father Manuel hasn't given me permission to allow Micaela to go anywhere with anyone."

I made to argue, but before I could say a word, Fray Ignacio took Antonia aside and whispered into her ear for several minutes. She kept shaking her head, but he must have finally said something that cowed her, for she took a sudden step back and furrowed her brow before agreeing to let him have me.

She gave me an odd look as he swept me out the door. I should've taken that as a sign to refuse to go with him—though he was so adamant I'm not sure what good a refusal on my part would've done—but I was so excited to venture to the plaza it never occurred to me how strange it was that my guardian's friend had shown up unexpected and ushered me into the streets.

Traveling almost due north, we made our zigzagging way toward Zocodover, avoiding the main roads for the sake of cutting through the crowds that grew larger the closer we got to our destination. I observed the city as the friar strode purposely toward the plaza with me tagging along behind him. I was reluctant to walk too fast because I liked to look at the many churches, the houses crowded in so close, the open-air vendor stalls, the narrow passages, and the taverns—all vacant so early in the morning.

Our route did not pass the Catedral Primada, but I asked Fray Ignacio if we mightn't divert so I could look at the rose window over the Puerta del Reloj, for the crimson reds and royal blues and bright golden yellows never failed to captivate me. The rosetón and the windows through the transept were my favorites. I loved to watch them play with the sun as it cast its rays through the stained glass all the way to the alabaster-and-ebony floor, reflecting colorful prisms in pools of light that moved across the marble. Father Manuel often allowed me to spend hours inside the church, staring at the glowing glass until the blazing light left imprints behind my eyelids, but I had no such luck with Fray Ignacio.

Caring nothing for the windows, the good friar said we were going to be late enough already and he had no intention of making pointless deviations. As we hurried through the city, he droned on about how the fires of this world were purifying and could save the souls of all heretics from the flames of Hell. I had heard all of this from him many a time before; he did so love the fires of both Earth and Hell, that man.

Thus, I paid him no heed, stopping often to stare at whatever captured my fancy. Between the pungent smells of fresh-baked bread and salted meats hanging in the open shop windows, the sight of the rust-colored roof tiles warming in the morning sun, and the sounds of braying mules and laughing children, I had plenty to catch my attention.

I stopped so much that Fray Ignacio doubled back and grabbed my hand, dragging me through the streets, though my shorter legs could scarcely keep pace up the steep hills. When we neared the plaza, we found ourselves falling in with an animated crowd headed in the same direction. An air of excitement permeated the throng and infected me immediately. With Fray Ignacio clutching my hand so tight it numbed my fingers, we squeezed our way through to the edge of Zocodover.

The plaza looked different at present than it would in later eras, for the whole thing burned to cinders a decade or two after what would have been the end of my natural lifespan, and it had to be rebuilt later. These days, the place usually served as an open-air market, as long as it wasn't a festival day. There were vegetable booths and a livestock auction and all sorts of vendors and people selling their wares. Today, however, none of the vendors or booths were here. Instead, almost everything in the plaza that was not nailed down had been moved to make room for two separate, unremarkable scaffolds hastily erected on the far end.

Fray Ignacio tried to maneuver us in front of this scaffolding, upon which someone was already standing and shouting, but he could not press himself through the mass of people. We had arrived late, as he'd said we would, which forced us to remain at the edge of the crowd and made it impossible for me to hear or see much.

If Father Manuel had been the one to bring me here, he'd have let me sit on his shoulders so I could see above the crowd. Yet Fray Ignacio, for all his efforts to get me to this place, did not seem all that interested in making sure I paid attention to what happened. Annoyed, I wondered why Father Manuel hadn't brought me here himself if this nameless ceremony was so important.

Unable to see anything but everyone else's backs, I paid little heed to the celebration. It was just as well, enamored as I was with the architecture surrounding the plaza and the energy of the city's residents. There was some scuffling and shouting in the crowd, and the man on the scaffold kept preaching his sermon, almost like an outdoor Mass, but none of it much interested me. When I grew tired of staring at my surroundings, I knelt and used my finger to draw pictures of butterflies and birds in the dust that coated the street.

I was surprised at how long the ceremony dragged on and how boring the whole thing was, and I wondered how much longer we were going to have to be here. I grew hungry and thirsty, but Fray Ignacio had obviously not thought about food. I did not dare interrupt the proceedings to complain, so I ignored my parched throat and my grumbling stomach, hoping it would all be over soon. No such luck—we stayed there for hours, and I sometimes looked skyward to note the position of the sun as it flew up and over the highest point on its track.

After a long time of that preacher and some other men harping from the scaffold, the ceremony ended, and Fray Ignacio grabbed my hand and led me away toward the northern wall. I tried to resist leaving the city so that we might find some hope of sustenance around the plaza, but Fray Ignacio jerked me along toward the nearest gate, where we followed about a third of the original crowd as it made its slow way from the plaza to our final destination a few hundred meters outside the walls.

I was disappointed we headed into the vega and not anywhere there might be food, but Fray Ignacio's powerful grip proved irresistible, and he cast not a single glance at the high walls or the intriguing façades on the gate towers. He wished only to get wherever we were going, and he was no more pleased with the façades than he was with anything other than whatever might impend outside the walls. He shook the dust from his robes and huffed at anyone who bumped into him, which happened with fair frequency since we walked in a crowd.

When we arrived at our station, we had a much better view, for we positioned ourselves right in front of the dirt road. Everyone was already chatting animatedly as they turned toward the road and made way for a procession of armed guards and clergymen surrounding a group of people in a single-file line.

I was shocked that the people who marched in the procession did not appear happy, as the participants usually did when they walked in the holy day parades. Rather, they looked sad and terrified. All of them were dressed in black robes made of sackcloth. These robes—which were called sanbenitos—upset me because they were painted with bright-red hideous-faced devils and leaping flames. The people in these robes also wore long, conical hats on their heads and carried candles in their hands. I made to ask Fray Ignacio about the frightening robes, but when I gazed into his face, I was cowed by the strange greediness of his expression. He looked like a starving man who'd just stumbled upon a colossal feast.

Thinking better of speaking to him, I turned back to the procession. The participants walked barefoot. The men kept their eyes downward as if in prayer, while the women trudged in silence or shed tears and attempted to avoid the admonitions of the Dominicans and Franciscans who marched beside them. Some armed men also carried hideous straw statues dressed in the same garb as the barefoot people and bearing ugly faces painted on their wax heads. At the end of the procession, a donkey pulled a cart full of bones.

One of the barefoot women shook so badly she could scarcely walk. She stumbled through the crowd and pleaded for mercy. I was thoroughly confused at this point, since I'd been under the impression this was intended to be a joyous occasion. Everyone, except the black-clad people in the guarded procession, was still delighted.

As the procession approached where Fray Ignacio and I stood, a flood of dread washed over me. The distraught woman passed me by, still begging anyone within earshot to help her, beseeching to be allowed to go home and raise her children, though everyone in the crowd ignored her pleas. Her eyes locked on mine for a split second; they were bloodshot and stained with hours of torrential crying.

She was in her thirties or forties, though her face was so swollen and tearstained I could not tell for certain. When her eyes fell on me, she begged Fray Ignacio to intervene for her, saying she had a young girl just my age, one who needed a mother. She even went so far as to maneuver through the guards for a split second and seize his hand. At this, Fray Ignacio spat on her and shoved her back into the waiting arms of the soldiers, using the hand not clutching mine.

As the guards seized the woman and forced her back in line, I became overwhelmed with an abrupt and visceral terror that whatever was to occur would be nothing good. The procession moved toward the front of the throng, and everyone's eyes followed it to its destination. There, in the center of the field I would later learn was called the quemadero, stood a platform I'd as yet failed to notice. From this platform jutted a row of stakes, lined like spikes around a city wall and already piled with kindling. With a horrid lurch of the stomach, I realized what was to happen.

"No!" I shrieked and tried to yank my hand away from Fray Ignacio.

He pulled me back, grasped me by my shoulders, and held me where I stood. The guards forced the condemned to mount the platform and tore their sanbenitos from their trembling shoulders before fastening them to the stakes, all whilst the clerics kept dogging them.

When all was ready, a clergyman or a city official—I could hardly tell the difference—ascended the platform and began reading from a long scroll, though I did not take in a word of it. I was so busy wailing and struggling to get away from Fray Ignacio, to get out of this place, to somehow stop this thing from happening, that I hadn't a care for the reading of the crimes or the fact that the people in our immediate vicinity had started to stare at us.

Finally, the friar had had enough of my outburst, so he squatted down to my level, turned me to face him, and shook me until I stopped screaming.

"Watch and learn what happens to blasphemers and heretics, you insolent little witch," he shouted. "It is to save their eternal souls from damnation. You of all the children of Castilla need to see this!"

There was a blaze in his eyes unlike anything I'd ever seen, a passionate fire that was much more than a reflection of the impending flames of the stake. He was loving this, breathing it in, as if both my own terror and the horror of the accused were more vital than air.

"This isn't right. No matter what they've done, it isn't right!" I cried.

He slapped me across the face with the back of his right hand and all the strength in his young man's body, knocking me to the ground with such force that the back of my skull bounced off the dirt. He yanked me to my feet and slapped me on the other cheek, this time with his palm. The only reason I did not fall again was he still held me by the shoulder with his left hand. I had never been struck before, not even once, but I had no time to register the shock or immense pain before he started shouting again.

"It is as the Lord your God commands. Nothing he decrees is wrong. Now, look upon your fate if you don't change your wicked ways."

"I haven't done anything," I cried, tears streaming down my burning cheeks.

"It's in your filthy blood."

He stood back up and jerked me around to face the stakes. Grasping a handful of my hair, he held my head still and forced my eyes upon the executioners as they garroted the repentant and then kindled the flames. With his other hand, he pinned my wrists behind my back.

I shut my eyes and screamed at the top of my lungs, but everyone ignored me now because my cries suffocated under the shrieks of agony from the impenitent condemned. Never in all my long life have I heard such a horrifying din as I did that day. Centuries later, I still can't forget it. No matter how I howled and wept, I couldn't shield myself from those wails, for Fray Ignacio's hold of my arms prevented me from putting my hands over my ears.

The most disturbing part of the ordeal was the misery I suffered in my own body. It was as if I somehow absorbed the pain and horror of the burning victims and felt it right alongside them. My skin seared from invisible flame; my lungs choked and my eyes watered from smoke that wasn't really there; I could feel my flesh shriveling and cracking, veins bursting from the heat and spilling their contents of boiling blood. I couldn't see much of this happening, as I was among the shortest in the crowd and kept my eyes tight shut, but I knew it happened because I felt it more keenly than I've felt much of my own pain.

I shrieked in terror and torture and frustration from being held immobile in Fray Ignacio's strong arms. I opened my eyes and desperately searched for help. Since my captor still gripped my head, I could only scan the crowd by moving my eyes. I looked wildly for someone—anyone—to help them, help me, utter even one word of protest. As I watched the spiteful joy apparent in the faces of almost everyone present, I deduced this hope was fantasy. No one would stop this madness, least of all Fray Ignacio.

Enraptured by the proceedings, he'd all but forgotten my presence, though he still held me, and I still fought him with all my might. It did not take me long to run out of steam. I screamed and cried myself into a near stupor, my kidnapper's strength wearing me down as I wrestled in vain to free myself from his grip. Fray Ignacio let go of me when I stopped struggling. He left me to slip to the ground and lie where I fell, my tears speckling the dust, making tiny droplets of mud. With my arms free, I could put my fingers in my ears.

A finger stuffed in each ear did me no good. I hadn't the energy to keep on screaming, so I lay still and listened to the cacophony of wails emanating from the stakes, shrieks so loud they overwhelmed all my efforts to drown them out. I squeezed my ears ever tighter, breathing in the hot dust the crowd kicked up as they jostled for position, some laughing, some watching, some even munching on refreshments they'd brought to the quemadero.

Somewhere nearby, a woman wailed right along with the condemned while a few of her compatriots tried to comfort her. I wondered if she might be the wife or mother of one of the victims. Unable to see anything but dirt and feet, I couldn't tell what she looked like.

It took the poor wretches at the stake well over half an hour to expire. When at last they succumbed to the flames, the final echoes of their screams bounced through the river gorge even as the dying embers of the fire kept on crackling. Still lying in the dirt, I couldn't move, couldn't breathe, couldn't even make myself faint, but my misery had no effect on Fray Ignacio.

He tried to force me to my feet, shaking me and plying me with vicious threats of flogging and starvation, but I didn't care. Eventually, he saw terrorizing me would rouse me from my catatonia no more than a bucket of cold water rouses a dead man, so he scooped me up, threw me like a corpse over his shoulder, and carried me all the way back to my home. There, he tossed me onto my tiny bed in the rear corner of the house and walked away without a backward glance, not bothering to speak to me as he swept off.

I stared at the ceiling in total shock, too numb to weep or even sit up. I could not move my limbs, but my heart still thundered in my chest, sending the blood roaring to my ears, where it beat a frantic drumroll. Even over that gory percussion, the sound of footsteps resonated somewhere nearby. Fray Ignacio still moved about the house, each step he took louder and closer than the last. I didn't hear Antonia anywhere around, and terror seized me once more as I realized I was all alone with this man.

The friar stalked back toward my bed and gazed at me where I lay. He said not a word. He only stood there leering. He was so still I'd have thought him a statue if he'd not been sucking in slow, deep breaths. I rolled onto my side, pulled my knees to my chest, and wrapped my arms around them as he took a sudden step toward me.

To my great fortune, Father Manuel's voice came wafting in from the rectory's entryway before the friar could take a second step. Fray Ignacio leapt away in an instant. Upon finding him alone with me, Father Manuel demanded to know why his friend had sent Antonia away and where the two of us had been all day. Fray Ignacio shamelessly admitted to having taken me to the auto de fe.

"Your miniature infidel needed to witness the wages of heresy." He smirked.

"I hardly think she's old enough to be capable of heresy," Father Manuel said, the volume of his voice ticking up.

"Original sin, my brother, means there is no age at which a child is incapable of heresy, especially a child like that."

"I will not have a vicious Pharisee who'd force a little girl to witness a burning explain the nature of sin to me!"

"Perhaps if you better understood the nature of sin, I wouldn't need to explain it. If you do not prune the fruit of the poisoned vine, will it not spread its venom to all who partake of it?"

"What do you mean 'prune'?" Father Manuel cried.

They argued for a long while, screaming and striking the walls. Fray Ignacio was a good bit larger than Father Manuel and nearly three decades younger. At a few points during their debate, I feared he might turn violent. Luckily, several of our neighbors showed up when they heard the shouting coming from the open window, and they urged the younger man to respect his elder. Fray Ignacio measured his tone but did not cede his position, happy to quarrel with Father Manuel and as many neighbors as need be.

While they argued away, I stared blankly at a shaft of light coming through the window shutters, the illumination turning a deeper and deeper shade of orange as the sun set, until it reached the same shade as the flames of the stake. I shook where I lay, but I was too weak to do anything besides watch the light and listen as the men's voices rose to shouts once more. I gazed at the motes of dust swirling in the blood-orange beam, trying to tell myself this was the light of the setting sun, not of the fires. Yet I couldn't get the sound of screaming out of my head. It nearly drowned out even the angry bellows that reverberated through the house. Barely daring to breathe, I remained motionless as the shaft disappeared and dusk descended.

Despite the hour, the fight dragged on. Though I could hear every vehement exchange, I did not understand many of them, for Father Manuel and Fray Ignacio were both educated men while I was but a girl who still needed to summon all her wits to get through a children's prayer book. However, I got the measure of the results: Father Manuel told Fray Ignacio in no uncertain terms he was no longer welcome in our home or our church.

At this, Fray Ignacio shrieked, "You have no authority to tell me which of God's houses I can and cannot enter. I gave that child nothing she did not need."

"Of course, it's appropriate for the girl to understand the proper fate of heretics," one of the neighbors said. "But it was not within your rights to take a ward from her guardian."

Another man's voice chimed in. "Agreed. Father Manuel should have been the one to decide when the girl was ready to see such things."

Other voices assented to this statement, and Fray Ignacio could do little but agree to leave the rectory at once. He, however, could not resist a last jab as he made for the door.

"I'll spend the rest of this night asking the Lord to deliver us all from such backslidden believers as you. Your lack of concern for the true faith borders on heresy." With that, he was gone, though he slammed the front door so hard he knocked a crucifix from the wall and sent it scurrying across the floor like a wooden mouse.

I did not think for a second Fray Ignacio's indignation had anything to do with a desire to remain in our company. He suffered no blow other than wounded pride. I cared not what he felt, for I was relieved beyond measure I was never to see him again.

By this time, dusk had become full night. Father Manuel thanked his parishioners for providing him with reinforcements, and they all agreed they couldn't be sure what Fray Ignacio might have done if they'd not arrived.

After Father Manuel showed them out, he came to me. He held an oil lamp, from which I recoiled. When he drew closer, I yelped, leapt from my bed, and flew to another corner that was not cast in the glow of the flame.

"Micaela? It's alright, child. This little light cannot harm you," Father Manuel said, drawing nearer.

He stopped short when he saw my face. His expression darkened.

"What happened? How did you hurt your face?"

I touched my cheek, having forgotten Fray Ignacio had struck me. The back of his hand had made its mark: a line of deep bruises left by his knuckles and the stone in his ring ran up the entire side of my face. I said nothing, fearing to tell Father Manuel in case the young friar ever found an opportunity to avenge himself upon me. My guardian reached out, and I shrank as far back into the corner as I could, mumbling something incoherent about how I couldn't bear the torment of the flames. Father Manuel tried to tell me it was alright, and he asked if Fray Ignacio had beaten me. I couldn't answer, couldn't even form a clear thought.

Father Manuel took the light away and came back in darkness. Though I would not eat, he coaxed me to drink some water where I sat on the floor. Once I'd had my fill, he picked me up and sat me on the bed. He made to leave after tucking me in, but he came back and sat down beside me when I started crying. He tried to go to bed several more times, but whenever he did, I begged and pleaded, and if he insisted on retiring, I screamed at the top of my lungs until he returned. I didn't have anything in my head except I couldn't let him leave me.

Eventually, he took me in his arms and carried me back to his bed. It was the only night in my life he ever let me sleep next to him. It comforted me to feel him twitch as he slept and to hear his breath, even though his snores were so loud they made my ears ring. I did not sleep at all that night or for several nights after, not until I was so exhausted I couldn't help myself; nightmares be damned.

The day after the auto de fe, Father Manuel scolded Antonia for allowing Fray Ignacio to take me, though he was not too harsh with her. She was little more than a girl herself, and he seemed to understand more than I did what the young friar had said to intimidate her into submission. Weeping and contrite, she tried to apologize to me. She explained Fray Ignacio had frightened her into letting him leave with me and admitted she should have been braver. I didn't blame her, but I didn't speak to her either. It took me several weeks to speak to anyone besides my guardian again.

For his part, Father Manuel attempted to console me as best he could, telling me the stake was only meant for heretics, blasphemers, and the worst of criminals, and I was never to be counted among such villainous characters. But the damage was done. I couldn't think of anything in the world so heinous it would make a person worthy of such a fate. What of that poor woman, crying and helpless, her face stained with tears and dirt? I couldn't fathom what crime she could have committed that was so great she deserved the fire.

I became fixated on her for a long time, imagining her pain and terror, unable to let go of the images of her bloodshot eyes and the sound of her raw, hoarse voice begging for her children. Father Manuel hadn't known her identity, but it was not difficult to ascertain. At my request, he'd asked for her sanbenito at the cathedral to get her name from the inscription.

She was María González of Ciudad Real, burned by the Toledo tribunal in September of 1513. I suppose I ought to thank our persecutors for that single consolatory favor. They thought they did no wrong; thus, they felt no shame. They recorded María's name, along with everyone else's, ensuring their victims would be more than forgotten piles of ashes abandoned in the smoldering vega.

Father Manuel recounted the crimes for which the accused had been burned: mostly heresy, including María. In addition to Judaizing, she had been executed for bearing false witness to the inquisitors. I would later discover she'd made her false statements under torture. Even before I learned this, I didn't believe that was a thing to be roasted alive over, but Father Manuel took the Crown's word for it and tried to put the matter to rest.

He said it was best not to question the laws of God and King and insisted that, as a child, I couldn't understand the essential nature of such violence, for orchestrated brutality was a necessary evil to bring about eternal good.

I could not put it to rest. Although I gradually began to communicate with those around me once more and regained the ability to tolerate the mere sight of a flame, never again was I to view Father Manuel in the same light. I still held him dear to my heart, for he was all I'd known since losing my parents in infancy, but it horrified me that he could not bring himself to call a crime a crime if it was committed in the name of his god.

I often wondered if he'd participated in this crime in a more direct manner than he'd admitted, for even at my tender age, it was not lost on me that he had spent the night somewhere else on the very eve of the burning. I did not ask him about his part in the auto de fe until over a decade later. There were many things I should've confronted him about much sooner than I did.

# Chapter Two

# A CLOSE ENCOUNTER

Ten years after that fateful day, in the spring of 1523, I found myself in a place far removed from the Plaza de Zocodover, the quemadero, and every vestige of my childhood. Father Manuel had been assigned a new parish perhaps a year after the auto de fe, and we'd moved all the way from Toledo to the northerly port city of Santa Colomba de la Bahía, a few leagues west of Santander along the rugged Cantabrian coast—La Montaña, as that region was called in those days. It was in this cool, green land of thick forests and migrating sheep that I blossomed into womanhood.

In the first few years after our relocation, I resented coming of age in La Montaña. I longed for the bustle and warmth of the city I'd left behind. Still, I was well aware that growing up under Father Manuel's guidance was better than being dragged half into adulthood in some foundling home and then either entombed in a convent or tossed into the world too young to fend for myself yet too old to expect others to do so for me—as my husband had been.

That spring, when the bizarre and mysterious events of my life first began, I had been married to Sergio for well over a year. Though he was a contramaestre on a merchant vessel and was gone for much of the warm season, I had not yet come to regret agreeing to be his wife. Thus far, we'd lived together if not in harmony, then in some passable attempt at it. I tried in those days to be a pleasing and obedient wife, serving him at his bidding and biting my tongue when it compelled me to argue. At this, I often failed, especially with my inability to grow accustomed to his habitual weekslong absences.

It was on the eve of one of these absences that my husband and I had another of what Father Manuel liked to call our "traditional predeparture quarrels." Sergio had been supervising the final preparations for a nearly six-month voyage to Bruges, and when the crew finished early, he and a couple of his mates returned to our house.

When he, Pablo, and Marcos arrived, I was not prepared for it. They burst into the house just as I was sweeping the kitchen, and they tracked caked-on mud with them as they filed through the door.

"Wait a minute," I cried. "Do something about your boots."

"Right," Sergio said, ushering the other two back outside so they could knock off their shoes. "Sorry about that," he added when they entered the house once more.

While they removed their outer layers and took their seats upstairs, I put the broom away and got something going for them to eat. I had to improvise, opening a wine cask and filling a couple of pewter pitchers, frying up some anchovies and dried cod, and serving the three of them cheese and bread while they waited for me to finish cooking.

Once I'd taken the cold refreshments up to them, I returned downstairs to the kitchen to mind the frying fish. I cut a slice of cheese for myself while I waited. Just as I opened my mouth to take my first bite, a booming knock sounded at the door. When I opened, I came face-to-face with the fleet owner and one of his pages.

"Don Armando!" I said, wiping my hands on my apron and ushering him in. "So sorry; I wasn't expecting you, or I'd have prepared something better."

"Sergio is upstairs, is he not?" Armando snapped, without acknowledging my comment.

"Yes, he is." I gave a slight bow and shut the door.

Armando turned toward the stairs, motioning for his page to follow and leaving me to ascend last. Upstairs, Marcos and Pablo stood and greeted the master. Sergio made to get out of his chair, but Armando commanded him to sit.

"Do you want to return to the estate house?" Sergio asked.

"Sara is there," Armando replied.

That was all that was necessary. Armando's wife had come to the country house from the town house where she spent most of her time, so he'd fled here to escape her.

After Armando settled into his seat, I went back to the kitchen to tend the food. Almost as soon as I set foot on the bottom stair, someone above set a glass decanter on a wooden table, which resulted in an immediate chorus of approval. Sergio called my name not long after, and when I returned upstairs, he waved me over to his seat.

"Micalita, after you finish cooking, I want you to go to the big house and fetch Gabriel. Then, see if you can stay up there with Gracia and Sara so we can work on this." He grinned and pointed to a decanter full of brandy now in the hand of Armando's page.

"Alright." I turned away without another word, hoping my inner fury hadn't burned through to my outer expression.

So tempted was I to resist this command that I had to run down the stairs and out the door with scarcely a goodbye to any of them. With the fish done, I had no reason to wait anyhow—let the damned page serve them.

I stepped outside into the uncharacteristically clear spring weather, wrapping myself in a thick woolen shawl to keep out the humid chill. My huge shaggy dog, Lobo, rolled over in his spot in a glowing patch of late-afternoon sunlight and gave me a look that almost begged me not to head for the road. I shrugged and made to go. He heaved himself off the ground with a grunt and a sigh, shook his charcoal fur, and followed, casting a forlorn glance at his warm place in the sun. When he caught up to me, I patted his head without slowing my gait.

Even though Sergio's and my house was the closest to Armando's country estate—and incidentally the farthest from Santa Colomba proper, being one of the newest houses in the arrabal that had spread out beyond the city walls over the last few decades—it was still a ways from the start of Armando's lands to the threshold of his house. If it had been dark, Sergio would not have sent me out alone. Yet, since the last light of the evening still held, I felt comfortable making the short trek with only Lobo for company.

Still fuming at Sergio's dismissal, I spent the entire walk growing ever more agitated. By the time I reached the big house, I almost had to grit my teeth to stop myself from shouting at Gabriel that my husband would prefer to spend his final hours on Spanish shores in his friends' company rather than in mine. Instead, I cordially informed Armando's younger brother that the master requested his presence at my house. Then I took Lobo to the kitchen and followed a maid into the parlor, where Sara and Gabriel's wife, Gracia, already sat drinking wine and chatting.

Sara had her mahogany-brown hair strung with a thin band of gold and pulled into a flowing half-up, half-down knot, and she wore a deep-emerald taffeta dress embroidered with matching golden thread that accentuated her green eyes. Gracia's auburn hair cascaded down her milk-pale shoulders in spiraling curls as it mingled with the twilight blue of her silk dress. She idly twirled the puffy skirts with the hand not holding her wine cup.

When I entered the parlor and both women's eyes fell on me, I became aware I'd not prepared at all for this visit. I wore a simple dress of tan wool that laced up the front, and my hair was neither brushed nor styled. Christ save me! I even had streaks of mud on my shoes.

My abrupt embarrassment overpowered me, and I froze where I stood. Living as Sergio and I did, in such intimate proximity to our betters, proved to be difficult for me, especially on occasions like this. Whilst he moved comfortably amongst the moneyed and well-bred, thanks to his close friendship with Armando, I felt awkward in their presence, their manners throwing into stark relief my own simple upbringing, their vast wealth putting my own humbler circumstances to shame.

I was often envious of the deep colors and soft fabrics of Gracia's dresses, jealous of the beautiful dishes and wonderful paintings Sara always collected, and annoyed when I was obliged to perform in my own home the duties that always fell to their servants. I might not have been so disturbed by the lack of such luxuries if they were not constantly paraded in front of me—and if Sergio did not spend as much of his time ashore making my life more difficult.

At the same time, if I could count on one thing in this world of rich ship lords and indulged merchants' wives, it was for Sara to be kind. For some reason, she'd taken a liking to me from the day we'd met. Because of her, the servants treated me as a guest rather than an intruder, and because of her, Gracia and I had become friends when she and Gabriel had married. A girl like Gracia mightn't have even spoken to a girl like me without Sara's intervention. In some ways, I almost felt Sara to be a sort of mother. It had been she, after all, who'd dressed me for my wedding and advised me on what to expect after. So even though I'd just burst into her parlor with hair flying and dress flecked with cooking lard, she welcomed me.

I sat down on the sofa farthest from the window so as to be in the darkest corner possible and hoped the wine would help me feel less self-conscious. Sara and Gracia informed me they had been talking about which tailors made the best baby clothes in town and what sorts of amulets and charms the midwives recommended for a healthy pregnancy.

When I asked what brought on that conversation, Gracia let out a demure laugh.

"I suppose I should catch you up," she said, her blue eyes sparkling. "Gabriel and I swore we would not tell anyone about this until we were certain the time had come, but a few days ago I felt the quickening."

I started, knowing what she would say next.

"I am with child." She beamed, flashing her brilliant smile.

That smile was one of the things I loved most about her. It always filled me with a warmth that evaporated my envy of her dresses and her beauty. Except today. Today, I turned my gaze to Sara, searching for what I ought to say. Under normal circumstances, a pregnancy announcement from a wealthy, married young woman would be met with nothing but joy and congratulations. But these were not normal circumstances.

"It's alright, Micaela, honestly," Sara assured me, with her characteristic half smile that never reached her eyes.

At this, I leapt from my seat to hug Gracia and kiss her cheeks, bursting forth with the expected congratulations and adulations that the mother-to-be looked radiant and Gabriel's son would be the handsomest child ever born. However, I couldn't shake the feeling Sara probably was not as alright as she claimed to be, and I wished we might talk about it alone.

"Don Gabriel must be thrilled to become a father," I said.

"He is beside himself," Gracia replied.

"Does anyone else know yet?"

"Gabriel told Armando earlier today, and I informed my parents yesterday. We've sent letters to Gabriel's mother in Santander, as well."

I don't remember much else about what we discussed that evening, things to do with the pregnancy and Gracia's family and other idle conversation. I stayed for several hours, trying to become more accustomed to the notion that this house would soon be filled with infant cries and infant toys—while mine would not. In all the time Sergio and I had been married, we had not managed to conceive. I tried to forget this uncomfortable fact and be happy for Gracia, but between my own barrenness and the grief I could only imagine Sara to be in at this news, it was difficult to avoid putting a damper on the situation.

For her part, Sara proved more adept at stoicism and empathy than I might've been if I'd borne four living children and watched them all succumb to illness within the first few months or years of their lives. Sara and I had never discussed it much, but I knew she'd delivered at least two stillborns and suffered several miscarriages on top of the babies that had died later. Despite so many pregnancies, she and Armando never had a child survive beyond the age of three. Not a single one.

While it wasn't unusual in those days to lose a young child, to lose all of them was quite another matter. Thus, Gracia and I kept our toasts and celebrations politely restrained. Indeed, Gracia acted almost ashamed to be too excited in Sara's presence, checking the intensity of her smile and allowing the conversation to drift away from baby things after a while.

It was past midnight when Sergio, Armando, and Gabriel all stumbled back to the estate. Sergio and Armando were tipsy, but Gabriel had gotten himself so falling-down drunk that Armando's manservant Tomás and one of the pages had to carry him into the house. Much less concerned about his brother's feelings than Gracia had been about Sara's, Gabriel ranted and raved about how his son was to be the richest ship lord and most desirable bachelor in all the land. He carried on like that until the servants took him up to his room to sleep it off.

Sergio and I fetched Lobo and went home to our own bed. The brandy hit my husband hard on the road back, and he tripped more than a few times, obliging me to help him navigate a relatively flat, straight path. He was a tall man—a full head and shoulders taller than me—which made it difficult to keep him upright and only increased my irritation. Try as I might, I couldn't help but snap at him.

"I hope you had a damn good time turning me out like a mule to pasture tonight."

"Why you want to ruin a perfectly nice evening, Micaela?" he slurred.

"It was nice for you." I stepped out in front of him and turned to face him whilst blocking his path. "How do you think I feel, with you deserting me the night before you sail, just so you can drink with the same lads you always do?"

Sergio rolled his eyes and swerved around me without a word, which only incensed me further.

"Sergio!" I shouted.

"I'm not going to do this in the middle of the road in the middle of the night," he said, staggering down the path toward our barrio.

I trotted after him. "When would you prefer to do it?"

"After I'm dead would be ideal." He chuckled and slowed his pace to let me catch up. "What would you have me do?" he asked when I once again strode at his side. "When my master knocks on my door, am I to turn him away?"

"No, but . . ."

"Should I insult my officers by refusing to dine with them the night before we'll be working together for weeks on end?"

"I suppose not."

"Should I keep my wife in a house full of drunken, cursing sailors making nasty jokes no woman should hear?"

"No," I snapped.

Though I remained unconvinced, I couldn't concoct much of a refutation, so we finished the rest of our journey in total silence. When we arrived home, Sergio lit a candle and fumbled through building a fire while I hung our cloaks and undid my shoes. We still hadn't said another word.

"If you want to pass this night arguing, I'd rather find somewhere else to sleep," Sergio mumbled, breaking the silence while he continued trying and failing to ignite the fireplace.

I sighed. "You know I don't like it when you run off the night before you sail."

"I know. Ha!" he cried as he finally set the kindling alight.

He then stumbled over to where I stood at the washbasin and planted a kiss on my forehead. He pinched my nose and grinned in the teasing, impish way he always did when he was good and drunk yet firm in the knowledge he could talk himself out of trouble. Just like that, our fight was over. I always pardoned him in the end; might as well not delay the inevitable.

When I smiled in return, he kissed me on the mouth, sliding his hands around my waist and lifting me off the floor. I undid the laces of his jerkin while he carried me to the bed and laid me on the wool mattress. He lost his balance when he moved his arm from underneath my body, falling on top of me. We both laughed.

After he undressed me, I ran my hands over his bare chest and shoulders, kissing his neck and wrapping my legs around his waist. I drew my fingers over the length of his smooth back and plunged them into his thick hair. I then shoved his hand between my legs so he could attend me with his fingers. While we kissed, he stroked me right where I'd placed his hand, slowly increasing the pressure until I moaned with anticipation.

I couldn't wait any longer, so I told Sergio to take me. He lifted me bodily, pulling me on top of him and flopping to his back, but he misjudged his position on the bed and slammed the rear of his skull against the wall behind the mattress.

Bolting upright, he gripped his head with one hand while holding me in place on his lap with the other. "Oh, shit!"

I pressed his face to my chest to get a look at his head. As I began to gently test the lump on his scalp, he snatched my nipple into his mouth.

A hot tingle zipped down my spine, and I smiled. "You're obviously fine."

He looked up at me. "I am. That just hurt."

"Serves you right for drinking all night." I chuckled and gave his cheek a playful slap.

Sergio laughed. "I guess it does. Still, you're going to pay for that." He flipped me flat on my back and plunged into me, making me gasp.

"As long as you don't whack *my* head on the wall, we're alright." I giggled.

His body shuddered with suppressed laughter. "Shh. I'm trying to focus."

Despite his intoxication, he automatically did what I liked, and I soon found myself groaning as he rubbed against me in just the right spot. I wound my legs around his waist once more. He kissed my lips and my neck and the space between my breasts, all while he intensified the pressure of his thrusts until we both climaxed.

Panting, I unwrapped my arms and legs from around his body and let him slide the blankets over my limp form, moaning as the wool brushed against my newly sensitive skin. Sergio pulled on his nightclothes, then gathered me into his arms for one last embrace before he drifted off.

Though I'd been annoyed with him all evening, I preferred to spend the night in his arms, listening to the melodic tinkling of a rain shower on the roof tiles and basking in the smell of his salty sweat and the feel of his hot breath on my skin. Besides the rain, the only sounds in the room were the occasional hiss and pop of the fire and Sergio's gentle snores, punctuated by Lobo's louder ones rising from the floor. Yet, even in this lulling atmosphere, I remained wide awake, running my fingers through my husband's mass of jet-black curls and wishing I could delay the dawn.

The embarkation always provoked in me a nagging and visceral dread, for despite Sergio's assurances that sailing in a convoy made the trip to Flanders safer than it might be otherwise, many things could still go wrong. In those days of ceaseless war and piracy and unpredictable weather, sailing could prove a dangerous business, convoy or no. I could never shake the anxious dream that one day Sergio's ship would return without him—or it wouldn't return at all. The very thought took my breath away.

I tried to push it out of my mind by reminding myself the officers did not do the dangerous work. What's more, I always got letters and presents from Sergio while he was abroad to let me know he was safe. But on the nights before the voyages, I couldn't force myself to let go of the worry that one day the letters and presents would stop. I never could doze off on those nights, though Sergio always slept them right away, sometimes snoring as loud as Lobo.

When dawn came the next morning, Sergio skipped breakfast like he always did before a trip. I was still privately smarting from his treatment of me the evening before, regardless of how easily he could trick me into feeling like I'd forgiven him, so I chose not to go to the docks to see him off.

Rather, I held him in the doorway, dreading that inevitable moment when I'd see it close on him. He squeezed me tight around the shoulders and bent down to lay his chin on the top of my head. I gave him one final kiss as we stood at the threshold, wrapped in each other's arms, the air thick with yet another goodbye.

"Don't worry," he said, cocking his head and flashing his wide smile. "It's only a few weeks. I'll be back before you know it."

"Last time I checked, six months isn't a few weeks," I mumbled, rolling my eyes.

"Sure it is. Any number more than two and less than a hundred is a few."

"So that's how you always 'only have a few' when you go out with the lads?"

He threw his head back and laughed. "Oh, I'll miss you."

Kissing me on the forehead, he swung his bag over his shoulder, gave Lobo a pat, and walked out the door. I shut it behind him and turned toward our empty kitchen. The fresh silence rang louder in my ears than a chorus of church bells, and the empty feeling in my stomach mixed with a tightness in my chest. I wondered if I ought to have gone to the harbor with him, but I was too proud to run after him now, so I went upstairs.

I didn't give in to tears. Instead, I sat down on the bed and stared at the embers of the fire Sergio had rebuilt upon waking—the last one he would kindle for me for a long while—and watched the ash as it spilled out onto the hearth. I curled up in a ball and fell asleep, exhausted from my wakeful night and lulled by the sound of Lobo's renewed snoring from his place so close to the hot coals, it was a wonder he wasn't roasted alive.

When I woke again around an hour later, I decided rather than stay cooped up inside my silent house, I'd go into the walled part of town and call on Father Manuel. I rolled out of bed and completed the chores that couldn't wait—feeding the chickens, collecting the eggs, and drawing water from the well near the house. I then dressed and made a halfhearted attempt to comb my thick, heavy hair into submission before giving up, tying it with a ribbon, and concealing it under a linen veil.

Almost to add insult to injury, Lobo and I stepped through the doorway of our empty home to find an equally empty arrabal. But I'd expected as much—it happened this way every sailing season. As I understood things, Armando had been obliged by his late father's debts to sell some of the family's land adjacent to the arrabal. The sailors and fishermen coming in to escape the plagues and fires that had ravaged other nearby cities in the preceding years had snapped up this land and built their homes on it. This meant when Sergio left, a good many of our neighbors did also, either to sail on one of the merchant ships that all liked to leave around the same time or to fish in open waters.

Marcos and Pablo happened to be our nearest neighbors, and since neither of the brothers was married, their house went even quieter than mine when Armando's ships set out. During the on-season, our corner of the neighborhood was sometimes all but deserted. I did not at all like that arrangement, but Sergio had built our home before we'd met, and we'd lose a significant sum if we were to sell it in exchange for a more expensive house within the city walls—if we found one at all. Thus, I tended to lose any argument I started about us moving into town.

Still, there were a few families scattered around. I waved hello to Susana as I passed her home. As usual, several of her five small children heckled her, whining like tiny dogs at her ankles, while she and her servant girl fed the family pig in the stall underneath their house. I called on Susana often enough, but since she never got a moment of peace, I always felt like just one more bother to her.

I also passed by Catalina's house as I neared the open city gate, though she wasn't anywhere to be seen today. I'd gone to visit Catalina a few times when I first moved to the arrabal because she was a blind, old widow whose teenaged grandson apprenticed on Armando's sole nao. However, her spinster daughter lived there with her, and I preferred to avoid Cecilia. Catalina was kindly on her own, but she and her daughter could whip one another into a frenzy over the conversos or the Alumbrados or the Lutherans or whatever other variety of assorted heretics happened to be the subject of collective ire at the moment. A couple of incidents like that were enough to put me off visiting their home too often.

When I arrived at Father Manuel's, he was in the church plaza, standing right in front of the main door and talking with one of the lads who was working on some repairs to the windows and the bell tower. I went inside the rectory without interrupting and took it upon myself to fry up some sausages before he returned. While I stood over the kitchen fire, fiddling with my apron and waiting for the fat to bubble, I mulled over whether to air my grievances about Sergio's and my argument from the night before or keep them to myself.

When he came into the rectory, Father Manuel sat down at the table and leaned his walking stick on the end.

"Father?" I hesitated, unsure what I might say next.

I laid a few salchichas in the pan before wiping my hands on my apron and turning to fetch him a cup of wine. He didn't answer. Rather, he waited to see what I'd say. Silently, I set the mug before him and turned back to my pan.

"Did you and Sergio have your traditional predeparture quarrel?" he asked at last.

"It is not a traditional predeparture quarrel," I said, annoyed he'd managed to deduce that much so easily. "It's more like a habitual predeparture discontent."

He smiled. "Child, I told you marrying Sergio would be more difficult than you anticipated. You've made your vows before God. Antagonizing your husband about his work is not what I'd call keeping them."

I sighed before replying, wishing he hadn't reminded me of my failure to heed his warnings about what marriage to a sailor would be like. Though he had ceded to my desires in the end, Father Manuel had had mixed emotions about Sergio's and my match.

On the one hand, I'm sure it was a relief for him to get me out of his rectory. I was a grown woman by the time I'd married, making it ever more inappropriate for me to remain housed with him. The rumors that he'd bought me for a concubine had been flying since the day we'd arrived in Santa Colomba, after all.

On the other hand, he'd always wished me to live a monastic life. I'd been in such fear he was going to force me through the doors of a nunnery that I'd found myself a husband at the first opportunity. Sometimes, I wondered if my marriage vows mightn't have turned out more burdensome than the vows I'd have taken at the convent, yet I couldn't bear even the thought of being cloistered for all eternity.

"I know I must keep my vows," I said after a long pause. "But does that mean I must always be pleased with it?"

"Yes," he replied. "You must put your husband at ease, make his life and his work as comfortable as possible. If that means biting your tongue when he leaves, then you do it."

I sighed. I'd expected Father Manuel to side with Sergio, my husband being the head of our household and all, and I almost wished I hadn't said anything. It was not as though I always made it a point to argue with Sergio about his departures. I simply wished him to spend more of the preceding days in my company rather than in that of the people with whom he was about to be trapped on a ship for weeks on end, and I wished the good Father had more to say about *that*.

While I was turning the sausages, Lobo gave a thunderous bark from behind me, and I jumped almost out of my shoes before laughing at his brazen attempt to startle me into dropping a piece of meat. That booming bark reminded me of why I'd chosen Sergio: he was a difficult man to be sure, but he could be tender and thoughtful if he had a mind to be.

It had been drizzling the day my husband brought Lobo home as a puppy, as it often did in the late winter when the storms rolled in off the Atlantic to drench the coast, sometimes for days on end. This particular storm had arrived a week or two before Sergio was set to depart for the first time since our wedding. He only had to travel to Santander and would be gone a mere two or three weeks. Even so, I was filled with dismay at the thought of our impending separation. I had not spoken to Sergio of these feelings, but he had sensed my dejection.

He'd shown up out of the rain that day holding a tiny bundle in his hand and using the folds of his cloak to shield it from the weather. I'd been trying my best with my needlework when he entered, and I thought he'd brought a loaf of bread from town. I rose from my seat, ready to make him a meal with this bundle, when he cast a glance down at it and a wide grin spread across his face. I looked at the half-soaked wrappings to find a shaggy head poking out from their center and a pair of round brown eyes staring up at me.

"Oh, Sergio," I said. "Where did you get him?"

"Found him outside the tavern. Couple of my seamen and I trapped him in a crate. I thought he might keep you company while I'm away." He handed me the tiny ball of matted fur.

The pup must have realized by this point that neither of us meant him harm, for he'd cooperated as we bathed him and fed him some dried cod. Of course, neither Sergio nor I had known at the time how huge this tiny ball of fur was to become. Now well over a year old, he stood as tall as me on his hind legs, his paws were as large as my own hands, and his neck had grown to be nearly as thick as my waist. He was a towering mass of charcoal fur that was almost indistinguishable from a wolf, so his name wasn't exactly unearned. Yet he was the gentlest of giants, and his happiness was almost tangible, aiding me and sustaining me on the nights when my bed was empty and my home would have been empty if he weren't curled up on the floor.

Father Manuel had never been all that fond of dogs, but even he had come around to Lobo. As we ate, he tossed a piece of sausage into Lobo's waiting jaws every now and again. I picked at a link, eating only half of it before dropping it to the floor. I always lost my appetite in the days following Sergio's departure.

After the meal, I remained in the rectory until Father Manuel went to prepare for Vespers. Not feeling up to seeing anyone else, I decided to head home as soon as I finished washing the dishes and tidying up the house. Father Manuel used to have a full-time housekeeper for that sort of work, and I couldn't help but remember her whenever I performed these tasks, for she and I had always done these sorts of chores together from the time I arrived in Santa Colomba.

Leonor had been an older widow when she came to work for us because she needed to help her sons pay off her late husband's debts. She'd stayed with us half the time and with her sons half the time in the beginning. However, as her sons married and their home became cramped with wives and children, she'd begun staying at the rectory more and more, sleeping on a cot next to mine in the maid's room.

It wasn't until much later that I realized there was likely another reason Leonor decided to move in with us. For propriety's sake, she and Father Manuel had always been so discreet that I had suspected nothing while she'd lived, but he'd mourned so deeply when she'd passed, I became certain she'd been much more to him than a housemaid.

She had been more than a governess to me, as well. I had Leonor to thank for all those afternoons spent washing with the laundresses rather than sitting cooped up in the rectory. I had Leonor to thank that I'd finally mastered the culinary arts, even if she'd not been able to do anything about my abysmal sewing talents. I even had Leonor to thank for my first meetings with Sergio, for if she'd not sent me to the good fish market along the harbor every day, I might never have run into him there. Thus, it never took more than a few strokes of the broom across Father Manuel's floor or a few dirty dishes on his table to make me miss her.

Once I finished the chores, I made a beeline back through the city, into the arrabal, and over the bridge that crossed the river before it opened into the wide estuary on which our town was situated. On the other side of this bridge spanned sprawling sheep and cattle pastures almost as far as the eye could see, flanked at last by the forests of beech and oak that marked the start of the rolling hills and baldíos—or wilderness lands—that began perhaps a league south of town.

In the far distance, wooded ridges rose above the hills, and beyond those loomed the high mountains, their barren peaks always visible on clear days. Today, they were still capped with snow, though down here along the coast, the same precipitation had fallen as rain overnight. Sometimes, when I returned to the arrabal from the old town, I took a detour so I could stand in the field closest to my house and enjoy the view of the icy spikes as they towered over the coast, basking in the glow of the sun whenever it managed to burn its way through the clouds.

It was on this evening's detour that I spotted *her*.

She stood stark still on the edge of a grove of shade trees that grew in the pastures along the river. I started, sure at first this woman had to be a hallucination. Everything about her screamed of unnaturalness: an inhumanly tall and slender frame, flawless lavender-colored skin covered intermittently with slate-gray runes, shiny silver hair that shimmered with a touch of lilac, and bright eyes gleaming with a hint of the same purple hue as her flesh.

Terrified at the mere sight of such a phantom, I turned from the fields, flew over the bridge, and ran to my house. Lobo tailed me the whole way, as shocked and frightened as I. I slammed the door as soon as we had flung ourselves inside, and when I snuck to the window and peered out, I found the apparition had not given chase.

Though my knees quaked and my heart pounded against my breastbone, I still somehow wished I'd had the courage to look at her just a little longer, if only to make sure she hadn't been a mirage. Now that she no longer stood before my eyes, I began to question whether she might have been a figment of my imagination after all, a delirium I'd created in my dismay at Sergio's departure.

I resolved never to ponder my fleeting vision again, and never ever to speak of it. Such a creature as that willow of a woman was not—could not be—real. The last thing I needed was for people to question my sanity. So when Lobo snuck up behind me and shoved his long snout underneath my palm, I laid my hand on his shaggy head, turned from the window, and tried to think no more of what I had seen.

I was not able to forget it long. The very next day, the phantom appeared once more. I had been doing the wash in the river that separated the arrabal from the sheep fields. Susana's servant Isabel as well as Constanza and Eulalia—two of the town laundresses—met me at our usual spot: a place near the shoreline that was shallow enough for us to gain purchase on the bottom but not so shallow that the mud churned up by our scrubbing rendered the exercise moot. Washing in these days was a difficult and arduous task, which made it no small wonder that people did not bother with it very often. At least it was not so bad when we did it as a group, for we passed the time chatting and laughing as much as working.

It took half the afternoon to get the wash done, and when I parted ways with the other women and reentered my house, my flesh had imbibed all the dirt and sweat I'd taken off the linens. I'd used the stream to rinse the mud off my arms and hands, but I noticed when I looked down at my chest that the exposed skin of my neck and collarbone was speckled with teeny brown dewdrops.

I set the basket on the kitchen table and went to the washbasin. While I stood with my back to the rest of the kitchen, leaned over the basin and pouring water from the vessel next to it, Lobo let out a low, menacing growl. Then a shadow appeared, blocking the dusty light streaming through the threshold of the door I'd forgotten to shut.

My stomach dropped, and I expected to see some stranger had followed me inside. Instead, a more horrifying vision greeted me: the phantom woman. Now that I could see her up close, her stature appeared even more unnaturally slim and tall—she had to duck to fit through my door. She still sported her pastel-purple flesh and her gray painted symbols. By far the most aberrational features were her eyes. They had neither iris nor pupil, uniform as the eyes of an insect. So bright did the eyes reflect the dim sun in the shadowy room that they glowed with a soft lavender-gray light of their own.

Lobo continued his threatening growl, but he remained uninterested in going anywhere near this apparition. I was even more fearful than him. Upon seeing the ghost, I collapsed to the floor, tears cascading down my face.

"Go away. Whatever you are, I want nothing to do with you," I shouted. Stumbling back to my feet, I drew the Sign of the Cross in the air before the demoness. "Get out! In the name of Christ, get out!"

I summoned the courage to look the woman in her evil eye, but instead of meeting my gaze with an expression of rage or terror, she seemed at a loss. She stood still as a winter forest, looking at me as one would a child throwing a tantrum. After a while, she turned to go, moving slowly and deliberately, as if beckoning me to follow. She swung her glittering lilac hair over her shoulders and slid toward the river, her footsteps so light she almost floated.

I bolted out the back of the kitchen and through the animal stall on the other side, scattering chickens as I dashed onto the road. I fled through the arrabal, sprinting until I found Isabel and Susana hanging their wash to dry.

"What on earth happened?" Susana said.

I couldn't answer, sweaty and gasping as I was, with red spots dancing all over my vision. By the time I caught my breath, whatever delusion I'd harbored of telling them about this woman had dissolved. If I ran to the townspeople shrieking about having seen a demoness, they'd think me a lunatic—or worse. Above all, I could not let Father Manuel get word I'd seen this spirit, now on more than one occasion.

"There was a rat, a big rat, in my kitchen," I said between gasps.

The pair of them burst into laughter.

"Well, I've never known you to let a little thing like a rat startle you," said Susana.

"It was the size of a rooster," I protested.

"I want to see the giant rat," screamed one of Susana's boys.

"Me too," shouted a tinier one.

Susana rounded on both of them and told them they were under no circumstances to go off looking for some awful rat whilst she and Isabel simultaneously kept on laughing at my foolish terror. Their mirth helped me calm myself. I needed a place to think without interruption, so I told them I'd go home and get Lobo to kill the rat.

I got back onto the arrabal street, walking slowly this time and keeping my head hung and my gaze low. As I trudged, a dark figure appeared in my peripheral vision. I whipped around, sure it was the demoness come to haunt me again, but it was just Lobo. Relief washed over me to find him standing there like a guardian angel.

When I made it back to the house, I barred the door, which had still been swinging on its hinges, bouncing against the wall as the breeze blew it about. I plopped down at the table to ponder my predicament. I certainly was not going to recount my visions to anyone, but I could not deny the presence of the she-devil now that I'd encountered her more than once. I tried to comfort myself with the faint and fading hope she was just an illusion, but I was sure I couldn't have imagined her. Lobo had spotted her first.

Yet, despite my fear, I found myself longing to know what this woman was and why she deliberately sought me out. I pictured the phantom in her preternatural glory, standing in the doorway, sun on her bare arms, sharp and bright eyes glinting.

Bare arms? I hadn't remembered that until now. She wore nothing but a floor-length, cloudy wisp of a gown, whitish-purple as her hair, with a darker purple sash around her waist, free as a Greek goddess of old. I imagined what it would be like to don that clean, sheer fabric, to be free of heavy cloth and sweaty layers and enjoy the pleasure of movement, of sun on all my skin, the wind about my whole body and not just my face.

I knew better than to think such a thing. Even the desire to emulate the fashion of a demoness probably constituted heresy. With the fires of the stake as fresh in my mind as the day I'd seen them kindled, I feared to give free rein to whatever natural bent toward unorthodoxy might dwell within me. Yet this icy woman had been as beautiful as she was unnerving, and an unwelcome desire to see her again sprouted in the depths of my soul, though I dismissed it instantly—or, at least, I tried.

***

A day or two after this incident, I still found myself unable to get the strange apparition out of my head, so I decided to go see Sara in her town house near the plaza mayor, hoping her company might provide some solace.

Originally from Burgos, she'd been born to a family of wealthy wool merchants and flock owners whose sheep numbered in the hundreds. Her marriage to Armando had been arranged, and she'd never even met him before their wedding. I often felt sorry for her that she'd had to leave her family and a beautiful city like Burgos when she'd been married off, but at least her home was lovely, if that was any comfort.

Sara's town house was one of the biggest in the port, a beautiful new building, architected in the elegant and symmetrical style that had become so popular in recent years. During my visits, I often stopped to admire its intricate decorations and arched windows before I walked to the front door.

Today, however, a biting cold front had moved in from the sea, obliging me to get inside without unnecessary delays. I tapped on the door, waiting for an answer as a chill, salty breeze blew my hair out from under my veil and into my face. I pushed it all back into place as a page opened the door. He was new. Sara tended to run through handsome manservants at a brisk pace.

"Yes?" he asked.

"I'm Micaela, Sergio's wife. I came to call on your mistress," I said.

The page ushered me in with a wave of the hand, beckoning me to go on ahead of him into the house. I loved the interior. It was exactly how I felt a dwelling Sara occupied was meant to be: fashionable and elegant, with every item in its proper place and every decoration meticulously chosen to create an atmosphere of class and luxury—not to the point of extravagance, but enough to let any visitor know this was the dwelling of a real lady with breeding and taste.

The servant led me up the stairs into the spacious parlor, which was sprinkled throughout with many inviting elements. A small fire crackled in its place, large enough to warm the room without overwhelming it with odor. A decanter of wine and glasses—real glasses made of actual glass—sat on a table in the center of the room, surrounded by a sofa and armchairs. Decadent paintings, mostly of beautiful horses and handsome women, hung in strategic spots along the walls to catch the light of the sun as it spilled in through the window and played tricks with their shapes and colors.

I sat on the sofa and kept my hands in my lap, standing again when Sara entered the sitting room. I couldn't help but grin at the sight of her. She was so regal in posture and mannerisms, her movements affected with an easy grace that even Gracia in all her daintiness could not match. If Armando was in his early forties, Sara could not be far behind. Perhaps she was even equal to him in years, but the harsh oceanic wind and summer sun had not cut lines into her face as they had so many others. She'd kept indoors most of her life, so her green eyes would not become speckled with sunspots and her chocolate-brown hair could stay forever tied in the elegant braided knot she liked to wear.

Yet Sara's outer loveliness was marred by that irreparable loss she carried everywhere she went. Every time she entered my presence, I recalled the instances I'd happened upon a blooming mountain daffodil that had come forth too early in spring, only to see its beauty wither in the storm or the frost at the prime of its short existence.

When we sat down, Sara beckoned Ana, one of her maids, to bring us drinks.

"It's wonderful about Gracia, isn't it?" she asked, accepting her wine cup from Ana.

Her words were right, but the tone was distant and impassive.

"How are you with it? Really?" I said.

She sighed, her eyes downcast and her lips pursed over what I thought might be her tongue between her teeth. Silence followed her sigh. I didn't break it, though I hated to allow it to remain intact.

Silence almost never found a place between Sara and me. Usually, our conversations lasted hours, sometimes all night. While the men drank and laughed, Sara and I would sit by the fire. She'd do her needlework, but I'd always clasp my hands together in my lap, in what I hoped was a delicate and feminine manner, because I was embarrassed to fumble about with a needle in front of her. We would talk of idle town gossip, of her husband's business, of the latest political scandals and distant wars, of her hopes for her family's future, of love and domestic responsibilities. We never spoke of her children, but that was understandable.

Now, however, we sat in the dread silence, listening to the thudding of the servants' footsteps and the indistinct chatter of voices as they prepared the afternoon meal in the kitchen below. When Sara broke the quiet at last, her tone was cordial but still distant.

"I suppose I should be excited to be an aunt. But I don't feel anything. Every time someone congratulates Gracia in my presence, I . . ." She trailed off and stared out the window.

"I hope people have been understanding," I whispered.

"For the most part, yes, though I'm sure when Juliana gets the news, she won't pass up the opportunity to remind me of my many failures as a wife and daughter-in-law."

"Forget what Armando's witch of a mother says. When has that woman had a kind word for anyone?"

"I almost dread her coming back to town for the birth more than any of the rest of it."

"I cannot imagine. I suppose that's one of the blessings I got when I married Sergio—no mother-in-law."

"I'd kill to be rid of mine, even if she does live two days' ride away." Sara went silent once more.

When she spoke again, she changed the subject, and I followed her lead. We talked of a possible gale; she thought the weather might turn foul now that the cold had returned. I hoped not, pondering what it might mean for the fleet. We moved on to idle gossip about some of the other townswomen's supposedly illicit activities while their husbands were away at sea. Eventually, the topic came around to Sergio. I commented this was his longest voyage yet and I would not know what to do with myself for almost half a year.

"It must seem long to you. You and Sergio still have some love left," she said.

I wasn't sure how to respond to that. The problems between her and Armando were another of those untouchable subjects she and I chose to avoid. I knew their troubles were severe, but I didn't know their cause and never wanted to appear too eager to find out.

"Do you prefer Armando to leave Castilla so often?" I asked.

"I'm not sure it would make any difference what I preferred; he'd leave all the same. But yes, I prefer it, and so does he."

"Perhaps he doesn't prefer it as much as you think?"

"He does. You doubt it because your husband spends his days onshore in your bed—and because he doesn't have a lovely young sister-in-law giving his brother the sons you never could," she added bitterly.

"I'm sure Armando does not blame you for"—I hesitated—"for that."

"I know *I* am not the one to blame, but I often wish I could have followed my children." She said this to the air more than to me.

She radiated such desperate misery I wanted to embrace her and escape her all at once. For a fleeting instant, I wished I could bring forth a healthy child from my womb just to give it to her. I slid my hands under my thighs and shifted in my seat.

Sensing my discomfort, she knit her brow and gave me an understanding look. "I apologize. I shouldn't speak of such things to one who is still young and has yet even to bear her first child. All this fuss over Gracia is making me feel ill at ease. I'm sure you and Sergio will have many healthy children. It won't be for you as it has for me."

I was unsure how to feel about this statement. Sometimes, I was secretly glad Sergio and I had never conceived, because ever since I'd met Sara, the fear of bearing children only to see them all wither away, one by one, had hung like a cloud over the prospect of motherhood. I didn't wish to learn of her pain firsthand, but in that day, it was difficult to keep all one's children living. I was fully aware it might very well be the same for me as it had for her.

I did not know what to say regarding this subject, so I apologized for her loss, silently asking myself what could be the matter with me that I could think of no better words of comfort. My eyes misted over as I sat pondering what the next year could bring and what such a loss as Sara's might do to Gracia.

"Mica, please," Sara said. "I didn't wish to upset you."

"You haven't," I replied.

This at least was true. She had not said or done anything to upset me. I grieved for what time and loss had done to her and what they had yet to do to the rest of us, for I still remembered the Sara of my youth. When I was a girl, I'd sometimes seen her at Mass before she and I had formally met, and she was always cuddling her only baby to make it out of the cradle. Back then, Sara smiled and laughed at everything that child did, failing to notice another thing in the wide world outside of that little girl with a head of chestnut curls.

Margarita made it to the age of three, and her requiem had been the last Mass Sara attended for a long while. I often wondered about the person Sara might have been if only that child had survived. There was still time enough to have another if she wished to give it one last try. But, of course, I knew better than to suggest such a thing.

# Chapter Three

# A CLOSER ENCOUNTER

In the days following my encounters with the phantom woman, every shadow in the corner of my eye took her shape. Every sound of unknown origin was her footstep. Every time Lobo cocked his head, I was sure he sensed her.

I remained uncertain of how to feel about the prospect of her return. Though I feared to let her tempt me toward whatever sin she might be peddling, that fear was equally matched by a strong curiosity to know her nature and what she wanted. I resolved that if she came to me again, I would not run off like a coward. I would ask her why she continued to pester and terrify me. Yet, day after day, no true hint of her appeared, and after a couple of uneventful weeks, I became sure I would never see this insect-eyed woman again.

By this time, spring was in full swing, and the sun bounced off the green leaves like tiny rain droplets leaping off the surface of a puddle. I was excited for the sheep to return to the fields, which would soon be filled with the sound of bleating and the sight of fluffy lambs playing near the creek. As the days lengthened and warmed, I spent my free time leaned against the fence surrounding my vegetable garden, watching across the river as the first arrivals filtered in from the shearing. Sometimes, a few of the shepherds I knew would pass by, and I'd wave at them or speak to them.

On the occasions when familiar shepherds were near at hand, I felt safe to wander all the way to the edge of the baldíos and walk in the forests that bordered the grazing pastures. Even with shepherds I trusted close by, I might not have taken these walks if not for Lobo. He offered me some freedom, for before he'd become such a formidable animal, I would never have dared to skirt the periphery of wolf and bandit territory—not even in broad daylight.

One morning, I wasted a few hours loafing in the dappled sunlight of a forest grove adjacent to the last sheep field. I sat tossing sticks into a creek and watching them flee downstream to the waiting sea. As I perched on a rock, stripping fat leaves from a fallen twig, I felt it: that aura I had known only twice before and had half hoped and half feared I'd never know again. I got to my feet and turned slowly. I cannot explain how I knew she watched me from deeper in the forest, keeping enough distance to avoid intimidating me. I just knew.

Lobo offered no resistance. Though the hair on the back of my neck stood on end, I took some comfort from his lack of fear and faced the visitor head on, studying her appearance and waiting to see what she'd do. I could not put my finger on the reason, but she looked less terrifying than I remembered—at least at this distance. After all my stewing in a dreadful cocktail of hope and fear of both her return and her abandonment, an odd sense of relief mixed in with my apprehension at the sight of her. She had come back after all.

She spoke not one word. Rather, she stood in the shadow of an old beech tree, her body speckled with sunlight and shade, waiting until I made the first move. I crept closer, ready to turn tail and run in an instant should she strike out but also ready to satisfy my curiosity.

As I inched ever nearer, it dawned on me why she appeared less frightening than she had before: she looked more normal. She was shorter, and her skin was no longer purple and gray but a natural-looking beige. When I saw it up close, though, I noticed it was still flawless, without pores or wrinkles, as if she were wrought from painted clay. Her eyes no longer resembled polished pewter either; they bore a white and a pupil and an iris of smoky gray. Her hair had lost its lilac glow. It now formed a whitish-silver sheet that veiled her back and shoulders. If I'd not known better, I'd have thought her human.

I had come within centimeters of her as I made these observations. Seized by a sudden desire to touch her, I reached out. I intended to grasp a handful of her silver hair, but she turned and glided from under the tree. This time, I followed.

She led me across the stream and through the fields until we came to a grove of large oak trees, farther into the forest than I'd ever ventured. We crept through these woods, sliding over the soft peat of fallen leaves from last autumn, not wishing to disturb the bustling birds as they went about their work. Finally, we came to a place where the trees weren't so thick.

She sat down on a flat rock underneath the oldest, tallest tree, shaking some dirt off the skirt of her gossamer gown: the same pastel sleeveless thing I'd seen before. She looked up as I stood before her in the morning sun. At first, I made to sit right next to her, but then I thought better of it. Still wary, I sat under a younger tree a short distance away.

She said nothing, so I spoke first.

"Are you a devil?" I blurted without pretense.

"What is a devil?" she asked.

"An evil spirit," I said.

"I have never heard of such things, so I suppose I cannot be a devil," she replied.

"That's exactly what a devil would say."

"It is also exactly what someone who is not a devil would say. Is it sensible to say one is a devil if one is not?"

To this, I had no response.

At this point, I must divulge I am giving her more eloquent speech than she exhibited during this initial conversation. When we spoke, her words were awkward, not devoid of meaning but also not aware of certain turns of phrase and unspoken rules that a fluent speaker would understand. Naturally, attempting to imitate this verbal clumsiness would be futile.

I decided to tell her my name after another moment of silence, though I was unsure if she could understand my words because of her clumsy manner of speech.

She looked at me with an air of confused curiosity before asking, "'Micaela' is your name or what you call your own kind?"

I hesitated; that was an odd question. "My name."

"Is that considered an appealing name?" she asked.

"It's a fine name. Why don't you give me yours?"

"I am called Jhasali."

"What does it mean?"

She inhaled. "In my language, the name means 'builder of useful structures.'"

"What language is that?"

"You wouldn't know of it."

Her low, even tone emboldened me, so I moved closer and sat down on her rock. Staring into her large eyes, I reached out and grasped a lock of her silver hair, just to ensure she was indeed corporeal. This time, she allowed me to touch her.

Now that I'd somewhat conquered my fear, I realized what a beauty she was. In addition to those large almond-shaped eyes, she had a long neck, high cheekbones, and a slender, straight nose, almost as if Donatello had carved her out of flesh and blood.

I gasped and let go of her hair, dropping my gaze from hers. I'd recalled something Father Manuel had told me long ago: Satan could masquerade as an angel of light. To test Jhasali, I removed the little crucifix I wore around my neck and held it out to her. She took it without hesitation. Staring at it in silence, she raised it to the light and turned it round and round between her fingers.

She looked back toward me. "Is this an image of some primitive mating ritual?"

"What? No," I said, but before I could scold her for blasphemy, she asked me what the symbol meant, so I explained it was an antiquated form of execution.

"Why would you carry an image of a member of your kind being killed in this manner?"

"Because it's Christ. The Son of God."

"What is a son? What is God?"

"The creator of the world. Haven't your people any faith?"

"I don't understand the question," she said.

It was I who didn't understand. I was on the verge of frustration, for I'd not decided for certain this woman was no demon, but her almost ludicrous ignorance made me doubt my initial impression that she must be. No demon could handle the crucifix with such apathy. Jhasali had given it another passing glance and handed it back as though it were nothing.

"You have lived here all your life?" Jhasali asked, bored of the current topic.

"Yes. The last ten years, anyway," I answered.

I raised my eyes to meet hers once more. Her gaze was intense, yet I could not bring myself to be afraid. Even though her bizarre looks had terrified me before, she now sat so tranquil that her demeanor, mixed with the sound of birdsong and rustling leaves, lulled me into lowering my guard.

Jhasali smiled so spontaneously I almost suspected she'd read my thoughts, but then it dawned on me I had been the one to smile first. I'd done it out of nerves, and she was merely imitating me, albeit poorly. Her smile was stiff and twisted, as though she'd never tried to do it before in her life.

"Why do you smile like that?" I asked.

"I cannot discern what this expression means. If it is a gesture of displeasure or a display of aggression or a show of amiability. I have never been in such physical proximity to one of your kind before."

At the time, I thought she meant Castellanos, so I asked her where she'd come from.

"A place very far from here," she said in a tone that made clear she was disinclined to discuss it further.

I asked her how she got to this country, and she told me she took a ship. This was not technically a lie, but her meaning and my inference were two different things.

While we talked, a chill wind blew out of the north, and I grew cold, though I'd thrown my cloak over my shoulders before leaving the house. Jhasali remained untroubled by the sudden drop in temperature, despite wearing next to nothing. I pulled my cloak tighter around my shoulders and tucked my hands underneath the thick wool.

Jhasali asked me what was wrong, and I told her the wind chilled me.

"We should get you indoors, then," she said, rising from her seat and making for the direction of my house.

I got up and followed her back through the woods, but when we reached the edge of the pastures, the thought occurred to me that if she accompanied me to the arrabal, there was a good chance we'd be spotted wandering across the open fields together. It wouldn't do at all for me to be seen with a strange, foreign-looking woman wearing nothing but a sleeveless chemise.

Being from Toledo in this region made me foreign enough. With a nickname like "La Toledana," I couldn't afford any more abnormalities, so when Jhasali made to step into the open, I hissed for her to wait.

"You cannot go to my house dressed like that. If anyone spotted me with you, I . . . it wouldn't be good."

She squinted her eyes but did not question why I took issue with her clothing. Instead, she asked if I preferred her to dress in a manner more similar to my own. When I affirmed, she doubled back and headed for the forest once more.

Before I could even get the words out of my mouth, she turned and said, "Don't worry. You shall see me again."

***

The woman was back a few days later, so early in the morning I'd just begun to stir. I would never have been aware she'd returned if not for Lobo bolting to the threshold from his spot on the kitchen floor, where he paced and whined for no apparent reason. When I opened the door, I found Jhasali looking at it with an air of confusion, pondering the solid wood almost like she expected an entryway to magically appear.

Once I told her to come inside, she passed me into the house, where she stopped and gaped at the kitchen fireplace as if she believed a fire would materialize there. I rolled my eyes and arranged the kindling while she stared at me with that intense gaze. When I struck the flint and set the fuel alight, she gasped and clapped as if I'd performed a magnificent feat.

"What's the matter with you? You never seen fire before?" I snapped.

"No, no. It is just amazing how you've all learned to get on with such methods."

"What does that mean?"

"Nothing," she said with a dismissive wave of the hand. "I meant it is different here. In my culture, we have servants to do manual labor such as this."

"My husband says we don't have the money to waste on a servant, leastways while we have no children."

"Where I come from, they are irrelevant to wealth. Everyone has at least a few."

I laughed in disbelief, for surely *all* the servants could not also have servants.

Jhasali followed me around like a dog, watching as I gathered eggs for breakfast and prepared to cook. She gasped and clapped again when the oil in the pan bubbled. Hoping to make her stop looking over my shoulder, I gave her a mug full of the milk I'd bought the previous afternoon and bade her sit at the table.

"What is this?" she asked.

"Try it," I said.

She took the cup in hand and bent her head down, smelling the milk before taking a sip. She winced.

"Oh. It's greasy." She wiped away her milk mustache.

"I like it."

"How can you like this? There's too much oil in it."

"What do you drink that's so great?" I asked, offended.

"In my home, we drink sweet or salty things. Never greasy like that."

I pondered what else I might have in the house. Then I went to the pantry and pulled out a wine jug. It was early, but I didn't figure she'd be concerned with that. When I handed her the wine cup, she smelled the stuff inside before sipping, as she had before. This time, after taking a sip, she gave her odd, almost forced smile.

"That's more like what I am accustomed to," she said. "But it's different—better even. What is it?"

"Wine," I answered.

"What is it made of?"

"Grapes. There are many vineyards around here and to the south."

"Grapes. Intriguing." She drained the cup. "You have more wine?"

"You should be careful. You'll get drunk if you have too much."

"What is drunk?"

I chuckled. "You know. If you have too much wine, you get silly and debaucherous."

"There is some sort of intoxicant in this?"

"Yes. That's why everyone likes to drink it."

"Let me see."

Jhasali stared at the cup. She swirled the dregs around the bottom and stuck her finger in them, using the wet fingernail to taste a single drop of wine.

"Is there something wrong with the wine?" I asked.

"I am analyzing," she answered, not explaining any further.

After a moment, she looked up. "I am not concerned with this. It should not affect me."

I stared at her, confused as to why she thought she could not get drunk. She seemed to take this the wrong way.

"If you do not wish me to have more, I will not." She set the cup on the table.

"Maybe the wine where you're from isn't as strong as ours. I don't normally drink a lot."

"Then how do you survive?"

"Wine, I mean. I don't usually drink much wine."

"Why not?"

"I don't know. I've never been drunk before. I don't wish to be."

"Why not?" she repeated.

That was easy. I'd seen Sergio and his friends crawl to the back of the wine cask enough times to know I had no wish to partake of the stuff the way they did. All they suffered the next morning put me quite off it.

"I have seen my husband do it on occasion, and it makes him sick after," I said.

"What is a husband?" she asked.

"Come now, you don't have marriage in your culture?"

"How can I say we do or do not when I don't know what marriage is?"

"It's the joining of a man and a woman together for life. When the vows are said, the two become one. They are free to share a home and a bed and have children."

She brushed her hair out of her face. "You are not free to do these things already?"

"Well, people do, but it's fornication—and that's wrong."

"It is a strange custom. But I suppose it is not too far beyond the realm of normal mating behavior."

"Then there is no marriage in your country?" I asked again.

"No."

"How do you have children?"

"You would not understand. My people don't mate. Our reproductive process doesn't work like yours."

"Try me," I told her, annoyed that she clearly thought me stupid.

She pondered her next words before speaking again. "Alright. Our Elders select certain specimens for reproduction, and they do it."

"And these specimens aren't married?"

"Of course not. Why should a simple act of reproduction bind them together for life?"

"But then they are committing a sin. A crime, I mean," I added, explaining myself before she got the opportunity to ask me what a sin was.

"Says who? There is no marriage in my culture; thus, there can be no fornication. If you do not define it as such, then it is not."

"But it's immoral."

"Why?" she asked.

"It goes against the natural order of things."

"Who defines that?"

I was silent for a long while before saying God did.

"Did you speak to this god?"

"Not in the sense that we're speaking now," I snapped.

She tilted her head to the side. "I do not wish to upset you. It's just I also do not understand your ways."

"No. I'm not upset. I want to help you understand," I replied.

"You do?" she asked, to which I nodded.

That nod proved to be a huge mistake, as she spent the rest of the morning bombarding me with a torrent of questions so relentless it felt like an Inquisitorial interrogation. She asked me about modes of transportation and why my people insisted on using animals to get from place to place. She plied me with more queries about wine and drinking and said she found it quite plausible certain members of my kind could become addicted to such tasty stuff. She questioned me about the pleasant sounds she'd heard coming from town, and I explained they were called music and came from the churches and taverns and streets.

She refused to answer when I asked how she'd heard music without going into town, but I didn't wish to press her about it, still fearing her on some level. Somehow, the topic came around to gold and silver, and it only intensified the interrogation when she learned metals were the basis of our economy.

"So your people use elements for money?" she demanded.

"We use what for money?" I asked, for she'd not used the word "elements," but a strange word I'd never heard before.

"Metals that . . . oh, nevermind. I have no words to explain it that you will understand."

"Metals have many purposes," I snapped. "We make things from them, like weapons and armor and dishes."

"So you trade these things for other things?"

"Sometimes, but we mostly use coins for trade."

"Coins?"

I got up without another word to fetch my purse. Sergio always left me a lockbox full of money to manage the household. We had no gold ducats, so the chest contained mostly blancas made of billon and reals of silver. I returned with an example of each of these coins and set them on the table.

"That's a blanca," I explained. "This is a real. Reals are worth much more than blancas, but blancas are good to have around for small purchases."

"So, these buy things," she said, more to herself than to me. Lifting her eyes to mine, she added, "Would it please you to have more of them?"

I raised my eyebrows. "Of course it would."

She took the coins and turned each of them in hand. "Can I have these, then?"

"No. I barely have enough to keep this house running."

"I don't wish to keep them. I have raw elemental metals for my own purposes. If you give me these, I can reproduce them. I'll come back with a thousand more like them."

"How can you possibly—"

"Never you mind about that," she replied. "But if you are willing to lend them to me, I will give you as many as you like."

"Truly?" I asked.

"Certainly. If it would please you."

I looked at the real as she twirled it between her fingers. I didn't really believe she could reproduce the coins. After all the terror she'd caused me and the endless questions she'd subjected me to, she was just wandering the countryside using magic spells to trick fools like me into giving her money!

I sighed. "I will give you one real and one blanca. Is that agreeable to you?"

A real was no pittance, but I offered it thinking if I played along, I could get her out of my house without a confrontation.

"Yes." She took the two coins to stow them in her pocket. Just then, she started and looked out the window. "Someone is calling your name."

I couldn't hear anything, so I rose and went to the window. There, I was able to make out Isabel's voice carrying through the half-open shutter.

"You should go," I said.

"Would you come to some harm if you were seen in my company?"

"I don't know. Possibly. People would talk for certain."

"And you do not desire this?"

"No!"

Without another word, she rose from her seat and slipped out the back door, leaving me with nothing more than an empty wine cup and a strong sense of relief at being rid of her. When the door shut behind her, I almost slapped myself for my stupidity, but at least I was certain I wouldn't see her again. A con artist like her wouldn't return now that she'd gotten what she came for. Once assured she was good and gone, I headed outside to see what Isabel wanted.

***

I wasted hours castigating myself for being taken in by a vagabond with the power only to delude and defraud. In my foolishness, I'd actually believed myself to be important enough for some preternatural entity to visit me, but I supposed that was how Jhasali—or whatever her real name was—tricked idiot townswomen into lightening our purses.

Trying not to ruminate, I spent the next few days focusing on my household chores, socializing with the neighbors, and attending to Father Manuel as often as I could. I also tried to visit Sara whenever possible, knowing how all Gracia's celebrations must be weighing on her.

I spent a couple of nights at Sara's town house that week because Gracia had invited all her and Gabriel's relatives to a family celebration of their news. Sara feigned illness to avoid attending, and she and I passed two quiet nights eating cocido montañés, drinking wine, and playing card games. We both preferred each other's company to huge parties, especially parties with a particular subset of Gabriel and Armando's relatives.

Like me, Sara still found herself treated like an outsider by much of her husband's family and even some of the townsfolk of her station. Her wealth and status were the only reasons she'd not received a nickname denoting her foreignness, as I had. Though no one was ever openly hostile to us—her because of Armando and me because of Father Manuel—and some even revered us for being from the big city, we still weren't often permitted to forget we were neither born nor raised in La Montaña. At least by ourselves, we could be outlanders together.

On the evening I returned home from my sojourn at Sara's, darkness had nearly fallen, so I decided every chore other than feeding the chickens could wait until morning. I awoke just after dawn and began sweeping the house. As I bent down to push dirt into the pan, Lobo barked and leapt to his feet. I rose to see what the fuss was about and found myself face-to-face with Jhasali, who stood not five paces from me.

"Hostia! Will you knock?" I cried, holding my hand over my heart and collapsing into a chair, broom still in my fist.

I couldn't guess how in hell she'd unbarred the door from the outside. Or had she floated in through the open window?

"What is knock?" she asked.

"When you bang on the door and announce yourself to the occupants."

"Is not to do so improper?"

"Yes. Christ! You cannot barge into people's homes like some kind of wild animal."

While my heart still raced, she walked over and handed me a silver coin: the real I'd given her the week prior.

"You didn't plan to steal it?" I asked. I'd been so certain she would not be coming back after taking my money.

"Why would I steal what I don't need?"

She cast a sack onto the chair beside me, lifting and tossing it like it weighed nothing, though it landed with such a heavy thud I worried for the chair's integrity. It was full of shining silver reals, all of them a carbon copy of my coin.

"This is . . . this is so much," I mumbled weakly.

"Nonsense. It's a fraction of what I have."

"Regardless, I cannot accept it."

"Why ever not? It is as meaningless to me as dirt."

"Yes but, well, my husband earns a good salary. We are not starving, but we are not wealthy either. If I suddenly show up with more money than the Holy Roman Emperor, people will start asking questions."

"Is this emperor meant to have the most metal of all?" Jhasali asked.

"Yes, well, that's not exactly how it works—can't you see how it might look suspicious for me to have this much coin all of a sudden? I am not ungrateful, but I fear being suspected of thievery or worse."

"Alright. I see," she said.

"I'm sorry. I don't mean to offend."

"Why would I be offended? Keep what you wish. I'll take the rest with me."

"How did you even get it here?"

"I have my ways," she replied.

Deciding once again not to push her, I took a real out of the bag to inspect it. Turning the coin over, I whispered, "How did you make them all the same?"

"I made a mold of the original. How else would I do it?"

Finally, an answer that made some damn sense. I marveled at the reals' impossible uniformity and sheer number, thinking I'd have to take a hammer to whatever silver I kept to make the coins look circulated. Even as this thought passed through my mind, it occurred to me that a shape-shifting woman offering me a fortune in counterfeited silver should give me no small amount of pause.

While I pondered what to do, Jhasali began wandering about the house, picking up different items and staring at them, as if doing so would magically make her understand what they were for and how they worked. She lifted a water pitcher and considered it before setting it next to the basin. She took up the broom and stared at it before leaning it against the wall.

"What are you doing?" I said.

"I am analyzing," she replied.

"What does that mean?"

She didn't respond.

While she continued to study everything in sight, I studied her. She'd undergone additional alterations since I'd last seen her. For one thing, her skin had taken on a fair olive tone that perfectly matched my own. She also did not look as flawless; her face and neck now bore fine lines and creases, and when I approached her, I could see many tiny pores just like those that dotted any human countenance. Her hair was less white and more bluish, almost the color of lead, as if she'd gone prematurely gray. Her nose and mouth had taken on a shape similar to my own, and her iris color had darkened to match my eyes as well.

She looked as though she could be my older sister or even my mother, if she'd borne me young. She also wore a dress more fitting to the style of the times: a deep chocolate brown, long and loose sleeves, full skirts, formfitting at the top, though she wore no head ornament and the entire dress was only one layer, which was odd for that period.

"How have you done this?" I asked.

"Done what?" she said.

"Changed the way you look so drastically. You were a sight to behold when we first met, and now I might not give you a second glance."

"Everyone from my home can do such a thing," she said. "It is a nonissue."

"Is it magic?"

"If you must call it that."

"So you're a witch, then?"

"I don't suppose I am a witch any more than I am a devil. My people are born with the ability to change our appearance, much as you are born with the ability to see or speak."

"Because fairies can shape-shift?" I asked.

I was still blindly scrabbling for some familiar category in which to place her. I'd always thought myself above belief in such superstitions as fairies, but her ability to alter her appearance with such apparent ease baffled me.

Ignoring me once more, she picked up the copy of *Amadís de Gaula* lying on my chair and studied it for a good ten minutes before asking me why everyone was always "smiting one another to the ground" and "cleaving one another down to the teeth" for no reason at all. I had to laugh at that one, though I had not a clue how she'd become literate, since she hadn't known how to speak my language properly last week.

"How did you learn to read?" I demanded. "You could barely even speak Castellano when we met."

"Everything is mathematical. Everything is related to something else. The relational laws make such a thing as this self-evident. My people place much emphasis on intuitive learning. Most things we don't need to be taught by anyone outside ourselves. How did you think I learned to speak your language in the first place?"

"You taught yourself?" I was stunned.

"But of course," she answered.

"No. I don't believe that. Someone had to have taught you."

"Why is that? I listened to people speak and figured out how to interpret the words into my own language. After that, it was easy."

"So you went to town, then?"

"No. You are the only person I've spoken to in this realm," she said.

"If you haven't gone to any town, how did you hear people speak enough to master our tongue?"

She paused and pondered her answer. Finally, she said she had items that could receive and transmit sound to her when she pleased.

"But that is witchcraft!" I cried.

"How can I perform witchcraft if I am still unsure of what it is?"

I huffed and ran my fingers through my hair. "It's spells, curses, that sort of thing. Like if you were displeased with the neighbors, so you put a spell on their cattle to make them all die. Or if you spoke some incantations to summon evil spirits to you."

She laughed in a most unnatural way, as if the act were nothing but an imitation of my own laughter rather than something she would have done of her own accord. She asked if I'd seen her do such things, and I had to deny it, for I had not seen her do them—yet.

She snapped *Amadís* shut. "The ability to transmit information is not witchcraft, nor has it ever been. If you don't wish to believe that, it is your prerogative. But do not waste our time asserting that I am a practitioner of such foolishness."

She looked back down at the book cover without another word. To test her reaction, I said if she were not a witch, she must be an angel instead, or perhaps the Virgin in disguise. She glanced up and replied she'd be whatever I wished if it would bring this conversation to a close.

I threw up my hands. "If you want to end this conversation, tell me what you are."

"I am what I am."

"Who am I, Moses? That is not a real answer."

"I am evidently a devil, a witch, an angel, a virgin, a fairy, and a thief. I know nothing of the first five, but I can assure you I am no thief," she replied.

"That is still not—"

"Make of me what you prefer. You ask too many questions."

"You can interrogate me for hours, but I put a few questions to you and that's too many?"

"I cannot explain it now," she said. "I admittedly know little of your kind, but from what I have observed of your behavior, it seems a bad idea to lay the truth on you. You're unlikely to be able to bear it."

"I can bear it."

"Really? I make one mere mention of sound transmission, and your immediate assumption is that I must be a cattle killer and a summoner of evil spirits. Does that sound like someone who can bear what I might say?"

I opened my mouth to tell her if she thought me too dimwitted to comprehend her nature, she should find another person to visit. But instead of uttering these words, I decided to test this spirit more thoroughly before dismissing it. I mightn't be able to determine what she was, but I could determine what she was not.

In a quiet corner of the house, I'd made a tiny shrine over which I'd hung an icon of Santa Bárbara: my patron saint. I'd grown fond of her after I'd witnessed the auto de fe. For many months following, I'd been tormented by a recurrent nightmare in which I sprinted through an open field during a thunderstorm. My frantic attempts to escape the lightning always resulted in my being changed into a dry, dead tree, rooted to the ground in the spot where I transformed. Inevitably, I was struck by the lightning from which I'd fled, causing me to catch fire. Unable to run or roll or even scream, I burned and burned until I was incinerated, my ashes pounded to mud in the rain that only arrived after I was already consumed.

Santa Bárbara had been my sole comfort during that blazing fever of dreams, which hadn't broken until I'd left Toledo. She provided me great comfort even now, on the rarer occasion when that same old nightmare invaded my slumber. At present, I could also depend on her to help me sort out my mysterious guest.

I told Jhasali if she wished to continue to visit me, she must offer some proofs she was not malevolent. I made her hold the rosary and the wooden crucifix that rested atop my little altar. I showed her how to make the Sign of the Cross. I had her repeat after me that Jesus Christ was God in the flesh and no other name under Heaven could save men.

Every one of these tests she completed without any issue, though she did so whilst uttering an incessant stream of complaints that she did not understand how engaging in these pointless procedures could offer me any assurance that she meant me no harm. Yet her inability to comprehend the need for the rituals did not at all curb my relief that she could and would perform them.

Once I was reassured she could not be anything demonic, I asked her why she wanted to give me so much money.

She smiled. "I wished to please you. You said you don't have enough metal. I have more than enough."

"You want nothing in return? Truly?"

"I don't suppose any of your kind has anything I might want."

I wasn't sure what to think, but even if she decided I owed her something later, she'd have no standing to claim it if she'd offered me the coins freely. And why should I refuse? Gracia and Sara shouldn't be the only ones to have nice things.

"What are you going to do with your new metal?" Jhasali asked.

"I would like a dress or two."

"I don't understand why you prefer to wear these ridiculous contraptions." She tugged at the collar of her own dress.

I did not respond to that. Instead, I said, "I'd also like a horse."

"Is that the animal your people think is an acceptable mode of transportation?"

"Yes. And when I buy mine, I'll show you how to ride."

"Oh no. I am not doing that." She retrieved the copy of *Amadís* once more.

I laughed. "We shall see."

"May I take some of these?" She motioned to the books stacked on the shelf.

I was loath to tell her she could. Printed material was expensive, and the books I had on that shelf were all the books I owned in the world. Yet she'd brought me more than enough coinage to buy them back, and after I'd spent all week thinking her a con artist, I felt I owed her a little trust, though I swore her to return all the books she borrowed.

When she left that afternoon, I also made her promise me in every tongue she knew that she would never ever enter my house again without knocking first. After she pledged this oath, she was gone. This time, I knew that, like the high tide, she'd always be back.

# Chapter Four

# PEPITO

J hasali continued to call on me sporadically over the following weeks, always at times when the arrabal streets were empty and the surrounding areas unoccupied. At least she'd taken to heart my request she avoid letting the neighbors spot her. During her visits, we kept up our pattern of playfully combative exchanges, in which I grew more and more flustered with her ignorance of things I considered common knowledge and she gave me ever more cryptic responses to any question I put to her.

Her completion of my spiritual examinations gave me leeway to presume she must be a divine messenger testing my faith for some mysterious purpose. Of course, there were many problems with this assessment, not the least of which was her persistent failure to actually give me a divine message. There was also the issue of my being forced to spell out everything for her every time she came knocking—and knock she did, after the initial fright she'd given me—but I wished her to be a holy apparition, so that was what I believed her to be.

Meanwhile, I didn't wait long to start spending her coin. I had let her leave just enough for me to make what purchases I believed would go unquestioned, plus some extra to feed the first item on my list for a good long while.

I'd already chosen where I would buy my horse. There was a stable a few blocks from the church, and the man who owned it dabbled in the art of breeding the beasts. I say "dabbled" because he never developed much of a reputation for his stock. He mostly boarded the mules belonging to the patrons of the inn across the street, and he only had one stallion and a mare or two of his own.

Yet his lack of stock did not affect his commitment. Each colt and filly born to that man (Alonso was his name, if I remember accurately) he raised as if it were his own child. He tended his charges with care and affection, broke them with a gentle hand, and trained them with a loving patience that rivaled that of the most devoted mother. The few foals he did have always grew up to be excellent mounts: intelligent, obedient, loyal, friendly—everything one could want from a working animal.

Unfortunately, Alonso's patience with his horses did not extend to human beings. With most people, he was terse, aloof, and blunt to the point of rudeness. Then again, I wasn't interested in buying his personality.

When I arrived at the stable, I told Lobo to stay at the gate post while I went around back, where Alonso was busy feeding the mules and horses. I knocked on one of the stall doors, and he stopped tossing hay into the troughs long enough to grunt at me when I told him good morning.

"I wish to buy one of your horses," I bellowed so he could hear me over the whinnying of the hungry equines.

He looked back at me long enough to say, "I'll show you when I'm done."

I returned to the front of the barn, where I leaned against the post with Lobo to wait for Alonso. When he emerged, he pointed to my wedding band.

"Does Sergio know you're making such a purchase?"

"Yes. I have his leave to administer our finances in his absence. I can even show you—"

"That'll do," he said.

He led me into the barn, where he had a dark chestnut mare, a dappled gray gelding, and a black draft horse for sale. The last one was not foaled to him, so she was out. I had him take his chestnut and his gray to a small paddock that extended from the side of the stable and wrapped around back. He saddled them up one at a time and allowed me to ride them in a tiny circle around the pen at the side of the barn. I felt no excitement for either of them, but the chestnut reminded me of the church cart mule I'd grown to love as a child, so I considered taking her.

While Alonso went to put the gray back in his stall, a commotion emanated from around the stable corner. Curious as to the source of what sounded like frustrated pawing at the packed earth and stone, I went to investigate. When I rounded the corner, I discovered that a golden-haired, black-maned horse had let himself out of his stall. He now leaned over the fence almost to the point of knocking the rails off, craning his neck to reach the hay cart, which sat half-full on the other side.

The wiry young stallion froze when he saw me, slowly backing his still-stretched lips away from the hay as if this act would reverse the fact that I'd just caught him pilfering it. I burst out laughing and jogged toward him. I would know this horse anywhere: Pepito. I had met him when he was a foal, and I used to sneak him apples and carrots every time I came back from the market.

It appeared he remembered me too. He turned from the hay he'd been trying to filch and trotted toward me, sun glistening along the ridges of his golden hide and bouncing playfully off his soot-black mane. When he put his head down toward me and rested his muzzle gently on my forearm, I noticed his raven locks were almost indistinguishable from my own ebony strands—like we two were somehow akin, no matter how distantly. He took the end of one of my braids in his mouth and nibbled it between his soft, flexible lips.

I had liked him from the moment I'd laid eyes on him almost three years ago. He'd been standing in this very pen, wobbly on his overlong newborn legs and swishing his awkward poof of a newborn tail. Never in a hundred years did I think I'd have the opportunity to own him.

I turned to Alonso when he rounded the barn. "I want this one."

"No," he said.

"How much?" I asked.

"Pepito is no palfrey, Toledana."

"I don't mind. I was never afforded such a horse before."

"Pepito's not for sale."

"Everything's for sale." I smiled and deposited a substantial sum of silver into my hand for him to view.

Alonso's eyes widened as he looked at my overfull palm and the still-stuffed purse hanging from my wrist.

"Oh, alright," he snapped.

He opened his mouth again, likely to ask where I got such a big bag of money, but then he must've thought better of it, considering a good bit of that money was about to be his.

I bought a saddle and bridle as well, and I asked if Pepito could stay in the barn until I returned from my other errands. Alonso made me pay for a day's board even though I had given him well over what he could have gotten out of Pepito at auction. Cheap bastard.

As I put Pepito in his stall and turned to leave, Alonso gave him an affectionate pat under his forelock. He was surely sorry to see such a fine animal go, but at the end of the day, money is money, and a horse is a horse.

I exited the stables to find an empty fence post; Lobo had vanished. Worried, I thought he might've spotted Gracia and gone to her. A while ago, I'd casually mentioned my intention to have some new clothes made, and she'd insisted on accompanying me to the tailor today—any excuse to shop for dresses. Thus, I hoped she might've arrived in the square already. That would explain why Lobo had wandered off.

I made a beeline for the plaza. As I turned a corner, I nearly bowled right into Rodrigo, one of Alonso's stable hands. I'd never liked him. He'd had his eye on me from our first meeting, and he always asked about my husband when Sergio was away, like he thought catching me alone might make a difference in whether I wished to talk to him.

I knew him to be a petty thief too. Everyone did, though no one had ever been able to prove it was he who had picked through their purses or lightened their steeds' saddlebags. These were just rumors, after all—rumors Alonso took no interest in. Dependable stable hands were hard to come by, and Rodrigo never stole from his employer. That was all that mattered.

"Morning, Toledana. Lovely day, is it not?" Rodrigo said.

Even the way he talked was unpleasant. He had an unctuous sort of voice that reminded me of the layer of oil that floats on top of the water in a dirty cup.

"Yes. It is a nice day," I said, wishing to keep this conversation short.

"I heard the *San Bruno* sailed a few weeks ago, but I have not seen much of you."

"Why would you see more of me just because my husband is away?" I snapped, before realizing I'd only meant to think that.

"I did not intend to offend. My master informed me you bought one of our horses. Pepito, isn't it?"

I failed to see what business it was of his. I just nodded, wishing to get away but now afraid he might hurt Pepito if I were to anger him. Funny things often happened to people who crossed Rodrigo, though, of course, he was never responsible.

"Where in the world would a girl like you get such a sum of money? I wasn't under the impression your husband had all that much," he said.

I felt the heat come to my cheeks at the insult to Sergio.

"He makes more than enough. He left me instructions we needed a horse," I lied, further outraged at Rodrigo's other insinuation: I might be doing something clandestine for money.

"I only meant—"

"Rodrigo, I'm sorry, but I have to go. I cannot keep Doña Gracia waiting," I blurted as I spotted her and a pair of her servant girls round the corner of a shop and stop just in front of the entrance. Lobo followed them, wagging his tail.

She waved and beckoned for me to come to her, so I slid between Rodrigo and the wall. He did not move to let me pass, forcing me to squeeze my belly in to avoid touching him. He did not say goodbye either; he just stared at me as I walked away, his gaze so intense I could almost feel it on my back.

"Thank Heaven," I whispered as I headed for the spot where Gracia stood.

Lobo barked and ran to me, slobbering and wagging his tail all the way.

"You scared me!" I cried, bending down to squeeze his face before looking back up at Gracia. "I didn't know where he went."

"I fear that's my fault. I called out to Gabriel before he went into the commerce house, and Lobo must have heard me. I turned around and there he was, like a big hairy ghost. He gave me a fright." She laughed.

"I'm sorry for that." I rose and kissed her on one cheek and then the other. "You look wonderful."

Gracia remained gracefully thin, but her belly had grown fuller and rounder over the weeks, and she beamed more freely since Sara was not with us. I looked past her to give a polite greeting to her maids, Ximena and Carlota, but she was impatient.

"Are you ready?" She grinned and inclined her head toward the dressmaker's shop down the street.

Without a word, I grabbed Gracia by the hand and led the way. I giggled the entire time, forgetting all about Rodrigo. I knew how silly I must have looked, but I couldn't help myself. I'd spent the last ten years passing by this tailor's shop and dreaming of being able to buy even one of its dresses.

I stopped outside the entrance and gazed through the open window, unable to charge right in. I'd never gone inside before. It seemed ridiculous when I couldn't afford to buy anything. I'd just wasted many a futile afternoon staring at the front door and watching people flit in and out. Now, it almost felt bizarre to flit in the same way.

Gracia, however, darted past me and into the shop without so much as a glance through the window. I followed only when Ximena beckoned me inside, but instead of finding the tailor, we found Teresa: his wife and seamstress.

Once I told her what I wanted, Teresa laid her sewing implements on the seat from which she'd risen when Gracia had entered the shop. The seamstress then began showing me cloth samples while Gracia rooted through the fabrics on her own. My dear friend had quite the penchant for pretty dresses, and while I was trying things on, she kept going for the dyed silks and the glass beads and the pearl strings, huffing and putting her hands on her hips whenever I turned them down.

"Come now, dresses need some decoration," she said, holding a farthingale hoop in her hand and tilting it from side to side.

"I know they do, but Sergio gave me permission to buy two reasonable dresses—and I mean reasonable," I added when she lifted a long ribbon of pure gold thread.

"Goodness, alright," Gracia huffed. "I suppose if he comes home to find you dressed like a countess, he might be perturbed."

Was that ever an understatement. The horse I might pass off as a practical purchase, but if I were to somehow get Sergio to accept such a frivolous purchase as dresses, I could not make them too fabulous. If I greeted him on his return wearing some bejeweled, damasked, farthingaled monstrosity, his heart might very well give out.

After I selected the cloth for the skirts, Teresa closed the window shades while I stripped to my chemise to begin the tedious process of measuring and tailoring. I grew bored as I stood at length on the stool, being wrapped and poked and prodded, all while Gracia drove Teresa mad with her running commentary on where my ideal waistline should go and what accessories would look best with my chosen colors.

One of the dresses was to be dark-sapphire wool, embroidered with white thread. I made sure Teresa knew to keep the neckline high to preserve my modesty and ensured she would put the laces up the sides so I might still tie them myself without them being front and center like they were on my current gray and brown dresses.

Though the blue would indeed be lovely, I had failed to realize my real color until this afternoon. When I tried on the wraps of soft wool that were to become a black dress, Gracia exclaimed, "It's perfect! Just needs a little pop of something brighter."

She had Ximena twirl a bit of burgundy ribbon through my braids. Gracia then held up a spool of burgundy silk thread, saying if I didn't at least get some embroidery, she'd steal the dress and have her maid Rosa stitch it herself. Vanquished at last, I laughed and agreed to have the black fabric embroidered with the thread in her hand.

The dress's waistline would sit just below the start of my ribcage, so as to make my waist look as tiny as it had been when I was a child, and, when complete, the skirts would ruffle out at the perfect angle to contrast my hips with my cinched waist. The slight dip of the collar would make my neck appear twice its actual length. I hoped when Sergio saw how radiant I looked in this dress, he might forget all about its cost. I almost grieved I'd have to leave it with Teresa while she did the embroidery.

When we took our leave of the dressmaker's shop, we returned to Gabriel and Armando's family tower house in the plaza mayor for a siesta and a late lunch of ham, cheese, bread, and a tart white wine from the País Vasco. While we sat in the courtyard sipping our summer wine, we spoke of baby names. Gracia said she wished to name it Eduardo, for her father, if it was a boy, and Juliana, for Gabriel's mother, if it was a girl.

"Even more reasons to hope for a boy." I chuckled.

"I know, but I had to compromise. We're naming for one of our parents, and Alejandro got a child named after him before he passed," Gracia said, before seeming to recall that Armando's father's namesake hadn't lived out the month of his birth.

She went quiet before adding, "I hope Papá makes it long enough to meet his namesake."

"I know he's been ill a long time. Is there any chance he'll recover?"

"The physicians aren't optimistic, but they're doing everything they can."

"I'm sorry." I fiddled with my dress.

"Thank you. I suppose this happens to everyone, but I want to give him a grandchild before . . . you know."

"I know," I said, taking her hand. "I'm sure he'll meet Eduardo."

She furrowed her brow. I asked if she was alright, and she affirmed she was, but we were certainly thinking the same thing. The nagging fear that her father's future namesake might go the same way as Alejandro's always managed to burrow its way to the forefront of everyone's mind, though, at present, neither of us articulated this sly anxiety.

***

As the weeks passed, Jhasali and I grew more adept at interacting with one another. I finally came to believe she possessed some power that let her transmit sound, for she asked me about things she couldn't have heard unless she lived within the walls of every building in Santa Colomba. She questioned me on songs and instruments they played in town, from the vibrating pluck of the vihuela to the soulful whine of the gaita. She recounted conversations between people I knew she'd never met because they'd surely remember meeting her. She even repeated the content of Masses I had attended and knew with certainty she had not.

Every conversation with her caused more consternation. Though I still told myself I believed her to be a divine apparition, each interaction of ours produced the same nagging doubt. At least I could be certain she was no hallucination. Aside from her money being as good as anyone else's, Lobo had taken a great liking to her, whilst Pepito mirrored her own revulsion every time they came into contact.

Despite their mutual dislike, I enjoyed the freedom of owning a horse. Gracia had permitted me to turn Pepito out in the estate pastures when I wished, so all I had to do was either descend to the stall under my own home or walk to the grounds and call for him, and then Lobo and I could go wherever we pleased whenever we pleased.

Pepito also made caring for Father Manuel easier. Now, whenever I visited him, I could throw the things I needed in the saddlebags rather than lugging them around on my own shoulders or tugging them along the rough, uneven roads in my hand cart. Best of all, I was no longer obliged to tramp through a hundred leagues of mud or dust on my own two feet.

One morning, as I often did in the early days of my foray into horse ownership, I decided I would go into town for no particular reason, just because it was so easy. It was a fine morning: breezy, warm, not overly humid, and sunny, though the sky was marbled with those high, long wisps of snow-white clouds that resemble sea-foam being whipped about by the currents.

I went to see Father Manuel, and we breakfasted on his porch, watching Pepito picking through a bit of hay in the courtyard between the rectory and the church. Pepito tried to bully the church cart mule, but that animal, though much smaller than him, was too tough to be pushed around by some pretty-boy stallion.

Pepe tried to chase the mule, but he wouldn't run. When Pepito tried to shove him, he would not budge. Pepito even bit him on the haunch. At this, the mule kicked so fast I could hardly believe it of such a stumpy thing. He narrowly missed Pepito's face, both his hooves flying mere centimeters from Pepe's muzzle.

I leapt up to separate them, but Father Manuel stopped me, telling me to let them work it out for themselves. The mule didn't move another muscle, nor did he seem keen on striking out again. After a while, Pepito lost interest in picking on the smaller animal. He trotted to the other side of the paddock, poking his head over the fence and whinnying for attention. I rose and patted him on the head, laughing at both the mule's unwavering stubbornness and Pepito's pointless harassment of him.

When I took leave of Father Manuel, I let Pepito stay with his new "friend" and went walking along the main street toward a tiny plaza near the harbor. I passed Alonso's on the way and stopped to admire his new foal: a lithe black thing who pranced circles around her mother in the stables' paddock, swishing her poofy tail and wiggling her overlong legs just as Pepito had in this very same pen. I didn't get to spend as much time observing the pair as I'd have liked, though, for Rodrigo watched me out of one of the stalls.

Once I reached the plaza, I bought myself a sweet roll and walked to where I could get a view of the harbor. I stood at the north end of the square, leaned against a wall, eating my roll and giving pieces to Lobo.

Suddenly, the woman who'd sold me the roll screamed and burst out of the bakery, swinging a broom and chasing a boy who couldn't have been more than five or six. Even at that age, he outpaced her, and she gave up as soon as she'd chased him into the street. He ducked into the alley opposite the bakery and was gone.

I was well aware what had just occurred wasn't any of my business, but I had a nosey streak and decided I might satisfy my curiosity since I'd just bought a cake anyway.

"That little ruffian tries to raid my stores at least once a week. They all do. Barbarians!" the baker's wife cried when I asked her what happened.

"Aren't they hungry?"

"I give them everything I can afford." She planted her floury hands on her hips. "But I can barely keep up, what with all the villages nearby having their abandoned children carted here. I can't exactly let them steal the bread from my own children's mouths, can I?"

I didn't reply. Rather, I looked down at the black wool and burgundy embroidery now stretched across my chest. I felt like someone had walloped me on the back of the head. What a perfect fool I'd been, buying myself pretty dresses while half the town starved. Of course I'm hyperbolizing, but even so, we in Santa Colomba had our fair share of hungry souls. Sometimes I found it easy to forget that, as I'd never been one of them.

Taking my leave of the bakery once more, I headed for the dark, narrow alley into which the boy had fled. I preferred not to go in, so I stood at the entrance and called to the back, telling the lad it was alright. No one answered. I paced the street, wondering what I might do.

When I'd distributed alms with Father Manuel in the past, we'd always done it right outside the doorstep of our church. Any time he'd gone to minister in other parts of the parish, he'd left me with Leonor or given me to Inés, the innkeeper's wife. Though Father Manuel had allowed me to give money on Sundays, he'd otherwise kept me well away from the impoverished to whom I gave it, so I had no notion of where the boy might've gone.

Once I turned back in the direction of the alley, to my surprise the same dirty little boy was poking his head out. This time, he had a few other children with him. They seemed to know I intended to give them something; they'd probably learned long ago to spot people from whom they could expect help. I'm sorry to say up until that point I'd not been one of them.

I walked toward the band of children and motioned for them to come to me. None of them budged, though I could not imagine why. When I tried to approach them, they retreated as a unit into the alley. I told them not to go, but then I realized they feared Lobo, for he remained glued to my hip as always. I took him back across the plaza and made him stay near the bakery.

As I suspected, the children were more willing to allow me to approach when Lobo was not a centimeter from my side. Kneeling, I reached for my purse. One by one, I distributed the coins inside, giving each child a coin in turn until every last piece sat in a tiny pouch or a stubby hand. I smiled at them and said nothing.

When I showed them my empty purse, they all scattered without a word, like a gaggle of frightened bunnies. No matter. I didn't need thanks. I'd been blessed with good fortune, and I should've realized I owed some of it to the people around me much sooner than I did.

Suddenly, I gasped and smacked my forehead. What if the money had been a test? I'd spent so much of this coin indulging myself instead of giving alms to the needy. If Jhasali really was a heavenly messenger assessing my resistance to temptation, my recent selfishness had done me no favors. However, I had not yet failed entirely. I'd realized my error in the end, though it had taken the sight of that poor child.

I returned to the rectory soon after distributing my alms. On the way, I decided to broach the subject of Jhasali with Father Manuel in as impersonal a manner as possible. I wished to glean some information on what I might expect next, for the nagging doubt of Jhasali's status as a holy apparition still wriggled like a worm at the bottom of my consciousness.

Father Manuel was tending the tiny vegetable plot Leonor had started behind the rectory. He hadn't cared one bit about that garden while she'd lived. After she'd passed, however, he'd begun to tend every onion sprout and spinach leaf with such devotion it made one wonder if he thought he might grow her very soul back from the ground through the seeds she had planted.

I walked to the edge of the garden, standing with my feet just on the border of the tilled dirt. "Father, I have a question. Well, perhaps more of a theoretical musing."

"Go on," he said, packing soil around a growing sprout.

"Recently, I have been reading." I hesitated to gather my thoughts. "About holy and demonic visitations. And I was wondering how one might tell the difference."

He looked up at me and arched an eyebrow. "One way to tell if you have been visited by a benevolent spirit or an evil one is if the apparition attempts to persuade you to do something immoral. If it leads you down the path of righteousness, it is likely of the Lord, but if it uses deception or the pretense of righteousness to lead you toward sin, then it cannot be holy. You must always be wary of anything you suspect to be supernatural, though it shouldn't be long before an apparition shows its true nature."

"How long exactly?"

"I cannot give you a specific number of hours or days, but not long."

I wished to ask what I should think if the apparition did not tempt me one way or the other for weeks on end, but I feared that would take this conversation beyond the realm of the hypothetical. In those days, nasty things happened to women who saw visions. Given my own family history, I needed to take special precautions if I were to avoid an unpleasant fate.

"What about other possibilities?" I asked.

"Such as?"

"I don't know. Culebres, anjanas, changelings, anything."

Father Manuel cleared his throat. "Micaela, I've raised you to know better than to put stock in fairytales and myths. If you see an apparition, it can only be divine or demonic."

"What about witches?"

"I doubt there is such a thing as a true witch. Witches are just superstitious women who imagine themselves to have powers—or else wish to make others believe they do."

I bit my lip and tried to ponder how much I might safely ask about a woman with demonstrable powers, but he intervened.

"Have you seen something you believe to be an apparition?"

I clicked my tongue. "No. This discussion is just the result of my readings."

"These readings wouldn't have anything to do with the strangely dressed woman spotted accompanying you in the arrabal a while ago, would they?"

"How did you know about that?" I'd thought Jhasali and I had been so careful.

I attempted to cook up a lie while he explained that being an old man didn't make his ears deaf to the grapevine. I told him the woman was a pilgrim on the road to Santiago de Compostela and she'd been in town for the day. I said I had met her at the market and invited her to my house for a sojourn.

Though I was unsure if he believed this story, he proved disinterested in turning my visit into an interrogation. He let the matter drop, but not before reminding me, as he often did, that members of my sex must take extra care to avoid committing the same sins as our original mother.

Fearful of divulging anything more, I dared not question him further. I took my leave and rode home, feeling like a fool. I wasn't in exact agreement with Father Manuel that witches were just superstition in light of Jhasali's prodigious shape-shifting and eavesdropping talents. I feared in my heart of hearts she was much more likely to be a sorceress than anything divine, yet for reasons I couldn't fathom, I continued to permit and enjoy her visits.

Of course, my curiosity had long ago gotten the better of my judgement, but there was something else. Until my tenth year, I'd had my feet planted unwaveringly on the straight and narrow, but ever since the incident with Fray Ignacio, those feet had begun to stray. I had tried to be as devout as I could in the aftermath of the auto de fe. I prayed; I received the Eucharist; I attended Mass; I went to confession; I'd kept my honor and my marriage vows; I avoided every hint of unorthodoxy.

Yet, from the autumn of 1513 onward, there was always a tiny voice inside my head, and with every devotional I read, every prayer I said, every morsel I took of Communion bread, it whispered three words: "Remember the quemadero."

# Chapter Five

# A BIRD IN FLIGHT

C onsidering the pleasantness of the summer weather, Jhasali and I had taken to walking out to the baldíos and wiling away the occasional early afternoon in the forest. I took more precautions now that I'd been spotted with her, meaning I had to wait for chances to slip away without being noticed. Whenever one presented itself, I would go out into the woods and wait. Wandering that deep into the wilderness set my nerves to prickling, even with Lobo present, but Jhasali never failed to appear when I made myself available to her.

Though I couldn't put my finger on why, being by her side gave me a strength and a confidence I'd only ever known when Sergio accompanied me. With her, I didn't feel so vulnerable, and we would often walk long distances along the rugged coastline on the other side of the river. I sometimes twirled around in the sunlight on these walks, smiling as my blue or black skirts flared and caught the rays of the sun, the light shimmering off the embroidery. This behavior confused my traveling companion, though she didn't make too much fuss. Like me, she was growing accustomed to a certain level of perpetual bewilderment.

Jhasali still visited my home, but only if there was no chance of her being spotted. One morning, she came to call before the sun rose. As the dawn approached, I rushed through my chores and fetched Pepito from the estate fields so we could get out of the arrabal before the roads became occupied.

Pepe had learned to come to my whistle just as Lobo did. He could even snatch a gate latch open if he were so inclined. Witty bastard. Tomás had had to put a stronger bolt on the estate's fence gate so Pepito couldn't escape and let the rest of the horses out with him.

I led Pepito by the bridle, walking between him and Jhasali, as we headed through the fields to the forest. The sheep bleated at us, hoping we had some feed for them. They followed us out toward the other side of a line of hills and only ran off when I permitted Lobo to chase after them. He amused himself by herding them into a tight ball, nipping at their heels and running circles around them as they packed themselves ever closer. I was thankful the shepherds were not within eyeshot, for this would have irked them mightily. When a pair of big sheep dogs appeared and lunged straight at Lobo, I called him to heel, and we all ran to the woods to avert a fight.

While we walked, I pondered how I might achieve my goal for this day. I'd spent much of my recent time with Jhasali cajoling her to learn to ride, for I desired us to be able to take Pepito in tandem to our destinations. Every time it took us too long to reach the coast, I would remind her our journey would be much quicker with Pepito. Every time we had to leave earlier to avoid being out after dark, I would inform her we could stay longer if we had Pepito. Every time she walked out the door of my house to go back to wherever she came from, I would tell her she'd get home a lot quicker if she had a horse, like Pepito. Yet she had thus far refused my each and every imploration. Today would be different, though. Today would be the day I finally changed her mind.

Once we found a secluded meadow, I rounded on Jhasali and told her she could at least sit on the horse. She had sufficiently warmed to him that she would now pat him on the face and even feed him a carrot. Still, she'd never wavered in her refusals to ride him, and her tune remained the same.

"I am not riding that animal," she repeated for the hundredth time.

"Come now. It's ridiculous for you to not know how to ride," I huffed.

"I don't care how ridiculous you think it is. I will not ride that thing. I cannot master this skill by analysis. There are too many variables."

"Jhasali, you have to get on the horse, alright? It's nonnegotiable. I am tired of walking on my own two legs every time we go out together. You can learn to ride, or you can go find another friend who'll have more patience with your stubbornness."

"Fine," she conceded. "I will sit on him, but you must keep him still."

Jhasali moved toward Pepito, and I demonstrated how she should mount. She swung herself up without issue, but as soon as I handed her the reins, Pepito decided now would be a good time to toy with her. He yanked himself free of my grasp and took off at a prancing, silly canter, kicking his heels out from under his haunches.

He slung her around, running under a few low-lying tree branches in a halfhearted attempt to scrape her off. He bucked and reared, gently enough, not intent on getting her out of the saddle.

Snorting with laughter, I jogged after them and tried to tell Jhasali how to rein him in. I also tried to stifle my giggling but couldn't help myself. I was unused to seeing my friend huffing and irate with her hair flying out of its ribbon. She was not afraid. In fact, she was becoming incensed at Pepito's disrespect, and he responded by escalating his misbehavior.

Before I could register what he did, Pepito took off in a full gallop. He then slid to a short stop and bucked, launching Jhasali over his withers. My laughter stalled midair. She flew high over his head and crashed down to the ground, the force of the fall hammering the top of her skull into the sharp rock awaiting her at the end of her plunge.

I screamed and sprinted over, sure she was horrifically injured, if not dead. Falling to my knees next to her, I squeezed my eyes shut and cried out for help, though I knew the forest animals would be the only ones to hear me. Pepito stood a few paces away, head down and ears forward, like he realized he'd taken things further than he'd intended. I sobbed with my head in my hands, not daring to open my eyes for a good minute or two, before calming myself enough to look down at my fallen comrade.

When I opened my lids a slit, the first thing I saw was Jhasali's face. She sat on her knees, hands in her lap, nose not ten centimeters from mine. I had been weeping so loud I hadn't heard her get up.

"You finished?" she asked.

"Oh, God! You're not hurt? I thought for sure you'd be dead," I cried. "That should have caved your skull in or broken your neck."

"Why should such a silly thing as falling kill me? You thought I'd been hurt? Truly?"

"Of course."

"Humph. It's good to know you'll completely lose your head in any emergency." Her tone was short, but her face was smiling.

"You didn't cut your scalp? Not even a bump?" I couldn't stop trembling.

"Of course not." She chuckled. "Now help me catch that beast. I won't be humiliated by a dumb animal."

She leapt from her knees with all the spryness of a jungle cat and jogged toward Pepito, who allowed her to approach, seeming to understand he had taken things quite far enough. I rose slowly, quivering, weak, and confused. She'd smacked her head on that rock hard enough to crack it wide open. Yet, there she went, strolling up to Pepito as if she'd only hopped off for a sip of water.

As I walked toward the two of them, trying to piece things together, Pepito began his protestations once again. He reared up when Jhasali stretched out her hand for his bridle, jerking his head a league out of her reach.

"I know you don't like her, but stop it," I cried, fed up with him.

Pepito brought his forefeet down hard, which forced Jhasali to step out of the way or be trampled. She moved aside as his hooves landed with a dramatic thud on the spot where she'd been standing. I shook my head, wondering if we'd done enough for one day.

I was about to express this sentiment when I caught movement out of the corner of my eye. I turned in the direction from whence it came just in time to see a terrifying specter: an airborne bulbous monster streaked across the clearing faster than a cannonball, hurling itself straight at Jhasali and Pepito.

Pepito panicked and parted company with both Jhasali and the ground, kicking her out of the way in his haste and bolting before I had time to react. He flung himself at full gallop into the woods in the direction of the far-off house, the stirrups flying out behind him as he fled.

"Look out!" I cried to Jhasali, urging her to flee too, so this giant bird wouldn't eat us, but she did not run.

Instead, she did the last thing I expected—she turned to greet this creature as if it was an old friend. It slowed its pace and floated to within centimeters of her outstretched hand, where it stayed put, benignly resting at her side, about shoulder height.

Lobo burst out to my front, snarling and baring his teeth, froth flying from his mouth as he lunged at the hovering thing.

"Stop that," Jhasali snapped at him, and he complied at once.

"Apologies, Micaela. I had a reflexive reaction," she said, as if huge shimmering birds pursuing horses through forest clearings were an everyday occurrence.

Rooted to the spot where I stood, mouth agape, body frozen, I stared at her and the raptor, which I now realized was no bird. It couldn't be, for it looked as though it were made of forged silver. About the size of a large cat, its most basic shape was that of an oval, though it contained many ruts and bulges placed symmetrically on both sides. From some of these ruts jutted thin arms, almost like the folded legs of an insect. In some of the ruts, there were deep holes that appeared to be emitting heat or an airstream. And some of the ruts, positioned in equal intervals all over the body, contained glassy black orbs that reminded me of the big dark eyes of grazing animals like horses and deer.

The thing seemed alive, yet it did not breathe. It seemed to perceive its surroundings, yet its "eyes" did not move or blink. I could not imagine how it remained aloft without any visible effort or why it obviously belonged to Jhasali.

I feared if I moved, I might provoke it to give chase, same as running makes a bear charge. Yet, as suddenly as it had appeared, it was gone, vanished into the woods in the same direction from whence it had emerged.

Flabbergasted, I stammered out a question as to what that thing had been.

"And don't you dare," I gasped, "don't you dare tell me you can't explain!"

Jhasali stepped toward me, and I backed away. I would have turned and run if I'd had anywhere safe to go, but she knew my house and my town. I leaned on my rear leg so if I got the chance to flee, I might take it.

"Please don't run," she whispered, holding her hands up near her face, palms toward me, signaling as best she could that she meant no harm.

My feet kept on taking me backward. I wanted to bolt, but I also couldn't help but wonder about that floating hunk of silver. Caught in a war between my terror and my curiosity, a battle of base instinct and conscious will, I bade my thundering heart be still. It didn't listen, but my feet stopped moving. I let Jhasali approach.

"I will explain," she murmured. "But I am going to have to lay a considerable foundation before I can make you truly understand. If I place such a burden on you all at once, I fear you will be too overwhelmed to comprehend. Yet if you trust me, I will make you see. Come, I wish to show you something."

I breathed through my nose and clenched my teeth, fearing if I opened my mouth to speak, I might vomit. Lobo's deep, rumbling growl rose from below. He'd slipped his body between mine and Jhasali's. The shuddering vibration in his ribcage rattled on my hip as he continued to growl, low and menacing. I put a hand on his head to steady him.

"I have to get Pepito," I said through my gritted teeth, searching for any excuse to escape.

"Let's go get him, then, and I will give you your first lesson tonight."

"No, not tonight. I cannot. I simply . . ." I trailed off.

I needed space to calm myself. I wished to hear her explanation, but I worried that being in the presence of that silver "bird" for even another second might become unbearable. I told her I must have some time to recover before I could learn whatever lesson she wished to teach. She agreed and said she would come back another time. Before I could respond, she disappeared into the woods, leaving me alone to fetch Pepito.

\*\*\*

I lay awake all night, mulling over the incident, searching for any reference in any dark recess of my memory that might help me understand. The silver bird was so unlike anything I had ever seen or heard of that my flash of contact with it had divested me of the comfortable notion that Jhasali was a holy apparition with some hidden message for me. Now, I couldn't make sense of anything. Despising the uncertainty, I decided to drink enough wine to quiet my roiling brain, until I fell asleep just before dawn.

I awoke two or three hours later, fatigued and thirsty, and gathered that I had little hope of getting any more sleep. I opted to go to town after I tended my vegetable garden and fed the chickens, hoping to distract myself from thoughts of what had occurred the day before.

Of late, I'd been trying to distribute alms to the poor children as often as possible. I'd informed Jhasali several weeks ago that I wished her to bring more blancas so I might give them away. She had agreed, saying she had no interest in what I did with elemental metals with pictures stamped on them.

I had been careful to give only what would be considered reasonable for my station and to avoid flashing a purse full of silver around town, as I had on the occasion I'd bought Pepito. I hoped these precautions might ensure my actions would go unnoticed. Father Manuel had taken note, of course, but he'd said he was proud of my decision to dedicate more of my funds to my Christian duties.

Besides him, the only person to make mention of my change in habit was Rodrigo. I sometimes got the impression he followed me when it pleased him. No matter how hard I tried, it proved damn near impossible to avoid "coincidentally" bumping into him. I had never considered telling Sergio of this behavior, though it happened every time he was at sea, fearing my husband might lay the blame for Rodrigo's attentions on me or else do something foolish to him in a fit of jealousy.

I'd spoken to Father Manuel of Rodrigo's unwanted interest, hoping the stable hand would leave me be if his confessor told him to back off. However, Father Manuel chided me, telling me I must repel the unsavory gazes of men; thus, I should remain confined as much as possible and keep my dress modest if circumstances dictated I leave the house.

I'd also tried mentioning the problem to Sara back before Lobo had grown, hoping she'd send a couple of her manservants to frighten Rodrigo. Sara had said she knew Rodrigo wasn't the pleasantest of fellows, but he was a harmless sort. At first, I thought perhaps she was right and I was just being paranoid. After all, Rodrigo had never done anything but attempt to engage me in small talk. Yet, every time he "happened" to run into me, the nasty sensation I got in my gut didn't feel like paranoia. So I decided never to let Lobo out of my sight, though I gave up on the idea of getting any human help.

On this particular day, however, I had locked my dog in the rectory because I wanted to be able to interact with the children without him frightening them. I thought I'd be safe without Lobo if I stayed near the parsonage. Thus, I went out alone, knelt in the plaza outside the church, and began giving the children their blancas.

Not long after I'd started handing out the coins, the children scattered, seeing something behind me I had not sensed. When I turned to look, Rodrigo stood centimeters from me, so when I glanced in his direction, my face was just below his belt. I leapt to my feet, not appreciating the position in which he'd publicly put me.

"You frightened them," I said.

"I only thought you'd have some alms for me," he replied.

"It doesn't look like you've missed nearly enough meals to qualify for charity."

"Your Toledan heart is blacker than those onyx eyes of yours."

"Don't try to be poetic; you only sound like a fool," I retorted, thinking I'd love to see him get poetic with me when the ships were in port.

His face darkened at this comment, and he stepped even closer. I retreated until my back pressed against the church wall. Rodrigo did not make an overt show of aggression, for there were potential witnesses not too far in the distance. Rather, he positioned himself in front of me, and when I tried to get past him, he shoved me around the corner to shield us from the eyes of bystanders. Then he lowered his face toward mine. At this, I no longer strategized about how I might deescalate. I just slapped him with all my might.

As soon as he'd recovered from the shock, Rodrigo grabbed my shoulders and slammed me hard against the church wall. I opened my mouth to scream, but no sound came out, so I threw up my knee and hit him in the groin as hard as I could. He grunted and buckled but didn't let go of me.

Thankfully, Father Manuel's voice called my name from the church door.

"He won't leave me be, Father!" I shouted, finally finding my voice.

Rodrigo released me as Father Manuel descended the church steps into the plaza and rounded the corner toward us, his walking stick thudding on the cobbled stone.

"I should think a steadily employed young man such as yourself could find a better place for his attentions than another man's wife," Father Manuel said to Rodrigo.

Rodrigo stared at the ground, avoiding both our gazes.

"You should have more care for your behavior toward married women," Father Manuel repeated. "Now go back to your work."

Without another word, Rodrigo slunk back to the hole he'd crawled out of, leaving me to catch my breath.

"Are you alright, child?" Father Manuel patted me on the shoulder.

I opened my mouth only to find I couldn't speak again. After a brief respite, I said in a wobbly voice, "Rodrigo accosted me while I was minding my own business."

"I'm sorry, my dear. If you wish to avoid such situations, you should try harder to keep out of the way of men."

"Keep out of the way of men? I was just standing outside the church, giving alms to the children."

"Perhaps you did something earlier to stir up lust in him. An unchaste gaze? I've noticed your dress has become more ostentatious of late. Maybe I should speak to Sergio about having you better chaperoned. I suppose Catalina mightn't object to you staying with her and Cecilia."

"If you don't like the job my current chaperone is doing, I'll buy you a looking glass so you can give yourself a good talking to," I spat.

Father Manuel put a hand on his hip. "I ought to be able to place more trust in *you* than I can in the ordinary female. I have enough unsupervised sailors' wives to keep on the straight and narrow that I shouldn't have to lay one eye on you at all times."

He turned and made for the rectory, and I steadied myself before taking off after him.

"I'm sorry," I said, once I caught up to him. "You make a fine chaperone. I'll try to do better in the future."

He nodded and beckoned me toward the rectory. I followed, trying to imagine what I might've done to lead Rodrigo to any other conclusion than I thought him a pig. Though I argued no more with Father Manuel, I remained certain, despite whatever he said to the contrary, I could lock myself in the house and wrap myself in sackcloth and it wouldn't repel Rodrigo.

Not wishing to dwell on what Father Manuel or Sergio might say if my honor came into question, I thanked my good fortune that Jhasali was a woman. Whatever rumors had flown about the way she had dressed or the timing of her visits, at least no one could accuse me of adultery.

*** 

The next time I saw Jhasali was a week or two after the silver bird incident, on a humid July night. I was sitting at my kitchen table and reading by firelight when she showed up unexpectedly. Her graceful steps made not the slightest rustle outside, but Lobo's tail started thumping on the floor just before she tapped on my door.

"Micaela, I know you're in there. I can see light under the door," Jhasali said, making Lobo jump up and bark.

"Come in." I lifted the bar and undid the latches.

She entered and patted Lobo on the head as she crossed the threshold. Wary, I searched for the silver bird, but it did not appear.

"It is a clear night," Jhasali said, not taking a seat. "Therefore, if you have no objection, I would like you to observe the heavens with me."

"Don't you think it's a bad idea to go anywhere at this hour?" I asked.

"Why should it be?"

"Terrible things can happen to women who walk alone at night. We might be raped," I said, hoping this would make an impression on her.

She looked at me quizzically. "Raped?"

"You know. Some bandits or soldiers might compel you to have sex with them against your will," I explained.

"Ha! They're welcome to try their luck." Jhasali scoffed. "Just come."

She turned and swept back out the door. Hesitant, I remained at the threshold. I didn't know how she rested so firm in the certainty she couldn't be raped, but her certitude gave me some confidence. Unsure if my choice would prove correct, I followed her despite my fear.

We headed down the road away from town before crossing the bridge and making for the sheep fields. I still had serious reservations about going anywhere at this hour, for it occurred to me how dark these pastures were and how utterly alone we were within them. No sound penetrated the stillness, save the occasional cries of night birds and the metallic tinkling of cowbells as a herd grazed and rested at a great distance. Soon, even this welcome ringing faded away, leaving me all the more disquieted.

Jhasali, however, sauntered down the path as if this were nothing but a pleasant afternoon stroll. As intimidated as I felt by this almost luminescent self-assurance, I couldn't help but also feel a twinge of envy. What must it be like to fear nothing and no one? Of course, I didn't understand at the time that Jhasali's lack of fear of humans in no way indicated she feared nothing. She simply did not fear the same things I did, and she showed it as she led me through the fields before ducking into the forest on the far end.

"Wait." I halted. "We're going in there?"

"How else are we to get where I wish to go?" Jhasali called, not looking back.

"I don't want to enter the forest alone in the dark. We are defenseless," I argued, still standing at the edge of the tree line.

Jhasali turned back toward me. "I am nowhere near defenseless. In fact, I am much more perilous than anything you may encounter in here. Now, come."

That was not a request, and her tone spurred me to obedience. Patting Lobo's wide head for comfort, I bowed underneath the low branches and entered the forest, tracing a path through Jhasali's footsteps.

The gloom deepened, for the moon's fiercest lances could not pierce the high-summer canopy. After a while, it became clear we made for the ocean because the sound of the waves grew ever more prevalent as we continued to pick our way through the undergrowth. Eventually, we emerged from the woods and arrived at a high coastal cliff that dropped about twenty meters before reaching a wide beach below, its white sands glowing silver in the moonlight. Jhasali turned right and led us another two hundred meters or so, until we came to an inclined embankment.

"How did you find this place?" I asked.

"My servants did. Listen, I will make one of them visible now. I expect you to remain calm and watch it. Then I wish you to meet it and perhaps one or two more."

My stomach tightened at these words, but I did not wish her to think me a coward, so I kept still. Jhasali left me where I stood and descended the embankment. As she slid down, the metallic bird that had come charging at Pepito during our last encounter appeared at her side. No longer debilitated with shock, I could take a deeper look at it.

I noted some discrepancies between my present and first assessments of it. For one thing, it had six arms—three on each side—which it folded and tucked in like a floating spider. It also had two large holes in its underbelly that emitted a soft hum, not many holes, as I had thought before. I assumed these holes must have something to do with keeping the bird aloft.

As I sat on the cliff observing this strange thing, my fear of it began to subside. My heart and breathing slowed while I watched Jhasali walking along the beach, allowing her bird to tail her just as Lobo always tailed me. Emboldened by this thought, I slid down the embankment.

"What is it?" I asked when I arrived at Jhasali's side.

"*Jhelák*. That is what my people call it. This particular model is an *irik eijhelák*."

"What does that mean?"

"There is no equivalent in your language. Thus, I cannot translate. That is just what this thing is called."

Though there was no proper translation at the time, I must note the closest modern human word to describe the device would be "drone," and I shall use the translated term for the remainder of this tale.

"Is it your pet?" I motioned to the drone, trying to get it to react to my movements.

"It cannot ever be much of a companion because it is not conscious. It is merely a mechanical mind. It thinks, but it does not reflect. It perceives, but it does not feel. It has no subjective awareness of its own, so it is more like a semi-independent extension of my corporeal form than a true comrade."

"What?"

"Think of it this way. I am connected to these things in here." She tapped her temple. "My consciousness dwells in their bodies same as it does in my own. They share their thoughts with me, and I share mine with them, and I can use their sensory receptors as I do my body's sensory organs."

"I don't understand." I shook my head.

She smiled and murmured, "I'm trying."

I remained silent, listening to the quiet whirr of the silver bird. It emitted a soft sound in addition to its own humming, a haunting, high pitch that rose above the noise of the breeze and the waves in an almost melodious way. It was unlike anything I'd ever heard, its unearthly peals too bizarre and beautiful to put into words.

"What's that sound?" I asked.

"Music from my home," she answered.

I then realized the haunting sound, so high it could pass for a whistle, was actually a voice, accompanied by no instruments and singing strange words.

"What do the words mean?" I breathed.

"It is a ballad about an ancient one who's had too much of life, and thus she's said her goodbyes and set her ship on a course to collide with a star that can give her an ideal death."

"How is that possible?"

"You mustn't ask such a thing now. Know only that it is."

"Well, it's horrible, anyhow," I replied. "Suicide is the most odious of deaths."

"On the contrary. It provides a beauty and a peace that only those of us who can freely choose the time of our existential cessation can understand. You cannot comprehend it because your life cycle has a defined and limited duration. But those of us who have an indefinite lifespan will one day welcome an end to our existence, even if we do not desire it at present. There is no such thing as immortality or eternity as your species seems to believe."

"But you cannot wish to end your life."

"I don't right now. I am quite young by the measure of my people, not near so old I am willing to lay down my life."

"But you will one day?"

"Of course. Take my word for it: the longer you exist, the worse forever sounds. Pure annihilation—that is the most desirable destiny. No matter how lovely and wide and wondrous is the universe, in the end, your perception of it will dull to monotony. It deserves to be thought of better than that."

"How old are you?" I asked.

"I do not know the measure of my age in your planet's years. But I would say many generations of your species, perhaps whole civilizations, have lived and died since the year of my hatching."

"So you *are* an angel!"

"Did it ever occur to you I could be nothing you've ever heard of?"

I did not know how to respond, so I stayed silent. Though her tone had been sharp, she did not chide me; instead, she said she would play me a song she thought might be more to my liking. Then the music changed from the mournful, haunting wail to something not only more pleasant but downright familiar. She'd captured the songs of the musicians who often played in Inés's inn tavern.

"How did you get this?" I asked.

"A surveillance drone recorded it and shared the sound with all of us." She pointed at the silver bird hovering overhead.

"What is record?"

"I told you before. These machines can recall sounds and play them back."

"That is not possible."

"Isn't it?" She pointed to the bird once again as the tune continued to play.

The music swelled, making me wish to take a respite from complicated concepts, so I laughed and pulled Jhasali into a dance. She was unwilling at first, but after some hesitation, she said she'd demonstrate how her people danced. She twisted and twirled her form almost into contortion. I couldn't believe the fluidity of her movements, the flexibility of her body, as if she could unlock every one of her joints at will and put it back in its place when she'd finished with it. Her arms moved in front of her torso, behind her back, above her head so seamlessly it looked as if she were suspended in deep water. Even her hair seemed to rise on end.

As I watched her move to the recorded music, a sudden thought occurred to me. "Wait a minute. Is this 'recording' ability how you know when I enter the woods?"

"Certainly." She ceased her dance.

At once the music stopped, and in its place arose the sounds of the conversation Gracia and I had had about baby names while we'd lunched in her courtyard. When my own voice coming from somewhere other than my own mouth rang in my eardrums, a jolt of terror shot through me before it rapidly transformed to rage.

"What kind of devilry is this?" I demanded, shouting over myself as I spoke from above. "You've stolen my essence and used it to make a mockery of me!"

"I was under the impression you wished to learn how my devices function, not teach *me* how they function," Jhasali said coolly.

Her dry demeanor did nothing to temper my fury. "I don't care how they work. I don't care what they're for. You've been spying on me this entire time?"

"Micaela, I really don't understand the problem. My people are surveilled and recorded all the time, and we don't get nearly this fussed over it."

"I don't give a damn!" I screamed, my anger overriding any fear I might've otherwise felt to speak to her in this manner. "I don't care if every last one of your people has one of those musical birds up their ass! You will never ever spy on me again."

I was loath to think what she might hear if she continued to listen when Sergio returned.

She raised her hands. "If I'd known it would displease you so, I wouldn't have done it."

"Well, it displeases me. Of course it does. And I am telling you, Jhasali, if I ever see one of those things around me when you're not present or hear my own voice coming from them again, I will cease to be your friend. Swear to me. Swear you won't send them to watch me."

"I swear," she said. "Although if this is your reaction to something this trivial, perhaps we should return to your house without observing the heavens."

"I can observe the heavens. The heavens weren't made using black magic," I snapped.

"No, they most certainly were not," she snapped back.

I breathed deep to soothe myself before speaking again. "Are we going to study the constellations? Father Manuel taught me a little about the *Tetrabiblos*."

Jhasali crossed her arms. "We won't be discussing any of that foolery here."

Stung, I made to argue, but she cut across me.

"Your books have led me to the understanding that your species believes your planet to be the center of the universe and all other celestial bodies to revolve around it. Is this so?"

I affirmed, and she continued without further comment from me.

"This is absolutely incorrect. The sky is a vast ocean of empty space interspersed with infinite suns, around which worlds just like yours revolve. No sun anywhere revolves around its planets; only the planets' moons do that. Your planet is no exception. It is not the center of your solar system, nor is it unique in its shape or size or positioning, though it is special in the sense that it is what my people call a living world, meaning it is full of sentient life. Do you understand?"

I thought I understood, but I could not bring myself to believe. It contradicted everything I'd ever been taught on the subject.

"I brought this particular drone from the observation deck of my ship." Jhasali pointed to a second silver bird approaching from a distance.

This one was larger than the first drone I'd seen and shaped like an oblong cylinder, with one end of it much fatter than the other. The fat end was nothing but a gaping hole, like the open maw of a whale. My stomach tightened when it neared, but I was determined to keep calm, my curiosity once again overruling my fear.

Jhasali twisted a lock of hair around her finger. "This type of drone can see great distances into space. I am accustomed to utilizing it free of the visual impediment of an atmosphere, but I have tried it here and it works well enough, even if the viewing is somewhat obscured."

Naturally, I didn't understand, but I'd become habituated to the feeling of bewilderment, so I didn't bother to question her. Jhasali closed her eyes and went quiet. At this, the fat bird tilted toward a minuscule point of light floating on the sea in the vast distance, which I could only assume was a cargo ship anchored offshore, its torches lit for the night's work.

"One more thing," she added, looking at me again. "The drone can project the images it sees into my mind. But for you, this will be impossible, so you must use this window."

She pointed to the smaller end, which housed another oblong hole. This opening was shallow and looked empty. Jhasali motioned for me to put my face into the portal. When I did, the empty void blazed with a sudden light, and moving images poured into my field of view.

I gasped in shock. Every detail of the ship at sea was visible through this window. I could see the men moving about the deck, a few mending nets, others placing and removing lamps from their hooks, some pouring themselves wine out of skins—everything. Even the glint of the moonlight on the metal of their belts and the handles of their sheathed shipmen's knives.

I scanned the decks one way and then the other, hoping it might be possible to catch a glimpse of Sergio, though I knew by looking at the vessel it could not be his ship. Now that I viewed it up close, I could see it was a whaling boat, not a cargo ship. Still, so great was my desire to see him I scanned the hard, tanned faces of each of the men, the details of their countenances so visible that every line of their faces, every gray hair in their beards, the color of every pair of eyes was plain as the back of my hand.

Jhasali allowed me to study the ship for a long time before interrupting. "Are you satisfied this device is for viewing real things at great distances and is not some type of illusion?"

I stared at the sailors as they laughed and dealt their cards by both lamp and moonlight.

"Yes," I answered.

"Then let us turn our attention to the heavens." Jhasali placed a hand on my shoulder and motioned for me to back away from the metal hunk.

I did not wish to leave it. Watching the sailors without their knowing was satisfying in a strange way, like peeking into Sergio's secret life. It was not lost on me that I now sat on this beach doing to them the very thing I'd just forbidden Jhasali from doing to me. At the same time, I noted the wisdom of her decision to initially show me something I could understand. If she'd shown me first what she showed me next, I would have thought it a trick.

The bird tilted itself vertically and hovered higher so I might look up into the portal. When Jhasali motioned for me to return to the window, I could see the edge of some great white cliff plunging down for hundreds, maybe even thousands of meters into a gigantic round canyon. Then the vision in the window moved so that it appeared I flew along at a great height above this mountainous silver surface. When the focus backed out, I found I had been staring at the cratered face of the moon. It seemed I only needed to stretch out my hand a few centimeters to touch it.

Jhasali shifted the angle away from the moon to a shining sphere surrounded by many shimmering rings that she informed me was a planet composed of gases, though I figured I'd take her word for it because I didn't understand what that meant. She showed me many features of our universe that night: a cloud of colored dust swirling in a strange spiral that she told me was a birthplace of stars; a beautiful image of two radiant blue suns she explained were mated for life in an interlocked orbit; a faraway white-blue planet she said should look familiar because it was covered in water, though this water was all frozen; a blazing orange sun with several planets orbiting it, each of them orbited by their own moons.

All the while, she talked of the vast distances we viewed through her contraption and how it took the light so long to reach our planet that we were seeing the corresponding number of years back in time, millions and even billions of years into the past. She said what we saw likely had nothing to do with how the thing we viewed looked in the present, and the only way to know the current state of the universe was to fill it with probes that sent images of their subjects' existing conditions through the void to their masters' waiting eyes.

I understood scarcely any of this; I was so overwhelmed with the beauty of the pictures in the window that I heard few of her words. As I continued to stare in wonder, leaning my face ever closer to the opening, I felt a dampness on my cheeks. I was crying.

Jhasali, bastion of kindness and sensitivity that she was, blurted that she did not understand why my people leaked from the eyes every time the wind changed direction and she found such behavior ridiculous. Ignoring her, I continued to study the stars.

She forced me to look in her direction by making the window go black, and I found her pointing toward the sky.

"I am from up there."

I jumped for joy. "Oh, I knew it! You're Our Lady of—"

"You are not comprehending me. I am not from some alternate plane of existence. What is up there is space just as this is space, and I come from it. I lived my whole life in it."

I threw my head back and laughed. "And how is that? Did you get here on a ship that sails on the winds of the sun?"

"Yes. Did you think this to be the only planet in existence to contain sentient life?"

I shrugged. "I'd not thought of it before."

"Of course not; apologies. My people come from a planet that was once similar to yours. It was just in another part of the universe."

I knit my brow. "How do I know you aren't lying? How do I know all this isn't an illusion?"

"Have you ever seen anything like that before?" She pointed over my shoulder.

I looked toward the embankment behind me and saw dozens of those things she called drones gliding over the beach toward us. Some were much larger than the ones I had seen thus far, even as big as Pepito, and they surrounded me on all sides, except the one facing the ocean. Terrified, I leapt back and turned to flee, only to find myself greeted by even more metal monsters. I screamed and fell on the sand, covering my head with my arms.

"No. No! Micaela, come now. I didn't intend to frighten you. I merely wished to give you some evidence I am not a trickster." Jhasali offered me a hand, though I did not take it.

"How? How can this be?"

I sat rooted to the ground, scanning wildly for an escape route that wasn't blocked by one of Jhasali's vultures. Lobo barked in every direction, turning crazed circles and snarling at whichever bulbous culebre moved closest to me.

"I told you they are extensions of myself. They exist to do my bidding. If you believe I mean you no harm, then you have no reason to fear them."

"No. They're demons. I know they are. They'll drag me to Hell!" I shrieked.

Jhasali groaned. "How many times must I tell you none of this is supernatural?"

I leapt to my feet, prepared to run, fight, anything to get away. I eyed the larger birds that looked like they could open some unseen mouth and swallow me whole. I balled my fists and positioned myself to flee.

Jhasali gave me a disappointed look. "I can see I have made a mistake in showing you all these at once. If you wish to get clear of me, I will not impede you. But I ask one thing: take this as a token of my goodwill. If ever you wish to contact me, squeeze the center."

She pressed a tiny white disk that looked like a coin into my hand, though this coin did not shine and appeared as though it were made of stone rather than metal. I took it and stuffed it up my sleeve, fearing refusal might cause offense to the hovering devils.

The floating hunks of metal made a path for me. I fled into the forest so fast I could barely keep myself upright, fearing nothing in those woods the way I feared Jhasali and her monsters. Lobo tailed me, turning back and barking sporadically in the direction of the silver gargoyles, though they did not pursue. I ran like a thief all the way home, sprinting so hard I fainted as soon as I slammed my door behind me. The last thing I sensed was Lobo licking my sweaty forehead while I lay on the floor, consciousness slipping away, heart pounding in my ears.

# Chapter Six

# A STRANGE BARGAIN

I woke on my kitchen floor to find Lobo lying on top of me, his weight pressing down on my chest, constricting my breathing but making me feel protected. The house was still shrouded in darkness. I patted Lobo's head before gently pushing him off me and staggering to my feet.

I couldn't move or breathe without pain from having sprinted such a distance, and my mind was so clouded I couldn't formulate a coherent thought. I stumbled through the dark house, though I scarcely made it up the stairs before growing weak and dizzy again. I half walked, half crawled to the bed and fell into it without even unlacing my boots. Lobo stalked over and took his place at the foot of the bed just before I fainted away once more.

When I woke again, it was nearly afternoon. The sun had been beating down on the house for a long while. The humid warmth inside had become stifling, trapped within the closed windows. Thirsty and covered in a thin layer of sweat, I rolled out of bed and wobbled across the room to the basin. I felt strong enough to clean myself up after a tall cup of water from the pitcher.

Trying to avoid thinking about the nightmare that had been the previous evening, I cursed myself for falling for Jhasali's lies. Of course she wasn't from the sky. Of course those demons weren't connected to her mind. She was nothing but a sorceress luring me in with cockamamie stories until I followed her to the beach for her black sabbath. She'd even deluded me into thinking she could be a holy messenger, and I'd believed it without so much as asking for a miraculous sign!

I balled up my fist and banged it on the table next to the pitcher, but I yanked my hand back and cried out in shock when something fell out of my sleeve. I'd forgotten about the tiny white disk Jhasali had given me. I picked it up and turned it over.

It was round and symmetrical, white on what I assumed was the bottom and light gray on what I assumed was the top. It must've been the top because the gray side was marked in the middle by a smaller, darker section that seemed to be somehow separate from the whole yet still attached. It looked almost like a bullseye.

I was too terrified to try to destroy this satanic talisman, lest it strike out at me to defend itself. So I took it outside and buried it on the other side of the river, placing a heavy rock over it to keep it from digging its way out.

As I continued to calm from the previous night's fright, I became overwhelmed with the enormity of my sins, and a terrible, burdensome guilt took the place of my lingering terror. A little voice somewhere in the back of my mind reminded me of what Fray Ignacio had said all those years ago: the stain of my history made me more vulnerable to temptation than the average weak and corrupt woman.

My first instinct was to counteract this sentiment by running to the church to confess my complicit encounters with this obvious fiend, but I dared not. I could never presume to lay bare my participation in the witch's sabbath and expect Father Manuel to do anything other than lock me in a cell until he was convinced he'd reconciled me—or exorcised me. Nor did I want him to conclude Ignacio had been right about me.

Thus, I got on my knees before my altar, pressing my brow to the hard wood, and confessed my sins to my God for myself. I told him of my innumerable iniquities, my dearth of understanding, and my deliberate unwillingness to see this villainess for what she was. Above all, I pleaded for forgiveness.

I begged the martyr Bárbara to hear my prayer, to please comprehend why I was unable to confess these particular sins to Father Manuel. I implored her to recall we were both women, so assuredly she could understand why some things could not be trusted to the confidence of a priest. I swore if this herder of demons ever came around again, I would do nothing but rebuke her in Christ's name. I pleaded with all my might for a sign, anything to confirm my entreaties had been heard and God had not abandoned me.

Yet for all my prayers, I heard only quiet. For all my supplications, I received no response. Only the silence of God. I figured if this continued to be the case, I must have put myself beyond forgiveness, but I decided I would perform any service, endure any penance necessary to atone for the failure of Eve, which I'd so readily allowed to become my own failure.

After a long while, I got off my knees and chose to fast. I fasted for days, letting nothing but water pass my lips. I suffered intense hunger whenever I fed Lobo or gave fodder to the animals. By the second day, even hay and chicken feed smelled appetizing. In subsequent days, witnessing the act of eating became utter torment, but I deserved it and had to endure it to receive a sign from God.

Yet, as the days ticked by one after the other, I received only the divine silence. Though I focused on meditation and mental prayer, the quiet began to weigh on my soul, and I feared that I might never achieve the reconciliation I so urgently desired without confession. Still, I couldn't bring myself to consider it, for I had no other priest to whom I might turn, and I feared the repercussions if I opened my mouth to Father Manuel. Thus, I kept on repeating that I would confess later if only God would forgive me now, hoping that my merciful and loving deity might see my desperate acts of penance and take pity on me.

After over a week of fasting, I became so weak from starvation I started fainting when I performed my more demanding chores. I supposed it would be a graver sin to intentionally starve myself to death, so I switched to a Lenten fast. From then on, I ate only vegetables, bread, and the occasional sardine. Even so, nothing broke the silence.

I feared I wasn't putting in sufficient effort. Perhaps my faith was not strong enough, my contrition not perfect enough. Maybe God refused to send me a sign of his presence because I didn't believe he would, even if I thought I believed it. Could it be that, in my heart of hearts, a little doubt persisted? If that was the case, maybe God deemed me unworthy to receive the sign I craved.

To chase away any doubt from my mind, I prayed even more, calling on the Holy Spirit every day and asking him for guidance. Rather than erase my misgivings, each day without a response only augmented my certainty that another day of unresponsiveness would follow. I knew this was not the reaction God would wish me to have to his punitive silence, so I tried to use the days and weeks of merciless quiet to discipline myself to greater faith.

As autumn neared, I grew weary of having no one in whom I might confide, so I chose to be more open with Sara. I returned with her to the town house one Sunday after another silent Mass and told her without prompting that the fast I'd informed her of in weeks prior was not going so well.

"Have you ever known the silence of God?" I asked as we sat alone in the parlor.

"In all honesty, I've known nothing but silence for a long time," Sara replied.

I did not ask how long; I already knew the answer.

"What do you think it means?" I said.

"I cannot imagine. I have mulled it over many times, and I suppose it must be to teach me to remain strong in the faith—or perhaps it is to punish my husband."

"Why would God punish you for his sins?"

"Did he not punish Bathsheba for the sins of David?"

I didn't know what sin Armando might have committed that deserved the punishment of Bathsheba and David, but I did not want to pry.

Instead, I asked a different question. "Have you ever received any sign from God in the first place?"

"There were times in my youth I thought I had, but now I'm not sure. I fear the instances I believed I'd received a divine sign might have been nothing more than delusion," she said. "I suppose I must keep waiting. Aren't all these years but a day to him?"

"But what if there's a reason we don't hear from him?"

She asked what I meant, but I didn't know. The words had escaped my lips before I'd even conceived of them, as if someone else had uttered them. I told Sara I only meant God could be deaf to me because of my sin.

Apparently, he was dumb as well, because the deeper I pondered what Sara had said, the more it dawned on me I'd actually never heard the voice nor felt the presence of God—ever. I'd always depended on Father Manuel and the Church to interpret such things for me, as was the custom in those days. Now, in the throes of the first spiritual crisis I'd suffered in which I could not turn to them for answers, I realized the closest I'd come to experiencing the presence of something divine was when Jhasali had appeared to me. This disturbed me more than anything else that had passed in recent weeks. I couldn't comprehend why God would abandon me the first time I sought him for myself. Did he not say, "Seek, and you shall find"?

I stayed the night in Sara's town house, and when I took my leave of her in the morning, I headed toward the church to pray. I carried a purse full of blancas—my own blancas and not the ones Jhasali had made for me—so the alms I distributed would be a true sacrifice rather than the appearance of one. After spending all night pondering my weeks of penance, I supposed it would be more useful to atone for my sins by helping others than by chastising myself.

I stood just outside the church and gave all I had to the children, noting the relief in their faces, and I decided however long the divine silence followed, I needn't hear a word from any god to know this was the thing I should have been doing all along.

***

A few days later, I went to call on Gracia in the afternoon. The trip to the estate was pleasant, and I breathed deep of the rolling ocean waves as their scent floated into my nostrils on the sea breeze. When I arrived, Rosa greeted me at the door, telling me to keep my voice down as I went into the sitting room. Everything was oddly quiet, and I began to fear something had gone wrong in the day or two since I'd last visited.

"Gracia," I said, "I'm sorry I did not make it out earlier—"

"Shhhhhh!" several voices hissed at the same time.

Gabriel and Sara sat on the sofa, staring at a tiny bundle wrapped in a yellow blanket and cuddled up against Sara's chest. She was smiling and crying silent tears all at once, while Gabriel gazed at the blanket as though he'd never seen anything like it. Gracia slept in a chair with her feet up, a heavy quilt draped over her, and pillows piled underneath her body. She looked pale but satisfied. I moved across the living room, taking care to ensure my shoes did not make a sound on the floorboards.

When I reached the sofa, I whispered, "May I sit?"

Sara nodded, spilling a couple of tears onto the fluffy yellow blanket. I sank down at Sara's side, opposite Gabriel, and stared at the tiny bundle. I could just make out a round face, pale as Gracia's, with the thinnest wisp of auburn hair peeking out from under the white bonnet that rested on top of the head.

"When did it happen?" I asked.

"It started early this morning, but it happened very fast," Gabriel breathed.

My cheeks burned in disappointment and shame that I hadn't been here. "Where is everyone?"

"Their own homes, I would assume," Gabriel replied.

"You did not send for them during her pains?" I asked.

"As I said, it happened so fast; it was over even before the midwife arrived," Gabriel murmured. "We'll send for the others later."

"Don't be too upset, Micaela," Sara whispered without looking up. "If I hadn't already spent the night, I wouldn't have been present for the birth either."

She was trying to help, but if anything, she made me feel worse.

"Is it Eduardo or Juliana?" I asked.

"Eduardo," Gabriel answered, still staring down at the tiny face.

Eduardo seemed like a good baby. Granted, I'd known him a grand total of five minutes, but he slept deeply and remained quiet. I liked that. I looked over at Gracia in the chair, her sleep as deep as her son's, her face almost as white as a new sail.

"Is she alright?" I asked.

"The midwife believes so," Gabriel said. "We tried to make her get in bed, but she preferred to be down here where it's cooler."

"Should we lay her on the sofa?" I asked.

"She wanted that chair," Gabriel said.

I wondered why Gracia would not wish to rest in bed after such an ordeal, but I couldn't say how I was going to feel after giving birth. Perhaps I wouldn't want to be abed either.

"Do you wish to hold him?" Sara leaned the tiny bundle closer to me.

I wasn't sure about that; he looked so fragile. Before I could respond, Sara had already passed me the baby. I pressed him to my breast. He was warm and soft, like squeezing a loaf of fresh-baked bread. He smelled like sweet water and clean cloth. I looked down at his pale face and imagined him with a slightly darker complexion and a head of curly black hair like Sergio's. It made me smile. I glanced at his mother and realized her blue eyes gazed back.

"I love him," I said, and she grinned.

I spent much of the next few days in the big house with Gracia and her relatives. Her parents came from their town house, and soon her entire family—father, mother, sisters, mother-in-law, and mother-in-law's new husband—was bustling about waiting on her and cooing over the new baby. Everyone was miffed she'd given birth so early and with no one but Gabriel, Sara, and the servants present, but what could she do? Hold him in?

I tried to stay at Gracia's house as much as I could to assuage my guilt for missing Eduardo's birth. Yet, once the baptism came and went, it proved increasingly difficult for me to remain at the estate. Though Sara and Gracia treated me well, their families were not so courteous. The extended family disapproved of our "circumstances;" namely, me, an orphaned sailor's wife, being treated as a friend rather than a housemaid. Whenever they were around, they did all they could to remedy the situation. The sisters and husbands ignored me. This I could handle, but the mothers always singled me out for abuse.

When Gabriel's mother arrived from Santander to celebrate the birth, I happened to be standing in the foyer as Tomás opened the door. Juliana bade the servants toss the luggage at me and asked why I'd not offered her anything to drink. Gracia's mother barked from the parlor, saying I'd proven just as useless to her, and the pair of them complained about my incompetence right there in front of me, Tomás, and several of the maids. Things did not improve from there.

Of course, I would not have objected to waiting on people of their station, but the manner in which they condescended to me—demanding I serve them each time they needed something regardless of whether there were other servants closer, snapping at me when I entered the room, becoming irate if I failed to move out of the way or give up my seat fast enough—it would bother anyone to be deliberately humiliated like that.

Yet I did not complain or resist. First off, it wasn't my place to defend myself against people of their wealth and status. Second, even if it had been, Gracia was weak and looking haggard. If anything, her condition was worsening rather than improving. With each day, her face grew paler and her voice frailer, and she was scarcely able to muster the effort necessary to thank all the guests who bustled in and out bringing well-wishes and presents.

Gabriel barely left her bedside. A day or two after the baptism, he brought a surgeon to tend her. The man bled her to relieve the inflammation in her still-swollen belly, and he ordered us to keep her bedroom toasty and her rest as tranquil as possible.

The evening after, I took Gracia her dinner while Gabriel and the family enter-tained visitors in the parlor in an effort to keep them from invading her birthing chamber. She sat propped up in bed, nursing Eduardo and crying, kissing his tiny brow and then wiping her tears from it with her sleeve.

I sat down in a chair next to the bed. "Are you alright? You look tired."

"I don't feel like I ought to complain," Gracia said, covering herself as her son detached from her nipple and settled in for a nap. "Every other woman might think it marvelous to have such a short labor, but it was disconcerting to me. One minute I was having breakfast by the fire, and the next I was screaming and bleeding on the floor. I didn't have time to even grasp what was happening. Just, suddenly, Sara was there and then Eduardo was in my arms. I love him, but now I hurt so much."

"What do you mean?"

"I just have this horrid pain in my belly. Like my travail never ended. And I'm so afraid he came too soon."

"Do you think he quickened late? Maybe he's not as premature as you think." I glanced at Eduardo and noted he didn't look like a small baby, but I was no expert.

"That's possible, but it was so awful. I couldn't even make it to the bedroom before he arrived. That's why I slept in the chair after."

I gasped. No one told me Gracia had given birth right there on the sitting room floor. "Oh, darling. I suppose I didn't comprehend how fast it happened."

"Sara's never seen anything like it. That's why I cannot shake the premonition something's wrong." Gracia sniffled and wiped her nose with her sleeve. "I feel like such a fool. Everyone told me I should start lying in earlier, but I hate it in here. I didn't want to spend so much time cooped up abed in the dark, and now look what happened."

She broke into sobs, waking Eduardo and setting him to screeching. She squeezed him to her breast, and the both of them kept right on weeping while I found her a handkerchief.

"I thought I had more time," she moaned, sobbing even harder.

I sat on the bed and put my arms around her. "Don't blame yourself. This might've happened no matter what. Maybe he was just excited to meet you."

"Can I tell you a secret?" she asked through tears.

"Of course."

"It hurt more than I ever imagined. It felt like huge claws reached inside me to shred my innards, and the blood exploded out of me like a cloudburst. I was so sure I'd die right there on the floor. Then after everything was over, the servants cleaned up so fast it was like nothing happened. Yet the whole thing's still in my head, and I can't do this again. They're all going to expect me to do it again, and I can't. I can't. I don't know how Sara did it so many times."

"Have you spoken to her about this?"

Gracia nodded. "She says the memory fades after a while, but I can't see how."

"If anyone would know, it's her."

"She didn't seem as confident as she wished when she said it, and she told me she'd help me if I don't want to endure this again." Gracia wiped her tears with Eduardo's blanket. "What will Gabriel say if I don't?"

"I don't know," I whispered.

Gabriel was a kind man, but I couldn't guess how understanding he might be if Gracia refused to bear him more children, especially if Eduardo didn't make it. Not to mention the pressure she would be under to give Juliana and her own parents more grandchildren.

Gracia pressed her cheek to Eduardo's brow. "You know, I used to pity you because you haven't conceived, but now I envy you. You've no idea."

"I'm so sorry." I squeezed her tighter.

"Just don't breathe a word of this to anyone. Sara is the only one who knows."

I promised Gracia of course I would keep her secret. She kept on crying and caressing her baby, while I silently thanked Christ we could both count on Sara.

For her part, Sara had attempted to aid me during those first few days by providing a buffer between me and all the in-laws without breaking the fragile peace between Gracia's family and Gabriel's mother and stepfather, but she was so enthralled with Eduardo she had eyes for almost nothing else. No one seemed willing to part Sara and her nephew either. Aside from his actual parents, she was virtually the only one to hold him for the first days of his tiny life, and no one dared upset this arrangement until an incident when she tried to hand him off to me.

It occurred the day after Gracia told me her secret. A few hours after the midday meal, Sara sat in a chair near Gracia's bedside, holding Eduardo in her arms. I sat on a cushion on the floor next to them, looking up at the fuzzy bonnet covering his tiny auburn head. She whispered she needed the privy and made to pass me the baby. At this, a shout exploded from behind me, and someone wrenched Eduardo from my grasp.

"You'd hand him to that Toledana rather than his own grandmother!" Juliana shrieked.

Eduardo wailed his displeasure. Though Sara stumbled on the verge of speech, her expression of rage burst forth like the first arms of a hurricane reaching out from the spiral to stir up the surge. I leapt to my feet and fled the bedroom.

Just before I slammed the door, Sara screamed, "You could have broken his neck, Juliana! If you wanted to hold him, you should have asked."

Without waiting to hear Juliana's retort, I flung myself out of the house and down the road to my own home, intent on keeping those people from seeing me weep.

I remained in my house until the next day, hoping if I stayed out of the way a while, the family would lose focus on me. That afternoon, I was dressing to go for a visit to the rectory when a knock sounded at my door. It was so quiet I believed I'd imagined it until Lobo started whining. Then Sara called my name. When I opened, she looked grimmer than I'd ever seen her, which was saying something, and it worried me she'd come herself instead of sending a servant.

"Come sit," she said.

I obeyed at once, taking a seat at my own table.

She took a deep breath. "I need to tell you something."

I shook my head. Whatever it was, I didn't want to hear it. From the look on her face, I thought Eduardo was dead.

"Gracia took a bad turn last night," Sara murmured.

"No, that can't be. I talked with her yesterday," I argued.

True, she'd been frail and wan, but I hadn't thought her in serious danger.

Sara knit her brow. "Childbed fever worsens very fast sometimes."

"What's going to happen to her? She can't . . ." I choked and couldn't say the word "die."

"You need to come see her. The surgeons came again; they say it's not good."

"No!" I jumped up and ran to the door. This couldn't be happening.

Sara and I went as fast as we could to the big house. The whole way, I castigated myself for having thought I could so easily escape my folly with Jhasali unscathed. Now, Gracia teetered on the very edge of paying the ultimate price for my failure to chase the Lilith from my hearth. Desperate, I searched my mind, trying to comprehend what utter insanity had possessed me that I would commune with this thing for almost all of Gracia's pregnancy and deceive myself into believing it could be something other than the evil it was.

When we arrived, I took the stairs two at a time up to the bedroom without a care what the family might think. I'd shove them out of my way if I had to. I found Gracia lying in bed with several heavy quilts pulled up to her chin. She was whiter than I'd ever seen her. I'd have thought her a corpse already if she hadn't been sweating so profusely. The surgeons had bled her again. They were still there, packing a bag full of horrid instruments. Rosa took a pot of blood out of the room as I entered.

I shuffled to the bed, barely daring to breathe as I looked down on Gracia. Her eyes were shut, and she didn't say a word. Kneeling beside the bed, I pressed my face to hers, not needing Sara or any surgeon to tell me her situation was dire. Aside from being sweaty and pale, she smelled foul, like an animal with an open wound.

"Gracia?" I whispered.

She turned toward me with her eyes still shut, moaning softly but not emitting any real words. Somewhere behind me, the surgeon whispered to Gabriel that though death was not yet certain, he should send for a wet nurse if he did not already have one. I bowed my head and wept, holding my breath to stifle my sobs. The soft thud of tears falling on the coverlet was the only sound to indicate my crying.

I started to pray, begging Christ or any other god who might actually be out there to please not take Gracia, to save her for better things than to die of childbed fever not even two years after her wedding day. I did not go home that night, nor did I sleep. Rather, I stayed on my knees in the parlor downstairs, feeling the flames in the fireplace on my back, praying incessantly as the heat receded while the fire died. Gabriel came down and prayed with me, saying he couldn't bear to look at her like that all night.

I returned to her bedroom early in the morning. The foul smell was stronger now, though its quality had not changed. She was not sweating as much, but she no longer moved much either. I hoped her fever had broken in the night, but when I pressed the backs of my fingers to her brow, she was burning up.

I prayed all day long, clutching a rosary to my brow. I begged God to not make Gracia suffer for my failures and to let her recovery be the sign I'd so desperately sought. I had hoped a miraculous healing would be the breaking of this absolute divine silence I'd endured for weeks on end, that Gracia's victory over illness could be the proof I needed that God had not forsaken me, nor could his power fail. By evening, that hope proved false. Gracia barely breathed under the coverlet. Her scent had changed too; she smelled like death.

Everyone was seated in a circle around Gracia for the deathwatch, and Gabriel tearfully sent one of his pages to fetch Father Manuel. People moved in and out of the room, taking turns holding Eduardo, for he had no desire to suckle from his wet nurse. If his mother died while he was so young, he might die too.

Finally deciding to do the thing I'd thus far not allowed myself to even consider, I went and knelt at the side of the bed, putting my face nearer to Gracia's as I leaned toward her pillow.

"I'm sorry. All this is my fault. But I won't let you die, not if I can help it," I whispered so only she could hear it. "Just hold on a little while longer."

As soon as I breathed these words, I stood to my feet, gave Gabriel a sympathetic glance, and left the room. I didn't have any idea if what I was about to do would help. I knew only one thing: no one would pay for my sins but me.

Marching to the sheep fields, I found the rock under which I had buried the talisman, dug up the pendant, and took it home. When I arrived, Lobo whined for food, and I threw him the last of the salted pork before preparing to use Jhasali's amulet. Ignoring the lurching in my stomach, I steeled my nerves and pressed the button.

Nothing happened for long enough that I feared I'd done something wrong. Either that or Jhasali had rescinded whatever this token was supposed to do. Just as I began to give up hope, her voice called my name from my open palm, breaking the cruel silence I could scarcely endure any longer.

"Micaela? Are you alright?"

Startled, I threw the disk across the room, where it slammed against the wall and bounced to the floor.

"What was that noise?" the voice snapped out of the talisman. "Answer me."

"I'm sorry!" I called to the amulet, afraid to approach it.

I'd expected it to make her appear before me or something awful like that, but when it actually worked, it had somehow still surprised me.

"Micaela, this is ridiculous. Talk to me," said the voice.

I swallowed hard. "Jhasali? Is that you?"

"Of course it's me. Who did you expect? Your King Francisco or Fernando or whatever the devil it is?"

Her sourness and ignorance of the current head of state assured me it really was her. I breathed deep, for the words I was about to say would spell my doom. Yet I had been the one to turn my face toward the devil. I had been the one to commune with Jhasali in the wilderness and open my door when I'd heard her voice. I'd be damned if Gracia would pay the price for it.

"Jhasali, I will surrender my soul to you if you'll undo what you've done," I said.

"I am unaware what it is you think I've done, and I don't need to know what a soul is to know I've no use for one," Jhasali replied.

"Gracia—you made her sick. You avenged yourself on her because I left you, and now no one will hear my prayers because you've already sullied my spirit." I started sobbing.

"What? I think some clarification is in order."

At this, I plunged into a tearful explanation that Gracia was dying, I knew it was the work of the devil, and if anyone was to be punished for my sin, it should be me. I told Jhasali she could take whatever she wished from me in exchange for Gracia's life.

"Are you home?" she asked.

I nodded before I remembered she could only hear me. "Yes. I'm home."

"Alright," she said. "Wait there."

The amulet gave a chirping sound and then went still. Even the background noise of the evening songbirds disappeared. I hadn't noticed it coming through the talisman until it was gone.

"Jhasali?" I said to the disk. More silence.

Nearly half an hour passed before she showed. Indeed, it took her so long to come I began to fear that I'd made a terrible mistake in calling her and that I was wasting my last chance to say goodbye to Gracia. I was on the verge of returning to the estate when Lobo spontaneously perked up. He barked when Jhasali knocked, but he cowered once she entered the house tailed by several metal birds that became visible as soon as I shut the door. I forced myself to remain calm when they materialized out of thin air.

"I was unsure of the nature of this problem, so I brought everything I might need," she said, while the birds dropped several large containers onto my kitchen table. "I suppose I don't need to ask whether I can just enter the house and treat her."

"Impossible," I answered.

She arched a brow. "I need to get into that house, but first, I need a drop of your blood."

I asked why, and she said she wanted to analyze a sample of my blood to make certain her medicines wouldn't poison my species. Not wanting to let any of her monsters pierce me, I got a kitchen knife, pricked my finger, and allowed the first drops of the soul I'd offered her to fall into a tiny cup no bigger than a thimble. Jhasali gave this cup to one of her companions, which pulled it inside its hull. She stared at it for a few minutes before saying she could be just shy of certain the meds she'd brought would function as expected.

"Now to access the house," she said.

"What are you going to do?" I asked.

"It's already done." She swept out the door into the darkness.

I followed her down the road and into the big house, which she entered without hesitation, opening the door for herself like she owned the place. No one greeted us or moved about the house, as if everyone had vanished in the time I'd been gone. When we made it to the bedroom, it became clear why: everyone was slumped in their chairs, out cold.

"Hostia! What have you done to them?" I cried.

"Relax. Once I finished analyzing your blood, I had a drone release a cloud of sedating gas into the house. They're only asleep."

Before I could respond, one of Jhasali's birds appeared and floated menacingly toward the bed. I leapt at it, driven by my instinct to protect Gracia, but Jhasali wrapped her strong arms around me.

She held me back and whispered, "You asked for my help. How can I give it if you're doing this?"

I stopped resisting. Instead, I watched anxiously as the living metal hunk stuck a silver pin in Gracia's arm and used it to take a few drops of her blood.

A mere second after it did this, Jhasali said, "Ah. Excellent."

"What is excellent?"

"When you said she was dying, I feared it would be something difficult to cure."

"So you will reverse the curse?"

"Whatever you wish to call it, I can heal her. What kind of hyperintelligent, multigalactic species would mine be if we couldn't even take care of a simple bacterial infection?"

"I didn't understand any of that," I stammered.

"You don't have to. Go sit over there." She pointed to a chair in the corner.

"I'd rather sit with Gracia." I moved toward the bed.

"Suit yourself, but do not get in the way."

She brought that terrifying metal thing to the bed again, where it hovered over Gracia, sweeping her with a white light from its underbelly. I only suppressed my desire to protest because I assumed Jhasali would not harm Gracia if doing so threatened her ability to take possession of my soul.

"This doesn't make any sense," she muttered. "I cannot imagine why this individual has these bizarre internal injuries."

"She did just have a baby."

"Have a what?"

"Come now, you don't know what childbirth is?"

"Oh, live birth. How horrible. Much better to lay eggs or use external means."

I didn't get the opportunity to question that statement, for another bird appeared from behind the bigger one. This one was so small it could fit in the palms of my hands if I held them together. It was cylindrically shaped, with two rings on either side that housed whirring blades and a narrow tail extending from its short, hollow body. The only thing I had ever seen that looked remotely similar was a dragonfly, or perhaps a damselfly. This tiny bird was a silver devil's horse with a long, sharp beak. This fact only further confirmed my suspicion that if Jhasali wasn't a demon herself, she was a summoner of them.

Before I could react, the little devil pierced Gracia with its beak and began pumping her veins full of a bright blue liquid from a clear bag that the larger metal bird had attached to a tube connected to the damselfly's rear end.

"Stop!" I jumped up and drew crosses in the air to repel the damselfly, though it didn't even notice.

"No. Don't touch anything," Jhasali hissed, forcing me back to my seat. "If she doesn't have this, she'll die. I don't understand why there isn't enough blood in her."

"The surgeons bled her, of course," I said, and when she shrugged, I added, "They let the blood out of her to balance her humors."

"Those idiots. Is their goal to kill her faster?"

"Well it does relieve the swelling," I countered.

Jhasali didn't answer, so I watched as the blue fluid pumped into Gracia's body. When the bag drained, the damselfly removed its beak and altered its shape to accept vials rather than a tube. It then injected three different vials of violet, then white, then orange fluid into Gracia's arm, with its companion swapping them out one after the other until the last was empty.

"That's it?" I asked, watching the bigger bird stow the empty vials in its hull.

"Why wouldn't it be?" Jhasali said.

Just as I was about to answer, the sound of footsteps resonated from the floor below. Then Father Manuel's voice called from downstairs, asking where everyone was.

"My God! He cannot see this. I'll stall him, but you must clean all this up," I cried.

There were instruments and tubes and open containers strewn across the bed, and several silver birds still floated nearby. I scurried from the room and flew down the staircase, nearly bowling over Father Manuel as he made his way up.

He gave me a compassionate look. "Child, you seem weary. Everyone must be worn out. I saw all the servants asleep downstairs. Where is the poor soul?"

"You cannot go up there." I winced as I said this, thinking I must improve at concocting lies on the spot.

"Of course I can. I must." He made to ascend the staircase.

I blocked his way. "No, no. Not yet."

"Micaela, come now, you are preventing your friend from receiving her final sacraments. I highly doubt I can come down with a case of childbed fever, don't you agree?"

"I'm not worried it's contagious. It's just if you go up there, that means it really is finished." I burst into tears, and they weren't even fake tears; I was exhausted.

Father Manuel wrapped his arms around my shoulders. "If it is the Lord's will, then it is finished either way. Please don't put your friend's soul on the line."

I moved out of his way, for anything else might arouse suspicion. I already felt guilty for being foolish enough to commune with some unholy creature while Gracia had been pregnant and then summoning the very same creature to save her life. I even felt guilty for not feeling guilty enough. I couldn't bear it if this final effort failed and I'd also prevented Gracia from receiving her last rites.

I turned to go up the stairs and was shocked to find Jhasali descending them. She did not look too out of place, for she carried no equipment, was accompanied by no metal birds, and was dressed in a style that accurately imitated my own. Yet my stomach still lurched to see her face-to-face with Father Manuel.

"Father!" I blurted before she could speak. "This is Juana. She is . . . from Bilbao."

I was aware it didn't make any sense, but it was the first thing that popped into my head. As soon as I said it, I grasped I'd made a mistake, as Jhasali had no idea what Bilbao was, much less how to answer anything Father Manuel asked her about it.

Jhasali flashed her odd smile. "I apologize for the intrusion. I am the surgeon they called to tend her."

"Surgeon? You mean midwife?" said Father Manuel.

I held my breath at her error, but she understood she'd made some mistake and attempted to correct it. "Excuse me. I must have used the wrong word. My Castellano isn't the best."

I breathed a sigh of relief that I'd said Bilbao rather than Santander. Father Manuel thanked Jhasali for her help, and he and I made our way upstairs while she left through the front door. When we entered the bedroom, we found a window open. Father Manuel closed it, complaining of quack midwives who didn't even know better than to leave their patients exposed to the air.

Otherwise, the room was as I'd left it before I called Jhasali: Gracia sleeping, Gabriel kneeling at the headboard, and everyone else keeping a silent watch around her bedside. Even Eduardo lay quiet in his grandmother's arms. No one had any inclination they'd just been put to sleep for half an hour. The servants had come up the staircase after us, and they evidently had not the faintest idea anything was amiss either.

I knelt at Gracia's side. The liquid she'd been injected with gave her skin a horrid green tinge, but it did something else too: she didn't stink of death anymore.

Father Manuel, who'd seen death countless times, whispered to the room he'd never seen a case like this, where the victim looked so green. Several of the watchers agreed and said they couldn't remember when she'd taken on that color, but they all seemed to take it as an omen the end was near. Gracia's mother and Gabriel both wept aloud while her father and sisters prayed. I didn't know what would happen. Jhasali had said she'd done what was needed, but it was hard to believe looking at this sweaty, pale, green thing that had so recently been Gracia.

"We should try to rouse her. See if she has the strength for a final confession," Father Manuel said.

Gracia proved too feeble to be woken, so Father Manuel blessed her and anointed her. He then managed to coax her into taking one last Communion, though she gave no response other than a reflexive movement of the lips. This done, he laid a sympathetic hand on my shoulder.

"You should pray, Father. Pray she has the strength to live," I said, though I barely got the words out between sobs.

He squeezed my shoulder, as if acquiescing to my desire to hold on a little while longer.

I don't know how long we spent praying, several hours for certain, but it was almost like a positive feedback loop. We began to pray, and Gracia got a little better, so we prayed some more, and she improved even more. We stayed on our knees, heads bowed, hands clasped, tears flowing freely, each making our own heartfelt plea for a young mother's life. I felt it blasphemous for me to pray after having summoned a demon, but I figured I might utter one final plea for reconciliation before I faced my eternal damnation.

The night progressed, and Gracia's condition improved so rapidly I almost believed our supplications were working, though I could see with my own eyes that it was no prayer healing her: her skin remained tinted green by Jhasali's medicine.

As the hours kept ticking by, her breathing leveled out, and the fever, which had grown so intense it radiated off her body, finally broke. Just before dawn, Gracia opened her eyes and looked at Gabriel.

"Where is my son?" she whispered.

Gabriel cried out and fell upon his wife, bursting into tears, kissing her face and neck. Sara handed him the baby. He held Eduardo to Gracia with one hand and helped her lift her head just enough to kiss her son's cheek.

"Thank the Lord for his ever-present mercy," Father Manuel cried, then turned to me. "Bless you, child, for having faith even when I did not."

He kissed my forehead, but his words stung me in a way he couldn't know, for my actions had sprung from a lack of faith, not a surplus. Everyone started offering praise. I played along, but now that it was becoming clear Gracia was safe, I feared the loss of my soul even more keenly.

After perhaps an hour, we shooed the men out and helped Gracia comfort her son and get cleaned up. Her sheets were soaked with sweat, as were her hair and garments. She still didn't have much strength, so I held Eduardo while his aunt rinsed his mother's hair and his grandmothers helped her get into a new dressing gown and crawl under a set of fresh covers.

Once Gracia was tended to, I got a moment of privacy with her and Sara. I don't remember how, only that all of a sudden, we found ourselves alone save one another.

"I don't understand it. I feel better now than since before Eduardo came. The last thing I recall was feeling so ill it made me afraid I might die." Gracia's voice was still feeble.

"We called Father Manuel for you," Sara said.

Gracia went paler at these words, which enhanced the lingering green tint in her skin.

"I suppose I ought to make that pilgrimage I've been pondering," she whispered.

"I suppose you ought to," Sara replied.

"And thank Santa Bárbara your fever broke. It was so high you were practically warming the room," I added.

Gracia ran a hand through her damp hair. "It must have been. I had the strangest fever dreams of giant silver bubbles poking me with tiny lances."

Sara said that sounded like quite the fever dream, but I squirmed, hoping neither of them would ever find out that those silver bubbles had been more than just a hallucination.

"I still cannot comprehend how I recovered," Gracia repeated.

Sara brushed an auburn lock off Gracia's brow. "It's a miracle."

I remained quiet, privately wondering if this would be the last time I'd see or speak to either of them.

*** 

Hours later, I stumbled back to my home, desperate for food and bed and wishing I might get them before my doom was pronounced. With a pang of guilt, I recalled Lobo had gone without a meal almost as long as I. Hoping Jhasali might at least give me time to feed him and take him to the estate before she dragged me to Hell, I opened the door to find her seated at my table, feeding Lobo strips of fresh meat.

"I suppose you want to collect your price," I said, trying to resign myself to my fate with a shred of dignity. The devil had wanted me, and now, here I stood.

"What price?" Jhasali asked.

"The price you must expect for reversing the curse you laid on Gracia."

She rubbed her brow with her middle fingers. "I haven't the patience for this. I want no price. I reversed no curse."

"But she was dying!"

"Of course she was. She had a bad infection. And I eradicated it."

"Well, you wouldn't have had the power to cure her that easily if you had no magic."

"*Well*, I have no magic. And I expect no payment for what I have done."

This I could not accept, for I believed she only wished to torment me as a prelude to her final triumph. For a long while, we engaged in a fruitless argument, with her insisting she was only a natural lifeform and me insisting that couldn't be true. To end the debate once and for all, I told her what I had seen on the beach looked awfully like a black sabbath and she'd better tell me right now what class of dark magic she'd used to falsely pass my spiritual tests.

"If you and your master want my soul, you'd better take it now rather than taunt me another second with these ridiculous lies," I shouted.

"Micaela, damn it! I am tired of all this nonsense. You cannot drive me like a peg into an ill-fitted hole," she shouted right back, slamming her fists on the table and leaping up. "I am no demon. I want no soul. I am still not sure I even understand what that is. Now, I am placing an embargo on this sort of talk until you can figure out a way to deal with me in terms that are not divorced from reality. I am beginning to grow truly impatient."

Her eyes flashed and spit flew from her mouth as she bellowed these words, and I feared to press her further, lest she show me the meaning of "truly impatient." Yet I still could not accept her assertion that she was just another natural lifeform because I could not make sense of one overarching question. If she were nothing but a lifeform same as me, possessing neither magic nor spiritual influence, how was it she had all this power? I was unsure if that question fell into the category of things that didn't test her patience, but I tried my luck and asked anyway.

"It has been a long time since my people discovered the means to manipulate and control most of the physical world, including our own bodies. One day, maybe sooner than you think, your species might make such discoveries for itself," she said.

"I don't understand."

"I know you don't, and I don't know how to make you. Every time I think I'm getting through to you, it turns out I'm not."

"If you want to make me understand, let's start from the beginning. What is this?" I pulled out the gray-and-white talisman, setting it on the table before taking my seat.

"A communicator. My species has no need for such primitive devices. I had it made for you, and I was going to give it to you with a more detailed explanation, but—"

"I ran off like a coward. I know." I glowered at her.

"I was going to say I made a mistake showing you so many of my drones at once and making you feel surrounded."

"Oh!" I exclaimed, surprised she'd taken the blame for what had happened.

She went back to feeding Lobo. "I assume you have more questions than this."

"I do. If your people are so powerful they can dominate all the world around them, what are you doing here?"

"Let me tell you a story," she said.

I leaned across the table. No matter how long it was or how little I understood, I wanted to hear it, especially now that it seemed I might not be on the verge of losing my soul. I must make note here that I interrupted this strange story on many occasions with my confusion and questioning, but for the sake of coherence, I shall recount it without disruption, as Jhasali wished she could have done.

Jhasali spoke softly, imitating the fairytale style from the books I'd lent her.

"A long way from here, in a civilization called Sartjyana, there was once a young individual born not a free citizen of her nation but an Ukdah'ni: a genetically engineered laborer eternally bound to the occupation she was created to perform. Like all her compatriots, she was taught this arrangement was necessary for the stability of her society, and any upset of the status quo could bring about another near-extinction event like the ones her people had suffered in eons past. In the beginning, she believed it.

"She did well enough for herself from the day of her hatching. She was bright and gifted, a talented master of drones and harnesser of stars. The world in which she lived rewards that sort of thing, and she rose through the ranks of her society, achieving as much authority as her young age and low caste permitted.

"In this place where no one perishes until they please, the old are free to linger and control all culture and governance, and they have formed a civilization in which there are two distinct classes: the powerful ancients and the oppressed youth, those of us born to fulfill the needs of the Elders. The more ancient the Elders, the more power they have and the closer they are to the most ancient of all, the ruler of young and old alike—the Adoruch.

"To ensure our obedience to the Adoruch and the Elders, each member of the Ukdah'ni is hatched with a twin to provide us stability and comfort, for those who have nothing to lose are likelier to rebel. The twin is more than a familial relation because the biological connection runs far deeper than anything I have observed on this planet. The twin is lover and friend and sibling and life-mate all wrapped into one, sharing the very synapses of her twin's nervous system from the instant the first of their brain waves blossom into being within their joint incubator.

"Because the twins are so close, when there is a cull of our kind, we are nearly always culled together to prevent upset. Yet Aenwi, my twin, did not have a particular experimental characteristic that I and a few others like me were imbued with during our development. Thus, she did not perform to the level I did and was slated to be culled without me.

"The Elders did not engineer me nor indoctrinate me as well as they had hoped, for the expectation was when the authorities came for the other half of my very essence, I would gladly surrender her, as was my duty to the Adoruch. But I did not. I barricaded myself in my chambers and refused to allow Aenwi to be taken from me, destroying much property and killing one or two of the station masters in the process. This one act of resistance broke through the aged, thinning crust and released the boiling caldera of Ukdah'ni wrath and hatred that had thus far only steamed below the surface.

"From my act of mutiny, a revolution flowered, and I became the de facto leader of a political upheaval that would last half my lifetime, rending the youth from the ancients, as two divergent classes warred against one another for supremacy. The revolutionaries became known as the Dissenters, and we waged a ferocious war, intending to depose the Adoruch and place in her stead a leader and a system that offered us better than to be hatched, used, and culled at the whim of an autocrat who likes to think herself almighty.

"Unfortunately for rebellions such as this, they only count as revolutions if they are successful. Ours was not. We were many in number, but still fewer than our opponents and disadvantaged in respect to resources. We failed in our attempts to resist and were scattered all over the universe, pursued by a furious and vengeful Adoruch.

"I took my own ship and drones, which the children of the insurrection had given me, and fled alone with all the supplies I might need to spend many ages in solitary exile in whatever distant shelter proved suitable. Despite my greatest efforts, Aenwi and I were parted in the end. As the originating spark, I would be hunted above all others, and all my companions would be endangered by my mere presence. Thus, I left my love with my closest comrades, hoping even if I were captured, she might at least escape with her life.

"After much time wandering through deep space in maddening solitude, I found a tiny planet in a far-flung and unexplored corner of some obscure galaxy well beyond the territory of the Adoruch. I hid there, waiting and watching for many of the planet's years, until my isolation compelled me to explore a world of primitives—maybe throw in my lot with one—anything to find a companion who might provide me solace after my greatest and most terrible loss."

She abruptly went quiet, and I realized she was finished.

"Your twin, where is she now?" I asked.

"I don't know. We were separated so long ago; she could be anywhere in the universe. Who knows if I'll ever see her again?"

"Do you miss her?"

"More than anything. My people have appendages that allow us to commune in a way nothing else in the universe can replicate. The prolonged lack of this communion has been, well . . . difficult for me."

"What do you mean?"

"If you must know, in my real body, I have many neural extensions that allow me to perceive the electrical pulses all around me. Being without them in this body is akin to you going blind, but even worse is the lack of ability to share synapses with a partner. If I physically connect with a close friend, or especially with my twin, I can share her thoughts and feelings on a corporeal level. It is common for twins to stay connected for long stretches; we go about our business attached to one another, and we learn to avoid breaking this bond. Going so long without it has been more uncomfortable than I anticipated."

"I'm sorry." I knew not how else to reply, for there was so much I couldn't comprehend.

"As am I. A wondrous reward I've received for all my troubles," Jhasali spat. "How I wish now I'd never been the chief of fools, leading them all on to hopeless rebellion. What did I think would happen? That I'd install myself in place of the Adoruch?"

"Perhaps you were ordained to come here. Perhaps you were fated to find me," I said.

"There is no such thing as ordination or fate. Indeed, if I had landed on some other planet or even some other location on this one, I would have been in proximity to someone else I might have thought a suitable companion, and you would have lived and died without ever knowing or desiring to know me because you'd be unaware of what you missed. You only feel like our meeting has some meaning because you're looking at it with your hindsight."

I shook my head. "I cannot accept that."

"You don't have to accept it for it to be reality. I can refuse to accept my home and my twin are lost to me, I am to be marooned on this planet for possibly hundreds more of its years, and the young of my culture are now worse off than we ever were, but it doesn't make it untrue."

"Why can you not leave Earth, then?" I said, trying to trip her into confessing something that would make sense without angering her by asking forbidden questions.

"I cannot do anything that might draw attention. I am guilty of treason; there is no denying that. If I am caught, I'll be killed, and it won't be a pleasant death."

"What can you do?"

"Lie low until the pursuit dies down. In time, I hope the Adoruch's rage will cool. Then I may be able to escape to some other corner of the universe to meet up with my comrades. We could spend our lives on a homeship or colonize our own planet."

"Why haven't they caught you yet? If you've been hiding so long?"

Jhasali sighed. "Space is vast, and the lives of my people are long. It'd take an eternity to do a grid search of the universe. In all likelihood, if I keep my head down and maintain rigorous concealment protocols, they will never find me."

"What of the people still trapped in your homeland? Are you to leave them to their fate?"

She smacked the table with her palm. "Yes, Micaela. I am. Things don't work like they do in your story books, where the knight on the strong horse always beats the evil monster in the end. In the real universe, the monster wins. If you don't accept that, you'll drive yourself mad."

"How can you be alright with that?"

"I am not alright with it, but I already tried to change it, and I failed. There is nothing left to do but look to the future and be thankful your planet lies far outside either of the cosmic realms. If I were captured by the enemies of my enemies, I'd likely fare no better."

"But if you—"

"I do not wish to speak of it anymore. Ever. I have explained to you the situation, and that is enough."

It didn't feel like enough, but I thought better than to push it. Rather, I asked, "How do I know this story is true?"

"I suppose you'll have to trust in the evidence I've already provided you. Under different circumstances, I could offer you more than a few drones and some simple medicines. I could tell you to pick a star, any star, and I'd pull my ship out of that dismal forest and take you as close to it as it's possible to get without melting. But as it stands, I cannot. I don't ask you to believe on my word alone; that would be foolish. I only hope one day I'll be able to give you more."

I didn't pay heed to the final part about not taking Jhasali at her word. All this sounded too much like the fall of Lucifer to be coincidence, and I feared for my soul again, though I didn't dare verbalize that sentiment. Instead, I asked Jhasali once more if she wished for something in return for saving Gracia, couching it in the most neutral of terms to avert her wrath.

Jhasali pursed her lips. "I wish for nothing more than what I wished for the day we met: a friend to ease the pain of separation and isolation. I've been interred within myself for eons, spent so long hiding in my ship without so much as a glance at the outside world. After such solitude, I feel I'm clinging to the last shred of my sanity, and if I don't have someone to speak to, I'll lose that too. I've already lost everything else."

For the first time, there was a whisper of softness in her voice, a hint of vulnerability. It both stunned me and stirred within me a deep empathy. If she'd wished to befriend someone who understood loneliness, she'd made the perfect selection. I smiled after a while and told her of course I would remain her friend. It was the least I could do after she'd saved Gracia—and certainly preferable to the loss of my soul.

# Chapter Seven

# AN UNEXPECTED BATTLE

I spent the following few days engaged in a raging internal war. Though I went about my business as usual, I still pondered the same points again and again, resolving as little as ever. Jhasali's apparent lack of interest in seizing my immortal soul allayed some of my fears, but her wild story of a fall from the heavens had done nothing but confuse me further. Try as I might, it proved damn near impossible for me to do as she'd asked and accept her as something outside of my mental repertoire. Never before had anyone spoken to me about the possibility of such an entity as the one she claimed to be.

I sat at my kitchen table one morning around a week after Gracia's "miraculous" recovery, obsessing over the same set of questions, when a loud banging on my front door interrupted my thoughts. Gabriel's voice resounded outside, sounding exuberant for the hour. I could not imagine what in God's name had gotten him so excited nor why he'd not let one of his boys bring me the message.

I hadn't yet dressed, so I yanked on a cloak to cover my nightgown before scurrying to the threshold.

"What in the world?" I flung the door wide.

"Guess what ship arrived ahead of schedule," Gabriel said.

I covered my mouth and jumped up and down. "Oh, God!" I slammed the door and turned to dress.

"Oh no!" I wheeled around and wrenched the door open to find Gabriel laughing at me.

"I'm so sorry about that, Don Gabriel. Just give me a few minutes to dress, please." I fled upstairs and left him standing in the open doorway.

I shimmied into one of my old dresses before hiding the new ones at the bottom of a trunk—best to save news of my purchases for later—and hurried back down to meet Gabriel.

When we reached the harbor, I first spotted Armando standing near the gangplank of the *San Bruno* and talking to a velvet-caped man carrying a thick stack of papers. Armando looked more disheveled than I was accustomed to seeing him. His chestnut-brown hair hung in unbrushed, loose waves over his shoulders, obscuring his face. His hands and cape were dusty, and his eyes had a glazed expression, like he'd rather be doing anything else than talking to this man with this paper.

Other than his darker hair (which was ruddy brown rather than sandy blonde), Armando looked quite like his younger brother. Same sturdy, slightly shorter-than-average build, same Roman nose, same hazel eyes. But he had a more serious aura about him that Gabriel lacked, and he often wore a somber expression—not a scowl, for it did not emanate an angry or disagreeable quality, though it was just as extreme in intensity.

Now, however, Armando cracked a measured smile as he saw his brother approach. He dismissed the man he'd been speaking with and pulled Gabriel into a tight embrace.

"How have things been on the home front, little brother?" he asked.

"Wonderful," Gabriel beamed. "I'll be introducing you to your new nephew as soon as we arrive."

"What? Why didn't you write to tell us?" Armando said.

Gabriel laughed. "I did. I suppose the letter will be waiting for you in Flanders."

"Congratulations, señor, on your first nephew. One of many, I hope," I added.

Armando squinted and turned away, continuing to speak to Gabriel as if I weren't there. I'd always gotten the feeling he was not as fond of me as I might have hoped. He treated me in a cooler, more distant manner than almost anyone else, and I thought it might have something to do with my friendship with his wife.

Whenever Armando was cold to me, it made me fear I'd inadvertently given him the impression I'd take Sara's side against him (I would) or that she'd complained of him to me (she had). Although I would never have breathed a word to indicate either of these things was true, I couldn't help but fear he'd caught a whiff of their certitude in the very air around me, much like a horse senses when its rider is afraid to fall.

As I pondered all this, Gabriel mentioned something about what I came for, though I didn't catch most of it, and he motioned toward the ship. It took me a second to realize his outstretched finger pointed at Sergio, who stood halfway down the gangplank, holding his feathered cap in one hand and a handful of his dark-blue cloak in the other.

He was looking back up the ramp at one of the boatswain's mates, and he'd not spotted me yet. I smiled as I caught a glimpse of the blueish beard line peeking through his skin. He'd been keeping a hat on his head, as I'd begged him to do before he'd left the last time, and it showed, for his face was not burned by the sun as it often was when he returned from the sea.

When Lobo barked, Sergio looked in our direction and spotted me standing next to Armando. He grinned and waved from his perch on the ramp, letting the folds of his cloak fall from his hand. He stuck the hat back on his head as he continued down. I made my way toward the end of the dock and met him at the bottom of the gangplank. He bowed his head and laid the end of his nose on my hairline, pressing his lips to my brow. I put my right hand on his stubbly jaw and pulled the hat from his head with my left, letting his black curls fall loose in the breeze.

"Cariño, I missed you so much," I whispered so only he could hear it.

He smelled my hair but did not reply. He just covered my hand with his own and pressed it harder to his face, breathing deep.

By this point, Lobo was beside himself, jumping up and down, wagging his whole body, and emitting that birdsong whine dogs make when they're over-whelmed with joy. Sergio squatted to greet Lobo, who kept up that embarrassing screeching, so unbefitting the descendants of Europe's most feared hunter, until Sergio patted him on the head and bade him hush.

It was all I could do to maintain some semblance of decorum while the men saw to the cargo and paid the wages and port fees. When afternoon arrived, I finally got Sergio into my bed. We were halfway undressed as soon as the door to our house shut. I hadn't gone so many months without being touched since I'd married, and it wasn't until I had Sergio's chest squeezed to mine and his lips on my neck that I fully appreciated how much I'd been yearning for him.

He seemed to sense how deeply I craved his touch, for he pressed his body against mine so tight he squished me halfway into the mattress. We were in such a hurry he didn't bother to remove my chemise, only pushing it up to my waist. He thrust so hard inside me that I could feel the wool garment bunching up underneath my back as my whole body slid up and down. I pressed his head into the curve of my neck, where he blew a hot whirlwind into my ear while I moaned in harmony.

It'd been so long since I'd last made love to him that I knew my climax would come hard and fast. I covered my mouth with my right hand to stifle myself but couldn't avoid shouting out loud, and I dragged the fingernails of my left hand across Sergio's back as he pushed between my knees. He reached his own climax within seconds, after which he collapsed on top of me. I welcomed his weight, enveloping his body in my limbs and letting the last waves of tingling pleasure linger in my skin.

"Oh, I'm so glad you're back," I panted.

"I know. Goodness. You were ready for that, weren't you?" He chuckled.

"What did you expect? It's been so long. I was almost desperate."

He didn't respond; he only laughed as he laid his head on my shoulder.

We didn't even eat the remainder of that day. Sergio was ready again within minutes, so we spent the whole night making up for the past months of separation until we were both so spent we fell asleep.

When I awoke, the bed was empty, though Sergio moved about downstairs. As soon as I shook the sleep out of my head, it occurred to me my husband should not discover on his own that I'd bought a horse. Nobody had any reason to avoid mentioning it since I'd told everyone he'd condoned the purchase. This wasn't technically a lie; it was within my rights to run our house as I saw fit whenever he was absent. Still, it was better I get on with telling him. The sooner I did, the quicker we could be done with the fight.

I snuck out of the house as Sergio was muddling around the pantry and went to the fields to call Pepito. When he came to my whistle, I let him out of the estate pasture and clambered onto his bare back, using my heels to guide him away from the fields toward our house.

He broke into a gentle canter, I suspected just to toy with me because I had no reins to stop him, and I gripped his mane and squeezed my legs around him with all my might. Sergio was outside feeding Lobo next to the garden, and we ran right up to the pair of them.

"What is this?" Sergio asked.

"A horse. What's it look like?" I blurted, but I backtracked fast, for sarcasm was not going to make Sergio more receptive to this news.

"This is Pepito," I added in a politer tone.

"And Pepito is?"

"My horse. I bought him from Alonso." I grimaced, recalling too late that I mustn't mention the stableman.

Sergio's eyes widened. "So this is one of Alonso's expensive hand-raised horses?"

I nodded.

"And you bought it?"

I nodded again, less vigorously this time.

Sergio did not say another word. Instead, he huffed and stomped back into the house.

This was not going well, though I didn't know what other reaction I could've expected. I slid off Pepito and led him by the forelock to the stall underneath the house, where I'd portioned off a box for him separate from the chickens. I put him inside and closed the gate, leaving him looking confused as to why I'd called him out to begin with.

I dragged my feet back into the house, dreading every step more than the last and regretting my decision to blindside my husband with Pepito. When I got inside, Sergio sat at the kitchen table, one arm slung over the back of the chair, the other hand twisting one of his curls around his index finger.

"So, I leave you in charge of our financial situation in my absence, and this is how you handle it?" he asked.

"I did not think it an unwise purchase. I need some mode of transportation."

"Why? Where do you need to go?"

"I don't know. Father Manuel is almost seventy; I have to take care of him."

Sergio rolled his eyes. "He can spend his own money to hire people to care for him instead of compelling you to spend ours."

"I'm not going to abandon him, no matter how much help he hires. He's all alone now."

"Regardless, it isn't like you cannot borrow the church cart mule if you must—or catch a ride with Gabriel. He and Gracia come back and forth often enough." The volume of Sergio's voice ticked up.

"I was tired of waiting around. And Gabriel and Gracia stay in town more than they stay in the country house. I need my own mount."

"And your own tack, too, I assume!" he shouted. "Did it ever occur to you we might need that money for other expenses? And now we'll have to feed that nag all winter."

"What do you care? I didn't use any of the money you left me to buy him anyway!" I shrieked, the words flying out of my mouth before I could stop them.

Sergio's jaw went slack before he gathered himself. "What did you say?"

"I only meant that—"

"No. No. You said you didn't use any of our money to buy the horse. So what money did you use?"

"Now, don't be angry," I said, well aware it was far too late for that. "But I earned a bit over the summer."

"Doing what?"

"What I did before we met: laundering," I lied.

"I cannot believe you would wash other people's clothes like a common peasant. You married better than that." He stood and leaned over the table with his hands splayed out on the wood. "How is it you earned enough for that horse?"

"I've saved up over several years. And I supplemented the rest with my dowry."

"I'm supposed to administer that."

"And you administered it to buy your wife a horse," I retorted.

"This cannot stand," he hissed. "We'll sell the horse and put that money to better use."

"No! He's mine. I bought him," I cried.

"You might have purchased him, but you know as well as I do I'm at liberty to sell him when I like," Sergio said matter-of-factly.

"You might be at liberty to sell him as you please, but if you do, I will never forgive you, Sergio. I never shall!" I flung a pewter mug off the table, slamming it on the wall behind Sergio's head and sending the water inside flying in every direction.

Sergio's anger seemed to render him incapable of speech. He leapt away from the table, swept past me, and marched out the door, not even bothering to close it. I stood my ground, fuming that he would threaten to sell the horse I'd bought with my money. Granted, it was actually Jhasali's money, but that was beside the point. I'd married with a minuscule dowry, so this was the first time in my life I had something that was *mine*, not just a thing I used that belonged to someone else. I was not about to let my husband take that away from me.

Sergio did not come back all day or that night, so I ate with Lobo and went to bed alone, as usual. I was still so angry I felt glad he hadn't returned. I did not bother even to go right down the road to the big house, where I was sure Sergio had holed up with Armando to fume about my defiance. No matter. Regardless of how long it took him to return, under no circumstance would I go after him. With that resolution swimming about in my head, I went to sleep.

I woke in the middle of the night to find my pillow wet with tears. I'd been crying in my sleep like a damned fool. Now more furious with myself than Sergio, I rolled to my other side, expecting to find empty bedclothes. Instead, I discovered him sleeping beside me, facing the other direction. I wasn't sure what to feel at this.

On the one hand, I was still livid about his earlier behavior, but on the other, I was relieved he'd not disappeared for days to go drinking with his mates from the ship, as he had after some of our past screaming matches. Realizing, despite my anger, that I wanted him near, I loathed myself for letting him get the better of me.

I gazed sleepily at Sergio, though he was almost invisible in the darkness, and my anger subsided as I stared at his peaceful silhouette. He was so handsome when he was quiet. I could just make out the mass of dark curls on the pillow beside me, now grown long enough to spill over onto my pillow and intertwine with the ends of my hair. I ran my hand through his ringlets, enjoying the feel of them when they were this length, wrapping them around my fingers like soft ribbons. Then I slipped my fingers down his neck and over his shoulder, letting my hand find its way under his nightshirt. I slid closer to him and pressed my breasts to his back, wrapping my arm around his warm body and laying my fingers on his chest.

I didn't wish to rouse him, only to feel this intimacy without it being corrupted by his sullen mood. He didn't wake, but he did roll onto his back and throw his arm over his face, blocking my hand from his hair. I would not be dissuaded that easily, so I curled up next to him once more and found a spot for my head on his chest. He took his arm off his face and wrapped it around me. Satisfied with this unconscious gesture of goodwill, I relaxed and went back to sleep.

I woke again a few hours later, facing away from Sergio once more. Without raising my eyelids, I rolled over and placed my hand on the spot where he'd been sleeping beside me. I was surprised to find not the warm flesh of his shoulder but cold, empty coverlet. Confused, I opened my eyes and looked around to see if he'd gone to fetch wood for the fire or to feed the dog. No. Lobo lay stretched out on the rug at the foot of the bed.

It was so early that the first light had just begun to cast a faint glow over the horizon, so I thought perhaps Sergio had descended to the larder without waking me. Yet a quick search of the house and garden turned up no trace of him. By that point, I could only imagine one place Sergio might be. Rolling my eyes, I dressed and went to the estate.

There, a couple of the staff moved about, but it was still mostly quiet. Gracia dozed before a fire in the sitting room, holding her sleeping child, who had obviously been crying until recently. Though it was fading, the green tint of Jhasali's medicine still lingered on her skin, and I hoped it would not be permanent.

Ximena attended her mistress, creeping around to bring hot broth and adjust warm blankets. I thought better of disturbing mother and child, so I edged closer to the young maid, not daring to squeak a floorboard.

"Where is everyone?" I asked.

"Don Gabriel is still sleeping," she whispered. "But the master and your husband left a few minutes ago. They set out for an early hunt."

I felt a fresh surge of anger erupt in my chest. Sergio had been either on that accursed ship or in Bruges with Armando for months, yet he'd been home a grand total of two days—one of which we'd spent fighting—before abandoning me to go gallivanting off with him again!

I huffed and thanked Ximena before sweeping back out the door. Livid as a goaded morlaco, I stomped straight into the grazing fields, which were mostly empty now that the shepherds had begun the annual drive south for the coming winter.

I'd let Pepito out to pasture again last night, so I stood on a short hill, whistling and waiting for him, fuming all the while about Sergio. Did he think me some accessory he could just discard at will when the novelty of its company waned? He was well beyond the age of obeying women, so I did not expect to be able to order him back to the house, but I had no intention of being so readily gotten rid of either. I'd stick to him like a barnacle if he thought he could cast me aside.

"Took you long enough," I snapped when Pepito crested the hill and trotted over, his pace too leisurely for my liking.

Though he did not understand my words, the tone was unmistakable, and he flattened his ears and flared his nostrils in indignation. I didn't have time to cater to his equine ego, so I led him by the forelock back to the house and saddled him without brushing him first, which only served to make him more annoyed.

When I swung myself into the saddle, I told Lobo to find Sergio. He turned south, toward the leagues of baldíos that stretched all the way from the end of the tilled farmland to the high mountains. The three of us entered the woods and trotted up a ridge. The men had not gotten too much of a head start, for soon I no longer needed Lobo's nose. I could see the indentations of their horses' hooves in the soft game trail as well as fresh horse droppings. I prodded Pepito to canter as fast as I dared push him through the thick woods, ducking under the lowest branches that dipped down from the red-and-gold canopy.

Pepe still smarted from my foul mood, and he expressed his displeasure by thrusting his rear feet out or throwing his head back to knock me about in the saddle. I didn't trust him not to scrape me off under a low-lying branch, so I leaned forward and held tight with my legs. Lobo flew on ahead of us, his smaller profile presenting less of a challenge on the wooded trail.

We ran on until we neared the peak of the ridge. It had not taken us that long, but the sun was already well above the horizon. I had begun to worry Sergio and Armando had moved off the game trail when someone called out from behind me.

"Who goes there?" a male voice shouted.

Looking back, I saw Sergio seated atop one of Armando's horses.

He lowered a crossbow. "Oh, Micaela. It's you."

"Who else would it be?" I asked.

"We didn't know." Armando appeared beside Sergio, seated on the tall red roan he always preferred.

"We heard a pursuer in the wilderness who didn't announce himself. What were we to think?" Sergio added. "You should not have chased after us without warning."

"I'll remember that for next time," I said, checking my anger now that I'd caught them.

"Next time?" Sergio laughed. "There's no *this* time. Go home."

"No."

"You're telling me no?"

"I have not seen you for months on end. I wish to spend these days with you. If this is where you want to be"—I motioned toward the wilds around us—"then I will be here too."

Sergio scoffed. "Good Lord, save me. I suppose you only tracked me down to pester me again about not selling that nag."

Armando laughed, and I shot Sergio a filthy look. He was trying to goad me into turning around, but I wasn't having it.

"If you want to be shed of me, you'll have to outrun me," I said to my husband.

Armando opened his mouth to form what I assumed would be a stiff admonition that the wilderness was no place for me, but he never got the words past his lips. Sergio shot me that impish smile he always gave when he was up for some mischief and took off in a full gallop without another word, barreling up the trail deeper into the woods.

I loosed Pepito's reins and told him to show these old mules the stuff he was made of. He needed no further provocation, flinging himself up the trail after Sergio. Armando chased after us, shouting words I couldn't make out, but his objections were soon drowned in the sound of rushing wind and pounding hooves.

Sergio had a head start, but his steed was taller and stockier than Pepito. His mount's size, accompanied by Sergio's own towering height, gave them a distinct disadvantage in these thick trees. Pepito's thin young body and my smaller frame fit better within the trail, and we soon outpaced our competition, whipping off the path and around a grove of large oaks before overtaking them. I laughed and taunted Sergio, calling out that I thought this was supposed to be a race. His cheeks flushed and he dug his heels into his mount's sides to no avail.

Laughing again, I slung Pepito's rein over my arm so I could tie my long hair back with a ribbon. Pepe took this as a sign to go all the faster, and he flung himself off the game trail toward a more open area to our left.

"Micaela, wait. Stop!" Sergio called.

I didn't listen. I guessed he was just smarting at losing our little competition.

Tying my hair in a messy knot, I kept going, allowing Pepito to set his own pace and choose his own path. Suddenly, we shot out of the forest altogether and nearly barreled into Lobo. Pepito slid to an immediate stop, and I did not realize why until I was hurtling over his neck—right toward the edge of a high cliff. I screamed and tried to stop myself, but I was already halfway over Pepito's head.

He realized just in time that if I flew completely over his head, I'd shoot right off the precipice, so he reared on his hind legs, slamming his skull into my face and sending me tumbling backward. All this happened so fast that by the time Sergio caught up to us, I was already on the ground, crying out in pain and holding my bleeding nose.

Pepito gave me a nudge with his muzzle, as if to say "Saved you."

"Coño, Micalita!" Sergio dismounted and ran to the place where I'd fallen.

I expected him to chide me about how foolish I'd been and tell me this was why I didn't belong out here. Instead, I found myself enveloped in a flurry of warm traveling cape as Sergio scooped me up and carried me to a huge flat stone farther away from the cliff's edge. He sat me down on this rock and took a seat beside me. There, he held me so tight he pressed my hands, which still clutched my bleeding nose, even harder into my face.

He was gasping for breath. "You scared me so. When you turned north, I feared you'd go over the edge before I could catch you."

The incident had happened so fast I'd not yet had time to register that I'd nearly catapulted to my death. Now, as I sat on the rock, my heart thundering in my chest and my ears and my throbbing nose, intense terror and relief welled up in me at the same time. Tears of pain and fear burned my eyes, but I tried to hold them back. I'd been humiliated enough already without sobbing like a child. One or two droplets spilled over the fingers that pressed into my cheeks, but I permitted no more.

Sergio unwrapped his arms from around me. "Are you alright?"

I didn't answer; I just kept cupping my hands over my nose. I didn't want anyone to see it, even though the blood ran down my forearms, dripping off my elbows.

Sergio slid off the rock. Kneeling before me, he pulled my hands away from my face. He then extracted a kerchief from a pouch on his belt. "Here. Use this."

I appreciated he had the decency to stuff it in my hand rather than mopping my face like one would a baby. He got back up on the rock once more and enveloped me in his arms again, squeezing my shoulders with one hand and pressing my cheek to his breast with the other.

He rested his jaw on the top of my head and said, "I don't want you to put yourself in danger to be with me. There's no need for that."

I wrapped my hand around his forearm but said nothing. As the pain in my face subsided, I looked about the place, holding the kerchief to my nose to stop the bleeding. Pepito and Lobo had both backed away from the cliff and now gave it a wide berth, Lobo smelling the base of a tall tree and Pepito picking at a patch of grass near the forest's edge.

"Hello? Where are you two?" Armando called through the trees, still at a distance.

"Here," said Sergio.

They kept calling until Armando found the spot where we sat, taking care as he picked his way through the trees. It appeared I was the only fool who hadn't known the cliff was so close. Armando didn't approach us. Rather, he dismounted and walked to the edge of the precipice, staring down at the forest and the rocky outcrop far below.

When I had composed myself and cleaned the blood off my face, I found my nose had dried up, though the congealed blood blocked it good and tight. Gingerly, I prodded it with my fingers. It felt bruised but not broken.

"Do I have a mark on my face?" I asked Sergio.

"Not yet. But you may later."

"Did you see what happened?"

"I did. That is a smart horse."

"It's why I bought him." I smiled.

Sergio rolled his eyes and snorted. Clearly Pepito's brains hadn't made my husband forget his price tag.

Seeing I had regained my composure, Sergio got up, walked back to where his own horse stood, and took up the reins. I expected him to say it was time to return me to my rightful place.

Instead, he looked at Armando, saying only, "Shall we carry on?"

"We'll carry on home! She shouldn't be out here. And neither of you should've run off and left me like that," Armando snapped.

"I know; I'm sorry," Sergio said. "We—"

"It was my fault, Don Armando," I interrupted.

The master glared at me. "I'm aware. Now, get on your horse, and we'll take you back."

"Come on, Armando." Sergio grinned. "If she was willing to jump off a cliff just to spend time with us, can't we let her stay this once? You promise not to run off again, right, Mica?"

I nodded emphatically. Armando opened his mouth as if he might deny Sergio's request, but after a second's contemplation, he mounted his roan and crossed his arms. Not wanting to keep him waiting, I stuffed the bloody kerchief in my sleeve and strode to Pepito, who turned to the side so I could mount.

With Pepito's body blocking me from the two men's sight, I chanced a look down at my chest and saw I'd gotten blood all over the front of my dress and sleeves. I cursed myself for being so careless, but staining my old dress was a great deal better than plummeting to my death. Making no mention of the bloodstains, I waited for Sergio to lift me into the saddle and then indicated I was ready to continue.

"Micaela," Armando said, "if you're going to be out here with us, you need to do as we say. No more mischief."

"Yes, señor. I'm sorry again," I replied.

Armando trotted off without another word, and I fell in line behind him and Sergio. We hunted the forest for several hours before stopping for a quick lunch of cured meat and bread. The afternoon wore on, warming enough for us to pull off our cloaks. We didn't have any luck with deer, but Sergio and Armando shot several hares while we rode through the woods. By evening, we had a sack full of them hanging from Armando's saddle, and we all chatted merrily about Rosa's famous rabbit stew as we rode back toward town.

"I feared you'd be angry with me for coming after you today," I said to Sergio when we arrived home after dinner.

"I was at first, but only for a minute." He lit the fire before kicking off his boots.

I poured two cups of wine and handed him one as he sat down on the bed. "Why did you change your mind?"

"I expected to have to look after you, and I wished to hunt. If I'd known you were that comfortable in the forest, I'd have invited you before."

"Really?" I said, disbelieving. "What about Armando?"

"You should always leave him to me. But it was I who assumed you had no interest in such things."

"I never said I had no interest."

Sergio took a deep draught of wine. "You never asked to accompany me either."

"I thought if I expressed a desire to go shooting rabbits in the woods like a bandit, you might think me unladylike."

He laughed. "I could have chosen a ladylike wife if I'd wanted one. I enjoy your little adventurous streak, as long as it's restrained. I'd prefer you didn't hurl yourself over any cliffs."

I was suspicious Sergio was so placating because he felt guilty for making such a fuss about Pepito the day before and for being partially the cause of my near-fatal accident this morning, but I decided against pressing him about his change in demeanor. I just smiled, feeling the bruises on my nose as it wrinkled. Pepito had marked my face after all.

As though he'd read my mind, Sergio put his hand on my cheek, laying his thumb on the side of my nose. "I can't see anything."

I was tempted to bring up the issue of Pepito once again, since I had still not gained Sergio's word we would keep him. Before I could broach the subject, though, he kissed me and pushed me backward onto the pillows. Undoing my nightgown, he took my nipple between his tongue and his front teeth and pinched it just hard enough to hurt. I moaned with both pain and pleasure; whatever else we needed to discuss could wait until morning.

Once morning came, however, Sergio jumped out of bed and dressed in his good clothes. When he started to leave, I thought he was headed into town to find a buyer for Pepito, and I pleaded with him not to go.

He told me he had no intention of selling my horse, seeing as I was so opposed to it, but he forbade me from working as a laundress again. He said I was nobody's servant and if I wanted to earn money that badly, I ought to improve my pitiful sewing skills so I could do something more respectable. Fearing he might renege on his tenuous promise to keep Pepe, I did not argue but swore to do a better job of obeying his wishes in the future. Seeming satisfied, he went straight out the door to meet Armando.

The pair of them continued to work in the same manner day after day, rising early every morning save Sundays and staying out late into the evening. It was odd because they'd just returned from a long voyage, which normally gave them plenty of time off, but I didn't question Sergio. If anything had to do with me, he'd let me know in his own time.

These daily absences proved both irritating and—as it happened—convenient, for they did allow me a chance to steal a few hours with Jhasali. Knowing it'd be difficult for us to snatch any time together when Sergio returned, I'd warned her beforehand that when the ships were in port, she mustn't contact me but wait until I contacted her. Now that I knew what to expect from the communicator, I could arrange to meet her at my leisure.

I also soon discovered that the less I pestered Jhasali about devilry and witchcraft, the easier it became to learn about her devices. We'd been able to see each other for an hour or two in the week between Gracia's recuperation and Sergio's return, and during those hours, Jhasali allowed me to explore her metal birds better than I had in my earlier encounters with them.

At that rendezvous, she had commanded the first drone I'd met to float at eye level so I could get a closer look at it. She'd also pressed me to touch it, as I'd thus far avoided contact with any of them, but I was still too frightened. When I'd refused, she'd reminded me that when she'd been too disgusted to ride my horrid animal, I'd forced her to do so anyway with threats of rescinding my friendship. Feeling guilty, I'd sworn the next time we saw one another, I'd touch her drone. Well, like it or not, the next time was today.

I arrived at our prearranged meeting location to find Jhasali already there. When I entered the forest clearing, she turned to greet me.

Before she could speak, however, I blurted, "Is Gracia always going to be green?"

"Who?"

"My friend. It's been weeks since you cured her, yet she's not recovered her normal color. Some of the green has faded, but it's still apparent. Sergio and Armando were shocked when they saw it. Even the physicians are baffled. They've thus far been afraid to bleed her, but if they decide to and her blood runs blue, I don't know how anyone will react. Isn't there any way to restore her complexion?"

Jhasali shrugged. "It will restore itself with time. However long it takes her body to filter out the alternative blood cells and replace them with its own is how long it will take her to return to her normal appearance."

"As usual, I don't know what that means."

"The alternate blood is . . ." She paused. "It's almost like a universal variant. The cells within it are neutral and won't cause an immune response in any animal."

"What?"

She threw up her hands. "I am trying to put it in terms you'll understand."

I rankled at this; it irked me to no end when she spoke as if she thought me a dotard.

"I had to make some modifications to the blood. So when I used it on your companion, it was more like veterinary medicine than something that would work for me," she continued.

"What does that even mean?"

"I believe your people use the word 'farrier'? Like a horse doctor?"

"You used animal medicine on her?" I demanded.

"Of course. Every treatment I utilized was veterinary. The bodies of your species function no differently than those of any other carbon-based species on any other oxygen-rich planet. I cannot treat any of you in the manner I would treat my fellows. We are not made of the same stuff you are. Not anymore."

"That doesn't make sense either. I don't understand half the words you say."

"I am trying to make you understand, but it is difficult to explain."

"It might surprise you to discover I'm not actually an idiot," I snapped.

"I didn't say you were. But there are so many words in my language that have no equivalent in any earthly tongue, and even an explanation of the concepts they describe requires more words than yet exist on this planet."

She paused for a breath, but before I could respond, she switched topics.

"All this is irrelevant, anyhow. You promised me on our last meeting you would be brave and touch one of my drones, so let's see it."

A small drone had been floating next to her the entire time, but I'd been ignoring it. I'd brought Gracia up because I worried for her, but I had also clung to the hope that if we discussed something else, the promise I'd made during our last visit might slip Jhasali's mind. It hadn't.

Jhasali pointed her finger in the drone's direction, and I crept toward the place where it hovered. Tentative but determined, I stretched out my hand and ran my finger over the outer curve of its body, tracing my nail along a ridge around its circumference. I didn't know how I'd expected it to feel, if I'd thought it would burn me or open a hidden mouth and bite me, but it did nothing of the sort. It just hung there, suspended in midair, like it sat on an invisible table. If I had my eyes shut, I mightn't have been able to distinguish its surface from that of a metal plate.

"How do they fly?" I ran my thumb across one of the drone's many black orb eyes.

Jhasali huffed. "It is even harder to explain than the horse medicine."

"Give it your best shot."

"Alright. The drones use the energy of their surroundings to keep themselves aloft. I can even get on top or inside some of them so that I can fly too."

"What? That's—"

"If I hear the words devil, demon, sorcery, or witchcraft, I'm going home."

"What about enchantment?" I winked.

She squinted her eyes, unamused.

"Alright, fine. How do they 'use the energy of their surroundings'?" I asked.

"My people get our power from many sources. The winds and the light of the stars. The entrails of the planets. The cores of our own ships. Energy is everywhere; one only needs to know how to harness it."

"How does your ship have a core?"

She scratched her head and then uttered a long phrase in a bizarre, warbling tongue that changed pitch and tone so much I could not even distinguish one word from another.

"You know I don't speak your language!" I cried.

"I'm trying to translate. My ship has a core of molten material, like the heart of a volcano, but your tongue hasn't the words to explain what it's made of or how it functions."

"If explaining is too hard, maybe you should let me see it instead," I said.

"It's a microstar. It would burn your eyeballs out of their sockets if you looked at it."

"Not the core, the ship. Let me see your ship. What harbor is it docked in?"

"No, you're not yet ready for that." She scoffed.

"Of course I am."

"It took you forever to work up the courage to touch this little attending drone, and now that you've done that, you think you're ready to see a ship with a core of fire and the power to traverse the universe?" She guffawed, her laugh more natural than the first time she'd uttered it.

"Don't act like I'm a coward. I just touched the drone, and I didn't even flinch. I only needed to ready myself in my mind, but once I did, I didn't panic or run away."

"I doubt you've readied your mind or any other part of yourself for a visit to Homeship."

"So now you're a better judge of what I think than I am?" I put a hand on my hip.

"That's not what I said. I just meant you have no idea what you're going to see, no idea what this is going to be like."

"The only way for me to obtain such an idea would be to see for myself, wouldn't you say?" I asked.

"That's not such a terrible attitude to have, but I still want you to spend more time growing accustomed to these smaller drones first."

"But why?" I demanded.

Jhasali groaned and threw her hands in the air.

We argued fruitlessly about her ship and her drones and how much I was ready to see and when I might be permitted to see it until the hour grew late enough that I could wait no longer. I had to leave if I wished to beat Sergio back to our house. Bidding Jhasali farewell, I slid out of the forest, part of me excited to see my husband and the other part resenting him for separating me from my new friend.

It was well after dark when Sergio arrived. I whipped us up a supper of bean stew, bread, and cheese, but he was strangely silent while we ate. After I cleared the dishes, he poured himself a cup of wine and went upstairs without a word.

I followed him once I'd finished cleaning up and found him perched in his chair, his hand stroking Lobo's head and his gaze far-off. Before I could ask him what was wrong, he spoke.

"Micaela, I need to tell you something."

"No. You promised you would not sell Pepito."

He waved the topic away. "This isn't about that. The work Armando and I have been doing for many months now: we did not just sail to Bruges to drop off last season's wool. We also went to Antwerp and took out loans so we could invest a substantial sum in a larger nao than the one we've got. The final correspondence arrived from Sevilla this morning. We are to sail for the New World."

"What?" I said, a note of panic in my voice.

"The permits to sail a couple ships' worth of cargo to La Española are being drawn up as we speak. We embark for Sevilla in March."

"So you lied to me about what you were doing all those months?" I demanded.

"I did not lie. I simply didn't correct you when you assumed we were doing nothing but hauling wool and meeting with Flemish merchants."

"But you should have told me everything!"

"I told you what you needed to know at the time."

"Where does all this leave you?" I asked, already knowing the answer.

"Where else? I am to sail."

I sank into a chair opposite him. "How long will you be gone?"

"We'll leave Sevilla around August and return there the following spring. So at least a year, maybe two." His speech was calm enough, but I caught a note of pain in his tone.

"Two years?" My voice was shrill, and my heart raced. "No! No! No! This cannot happen. You've never been gone nearly that long before."

"That's because we've never had business so far away before. You think other wives of men who sail to the Far East or the New World don't have to learn to make do?"

"I don't know. What have they got to do with me?"

"Micaela, I don't like the idea of being apart from you for so long, either."

"Then why do you have to go?" I shouted, on the verge of sobbing.

"Because Armando needs me. Not only that, but these long voyages are profitable. I'll be paid even better than before, and I might be promoted to shipmaster soon. Finally!"

I lowered my voice. "I know you've been waiting for that position a long time, but is it really worth—"

"Yes. If I do well at mastering one of the vessels, when Armando retires from the sea, he'll be able to convince his investors to let me sail the fleet. Think of it. If I spend a few years commanding the fleet, we'll have enough money that I won't ever need to leave you again."

"But you're leaving me now!"

"I'm not leaving right now. As I said, we aren't sailing until spring."

"So I have a few more months with you before I'm never to see you again?" I snapped.

He sighed. "Don't be melodramatic."

"Why does Armando have to go? Why can't he send someone else so you both can stay?"

"He's never been one to trust his money to less capable hands. As long as he's fit, he'll sail. Regardless, how does this surprise you? How many times have you heard us speak of our wish to see the colonies? It's the other side of the world, Mica."

It was true; Sergio and Armando had harped about all the wondrous rumors of the New World a thousand times before, but I'd always thought it empty chatter. I'd never for an instant taken it seriously.

"Apparently, you both wish to be on the other side of the world more than you wish to be home with your wives," I said.

"Now," he replied, a hint of anger in his voice, "I expected you to be unhappy with this news, but I say again, all sailors' wives must learn to live with their husbands' long absences. I don't know how you believed you'd be spared forever. Did you think Armando or I would be satisfied with running cargo back and forth from Flanders until we die?"

I opened my mouth to argue, but he cut across me. "I don't wish to spend the next few months fighting about this. It is done. Please, let's speak no more of it. Let's just enjoy the time we do have together."

His tone was gentle but final, and any further argument from me would serve no purpose but to anger him. Of course, I had no intention of letting him sail without a fight, but I decided to save that for later.

***

During the weeks after Sergio informed me of his plans, I made subtle arguments against his departure. I reminded him of the terrible wound he'd received fighting corsairs who'd tried to commandeer his ship many years before we'd met. I dropped the words "hurricane" and "disease" into every conversation possible.

I even considered informing him of Rodrigo's behavior during his absences and insinuating I might initiate an affair with the stable hand if I were deprived of my husband for years on end, though I ultimately thought better of this strategy. The one thing I avoided was starting an actual fight, for confronting Sergio outright about his intentions would only further his resolve to carry them out.

However, one evening, as I was curled in my chair attempting to mend a tear in my husband's cape, he entered and laid a piece of paper on my lap. Then he handed me an inkwell with a quill already inside it.

"I need you to sign this," he said.

"What is it?"

"Doesn't matter. Just sign it."

I perused the form as I reached for the quill. Sergio himself had gotten me into the habit of never signing something unless I knew what it said.

"Will you hurry? I don't have time for this," he snapped.

"Sergio! This is an authorization letter stating I give you my permission to travel to the New World. I was unaware you need my consent."

"I don't need your consent. It's not an authorization letter. It's only your acknowledgment that we're not separating, so Armando and I can satisfy the authorities that the married men in the crew aren't abandoning our wives, financially or otherwise."

"But you *are* abandoning me!" I shouted.

"No, I am not. I am not a migrant. I am not a conquistador. I'm taking goods to the New World, turning around, and coming back. I shouldn't have to deal with this ridiculous nonsense at all. I get so sick of these accursed bureaucrats forcing us to jump through hoop after hoop so they can wallow in their own petty authority. Now sign it."

"No. I don't want to become a viuda de los vivos. I don't agree that you're not abandoning me. And I won't sign this ridiculous letter." I rose from my seat.

"You will sign it, one way or another. Don't be difficult," he growled.

I shook my head without a word, determined to refuse no matter what.

So began the longest and fiercest conflict of our entire marriage. Sergio ranted for hours about how I had forgotten my place, how I should respect his authority as the head of our household, and how ridiculous it was for him to have to ask me to sign anything. I did not budge. He upbraided me for foolishness and rebelliousness and stubbornness. Yet I did not cave. He pleaded with me that if I wished him to maintain his position as Armando's right hand, I would obey his wishes. He accused me of hating him. Still, I would not sign.

How could I? Sergio would be on the other side of the world for two years. On top of that, the crossing was so fraught with peril that almost every sailor drew up his final will and testament before departing. I'd never recover if I received the dread news that his ship had sunk or that he'd died of some horrid foreign disease.

We stayed up all night in a towering screaming match that assuredly carried through the arrabal. We shouted ourselves hoarse, but it resulted in nothing more than a continued stalemate. Sergio would not accept my refusals, and I would not sign. When morning came at last, he swept out the door in a roiling fury, leaving me alone.

I had been quite afraid throughout our confrontation. Sailors' reputation for being a rough bunch was well-earned, but in all the time Sergio and I had been together, he had never once hit me. That night, he'd been so furious I'd feared he might break his streak of nonviolence. He'd managed to restrain himself toward me, but he'd struck the wall many times and slung a chair across the room. I, in turn, had thrown several pewter dishes at him and broken a pitcher Armando had given him—the only glass item we owned.

Poor Lobo had been so distraught I'd had to put him outside so we could continue shouting without further upsetting him, but he stood at the door and barked all night until Sergio let him in when he left. Lobo now sat at my bedside, and I let my arm dangle over the edge of the mattress so I could pat him while he lay on the floor, agitated and panting, his head held high and his ears erect.

With my fingers in Lobo's fur, I fell asleep for a few hours but awoke when Sergio returned that afternoon. I did not dare say anything. After everything that had happened the previous night, I was no longer afraid he would attack me, but he had plenty of ways to punish me aside from that.

From that day on, he refused to share a bed with me, spending his nights out with Marcos and Pablo or at whichever house Armando occupied. He did not speak to me unless it was to admonish me to sign the letter. He reclaimed all the money in the house and refused to give me any funds, not even to go to the market, so I often went hungry when he ate somewhere else.

Sergio also got Armando and Father Manuel involved. Armando told me he did not appreciate my interfering with his business, and Father Manuel reminded me God had ordained for me to submit to my husband in all things, even if I did not agree with them. I knew it was a sin to deny the will of my husband, but keeping Sergio safe was worth whatever penance might be required for my insubordination, so I still refused.

Even Sara, the one person I thought might be on my side, proved of no help. I sometimes called on her for supper when Sergio left me hungry. When I complained to her of our conflict, instead of agreeing with me about the insanity of this New World nonsense, she told me the prize of Sergio's company wasn't worth the pain I was enduring to win it and I'd be better off rid of him. At the time, I'd thought she was applying her own feelings about Armando to Sergio's and my situation, so I didn't heed her advice and continued fighting a war I knew I couldn't win.

Jhasali had little clue about our weekslong conflict. After the battle had commenced, I'd used the tiny disk to warn her she might not see me for a while, but I would call on her when I could. She and I passed several weeks without speaking. Sometimes, I worried she'd forget about me if we went too long without contact. I also wondered what she might think to see me in such a state, if she'd judge me weak and foolish or if she'd tell me I cared too much. As boorishly as Sergio had been behaving of late, I wondered if I did.

One sleety, frigid evening perhaps halfway through Advent, I spent a long while down in the stall brushing and feeding Pepito. Sergio had not lifted a finger to help with Pepe since he'd returned home. He said if I could manage to purchase the horse, I could manage to care for him, though I noticed my husband had no problem taking him out on the hunt or to town whenever it pleased him.

I left the stall freezing, covered in hay, and trying not to feel bitter that Sergio had ridden Pepito to town that very day and had not even bothered to groom him once he'd returned. Opening the kitchen door, I peered through the threshold.

Sergio sat next to the fire, leaned back on the two hind legs of his chair, boots on the table, a leather-bound book in his left hand. He had a quill in his right hand and was scribbling all over the pages. He had to know I'd returned from outside. The blurry light from the unimpeded doorway spilled across the room and cast the shadows away from the table where he sat, but he did not acknowledge my presence. As I entered, he stopped writing and stared at the book, his eyes darting fast, as if focusing with all their might on each word.

I lifted my skirts to keep them noiseless and crept farther into the kitchen. I did not wish to disturb his reading nor to start a massive fight that would do me no good. Yet I still couldn't subdue the thing I was so desperately bursting to say.

"You cannot leave me for two years," I blurted, after glaring at him in silence for a long time.

Sergio did not look up, but his eyes stopped moving at my words. "Certainly I can. And certainly I shall."

"You will not. I forbid it. I will never sign that stupid letter!"

I knew instantly I'd made a mistake. His eyes rose to meet mine, and there was a coldness in them I'd always known lay dormant there, reserved for others but not for me. Taking his feet from the table, he gave a mirthless chuckle.

"And on whose authority do you forbid me to do anything?" he asked in a distant, apathetic tone, as if requesting directions from a stranger. "That 'stupid letter' is an illegitimate hurdle that only exists because certain men run off and shirk their financial responsibilities. If not for them, we wouldn't be having this conversation."

I couldn't think of anything to say in reply. Sergio, however, had plenty to say.

"I give you more freedom than is my obligation. I allow Father Manuel to serve as your chaperone. I permit you, perhaps against my better judgement, to hold the purse strings of this house in my stead. Don't you understand how much trust I place in you?"

"I do, but—"

"But nothing. I won't let you think for one minute you have the right to command me. Only Armando, my king, and God have that power."

"I don't think I can command you. I only want you to stay. Don't you love me at all?"

At this, he slammed the book on the table with such force I thought he'd thrown it at me. The crack of cover hitting wood made me jump and duck.

"Love won't pay our debts! It won't feed that horse you so unwisely bought and refuse to consent that I sell. It won't keep wood in the stove or the roof from leaking. I don't deny I love you, but you don't know what it's like to bear the financial burden of this household. I must go on this voyage, but more than that, I want to go on it. No love can keep me from it. I know you lack the capacity to comprehend this, so I won't make you try."

"Take me with you then."

Sergio let out a real guffaw. "You know what sort of woman makes that crossing."

"You would accompany me."

"And what use does the crew have for you? Are you going to dive down and patch the hull if it leaks? Will you man the cannons if we're attacked—or should I say 'woman' the cannons?" His black eyes gleamed at the absurdity, and his lips curled in a fresh peal of laughter.

"I could do something. It isn't like a woman was never a passenger before."

"I will hear no more of this!" he barked, pulling the wrinkled, folded letter out of his book and slamming the paper so hard on the table it made me jump again. "I have decided. If you do not sign, I will sell Pepito, I will forge your signature, and I will have you shut up in a convent from the time I leave until the time I return."

"You cannot do that!"

"Yes, I can. Father Manuel thinks it'll be good for you. Remind you of your place."

I was defeated; I couldn't continue this battle with no one on my side. I dropped into the chair across from Sergio and signed the letter. Once I did, he ripped the paper from under my hand and stuffed it back into his book. I began to weep, turning away in shame so he would not see the tears that streamed from my unwilling eyes.

It is a strange thing to hate the one you love, but for the first time in our marriage, a burning revulsion for my husband radiated out of my beating heart, hot as the tears that dripped from my jaw to my breast.

Sergio seemed to have realized he'd been crueler than he'd intended, for his voice was tender when he murmured, "Micalita, buck up. I was beaten bloody on a regular basis from the time I was a little child, and I never did this much. caterwauling."

He was trying to comfort me in his own fumbling way, but, of course, this was the exact wrong thing to say. I threw my hands up in exasperation, leapt from the table, and swept back out the door. He did not come after me. I hadn't expected him to, though I did desire it.

Back in Pepito's stall, I curled in a trough already cleaned of hay. Pepe rummaged through the bale in the other manger, picking apart the tufts of pungent dried grass and tossing the parts he didn't like to the ground. I sat there and cried silent tears that came every so often as I listened to the rustling of hay and the gentle clomp of hooves and the tapping of the freezing rain on the roof. It sounded like it might be turning to snow.

Sergio's condescension rang in my ears, and it made me yearn for the times when I'd been new and exciting and he hadn't thought the very idea of having me onboard his ship so ludicrous. In fact, the autumn before we'd married, he'd snuck me onto the *San Bruno*.

I'd never been on a ship before. I'd only seen them from the docks, so I'd begged Sergio to bring me onto his. He was hesitant, for usually only the masters' wives, female passengers, and women of the most unsavory sort were allowed onto the vessel. Yet I'd cajoled him into concession, and he'd reluctantly agreed to meet me at sundown soon after the *San Bruno* made its final berth of the season.

Night was falling fast that crisp evening, and I giggled as Sergio led me up the gangplank, shushing me the entire time. When we reached the ship's railing, he rounded on me.

"Quiet, Micaela. Really, I hope you realize the ship's master will probably have me whipped for bringing you here."

"Oh." I stopped short of the deck. I hadn't realized the penalty might be that serious. "We should go then. I don't need to see a silly boat."

I pulled my hand off the railing and turned to walk down the gangplank.

Sergio grabbed my wrist. "No. We don't have to go. Nobody is here but Marcos and Pablo. Just keep it down."

"I don't want to get you flogged."

"I never let that stop me from getting into trouble before. I don't intend to start now."

He smiled with the tip of his tongue between his teeth. His casual demeanor made me question if he might truly be lashed or if this was just a ruse to make me keep my voice down. I was unaware, at the time, that the owner of the fleet was Armando, who would never have allowed such a thing to be done to Sergio even if he'd set the harbor on fire. As it stood, I wanted to see the ship, so I followed him onboard, silent as a mouse.

I'm not sure where that phrase came from. The ship's mice were a rather rambunctious crowd. A couple of them scurried up and down the deck, squeaking as a great orange cat stalked by on the railing.

Sergio led me around the decks, showing me the knotted ropes they used to climb the masts, the mechanisms for pulling the sails up and letting them down, and the long pole—called a whipstaff—that the helmsman used to steer the vessel.

His mates were onboard that evening "guarding" the ship while the rest of the crew were off gallivanting around the port. Since the vessel contained cargo yet to be unloaded, they'd been assigned to remain with it. They didn't seem to take this charge all that seriously, for they sat on the empty deck, drinking wine and roaring with laughter that Sergio had brought me aboard. He took their jabs with good humor; I assumed, since they were covering for him, he hadn't much choice. They were kinder to me than to him, each bowing and kissing my hand in turn when introduced.

Both Marcos and Pablo were a bit shorter and stockier than Sergio. They also had longer, looser curls and darker complexions than him. The pair of them looked so alike I deduced they were brothers well before being informed of this.

We did not stay long in their company. They went back to drinking away their guard duty, and Sergio helped me down the ladder into the belly of the ship so he could show me the storage areas and some of the corners where the men preferred to lay out their sleeping mats.

As the contramaestre, he had partitioned some prime real estate for his own bedchamber, though it was little more than a pallet tucked behind a bit of wooden sheeting. He explained the shipmaster and the pilot were typically the only officers provided with staterooms. Then he took me deeper into the hold, where he showed me more sleeping corners and demonstrated how the men liked to arrange their sea chests to create some semblance of privacy.

As I observed the ship's guts, I became aware Sergio and I were quite alone in the recesses of the hold. The voices of the brothers had died away, and even the sounds of the breeze and the sea were quiet down here. The only noise that broke the silence was the creaking of the ship as it rocked back and forth with the waves.

I no longer heard Sergio nearby. Thinking he had gone on to a different room, I made to find him, but when I turned, I saw nothing but the laces of the jerkin stretched across his chest. He'd been so silent I hadn't realized he'd never left my side.

Bending down, he kissed me deeply. I ran my hands over his neck, sliding them under the linen shirt beneath his jerkin, then into his hair. He pressed me to the wall and held my arms against the rough wood. Burying his face in my neck, he positioned his hips between my thighs and lifted me off my feet. I inhaled sharply at the feeling of his strong limbs hoisting me up as if I weighed nothing, and my legs wound themselves around his waist of their own accord.

I wrapped my arms around his shoulders and arched myself into his body, but when he moved his left hand to undo the laces of my dress, I realized he intended to make love to me then and there. I shook my head, but he didn't notice. Desperate to stop this before I lost control of myself, I pulled my lips off his skin.

"No, Sergio. Not this way. We aren't even betrothed, and I must keep my maidenhead for my wedding night," I panted.

He let me drop to my feet, though a spasm of disappointment passed through my body as he removed his hands from my hips.

Sergio cocked his head. "I don't understand. I thought this was the entire reason you wanted to come here."

"Are you serious? You think I want our first time to be like this?"

He glanced around the gloomy hold, eyeing its weathered floor and sniffing its musty air. "Of course not. Apologies. I don't know what I was thinking. Come on. I'll escort you back to the parsonage before Father Manuel finds you're missing."

"But I haven't seen the rest of the ship."

"You actually want to see the whole thing?"

"If I didn't come to 'sample your chorizo,' why else would I be here?"

Sergio gathered me into a tight embrace, his body quaking with quiet laughter. I laid my brow on his chest and laughed too.

After we'd composed ourselves, he tightened his jerkin laces and said, "Well, then. Shall we continue our little tour?"

He guided me back up to the deck, where his mates were now drinking so much it seemed they intended to pass out before the moon had risen. We went down a passage that started under the bridge and led to the master's quarters at the stern. Though they were locked, Sergio had me peer through a crack in the door so I could see the cozy room with its bed and its desk and, from what I could make out, a view of the sea.

I pushed him against the master's door to kiss him, standing on tiptoe so I could wind the loose ringlets of his hair around my fingers and slide my palms over his neck and shoulders. Then I took his hand and let him lead me along the passage.

When we neared the deck, he balked and jerked me backward into the enclosed space underneath the bridge. I had heard it too. A strange man's voice, deeper and more serious than Marcos's or Pablo's.

Sergio groaned. "Oh no. It's the master of the *San Baco*." (This, I would later learn, was a smaller ship in the fleet.) "I can't let him find you here with me."

"What will happen to me?"

"Nothing will happen to you. But Armando—the ship lord, I mean—he'll be angry I brought you here. He cannot find out."

"Is there any way off the ship besides the gangplank?"

"Not unless you're willing to jump the railing into the water." He scoffed.

"Let's do that."

"Are you mad? We'll just have to hide until he leaves and then sneak off."

"Come, I can swim, and it's better than you being punished on my account. How do we get to the starboard side?"

He pointed over my shoulder without thinking. I grabbed his hand and ran in the direction he'd indicated. We came on deck facing the sea, which was darkening now that the sun had set. The men's voices were far-off, and the master was so busy upbraiding the brothers for getting drunk on their guard duty that he left no silence in which to hear any movement on our part.

I feared if I hesitated, Sergio might take a whipping rather than allow me to jump the ship's railing. Before he could react, I ran straight to the rail and leapt overboard. He flung himself off a second after me.

I fell through empty air longer than I'd expected, feeling my innards fluttering up inside me as they tumbled around within my body. When I hit the freezing water, I popped up like a cork, my simple dress offering little in the way of extra weight. By the time Sergio popped up beside me, I was laughing as quietly as I could.

"I cannot believe you did that," Sergio said as I kicked for the shore.

"I didn't want to see you whipped on my account."

"That would never have actually happened. I just said it to keep you from giggling like a damn child and announcing your presence to the whole harbor."

I laughed out loud this time. "Well, it's too late now. I already jumped and I'm already giggling like a damn child."

Sergio rolled his eyes and took off. He was a faster swimmer, so he went ahead and found us a spot where we could dry off undisturbed. He helped me out of the frigid water onto an outcropping of rock that hung much lower than the main shore and was therefore hidden from view. There we sat, shivering and waiting for our clothes to dry in the chilly, humid night.

Sergio huffed as if in anger at me for literally jumping ship, but he flashed a broad smile.

"Where in the world did you learn to swim?" He wrapped his arms around my body to warm me.

"Father Manuel used to leave me with our housekeeper, and she sometimes let me go to the river to help the laundresses. They showed me how to swim. Don't tell him! He still has no idea they taught me such a thing."

Sergio chuckled. "I didn't think you would really believe me, by the way. I'd never have told you I'd be whipped if I had known it would make you walk the plank with no plank."

"I didn't know it wasn't true. How would you expect me to know?"

"Well, now you do." He shook the water out of his hair and breathed deep, smelling the salty air. "You are one insane little thing."

I giggled. "Why wouldn't I jump in the water if I know I can swim?"

"I suppose you've no reason not to. Now, let's get you home." He squeezed my shoulders, lifted me off the ground, and set me on my feet.

"Yeah. The master mightn't have you whipped, but Father Manuel may penance you with a bit of self-flagellation if he discovers you snuck me out aiming to have your way with me."

That comment had made Sergio lose his composure. I rarely saw him laugh now as freely as he had back then, under the emergent stars, our hair and our clothes still dripping.

It pained me to remember the good times as I curled, stiff and cold, in my manger and compared the way Sergio and I had been at the beginning of our relationship to the way we were now. He'd been kinder to me before he was my husband; then again, I supposed I'd worked harder to appeal to him before I was his wife. Or, perhaps more accurately, he'd found certain traits of my personality more pleasing before we'd married.

I put my hands inside my apron pockets and felt Jhasali's tiny amulet fold into the curve of my palm. I'd revealed its hiding place the night I'd been throwing things during the first fight about the damned letter, so I'd slipped the disk into my apron to conceal it in a place Sergio would never look.

All this time, it had sat in my pocket, lonely and abandoned. I pulled it out and turned it over, and the feel of it in my hand made me realize that if Sergio didn't want me on his ship any longer, I now had other nautical options. I pressed the button.

As soon as Jhasali's voice materialized on the other end, I said, "I want to see your ship."

## Chapter Eight

# THE LANDLOCKED HARBOR

J hasali sighed. "I still don't think you're ready."

"I am!" I cried.

"Like you were ready to see my drones that night on the beach?"

"You caught me off guard then. I'm not having a problem with them now, am I?" I motioned to the half dozen that floated in the vicinity. "You explained it already. Your ship is like one of them, only it's the size of a palace and you live in it. I got it."

I'd had to let the Christmas season come and go before I could snatch an afternoon away again. Once the celebrations died down, I'd begun looking for opportunities. This morning, I'd called Jhasali as soon as Sergio had left the house, telling me not to expect him until late.

Now, she and I stood in the baldíos far from my home. We'd been arguing for a solid hour over whether I was going to panic as soon as I laid eyes on her ship. She had initially contended that the weeks between our last encounter hadn't done much to change her mind about my preparedness, but after relentless badgering on my part, she finally seemed to be yielding.

"You say you've 'got it' now, but whether that'll stand when you get a look at the ship remains to be seen," Jhasali said.

"I swear, I won't disappoint. Even if I'm afraid, I won't seem so."

Jhasali paused and pondered before asking, "Do you trust me?"

"Of course," I replied, prepared for her to tell me that if I trusted her, I'd heed her word.

Instead, she shrugged. "Then let's go."

I felt a sudden leap of elation as it dawned on me what she meant. I called Lobo, and he came bounding over from under an old oak tree. Pepito was picking through the undergrowth nearby, his bridle hanging from a branch and his stirrups hitched up to the saddle seat.

Jhasali took her place behind me once I'd bridled him and mounted. When I turned Pepito toward the road, however, Jhasali bade me not to head for it, telling me to plunge deeper into the woods instead.

It was a long way to her . . . whatever it was, and the farther we rode into the hills, the more confused I became. Jhasali had kept using the word "ship" to describe her home, so even though she'd told me it was metal, and even though she had tried to make clear it could do all the things her drones could (including fly), I still did not get it, though I'd thus far failed to appreciate that fact. Expecting us to make for a harbor, I wondered why in the world we kept heading away from the coast and deeper into the mountains. I thought at some point we would *have* to turn toward the sea, but we never did.

We rode hard up a slope, across a plateau, down a gulley, up another steep ascent, and over several more rises. It was tough going through the winter sludge, and sometimes we got to such a high elevation as to see thicker ice. If we'd continued south, we would have climbed to the alpine altitudes that bore the serious snow, but we did not.

Once we'd dipped south for a bit, we then continued east, almost parallel to the coast, more than a league through the deep wilderness, until Pepito balked at a large sinkhole near the top of a ridge, panicking inexplicably at the sight of it rather than going around. He reared and stomped, and Lobo gave a low growl, every hair on his shoulders standing on end.

"They must sense the ship's cloaks," Jhasali said.

"Your house is a ship that wears a cloak?"

Jhasali laughed. "No. It is a ship that carries cloaking devices: shields to make it undetectable within a certain boundary. Inside the perimeter, the ship is imperceptible to any external artificial sensory medium, and the signals of my isolated network are confined—you'll see. Though, I think it best we leave the animals out here. At least until they get used to it."

Unable to see anything unusual, I wasn't sure what "it" she referred to, but I slid off Pepito and removed his tack, placing it in the lowest tree branches I could find. I clutched my winter cape tight around my shoulders and followed Jhasali, wondering why she walked straight toward this massive sinkhole. We only went a few more paces before we came to a stop.

Pepito trotted off to rifle through the dusting of snow in search of grass, but Lobo did not leave my side. I patted him to quiet his displeased growling.

Jhasali turned to me. "You may want to take hold of his collar. And I need you to promise, no matter what happens, you will not scream or run."

"I promise," I said.

As soon as I agreed to Jhasali's terms, the air itself began to ripple like a pool pierced by a stone. It only did this for an instant, but when it finished, the sinkhole disappeared, revealing a hulking silver mass that materialized in what had once been empty woods.

Of course, I instantly broke my promise, not only crying out but falling to the ground.

"Stop that!" Jhasali snapped between gritted teeth.

With great effort, I obeyed, but it was all I could do to contain myself as I sat on the cold earth and stared at her ship, which was no ship at all. It was a sleek palace that looked similar to the drones I had seen before, just a hundred times their size—no, a thousand times. It was bigger than any castle or cathedral in Toledo, only instead of towers and turrets, it boasted a gleaming oval-shaped hull, dotted all over with round windows and striped at the top with rows of large glass panes that curved around what I could only assume was the front, though I'd later learn its multidirectional engines meant it had no real front. Jhasali had told me it was essentially a giant drone that housed living beings, but I could never have fathomed what that meant.

For his part, Lobo took a look at the ship, seemed to decide it didn't smell like much after all, and began sniffing the ground.

Jhasali was laughing. "Well, you managed not to run."

"What is this thing?" I asked.

"Homeship, of course." She helped me to my feet.

"But how does it sail?"

"It doesn't sail. It flies, like them," she replied, pointing to her drones. "I have said that before. Now come."

She turned and walked toward this outrageous ship, expecting me to fall right in line behind her, though I couldn't because my heart was trying to claw its way out of my chest. Jhasali had been right to make me promise not to run; the temptation to do so was agonizing. Lobo sensed my trepidation and shoved his head under my hand to steady me. Unable to move, I kept staring at the ship.

I hadn't really believed her. Despite all the time she'd spent telling me she was no supernatural thing, even after I'd decided to try to think of her outside my own preconceptions, I'd always suspected that one day I'd be proven right. One day, she'd turn out to be something familiar and explicable within my existing reality. Yet, as I trembled on my wobbling knees, gripping a fistful of the fur on Lobo's head, I grasped the piece I'd been missing.

Nothing in my education nor the insufficient knowledge I possessed on any subject had prepared me for this. I imagined no one in the world, no matter how educated or knowledgeable, could be prepared for *this*. Now, I comprehended what Jhasali had meant when she'd said to think of her outside the terms I'd been taught, and I finally believed her.

Jhasali did not offer so much as a backward glance before stepping onto a tilted platform I could only describe as a gangplank and walking straight toward a sealed portal like it was already open. As soon as she approached the threshold, a piece of the wall slid up into the portal frame to reveal a wide entryway, much larger and taller than necessary for humans. No wonder she'd acted like she'd never opened a door when we'd first met.

Jhasali turned back in my direction. "I need to restore the visual camouflage."

Without warning, the same waving effect from before rippled through the air again, and when it finished, there stood a faint barrier to my rear, invisible except for the odd blur it cast over the woods beyond it. She'd expanded the boundary around me, though I hadn't moved a muscle, and I now stood within it.

"I only put the visual concealment down to show you the cruiser from a distance. I shan't next time. We will just pass through. Come, now," she repeated.

I wasn't sure there was going to be a next time of me coming here. Lobo growled again in the direction of the optical barrier. Whatever it was made of, he could clearly feel it.

Jhasali passed through the ship's threshold and into what I guessed was a hall beyond. The doorway loomed too high above my head for me to see inside this vast metal vessel. Steeling my trembling nerves, I told myself Jhasali had brought me to no harm thus far. I wished to follow her inside, but I couldn't make my legs move, nor could I forget the phrase "All hope abandon ye who enter here," though only much later did I remember where I'd read it.

From somewhere inside, Jhasali whistled for Lobo and asked if he wanted food. He bounded up the platform and entered the ship without hesitation. His lack of fear gave my failing courage a boost, and I lifted each unwilling foot one at a time and put it in front of the other up every terrifying centimeter of that gangplank until I stood at the threshold, on the edge of a long, tubular hallway.

As I peered into the passage, my panic all but conquered me. The sense of the unknown was so terrible that even death itself felt more familiar. I needed all my pride and defiance to help me cross that threshold. I'd been so confident about coming here, telling Jhasali I was ready and unafraid. I wasn't about to prove myself wrong. Feeling a sudden wave of anger at my own cowardice, I forced my frozen feet to move and dragged my reluctant body inside the ship.

The door, which I'd half expected to slam shut behind me, remained open. My breath came in great gasps, but I forced myself to stay calm, determined to master my own body and will. After a few shaky inhales, I became convinced this place was not poised to swallow me alive, so I crept down the hall. With its rounded walls and straight, narrow passage, it felt like I was walking down the barrel of a giant cannon.

A loud clicking noise resounded through the hallway, and the corridor filled with unnatural white light. I ducked and prepared to make a run for it, but nothing else happened. I looked down at the illuminated floor, then up at the ceiling, trying to find the source of the light, but it wasn't apparent.

It was as if the ceiling was made of one sheet of softly glowing glass. I could not understand how the glow was generated, but it appeared its only function was to illuminate the hall. Repeating to myself there was no danger here, I made my way down the passage, calling Jhasali's name as loudly as I dared.

She replied from somewhere deeper within. Lobo came bounding out from a room on the left, several doors down this gun barrel of a hallway, his tail wagging and his tongue hanging out. I followed him back into a room I immediately designated "the kitchen" because that was the closest reference I had for it.

It appeared empty except for a long storage counter that looked similar to the preparation table in the kitchen at the estate house. Since this counter was much too tall for me to see over, I had to let Lobo lead me to Jhasali, who sat on a huge, curved stool hanging from the ceiling. Lobo ran to her, whining for another cut of meat.

"So, you got hold of yourself yet? Convinced the place isn't going to eat you alive?" Jhasali laughed.

I kept quiet, not wanting her to think me foolish, but I didn't dare consider this place as benign as any old town house either.

"Come. Let me show you around." She rose from her seat.

Jhasali brought me back to the passage and led me even farther into the interior of the vessel. I forced myself to breathe and clenched my fists to stop my hands from shaking, but there was nothing I could do to soothe my thundering heart, which remained determined to batter its way through my sternum.

I followed Jhasali down the hall, the walls of which were streaked throughout with veins of iridescent purples, pastel blues, pearlescent ivories, and pale yellows, giving the passage the air of a fairytale mine. Indeed, when I stopped and took a closer look at these veins, they turned out to be deep fissures filled with colorful crystals and glazed over with a glassy polish.

The light glowing from the ceiling enhanced their sheen, making it seem as if we strode through a giant geode. I placed my hand on the wall. It was smooth and hard as granite, yet if I could only peel off this top layer of clear resin, I could feel the roughness of the crystals underneath and place my fingers in the cracks.

I started as a set of strong, cold fingers clasped my right hand in an unintentionally viselike grip.

"Why are you obsessed with the walls?" Jhasali asked, leading me away.

On the lowest level, she took me through the escape-pod bay: a huge passageway lined with stalls housing drones large enough to carry passengers. There were also several empty spaces, which she said were meant for the drones that currently sat outside to shore up her defenses.

On the next floor, she showed me the communal washrooms and waste disposal stations, and she demonstrated how the chamber pots ejected themselves from the wall at the perfect height to receive her people's waste before sliding back into their respective repositories. She also showed me how her people bathed: by entering a huge glass tube that sealed itself and filled with water that fizzed and bubbled. Such a bath sounded like a pleasant experience except, at my height, I'd drown taking it.

I wished to see the ship's core that we'd previously discussed. Though Jhasali told me this was pointless, I would not let up until she led me deeper into the vessel to view a section of the uninteresting bare wall that encased the blazing reactor on the other side.

We continued the tour, ascending to each subsequent floor. We did so by hitching a ride on enormous free-floating platforms that rose and descended from one level to the next. In times gone by, my first instinct would have been to refuse to ride such a platform. Now, already saturated with the bizarre and unsettling, I'd become so numb to novelty that I accepted the platform without hesitation.

Heading down the hallway on a middle floor, we came to what Jhasali called the medical ward. As we passed yet another doorway—one of the few open ones—I peeked through it and gasped. The room was like most of the others in that it appeared almost empty, but it contained a huge hole in the middle with a drain in the center. The depression was large enough to swim in and had many seats of different depths around the sides. It looked like the image I'd always had in my mind of the Roman baths of antiquity, though it was dry.

"What is this?" I asked, approaching the depression.

"It's for radiation burns. If the injuries are severe enough to require it, several victims at a time can float in medicine until it heals them," Jhasali replied.

I didn't know what she meant by the word "radiation," but I knew what burns were well enough, and it almost pained me that this beautiful huge pool was meant for something so far removed from the luxurious.

"Can you put plain water in it?" I said.

"Of course. Free-floating nanos need a medium. The water comes up from the bottom."

"Nanos?"

"Yes. They're like creatures so tiny you cannot see them. They communicate and cognate, but they're machines, not animals, and we can tell them what to do. We put nanos inside our bodies, and they integrate with our systems to make them function perfectly—without disease or defect. They work in tandem with our brain implants to allow us to command our own bodies just as we do our external devices."

"External devices? So you couldn't make anything on this ship work if you didn't have these implants?"

Jhasali shook her head. "Very little of it. Almost nothing functions here if you don't have cerebral sensors—the brain implants, I mean. You cannot issue commands if you're not on the network, and you cannot be on the network without the implants."

"Meaning nothing will work for me."

"The common area doors open for movement unless they're locked, the lights come on automatically, and the ship performs its basic functions. Besides that, nothing will work for you unless I direct it to."

"Can you give the implants to me so I can issue commands?" I asked.

"No. I could never do that."

"Why not?"

"All my people are implanted during fertilization, and the nanos integrate with our bodies as they gestate. If I did such a thing to you now, you would likely die."

I didn't respond. It had just been a passing fancy, but Jhasali seemed to sense my disappointment.

She laid a hand on my forearm. "Even if you would not be in danger, I still couldn't offer the implants to you. My people jealously guard our achievements. If I were to share them with an outsider, many of my peers would consider that an abominable act."

"I understand."

Jhasali interlaced her fingers with mine. "Come now, let us continue."

After a pilgrimage of passageways in which we ascended several floors, we reached the penultimate level and came to a long row of rooms designed to give the ranking members of the ship's crew some privacy. I likened these to bedrooms, though they were not exactly. They all contained two semicircles of tilted, backless benches that dipped in the middle like soup spoons and a large storage chest that was topped with a thin, flat mat and pressed against a picture window that took up the entire outside wall.

Opposite the chest was a deep nook in the corner that housed an odd egg-shaped apparatus—like a short peapod on a post—tilted about halfway between vertical and horizontal. It seemed to be without opening, but further inspection revealed it did, in fact, have a seam running through the center and all the way around the circumference. This seam popped as I moved closer.

I jumped back in fright before realizing Jhasali herself had silently commanded this; she was laughing at my startled reaction.

"Don't do that!" I snapped.

"I shan't again, I promise. But I couldn't resist this once."

I shot her an exasperated sigh. "What's this for?"

"My people don't need sleep anymore, but we sometimes shut down for pleasure or relief, and this is where we do it."

The inside was spacious enough, about five meters long by three wide, and the chamber within was stuffed with squishy cushions, making it almost a nest within the egg. Though it was made with the comfort of her people in mind, it looked to me like an oval-shaped sarcophagus.

I shuddered. "Why would anyone sleep in this?"

"If the ship is in motion, you can get knocked about or thrown from your bed. The sleeping chamber is a more comfortable option than strapping your body down."

"It closes like a coffin."

"A what?"

"A box you put the dead in before you bury them."

She burst out laughing. "Why on earth would you put a dead body in a box to bury it?"

"I don't know, Jhasali. Some people just do if they have the money for it," I snapped, more harshly than I'd intended, for her constant derision of my planet annoyed me.

She cocked her head like a dog listening to a strange noise. "Sorry. I only find it odd you'd try to preserve something that belongs to your planet."

"I suppose it is odd if you don't know why we do it," I admitted. "But what do your people do with their dead?"

"If someone dies in space, we recycle their nanos and then burn what's left of their body in the reactor."

I shuddered. "Why would you burn bodies like a pagan?"

"Because that way, we can dispose of them, yet they'll always be with the last ship to shelter them. It is right that the dead should be incinerated." She pointed to the pod. "This is for sleeping. Not for the storage of dead bodies for who knows what."

"I don't care what it's for. It's horrible. I could never learn to sleep in it."

"Forget it. We'll go look at something more to your liking," she said, leading me to the hallway once more.

When we made it to the top floor, we entered a vast chamber with no seating, no shelving, no storage, no furniture of any kind—but that did not matter. The room was surrounded by a 360-degree glass wall and covered with a ceiling made of crystal so clear it was invisible. Standing in this place felt like being housed in a giant bubble, looking out to the snowcapped mountains on the southern side and the wide, sprawling sea to the north.

"This is where we steer the vessel. Well, it pilots itself or can be navigated by the captain from any point, but this is traditionally where we perform most of the piloting activities on a craft like this," Jhasali explained.

"It doesn't look the way I'd imagined. Where is the whipstaff? Where does the helmsman stand? How do you let down the sails?"

"There are no sails, and I control the ship the way I control the drones." She tapped her temple. "In here."

"It's just, there's nothing in this room. Not even any seating. How can you—"

"That can be remedied."

A chair popped up from the floor just under my legs and swept me off my feet into its deep seat. It was much too big for me, like everything else in this place. It was also oddly shaped, looking more like a giant tilted teacup than a chair.

"We keep most everything stowed when it's not in use," Jhasali said while I labored to right myself.

After a short struggle, I slid out of this painful contraption, wondering how I'd ever learn to be comfortable in this place if I couldn't even find a seat I could bear to use. I walked back to the glass wall and pressed my face to its smooth, cool surface.

The glass, if you could call it such a thing, was unlike any glass I had ever beheld in my life. Assuming one could afford glass at all in those days, even the best of it was thin, uneven, wavy stuff that you could never really see all the way through because it distorted everything.

The glass in front of me, however, was of a different class. Clear as the air itself, I was struck by how easily I forgot it was even present, for it made no distortion of the world beyond it. When I smacked it with my palm, it made the same slapping sound one might hear when tapping on a wall of solid rock.

"What is this?" I asked.

"A window," Jhasali said from her perch in the chair she'd summoned for me. She curled in a ball in the center of its cupped seat, like a cat stuffing itself into a box.

"Thank you. I never would have worked that out," I snapped before I could stop myself.

I bit my tongue, knowing she had not intended to be sarcastic. Indeed, she had answered the question I'd asked in the most literal sense.

I tried again. "What's it made of? That's what I meant."

"It's a modified form of crystallized carbon."

"Crystallized what?"

"This glass is basically one big sheet of enhanced diamond. We mine them from planets where they're as common as dirt. Then we process them and compress them into big sheets to use for windows. Better than synthesizing them. Naturally occurring ones are easy to collect where they fall as rain, and when they're treated, they grow even clearer and stronger."

I pretended I understood (though she knew I didn't) and turned back to the window. This room was not so bad. The view was fantastic, for we sat high on the ridge and well above the canopy, overlooking the ocean from a good distance. The perch offered an unimpeded panorama of the oscillating sea on the horizon, flanked on either side by cool winter-brown cliffs that were dotted here and there with tiny gray blotches of afternoon mist. If you ignored the floor and stood with your back to the room, it looked almost like being outside, standing on the very edge of a wild, high precipice—except for the fact that there was no breeze, and this precipice remained unsettlingly silent.

"You could stay here, you know," Jhasali's voice whispered somewhere behind me.

I chuckled. "No, I couldn't."

"Why not?"

I hesitated. What was I to tell her? This place was too sterile for me, the hallways too heavily monitored and the climate too tightly controlled. Aside from a few stunning decorations, this ship was an inescapable utilitarian nightmare. The scentlessness, the stillness of the air, and the silence were all too complete. I could never grow accustomed to this.

I traced my finger along the glass. "Sergio would probably notice if I didn't come home. But even if that weren't an issue, I couldn't stand to live here."

"Why not?" she asked again.

"It's not like my home. It is too uncomfortable. There are no chairs—not a seat worth sitting on in the whole place. There's no bedroom with a proper bed. There are no doors I can open nor lights I can work on my own. And I don't know how you stand the silence."

"You grow accustomed to it. Space is very quiet."

"I could never grow accustomed to sleeping in a bedroom where all I could hear was the ringing in my own ears."

When Jhasali did not reply, I sat down on the floor and leaned against the wall with my face pressed to the glass. She remained silent, and I allowed my eyes to scan the horizon, watching the sun glittering on the ocean, the shadows of the clouds sweeping over the water, the distant waves rippling and whitecapping.

"I didn't believe you," I whispered. "Not until now. Before today, some part of me still thought everything you said was a lie."

"What do you think now?"

"I don't know what to think. Maybe God is testing me."

"Not this again. You promised you'd leave me in peace about your people's superstitions," she moaned.

"How can I leave you in peace if I can get none? I keep asking the same questions and getting no answers."

"Perhaps that is because you are asking the wrong questions, questions that aren't worth asking." She rose from her chair and took a seat beside me on the floor, pressing her back to the glass and facing the interior. "My people are constantly working to discover the truth of things we think we know, but if a question is unanswerable, we set it aside. We don't mull over unverifiable conjecture until we drive ourselves mad."

I rolled my eyes. "You know, since your people selectively breed babies to exploit them until they're culled if they prove useless, I think there's a remote possibility not all their ideas are pure gold."

She laughed. "The fact that my people are victims of our imposed regime does not automatically make us wrong about everything. The Tanmorayans don't genetically engineer themselves a slave caste, but they've also abandoned such speculation on the unknowable."

"Tanmorayans?"

"Yes. They are the only other species in the known universe that has achieved anywhere close to my people's level of hyperintelligence. They are our traditional enemy, and I used to despise them. Although now that I've passed so much time on the other side of a failed revolution, I cannot help but wonder how much of what I thought I knew of them was propaganda. Likely most of it. That's why I ask you to question your own people's propaganda. Don't you see the dangers inherent in communal dogma—of any kind—not just your species' unfortunate brand of it?"

I didn't answer. She'd struck a nerve without realizing. I could think of one big danger, and his name was Ignacio. I also supposed the auto de fe to which he'd dragged me could serve as a second, albeit subtle, indicator of the perils.

I rubbed the space between my brows. "My whole kind all over the world asks these questions without cease. We wouldn't spend so much time on them if they were nothing but unverifiable conjecture, would we?"

"Maybe. From my own observations, your kind is collectively incapable of uncertainty, to the point that you'd rather invent absurd explanations for things you don't comprehend than spend the time comprehending them."

"Why would we do such a thing?"

"I don't know why. Perhaps because your lives are so short and difficult, you need to feel there's some meaning to all this meaningless happenstance that is the universe. It isn't like I cannot empathize with such a need, even if I don't agree with how your people fulfill it."

I bit the tip of my tongue. "I just—even if everything I've been taught is wrong, I cannot abandon it."

"It appears you may have already."

"How?"

"If the first time you saw me, I seemed to you a thing forbidden by your people's gods, why did you follow me?"

In truth, I didn't know. It was a question I'd scarcely dared to ask myself.

"I suppose I was merely curious," I said after a pause.

"That is the most pitiful circumvention of all the pitiful circumventions you've had the nerve to offer me," she snapped. "You've got a perfectly good brain, and I cannot imagine why you insist on not using it."

"That is not fair!" I spat.

Before I could scold her for insulting me, she apologized. "I don't wish to be harsh. I suppose I'm averse to any display of herd mentality. After all, it is why I rebelled. I'm disposed against it on a biological level, thanks to my masters' unchecked experimentation. A happy or unhappy accident, depending on who's looking at it. But maybe I am wrong; maybe collective delusion does your species a good it doesn't do mine."

I wanted to agree with that last statement, but between Ignacio's bitter words and the shrieks of the condemned at the stake suddenly ringing in my ears all over again, I couldn't.

"I don't know if it does us all that much good, now that I think about it," I said.

Jhasali laughed. "Certainly prevents you from learning. I mean, you spent so much of our first encounters insisting I must be something you'd already heard of that it took you ten times longer to discover what I *am* than it would've if you'd just asked."

"I did ask, and you said, 'I am what I am.' Like that's a real answer."

"I only said that because I'd not yet worked out what I needed to do to make you comprehend. It was right for you to demand proof of me, but even after I offered it to you—after I showed you my drones and the heavens and explained to you where I come from—you still refused to believe me. You've spent half our time together accusing me of being a sorceress or a spirit, and it took seeing a spacefaring vessel to make you believe I am what I say I am rather than what you thought I must be."

"Well, it was hard not to be satisfied when I saw this place," I admitted.

"I am glad you're convinced—at last. Though, it now occurs to me that if you required a literal shipful of evidence to believe a word I said, then you should not be so resistant to subjecting your own people's ideas to the same standard."

I pondered it and realized, once again, she was more accurate than I cared to admit. Neither Father Manuel nor any other clergyman had ever offered me a shred of proof their words were true—not that I'd asked for any. They'd expected me to believe what they said, and I'd happily obliged. Blessed are those who have not seen and yet have believed.

Doubly blessed are the deaf, for they shall never know their gods are silent. My god had been perpetually so, and I had no indication that he would not remain so. I'd expected external proofs and internal helps, yet I'd received neither—only that same empty muteness.

Jhasali, on the other hand? I'd not been able to shut her up since I'd met her. That did not prove her right, but it did prove she existed. Could I say the same of my silent god? My hushed Holy Spirit? I remained unready to consider that question.

"Look," Jhasali said when I didn't speak. "I wish I could offer you more than a cold rejection of the whole mess, but I cannot. What I can offer you is a piece of advice: search for reality and not just reinforcement of your existing beliefs. If you seek it, you will find it, whatever it may be. Your reality is only as good as your perception, after all. But you'll never find any version of truth if you spend your life pretending you already have the only version."

Deeming it sound advice, I looked over the tranquil ocean, its waters shimmering to my left as the sun marched on its westward track. Sunset! We'd been talking so long I hadn't noted the time, and I suddenly remembered how far I was from home and how Sergio could be there any minute.

"I've got to go home," I cried.

"Whatever for?" Jhasali said, not moving a muscle.

"Because if I don't make it back soon, I'll be missed. Sergio won't know what to think if he returns to find me gone."

"How could that possibly matter?"

"It matters. Don't ask me why. Just trust me."

"If you say so. I'll see you to the door."

"No. You are taking me home."

Jhasali gave an exasperated sigh. "Micaela, you rode all the way here and now you're telling me you don't remember the way back?"

"It is not about that. You brought me here. You take me home. We're much too far into the wilderness for me to go back by myself."

"Fine. But next time, you're coming on your own. You made me learn to ride that horrid beast. Now it's time for you to learn to do something that disquiets *you*."

"Alright," I assented. "Tomorrow. Later. Not now."

Jhasali rolled her eyes and dragged herself to her feet as though it cost her tremendous effort. In the end, she took me home, though she bombarded me with an endless barrage of complaints along the way.

***

I went back to town a day or two after seeing the ship, deeper in crisis than ever. Whether it was the vessel's size or its bizarre interior or the fact that it obeyed Jhasali's telepathic commands, some quality about it had made a believer of me, though I still could not explain why. Yet this hard-fought acceptance had left me, once again, with more questions than answers.

My sudden belief in Jhasali's assertions had made me doubt certain aspects of the things I had been taught. Following our night observing the heavens, I'd brushed aside the images of the magnified stars in the viewing window, especially after the terror I'd endured facing her swarm of drones. Yet Jhasali's and my latest conversation had brought that night roaring to the fore of my consciousness, and it opened a Pandora's box of misgivings. If one or two of the things I'd been taught were demonstrable falsehoods, how was I to know all the others were not as well?

I hoped Father Manuel might comfort me; maybe he could calm some of the disquiet in my soul by proving himself a worthier intellectual opponent of Jhasali than I was. So I paid him a visit. When I arrived at his house, I loosened him up with some wine and fresh chicken, just to ensure he wouldn't become too distraught when I asked him certain questions. His heart was not the strongest, and I didn't want to upset him too much. Thus, I waited until he was full of a lot of chicken and a little wine to bring up some of the things Jhasali had asserted—and had used her devices to demonstrate—were false.

"Father," I said, "could you explain why we believe the sun revolves around the earth?"

"Of course, child. We believe the sun revolves around the earth because this is what the Holy Mother Church teaches. There are many instances in the scriptures that describe celestial bodies moving in relation to an immobile terrain. For example, Ecclesiastes speaks of the sun rising and setting and returning to its place of origin to rise again. Also, you recall the story of Joshua, and how he commanded the sun to stand still at Gibeon. The scripture says the sun stood still, not the earth. Now, how can the sun stand still if the earth is doing the moving?"

"Alright, but what of science? What does it say?" I pressed.

"Science backs up the scriptures. Aristotle pointed out that if the earth truly revolved around the sun, we would see a parallax effect in the stars. If the earth moved, the stars closer to it would appear to move in comparison to the stars farther off, yet this does not occur. That can only mean the earth isn't moving."

I had no answer for that. I wasn't smart enough to argue with Aristotle, nor did it appear to me the stars altered their positions. I was unaware at the time that this is because the distances in space are so vast the effect is undetectable to the naked eye. Regardless, I couldn't just dismiss what I'd seen through the conical drone.

"But if we were to assume this science is wrong, would it be a sin?" I asked.

"Of course not," he replied. "Science turns out to be wrong all the time."

"What if we assume the scripture is wrong? Is that a sin?"

"Of course it is, darling. We would be creatures of little faith if we presumed the scriptures to be fallible."

He said this with such unwavering certainty. Yet Jhasali had shown me! She'd shown me that night on the beach multiple instances of planets revolving around suns, and she'd been clear this was the way of the universe. If every single other planet in the cosmos revolved around its sun, I had no reason to assume Earth would be any different.

My first instinct was to doubt my memory of the event. Perhaps she really *had* tricked me with magic. But I'd thought that about everything else she'd shown me, and I'd been wrong. Why would I deny what I'd seen with my own eyes in favor of something I'd only been told and expected to believe?

"But what if the scripture really *is* wrong?" I said, knowing I was pushing this discussion to the limit of what he'd tolerate. "And I'm not saying it is. Just, if the Bible is infallible, shouldn't the Church be accurately telling astronomers what is and isn't correct?"

He squinted. "Where is all this coming from?"

"I haven't any doubts. I simply need some help to defend the faith."

Father Manuel's attitude changed instantly at that statement. "Defend it from whom?"

"Oh, I . . . nobody."

"Micaela, you should not be spending time with anyone whose heresy gives you cause to defend the scriptures. I'd think you of all women would know better than to fraternize with people who might put unorthodox ideas in your head."

"But I—"

"No buts. You need to stay away from anyone who spouts such profane nonsense. With any luck, the Holy Office will start putting those heretics to the fire. That way, they might be spared the eternal fire to come."

I didn't like to hear such words escape his lips, for I'd heard them before from the lips of Ignacio, and I hated the notion that the two of them might have anything in common. I ceased questioning Father Manuel, fearing to upset him further. Instead, I kept my mouth shut and decided any more study I needed to do on this particular subject, I'd have to do myself.

For the rest of that day and much time after, I pondered both Jhasali's and Father Manuel's words, slipping further into doubt all the while. I must clarify that the positioning of the celestial bodies was not the crux of my crisis. That alone did not make an apostate of me in the end, for that alone was never a foundational tenet of the Christian faith. However, it did open the door to many questions, not the least of which was why I should believe an entity that claimed to be infallible in matters of doctrine when it was provably wrong on an issue it asserted was settled by scripture.

That is the danger of absolute assertions: a refutation of one part of the whole automatically refutes the whole itself. Heliocentrism might not have been foundational to my faith, but it was now foundational to my ever-augmenting distrust of its dogmas and its authority figures.

I liken this slow decay of confidence to tugging on a loose thread in a knitted shirt. If you pull too hard on the single fiber, it starts to unravel the others, and the garment soon falls apart. I did not know it at the time, but the loose threads that would prove to be my garment's undoing had already been tugged beyond repair.

# Chapter Nine

# THE WRONG ROBBERY

Though I wanted to visit Jhasali's ship often, Sergio's presence made it next to impossible to steal an afternoon away. The fact that he spent so much time outside the house was no guarantee someone would not notice me missing. I'd thus far been able to prevent my absences from being detected through a combination of obsessive planning, meticulous observation of my surroundings, and sheer dumb luck, as well as only considering an outing when Sergio told me not to expect him for supper. Still, I worried that no amount of caution could keep my excursions from being discovered indefinitely, especially when the arrabal was full. Thus, another few weeks passed before I was able to see Jhasali again.

In that time, my resentment of Sergio intensified. Though I had signed the damned paper, I regretted my momentary weakness in doing so. We had several more towering altercations, which always devolved into me begging him not to go to the New World until he tired of my pleas and left the house. Eventually, I gave up and decided to salvage whatever dignity I had left. I stopped begging and pleading. It was too late for all that anyhow.

So I began to drink. I never got belligerent, but I maintained a steady state of mild inebriation virtually all the time. The feelings of tingling warmth and fuzziness in my face helped me forget that I'd been forced to condemn myself to living in an empty home for the next two years. If Sergio noted my increased consumption, he said nothing. He would have been quite a hypocrite to lecture me for drinking away my misery anyhow.

Consequently, the next time I got an opportunity to snatch a few hours with Jhasali, I'd already been drinking all morning. I called her on the communicator and told her to meet me halfway between her ship and my house. To keep out the late winter chill, I drank away the ride there. By the time I met up with her, I was still able to keep my seat, but only just. I was also drunk enough to forget to be afraid of how far I'd come into the wilderness on my own.

Jhasali said we should walk around to sober me up. I dismounted and unsaddled Pepito, allowing him a respite to graze while she and I sauntered deeper into the forest. I stumbled more than once on the loose pebbles and slippery leaves underneath my feet. Without fail, Jhasali caught me as I teetered on the brink of falling.

I giggled like a child, but she didn't mind. Indeed, she found my current state of inebriation amusing. We got into a pattern: I'd stumble and burst into laughter. Then she'd grin and shake her head before helping me to my feet and urging me on, and a few paces later, we'd do it over again.

Lobo ran in circles around us, barking and whining his displeasure at the situation. He was unused to seeing me drunk, especially in the forest in the middle of the day. He licked my face, panting and shooting whiffs of hot breath up my nostrils whenever I fell guffawing to my knees. We traveled on like this through the woods and into the foothills of the ridge that played host to Jhasali's temporary residence.

When we approached the slope, the hair on the back of Lobo's neck stood on end, and he emitted a soft, rumbling growl. I went rigid, finding myself suddenly sober. I'd sensed it too, or rather, I'd heard it—a rustling in the trees that could not have been any forest creature.

"Greetings, ladies," a male voice called.

My heart leapt so far into my throat I envisioned it crawling out my open mouth and fluttering away. The sound of hooves thudding over the mud and peat resounded through the forest as this unknown man rode up the slope to greet us. Lobo made to run toward him, but I grabbed him and forced him to stay still, fearing they might shoot him. Several more men appeared through the trees, most of them armed with bows or crossbows.

Jhasali stood her ground, fearless, disinterested even. At the time, I thought she did not understand our predicament. She had yet to demonstrate why humans posed as little threat to her as she claimed we did.

"What is a pair of lovely damsels like you two doing all the way out here?" one of the men asked.

"What makes you think it's any of your concern?" Jhasali folded her arms and leaned against a tree.

My heart was racing, but she sounded almost bored. I took her hand and squeezed it hard, hoping that would somehow communicate to her to let me do the talking.

"We're enjoying the forest, same as you," I said in what I hoped was a nonconfrontational tone.

The man laughed and patted his steed's neck. "Don't you know there could be bandits in these woods? A couple of lone women such as yourselves could get hurt out here."

"We haven't done you any harm. Why hurt us?" I replied.

"We won't hurt you, love," said another man. "Just give us whatever you're carrying, and we'll be on our way."

I carried a bag with a few coins, and I much preferred to give that up than to be raped and murdered. I pulled it out and tossed it to the man who'd asked for it, telling him it was all we had, while hoping Pepito was far away from here. I doubted that these men had bought the horses they currently rode.

Jhasali shot me an odd look, and I couldn't tell if she understood we were being robbed. I feared the men would want more or might not believe the purse to be my only valuable possession, but to my surprise, they were courteous (as robbers go). They did not ask for anything further and had actually turned to leave when Jhasali called out for them to wait.

"Where did you come from?" she demanded.

"Why do you want to know?" one of the bandits asked.

I tugged on her sleeve for her to please, please keep quiet.

"Do you live in these woods?" she said.

The men's faces hardened, and I guessed they thought she asked these questions because she planned to report them. I, however, knew she intended no such thing, but I had no idea why she would want to know this information. Gripping her wrist, I shook her arm to hush her.

"Please pardon my friend. She's French. She doesn't know our customs," I said, desperate to think of any excuse for her prying.

She would not be dissuaded. "Have you seen anything strange in these woods lately?"

At this question, all the men perked up.

"Yes, we have. A small silver creature that floated in the air unlike any bird we've ever seen. It went off that way." The bandit pointed in the direction of the ship.

"We tried to follow it, but when we got close, it disappeared," another man interrupted. "We thought we were going mad. But you must've seen it too!"

"When did you see it?" she asked.

"Yesterday, around noon," the first man answered, and I believed I heard her whisper that was what she thought.

"And you followed it a long way," she said. It was more of a statement than a question.

"Of course we did. We wanted to know what it was," a third bandit replied.

Another chimed in. "We came back here hoping to see it again. When did y—"

A thundering of high-pitched, resonant cracks echoed through the forest. I dropped to my knees and covered my ears as best I could with my arm wrapped around Lobo's neck. I deafened myself with my own terrified cries as I held my fingers tight inside my ear canals while Lobo barked and yelped.

The cracks went on and on, and though they lasted mere seconds, to me it seemed time stood still. The horses shrieked and tried to bolt, but they fell where they stood, blood bursting from their necks and sides. The riders slumped over dead in their saddles before they even knew what hit them. Human and horse blood gushed in dozens of fountains, spraying the trees and soaking the dirt to the point it turned to mud, which the flailing horses slung in every direction as they suffered their final death throes. All I could do was curl up in a kneeling fetal position and pray whatever was attacking us would go away.

After a few more seconds, the cracking ended, and the last echoes of the dead horses' shrieks bounced out of earshot. I lifted my head to find Jhasali's silver drones hovering all around us. At once, I knew they had slain these men. Several of them hovered at the edge of the area we occupied, and they all had long, smoking barrels dropped from their undersides and trained on the lifeless bandits.

Jhasali paid no heed to the bodies of men or horses, not even bothering to look down to ensure she didn't step on them as she walked out of the circle of corpses. I couldn't wrap my head around what had just happened; she'd commanded this slaughter and done it standing there like a statue, as if their lives weren't worth conjuring a hint of interest.

"You coming?" she asked, walking up the hill.

I followed, still reeling. It had been readily apparent when I'd met Jhasali that she had no fear of humans, but it had never occurred to me this was why. We walked up the ridge, she a long way ahead of me, until she called down and asked jokingly if I wanted a little more wine. The question snapped me out of my stupor.

"What was that?" I shouted.

"What was what?" she yelled from up ahead.

I sprinted to catch up and wheeled around her, blocking her path. "Why? Why the devil?"

"You mean why would I kill them?" She shrugged. "They were too close to Homeship. One of the unarmed drones spotted them yesterday, and they saw it too. I didn't think much of it. I even decided to let them be if they moved on from here, but they obviously had other ideas."

"We are still a hundred leagues from your ship. You killed them all because you didn't like where they were standing? Are you joking?"

"Micaela, stop shouting. I don't understand why you're making such an issue of this."

"Because it's crazy!"

She looked puzzled. "Is it? They kept looking for my drone yesterday. They made it clear just now that they had no plans to leave my refuge until they found it."

"That doesn't matter. You can't just kill people because you don't like their current geographical location!"

"Why not? If you found a bees' nest in your home, you'd wipe out their entire civilization without a second thought."

"This is different!"

"How?" She whipped past me and continued on her path before I could answer.

"If they're bees, I'm a bee too," I cried, unable to think of anything better to say. She turned back toward me and smiled. "But you're my bee, remember?"

"You can't leave them there to rot." I planted my feet.

"Sure I can. Makes more sense than doing anything else with them."

"No. You can't."

Even though these men had technically just robbed us, they hadn't done us any real harm, and Jhasali's flippant murder of their whole group frightened me much more than anything they'd done. I ran after her as she resumed her trek up the slope.

"You can't kill people like that. The only time you kill a person is for self-defense," I said once I'd caught up.

"I defended my perimeter."

"That's not the same!"

"Yes, it is. I do not wish to be forced to move my ship nor engage my larger weapons nor do anything else that could put a noticeable signature into space. What if they'd penetrated the visual camouflage and then brought some torch-bearing rabble into these mountains? I'd be obliged to deploy my primary munitions, and then I'd have to find a new planet to hide on."

She paused, thinking things over. "I've been too careless of late. Flitting out whenever I pleased, allowing myself to be seen by whatever member of your species laid eyes on me."

"What do you mean?"

"I mean I shall not enter into your arrabal again, or any other populated area of your people's civilization—if it can even be called that."

If this pile of cadavers was how she planned to interact with my people, I found myself disinclined to protest her decision to avoid us. I was tempted to call for Pepito and abandon her right then and there. I feared how capriciously she'd slaughtered those men and the triviality of the reason she'd done it. If she thought my kind equal to bees, I might take that fact as a reason to no longer keep her company—or it could be all the more reason to stick with her.

If she did think of humankind as nothing more than a bees' nest to be exterminated if it inconvenienced her, and she thought of me as "her bee," might I be the only thing standing between her and the rest of my people? I remained in the spot she'd left me, looking first at her as she continued to climb the slope, then back down the hill at the bleeding corpses still lying uncovered in the dead winter grass, and I wondered how much of a mitigating force I could be against one so strong and so unsympathetic to human life. Yet I couldn't leave her to her own devices when she'd just proved how dangerous those devices might be.

I won't pretend my motives were entirely altruistic. I admit I was curious and almost thrilled to witness my first demonstration of the magnitude of her power. I wondered what its limits were, but I decided that if I was to stick with her, I must establish some rules for when and where she might use it. I called to her, asking her to return to where I stood.

"Listen," I said once she'd appeared at my side. "I understand you wish to protect your security perimeter, but I cannot have you slaughtering everyone within a ten-league radius of it. Understand?"

She laughed and took a breath to speak, but I did not allow it. "It is not funny. You must bury these bodies in a proper grave—a hole in the ground, I mean—and you must promise me you won't kill again, leastways not without a better reason."

She raised her eyebrows. "I don't understand. According to all the literature you have given me, the top members of your social hierarchy are allowed to murder as they see fit, for reasons even less valid than mine, and your species does not protest. Yet you expect to hold me to a higher standard when I am not a member of your species and therefore no more obligated to preserve the lives of its individuals than you are to preserve the lives of chickens or pigs?"

"I don't care if it makes no sense to you. You cannot slay a half dozen men and their horses because you feel like it. There will be no more of that!" I pointed at the corpses. "And speaking of that . . ."

She tilted her head back and groaned. "If it means that much to you, I shall dispose of the bodies, but I still find such requests ridiculous. Go get your horse. Wait for me by the stream."

I didn't argue further. I feared I'd already stretched the limit of what I could demand, and she acted as though obeying a prohibition on homicide whenever she arbitrarily felt like it would prove an intolerable challenge. I climbed the slope and went to find Pepe, who came to my whistle not long after I uttered it. He, Lobo, and I all waited by the stream as Jhasali had asked.

"I still don't understand why you have a problem with what happened back there," Jhasali said when she found us.

"You killed a person," I replied.

"So? You kill members of other species all the time. Every time you eat meat, something has to die."

"That's different."

"Again, how?"

"They aren't human."

"Neither am I. I don't know how many times I must say it."

"Are you saying I should never eat meat?" I asked.

"Goodness, no. Eat as much meat as you wish. Natural selection is essential, and predation is an indispensable cog in that machine. I am simply saying your species kills individuals of other species it deems beneath itself all the time, so don't get picky when I do the same thing. It's hypocritical."

"I don't care if it's hypocritical. I don't care if it doesn't make any sense to you. I won't tell you again: I forbid you to hurt a person unless one of us is in serious physical danger."

Jhasali sat on the ground and put her chin in her hand and her elbow on her knee. She seemed to be sizing me up, trying to decide how serious I was.

"I will agree to those terms," she said. "But I am still no longer going to allow myself to be seen amongst these primitives. Clearly the drones have not maintained the level of discretion I intended. Or perhaps your species is more observant than I appreciated."

"Fine," I snapped.

I did not like the idea of her never visiting me in the arrabal again, but I liked the idea of another incident like this one even less.

I rode home later that afternoon to beat Sergio back to the house. I'd barely done any of my chores for the day. There was no water drawn, no meal prepared, no wood cut, no fire lit; I hadn't even dusted the mantlepiece, but I didn't pay it any heed. My husband was to depart in a matter of weeks, so who'd be around to be inconvenienced? I figured I might as well not bother with more than drawing us some water and trying to warm the house for the night.

Sergio arrived just after I'd gotten a fire started in the upstairs hearth. He said nothing, and I did the same. He did not ask for food, which made me assume he had eaten with Armando. Instead, he walked right by the chair where I was sitting and went straight to preparing for sleep without saying a single word.

I hated myself for doing it, but I rose and unlaced my dress while he had his back turned. I derived great pleasure from making love to him after a fight, and the last few months had been a marathon of shouting matches followed by stone-faced silences, then bouts of tentative calm before another inevitable shouting match erupted. We were at an impasse: I knew I'd exhausted all my options for convincing him to stay, and he knew I'd never accept his leaving.

I stripped down before Sergio turned around. When he did, I caught a hint of surprise on his face before he forced it back to an expression of indifference. He took me in hand and flipped me around. Thrusting me onto the bed, he entered me from behind. I gasped at the sensation of pressure between my hips as he grabbed a handful of my hair and pushed my head and shoulders all the way down. It hurt at first, but the feeling of being filled up and relieved of tension was well worth those initial seconds of burning pain.

When he was ready, my husband decided to finish by turning me onto my back, pulling me to the edge of the bed, and pushing himself into me while he was still standing. He wasn't any gentler, but in that position, he could lift my hips and grind me against his pelvis. I only needed a few seconds of that intense friction to reach the pinnacle of my pleasure. As I climaxed, I screamed and squeezed his forearms so tight I left fingernail impressions in his flesh.

Sergio rolled me back to the middle of the bed once he finished, then walked away to clean himself up and put on his sleeping clothes. I pulled the covers over my shoulders, realizing as soon as I'd finished just how cold it was in here despite the fire.

I also realized my face was wet and wondered when I had started crying and if Sergio had noticed. Even during, I hadn't been able to avoid thinking of how long I was soon to be deprived of the warmth of his breast, the strength of his hands, and the thumping of his heart in my ears when I curled up inside his arms.

"I don't want you to cry," he whispered as he took his place behind me, folding me into the curve of his body.

"I don't want you to go," I said, barely able to squeak out the words.

"I'm too tired to keep fighting you over this. I am going. I must. Please don't speak of it any longer."

The words weren't all that different from what he had been saying since we'd begun this battle, but there was something so fatigued and defeated in the tone that it drew my heart to him. I had been so caught up in the idea of losing him for such a long span, I hadn't spared a passing thought for how exhausting and terrifying and difficult such a voyage must have loomed in his mind. He was the one risking life and limb; he was the one who was leaving everything safe and familiar.

Now, the tears I shed were more for my own shame than for whatever crime I felt Sergio had committed against me. I resolved from this night forward I would do my best to ease his passing into the New World and not make myself an added burden on him. I rolled over and snuggled up to him.

"I'm finished trying to prevent your departure. I know you have to go. I hope you understand I only fought it so hard because I cannot stand the idea of losing you." I breathed in the scent of his warm sweat in the chill air.

"I know. I get the feeling you think I'm trying to escape you, but you're wrong. If I wished to avoid you, I would not have married you."

I kissed his chest. "I suppose I'll just have to give you as much of my company as you can stand to tide us over."

"I would like that," he whispered.

***

The days ran away from us at a pace I'd not known possible. The more I tried to slow them down and savor them, the faster they fled. Before I blinked, the mid-March departure date had arrived, and the ships were ready and waiting.

The day Sergio was to disembark, I went with him to the harbor to say my last goodbyes. We were obliged to rise early that morning, before the sun, and take Pepito into town in the dark. By the time we arrived, the sun had peeked over the horizon. It now shone on us from the east, softly illuminating the two naos: the smaller, older *San Bruno* and the gleaming new *San José*.

I walked to the dock with Sergio, silent all the way, watching the early morning light reflect off the rippling water. When we reached the *San José*, he held me tight and rested his jaw on the top of my head, wrapping his arms around me and squeezing me to himself. He drew in a deep, slow breath.

I looked with loathing at the ship that was to steal my husband and impose a sentence of what felt like a hundred years of solitude upon me. In Jhasali's view, a two-year span was little different than a single day. In mine, it was an eternity. Perspective is everything.

"I ask only one thing," I murmured to Sergio, trying to measure my words and yet prevent the bustle of the harbor from drowning them out. They could very well be the last I would ever speak to him. "Come back to me in the end. Don't leave me here all alone."

A pained look crossed his usually collected countenance. "Never."

He cupped my face in his hands, running his fingers through the hair under my veil one last time. With that, he kissed my forehead and boarded the ship.

I turned back toward Lobo and Pepito, who waited for me across the street. Despite myself, I shed no tears. I only lifted the sleeve of my dress to my nose so I could catch one last whiff of my husband's scent.

I didn't stay to watch the ships depart. Not wishing to see them sail into the glistening water and turn west on the way to Sevilla and then that incomprehensibly long journey, I swung myself into Pepito's saddle and trotted off without looking back.

I made it into the horse stall at my house before the tears broke through, blurring my vision and racking my body with sobs. I slipped to my knees in the packed dirt and buried my face in my hands. Pepito leaned down and gave me what he must've thought was a gentle nudge, though it knocked me backward and obliged me to put out a hand to steady myself. I let out a halfhearted chuckle at this and leaned forward against Pepito's face. Wrapping my arms around his muzzle, I buried my nose in his forelock. I held him tight, leaning my body against his head and neck, with Lobo's hot fur pressing to my back and the weight of his whiskery snout falling on my shoulder. I sat there and cried like that for hours.

It took me a few days to recover enough from Sergio's departure to leave my house. The first day, I barely got out of bed. Once I regained some of my spirits, however, I sought comfort by riding to see Jhasali, arriving just before noon and turning Pepito out at the edge of her security perimeter. I'd not dared make the ride alone, so I'd asked her over the communicator to send a drone to serve as my artificial anjana, guiding me through the wilderness to the ship.

I passed through the boundary to find Jhasali in the yard just outside the vessel. She was staring at a huge drone that she'd told me before was an escape pod, making me understand it by likening it to a ship's boat. She stood behind one of the holes in the rear while loud banging noises erupted intermittently from inside.

"What's all that racket?" I said.

"The exhaust vent is clogged with something," Jhasali replied. "But the pod can't expel it. I think it's alive. It keeps giving the maintenance drones in there the slip."

I couldn't imagine what an exhaust vent was, but the drones continued their noisy attempts to dislodge whatever plugged it. Jhasali threw up her hands and said she had no idea how anything could have found its way so far up the pod's innards.

Hungry, I headed toward the ship to find some lunch. Just as I approached the gangplank, a deafening explosion ripped through the spring morning and nearly blew me off my feet. I whipped around to see a column of fire gliding away from the pod. It was Jhasali, fully engulfed in flame.

I shrieked and flung myself toward her without a clue as to how I'd extinguish her. Before I reached her, however, she stopped and extended her arms like a burning scarecrow, allowing a drone to quench her with a cloud of white dust. By the time I got to her, she was brushing powder out of her unsinged hair.

In shock, I tried to speak, but nothing came out. Meanwhile, an almost inaudible scraping sound floated from the smoldering engine. We both glanced in the direction of the pod to see a fat red squirrel wobbling her way out of the vent like a drunken dust clump. Lobo lunged at the squirrel, but I grabbed his collar and bade him be still. Jhasali burst into laughter and ran to help the poor, heavily pregnant animal escape the opening, taking the squirrel and placing her at the base of a thick tree trunk.

"I don't believe it's hurt. It must have decided to build a nest inside one of the auxiliary vents." She laughed again as the reeling animal came around and started trying to climb the tree. "I suppose I should put these pods in maintenance mode rather than sleep mode if I'm to keep them outside."

The squirrel finally got a foothold and scurried up the trunk.

"They bounce back quick, don't they?" Jhasali put her hands on her hips and watched the squirrel climb higher, as though it hadn't occurred to her that she had just been on fire.

"How are you not hurt?" I cried.

This was the second time she had received what, in my mind, constituted a mortal injury and walked away unscathed.

"Why would I be hurt?"

"Because you were just on fire!" I shouted, making the dizzy squirrel scurry even faster.

"That's nothing to the nanos. They act as a shield."

"How?" I squinted my eyes and scanned her skin for any sign of their presence.

"There are many nanos in my system. My body would be as fragile as yours if not for them, but they bond with all my cells to make my bones stronger, my organs tougher, my muscles harder, and my skin less vulnerable to trauma. They can't keep out everything, but they can handle mild to moderate hazards."

"Such as?"

"For instance, if you blasted me into space, they couldn't protect me from such intense exposure forever, but their melting point, and thus my melting point, is much higher than yours. Also, if you shot me with one of my own weapons, it would kill me, but if you stabbed me with one of your swords, it would hurt the blade more than it hurt me."

"I want them—the nanos, I mean," I blurted.

"When last we spoke of this, you conceded it isn't worth the risk," she replied.

"That was before I knew they could make me fireproof."

"Correction. They make *me* fireproof. Who knows what they'd do to you?"

"Only one way to find out," I said.

"No, Micaela. I already told you there's a high probability the nanos would kill you if I tried to integrate them with you, and it likely wouldn't be a pleasant death."

"Isn't it my choice as to whether I think it worth the risk?"

"Isn't it *my* choice as to whether I share my technology with you?"

"I suppose, but if you—"

She raised a hand. "But nothing. I'll never risk your life on the remote possibility one can integrate nanobots with an adult lifeform. Maybe we can restart this conversation when you're closer to the end of your natural lifespan."

"And you'll offer them to me then?" I asked.

"I don't know, but I'll be much less concerned about killing you when you're already dying. Since you're not at the moment, please drop it."

I didn't wish to drop it, but she walked away from me as if to say she would hear no more. She returned to the hole in the rear of the escape pod, giggling again as a pitiful drone emerged, sooty and still smoking. It looked almost humiliated as it floated past her.

Disappointed but fearing to further irritate my companion, I let my eyes wander to the place where she'd been burning: a blackened circle full of scorched leaves and smoldering twigs, some of them still glowing orange. I looked back to her.

Her clothes weren't even singed, and she acted as though being set on fire was as unremarkable as an afternoon stroll. I wondered what it must be like to be able to stand inside all the pyres of all the churches in all of Christendom and have nothing to fear, to never have had anything to fear. I supposed I would have to wait to find out—if I ever did.

The image of my torched friend popped back into my head, bringing along with it a plethora of other images. I sat down under a tree and breathed deep, cupping my hands over my mouth and nose, trying to pretend I'd forgotten the memory of the auto de fe from all those years ago. Sometimes, the recollection was still so fresh it caused me to panic. I pressed my hands tighter over my face, digging my nails into my skin.

"What in all this little galaxy is wrong with you?" Jhasali asked.

I looked up to discover she now stood just above me, looking down. For some reason, I opened my mouth and the tale of how Ignacio had dragged me out of my home and forced me to witness the burning came pouring out. I wasn't sure why I told her. No one in my life besides Father Manuel knew of that fateful day. Yet here I sat, in the shadow of the budding forest canopy, recounting the miserable experience to Jhasali in great detail, feeling relief in the act of retelling it to one who'd not be able to infer anything from it I didn't want inferred.

When I was finished, she looked stunned. "I assume burning is painful for your people?"

"Terribly. Possibly worse than any other pain."

She was silent a long time before speaking again. "I knew you humans had a bit of a silly fixation with the supernatural, but I did not realize you'd carried it so far."

"Well, we have. I wish you could use those primary weapons you've spoken of to put a stop to things like the trials and the burnings."

"I certainly could, but I never would. You humans may not be able to threaten me, but my own species can. That is why I cannot use any device that can send too many signals out of the atmosphere. If I surround this planet with indicators of a large spacecraft, it will eventually draw attention. Aside from that, why would it be in my interest to save any of you?"

"Sometimes we must do things because they are right, not because they benefit ourselves," I said.

"Oh, my darling, I quite enjoy your innocence. It is part of why I have grown to love you so. But you're mistaken if you believe your species' ideas on morality are akin to those of my people. It is right in your eyes to save human lives. In my eyes, it is right to allow your nature to have its say. If you pose excessive danger to each other, it is right that your environment should select you for extinction."

I shot her an angry look. "I think my species is worth preserving."

"Of course you do. You're still subject to the biological drive to pass on your genetic material, are you not?"

I threw up my hands, not comprehending.

"Look Mica, you can't fix everything. I learned that the hard way. Even if I were to install myself as Lord of the Earth tomorrow, it would not make your species less violent or stupid. Forcing them to change their behavior wouldn't change their nature, and as soon as I abandoned the planet, they'd go right back to warring amongst themselves. Do you deny that?"

"No," I huffed.

"Then what, pray tell, is the logical point in bothering at all? What is rational about saving the life of an individual when its own kind doesn't even deem it worth preserving?"

"Sometimes you cannot base things on logic," I said, exasperated. "The life of the individual is valuable because the individual who possesses it values it over all else."

"Then why do humans seem to consider their lives so worthless they'd throw them away for nothing? Burn and be burned for deities they've never seen?" she asked.

"So you're lifting the embargo on the god talk?"

"Of course not. I am merely pointing out the fallacy of your argument. You say humans value their lives, yet they seem all too willing to kill and die for the silliest of things. How is that value? Savages! Mindless savages, the lot of you."

"You say we're savages because we have many cruel ways of killing one another and reasons for doing so that are admittedly foolish. But what would your Adoruch do to you if she caught you?"

Jhasali pursed her lips. "I shudder to think. I'd be made an example of without doubt."

"Yet it's different because it's for a reason that makes sense to you?"

"I suppose it is not. Technologically savvy savages we are."

I wished to pause and savor the pleasure of finally having talked her into a corner, but I instead uttered, "You no longer have to place an embargo on the god talk, by the way. After everything I've seen in the last year, I hardly believe a word the Church says anymore."

I had not expected those words to ever escape my lips, but given all that my family and I had endured at the hands of ecclesiastics, I supposed I shouldn't be surprised at my growing suspicion of the institution such men represented.

As I was telling Jhasali my tale of the auto, I'd let her believe that I recounted every detail exactly as I recalled it. But I'd left one thing out. After the incident in the quemadero, I was tormented by what Ignacio had said to me. Why had he thought I, of all the children of Castilla, needed to witness such an event? What had I done that made me so wicked? I did not long endure before I felt compelled to put these questions to Father Manuel.

At first, he told me such things were not for young ears and I was still not old enough to know the truth. But I'd been damn well old enough to be dragged to the quemadero, so I refused to take no for an answer. I kept at it for days and weeks: every night after Vespers, every morning when he awoke, every evening when Antonia was making us supper, every afternoon when he sat down to read or write his letters. Until one day, he finally gave in.

That was the day I discovered my parents hadn't died of illness nor had they abandoned me on the steps of Father Manuel's church, as he'd always said. They had been Muslims until they were forcibly baptized at the hands of the queen I had hitherto admired. Soon thereafter, my father must have decided he could no longer pretend he'd abandoned his faith, for he and my mother had been accused of spreading their infidel beliefs by disseminating Qurans to Old Christians, and they'd been arrested while she was pregnant with me.

I'd been born in a dungeon, and mere weeks after, when Father Manuel had come to give one of his ailing parishioners her last rites, my mother had begged him to take me from her very arms. Fearing I might perish if I remained with her in the Inquisition's jail, she'd convinced him to sneak me out under his cloak after he'd finished ministering to her dying cellmate.

She'd been right to fear a long imprisonment, for she'd languished for several years before appearing alongside my father in an auto de fe much like the one I'd observed. The day I wore down Father Manuel was the day I learned why Ignacio had beaten me and forced me to witness the burning. It was the punishment my parents had suffered, the punishment I deserved as the spawn of heretics.

Yet Father Manuel swore on all the saints that my parents had not been burnt, that they'd been spared the fire in exchange for lashes and exile. He guessed they must've made their way to the lands of their coreligionists as soon as they'd escaped the claws of Castilla, though he could not be sure of anything except that they'd never returned for me, not even after the term of their exile had ended.

I couldn't accept that. How could they have been spared the fire? For if they had, I'd be with them! Anything else was unfathomable. Still, I didn't press Father Manuel further on the subject because I feared to push him until he confirmed my parents had been burnt alive. I couldn't bear that thought, so I kept repeating to myself the pleasant lie he'd told me: my mother and father had fled to the Barbary Coast and been unable to return for me. That was all I needed to know—all I wanted to know.

After Father Manuel's revelations, I deduced that I probably never knew my parents' true names, the Moorish ones they'd been called before they'd been forced to accept Christian monikers, so I demanded these of my guardian. He told me he had never met either of my parents before stumbling across my mother in prison, nor had he spoken to either of them again after that encounter, so he couldn't offer me any other names than the ones he'd given me my whole life: Miguel and Josefa.

At first, I was devastated at this news, for though I believed Father Manuel had lied when he told me my mother and father hadn't been burnt at the stake, a small part of me still held onto the hope that he was telling the truth. Yet how could I ever find my parents one day if I didn't know their given names? I thought at least I might have a chance if I knew what my mother had called me—my *real* name. But when I asked Father Manuel, he informed me my mother had never told him to call me anything but Micaela.

As a child, I had believed him. As I matured, however, I began to suspect he was deliberately keeping this vital piece of myself from me. Of course, it was possible my mother had thought it would be to my advantage to receive a Christian name and be raised in a Christian household. Yet it was equally possible she'd told Father Manuel my real name was Fátima or Nafisa or something and that he was to take me to my relatives. Maybe *he* had been the one to decide I'd be best off in a Christian house. After all, he'd said things to make me suspect it.

For one, he'd told me on multiple occasions I ought to be grateful I hadn't been raised in a heathen cult. I'd also once overheard him in a heated argument with another parish priest who espoused expelling the moriscos of Castilla rather than trying to evangelize them. Father Manuel had told Father Enrique he'd best think twice about sending a horde of crypto-infidels to the Berbers or the Turks, and if they would not abandon their heresy, it'd be better to see to it their children were placed under the care of people who would nurture them in the true faith—raising them to be soldiers of Christ rather than assets to an unholy empire. It was this conversation above all else that made me question his motives for our own relocation.

Not long after Father Manuel and I had left Toledo for good, I learned we had been transferred out of our old parish at his request. He assured me we'd moved so the stain of sanbenito might never again bring me such calamity as that which Ignacio had inflicted. Yet, deep in my heart, I wondered if Father Manuel had chosen to leave the city because he feared I might start looking for my parents or that one of them might return looking for me. I'd never dared to ask him or to suggest I suspected such a thing.

On the other hand, Father Manuel had never given me reason to believe he didn't care for me. He could've refused to ferry me out of the Inquisition's prison. He could've let the Holy Office rip me from my mother's arms and send me to die in some overcrowded foundling home. He could've dumped me there himself, for there I'd have died a Christian—heretic-spawned and dirty-blooded, but a baptized

Christian, nonetheless. If that were all that mattered to him, he wouldn't have raised me, educated me, found governesses to tend me, or tried to comfort me as I grieved my own suffering and that of my parents.

For the first few months after learning of their misfortunes, I had mourned deeply, my tears all but incessant. I wept for my mother and my father and the realization that, even if whatever had happened to them hadn't been fatal, it had been the most awful, traumatic experience of their lives. I wept for my lost family and the life I could have had if I hadn't been forced from their arms when I was only a babe. I wept because I didn't know Father Manuel's true motives for keeping me during my parents' exile. I wept because the pleasant lie I'd clung to my whole life—my dying parents had given me up to protect me from their own sickness—was shattered.

In my anger and grief, I often resented my parents above all, for the churchstate had been so busy murdering Jews in the early days of the Inquisition that they'd had almost no time for moriscos. The appearance of a morisco in an auto de fe was practically unheard of until long after my parents had endured theirs. So I believed they must've done something outrageous to bring such trouble to our house and if they'd only kept their Qurans to themselves instead of hounding Old Christians with them, nothing would've happened to us. It enraged me that they'd thought spreading their faith was worth inflicting such pain and loss on their infant daughter.

Despite my fury at their supposed placement of their religion above me, I still couldn't chase the little voice of doubt from the back of my mind: the voice that couldn't accept the injustice and the unrighteousness of it all. Now, I wondered if it was this voice that had led me to rebel by taking up with Jhasali. Perhaps it was the thing that had drawn her to me, as well. She knew I, like herself, was a Dissenter.

As I sat on the cold forest floor inside her security perimeter, pondering the past I still kept hidden, that familiar voice of dissent howled like a hurricane inside my head. Yet, even in the midst of the tempest, I was so ashamed of my history that I could not bear to tell a single soul. So I'd kept up the lie that my parents had died of illness, the lie I'd been telling everyone my entire life.

Beyond repeating this falsehood to Jhasali, I'd also maintained it with Sara and even with Sergio. I had lain with him more times than I could count and he still knew me not—nor would he ever. There were few greater humiliations in those days than having a parent who'd worn the sanbenito, and if it was a terrible crime to be born a woman, it was a doubly terrible crime to be born a morisca.

***

I allowed myself some time to grieve for Sergio during the next few weeks, for I was plagued by a feeling of loss akin to real bereavement. I feared for his physical well-being, but I also mourned a much more tangible and sure loss than some illness or injury that might not ever come to pass: this single voyage would span more than five percent of my remaining life expectancy—if I was lucky. No matter how much money he made or how good a condition he returned in, it was time the two of us would simply not get back.

To comfort myself, I tried to focus on the silver linings around this dark cloud. With Sergio gone, I could resume giving alms to the destitute children, though Rodrigo made this more difficult than need be. As anticipated, his unwanted attentions had recommenced the second my husband's feet left Spanish shores.

I could also pull my lovely new dresses from their trunk again. Between our fights about Pepito and the accursed New World, I couldn't risk showing them to Sergio, so I hadn't been able to wear them in months. Not to mention I'd only gotten to see Jhasali on a handful of occasions during Sergio's entire stint ashore, and now we could make up for lost time. In the early period of his absence, I rode out to her as much as I dared, but I visited my neighbors and called on Sara, Gabriel, and Gracia much more often.

One fine May afternoon, I was in the plaza mayor when I decided to visit Sara. Rosa let me inside the town house, and I didn't understand why Gracia's matronly housekeeper was answering Sara's door until I heard soft music floating in from the sitting room. I went there to find Gabriel playing a slow tune on his vihuela: a lullaby for his infant son.

Gracia lay on the sofa, holding the baby on her chest, and Sara sat in a chair near the window. I did not wish to interrupt this quiet scene, and I felt awkward having stumbled upon it at all. I made to back out of the room, but Gabriel looked up from his instrument. Smiling, he whispered for me to enter.

Then he looked back down at the ruddy wood of his vihuela and kept playing his serenade, a soothing version of "La nodriza del rey." I found it ironic that Gabriel would play a song about a nursemaid who fell asleep and accidentally let her charge burn to death. Though the child was resurrected in the end, the tale was still unpleasant, and I did not fail to recall Gracia had remained steadfast in her refusal to keep a wet nurse for Eduardo. Perhaps she'd taken the lyrics a bit too seriously. I chose not to listen to the words; the tune was pleasing to the ear, and the domesticity and fatherliness of playing it suited Gabriel.

As the notes drifted into my ears, I recalled Jhasali had enjoyed the music she'd recorded all over town. I already had the tiny communicator stuffed up my sleeve, so I pressed the button. Before Jhasali could speak from the other end, I whispered for her to just listen.

"What?" Gabriel murmured.

"Nothing," I answered.

He didn't look up. He must've thought he'd imagined me speaking. I sighed and remembered how much I loved to hear Gabriel play. He'd gravitated toward songs with a slow, tender tempo long before he'd had a son, as if he'd been nesting in preparation for the day he'd need them.

Eduardo seemed to be enjoying the music. His head was pressed between his mother's breasts, his dimpled arms limp by his sides, and his slumber so deep he'd leaked a pool of drool onto the fabric of her dress. I laughed softly at this. I wished to hold him, but I dared not try. That might wake him and break the gentle spell of the sleepy, plucking melody.

Leaning back in my chair, I did as I'd commanded Jhasali. I just listened. The music, like fine wine, permeated my whole body with a tingling sensation that traveled from my ears down my spine and made the hairs on my arms and legs stand on end. I sighed and wished the back of my seat were Sergio's chest. I enjoyed resting on him like a chair when we sat together in bed.

"You've been alright lately? We have not seen you around as much in recent days," Sara murmured, staring at me with those dark-green eyes.

Though I knew better, I wanted to tell her everything: my wilderness wanderings, the drones, the ship, and Jhasali. Jhasali! With a start, I recalled she was still listening. As clandestinely as I could, I reached into my dress and pressed the button to cut her off so she couldn't eavesdrop if Sara wished to talk.

"I am aggrieved Sergio's gone, but I'll manage," I replied.

Gracia nodded without a word, I assumed for the sake of not waking Eduardo. Sara gave me a sad look. I knew she wished me to be stronger in the face of Sergio's absence. She'd spent so much time saying what a boon it would be for me when he was gone, but I couldn't agree. I didn't hate my husband as she did hers.

"You'll get used to it, Micaela. Sooner or later," Sara muttered.

"I don't think that's possible," I whispered.

"Give it time. If not this voyage, then the next. Or the next after that."

I wanted to say Sergio had assured me he'd not sail forever, but part of me wondered if death might be the only thing that could truly part him from the ocean. His heart beat to the rhythm of the tides and pumped sea-foam through his veins. Even when his body was onshore, his soul never pulled its feet from the surf. How could I ever offer him anything that might compare?

# Chapter Ten

# THE INVASION

A week or two later, I spent Sunday evening having dinner with Father Manuel after he'd concluded the day's services. As I stared at the glowing coals from my cook fire, I thought about Jhasali's inadvertent conflagration and my subsequent recounting of the incident in the quemadero. Ever since her accident, I'd been thinking almost nonstop on Ignacio and everything that had happened at the auto de fe, wondering if Father Manuel might've spared me that day if only he'd seen his former friend's true colors sooner. Though I knew it would displease him, I couldn't resist bringing it up.

Without turning to face him, I asked, "Was Ignacio always so unpleasant, or was he different, somehow, before I knew him?"

"Micaela, is it really necessary to rehash that old affair? It's been over ten years; can you not just forget it?" Father Manuel groaned.

"Surely you're joking."

"No, I am not."

"I'll forget it the day the Crown forgets my parents were heretics and takes their sanbenitos off the cathedral walls. I'll forget it the day I have my mother and father in my own house," I snapped.

Father Manuel sighed. "Alright, I give you that. But why must we discuss Ignacio now?"

"I don't know. I guess because in all these years I've never understood why he felt it necessary to do as he did."

"I see. Well, Ignacio wasn't always as he is now," he said as I sat down and handed him a plate of cod. "I baptized the boy and took his first confession. Until you and I left Toledo, there was not a day of his life he and I weren't acquainted. I always liked him; he was a timid, gentle child, much like myself at that age. He held his mother's hand through Mass and read devotionals to the younger children on the church steps afterward—every Sunday without fail."

"What happened?" I asked.

"His mother died when he was ten. He was so aggrieved he asked me if there wasn't any prayer that could convince God to restore her life in exchange for his father's. She'd always been the only thing standing between him and that man."

"What did his father do to him?"

"Nothing terrible. But he thought the boy was too tender and too close with his mother and sisters. He only tried to toughen him up, though I often warned him about humiliating his son in the manner he did. I didn't think it best for the boy to live in fear every moment he spent in that house. I worried such treatment would do much worse than toughen him up."

"So that's when Ignacio changed?" I took a sip of wine.

"I saw the beginnings of it then, yes. But when it turned out his mother willed her dowry to pay for him to join the Dominicans, I thought I was doing him a favor by convincing his father to honor her wishes. Once his schooling commenced, though, things only got worse. He began scolding the younger children rather than reading to them. He got rough with his sisters and hounded his father to marry them both off as soon as possible. He became interested in . . . darker things.

"Once he completed his education, I tried to keep him away from the likes of the familiars and officials of the Inquisition, but he wouldn't be dissuaded. I suppose it made him feel powerful to be near such characters, but I always hoped his association with them might prove temporary." Father Manuel cleared his throat.

"If you knew what kind of man he'd become, why did you not send him away from us before he dragged me to the quemadero?" I asked.

"Because I didn't know he'd become that kind of man, or at least not to *that* degree. I spent many years looking for the boy who'd read picture books to the little ones after Mass. In the end, I suppose I only wished to avoid admitting he wasn't there anymore."

Much as I hated it, I couldn't help but feel a twinge of pity for Ignacio. His father had been trying to make a man of him. Instead, he'd made a monster, and I understood all too well the rage that dwelt in the heart of such a monster, the impotent fury over long-past hurts that would remain forever unavenged.

Despite this new information, my compassion evaporated as quick as it formed. I, too, had lost my mother and much more, yet I'd never attacked a child, nor did I derive pleasure from wanton cruelty. I also didn't understand why Father Manuel had wanted to keep Ignacio away from the tribunal in Toledo, since he himself wasn't exactly unacquainted with it. It was how he'd met my mother, after all.

"Why were you so interested in keeping Ignacio away from the familiars?" I said.

"You know my stance on the Inquisition. Their mission is a necessary evil, but the kind of person who would volunteer for such a mission . . . I suppose someone has to do it. If heresy is allowed to take root—"

"So I guess that means my parents got what they deserved," I snapped.

I'd never before dared to ask his thoughts on that topic. I was afraid to know the answer.

He shook his head. "That's not for me to say. There are so many false accusations."

"But if it were true, if they did what they were accused of, they deserved what they got?"

"Again, heresy cannot be allowed to spread. It sows discord among the populace."

"That's not an answer."

"Well, everyone who breaks the laws of the Church deserves punishment."

"It's interesting you would say that." I rolled my eyes.

"Why?"

I didn't reply. Father Manuel was still unaware I knew about him and Leonor, but supporting my family's persecution whilst simultaneously having lived in sin with her until the day she died was not a good look on him. Not wanting to open that door, I deflected.

"Because even if my parents did what everyone said they did, it's not a thing to be punished for. They were only evangelizing, same as you."

"For a false god."

"How do you know he's false? Allah could be true, and Christ could be false. Or maybe they're both false."

"Micaela! How dare you!" Father Manuel stood up and smacked the table.

"How dare I? I was ripped from my home and my family and everything I could've ever known, and how dare *I*?" I suddenly hesitated, cowed by the look on his face. "I'm sorry. I just get so angry that sometimes I forget myself. I don't believe what I just said."

He sat back down. "It is a very good thing you don't, child. I wish I knew what really troubled you."

"I cannot tell you."

"You think there's a thing in this world I won't understand?"

Images of Jhasali and the drones and the ship flooded my mind, and I wanted to say there were a great many things in this world he wouldn't understand. Instead, I told as much of the truth as I dared.

"I've been praying about the problem for over a year, and I've not gotten so much as a syllable in response. I ask for a sign and receive nothing."

"Keep praying, then. Call on the Holy Spirit and keep a lookout for his reply. But always remember that God sometimes uses silence to teach us."

I shrugged. "Feels like silence is the only teaching method he's ever used for me."

"Perhaps there's a reason for the silence. Is your heart far from him? Is your faith weak?"

"I suppose it's possible," I conceded. "But if God wished to strengthen my faith, isn't allowing me to find him the appropriate response to my seeking him? Whatever happened to 'everyone who asks receives'?"

Father Manuel chuckled. "God isn't a waiter at a tavern. You cannot presume to have every demand you make immediately met."

"But I'm not asking for anything. I only wish for a sign—some kind of signal that he's listening to me or is somewhere out there. How long must I stand and knock at an unanswered door before I accept no one is behind it?"

I'd only meant to think that, and from the look on Father Manuel's face, I should have.

He leaned across the table. "Micaela—"

"That came out wrong. I just meant . . . am I to die on my knees waiting for an answer?"

Whatever Father Manuel said in response, I was now too worried about my damned loose tongue to hear it. I'd become too open with my thoughts as we'd continued talking, and I didn't want to say anything else as stupid as the things I had said already. Though Father Manuel had always indulged me to an extent, he was still my chaperone and our parish priest, meaning he could exert a great deal of power over me if I pushed him too far. So, quickly as politeness permitted, I excused myself and fled out into the humid June evening.

When I got home, I poured myself some wine and went to bed before the sun even set. Yet sleep eluded me, so I rose to sit in my chair. There I sat, head tilted against the back, blinking toward the ceiling. I mulled over the question of why I should keep praying to an absent god until my lungs gave out. Truth be told, I was running out of reasons.

Fearing to think on it anymore lest I decide I should waste no more words on deities who wouldn't or couldn't reply, I downed several more cups of wine, hoping to tire myself enough to sleep away this lonely night. Jhasali's offer to let me stay with her on the ship popped into my head while I drank, and I wondered, as the hours ticked by, one after the next, whether it was alcohol or lonesomeness making me feel a twinge of regret for not taking her up on it. The ship might be too quiet and too unfamiliar, but at least I would not be alone tonight.

Stumbling to the bed to fetch her communicator from where I'd placed it under the pillow, I descended to the dark kitchen for another wineskin. Once I'd poured a fresh cup, I set the disk on the table without pressing the button. Though it would be impolite to call Jhasali in the middle of the night, the boredom and frustration of insomnia began to creep up on me as time continued its glacial march toward dawn. I hated to be awake all alone while everyone else slept, when even Lobo snored away before the huge hearth upstairs.

The press of a button was all it would take, but that one movement of the thumb felt more difficult than a voyage around the world. I wanted Jhasali's company, but I feared to be rude by demanding she descend from the mountain at my whim for no other reason than to entertain me because I couldn't sleep.

As I sat alone in the dark, wishing for the happy chirping of this tiny device to ring in my ears, there came a sudden knock at the door. My heart leapt. Jhasali had come to visit me, despite her recent rule against entering the arrabal. My apron lay on the table, so I put the disk inside the pocket before I unbarred the door and threw it open to let her in. But the face that greeted me at the threshold was not Jhasali's.

"Rodrigo?" I asked.

His strong hand clapped over my mouth and shoved me back inside. Another man pushed in behind Rodrigo, slamming and barring the door. This one I didn't know. I'd seen him with Rodrigo a time or two but had never learned his name.

"If you wake the neighbors, we'll kill you," the unknown one whispered, coming within centimeters of my nose as Rodrigo held me immobile.

Just as he said this, Lobo flew into the kitchen and lunged at Rodrigo's face. Rodrigo reached up to deflect him, and Lobo latched onto his left forearm. I wrenched myself out of Rodrigo's grasp as he pummeled Lobo's head with his free fist, but Lobo did not unclench his jaws. I swung around and yanked the fire poker out of the ashes, rushing back to defend Lobo from the other man.

"No!" I shrieked at the man as he sliced at Lobo with a long dagger, stabbing him over and over in the back and sides.

Lobo had still not released his hold on Rodrigo. If anything, he bit down harder, shaking his head so ferociously it made his blood-soaked body writhe from side to side. Rodrigo howled through gritted teeth, still beating Lobo about the head.

"Stop it!" I swung my poker, striking the strange man on the back as hard as I could.

I knocked the breath from him, but he did not collapse, so I hit him again. He turned on me as Lobo slipped to the ground. Rodrigo sank to his knees, holding his bleeding left arm to his body. I swung again, but this time, the stranger dodged the blow and backed up a step.

The man brandished his bloody knife and pointed to the poker. "Give me that. You'll make things much easier on yourself."

I held the poker with both hands and positioned the sharp end above my head, ready to swing again. I intended to beat this man to death if I had to, but he was careful not to put himself in range of the iron rod. We stood in a stalemate: he did not dare accost me lest I get a blow in, and I did not dare approach him lest he wrest my only weapon from my grasp.

Suddenly, I lurched forward as something shoved me from behind. In my terror of this unknown attacker, I'd let Rodrigo sneak up on me. I fell to the floor on my hands and knees. Before I could get up, the stranger stepped on the poker and wrenched it from my grip. The two of them dragged me away from the door and threw me face down on the kitchen floor at the foot of the table. I thrashed and kicked and scratched like a cat in a flour sack when they caught me by the ankles, but the strange man struck me several times across the back with the poker, knocking the breath from my body and rendering me still.

Rodrigo's mangled left arm bled from countless ugly lacerations. I hoped such an injury would deter him, but if anything, it made him more furious. He flipped me onto my back and pummeled my face just because he could. Grabbing a fistful of my hair, he slammed the back of my head on the floor.

I lay there stunned for a long while as they wrapped Rodrigo's arm and discussed this unforeseen resistance. It seemed they'd expected to be able to incapacitate Lobo before he harmed them. Nearly senseless, I couldn't move. I just listened to their conversation. I could see nothing save a mass of red and white spots swimming in haphazard patterns all over my field of vision, a flock of glowing birds swirling through a dark sky.

I heard what I could not see: they tore through my house, searching for the money that Rodrigo had seen me spending in town. They found a couple of silver cups and a few pieces of jewelry from Flanders and Bilbao, but there was not much money; I had only what Sergio left me to cover expenses and a few blancas of Jhasali's. Something heavy dropped beside my head—the lockbox that contained all the coin in the house.

"Where's the rest?" Rodrigo said.

"I didn't realize you'd moved up from petty theft to armed robbery," I mumbled, still lying dazed and paralyzed on the floor.

Rodrigo stomped on my hand.

"That's all there is!" I bolted upright, jerking my hand from under his boot and squeezing it to my chest.

My injured head spun so badly I almost vomited. I started to fall backward, but Rodrigo caught me by the back of the neck and held me in a seated position.

"That can't be all there is," the other man snapped when he came into the kitchen. "You said she had more."

"You think if I had more, I wouldn't give it to you? What use will it be to me if you kill me?" I asked.

"Where is the horse, then?" Rodrigo demanded.

"Don Armando's estate."

"Shit!" he roared.

Rodrigo's friend squinted at him. "Let's just take the box and go. We should get out of town before they come looking for us."

"Felipe, you know they won't find us here. Not for a long while," Rodrigo said.

I wondered who "they" were and what Rodrigo and this Felipe had done to cause "them" to come looking, but I was never to know. Obviously, Rodrigo had thought I would be an easy target for quick loot, for I was all alone without Sergio.

Rodrigo put his face closer to mine, and I tried to recoil. I knew the expression he bore. It was the same cruel, greedy look I'd seen on the face of Ignacio as we'd witnessed the burning all those years ago.

"You will give us more than this," Rodrigo said.

"You already have everything I can give," I replied.

"Not everything." Clutching my wrists, he yanked my arms away from my chest.

"Rodrigo, let's go. Let's just leave," Felipe pleaded.

"No one will be looking for us until morning," Rodrigo repeated. "If this pathetic box is all the money she's got, I intend to make this stop worth my while."

I had feared this was why he'd come; it was why I'd fought back instead of offering them the lockbox. Yet, as I sat on the floor of my own kitchen, head full of rocks, unable to get a proper breath for the pain in my back, Lobo dead a few meters away, I found I could fight no further. All the strength I had left slid through my pores and puddled under my body.

Suffice it to say, Felipe did not prove all that difficult to convince, and he and Rodrigo did as they would with me. As I had when I'd witnessed the auto de fe, I focused on the dirt rather than what was happening. In the quemadero, the dust on the ground had clumped up in my tear droplets. This time, the dust on the floor was held together within a congealing drop of my blood. I stared at this clod of dirt at every opportunity, noting all its intricacies, the tiny pores in its surface, the infinitesimal outline of each grain of grit as it clung to its neighbor.

When Rodrigo and Felipe stripped me, I imagined a world of tiny, invisible creatures occupying this speck. When one of them invaded my body, I worried all the creatures didn't know their universe could be wiped away with nothing but the sweep of a broom. When Rodrigo tried to make me look at him, I cast my gaze to the floor and fantasized that all the minuscule animals in this minuscule world were my friends, beings I had known my whole life, who'd occupied my house longer than I. Maybe they'd been here before the house itself. Maybe they'd be here after I was gone.

I was on the point of protecting this speck of dust like a madwoman when my attackers took a respite at my kitchen table. They even had the nerve to pour themselves some of my wine as I lay motionless at their feet. I stayed on my belly, staring at my clod of dirt and hoping it would be the last thing I saw instead of one of their faces. In the vast distance, Rodrigo said something about checking my purses and clothes for more coins.

My heart skipped a beat. I made to jump off the floor, but what I'd intended to be a leap and a bound turned out to be me staggering to my knees only to sink back down on my side instead of my belly. I was trying to cover myself with the hem of my nightdress, which they'd discarded under the table, when a hand grabbed me by the hair, lifted me back to my knees, and tilted my face up. Someone shoved Jhasali's disk in front of my eyes.

"What is this?" Felipe demanded.

I stretched out my hand and pressed the button before he could react, screaming into the communicator, "Jhasali, help me! They're in my house!"

Felipe balled up his fist and struck my face, sending a spurt of warm blood shooting from my nose and a fresh wave of white sparks flashing before my eyes. He smashed the disk on the floor and stomped it, shattering the casing and revealing its metallic guts. I did not have any inkling of whether I'd made contact.

"Witch! She's a witch," Rodrigo cried upon seeing all the strings inside the disk. "She was praying to that thing like it could hear her. It must be a charm or talisman of some kind."

"No!" I shouted.

At this, Rodrigo clamped his hand over my mouth before looking at Felipe. "I say we cut off her head and leave her here. If anyone finds out it was us, we show them that thing and tell them she tried to murder us with her magic."

I wriggled like a fish in a net, desperate to break free. When I gripped Rodrigo's wounded left forearm with all my might, he wrapped his right hand around my neck and squeezed hard enough to press the life out of me. I dug my nails into the puncture wounds, but he jerked his arm out of my grasp and started strangling me with both hands.

As I began to faint, a tremendous bang boomed at the door. Immediately after, Jhasali entered the house and looked around, bewildered at my bloody face and these two strangers in my kitchen.

Felipe lunged at her with his dagger, but she raised her right hand toward him, tilting her fist downward. A second later, a flash of light burst from her wrist, and his head exploded in a spectacular spray of blood and brain and fragmented bone.

Rodrigo shrieked and pushed me away. With another flash from her wrist, Jhasali shattered his head before he could take a single step, popping it like a soap bubble and spattering its contents all over the walls, floor, and ceiling. She brushed a piece of brain off her skirt like it was nothing more than a speck of lint.

"What happened?" she asked.

I did not answer; I sank all the way back to the floor and knew no more.

***

Next I knew, I woke from what seemed a short nap to find myself curled at the bottom of a gigantic pitch-black bowl. My nightgown had blessedly been slipped back onto my battered body. Hoping to see a light or a window, I uncurled and sat up, but there was no apparent escape from this dark cell.

Confused, throbbing from head to toe, and overpowered by thirst, I began to panic. Finally grasping where I must be, I cried out for Jhasali, wondering if she could hear me through the thick walls of the egg-bed. Just then, the lid popped open with a snap. I tried to scramble out of the gap, but I was too feeble to lift myself over the edge, so I slid back to the bottom.

"Help. Please," I murmured.

At these words, Jhasali reached into the egg, grasped me under the armpits, and lifted me out like I weighed nothing. She sat me in a chair—a real chair—but now that I was no longer in terror of being trapped in the pod, I turned out to be too weak to hold myself up. Lifting me once more, she carried me to the chest of drawers and laid me on top of the mat.

"I need water," I said.

A long, flat drone entered the room bearing a pitcher. Jhasali handed me a cup of water, and I drank one after another until my stomach felt like it might explode.

"Why did you put me in that horrid thing?" I whispered.

"It's where I would've wanted to be," Jhasali said. "I considered placing you in the bed, but I was unsure what was best while you were unconscious, so I went with what I knew."

"What bed?"

Without a word, Jhasali laid me on the flat drone that had brought me water. I was almost too lethargic to register that I hovered about a meter off the floor as she swept me out into the hall and then to the room next door. I didn't notice much about this room, but my body sank into a soft and springy mattress while Jhasali pulled a heavy blanket over me.

"You said you wished for furnishings more to your liking. Should I have put you here to begin with?" she asked.

"Yes. You should have."

"If you'd only been sleeping, I would have, but I couldn't wake you, no matter how hard I tried. If you hadn't been breathing, I'd have thought you dead."

"Where's Lobo?"

"Micaela—"

"Don't say it," I begged, recalling why he wasn't near. "What did you do with his body?"

"I put it in a hole in the ground—a grave, as you called it."

"Did you mark it?"

"No. But I can show you where it is."

"I wish we'd had some flowers. I wish I could have said something."

What could I have said for poor Lobo after such a nightmare? Goodbye, old friend; because of me, you died for nothing?

Jhasali laid her hand on mine. "Pepito is outside. If that brings you any comfort."

"I'm glad to know he's safe," I replied.

"And I had the drones clean up your house."

"Did you bury those men too?" I asked, worried what might happen if someone came calling and found two headless bodies in my kitchen.

"No. I disintegrated them, as my people do space junk. It is a dishonorable manner of disposal. Like refuse."

"Good. It's no more than they deserve."

"Did I do well to kill those members of your species?"

"Yes. This time, you had a valid reason," I answered. "How long have I been sleeping?"

"Something like twelve or thirteen hours. Why did they do that to you?" she asked.

"They came wanting gold. So they beat and robbed me."

"They didn't rob you. I have your element money here in Homeship."

"Thank you," I said.

"Micaela, did they rape you?"

I held my breath at the question. It was so direct it caught me off guard, not the least because the fact that she'd found me naked and pummeled with two strange men in my kitchen should have made it obvious.

"No, they didn't. They were trying to make me tell them where I hid my valuables. They thought I had more than the box." This lie came automatically. I felt a sudden, overwhelming desperation to avoid further humiliation.

Jhasali gave me a quizzical look but kept silent.

"You don't believe me," I whispered.

"It isn't for me to believe or disbelieve. If you don't wish to speak of whatever happened, I won't force you."

I coughed and almost cried out from the pain, sure several ribs on the right side of my back had to be cracked. I hadn't noticed before because Jhasali had laid me on my left side.

"I have to sleep," I said, wishing only to avoid speaking of this anymore.

Jhasali squeezed my hand and left without another word.

Unable to fall asleep because of the throbbing in my back, I removed my nightdress. Its fabric pressed on my bruises, and it felt better to leave them bare. I wrapped myself in the thick blanket, keeping it as loose as I could, though I had to remain on my left side so it would not touch my back.

The next two days passed in a blur. I spent them doing nothing but lying in bed sleeping or crying, sometimes both at once, for I'd wake intermittently to find my pillow soaked with tears. I wished to feel nothing, to think nothing, and indeed I was so spent that I often achieved this desire with no effort. I did not even dream.

On the occasions when I did let my mind wander, I replayed the scene of my attack over and over. Why hadn't I thought to get a kitchen knife? Why had I not gotten hold of the communicator before they'd raped me? Why hadn't I swung the poker harder or remembered there were two of them or, for God's sake, at least *asked who was at the door?*

I tried to drown these thoughts in wine, but if I drank too much, it made me have to use the chamber pot that I'd brought with me following my initial visit to this place, as the ship's waste removal system had proved too bizarre for me to tolerate. Scarcely willing and scarcely able to get out of bed, there were times I considered just pissing myself, so I stopped voluntarily drinking anything. Instead, I tried to sleep round the clock.

Jhasali interrupted my slumber several times a day to force me to eat or, when I refused, to drink as much as I could. I would have lain there like a slug and starved if she hadn't, but I hated her for it at the time. When I kept refusing food, she tried to put a tube into my arm like she had with Gracia, but as the damselfly approached me, I screamed and swatted at it as hard as my physical condition would allow. Not wishing to force a needle into my arm, she reverted to making me take water and milk by mouth.

Her patience proved to have its limits, though, for it only took two days of waking me for the sole purpose of getting enough fluids into me to keep me alive before it seemed she'd had enough. She came to rouse me in the afternoon of the third day.

I knew it was afternoon because I'd been watching the sunbeams stream through the glass behind the bed and creep across the floor and the walls, making their slow march from the left side of the room to the right, every now and then their bright glow interrupted by a passing cloud that cast a long shadow between us and the mother star.

Jhasali sat at my bedside. "You need to get up."

"Why? Caring for me has become too inconvenient?"

If she expelled me from the ship, I'd go sleep in the woods. My only regret was that the weather was not cold enough to freeze me to death overnight. No matter. I could find a spot to lie down until autumn rolled around.

"No, it isn't that." Jhasali sighed. "Can I tell you something?"

I nodded without speaking or turning to face her.

"During the war, one of my closest comrades was captured and held prisoner for a long time, even by my people's standards. We Dissenters are a tough sort, but we can be broken, and our enemies revel in the process. They interrogated my friend as long as it took to force our secrets from her mouth.

"Though we managed to get her back alive, she was a shell of what she had been. She stayed inside the sleeping chamber for ages. She didn't speak to anyone. She didn't even act like she knew we were there. We stopped trying to rouse her, thinking she'd come around on her own. Yet, when she did, it was like another person was living in her body. Her interrogators snuffed the fire out of her, and I always thought if I'd done something differently, if I'd pushed her out of that catatonia sooner, maybe she mightn't have changed so much."

Jhasali hissed between her teeth. "Look at me. I did the same thing after I was separated from Aenwi. Who knows how many Earth centuries I spent entombed in my own sleeping chamber once I landed here? I'm terrified to ask Homeship how many times we swung around this sun while I lay in the dark. Now I feel different too."

"What's your point?"

She rose to her feet. "That lying in bed curled up like a stone didn't do my comrade any good, it didn't do me any good, and it won't do you any good. I don't know exactly what was done to you any more than I know exactly what was done to my friend. I don't need to, but I do know you must get up, and you must do it soon. You'll no longer recognize yourself if you don't."

I said nothing in response, so Jhasali squeezed my shoulder and left.

Though I detested her for it, she was right. What was I to do, lie here and let myself die? Was ruining my whole life not precisely what Rodrigo would have wanted? I'd never give his shriveled, spiteful spirit the satisfaction.

I slept all that night, but next morning, I rose and put on real clothes, which Jhasali's drones had brought for me. As lethargic as I'd been these last days, I'd not done much more than stare at the wall, so I'd thus far failed to scan the place she had converted into my bedroom. As I combed my hair with my fingers and gingerly laced my dress, I took a look around.

This whole time, I'd assumed she'd only gotten me this bed and perhaps an oil lamp, but she'd outdone herself. The old furniture, including the awful peapod bed, had been removed. In its place was the four-poster I now sat on, flanked on either side by an ebony end table. The crescent couches had been replaced with human-sized, human-shaped furniture: a low sofa and two matching armchairs, similar to the ones in Sara's town house.

Sconces full of candles hung from the walls, along with a half dozen oil lamps strung from the ceiling. If I lit them after sunset, I would have the kind of oscillating golden glow to which I was accustomed. I also noticed Jhasali had retracted the sliding doors typical of this place and installed a wooden door, on actual hinges with an actual latch, that I could open and close myself. She'd hung curtains I could draw over the glass wall behind the bed, as well. At the far end of the room, she had positioned a table with a pitcher and a washbasin.

Jhasali had given me everything a human might need, and she'd been so attentive to detail that if I shut the door to the hallway, I would scarcely be able to tell the difference between this room and a bedroom in a luxurious human house. I let a single tear fall as I contemplated all the trouble she'd gone to just to please me, and it comforted me to be in such a beautiful, cozy place instead of the kind of room she liked.

I went down to the galley for breakfast, noticing, as I walked the ship's halls, I felt much better. My back and ribcage still pained me, and the rear of my skull hurt at the slightest touch, but the bruises and wounds seemed to be healing at an accelerated pace.

A drone set out some fruit and ham when I arrived, and I helped myself to it.

"How did you cure me so fast?" I asked Jhasali, easing myself into a human-sized chair.

She didn't have a table yet, so this chair was positioned underneath a flat drone that hovered at the correct height.

Jhasali sat across from me. "I have medicine that stimulates cell renewal. For my people, it would work within hours, but since you're biological, it's slower. Your external injuries should heal in a few more days, but it could take a couple weeks to fully mend your internal ones."

"Wait. You put stuff inside me?"

"I had to. You had a significant head injury that could've been fatal had I not treated it. You had several broken bones, too. I healed them and your outer wounds as well."

I didn't reply, unsure how to feel about that.

When Jhasali had healed Gracia, things had been different, for I'd truly believed her to be lifting a curse brought on by my sin. Now, I knew better, and her powerful alien science frightened me. I'd grown accustomed to her drones floating around, but the idea of them touching me, much less injecting me with unspecified substances, was still unpleasant. I feared the unknown of what she'd done and the unintended consequences it might have, and I would never have consented to it if I'd been awake.

"Is something wrong?" Jhasali said.

I didn't know how to respond. She'd helped me in the way she knew how, but I shuddered at the thought of those drones handling my unconscious form as it lay defenseless in their grasp.

"Nothing I . . . just need to be alone for a while," I muttered.

I left the ship, exited the perimeter, and went searching for Pepito. I did not whistle for him but walked deeper into the woods. This close to the ship, I felt safe to wander. Jhasali's drones patrolled the area surrounding her perimeter, and I took advantage of their protection to enjoy the misty, dewy morning, feeling the wet moss and decomposing leaves from the previous autumn squishing beneath my bare feet as I pulled great gasps of forest scent into my nostrils.

In a thicket of wild cherry trees, I discovered Pepito pawing at the base of an older one that had already begun to fruit. A smile spread across my face, my first in what felt like an eternity, as I watched him snorting and stomping at the roots of the tree, greedy for juicy cherries.

"You want some?" I asked, not wanting to approach too quietly and spook him.

He swung his thick neck around and looked at me as though I'd fallen from the sky. Then he turned back to the tree and kept pawing. I unwrapped the shawl from around my shoulders and looked for a branch low enough to give me a foothold.

I'd never been much of a tree climber, and the trunk was free of branches up to around two meters off the ground. There was no way I could get up the bare trunk without help, so I crept up to Pepito and took him by the forelock. He yanked his head out of my grasp and backed up a few paces, resisting my implied attempt to lead him away.

"I don't want to go anywhere. Get me into the tree and I'll get you the cherries."

Of course, he didn't understand me. He stood stock-still, head well beyond my reach, tips of his hooves digging into the soft ground.

"Fine." I marched straight up to him and grabbed a handful of mane farther down his neck. "Come, now."

He acquiesced and followed me begrudgingly. I led him around to the side of the tree with the lowest branches and bade him lie down for me to mount. I didn't feel like scrambling up, and I couldn't lift my arms above my head without some pain in my right side. Still, whatever medicine Jhasali had used was working. I would not have been able to mount Pepito, much less a tree, if she hadn't treated me.

Once I was on, I asked Pepito to stand again. When he did, instead of giving him the heel and turning him from the tree, I placed my hands on his withers and used them to help myself stand up on his back. He finally sensed what I intended to do and stood rigid as a statue so I could maintain my balance.

I caught hold of a branch that jutted from the trunk about the height of my belly and scrambled into the tree. Pain shot through my side and back, but I groaned and kept going, unwilling to be deterred now that I was here. Once I had planted my feet amongst the branches, climbing became easier, though I had to watch my head to avert any limbs touching my sore spot. Within minutes, I'd made it to the cherries. Many were pink and orange, only half-ripe, so I rifled through the clusters, looking for more mature fruits.

Knowing he shouldn't eat too many seeds, I plucked the first one and used my fingernails to tear it open and remove the pit before tossing the flesh to the ground below, where Pepito all but tripped over his own tail to get to it. There were more clusters of pink and even red cherries on the branch, so I kept picking, harvesting only the ripest ones I could find. Soon, the sound of falling fruit and tromping hooves filled the air as I plucked, pitted, and tossed faster than Pepito could catch and eat. It was not long until the base of the tree was covered with shining cherries.

When I'd plucked all the fruit I could reach, I gingerly climbed back down to the lowest branch and realized the jump to the ground was longer than I intended to make. I whistled to Pepito, who stood nearby, munching on a cluster I'd seeded and tossed into a heap. He turned his eyes toward me but did not budge or release his prize. I whistled again and banged my palm on the tree trunk.

"Come help me. I got you all those," I demanded.

This time, he raised his head and came toward me, still chewing on a mouthful of cherries. I got hold of his forelock and positioned him so I could slide from the branch onto his back, then from his back to the forest floor. When my feet hit the ground, he turned right around and went back to eating his fruit.

I picked up a juice-coated cherry, wiped it off with my fingers, and took a bite, wincing as I sank my teeth into its flesh. Though it was quite red, it was still painfully tart.

"How are you eating these?" I asked Pepito, spitting out the bite I took.

I went to the base of another tree and tossed the rest of the cherry back to the ground; let him have the lot of them if he could stand the taste. Sliding down and positioning the left side of my back against the trunk, I squished my sweaty dress to my skin. The day had grown warmer once the fog had lifted, and the dew had evaporated from the grass, leaving my seat on the forest floor dry and dusty.

I closed my eyes and listened to the sound of the birds calling, the calm rustling of the topmost tree branches in the almost nonexistent breeze, Pepito crunching away on his cherries. This was what I had needed: the noisy silence of the forest, the busy stillness of all the creatures bustling about as they enjoyed the approach of summer, the distraction of a form of work that was difficult enough to drive the thoughts from my mind with the sweat of my body. I felt peaceful for the first time in days—truly peaceful, not just beaten down with exhaustion—almost like things might be alright someday, somehow.

Pepito kept stomping and snorting in his contentment, his lazy tail swishing away a fly here, a gnat there, as he crunched through the remainder of the cherries. I shed a few quiet tears while I watched him, more for the release of doing so than anything else.

Somehow, weeping always made me feel better and worse at the same time. Emotionally, I got a sense of pressure relief, as if the weight of my feelings splashed to the ground with each drop from my eyes; but physically, I suffered fatigue and pain behind my brows after too long a bout of tears. In the end, weeping proved a mere act of trading one form of pain for another and deciding which was worse, like most things in life.

As night approached, I rose and headed back to Jhasali's home with Pepito tailing me. As we neared the ship's perimeter, he diverted for a drink from the stream. I didn't wait for him; he'd grown accustomed to passing through the barrier now. He reappeared behind me just as I set foot on Homeship's ramp, making a beeline for his hay trough. I left him there and entered the ship.

When Jhasali came down from wherever she'd been hiding, she found me in the kitchen, washed up and cutting a fillet of venison for our dinner. I stood on a high stool to reach the countertop. She mounted a platform drone to augment her own height.

"You know my devices can do that," she said.

"I wished to do it myself. Doing something with my hands makes me feel better," I replied and kept chopping.

She glided to the counter and watched me slice the meat for a stew, somehow still fascinated by the act of cutting food by hand.

I didn't look up from my work. "I need to get back to my husband's house. I've been gone four days already. There's no way I haven't been missed."

Of course, I didn't want to return to that house after what had happened there. I didn't wish to walk the floors that had been stained with my blood nor stoke the fire with the poker that had beaten me. Yet, loath as I was, I had no choice unless I wished to move into the ship and disappear for good. How could I leave Father Manuel, Gracia, and Sara?

Sergio had left me already, but when he returned (if he returned), I still wanted to be there for him. I wondered what was wrong with me that I wished to wait for a man who'd abandoned me at the very threshold of the door that had failed to keep out the men who'd attacked me. I shook that thought from my head and tried to focus on my work.

As I continued slicing the cut into bite-size pieces, I tossed a glob of fat from the counter to the floor.

"What did you do that for?" Jhasali asked.

My breath caught. I'd forgotten Lobo wasn't wedged between the stool and the counter, waiting to eat my trimmings.

"Must have dropped it." I got down to retrieve the morsel that would never be eaten, and I stifled a fresh sob.

Jhasali gave my shoulder a gentle squeeze and went back to watching while I resumed chopping, trying to keep my tears from falling into the meat.

***

When I returned to my house before sunup next morning, I discovered Jhasali's drones had scoured the place so thoroughly it was as if Rodrigo had never led his friend to my door. My armed escorts went back to their master as soon as I entered, leaving me to wander around like a ghost haunting the rooms that had once been mine.

The table where Sergio and I had spent many a night laughing over wine and dinner was now the table where Rodrigo and Felipe had relaxed after they'd violated me. The bed where Sergio and I had shared our pleasures was now the bed my assailants had stripped and ransacked. The stains of my brutalization might've been scrubbed from the floors, but my eyes still saw them everywhere. My new bedroom back in Homeship felt more like home now.

Isabel came knocking after sunrise. She and Susana had thought I was spending the night with Sara during the first few days of my absence, but they had begun to suspect something was wrong when I never returned to feed my chickens, even when the birds had completely run out of forage. They'd spent all yesterday evening trying to make me come to the door, and they'd decided if I didn't show by morning, they'd call the alguacil and find some townsmen to break it down.

"Where have you been? Why didn't you answer us?" Isabel demanded.

"I never left. I've been ill the last few days."

"You couldn't have told someone that? We would've taken care of you."

"I was too weak to get out of bed," I replied.

"What happened to your face?"

"I tried to get up to use the chamber pot, and I fell on the floor and hit my head."

Isabel's eyes bored into mine, but I only had the remnants of a black eye left by this point, so she had no real reason to suspect I lied. When she asked about the animals, I explained Pepito had been in the estate pastures, like he often was, and Lobo had taken ill at the same time as I, but he'd not made it. I told her—as I would soon tell everyone else—that I'd buried him this morning at first light. Though she didn't seem to entirely buy this story, she had no evidence to contradict it, so she asked no more questions.

The next couple of weeks passed in a blur of misery and shock. My physical pain faded so fast I would not have believed I'd been injured if I hadn't possessed the memories of the ordeal. Those I ignored, forcing them to the back of my mind every time some incident or item brought them to the fore. I soon became so adept at suppressing any sort of negative thought that I spent every day walking around in a haze of self-enforced numbness.

This numbness contrasted sharply with the celebratory mood around me. Noche de San Juan had snuck up on me as I mourned. As usual, everyone was excited for the feast day that coincided with the summer solstice. Gracia harped about how this would be Eduardo's first bonfire. Susana and Isabel called on me nonstop, pressing me to prepare herbal water and hunt for four-leaf clovers with them and then dragging me around the arrabal to visit all the neighbors who hadn't sailed away somewhere. My laundress friends, Constanza and Eulalia, invited me to their friend's home for a preholiday fiesta with dozens of the other townswomen.

I wished it would all just stop. I'd always hated this particular celebration, for when the hogueras were lit, I could never prevent myself from imagining shrieking women bound to stakes in the midst of the flames, especially if the throng incinerated a dummy or two. It reminded me too much of the effigy I'd seen burned all those years ago.

On the night of the bonfires, Isabel led me into the ocean so we could bathe in the waters and leap over the waves. Listening to everyone else carousing and hooting, the old people guffawing as they took to the surf, I began to weep, thankful the crowd was too excited and the night too dark for anyone to note my "laughs" were actually sobs.

I didn't jump the waves. Instead, I sat in the freezing sea while everyone else leapt around me, and I prayed for the curative waters to wash away my assailants' filth from my body and the memory of all they'd done from my mind. I knew the waves would fail, whether they were nine or ninety, for nothing could ever wash me clean again.

It wasn't long before Isabel dragged me to my feet and cajoled me to jump the waves too.

"Come, Toledana," she chirped. "I know there's no ocean in your city. But I'd think you would have learned to leap a little water after all these years."

Though I didn't reply, I had no choice but to play along. Anything to avert suspicion.

That eternal night did end, but my torment did not. My heart ached for vengeance. My soul cried out for justice and wept with despair whenever it recalled I should have none. I supposed one might argue I had received better justice than most people in my position, for Jhasali had slain both my assailants on sight.

Still, a quick and painless exit was hardly fitting of what Rodrigo and his friend had done to me. A single second of terror before the end felt nothing like punishment befitting the crime. It felt more like the elimination of a thing that inconvenienced Jhasali rather than the chastisement of someone who'd hurt me. Never had vengeance been so mercilessly inflicted and yet tasted so bland; its honey turned to vinegar in my mouth every time I recalled the ease of their demises.

To my dismay, the injustice of my assailants' swift ends was soon to be the least of my worries. As the bonfire celebrations came and went, the time of my monthly bleeding came and went with them. The first day without blood, I swore I'd miscalculated the timing, just forgotten the day I'd started last time. On the second day, I assured myself it wasn't altogether unusual for me to be a day or two late.

By the third day, I was praying with all my might for the flow to start. I promised my mute god if only he'd break his silence to spare me this, the worst possible result of Rodrigo's attack, I'd take up the mantle of the faith with renewed vigor and never backslide again. Over and over for days, I whispered only the words, "Please, please don't let me be with his child."

I managed to keep a good hold of myself as the blood-free days continued to tick by—first seven, then ten, then fourteen—by telling myself I'd skipped menstrual cycles before and been thrilled by the prospect of bearing Sergio's child only to suffer bitter disappointment at the next month's flow. This event would be no different in practice, just the emotional responses would be in reverse. I prepared myself to be overjoyed by the arrival of the blood. I'd revere it as a potion of healing and purification, more precious than gold, and never again would I revile the pain and troublesomeness of it.

However, the lack of blood was not my sole symptom, and every time I vomited or felt too fatigued to get out of bed, I knew deep down what that meant. Yet another invader of my body now colonized my womb, consuming me alive from the inside. In mere months, my belly would bloat up and burst open, after which this leech that had been feasting on my blood from within would crawl to my swollen breasts and suck me dry from the outside.

These awful feelings brought an even deeper sense of loss to my already soul-crushing grief, for I'd thought when this time in my life came around, I would be jubilant. I'd always anticipated watching Sergio build us a crib and offering Sara a godchild and finally becoming halfway decent at sewing so I could make my first set of baby clothes and a tiny baby's hat.

Not only did Rodrigo steal my honor and my pride and my sense of safety in my own home; he stole my first pregnancy. He had convinced his friend to stay and violate me when Felipe had wished to go, had *begged* to go. No matter which one of them had ultimately sired the enemy within my womb, its existence was Rodrigo's fault, and I hated him for this more than anything else. I never imagined the only thing I'd want for my first child would be to rip it out of my body with my bare hand.

When the week of my bleeding remained bloodless for a second time, I devolved into a state of real panic. I'd told no one of the attack, and now, there was no question Rodrigo had forced his child inside me. What would everyone say when I turned up pregnant whilst Sergio was away? If I were arrested for being with child in his absence, I could be imprisoned or whipped through the streets or worse.

If he were so inclined, my husband had the legal prerogative to shoot me for adultery. I did not think Sergio capable of such a thing, but neither did I think he'd believe I'd been forced now that it had resulted in a conception. How could I explain why I'd failed to bear him a child for years, yet I'd given birth to a total stranger's baby?

There were remedies for my problem back in those days, certain brews one could drink to induce menstruation, but I did not know anyone who might be able to procure one for me or tell me how to make it myself, and I was too terrified to try to find someone. I could meet the wrong person and, instead of getting the herbs I needed, I might find myself accidentally poisoned or outed as an adulteress—not to mention what Father Manuel would do to me if word reached him that I'd ended my pregnancy, no matter how it had begun. Thus, I tried to do it on my own first.

I went into the woods and rolled down a steep hill, trying to hit my belly as hard as possible, though I could barely prevent myself from curling into a ball. I drew an agonizing bath, walking pails as heavy as I could carry from the well to the house, then boiling them as fast as I could to keep the water almost scalding before I submerged myself. Then I beat my belly with the fire poker, blackening my flesh with bruises until the skin cracked. Yet that was the only blood I drew.

As my desperation amplified, I even took Pepito into the baldíos, where I goaded him to a gallop and deliberately threw myself out of the saddle, trying to land right on my belly. The first time I did it, he thought it an accident and returned to the spot so I could mount again. By the third time, he realized I did it on purpose and became agitated.

On the fourth try, I fell flat on my face, bouncing it off the ground and sending blood gushing from my nose. No matter. I held it shut until the bleeding stopped and mounted to try again. This time, however, Pepito refused to run, braying like a mule and stomping in distress every time I squeezed him with my heels. I gave up. I had never ridden with spurs or a crop, so I did not have much of anything to pressure him to gallop. I was aware falling on purpose was not going to work anyhow; I'd only kept at it because I was so frantic.

Despite how my distress augmented by the day, no matter how much weight I lost or how much hair I found scattered in clumps on my pillow every morning, I still resisted seeking out Jhasali's powerful medicines. I recalled her statements about how her people's reproductive process was different than ours. Though I remained unsure of specifics, I now understood the distinctions went far beyond the simple matter of unmarried parents.

Worse still, my recent humiliations had already been paraded before her in graphic detail. She'd not only seen my naked, battered body as I sat helpless within the grasp of my attackers; she'd also held that same body as she'd transported me to the ship, touched it as she'd healed me, and handled it as she'd dressed me. I didn't blame her. I would never have expected her to just leave me there, injured and unconscious, but I also couldn't bear the thought of her knowing of this latest and most horrendous degradation, especially since there was a good chance she wouldn't know how to fix it.

Yet I couldn't concoct anything else to do on my own, so I went to Sara. I wasn't sure if she could do much for me herself, but she was the only person I trusted enough to ask. At least she might know of a sympathetic midwife who could help a pitiful adulteress keep her secret.

When I entered the town house, I asked Sara to send the servants out of the parlor so we could talk in private. Instead, she took me upstairs to her bedroom and shut the door. She motioned for me to sit in one of the chairs near the closed shutters of the balcony.

"This is the most private place in the house. What's happened?" she asked.

"I wouldn't have bothered you at all with it, but I didn't know if I could trust anyone else." I steeled myself to force the awful words from my throat. "I am with child."

I burst into tears, expecting Sara to chide me for adultery or ask me with whom I'd sinned, but she did nothing of the sort. Rather, she took on an almost business-like tone, standing up straight and asking me how far along I thought I was.

"I don't know, maybe three months," I said.

"Three months? Why didn't you tell me sooner?"

I wept even harder. "I'm sorry. I was so ashamed."

"There's nothing to be ashamed of. What woman in our position hasn't had a dalliance or two? I knew something was going on with you."

"How did you know?"

"If you want to keep your affairs a secret, you don't disappear for days at a time."

"I guess so."

Back in June, the news that I'd gone missing had spread all over town. As long as it was just idle, unproven gossip, it didn't matter much, though it had taken a long discussion to convince Father Manuel I'd simply been sick in my bed the whole time. A child would be the proof everyone needed of my—as Sara put it—dalliances. Still,

I couldn't bring myself to tell her I'd been raped. Putting the horns on my husband was less embarrassing.

Sara patted me on the back. "Don't worry. We'll see if we cannot take care of this."

"You know how to make what I need?"

"Not really, but I have some left over from . . ." She stopped.

"You don't mean?"

"Yes. When I discovered certain things about Armando, I was newly pregnant. I decided then I'd never again bear another child of his. Thankfully, I hadn't yet told him I was expecting."

"What things did you discover?"

She hesitated before saying, "Nothing. It's not important."

"I'm sorry. I don't mean to pry."

"Don't be sorry. Just take this." She handed me a small wooden box full of pungent dried herbs. "You have to mix it in hot water and drink it all at once. It's going to make you sick, but it will hopefully make you bleed too."

"Hopefully?"

"Well, it worked for me. But I was not three months along."

"You mean I'm too late?" I cried.

"Keep your voice down. Do you want to be arrested?"

"Oh no. No!" I sobbed afresh and buried my face in my hands.

"Shhhh, Micaela, come here." She took a seat on the bed, and when I went to her, she put her arm around me. "We won't know whether it's too late until we try it."

"What if it is?" I asked.

"There are things we can do. You can go away with an 'illness' for a few months."

"Come on. You don't think Sergio will find out I was 'ill'?"

"Don't worry about Sergio. You'll find him more understanding than you anticipate."

"Why?" I raised a disbelieving eyebrow.

"He loves you a right sight more than Armando ever loved me. Men will bear quite a lot for someone they love, I hear."

"He won't love me anymore after this."

"With any luck, he won't ever find out about this," she replied.

Sara asked me to stay the night while I took the medicine, but I'd already been humiliated enough just by having to ask her for it. I couldn't stand the added shame of an audience watching me puke. Thus, I drank the herbs in my house.

Sara hadn't been lying when she said they would make me sick. I vomited all night until I had nothing left to give but my soul, and yet my stubborn blood refused to flow. Eventually, I just lay on the floor with my face over the basin, dry heaving and dry sobbing. I couldn't produce any more tears with all the water squeezed out of me. It seemed I could make myself expel any conceivable fluid from any conceivable orifice save the one I needed.

Next day, I sat in my house, weak and ill and still pregnant, and I realized I had the choice between grabbing that horrid fire poker and tearing my whole womb out of my body or going to Jhasali. I would have used the poker, too. At that point, I'd decided I'd rather die by my own hand than in childbirth, suffering as I'd seen Gracia suffer for a child that would be no more loved or wanted than an outbreak of the plague.

With every other option exhausted, I gave up and decided to do the thing I should have done from the start. I got the new communicator Jhasali had made to replace the broken one and called for a drone to escort me to Homeship.

# Chapter Eleven
# THE METAMORPHOSIS

"I am with child," I said to Jhasali upon finding her in one of the common rooms on a lower deck. Unable to look her in the eye, I pressed my brow to the window as I uttered the dread words.

She rose from her seat and turned me to face her. I still couldn't bring myself to gaze into those deep black eyes, so I stared instead at the dark gray hair cascading down her shoulders.

"Is that what you want?" she asked.

"Of course not. You think I want to bear the demon spawn of the bastard who raped me? Not to mention what Sergio will say if he returns to find some other man's babe in his house after he trusted me."

"I assume he would understand if you were forced against your will."

"How can I prove that? How can I prove I didn't willingly bring some stranger into his bed? All this time I've thought myself barren. Yet now I'm with child? God forgive me. I never wanted to bring another orphan into this world! I don't know how this happened." I buried my face in my hands.

"Well, it's clear your mate is the one with the issue, not you."

I looked up at Jhasali, aghast.

She laced her fingers together. "Think about it. You have been married to him for years now, and never have you become pregnant by him, even though I must assume you have mated with him with significant frequency. And you informed me he mated with many other females of your species before marrying you. Yet do you know of any products of all those pairings? You have been fertilized by another male only once, and it succeeded on the first instance. Thus, it stands to reason the problem lies with him, not you."

I gaped at her, not ready to believe the obvious truth. In that day, barrenness was seldom the fault of the man. It was typically assumed the root of the problem must lie in some defect or deficiency of the woman.

"Putting that aside," she said, disrupting my musings on her previous statement. "Clearly, you do not wish to birth this offspring, so would it not be better, then, to get rid of it now?"

"I've already tried, to no avail. I thought you might have a better way."

"Of course. If you wish to be free of it, I will terminate it for you by my own means. I don't understand why you didn't come to me first thing."

"I hoped I could do it on my own and spare myself the embarrassment. And I also—well—if you cannot do it, there's no hope left, is there?"

"None of that is in the least bit rational, Micaela."

"I'm sorry, I haven't been in the most rational state of mind the last few months!" I snapped. "I'll flagellate myself when I get home. How's that?"

"Don't work yourself into a frenzy. I must consult with my drones as to how to go about the procedure, but I see no reason I cannot help you. My guess is I'll have to send some nanos in to eliminate the foreign body and then extract them once they've expelled it from you."

I gasped. "You've got to send them inside me?"

"Yes. I did it before when I tended your injuries, and it went well. Don't worry. The bots will all be extracted as soon as their job is done. I suppose we could try to find some other way if you really don't want them—"

"No! I do want them, but I don't want you to extract them. If you put them inside me again, you're not pulling them out."

"How many times must I tell you no?" She sighed.

"Not even once more. I will gladly accept these things if that's what I must do to be rid of Rodrigo's accursed seed. But if they enter my body again, they are mine."

Jhasali held up a hand. "I say again, my people are fitted with our nanos early in our incubation, not well into our physical maturity. I don't know if the bots will integrate with your system, nor can I predict whether the sensors can be placed. I do not wish to kill you."

"But if it were to succeed, would I be like you? Able to resist flames and blades and blows? Able to withstand Hell itself?"

"It is likely that if the implantation succeeds, you will be closer to my state of being than you could ever hope otherwise. Still, there is no way to know what will happen before we do it. It could just as easily end your life or maim your mind or body."

I stared at the drizzling rain and deepening twilight beyond the window. The prospect of dying during the implantation did not frighten me as much as the prospect of continuing to live in the manner I had all my life: always at the mercy of whatever man looked my way. Now, I was even at the mercy of my own body and the unholy hijacker within it.

"I don't wish to be afraid anymore," I stated.

"There is no need to be afraid. The men who attacked you, I rent their heads from their shoulders. You saw me."

"What good does that do me when there are a thousand more just like them everywhere I turn? Are you to kill every man on Earth who might pose a threat to me? There'd be precious few of them left if you did."

"I cannot do this. You know that. I don't want to risk losing you. Who else do I have on this miserable planet?"

"If you don't do this, you'll lose me anyhow. I'll throw myself from a cliff! I'll drown myself in the sea! Whatever I must do, I won't go through anything like this again. I mean it, Jhasali. Give them to me."

Before I understood what I did, I ran to the metal wall and slammed my head against it as hard as I could. Right then, I felt betrayed by everything I'd ever held dear. My city and my guardian had betrayed me when I was a child; my husband had betrayed me when he'd abandoned me; my home had betrayed me when Rodrigo had come knocking; and my body betrayed me now. I could do little about the external traitors, but I had an opportunity to exert some control over the internal one, and I was not about to let it pass me by.

I thought all this even as I kept slamming my head against the wall. Jhasali leapt to stop me, grasping me in her arms and dragging me to the floor. Wrestling against her with all my might, I kicked her shins and elbowed her belly, but she was as strong as a bull and as hard as brass. She held me away from the wall and left me to struggle in vain. After a while, I grew exhausted and inert, though I wept uncontrollably.

Jhasali let me go and sat by me on the floor, looking more distressed than I had ever seen her. "I don't understand. I thought you agreed the danger outweighs any potential benefit."

"I didn't agree, not after I saw you withstand the fire. But you told me to drop it, so I did," I moaned, gasping for air. No matter the depth of my inhales, I was suffocating.

Jhasali knit her brow. "There's no need to gamble with your life. I can protect you."

That did not feel true anymore. She was just another in a long line of people who'd been charged to defend me and failed. Father Manuel had failed me when Ignacio came, and Sergio had failed me with his absence in my hour of need. Even though I owed Jhasali my life, she had still failed to save me from being robbed, beaten, and raped. The only one who'd come through for me in my darkest hour was Lobo, and he was gone.

"You didn't protect me. Where were your little spies when Rodrigo was raping me? Where were you? You stopped him killing me, but you stopped nothing else," I said.

"The surveillance bots aren't omniscient, and I have not sent them anywhere near your home since the day you told me not to. You wish me to resume observing you?"

"No!" I bellowed. "I don't want to be spied on or coddled. I just don't want anyone to hurt me again."

There lay the truth of the matter. I wanted so desperately not to hurt anymore that the past and future ceased to be. Reservations about risks or repercussions were all blown away like dandelion seeds. Nothing existed beyond these feelings of ultimate powerlessness and reckless abandon.

"You're bleeding," Jhasali whispered.

She looked at my belly, so I did too. Sure enough, a dark-red stain was spreading across the fabric covering the cracked and blackened bruises of my lower abdomen, where I'd been beating myself almost every day since my near-boiling bath. I must have torn one open during my struggle. I hadn't noticed, and it did not pain me even now.

Jhasali's drones brought water to clean my wound. As I was wearing only a white linen blouse and a dark brown skirt, it was not difficult to raise my shirt to wash the ruptured contusion.

Jhasali looked at my lower belly in horror. "What happened to you?"

"I'm going mad," I replied, still bawling.

When she looked at me in confusion, I explained I did it to myself as I was trying to end this agonizing pregnancy. Jhasali stayed silent for a long time. The drones hummed from their places behind us, but other than that, the ship was quiet.

Finally, when I'd begun to wonder if she planned to tell me she'd never implant me and I was welcome to fling myself off any cliff I chose, she spoke again.

"So, this is truly what you want?"

"It is. I can't stand this wretched worm inside my belly one more second," I whispered.

"I suppose it would be good to have another pair of hands around here. Useful ones, I mean, in case something happened." Jhasali furrowed her brow and cast her eyes away from me. "And I guess I'll lose you anyhow not so long from now. You'll grow old so fast."

She went quiet, but after a long silence in which she seemed lost in some internal debate with either herself or one of her many telepathic consorts, she turned back to me.

Heaving a deep sigh, she said, "Alright. Let's try it."

Late into the night, Jhasali consulted with the same drones she'd once used to tend Gracia. I knew she communicated with them because, even though they all remained quiet, she would change her expressions at random: a pursing of the lips, a raised eyebrow, an eye roll. Several times, the drones hovered around me, scanning my body while she gave audible sighs and threw me looks of deep concern.

"Stay still. They need a blood sample," she finally said after hours of silence.

The tiny needle-beaked damselfly floated toward me. Not long ago, I would have been terrified of its approach. Now, I felt nothing of the sort. Perhaps I even experienced a twinge of affection for the thing. I held out my arm and stayed still as the drone pricked me at the elbow and drew several vials of warm blood from my veins. A larger device switched them out, and, when the damselfly got its fill, the big drone spirited away with the vials.

"It needs to analyze," Jhasali said.

It did not take long, and the drone returned before I'd had the opportunity to collect my thoughts enough to properly ponder what I was about to do.

"The nanos wish to do an exploratory mission," Jhasali told me.

When I assented, she grabbed my wrist and turned my forearm toward the ceiling. The damselfly injected me with a shimmering gray liquid, viscous as gravy. I gnashed my teeth as this liquid entered my veins, but the burning pain and subsequent frigid chill only lasted a few seconds.

We sat in silence for much longer than we had when the damselfly drew my blood. I could not feel the liquid moving inside me. However, I imagined my veins bulged and squirmed as the tiny creatures moved through my system like infinitesimal parasites swimming upstream through the rivers of my blood to find a nesting place inside my heart. I shuddered.

When Jhasali spoke again, it was with more confidence and more seriousness. "The drones are reasonably certain the nanos will be able to integrate with your body. They say you have a strong heart. Good veins. No defect to speak of. You are the ideal specimen for such an attempt."

She looked away from me and toward a large drone before adding, "We will need to insert more of the nanos first so they may bond with your organic tissues and find the ideal spots in your brain for the placement of the sensor chips. They'll decide the best approach for positioning these implants after they've done a more thorough exploration of your physiology.

"I warn you, Micaela, the change you are about to make is a permanent one. Once the nanos have integrated with your body, you will no longer be purely biological. You will be a hybrid of organic and synthetic material, a true human and yet a true machine. From that, there will be no turning back."

"I'm ready," I blurted, understanding not a word she said but nevertheless wanting to begin the process before I lost my nerve.

The drones needed no more permission and herded me into a room I'd only been in once before: the medical ward. There, Jhasali told me they wished me to sit on a table that popped out of the floor and floated to the center of the otherwise empty chamber. I obeyed their command, my eyes darting around as several more damselflies appeared alongside the first one. Though this new development set my nerves to prickling, I held my arms out whenever the tiny drones bumped them to demand access to my veins.

They injected hundreds more rounds of the gray gel into both arms, poking holes in me from wrist to shoulder, filling me with trillions of bots over the span of about an hour. Upon finishing, they floated into a semicircle around me, waiting for I did not know what.

At first, nothing happened. Then, I sensed a lurch inside my veins. The flesh under my skin crawled with invisible fire. I'd been injected with molten metal. I shrieked and made to leap off the table. The bigger drones charged at me, but as I raised my arms to defend myself, Jhasali's hands intertwined with mine.

"Micaela, they do not wish you to leave this spot," she said as I moaned in agony. "What you're feeling now is the bots bonding with your oxygen-bearing blood cells and eliminating your immune system. They have no use for that. They will provide far superior immunity than your own body can. Just stay calm."

I tried to do as she said, but I hadn't anticipated such pain. To top off the anguish that intensified by the second, I developed a high fever, which Jhasali had not foreseen. Soon, I slid off the table and gripped either side of it, bending over into a sort of standing fetal position that made me more comfortable because it allowed me to tense my limbs against a solid object. There, I shook and moaned for hours, burning and freezing all at once.

The pain moved from my veins to my muscles, then inward to my very bones. Huge beads of sweat dropped from my face to the metal table, and I sank to my knees, hugging myself. This was by far the worst pain I'd ever endured; I could not even manage to scream. I just grimaced and gritted my teeth, never having imagined it possible to hurt so much yet live on.

Jhasali sat cross-legged on the floor beside me, her hand on my shoulder, telling me everything the bots in my body told her. She said the nanos were integrating with my muscle fibers, my organs, my marrow, fusing with every atom of my being, eliminating impurities and reconfiguring much of my system.

I heard Jhasali talking, but her words took so long to reach me through my fog of pain that I only caught the ones she repeated: focus on breathing. I counted the seconds of each inhale, each exhale, until I brought myself almost into a trance with the rhythm of my own respiration. In. Out. In. Out. It was the only thing that helped.

After what felt like an eternity, the pain subsided. I allowed my consciousness to emerge from that safe place deep within the recesses of myself to find Jhasali bathing my face and stroking my sweat-soaked hair.

"How are you feeling?" she asked, sounding worried as ever.

Truthfully, I felt horrible. I was weak, trembling from pain, and nauseated to the point of vomiting, but I managed to give Jhasali a feeble nod to tell her I was alright. She took me to my bed and laid me down, saying the newly integrated nanos would inform her when the next phase of the process was to begin. Damned if I knew what that meant, but if the next part of the process turned out to be as painful as the last, I would've preferred to die instead.

Die I did not. Rather, I drifted into a deep, dreamless sleep that lasted until Jhasali gently shook me awake several hours later. I sat up slowly, letting a drone support me from behind.

"The bots are done integrating with your brain matter. They're ready to implant your sensors." She beckoned me off the bed.

"I'm thirsty," I said as I rose to follow.

"It's better you don't drink now. They're saying you must be sedated for the placement of the nanochips."

When I turned out to be too weak to walk, Jhasali placed me on one of the flat drones and had it carry me down to the medical ward. We entered a different, larger room with a heavier table that contained a drain in the center. She had me lie down on this table.

"Your internal bots have decided it would be best to inject all the sensors into the large arteries that feed your brain. However, too much brain activity could hinder the placement process, so I am going to put you to sleep now." She stroked my hair.

"Thank Heaven for small favors," I said.

One of the damselflies held a tiny smoking marble underneath my nose, and next I knew, I was opening my eyes and looking up into Jhasali's face. She did not seem any less concerned.

"It's done," she said flatly. "Take it easy; the implants will have impacted your senses."

I tried to sit up but began reeling. The intensity of every sensation, every color, every sound was multiplied by a hundred. The feel of it overwhelmed me, making me dizzy and ill. I could sense every tiny electromagnetic pulse of the Earth, beating like a giant planetary heart pounding in my ears, my eyes, my very soul.

"What's wrong with me? What are they telling you?" I asked.

"You mean your nanos? They say it might take some time for your implants to configure your new sensory baseline," Jhasali answered. "Speaking of what they say, when your integration is further along, your internal devices will become yours alone. They'll cease to obey or communicate with any living being save you. So you need to start trying to commune with them on your own as soon as possible."

Jhasali spoke softly, but I heard bellowing. I covered my ears, leaned forward, and fell off the table. She caught me before I hit the floor, letting only one of my knees graze the tiles. I cried out in asphyxiating discomfort as my overwhelmed senses resisted their heightened strength.

Jhasali lifted me up. "Come on. We'll get you to sensory deprivation."

She carried me down the hall into a dark, windowless room with an even more unnaturally silent air than the rest of the ship. There, she placed me on some cushions on the floor and sat cross-legged behind me, laying my head in her lap. She tried stroking my hair, but even this sensation was too intense, and I had to ask her to stop.

The darkness and silence allowed me to rest without overwhelming my senses. It took me hours to gather the courage to permit Jhasali to start pricking me with small stimuli: a snap of the fingers near my ear, a burst of dim light, a soft brush of her fingertips. None of it worked, and I remained in a state of pained, miserable sensory overload.

She took me to my room, where I managed to drink some water, but if I tried to eat anything, the flavor hit my mouth so hard I preferred to go hungry rather than endure the sharp, shooting pain that ran through my tongue to my teeth and jawbones. Viewing any light at all felt like having my eyes pierced with needles, and hearing even the gentle hum of the drones passing through the hall felt like having my eardrums pounded with a hammer.

Despite my misery, I had to get back to town. I couldn't stay for more than one night if I wished to avoid being missed again—if I'd not already been missed. Jhasali had to blindfold me and stuff fabric in my ears just to take me back to the house in the middle of the night. She did not leave me when we arrived. Instead, she got me into bed and didn't touch me again (thank goodness), but she did ply me with fluid when I was reluctant to drink.

Sara knocked on my door the next morning. Her gentle taps on the wood sounded like cannon fire, and my light aversion obliged me to blindfold myself before I could even think about descending from the shuttered upper level.

When I rose to get the door, Jhasali protested. "Mica, let her knock until she gives up and goes away."

"Not so loud," I hissed as the spike of her whisper skewered my eardrums. "If I don't answer, she might have my door broken down thinking I'm dead."

At this, Jhasali rolled her eyes and huffed, "Fine. I'll keep the drones up here. Just get rid of her."

I crept downstairs to the kitchen, feeling like a thousand nails pierced my feet with each step I took.

"Are you alright?" Sara said when I opened the door.

I raised the blindfold but had to lower it after a second. She stood outside with two handsome pages and a carriage drawn by a pair of gleaming palomino draft horses. Without waiting for an invitation, she swept past me and bolted the door, leaving her servants outside.

"Why are you blindfolded?" Sara asked.

"My head has been pounding for days," I said.

"The medicine did that to me too. Did it at least work?"

"I think it is working, but I'm so sick."

"It isn't supposed to make you sick this long. Maybe I should send one of the boys for the midwife." Sara glanced back toward the door.

"No, don't! I don't want anyone else involved in this. Please."

"I was going to get more medicine from her anyhow, in case I ever need it again."

"No. No. I cannot risk Sergio finding out. The more people who know, the more people there are to talk about it. Please, don't tell anyone," I moaned.

"Micaela—"

"I'm begging you, please don't."

"Alright, I won't tell anyone. But what if you're still sick tomorrow or the next day?"

"It doesn't matter. However long I'm ill, it'll be worth it, if only you won't tell."

"I already said I wouldn't," Sara snapped. "Why don't you come to the estate for a day or two? I'm headed there now. That way, we can keep an eye on you. No one has to know why you're ill."

If Jhasali hadn't been present, I might've taken Sara up on the offer. But right now, my sole goal was to get her out of this house before she ran afoul of my bandit-murdering guest. In terror Sara might want to help me back upstairs, where she would then come face-to-face with an armed and agitated Jhasali, I thanked her profusely and told her I only wanted to be left alone. After much protest, I was able to get her out the door, though she said she'd send someone to check on me in a couple of days if she didn't hear from me.

My heart pounded so loud in my throat and ears that after Sara left, I sat on the stairs, unable to work up the strength to climb. Knowing I had little choice, I started crawling up them. Jhasali came down after I'd ascended the first few steps and made to lift me.

"Don't," I said.

I didn't want to let her touch me after I'd just gotten such a stark reminder of how dangerous she was. I feared I'd made a terrible mistake and that my first instincts about her devices had been right. What had I so impulsively asked her to do to me?

"I need your assurances of something," I said when I got myself back into bed. "I need you to promise me, no matter what, you won't hurt another person."

"I've already sworn I'll only kill to protect you or myself. What more could you want?"

"Next time a neighbor comes knocking while you're here, I want to be able to open the door without being petrified. I want to be able to trust you around the people I love."

"Fine, I assure you I will never kill again," she said, without anywhere near a convincing level of conviction, and then she added, "Not even in defense of you?"

"If the implantation works the way it should, I ought to be able to defend myself."

However, the question of whether the implantation was working as it should remained to be answered. Jhasali's obvious nervousness intensified my own worry that there would be no reprieve from this incessant inundation of the senses. She did not verbalize her fear, but she was not so good at hiding it either.

Her pacing never ceased, and her soft strides made such an awful racket I told her she could sit down or leave. She whispered that her devices had said it would not always be like this, but she didn't sound like she believed them, which further augmented my terror that death might be the only cure for this self-inflicted malady.

To my tremendous relief, the devices turned out to be right. After a few days of extreme suffering in which I became starved and dehydrated because eating and drinking were still too painful, the misery began to subside. It decreased little by little, until I did not mind the light so much when it managed to flit through the closed shutter and I regained the ability to eat without suffering the shooting pain in my mouth.

Sara kept her word and sent one of her manservants to check on me every couple of days. Though I could scarcely bear to open the door to the first messenger, talking to each subsequent one proved less and less painful, until, finally, I told the last that his mistress needn't worry anymore. She could expect me to call on her soon.

One evening, almost a week after Jhasali's and my return to my house, I stood at the window, peaking intermittently through the shutter and trying to grow more tolerant of the light of the setting sun. Taking sips of wine, I tried also to reacclimate myself to its intense flavor. The first sip hurt the most, but after subsequent mouthfuls, I started to adjust.

"Right! I had forgotten," Jhasali cried so randomly I jumped.

"Forgotten what?"

"The drones say your nanos still need to remove the foreign body from your system."

With a jolt, I recalled the pregnancy. I'd been so ill and in such pain since my implantation the thought had been all but chased from my mind for the first time in months.

"Why haven't they done that already?" I asked, surprised they hadn't. It was why I'd taken them, after all.

"The foreign body was not their priority—the holistic integration needed to be at a later stage before they started making more granular alterations. They say they're expelling it now. They are not programmed for sexual reproduction, you know."

As she said this, a pinching pain clamped the inside of my womb. Not long afterward came the familiar sensation of warm liquid sliding out of me, only the amount was far greater than I'd ever experienced before. It dripped all the way to the floor in a matter of seconds. At long last, I seized the prize I'd been so desperately seeking: that magnificent blood to wash me clean on the inside. I wept with relief at the feeling of it running down my legs.

"Oh! I didn't realize it would be so quick. Come. Stand on this," Jhasali said while one of the drones brought an old sack from the kitchen and tossed it at my feet.

As I stepped onto the bag, I took a glance at the floor beneath me and gave a reflexive cry. The soaked sack on which I stood lay next to a shining pool of my blood mixed with a substantial amount of water. Not until that second did I realize I'd lost so much—and I was still bleeding! A sudden thread of fear wove itself into the mantle of my delight and relief.

"It's alright. Nothing to fret over. It looks like more than it is," Jhasali assured me.

I did fret, however. I fretted as a small drone used a hose to suck up my blood from the floor. I fretted as a different drone handed me a glass of the strange liquid they'd all been making me drink. I fretted as I drank that obnoxiously sweet bright-white fluid. I fretted right up until the blood flow abated and I was able to step off the sack.

It was done, then. Now that the bleeding had stopped, that same relief—so intense it left me breathless—flooded my system again, its radiant warmth pushing out the fear I'd felt when I'd seen that dark stain on the floorboards.

The drones scooped the sack off the floor and removed it. Meanwhile, I took my leave of Jhasali, asking her to wait downstairs while I cleaned myself up. As I poured water into the basin, I began to weep again. I put my hands over my mouth and cried quietly. I didn't want Jhasali to mistake my tears of relief for tears of sorrow, nor did I wish her to take my laughs for sobs. She had grasped that humans weep for sadness and for pain, but she'd not yet understood we weep for joy too. Crying and laughing all at once, I glanced out the slit between the window shutters to find the sun shone brighter, and it didn't even hurt my eyes.

Once I finished washing up and changing my clothes, I invited Jhasali back upstairs. Now that I'd achieved the blessed miscarriage, I thought it a good time to bring up something she had said earlier that bothered me still.

"What did you mean when you said the nanos are not programmed for sexual reproduction?" I asked.

"It means they don't do that. They're programmed to prevent any function that could be harmful to your physical form. If your system attempts to do something dangerous to itself, they won't allow it. That's true of both biological malfunctions as well as functions that might be considered normal but hazardous."

Jhasali's tone was flat, informative. She failed to understand the impact of these words.

"And procreation falls into that category?" I said.

"Naturally. Why ever would we need such a thing as pregnancy when we can reproduce outside our bodies?"

I flushed with conflicted emotions at this statement: joy at my newfound freedom from the crippling terror of childbirth I'd carried like a weight in my gut since Gracia's nearly fatal experience; despair at being robbed of the chance to hold Sergio's child or twist my fingers around what I was sure would have been its curly dark hair; pain at the thought of being barren and alone whilst Sergio remained incessantly away at sea; and fear, above all, that he'd leave me lonelier than I'd ever been if he found out all hope of my ever bearing him a son was now lost.

"How can this be?" I murmured.

"I don't understand," Jhasali snapped. "I thought this was what you wanted. I fail to see the attraction of this thing, pregnancy, anyway. To carry a parasite inside your body while it grows to a size that makes your belly swell and your legs fail and your entire system start shutting down until you are seriously injured or killed in the act of expelling it—you could not find that appealing."

"Of course not when you say it like that."

"How else am I supposed to say it? It is disgusting."

My anger exploded, erasing all other emotion. I could scarcely believe her dismissiveness, for she was the one who'd assented to implant me without bothering to make me understand the full cost.

"How can you say that?" I shouted, despite the pain it caused my ears. "How can you mock me when these creatures you've filled me with mean I can never bear my husband's children?"

"Calm down. We've already established he is the barren one anyway."

I felt like she'd slapped me. Of course. I'd forgotten she had deduced this truth even before we'd decided to go through with the implantation.

Jhasali continued. "Besides, the fact that something is against their initial programming does not mean you cannot alter it. The point of these things is for you to control them. Not the other way around."

"So I am not barren?"

"Don't be silly. If you wish to carry a fetus, all you need to do is tell the nanos to support it rather than eliminate it. They won't treat it as a foreign body if *you* tell them not to."

I looked down at my belly and said, "Just because I didn't want this one doesn't mean I don't want others. You understand?"

Jhasali laughed. "That's not how you're supposed to do it."

"I don't know any other way!"

Jhasali rolled her eyes. "I'm going to teach you."

***

Unfortunately for me, my integration with the nanos was far from over. During the next few months, they spent much time making subtle but perceptible improvements to my system. After my sensory baseline finished resetting, the first thing I noticed was a constant, intense hunger. I lost so much weight in the first couple of weeks after my metamorphosis that Jhasali became quite alarmed.

By this point, the nanos had stopped communicating with the outside, and it took her much consultation with her drones before everyone realized one of the main issues with humans taking the nanos of an intergalactic civilization is that the bots cause our bodies to need more food to make up for the extra energy they use.

As a result, I was forced to change my eating habits to consume almost thrice as many calories as I had before.

Most of these calories I got from *av'vysh*—the white fluid Jhasali had begun giving me after my transformation. In addition to dense fuel, *av'vysh* contains the liquid form of the element the nanos are composed of: *vydhris*. This element does not occur on Earth, and while the bots are programmed to make do with other elemental metals in its absence, they need *vydhris* to operate at optimum capacity. *Av'vysh* tasted like shit when I first started drinking it. It was thick, textured like sand, and saccharine to the point of unpleasantness. It took me some time to develop a taste for it, but I had no choice. There wasn't enough food available in town to sustain my ravenous new body without it.

Along with my altered eating habits, the nanos gifted me with a new set of eyes. One night, not long after my transformation, I woke up to find my eyeballs burning like invisible phantoms were digging them out of their sockets. A change came over them even as my tears flowed, dripping off the end of my nose and dotting the blankets on the bed with dark water marks. My eyes grew hard beneath my lids, and an opaque film glazed over them, clouding my vision. Then, swift as it had come, it cleared and solidified, forming a protective barrier.

After my vision cleared, the discomfort became even worse. I sensed every contraction in the muscles of my irises as the bots worked to change what had once been a human eye into a biomechanical lens, sharpening my vision even beyond what the sensors had already accomplished and expanding both my tolerance for bright light and my ability to see in darkness.

Many similar alterations bombarded my system over the following weeks. Although Jhasali had told me all I needed to do to command my nanos was to give them a conscious directive inside my mind, my menstrual cycle never restarted, no matter how I begged the bots to give me back my fertility. My fingernails, no longer necessary to protect my fingertips, popped off at the slightest provocation, though, for some reason, I was able to correct *this* problem with a single conscious command.

My flesh also slowly hardened, whilst remaining an accurate enough imitation of what it had been before I experienced "the change." It felt almost like my body was carved out of supple, porous wood. I feared people might feel the subtle difference in the texture of my skin when they touched me, but no one seemed to take note of it. There'd been no alteration in my appearance, so perhaps they never thought there was any change to notice.

One of the more annoying physical alterations I experienced was my sudden inability to get drunk. I could drink all day long, yet because the nanos' baseline programming was to filter out all poisons, the only effect alcohol had was to make me urinate so frequently it became downright inconvenient to bother drinking wine or ale except in small amounts. Jhasali told me I should be able to order the bots to allow me to get drunk, but no matter how much I desired it, I couldn't get them to listen. The inconsistency in my ability to command them was to be an ongoing problem for many years.

Alongside the physical modifications, I also found, as my brain began to accept the sensors inside it, that I had been uploaded with the knowledge of Jhasali's people. This somewhat caught me up to her society's understanding of the universe.

Jhasali spent much time explaining all this new information, teaching me how to access, contextualize, and process it. She and my sensors, in tandem, taught me of the grandest spectacles: the nature of the movements of galaxies, the life cycles of the stars, the force of gravity, the slow march of the ever-expanding universe toward its inevitable end. They taught me of the minutest phenomena: the behavior of subatomic particles, the machinations of microscopic life, and the ways in which Jhasali's people wielded the quantum against disease and death.

I could ask my own brain questions and learn the answer. Sometimes, I might even wonder about something and then find the knowledge of the thing I'd wondered about spontaneously there. This trick only worked with Sartjyanan knowledge, of course. As far as information about my own planet, I discovered that, like Jhasali herself, the sensors possessed a woefully inadequate understanding of my world.

This unfortunate detail limited me to questions about space and time and the nature of the physical universe. Much of this information was applicable to Earth, as it is to all planets, but if I needed to know something that pertained only to my planet or my species or my country, I was on my own.

Though I could ask my sensors for answers to questions, I still preferred to converse with Jhasali—getting verbal answers from her was less confusing, especially now that I could speak Sartjyanan. When Jhasali first spoke to me in her people's tongue after my metamorphosis, I noticed I could comprehend her and respond to her as if I had always spoken this language.

We began to converse in her native idiom so we could communicate without the restraint of nonexistent words. Soon, she started steering me back to her language whenever I tried to switch to my own. Once it became clear I was just as fluent in Sartjyanan as I was in my mother tongue, we seldom spoke Castellano to one another again.

# Chapter Twelve

# STEEL DAFFODILS

I t took me a long time to grow accustomed to all the new information in my mind and all the new ways of accessing it, but I improved. Not only did I get progressively better at retrieving my stored files, but I grew adept at the analysis trick Jhasali had always harped about.

I discovered how well it worked when I visited Father Manuel one afternoon. He was not in the rectory when I arrived. Thinking he would soon return, I waited in the sitting room. Bored, I picked up his copy of the Bible and found I could read Latin. It was not an immediate realization, but I gathered that if I examined the words within their greater context, I could translate them into my own tongue based on the familiar ones and deduce the ones I did not know based on the ones I did.

I only needed to understand one or two words before I could correctly guess the others, and once I had construed the meaning of a word, I remembered it forever. No need for memorization or repetition. Of course, normal people can do this, too, but the speed with which the sensors process information is beyond human parallel. Within an hour or two that afternoon, I went from being illiterate in Latin to reading it fluently.

For knowledge that could be acquired by study alone, analysis was remarkable. I could look at the alphabet of an earthly tongue in comparison to my own and by the next day be fluent in it. I could ask my own brain about complex mathematical concepts and be able to solve any of them my heart desired as soon as the question materialized in my mind. I could request all sorts of data, from the number of bacteria inside my own gut to the number of stars in the known universe, and I'd receive it on demand.

However, for things requiring true practice or talent, the implants fell far short of that standard. Jhasali had not been able to learn to ride Pepito at the drop of a hat. That required her to develop muscle memory, to learn to feel and move her body with the movements of the horse. It also required her to guide and manage something with a will of its own rather than just a mechanical mind directed by her consciousness. And it required her to build trust instead of commanding and demanding as she did with her devices.

Learning to do something the old-fashioned way frustrated Jhasali to no end, for she had never had to gain new knowledge without mechanical aid. Everything she wanted to know had been uploaded to her mind before she was hatched. Everything she needed done was done for her by drones. As far as new skills were concerned, she did not know how to learn things in the absence of technological assistance, which made me all the prouder of her when she picked up the vihuela.

I found out just before the start of Advent, when I rode out for a short visit. Upon entering the ship, I made for the observation deck, where Jhasali liked to watch when it snowed. While the rain still buffeted the valleys, at this altitude a good coating of snow had already fallen around Homeship.

At first, I thought the music I heard as I wandered the halls was coming from a drone, but when I ascended onto the domed top deck, I found Jhasali sitting on the edge of an armchair and playing a real vihuela. She strummed a tune I did not know; I wondered if she'd made it up herself. Regardless, I was familiar with the words. They were from a song in *Amadís de Gaula*—composed by the protagonist himself, no less.

Jhasali's voice cracked and her hands trembled as she sang the lines:
*I little joy in any other's sight,*
*My heart is thine, thyself my chief delight.*
*But yet I see the more that I do love,*
*More smart I feel, more pain, more grief I prove.*
*Well! let Love rage, though he be angry ever,*
*I'll take my loss for gain, though I gain never.*

When she paused, I asked if she played these lines for her twin, but she said she'd rather not discuss it. So I listened, feeling no small amount of surprise at how good she was. Her timing and notation were perfect. More than that, she'd infused something of herself into the song, striking the right chords and placing it in a minor key to insert a feeling of listlessness and loss into the melody that was palpable even without lyrics.

I looked around as she played, noting the furnishings from my bedroom had multiplied and were spreading across the ship. Jhasali had brought in several arm-chairs, including the one on which she sat, as well as another sofa. Favoring these fixtures, she now seemed to have permanently stowed the seating that popped out of the floor.

I sat down opposite her and listened to her play this song as if she understood as well as any earthling what the lyrics meant. I couldn't help but think of Sergio while I listened to her sing the ode by the Child of the Sea. My husband was a child of the sea, too, separated from his Oriana by much more distance than Amadís ever was from his. I stared out the glass wall toward the ocean, imagining I'd spotted Sergio's ship on the horizon and I did not have many more solitary months to endure until his return—I'd go to our house and find him waiting for me.

"What's wrong?" Jhasali yanked me out of my daydreams.

I stared down at my hands. "Nothing. It's just about to be my first Christmas alone. Sergio's never been gone during winter before, and now I don't even have Lobo."

"I'm sorry."

Wanting to change the subject for fear of awakening memories of how I'd lost Lobo, I asked where she'd gotten the vihuela and the furniture.

"I used my drones to make them. I have many drones designed to repair ships in deep space, so I would think they can handle a little thing like carving wood. Whatever they cannot make, either through lack of knowledge or materials, I have them fetch for me," she said.

I knew what "fetch" meant, and I considered discussing with her how taking things from people while they were away or sleeping wasn't exactly the behavior of one who was no thief. Yet I decided, much as I'd already tested the limits of my ability to admonish her, my remonstrances might be better spent on the next time she did something dangerous.

"How did you learn to play so fast?" I asked instead.

"Fast? No. I have been practicing for months now. Ever since I heard your Gabriel play. I don't know why it's taken me so long."

"Of course it's taken you a long time. This isn't something your drones can just analyze and tell you how to do. You have to feel it in your soul." I laid a hand over my heart.

"What is a soul? I've heard the word, but I'm not sure I grasp its meaning."

"I suppose your people would call the soul 'consciousness.' On Earth, we call it the spirit, the essence which lives within the body and makes the person who they are."

"I see. I do feel it in my soul, though I don't know why. I've never felt such a thing for much of my people's music," she said.

"That's because you don't belong with them. You belong here with us."

She just smiled and shook her head. "If you would stay here in Homeship, you'd see it's actually the opposite. Especially now. What's more, if you remained for longer periods, you might begin attempting to link up with one of the base-model drones."

I should have seen that coming. Ever since Jhasali had discovered I'd become somewhat adept at sorting the data in my sensors, she had been pestering me to learn to connect with a drone, but I'd thus far resisted. The idea of the telepathic interface still felt too foreign. I'd allowed the nanos to invade my body on a despairing and desperate whim, but now I couldn't bring myself to allow a drone to invade my mind. The very thought of such a violation made me squirm, though I'd never been able to figure out a way to make Jhasali understand why.

"I'm still not ready for that," I said.

"Why?" Jhasali demanded.

"Because I'm not. Besides, I cannot stay here anyhow. It's almost Advent. This is probably my last time here until after the Christmas season."

When she asked what Christmas was like, I explained how the season started with the more temperate Advent and then continued through Epiphany, with special traditions like feasting, caroling, gift-giving, and the Misa de Gallo.

"That sounds pleasant," Jhasali said.

"It is. Or at least it used to be. I cannot be sure how I'll feel about it now. With Sergio gone and everything that's happened, I . . ."

I trailed off and stared out the window. I couldn't spend Christmas alone in that house; I could scarcely endure being there during normal days now. I was tempted to invite Jhasali down to stay out the holiday, but I knew better. Even assuming she didn't turn me down, I'd pass the entire season in a constant state of anxiety that she might do something irreparable.

I thought of spending more time with Susana, but her husband, Andrés, was home this time of year. I couldn't stand the idea of passing all the festivities alongside her whole family—not when the other half of my heart passed his Christmas on the other side of the world.

Sara was the logical choice: her husband was gone the same place as mine; she was childless same as me; and, like me, she preferred to spend her time with smaller groups of intimate friends rather than at crowded parties. If I could pass as much of the holiday with her and Father Manuel as possible, I might make it through the next few weeks.

Fortunately, Sara had not gone to Santander with Gabriel and Gracia for the Christmas season, as she and Armando had done since Juliana's remarriage, so I did wind up spending a great deal of Advent with her. I was apparently not as excited for the festivities as she had expected, though, for a few days before Christmas Eve, she asked me what was wrong as we took refreshments in the parlor.

"Nothing's wrong. Why do you ask?" I said.

"You're just typically not this glum," she replied.

"I suppose with Sergio gone, I—"

"What about your mysterious paramour? Is he not still around?" she whispered, leaning toward my ear and winking.

At this, I burst into tears. I'm sure this must have shocked her, but I didn't wait for her to respond before I fled the parlor and ran downstairs. There, I hid in the wine cellar and wept.

I'd been doing alright until now. In the weeks following my metamorphosis, my relief at being free of Rodrigo's spawn and my blossoming feelings of security in my newfound corporeal resilience had allowed me to begin the slow process of trying to leave that awful night behind me. But hearing Sara call Rodrigo my "mysterious paramour"—I didn't even know what to say. It had pricked the right spot in my still-unmended heart.

If Sara did not know what she had said, the fault lay with me. She believed I'd committed adultery, and I'd never said anything to relieve her of that notion. Even remembering that night was a pain unendurable, but to talk about it would be impossible.

Eventually, I dried my tears and went back up to the parlor again, passing a confused and gawking manservant on the way.

"I'm sorry, Sara," I said upon my return.

She rose and shut the parlor door. "Don't be. I should have known better than to ask. But you would do well to avoid catching feelings for your lovers in the future."

"I didn't catch feelings for him," I snapped as loudly as I dared.

Sara raised her eyebrows but did not reply.

"I didn't! I just—after everything I went through to rid myself of his vile seed, I . . . I love Sergio. I never wanted anyone else." I sank onto the sofa opposite Sara and stared at my hands.

Sara squinted. "It was an affair, right? A consensual affair?"

The tears filled my eyes until they blinded me, spilling down my cheeks when I silently shook my head to indicate, no, it hadn't been an affair.

"Oh. Fuck," she whispered. "I'm so sorry. Why didn't you tell me before?"

"I feared that since I turned up pregnant, you might not believe me."

"You think I don't know one needn't enjoy it to conceive? What happened? Who was it?" she asked.

"You don't want to know," I said, wondering how much of a difference it would've made if she or Father Manuel had done something to make Rodrigo stay away from me before he'd come knocking that night.

"Of course I want to know. Tell me. Who was it?"

"No. I can't."

"Micaela, he shouldn't just get away with—"

"No. He's gone now, for good. Don't make me speak of it. I only want to forget about it. Alright? It never happened."

"Alright, but why don't you stay with me for the rest of the holiday?" she said.

"What?"

"Yes. Just stay here. Whatever happened, it never happened, I promise. But you shouldn't spend your nights alone at Christmas."

I concurred. I slept in one of the guestrooms that night, and the next day, I rode to my house to retrieve a few things. I got my new dresses out of their hiding place once more. I'd put them away again after Rodrigo's attack, fearing to wear them lest they attract some other man's attention. Now, after all these months, I finally felt like celebrating, so I packed both dresses and stayed with Sara the rest of the holiday. She even had her servants go and feed my chickens so I needn't ride to the arrabal again.

Even though I missed Sergio, it was still one of the most pleasant Christmases I ever celebrated. Sara had always been happier without Armando around; now that his absence was combined with the Christmas festivities, she was practically giddy—comparatively speaking, of course. She hosted many parties, much smaller affairs than the grand fiestas Gracia liked to throw, which made them all the lovelier.

Many an evening, a few of her friends left their husbands where they sat and brought their children over, filling the house with the sounds of laughter and play, brightening Sara's mood, and even lifting my spirits. Sitting in the parlor, bouncing a laughing toddler on my knee while gently pinching the end of his nose until he squealed with glee, I could feel something of the way I'd been before "nothing" happened, the way I might one day be again if I could find a way to let myself.

Everyone but Sara and I swapped stories of funny things their children had done. And we each took a turn complaining about our husbands. Even I, though I'd been mostly silent, had plenty to say on that topic. Poor Sergio wouldn't have been too pleased to discover he'd been the subject of so much grumbling, but if he would've ever learned how to act, I'd have had no reason to complain.

One night, close to the end of the season, Sara and I came home late from feasting and stayed up almost until dawn, conversing and drinking before a crackling fire in the parlor. Somehow, we got on the subject of our parentage. I told her I wished I'd known my mother and father before they'd succumbed to illness, but Sara replied with something to the effect of having one's parents around is not always a blessing.

I asked why, and she gave me an odd look and laid down her needlework.

"I'm not sure anyone in this world has the power to hurt you like your parents," she said. "You're so much more vulnerable as a child. My father always doted on me when I was a girl, and it deceived me into believing he truly cared for me. But when the time came, he bartered me up here for nothing more than higher shipping priority than his competition. I guess he'd already sold my sisters at a better price, so he didn't have to bargain as high for me."

She stared into the fire. Not knowing how to respond, I waited for her to continue.

"I begged Father night and day not to send me from Burgos, or at least to send me to Toledo or Antwerp to be with one of my sisters. I pleaded with him not to pawn me to a man whose father only offered him to me because he'd failed to find him a bride from some higher-ranking family. Father didn't listen.

"I accepted it was within his rights to find me a match; I even accepted I could be married to a man I did not care for. But I wished to be farther north. In Antwerp, I could've been near my sister Beatriz. I told my father that, but he said I should be grateful he'd given me a dowry almost as handsome as that of my older sisters and found me a husband of wealth and halfway-respectable breeding."

"Don't you tire of men telling you what you should be grateful for?" I asked.

"What do you mean?"

I opened my mouth to answer but thought better of it. In truth, I'd been thinking of all those times Father Manuel had told me I should be grateful to have been raised in a good Christian household. Listening to Sara speak of her girlhood misfortunes made me wish to tell her of my own childhood calamities, but I couldn't.

Unlike Jhasali, Sara might very well infer the real reason Ignacio had done as he did, even if I didn't repeat the insults he'd hurled at me in the quemadero. So I cooked up a different response, something about Sergio telling me I ought to be grateful he provided so well for me though I'd come to him with a pittance for a dowry, which he really had said on more than one occasion.

"I was angry when my father told me to be grateful," Sara replied. "When Armando and I became as we are now—and it did not take all that long—I was even angrier. I suppose I never forgave my father for giving me away to a man like him."

"Does he hurt you?"

"Not in the way you mean. Not anymore. But there are many ways to hurt someone besides that."

"Do you tell your father what he does?" I asked.

"I haven't spoken to my father in more than sixteen years. I told myself I'd let him die before he ever heard from me again, and that is one vow I intend to keep. Sometimes I miss my brothers, but my father will rot before I go back to Burgos."

Now, it made sense why she had never gone with Armando and Sergio on the occasions they'd ridden down there to do business with her family.

"Perhaps I'll be able to visit when he dies," she continued.

"I don't understand."

Sara's face hardened, and I feared I'd offended her, but she bitterly spat, "It was my father's fault I lost all my children. If he'd married me to someone besides Armando, I might've been spared one or two of them."

I almost took that to mean Armando had killed his own offspring, but he wanted legitimate heirs more than anything, so that couldn't be right. Then I remembered what she'd once said about God punishing Bathsheba for the sins of the man who'd forced himself upon her. Wondering if that was what she meant, I opened my mouth to ask but then decided that would probably be an insensitive question.

"I'm sure the deaths of your children must be an unfortunate twist of fate, not some divine vengeance. I cannot fathom anything Armando could do that would be worth God murdering every last one of your progeny," I stammered.

Sara huffed. "You only say Armando isn't to blame because you don't know the reason I believe him to be."

Bursting to ask the reason but not wishing to be a gossip, I instead said, "Armando should spend more time here and try harder to win your affection."

"No. I am partly responsible for why he stays here so infrequently now. After our last child died, I told him it was best he take up residence in his family houses while I found my own. This is *my* house. I bought it with *my* dowry. And I don't want him here."

My eyes widened. How had I not known after all these years that she'd bought this house with her dowry? I'd always thought Armando kept her here because he wished it. Until now, I'd never known just how much power she wielded in her marriage.

"But how do you make him obey like that? How do you stop him from moving in if it pleases him?" I asked.

"You don't want to know such things. It's better to keep an amiable marriage if you can."

"I'm not sure 'amiable' is the word I'd use to characterize it. I mean, we do love one another, but he's so imperious. It'd be nice if he'd at least listen to me once in a while. He didn't sell Pepito, so I suppose that's something. But he threatens me with it if I contradict him. I wish I could make him treat me better."

"In that case, I would not advise you to go the same route as I have. You don't wish to wreck your marriage, only to improve your husband's behavior."

"Yes!"

"Then I would tell you this: hold your ground. He'll fight at first. He'll act like he's dying of humiliation. He'll probably scream and curse and disappear for days. He might even beat you. Though if he goes that far, let me know."

"He won't do that. He didn't even when I refused to sign his damned letter."

"Regardless, he might sell your horse. He might find other ways to make your life miserable. Don't give in. No matter how he howls, don't bow to his demands. If you stand firm, he'll wear himself out," Sara said.

I had to laugh. Crazy as it sounded, it just might work. I had already tried something to that effect with his letter, but I had caved when he'd threatened to sell Pepito. I supposed I'd have to make my peace with that possibility if I were to ever learn to hold my ground with Sergio. I dearly desired to keep our marriage amiable, but the version of amiable I'd found acceptable before did not work for me any longer. I wanted a new amiable, one in which I had a damned say in my own life. I wished I'd had Sara's dowry; then I might've also had Sara's bargaining power.

"You'd better be ready to pluck me off the street if I give your advice a try." I chuckled.

"Of course."

"Really?"

"Naturally. I'd best be prepared to deal with the possible results of my own counsel. Besides, having you around so much lately, well, it's been rather nice."

"To tell you the truth, I was afraid I'd be an imposition staying so long."

"My husband was an imposition, and I turned him right out. If you were an imposition, you'd already know it."

I took her hand and smiled, saying, "I hope one day I'll have your self-assurance."

She smiled in return. "Don't worry, Mica; you'll learn in time."

***

Most everyone stayed bundled up and indoors after Epiphany, giving me leeway to visit Jhasali more frequently and stay longer with her than was my normal custom. One gloomy evening, I rode out in the dark, guarded as always by the invisible escort I requested through the communicator. After months of metamorphosing, I no longer needed to dress for the cold, and I rode through the snow on the mountain in nothing more than a pair of pantaloons and an old linen shirt of Sergio's that I'd pitifully hemmed to fit myself.

Jhasali and I had argued over the communicator when I'd requested my escort. She'd refused to send me a drone at first, insisting I'd had many weeks to prepare myself to make the brain-to-drone link and if I'd only learn how to do it, I'd need neither the communicator nor her intervention to acquire an escort; I could call my own drone for myself. Still unready and unwilling to endure the telepathic penetration of my mind required for the master-drone connection, I'd had to all but beg her to send me something to defend me in case I was waylaid on my journey to Homeship.

Begrudgingly, she'd agreed. She'd also promised to show me other things besides the drones—things that might prove adequate intermediate steps between my current disconnected state and a full brain-to-drone interface. Apparently, the lessons she planned to impart would have the added benefit of helping me protect myself without suffering the bond.

Once I arrived at Homeship, I passed the rest of the night in my bedroom because Jhasali had gone to wander the woods alone to express her displeasure with my stubbornness. Though the nanos made it so that I no longer needed sleep, going to bed in the dark and awakening in the light was familiar and comforting, allowing me to both keep to a normal schedule and pass the loneliest hours of the night. I drifted off staring out the window at the forest, and when morning came, Jhasali entered my chamber before I awoke.

She beckoned me outside without a word, leading me beyond the security perimeter to one of the clearings we liked to frequent.

"Since you still refuse to learn how to utilize superior devices, I've brought you out here to teach you to use IDOS," Jhasali said, giving me quite the side-eye.

"IDOS? Oh. Integrated Defense/Offense System," I exclaimed as the sensors answered the question inside my head.

"Yes. Its primary purpose is to alter its shape and attach to our bodies so it can defend us from a variety of threats. You've seen how effective it can be."

I recalled what that "effectiveness" had done to the bodies of the men who'd attacked me. I wasn't sure I wanted to be the kind of person who regularly carried a weapon capable of inflicting that sort of damage. When Jhasali had said she would show me how to protect myself, I didn't know what I'd thought she'd meant, but it wasn't this.

"You want to see how it works?" she asked.

Without waiting for an answer, she stepped closer, her bare feet crunching the wet snow. She stretched out her arm, which now shone with a bright bracelet of the same silver hue as the drones. The cuff covered her from wrist to elbow. It had many ruts running up the underside, and a long ridge ran down the top, culminating in a horizontal slit above her wrist.

"If it's a defense *and* offense system, what's the defense part?" I asked.

"The defense lies in the quality of the offense," she replied.

I had to laugh at that. "Where do you load it?"

"You don't. It integrates with your forearm," she said, pointing to a section of slits that almost looked like gills. "Then it gathers the free-floating metals in your system, which your nanos bring to it. These it mixes with concentrated hydrogen from either the environment around it or the water in your body to create an explosive projectile that it fires from here." She pointed at the rectangular slit along the ridge just above her wrist. "It can perform this task without any reload mechanism. Though, of course, it will eventually deplete you if you use it over and over without replenishing yourself with *vydhris* or other elements."

"It must take forever to fire," I said.

"The projectiles are tiny, so they don't take long to produce. We have plenty of more effective weapons than this. But it's good to have one that's part of the body so you're never caught disarmed. We typically wear them on both wrists for good measure, but for now you only need one." She lifted a second cuff in her other hand and motioned for me to put it on.

"I don't know about this." I eyed the bracelet warily.

"You'll be fine. This is a good introductory step to the interface because you do not need to bond mentally with this one since it is attached to your body. Here," she said, demanding my wrist, pulling up my sleeve, and clasping the cuff over my bare flesh.

At this, I felt a horrible sensation in my right forearm, like the very sinews and tendons of that limb were digging through my skin and reaching out toward the silver bracelet on my wrist. The sensation was not painful, but I shuddered and tried not to think on the image that popped into my head of my arm turning itself inside out to attach to the device. Unable to make that image recede, I tried to peel the cuff off with my left hand. Jhasali grasped my wrist and told me to let it work. It must be fully integrated into my body to function, but once it was on, all I had to do was think "eject" to get it off.

I calmed down and made myself watch the integration. It took a few more seconds for the sensation of digging down to my very bones to abate. In those seconds, the cuff expanded some parts of itself and shrank others, molding to my arm. As a final gesture to its new master, it hid all its grooves and ridges and changed color and sheen like an octopus, blending itself with the tone and consistency of my skin. As long as I didn't clasp my forearm with my other hand and feel the hard plating of armor over my flesh, I could barely distinguish the cuff from my arm.

"Camouflages well, does it not?" Jhasali asked. "It really isn't supposed to go all the way up to your elbow like that. It's only meant to cover the wrist, but it cannot flex its length like it can its circumference because it needs the length for the microreactor."

"Makes sense," I said.

"So this weapon fires two types of rounds, which we call a hard and a soft. The soft is only an expulsion from the cuff's incendiary mechanism; it has no solid component. We use this to start fires in our enemies' spacecrafts. You flood the whole ship with oxygen and hydrogen and spark it. Everything is fireproof in space, so it doesn't do much damage, but it works well as a diversion. The hard round is the one that contains the solidified explosive projectile."

"Can it penetrate our defenses?" I asked.

"It fires at an extreme velocity. It's difficult to outright kill one of us with this weapon, but it can seriously injure us. Be careful with it."

Only now did I comprehend the trust she placed in me. A weapon that could pose a threat to her was not a thing to be offered to just anyone.

"You must point and think 'spark' to expel a soft round and 'fire' for a hard one. This will bring the weapon into the firing position and cause a discharge, so make sure it is pointed at your target before you tell it either way. You should be able to find all this information in your sensors if you wish to learn more. Right now, just give it a go." She slapped me on the back.

Pointing at a young sapling, about the width of a broom handle, on the opposite edge of the clearing, I straightened my arm and lowered my fist, as I'd seen Jhasali do. I thought not of the word "fire" but of the act of a glowing, molten ball of liquid flame exiting from above my right hand and disintegrating the tree at which I aimed.

In a split second, the cuff's grooves reappeared, the ridge popped into position, and an intense heat welled up around the part of my arm encircled by the weapon. Had I not been in possession of the nanos, I would have been burned, perhaps to the point of amputation. However, with them, I simply endured the painless sensation of having my forearm trapped inside a brick oven. This sensation lasted less than the blink of an eye before a recoil of energy passed at immense speed from my elbow to my wrist and over the back of my hand. Then a good portion of the sapling's base shattered into a million splinters. The tree fell to the ground with a snap and a thud.

In the instant it had taken me to fell that tiny tree, I'd gone from being a thing that should feel fear to a thing that should cause fear. I pressed my right wrist over my breast and clasped my left hand around IDOS, wondering why I'd ever felt any hesitancy toward it. There would not be another Rodrigo. There would not be another Ignacio. Not now. Not ever.

I smelled smoke all of a sudden and looked down. I was on fire! I'd not even noticed until my arms and chest were already engulfed. I shrieked and flailed, but Jhasali grabbed me and held me still.

"Let yourself burn. You are in no danger. Your clothes just caught fire."

She released me and backed up a few paces. I noticed *her* clothes weren't on fire, but I held firm and gritted my teeth, putting forth every effort to suppress my instinct to flee a pain that never appeared. I looked down to see bare skin appearing as the fabric of my linen shirt burned away. Jhasali was right. The flames spread in tiny blackening lines over the sleeves and up the seams, but they were contained to my clothes and impotent against my skin. Within minutes, the whole garment burned off me and left me naked to the waist but otherwise unharmed.

"Hang on." Jhasali grabbed my hair so abruptly I flinched. "Your hair's singeing."

She twisted it in a knot and fastened it to the back of my head—too late. The smell of burning hair floated into my nostrils.

"I suppose the bots won't protect dead protein cells of their own accord. You must tell them if you wish to keep your hair safe," she said.

I wasted no time but thought with all my might of making my long tresses as durable as my body. I was unsure if it worked, for the flames had died before they could reach the knot on top of my head.

Jhasali began to speak again somewhere behind me. At the sound of her voice, I tried to cover my bare breasts. Then I recalled she often walked these woods unclothed and unashamed, for her people would forgo clothing unless it had a practical use.

She'd begun to practice this habit in my presence after I'd taken the nanos. I'd been shocked and appalled at first, but now I'd grown accustomed to seeing her in little to no clothing. So I dropped my arms to my sides as I turned to face her and tried to forget my nakedness.

"I should have treated your clothing with a fire retardant before we started. Apologies. I forgot the ambient heat of these things can set even the hardiest of fabrics alight," she said.

"You can do that?" I asked.

"Of course. We make our clothing out of fireproof fabrics, but there is a treatment too. A liquid that will protect this kind of thing." She pointed out the few shredded remnants of the shirt as they blew around in the snow. "Though it isn't as effective as fireproof cloth."

"If I am to spend much time wearing these cuffs, you'll have to treat everything I own."

"I shall." She turned and headed for Homeship.

"What can harm us?" I asked on the journey home.

"Everything that can harm humans can harm us; the degree just has to be much greater," Jhasali answered. "We can be burned if something's hot enough. We can be wounded by sharp objects or projectiles if they are moving fast enough. These nanos make our bodies less vulnerable than they would be if we were purely biological, but they don't make us impervious to everything that could be dangerous. Think of it like being made of a suit of heavy armor instead of just wearing one. You are flesh and bone, but you are equally *vydhris* alloy. You are not indestructible, but you are no longer frail as a daffodil before the frost either."

"How can I know what can and cannot hurt me?"

"Your sensors will have most of that information, though for earthly weapons, I suppose we might have to experiment. There is no way a sword or lance could pierce us, but some of your other weapons that launch projectiles, I'm not so sure. It would depend on the velocity."

I bit the nail of my pinkie finger. "So like a crossbow or arquebus could kill us?"

"Maybe not kill. Probably just wound. If the projectiles pierced us, my guess is we could self-heal. But who knows? If they hit the right spot? That's why I always have my drones accompany me when I leave the perimeter. As long as I have them, I am unassailable."

While we walked back to Homeship, I imagined myself a daffodil encased in ice or, perhaps more accurately, a daffodil over which molten steel had been poured. Would there be anything left of the daffodil inside such a cast?

"Listen, Micalita," Jhasali said when we arrived at the ship's perimeter. "I was thinking on the walk back, the way you reacted to catching fire—"

"Please don't call me a coward."

"Let me finish. I was going to say you need to accustom yourself to being more durable than you were in the past. You've no reason to fear many things that might've harmed you back then, so it's best you learn not to overreact."

"How?"

"I don't know. More exposure? Jump off a cliff. Sit in fire. Do things that could have once killed you and now can do you no more harm than being struck by a dandelion seed."

"Alright. I'll try," I agreed.

"The training chamber might help," Jhasali mused as we entered the ship.

Later that same afternoon, after I'd found myself another shirt and we'd eaten a colossal lunch of drone-slaughtered venison, Jhasali took me back to the empty, uninteresting room she had used as a makeshift sensory-deprivation chamber during my metamorphosis.

Jhasali gave me a stern look. "Before we begin, I must warn you: do not enter this chamber on your own. It is for training; thus it is meant to challenge and terrify you to make you stronger. It is easy to forget everything you see within is unreality. If you become lost inside it or are not able to override the scenario, you could go mad."

My nerves prickled as my sensors simultaneously explained the concept of virtual reality inside my head while Jhasali continued speaking.

"Whatever happens, I need you to remain calm and remember all of this is an illusion wrought by the cooperation between your sensors and the chamber's own internal mechanisms."

As she said this, the door slammed shut with a dull thud, and the lights went out, plunging us into total darkness. The silence roared in my ears, and the lack of any point of reference disoriented me.

"Jhasali!" I cried.

She remained mute, but she took my hand in hers. The lights came back on after a second's delay to reveal a world utterly apart from the unremarkable room we'd entered.

I gasped and reeled backward, ready to turn and run. But to where? The door was gone; indeed, every part of Jhasali's ship had been replaced by the huge cylindrical atrium in which we now stood. We were in the middle of a long circular hallway that curved ever to our right. To our left were dozens of doors, windows, and other passageways leading away from the atrium and on to some other part of the structure.

To the right there was a silvery railing, and beyond lay a towering hollow space that reminded me of the inside of a huge cathedral bell tower. Only this was ten thousand times more massive than any belfry I'd ever seen, and it was filled from top to bottom with hallways and railings just like the area in which we now stood. The view from our vantage in this silo gave the impression that the entire thing was one gigantic vertical tube full of balconies.

Like Jhasali's ship, this place was built for people much larger than myself. The glowing hallway ceilings rose at least fifteen meters over my head, and I had to stand on the tips of my toes just to see over the railing, though there wasn't much to look at. The whole place was empty.

Since Jhasali appeared unfazed, I took some latitude and looked around. The railing blocked my view unless I strained to look over it, so I dropped to my knees instead and stuck my face between the bars that held it up. When I looked down, I almost fainted in shock.

At the very bottom of the silo—hundreds of meters below me—sat a floor made of glass. Beyond this glass lay a vast sea of stars. I turned my head upward to find a flat, clear ceiling that displayed the same sight. I pulled my head back through the bars and sat on my knees, looking up at Jhasali as she stood by the rail.

"We're in space, aren't we?" My bottom lip trembled as gooseflesh crawled up my arms.

"Not in a physical sense. This chamber was built to project training scenarios. Right now, I am having it project my memories," she said.

"What is this a memory of?"

"A voyaging vessel of my people, meant for colonizing new harvesting stars. It is, indeed, in space. In fact, this ship was constructed in the void and permanently resides there."

"It cannot land?" I got to my feet.

"It is much too large to land. It is not even equipped to do so. It can orbit, if need be, but it is designed to journey through deep space and replace the home world, not supplement it. Thanks to vessels such as this one, it is possible to be hatched and live and die without ever setting foot on a real planet."

"That is what you all do?"

"No. Most don't. Most take smaller vehicles in and out of the big ships. I know of no one who stays on permanently."

"You were born here?" I asked.

"I was," she replied.

"Why is it so empty?"

"Because we're in the chamber's full-control mode. This is an illusion of my creation. I wished you to see the place before the people."

She turned her eyes toward the doorway nearest to us and pointed at it. The door slid open to reveal a being so strange I would have plunged straight over the ledge at the sight of it had it not been for the railing. Of course, I had the information on what Jhasali's people actually looked like stored in my cerebral databases, but I'd never accessed it. She had become human to me so quickly, but the thing that stood before me now was far from human.

A pale-lavender-colored being, around three meters tall, stood at the threshold. It leaned slightly forward on long legs that had double-hinged knees and splayed, taloned feet like those of some gigantic raptor. Its bare, muscular torso contained no breasts or belly button, but it did have two pairs of arms. The lower pair was thinner and shorter, with hands similar to my own. The higher pair was thicker and longer than the lower, with clawed hands instead of fingers—it was obvious this pair was meant to allow the creature to run on all fours. Its long, thin tail ran in a ridge all the way down its spine until it fell to the floor, where it coiled once over the right foot like a resting serpent. The end of the tail was covered in a cluster of shining globules that looked like the beady black eyes of a shark.

All of this would have been shocking enough without the head. Atop the long, skinny neck sat the strangest face I'd ever seen. The mouth was lipless. The nose was flattened to the face, where the slit nostrils sat on the sides of the nasal bone rather than underneath. If there were any ears, I'd be damned if I could spot them. The eyes were the strangest feature of all. Huge and rimmed with heavy black lines that formed three separate wings flaring out across the face, they had no pupil, no iris, and no white. Rather, they were uniformly metallic gray, like pools of shining molten lead—just as Jhasali's had been when I'd first met her.

From the top of the head jutted hundreds of tiny tentacles that reminded me of the snake strands of Medusa. These tentacles fell from all over the head down the back and shoulders, stopping at the elbow of the first set of arms. Each strand was tipped with a tiny ball of flesh. Each strand could also move independently of the others, for they all pulsated in different directions, and many of them stood at attention, rising another meter or so above the head.

The creature wore no clothing but was covered in muted blue ink that formed strange symbols all over its body. These markings I understood to be little more than decoration, and I recalled Jhasali had worn a less obvious version of them when I'd first seen her.

As I stared at the creature, I backed away from it and moved behind Jhasali, placing her between it and myself. She was giving it the strangest look—an expression of longing.

"What do you think?" she asked.

"It's horrible," I blurted.

She hesitated before smiling. "That is my real body, my default DNA."

"You changed yourself to look like us from that?" I asked, wondering how.

At that, a massive clear tube appeared in my mind's eye, and I understood this tube to contain a medium in which the nanos could work to alter the shape of the body. Everything could be taken apart and put back together: bones lengthened or shortened, tissue added or subtracted, features altered, organs moved around, all at the cellular level. Christ! How much of us was actually made of meat?

"You really believe I'm horrible?" Jhasali said.

"Well, no. I just . . . I am unused to this." I pointed at the creature. "May I touch it?"

"You mean me? Yes, you may touch me."

I approached the thing, willing myself to remember this was my friend, regardless of how she looked. I stretched out my hand to touch the clawed fingers, for they were the closest. Then, I decided I'd rather touch the soft hand, the one that looked more like mine. The main differences were that this hand had no fingernails and six fingers instead of five.

I took the large hand in both of mine. It felt soft to the touch. As with myself, the nanos did a superb job of creating the illusion of flesh. The soft hand clasped my left one. I moved my right hand up to the four-fingered clawed one, where I pinched one of the prehensile black talons between my fingers. They were cold and hard as steel, sharp as razor blades. One of the fingers twitched. At this, I gasped and leapt back.

The human form of Jhasali giggled from behind me and pressed a hand to my shoulder. "It's alright. Neither of me will do you harm."

She smiled and motioned for me to turn once more toward the interior of the silo. When I did, the chamber had transformed. It practically buzzed with the humming sounds of people's conversations and drones bustling about. A surveillance bot—a tiny spherical drone with dozens of antennae sticking out of it—streaked past my head and veered into one of the side passages. To our right stood another of the creatures that possessed Jhasali's true form, only this one was a wild calico pattern of blue, green, and yellow.

Without warning, this stranger stepped onto the railing and leapt over the side.

"Oh!" I cried, running to the rail.

I needn't have worried; the creature fell less than a meter before a long, flat drone that looked like a diamond-shaped board with holes in the bottom caught it midair. The creature stood upon the board as if it were a solid platform, and the drone spirited its rider over to the other side of the atrium and down a hallway. In fact, many of these people leapt off the rails to catch the magical flying planks as if such behavior were as natural as walking.

"Couldn't they just go around?" I asked.

"Why? That would take forever. Flying is immediate," Jhasali answered.

She was right. The size of this place meant a walk just to the other side of the atrium could take fifteen or twenty minutes, assuming I'd accurately guessed the distance. Looking at one of the flying boards again, I wondered if this was how Jhasali got around my planet without a horse and realized of course it was.

"Does everyone choose their own markings?" I asked as another pastel-purple being, so like Jhasali that it was almost indistinguishable from her, strode past us. Her own form turned and hurried after that one.

"We are all hatched a neutral gray. When we gain the ability, we choose the color and patterns we believe suit us best, but many of us change our looks based on our summation of our lives," she said.

"So your feelings?"

"Not feelings. Those change moment to moment. We choose colors and markings based on our personalities, experiences, that sort of thing. For instance, if some cataclysmic or wonderful event happens to us, we might change our base colors. If we become close with one of our comrades, we might match their looks. But not for something like feeling sad one day."

"So that's why you made your human form look like me."

"Yes. Did it not please you?"

"Back then, it confused me more than anything else." I paused before adding, "Why did you choose purple for this body?"

"I felt this pale purple was a peaceful color, calming to behold. I used to be a bright green with orange markings, but I have mellowed with age."

I was tempted to laugh. If she considered her current disposition mellow, what had she once been? I walked farther down the passage, watching all the creatures hustling through the hallways atop their metal mounts.

"Can they see us?" I asked.

"They cannot see. They are merely projections of the room. They can interact with us for our benefit, but they do not sense anything. Watch. I'll show you."

As soon as she said this, our surroundings changed. We were now back in the empty, windowless room we'd first entered.

"See? Nothing in this chamber exists. It's all in our heads."

"So, it really was an illusion," I whispered to myself, but Jhasali heard me.

"An illusion representative of reality. That place might not be real inside the room, but it is a real place." She looked toward the chamber door, and it opened. "Let us forget all this for now. I want to go outside and see if your planet's sun is still up."

"But I want to see the rest of that giant vessel, and I want to try the—what did you call it? The scenario," I argued.

"Maybe later. All of this is just . . ." She trailed off.

"Just what?"

"I don't know, bringing up too many other memories, things not valuable to the present."

We went outside into the crisp mountain air, and Jhasali bade some drones build a fire. She played vihuela while I cooked our supper over the open flame, telling her to make the damned drones let me do it myself. While I prepared the meat, I remembered Lobo; he'd loved to laze about next to any fire, letting the flame heat his fur so hot his back became almost untouchable. The familiar burning sensation filled my nose, signaling I was about to start welling up, so I pushed the memory down and kept sliding cuts of deer meat onto skewers.

I missed Sergio as much as I missed Lobo, and I wished he were seated next to this fire making music with us under the open sky. Whilst listening to Jhasali play,

I had this fantasy that one day she would accompany Sergio, and he would finally abandon his habit of never allowing anyone to hear him sing.

He had a beautiful singing voice—rich, deep, and vibrating—but he never sang if he knew anyone was near. When we first married, I'd had to sneak around my own house if I wished to catch a hint of him humming a tune, though he'd warmed to singing around me after a time. That night, I told Jhasali of his lovely voice and that I would enjoy seeing the two of them play together, him singing, her strumming, me dancing to their rhythm, whilst we all looked ceaselessly to the heavens.

When dusk melted into darkness, Jhasali left her vihuela and stood, staring up at the night sky and sighing. The weak light from the crescent moon gave her gray hair an almost translucent quality that it had never possessed under more direct light. I approached her, unsure of her mood.

"You miss it?" I whispered.

"It's so quiet here. All the planets I've ever set foot on had occupied skies. Drones flying overhead. Cruisers coming in and out of orbit. Satellites passing by every few seconds. I've never been on a planet where the skies were empty. Not even an air transport flies by."

"Your home planet doesn't have empty skies?"

"I don't really have a home planet. If you mean the planet of my birth, I was hatched in space. If you mean the planet upon which my species originated, I have never been there. I don't even know what it used to look like beyond my ancient ancestors' uploaded data. You are lucky—to have a home planet, I mean."

I did not know how to respond, so I said nothing. She was always going on about the beauty of earthly music and the wildness of the forests and the splendor of the vast oceans, and it gave me hope that she might be coming around to the idea of making this her new home planet. I thought perhaps I might even help her transition to her adopted world.

How I wish now that I had not been so naïve as to believe she could ever think of any single planet as home. Although she could appreciate the beauty of Earth, the feet of one who wanders the stars cannot set themselves forever upon the ground. That was something no sensor could have told me.

# Chapter Thirteen

# LANDSLIDE

O ver the weeks, Jhasali took me into the chamber for some beginner sessions in which we trained together, either fighting a few lightly armed foes or working through survival situations where we were placed into fake forests or illusionary deserts and forced to fend for ourselves. The chamber was able to manipulate the passage of time, making a few hours feel like days and sometimes even weeks. At first, I'd been concerned the chamber sessions would ruin all my careful planning to escape and return to the arrabal unseen, but I soon learned not to worry. Jhasali always put everything on a timer so the scenario could only last so long.

The combination of my training sessions and IDOS meant I did not fear the darkness or anything hiding within as I once had. I started making my journeys to and from Homeship between midnight and dawn, when I was least likely to be spotted crossing the vega, and I rode with no escort.

My new courage also allowed me to stay with Father Manuel later and later with each visit, since I no longer had to choose between leaving before sunset or staying the night in my tiny childhood bed. Though I carried them for protection, I couldn't bear the thought of wearing the IDOS cuffs into Father Manuel's home, so I usually removed them and stowed them in my saddlebags, leaving them by the door when I entered the house.

One of these visits, I stayed into the wee hours of the morning. Father Manuel had not gone to bed, so I thought I'd stick around until he did, planning to show myself out once I heard him snoring. He drank wine at the table and read from his Bible by the light of a few candles. I sat on the hearth of the fireplace that heated both the dining and the sitting rooms, letting the radiating warmth of the flames relax my shoulders as I once again fiddled with a bit of needlework that looked like it had been done by a five-year-old.

As I stitched, one of the flaming logs behind me fell off the grate and broke into many different pieces. The force of the log's fall allowed several coals to bounce out of the fireplace onto the hearth and the stone of the floor. I should have grabbed the fire spade, but as I'd promised Jhasali, I'd spent several weeks conditioning myself to no longer fear flames.

I reached down without thinking, swept the white-hot coals off the hearth into my palms, and tossed them into the fireplace. Then I picked up the pieces of burning ember from the floor to stick them back in their place, moving a blazing log with one hand so I could position the coals underneath and make a nice bed for them. I made to go back to my pitiful excuse for needlework when I heard the clang of metal hitting the floor.

I started and looked up to find Father Manuel beside me. He'd gotten the poker and the spade to gather the coals and had dropped them both at his feet. The width of his eyes was exceeded only by that of his gaping mouth. A cold chill ran up my spine as I realized what he'd just seen me do. My body froze; I dared not move or speak, fearing if I frightened him much more, his heart might have another episode.

"What do you want of me, demon, and what have you done with Micaela?" he said.

"I am no demon. I'm Micaela," I replied.

"LIAR!" he barked with such force I jumped.

Before I could react, he swept the fire poker from the floor and swung it, whacking me across the side of my face. It didn't hurt; I barely even felt the pressure of the impact. Seeing this blow did no good, he raised the poker and brought it down across the top of my head.

"Stop it, Father," I said, though my words fell on deaf ears.

"Get back to Hell where you belong, devil!" He swung the poker again.

"I told you *I am* Micaela."

"No, you're not. Tell me what you've done with her, succubus!"

Father Manuel bludgeoned me several more times across the head and shoulders, screaming about how the power of Christ would defeat me. I tried to remain calm, but every blow of that fire poker bruised my heart in a way it could no longer bruise my body.

Before I became aware of what I did, I stood up, caught the poker, and pushed back on it, shoving Father Manuel to the floor and wrenching it from his grasp. I raised it over my head before realizing what I was about to do and letting it fall behind my back. I kept my eyes fixed on Father Manuel. If I closed them, I saw Rodrigo's face instead.

"I'm sorry. I didn't intend to shove you," I said.

I reached down to help him up, but he crawled away from me, turning and struggling to his feet once he'd put the table between us. He splayed his left hand on the wooden surface and clutched at his heart with his right, coughing and gasping for breath.

Knowing I had to act fast if I wished to convince him I was not some sort of shape-shifting demon, I waited until he regained his breath. Then I inched away from the hearth, trying to give him as wide a berth as I could and make no sudden movements. He stood rooted to the floor like a cornered animal, his eyes following my every move.

I knew what I must do; I must pass the same test I'd originally put to Jhasali. Walking to the table, I picked up the copy of the Bible that lay open there. I pressed my face into it and smelled the worn pages. I closed the book and kissed its cover. Wrapping my arms around it, I pressed it to my breast and strode out the rectory door into the misty night. I went straight across the courtyard to the church and waited at the rear entrance.

Father Manuel followed me, keeping his distance. When he crept nearer, he said nothing, waiting to see what I might do.

"Open the door," I said. "I wish to prove to you I am no demon."

He did as I asked, still wary, as I gave him room to maneuver around me and push the door open. As soon as he did, I walked into the empty church and straight to the main altar. I knelt, crossed myself, said the Apostles' Creed and the Pater Noster, and kissed the Bible once more. I then took the crucifix necklace Father Manuel had given me as a girl out of my collar and kissed it as well, making sure he saw I still wore it.

Suspicious and frightened, Father Manuel snuck up behind me as a newborn foal approaches the first human it has ever seen. Keeping his distance, he knelt before the altar.

"Micaela?" he said.

"Yes?" I replied.

"Is it really you?"

"What must I do? Pray the whole rosary? Receive the Eucharist here and now?"

His face hardened. "You should not be in here."

He got up, motioned for me to leave the church, and escorted me back to the rectory. I handed him his Bible when we reached the door. Once we entered, he bade me sit down at the table, then stood over me with his arms crossed, looking at me in a way I'd never seen.

"Explain yourself," he demanded.

"Bless me, Father, for I have sinned," I blurted involuntarily. "I've taken something into my body that I did not understand before I accepted it. All I can tell you is it is neither of God nor of Satan. It is neither evil nor good. It just *is*, and I don't have the words to explain it."

"If you have defiled your body, you have sold your soul to the devil also. Does your husband know you've brought Satan into his bed?"

At this, I burst into laughter. "I have not sold my soul to Satan, nor have I lain with him, for many reasons, not the least of which is that he would have to exist for me to do either."

"You'll be punished for insulting your master, witch."

My laughter died instantly. "I have no master, and I am no witch."

"You must be. That's the only possible explanation for this."

"The only explanation?" I scoffed. "You don't even believe in sorcery. How many times have you said witches' powers are only imaginary? How many times have you mocked the townswomen up here for fearing for their children? You call them superstitious montañesas. What does it make you if you believe the superstitions you used to despise the instant you see something you don't understand?"

"I don't have to understand this to know it's wrong!" he snapped.

"Well, you must be quite the prophet, then, to be able to label all the phenomena of the known universe as good or evil at the snap of a finger," I clapped back.

"Don't try to confuse the situation. This is about you and your unnatural abilities."

"They cannot be unnatural if they exist in nature."

"Silence your forked tongue this instant. I won't hear another word."

"But Father—"

"No!" he roared. "Ignacio tried to warn me, and I didn't pay him any heed. Now look at you! This is my reward for thinking I could make a proper believer out of the child of heretics."

I leapt to my feet. "You certainly took it upon yourself to try, regardless of what those heretics or their child wanted. It turned out mighty convenient for you that your brothers burned my mother!"

"I told you a thousand times your mother was not burned, nor your father. I thought we'd put this issue to rest long ago. Why must you constantly harass me with it?"

"You think there will ever be such a thing as putting it to rest for me?" I shouted. "All this time I've spent never ever knowing, and you thought it was put to rest! It was at rest enough for you to attend more burnings. You abandoned me to run off to the auto de fe and let Ignacio have me."

"I had to go to the auto de fe. One of my parishioners was to be burned, and I wished to try one last time to save his soul from damnation. But that is beside the point. You cannot blame me or Ignacio or anyone else for *your* moral failings, Micaela."

"Who do you blame for yours?" I asked.

"I suppose your new master probably has something to do with them," he answered.

"I am the master of myself. I shall call no one master any longer: not the devil, not you, not my husband, not Christ himself. No one."

"We'll see what the authorities have to say about that." He made for the door.

I charged at his back, swinging myself around him and placing myself between him and the exit. "You will not denounce me."

"How do you plan to stop me? Murder me?"

"That's what you think of me now? I don't want to hurt you. I've never hurt anyone in my life." I wiped the unbidden tears that spilled out of my eyes.

At this, his expression softened, and he let his hands drop to his sides.

"I could harm you if I wished," I whispered. "I could burn this house down with the pair of us inside and walk out like Shadrach from the fiery furnace, but I have no desire to do such a thing. Don't you see? I've been this way for months and you didn't suspect it. Did I ever stop coming here to visit you damn near every night of the week? Did I ever stop giving alms to the children? Nothing about me has changed, so your opinion of me shouldn't either."

"I don't care. I won't abide a—whatever you are—living in my parish and practicing her devilry under my very nose."

I sighed. "I practice no devilry, and no matter what you do, I'll never lay a hand on you. But if you fetch the alguacil or write to the Inquisition, you'll give me no choice but to take you down with me. I'll say you led me to the devil's sabbats and taught me every heresy I know."

"No one will believe you," he said. "They know better!"

"Are you willing to bet your life on it? Of the two of us, who has more to fear from the stake?" I asked.

As a reminder, I strode to the fire, grabbed a blazing white coal from underneath the logs, and shoved it in my mouth. There, I held it between my tongue and my palate until I smothered it, at which point, I spat it out and crushed it underfoot.

Father Manuel faltered at the sight of this. Just like that, I had him. While it was unlikely enough people would believe my version of events to send him to the stake, once everyone found out I was an incombustible witch, I could make up whatever nonsense I liked. I could say he'd been the one to give me to the devil or he was making monsters out of normal girls through experimentation in alchemy. Such rubbish might not lead him to the quemadero, but it could get him interrogated, imprisoned, and perhaps even defrocked. He knew it. I knew it. And it put him in a real bind—hopefully enough of a bind to keep him quiet.

"Well? Weren't you leaving?" I pointed at the door.

"I don't suppose. I mean, I could . . . oh, just get out," he replied.

I slid past him, grabbing my saddlebag as I swept out the door into the fog.

When I got back to my house, I gravitated toward my tiny shrine with its icon of Santa Bárbara. I realized as I approached that my altar was covered in a thick layer of dust, fading under the gray powder after languishing in disuse. How long had it been since I'd last prayed? How long had it been since I'd stopped believing there was anyone out there who could hear me?

Standing before the altar, I tried to answer these questions—to put a precise date on when I'd become an apostate. I guessed it must have truly occurred long before I'd met Jhasali, for she'd been right about one thing: if I'd genuinely believed as I'd been taught, I would never have befriended what I suspected was a demon.

I supposed she'd only shone the sun on the mustard seed of doubt that Ignacio's ilk had planted before my birth and he himself had watered. However, there was no single, overwhelming instant of clarity that stood out in my mind as being *the* instant in which I became an unbeliever. This was simply the moment I knew for certain I was one already.

I likened the feeling to a landslide that starts off with an almost imperceptible rumble deep in the mountain's crust and the plummeting of a few small stones down its slope. Yet, before I'd even noted the tiny tumbling stones, the entire slope had slid down and the mountain had collapsed. Now, I stood in the dust and rubble with no clear notion of how I'd gotten here but with an overwhelming sense of certitude that there would be no salvation for the yawning crater that had once been my mountain.

***

Though he didn't denounce me to either secular or ecclesiastical authorities, Father Manuel did not exactly take in stride my sudden transubstantiation into a fireproof aberration. He wasn't cruel to me, nor did he retaliate against me, as I feared he might. Instead, he attempted to act as though nothing had happened between us, I guessed for the simple fact he knew of naught else to do.

I still went to Mass and wore my crucifix, at the very least to keep up appearances. He did not attempt to prevent my entrance into the church, though for his sake, I stopped taking Communion. Up to this point, I'd still continued to go through the motions so Father Manuel might not suspect my reservations about them. However, now that he knew of my "condition," I felt it best not to push my luck. I was unsure if he might take my acceptance of the bread or wine as profaning the Host—a crime I doubted any amount of fear would compel him to tolerate.

I despised how our dispute had ended that night. So many things had surfaced during that argument, so many issues so shallowly considered before we'd shoved them aside in the heat of our fury. I wanted to ask him if he truly believed me to be as unsalvageable as Ignacio thought, and I wanted even more to discuss my parents without the veils of deception and decency. I longed to know what had become of them and why he'd never returned me to them if they hadn't been relaxed. Most of all, I wished I could believe the answers he'd already given me. Perhaps I might, somehow, if he offered me some proof.

Hoping to make amends and discuss things with more civility, I attempted to do what I could to assuage Father Manuel's terror. I waited a week or so to give him time to cool off before going to the rectory, but he wouldn't say more than a few words to me.

Though he opened the door, he kept his distance even after I entered his house. He refused to touch me or sit anywhere near me, declining to drink the wine I brought and casting furtive glances in my direction every time I moved a muscle. To avoid causing him even more discomfort, I ceased my visits to him for the time being, which left me lonelier and more isolated than ever.

As spring blossomed in the vale, I tried to fill the void left by our sudden rift with more frequent visits to Sara and as many clandestine trips to Homeship as I could get away with. I became obsessed with trying the training chamber alone—anything to keep my mind off mine and Father Manuel's seemingly unresolvable problems. Though Jhasali had warned me to stay away from it without her, that just wasn't going to happen. She failed to realize the most surefire way to get many humans to do something is to tell us not to do it.

I waited until she left for a solitary walk one afternoon, abandoning me alone inside Homeship. As soon as she was out of sight, I ran through the bowels of the vessel to the empty room with its drab gray walls and dim white tiles. I entered the chamber with nothing but the clothes on my back, no weapons or supplies, as Jhasali had said was necessary.

Taking a deep breath, I told the room to begin the scenario. At that, the door slammed behind me and the lights shut off, plunging me into darkness. I had expected this; it happened in the same manner as it had when I'd been here with Jhasali. Only this time, she did not control the scenario. No one did.

I stood in the pitch blackness, hearing no sound, seeing not the smallest pinpoint of light on which to focus my vision. Darkness. Silence. The inaction lasted far longer than I remembered from last time. I wondered if the chamber was trying to torment me with sensory deprivation in order to unnerve me. I could not see well enough to find my way out, and I was seized with terror that the room had pulled away the floor to trick me into falling into the blackness if I took a step.

When I began probing my surroundings with my foot, the room kicked into action. The lights roared on, blazing into my eyes. I squinted them shut and threw up my hands to shield against the glare. Shrieks and wails unlike anything I'd ever heard bombarded my ears. I dared not look at first, terrified I would find some hellscape where I'd see the tortures inflicted on the damned. However, when I did peer beyond my eyelids, I found not a hellscape but a forest.

This alien place could not be anything that had ever existed on Earth. I stood on a high cliff of dark-blue stone, looking down at an immense wood made of sky-blue trees that grew out of the dirt and looped back down to it in steep arches, spreading their branches into the soil itself, like a second set of roots. The forest of blue arches stretched as far as I could see, bathed in a bizarre red light. I realized the shrieks and wails I'd mistaken for the damned were actually coming from creatures that resided in this eerie baldío.

When I raised my face to the horizon, an even stranger sight greeted me. The pink sky was filled almost to capacity with a glowing red planet, marked here and there across its shimmering surface with swirling clouds of white, yellow, and violet. But no planet could emanate such powerful light on its own, so that had to mean there was a sun around somewhere.

Sure enough, behind me blazed a brilliant star, farther away and hotter than our earthly sun, raging in a calcium-white fury and beating everything on the surface with its ferocious radiation. No wonder the trees wished to dig back underground. Yet it seemed the planet's atmosphere was too thin to hold much heat from the mother star. Even though its light reflected starkly off the shiny surface of the bare cobalt-blue rock beneath my feet and the gigantic gaseous planet in the sky, there was a chill in the air.

As I peered over the cliff, the brush rustled behind me. I turned to look but could see nothing but the naked rock on which I stood and, beyond this bare spot that extended just a few meters between the long drop and the tree line, another endless waste of arching trunks. Still, something living must have made that rustling noise. There was no wind.

I heard it again, behind me once more, but that did not make sense because behind me loomed only the sheer, towering cliff. I glanced over my shoulder toward the precipice to ensure the noise was not some colossal bat rising from below.

When I turned back to the part of the forest on top of the cliff, such a hideous sight greeted me that I wished the rustling had been a colossal bat. A giant beast had come up to within centimeters of my face while I'd had my head turned. This massive serpent seized my ankles with its forelegs, toppling me over before I could react.

The body that now writhed beside me was at least six times my length, its sides lined with hundreds of thin, long legs like some titan of a centipede. The two pairs of front legs were thick and powerful, studded at each of their ends with prehensile claws. Its coiling back was covered in patterns of sky blue like the trees and cobalt like the rock. These patterns could only be for one thing: camouflage. The effect was so spectacular it had rendered this creature, huge though it was, invisible until the instant it'd taken hold of me.

Never in my most unbearable nightmares could I have dreamt of a demon with a face like this animal's. From the top of its square skull sprang dozens of short coal-black spikes and, below these, row upon row of yellow pupilless eyes. It possessed no teeth. Instead, a pair of razors jutted from its top and bottom jaws and curved around its mouth, clamping together like two opposing guillotine blades.

I screamed in fright as this thing caught me up with such ease I might as well have been a ragdoll and dragged me toward its open maw. I shrieked and cried for help, realizing I now viewed the gaping mouth through a haze of tears.

What was I doing? This was no time for shrieks and tears! I dug into the ground with my hands and tried to tear myself away from the creature's grip, but to no avail. I wished I had a blade to cut myself free, and the instant that wish formed in my mind, a long dagger appeared right under the belly of the beast.

I rolled toward the dagger, coming dangerously close to the snapping jaws. Spinning onto my back to face the creature, I drove the blade deep into the flesh of its neck, surprised to find it was indeed flesh and the liquid that poured from its wound was indeed blood—viscous blue blood, but blood, nonetheless. So this dreadful thing was not like Jhasali or me. It was a biological lifeform, as vulnerable to being pierced and torn as anything else.

I pulled the dagger from its neck and slashed at its forelimbs, slicing deep cuts into the flesh there and revealing the horrible black bones. The beast loosened its grip but changed tactics, attempting to wrap me in its serpentine body and constrict the life out of me instead. To prevent it from cocooning me, I gouged at its beady eyes. Blood spurted out of half a dozen sockets, and the fiend let me go. Without a second's hesitation, I threw myself away from it and unintentionally toppled over the cliff.

Down I plunged, not daring to loosen my grip on my only weapon. I closed my eyes and curled myself into a ball as a rocky outcropping flew closer. I braced for impact, feeling a bone-crushing blow to my left side as I hit the rocks, bounced up, tumbled down, and hit them again and again.

When I came to rest at the edge of the forest, I was amazed to find myself uninjured. For an instant, I'd forgotten I was still in the scenario (though the impact had hurt like the real thing). I didn't know if a fall from such a height could break my bones and tear my flesh in real life, so I made a mental note not to ever find out.

I looked to the top of the cliff and, with a thrill of horror, saw the beast scaling down the sheer rock wall with the same ease as I would have walked a paved road. Its skin glistened, slimy with its own blood. I turned to run but stopped myself. This was the scenario, after all, and in the scenario, you're not meant to run and hide. You're meant to fight and win.

Thus, I studied the creature as it made its way down. I watched the way it moved, how the forelimbs, independent of the tangle of legs behind them, felt for purchase for the limbs yet to come. The tangle of legs behind the forelimbs moved in long waves from the rear, the body between them a narrow mass of lithe muscle.

With another, equally unpleasant thrill of horror, I remembered something else I'd learned during one of Jhasali's and my tandem sessions: this training chamber didn't make things up. It pulled everything in its arsenal from real life—meaning somewhere, in some solar system, no matter how unfathomably distant, this creature existed. Maybe even now, in a dense extraterrestrial forest like this one, it slithered and slammed its guillotine teeth down on the necks of helpless prey, perhaps beheading them in one fell stroke.

It suddenly occurred to me I was just standing out in the open waiting for this thing to come down. I slipped my knife into the belt of my pantaloons and ran into the forest, where I climbed one of the largest arched plants I could find.

The climb presented a serious challenge, as the trunk of the tree was smooth and hard as granite, and the highest point of the arch towered over fifteen meters before looping back down. It took me almost as long to scramble to the top as it took the creature to get to the cliff's base. The beast could climb this perch in a heartbeat, but I did not plan to give it the chance.

I watched the reptilian monster finish its descent to the bottom of the cliff and slide down into the forest, once again disappearing, thanks to its excellent camouflage. I turned in frantic circles, trying to leave no centimeter of the forest unviewed for long. I was somewhat confident this thing could not really hurt me, but what did I know? Maybe the scenario could be lethal to weed out weak members of the crew.

Hearing the telltale rustling, I turned just as the beastly head emerged underneath the trunk on which I stood. I leapt from my perch like a diving falcon, landing in a straddling position across the brute's ugly snout and using the weight of my body and the force of the fall to plunge the dagger deep into the back of the neck, just behind the horns.

The beast let out a shriek and reared half its body into the air like a huge cobra, slinging me off its snout and catapulting me a good ten meters across the forest. I landed in soft mud, but by the time I'd rolled over and struggled to my feet, the serpent was on top of me again, bleeding and bellowing, but still alive.

"I need a better weapon!" I cried.

Sure enough, as soon as I'd said it, the chamber reacted. Out of the corner of my eye, I saw an IDOS cuff. I rolled out from under the creature and dove for the cuff, slamming it on my wrist while the beast dragged me backward by my ankle.

I turned and thought "fire," but I missed and blew a hole in an arching tree behind the creature. I aimed again—too late. The beast hauled me headfirst into its open maw and clamped its iron teeth around my waist. I cried out, sure I'd been cut clean in half, but after a second, I discovered I remained unhurt. Thank you, nanos.

The brute chomped on me several more times before deciding to swallow me whole instead. I was not about to let that happen. Though my right arm had been pinned underneath my body while the creature busied itself trying to chew me, I managed to wriggle it free once the animal positioned me to go down in one gulp. I pressed the cuff to the roof of the huge mouth and fired.

A dreadful explosion of blue blood engulfed me, filling my eyes, my ears, my nostrils, and my open mouth with a disgusting smell and sour taste. The creature fell with a thud onto the forest floor, trapping me halfway inside its mouth and pinning me under the weight of its massive head. I thrust and kicked with all my might, but my best efforts to lift the head or push the jaws wider apart proved futile. I couldn't see or breathe. There was only one thing to do.

Dreading it, I squinted my eyes tight and turned my face away from the back of the throat. Then I fired a volley of rounds toward the top of the head, partially severing it and making a hole large enough that I could slide my legs through the gap in the teeth and drag myself out through the back of the neck.

I spat the blood out of my mouth and wiped it from my face. Too exhausted to look down upon my defeated conquest, I fell beside the dead creature. There, I lay still for a long time. I was terrified there might be more of them, so I listened for rustling sounds as I continued to rest and try to regain some strength.

I assumed the forest must have plunged into night, for the light outside my eyelids dimmed to darkness, and the calls of the creatures faded to silence. Still drained, I hoped when I opened my eyes I'd find the scenario had faded away and left me on the floor of the chamber.

Alas, when I did open them, the sight that greeted me was not the extraterrestrial forest floor or the empty training chamber but a woodland not unlike that just outside Homeship. Without a clue as to how, I was now upright, my hands were bound, and I was being tugged along behind a horse and rider, with the end of my rope tied to the cantle of his saddle. I tried to jerk myself free, but laughter broke out to my rear. Several armed men escorted the rider and me.

I couldn't imagine where we might be going, so I leaned to the side to see around the horse's hindquarters. Some distance ahead, a stake had already been driven into the ground and piled with kindling.

I felt violated upon realizing the scenario had read my memories like that. I'd thought it could only access Jhasali's memories, not mine! The chamber had not gotten everything right as far as the scenery or the likelihood that some random stake would be set up in the middle of a forest, but it was enough to make me lose my cool.

I tried to heat my cuff only to discover IDOS had been taken away. I became even more alarmed when I tugged and twisted at my bonds but managed to accomplish no more than to set the foot soldiers behind me laughing again.

The rational part of me knew I wouldn't burn if they put me on a pyre of a hundred stakes, but the ten-year-old girl still inside me somehow didn't believe it. Seeing that black spike growing ever closer set her to panicking in earnest. I screamed and threw myself to the ground, rolling around in an attempt to wrest myself free. The more futile the effort proved, the louder I sobbed, the harder the men laughed, and the closer we moved toward our destination.

The alien creature and the bizarre otherworld had only unnerved me for a second, but this was another level—if the goal of the scenario were to make me melt into a puddle of frantic weeping, it had succeeded.

As I kept struggling, a voice broke into the chamber, emanating from nowhere and everywhere all at once. It was Jhasali.

"What are you doing? Get off the ground. You're making an ass of yourself, and you know the scenario will only intensify if you refuse to train."

I stopped squirming and realized she was right: I'd better fight back if I did not wish the chamber to punish me for cowardice. I leapt to my feet and charged at the horse, using a boulder to spring onto its haunches and looping the rope that bound my wrists around the rider's neck.

I twisted the rope into a makeshift noose and pulled with all my might. The horse took off at full gallop, but we didn't fall. Meanwhile, the rider resisted, swinging his hands up to pummel my head and trying to get his fingers between the rope and his throat. He even pulled out a knife to stab me, but it turned on my flesh as though the blade were made of paper.

Only now did it occur to me how difficult it is to strangle a man. I'd never had reason to think on such a thing in the past, but in this instant, with my hands clenched around the ligature and my arms pulling with all their strength, I realized it would take several minutes for this damned fool to die. Yet I didn't have several minutes, for bullets whizzed past my head as the foot soldiers fired from behind me.

Desperate to speed things along, I grasped the rope and heaved, flinging my captor and myself off the horse. The idea had been to use the force of the sprinting animal to break the rider's neck, but his accursed foot got caught in the stirrup, preventing his neck from snapping when we fell. The horse kept fleeing, dragging him along face down. I tried to keep my weight on top of him so he might be killed by striking his head on a rock, but he kept on struggling.

I attempted to reach my hands toward the rider's calf, but they were still attached both to one another and to his neck. I jerked my weight around, wriggling from side to side, trying to shift our bodies in such a manner as to loose his foot from the stirrup. Somehow, I was able to get my foot under his shin bone and lift his leg up just enough to wiggle his foot free.

As soon as I accomplished this, the backward pull flipped us around and slung us out behind the horse. The man's neck took the brunt of the force when the rope pulled taught, and the bones finally broke.

I'd managed to get hold of the dagger he'd been using to gouge at me when we were still in the saddle. With this I cut my bonds. Then I used the body of the dead rider as a platform to get myself into position to mount the fleeing horse.

Dragging myself up the rope, I tried and failed several times to gain a grip on the animal. I was much stronger in here than in real life—the scenario was helping me so I might continue my training rather than failing and having to start over. Even so, I struggled up and slid backward over and over, each time barely maintaining my grip on the rope while being dragged along the ground, before I managed to catch hold of the saddle and heave my body onto the horse. The animal still sustained a full gallop, bucking and kicking as I mounted.

When I positioned myself on the back of the sprinting horse, the rider's stirrups were much too long for my legs. No matter; I could cling to the saddle with my thighs. I cut the dead rider free, allowing the horse to race all the faster. The men behind us were unmounted, so I could have fled, but that was not the point.

The chamber was trying to unnerve me, and I was not going to give it the opportunity to discipline me for fleeing. I wheeled around and ripped the rider's sword from its saddle-mounted scabbard, and my mount and I charged back toward the foot soldiers.

The four-man company readied to fire, but I was too quick for the initial two, throwing the knife straight into the chest of the first and flinging the sword into the neck of the second. I thought this might decapitate him, but it didn't. The blade sliced through enough of his flesh to start a fount of blood pouring from his neck, and he fell to his knees, clutching at the hemorrhaging wound.

Once again, I figured the chamber must be helping me, for I didn't know how to throw a blade at an attacker. Yet here I was, doing it all the same. Out of time to think, I focused on my final two foes, who both raised their arquebuses and fired at the same time, shooting my mount out from under me. I toppled to the ground and rolled out of the way to avoid the horse crashing down on me.

The first man did not bother to reload his long gun. Instead, he threw it to the ground and pulled a pistol from his belt. In those days, the pistol was practically unheard of, and I'd only seen what it looked like in pictures. Sergio and Armando had occasional dealings with German metal merchants, and they'd returned from Flanders a year or two ago with stories of firearms manufacturers in Germany who were working on a shortened version of the wheellock rifle—a version that could be fired using only one hand. Sergio had shown me a rough drawing of what one was supposed to look like.

Now, my fake foe brandished a stubby wheellock pistol that looked similar to the one I remembered from the drawing. Before he could fire, I swept up the long gun, flipped it around, and struck him in the face with the stock, knocking the pistol from his hand. I caught the pistol in the air and shot him dead.

At the same time, the other man finished loading his long gun and fired, missing me by centimeters. I wheeled around and sprinted toward him, reaching him before he got the chance to pull a pistol from his belt. I smashed the butt of the unloaded arquebus into the bridge of his nose, bowling him over. Leaping on top of him, I hit him again and again with the stock.

"Stop! Please, I surrender!" he screamed.

I halted. "Throw away your gun."

He took the pistol from his waistband and tossed it to the ground behind me. I picked it up and threw away the long gun. Training the pistol on the bruised and bleeding face of my single remaining foe, I wondered what I might do with him. He rose from his back to his knees, holding his bloody nose with his hands.

"What to do with you," I mused aloud.

"What in all the wide universe do you mean?" a voice snapped behind me. I turned to see Jhasali had entered the scenario. "You kill him. That's what you do."

"No!" he shrieked. "Please don't. I have a family."

Thus far, the chamber had been toying with me, trying to make me lose my nerve, but I couldn't imagine the purpose of this. I would never shoot a man in the face while he sat before me and begged for his life.

Jhasali didn't even glance in his direction. "Who gives a damn about his family? Prisoners like him are useless. What else will you do with him? Let him go?"

"Yes! Please, let me go!" the man wailed.

"You think if you'd asked the same thing of him, he'd not have lit the stake anyway? Slay him now," Jhasali said.

"I can't," I replied.

"You will do it. I swear, Micaela, I am going to harden that tender little heart of yours if it kills you. Now *slay him*!" she cried.

She screamed in one ear for me to fire, and he screamed in the other begging me not to. I tried to repeat the words "not real" in my head, but this felt as real as real could get. I couldn't look the poor man in the eye, so I looked at the ground. I raised the pistol, still unable to squeeze the trigger. Jhasali yelled for me to get on with it, and the man shrieked for mercy.

I broke into sobs, caught between her demands that I slaughter this helpless and defeated man, my own desperate desire not to, and his frantic entreaties that I spare his life. She cried once more for me to do it. Almost before I knew it, I fired, surprising myself with the cracking recoil of the gun. The pleading ceased.

I fell to my knees, weeping and dropping the pistol in the grass, unable to look at the body of my fallen captive.

"Well done." Jhasali turned from me.

When she did, the lights—the real overhead lights of the chamber—came back on, leaving everything within the same as it had been before the scenario began. I glanced at the wall and saw Jhasali standing near the open door, collected and indifferent.

"Why did it make me do that?" I sobbed, my emotions failing to catch up to the fact that everything I'd just done had been a virtual act.

"I would guess the chamber believes you to be a naturally nonviolent person, and it wishes to train some of that out of you."

"What if I don't want it trained out of me?"

Jhasali shrugged. "I'd suggest you not prepare for combat."

"But I want to defend myself."

"Then you need to make your peace with killing whenever necessary."

"That wasn't necessary." I wiped my tears.

"I disagree. If you had let him go, he'd have still posed a threat to you. Dead men can do no harm."

I didn't agree, but it would do me no good to argue.

"Are you angry with me?" I asked, recalling she'd warned me not to come in here.

"Quite the contrary." She smiled.

"Even though I used the chamber alone?"

"Well, you disobeyed me; it's true. But you fought infinitely better than I ever imagined."

"You saw all of what happened?" I said.

"Through virtual view, yes. I came in just as you had thrown yourself from the cliff, so I decided to let the scenario run its course and see what you'd do."

"And you thought I did well?" I felt I'd been shamefully incompetent.

"Oh, yes. In fact, you've done so well I wish to train with you as an equal."

"What does that mean?"

"It means instead of me limiting the scenario, you and I shall enter it as a fighting pair and let the chamber run in zero-control mode. I will have as much idea of what is to happen as you do, but it will be a more intense situation than you have experienced today. The chamber made things much easier for you than it will for me."

"Easy!" I stammered.

"Of course. It challenged you according to your ability and aided you in a manner conducive to the lessons it wished to impart. It can get much worse than that."

"How?"

"Well, the battle sequences are more intense. Many more things go wrong. It's harder to access weapons."

"But if the chamber takes from your memories—"

"It doesn't take solely from your memories. You know that. It contains almost infinite datapoints and billions of possible situations," she said.

"It clearly accessed my memories for the last scenario. I thought only the drones do that, and only if you bond to them," I replied.

"If you'd asked your sensors—"

"I'm asking you!"

She sighed. "The chamber accesses data you've shared with your implants, but it only uses it against you for the time you're inside. It doesn't store it or share it with anyone."

"That's comforting."

"Look, there are ways to keep your data private. You can store sensitive memories in locked sensors that don't share anything with entities outside your living body. You can tag data as restricted to the isolated network of your brain and bonded drones. My people do that by default. That way, our thoughts are never shared because they get deleted from a device if we unlink. In fact, you don't even have to upload data from your brain at all. It's possible to route certain thoughts or memories out of your implants entirely."

"I want to do that," I blurted.

"It's best to avoid routing too much of your mind out of the sensors. If the data is only stored in your brain itself, it won't be accessible to your bonded servants nor uploaded to them if you die. If you lose your body, you'll lose whatever data didn't exist in a backup."

"I don't care. How do I move that data out of the implants and put it back solely inside my mind?" I asked.

"I'll have to teach you. It's a tough trick to master. We Ukdah'ni only learned it to get around the cerebral monitoring systems our masters had in place before the rebellion," she said.

"Well, I need to know it too."

"No, you don't. All the chips we manufactured for ourselves during the revolt were made without cerebral monitoring capabilities so the authorities could never read our thoughts again. None of us can even connect our sensors directly to those of another person because they're built without that function. Every layer of the system we have created is designed so that the only living being who can know your thoughts is you."

"I don't want the chamber to know them either," I huffed.

"Then restrict them. Labeling data is easier to learn than routing around the implants. But if you wish to continue training in the chamber, you can't restrict everything because the room needs to access at least some of your memories to build custom scenarios. Do you not want to continue training?"

"If I didn't, I wouldn't have snuck in here," I snapped.

"You know, at some point we need to start your lessons with the drones, as well," she said, slipping it into the conversation.

"No. That is still too much. I've told you a thousand times I don't want every computer in the damned universe knowing my every thought!"

Jhasali threw up her hands. "That's not how it works."

"I don't care. I don't know if I'll ever be ready for all this. I need more time."

"Take it, then." Jhasali inclined her head and left the room without another word.

I didn't follow her. Instead, I went to my bedroom, put on the IDOS cuffs, and returned to Santa Colomba. I wondered the whole ride back if I'd ever figure out a way to make my peace with all this. I also wondered if, in taking the nanos, I'd already divested myself of the option.

## Chapter Fourteen

# THE ROAD SOUTH

I didn't return to the ship for over two months. In the beginning, Jhasali attempted to contact me, but I begged her to leave me be. After that, I heard no more from her, for which I was grateful. I needed time to gather my thoughts.

The training chamber's use of my memories had deeply upset me. Until that point, I had given Homeship only spoken directives, and Jhasali had commanded a couple of her bonded drones to serve me when I asked. So I'd never made mental contact with an external device. My independent use of the chamber was the first time I'd had a computer commune with me in a manner that made it undeniable I was no longer the sole entity inside my own head, and I found it unbearably unnerving.

Much time as I spent sifting through the information on my sensors, I still didn't exactly believe them when they told me the Dissenters' system was designed so my thoughts would be mine and mine alone. I understood the intent was there, but there were too many potential weak spots that worried me in ways I could never have hoped to comprehend before I'd already made myself vulnerable to them.

These possible holes were not applicable to the Ukdah'ni themselves. They'd spent their lives designing and operating within a new system that gave them an extraordinary amount of freedom compared to what they'd had in the past, and they possessed a much more solid grasp of how to keep their minds protected than I did. For them, this network of shared and private brain-to-computer interfaces was a liberation. For me? An invasion much more severe and disturbing than the integration of IDOS with my body.

Free of the need for sleep, I often sought relief from my anxieties by stalking the baldíos on my own in the dead of night, armed with my heightened senses, my perfect night vision, a hunting knife, and, of course, IDOS. Over the weeks, I became skilled at marking my quarry—hitting it squarely in the head so as to avoid damaging the meat. The IDOS projectiles expanded on impact, meaning if I hit a hare in the body, it would leave little usable muscle. Deer and boar weren't as difficult. If I hit the body, it only damaged the flesh surrounding the entry wound.

I'd helped butcher enough pigs during the annual slaughter that learning to skin and clean my kills in the field proved easy. That spring was the first time I ever ate meat during Lent. Because my nanos were still making alterations to my system, I ate a lot of it, cooking over an open fire and stuffing my face in the predawn hours while everyone else fasted.

Throughout that Lent and the period following Easter, I spent a good deal of time with Sara. I was keen to hear news of Sergio, for the fleet's expected arrival drew near. She and I passed many a visit dancing a verbal fandango, in which I would attempt to bring up Sergio's homeward journey and she would speak of whatever other topic proved necessary to get me off the subject. She would just as soon pretend Armando was never coming back, but it had been over a year since I'd held my husband and many months since I'd even heard from him, so I didn't appreciate her unspoken prohibition on the mere mention of his name.

One morning in late May, Sara and I were taking some wine and cheese in the parlor of her town house when one of her manservants came to us, bowed, and handed her a stack of letters. Of that stack, almost all the letters were mine. Sara and I began to open them, and I went to the window for better reading light.

To my dismay, the first letter of Armando's that Sara opened contained not news of a homecoming but news of the most devastating sort. The fleet had indeed arrived in Sevilla, yet since the ships had not sustained too much damage and Armando expected to find enough cargo and passengers, they were to make another run as soon as possible. They intended to load up and set sail again no later than August.

Several of Sergio's letters to me contained varying versions of the same excuse for this decision: Armando and his investors had made no money with last year's run, since they'd been paying down debts. This time, they hoped for at least some profit. Of course, I should've anticipated that, in their avarice, Sergio and Armando couldn't be bothered to delay their voyage for such a silly thing as seeing their wives.

I shouted in anger, but Sara broke into a broad smile. Before she could stop herself, she chuckled and said how wonderful it was that we wouldn't have to endure the men for another year.

"You're selfish to say such things. Some of us don't have a smoldering pile of ruin for a marriage." I slammed myself into my chair and balled my fists.

The smile fell off Sara's face. "You wouldn't speak so if you knew anything about anything! Let's have damn near twenty years of barrenness and death pass by you and see where your marriage stands."

I buried my face in my hands and burst into tears. "I'm sorry. I'm so sorry. I shouldn't have said that. I just—this wasn't what I was hoping for. I didn't mean it. Really."

Sara crossed her arms. "I know you love him, but this isn't so bad. Another year will pass before you know it, and you'll see Sergio then."

I couldn't bring myself to accept that. Perhaps Sara didn't understand what it was like to be so deeply in love you felt like you were missing a part of yourself. Perhaps she did understand but didn't think it such a good thing.

Suddenly, a thought germinated, blossomed, and fruited all at once inside my mind. If Sergio could not come to me, why could I not go to him? The fleet didn't sail until August, which would give me five or six weeks with my husband before he set out, assuming I rode for Sevilla immediately.

"How stupid do you think it would be for us to go to Sevilla to see them?" I asked Sara.

"Very. How could the carriage even make it? What's more, I won't ride a couple dozen leagues to see my father in Burgos. So what makes you think I'd ride across the peninsula to see my husband? Especially since I have a smoldering ruin for a marriage."

"Please, please forgive me for that. I really did not mean it. I lost control of my worthless tongue. Sometimes, I want to rip it out of my head," I said.

Sara sighed. "It's alright. If there's one thing I understand, it's speaking out of grief."

Taking her by the hand, I apologized once more. She told me to forget it unless I didn't believe that she forgave me. I nodded and dropped it, instead asking her how stupid she thought it would be for me to go to Sevilla alone.

Her eyes grew big as saucers. "Micaela, are you mad? Going with a horde of manservants probably wouldn't be enough to keep us from being raped and murdered somewhere on the road. For you to go alone? You're not actually considering such a thing. Please, tell me you aren't."

I didn't answer.

"Mother of God!" she cried.

I didn't know how to respond. She had no idea I'd be going heavily armed. Not to mention I'd be traveling all alone with little baggage and only one horse. I'd stay off the road, eat what I killed, and never ever sleep. If I wished, I would not see another person from the time I left Santa Colomba until I got to Sevilla.

"I just miss him so much," I whispered.

"I don't care how much you miss him. It's not worth your life. Think of the possibilities."

I'd thought of them alright. I wished to see Sergio—honestly, I did—but more than that, I wished to shed the shackles that had been clamped on my wrists the day I'd been born a girl, chains that had been tightened when Ignacio had burned his way into my nightmares and tightened again when Rodrigo and Felipe had violated my home and my body.

Maybe I also wished to prove to myself I wasn't the helpless fool Sara and Sergio and everyone else seemed to think me. Aloud, I told Sara I'd heed her words and not do anything foolish. Inside, I'd already started making a mental packing list.

I had to make one call before I left for Sevilla; I had to see Jhasali. I'd been meaning to make up with her after my months of absence, and I did not want to ride all the way to Andalucía without speaking to her. Thus, when I took my leave of Sara that afternoon, I stopped at my house to gather everything valuable that I'd not be taking on the trip so I could deposit it at Homeship. After dark, I rode hard and made it up the mountains in less than two hours.

When I found Jhasali on the observation deck, I told her of my intentions without making any apology for my previous absence or my impending one. Once I'd finished, she gave me a wide smile and turned her gaze downward without speaking.

"What?" I asked her.

"Nothing. It's just that when I first knew you, you were in a panic over riding from your house to here. Now, you propose to undertake a ride of many weeks all alone," she said.

"I feel no need to remain cloistered in my husband's house. I stayed at home in my bed, like they all said I should, and it didn't keep me safe, though they all said it would. Why ought I assume I'm any worse off on the road?"

She raised her eyebrows. "I suppose there isn't much on this planet that could make you unsafe now. Your new friends are doing their job well."

"You don't object to my going then? Though I might be gone for months?"

"Your time is not my time, love. Do not forget I was on this planet for many of its years before venturing out into it. Those years were but a few days to me. What is an absence of mere weeks, then? Though, you must go armed. I want you to return at some point."

"I already planned to wear the cuffs. You wish me to take something more?"

"I think IDOS should suffice, I simply wished to ensure you were taking it."

"Hopefully, I won't have to use it. I'll ride dressed as a man so I don't attract as much attention," I said.

I hadn't thought of this before; the words escaped me involuntarily, but they sounded right. Such a disguise seemed a reasonable precaution, and it'd be easy to accomplish. If I bound my breasts tight and tucked my braid into a cap, I could pass as a thin older boy who'd not yet crossed the threshold of maturity.

"By the way, I have something for you," Jhasali said. "A Christmas or Magician King present or however you call it."

"It's a bit late, wouldn't you say?" I asked.

"I meant to give it to you once I finished making it, but you disappeared."

"I'm sorry for that. I'm not ready for all the mental bonding that goes on around here."

She shrugged. "It was no bother. I think things will go more smoothly if I don't put an inordinate amount of pressure on you. It isn't like we don't have time."

"What things? Time for what?"

Before I got an answer, a drone entered the room, bringing with it a package wrapped in deep-red cloth. When the drone pressed this package into my arms, I unrolled the cloth to find the crimson wrapping was actually the long, wide skirt of a dress rolled up around itself. It was without a doubt the most dazzling dress I had ever seen in my entire life. All the queens in all of Europe would've killed for it.

In its most basic form, it was an imitation of the black gown I already owned—only the ruby fabric was woven of living fire. It blazed iridescently, catching the light and alternating shades of pink and purple and orange. The areas where my black dress was embroidered with silk shone instead with intricate networks of infinitesimal white crystals—like the whole front was covered in dewy spiderwebs. I let go of the skirts to examine these crystals, and the fabric fell to the floor in a bloodred waterfall.

"Why a dress?" I asked.

"You were so impressed with the others, especially when you first bought them."

"Why this color?"

"I haven't seen much of it during my observations of the area. I've never seen you wear it, so I hoped you'd like something so unique," she said.

"It is unique. I adore it. Thank you."

I had not the heart to tell her I could never wear it in public because there was no way a dress as luxurious as this glittering scarlet jewel-encrusted gown could be legal for a woman of my station. If I wore it, I might be fined or mistaken for an expensive harlot. Still, I had to try it on at least once.

When I donned the gown, I noted it was made of the same inimitable fabric found nowhere but on this ship—sturdy yet flexible, strong yet light—I could move more easily in it than in my other dresses. Somehow, the skirts kept their flare without needing a farthingale. The gown also had pockets so deep I could stuff my arms in them up to the elbow. The outermost layer of the skirts was gossamer and frail, a touch of Jhasali's.

I twirled around and grinned, running my fingers through my long tresses and staring at myself from the front and rear as one of the drones projected my hologram back to me. I was disappointed no one would ever see me in this dress. It was twice as beautiful on my body as it was in my hand.

When I thanked her again, Jhasali said she was glad the dress pleased me before she sat down and pulled her vihuela off the floor, showing no more interest in what I thought of her gift.

After she played a few songs, I told her I must take my leave, and I tied the dress in a brown sack so I could attach it to the saddle. Jhasali gave me a capsule form of *av'vysh* to ensure any shortage of food along the way would not be as much of a problem. I had her string the white beads up like pearl necklaces to make them easier to carry.

Pepito and I got to the arrabal just before sunrise, and I stalled him to rest for the day. Meanwhile, I packed two saddlebags with food, clothing, and every coin I had in the house. It was a lot of money to take on the road, but I didn't know how much I'd need. I wasn't too concerned about it; if anyone tried to rob me, IDOS would deal with them.

I changed into my men's breeches and shirt, but I also packed my black dress as well as the scarlet one, unable to part with such a magnificent gown so soon after obtaining it. Maybe I could wear it somewhere no one knew me—somewhere they might mistake me for a princess. Before I departed for good, I barred the door from the inside and hopped out the window, though there was no real need. With all my valuables at Homeship, there wasn't much worth stealing in the house.

It was well after midnight before I rode to town and left Pepito to graze in the vega. Intending to leave a note for Father Manuel, I snuck through a gap in the city wall near the estuary and headed for the rectory.

I'd made several unsuccessful attempts to speak to him in the weeks after our initial confrontation, but I'd given up after he'd rebuffed me once too often. Still, I couldn't embark on such a long journey without leaving him some sort of explanation. My note apologized to him, Sara, and everyone else to whom I'd not said goodbye, but it rationalized that if I'd told anyone of my plans, they'd have stopped me for certain. It also asked Father Manuel to tell Susana she and Isabel could have my chickens.

I took the note and pressed it to the rectory door, holding a nail with my left forefinger and thumb so I could pound it into the wood with my right fist. Just as I raised my hand to strike the nail head, I caught the sound of footsteps behind me. I turned and rolled up my sleeve, ready to put IDOS into the firing position, but as soon as I laid eyes on the figure, I realized it was none other than Father Manuel. Balling up the note, I thrust it in my sleeve and stepped into the street.

He wobbled on his feet and would've fallen down if not for the walking stick in his hand. Unsure if I might frighten him by striding toward him, I stood in front of the rectory and waited for him to come to me.

"Who goes there?" he asked when he got within a few paces.

"Me, Father," I replied, wondering why he hadn't recognized me.

"Micaela? What are you doing out here in the middle of the night? Why are you dressed like that?"

Christ! I'd forgotten about my clothing. But it didn't matter now. I thanked my lucky stars I'd caught a strong whiff of brandy even before Father Manuel reached the place where I stood.

"I might ask you the same question. What are you doing out so late?" I deflected, hoping he was drunk enough to fall for it. "You were playing cards with Sancho and those other guys at the inn again, weren't you?"

"Yes."

"And you're drunk."

"Yes." He leaned forward and put both hands on his walking stick.

I couldn't help but chuckle. "Did you at least win?"

"No. And stop that dreadful giggling," he snapped. "Take me inside. I need to sit down."

"Do you want me to open a wine skin?" I teased as I helped him into the rectory.

"Unlike some people, I know when to stop." He swayed so badly I had to ease him into his chair myself.

"Are you sure about that?" I handed him a cup of water, which he downed in great gulps.

"Don't you dare think I've forgotten about your infernal abilities," he said.

"I didn't think that, though I notice you don't seem to take issue with them when you need my help." I pulled off his shoes and moved his cane to the side. "I can't believe those idiots let you stumble home alone at this hour."

"They all passed out, and I'm too old to sleep anywhere but my own bed," he slurred.

"I can take you there before I go."

"Not yet. Don't go."

"What is it?" I set the empty water cup aside.

"I've been thinking."

"That's a hazardous hobby."

He smacked the chair with his hand. "Just listen, damn it all. I hate how we left things a few months ago. I've had a lot of time to ponder what happened that night, and I don't wish to believe such horrible things about you. Yet how is it possible for you to be as you are without demonic intervention?"

"Would you believe it if I said I just woke up like this one morning?" I asked.

"How drunk do you think I am?"

"Not as drunk as I would've hoped. But think about it. What do witches do? They fly. They kill cattle. They conjure lightning and ruin crops with storms. They murder children. Have you ever seen me do any of those things?"

He shook his head.

"And are the poor children of this town afraid of me? You'd think they'd be terrified if I'd picked off one or two of them," I said.

"No. They love you. Whenever you go to market, they follow your every step."

"Because I always give them something. Does a witch who lies with demons take care of vagabond children?"

"No," he admitted. "I wouldn't think so."

"Answer me this. The penalty for witchcraft is burning or hanging, depending on the circumstance, is it not?"

He nodded silently, so I went on.

"Now, I've already demonstrated I cannot be burned, and if I'm fireproof, it isn't outrageous to assume I cannot die from hanging either. So what motive do I have to deny being a witch if I am one? I fear no consequence," I said.

"To deceive me, I suppose."

"To deceive you into following a devil I've already repudiated or abandoning a god whose symbol I still wear around my neck?" I asked, hoping he might not wish to see my necklace, which I'd left at Homeship in preparation for my journey.

"You could be using false orthodoxy to avoid detection," he argued.

"You've already detected me. And the unfortunate necessity of my blackmailing for your silence assures me you won't go running to the authorities. So, again, I assert I have no motive to prevent you from believing I'm a witch—unless I'm not one."

"But, well," he stammered, "I'm too drunk for this."

"I'd say being drunk makes you more open to the truth. And the truth is I'm neither demoness nor sorceress and never have been."

"Then how is it you came to have these abilities?"

I sighed. "If I wished to ingratiate myself to you, I'd say the archangel Gabriel appeared to me and gave me these powers to use them in the fight against heresy, but he did not. Nor did the devil give them to me in exchange for my body or my soul. As I said, my abilities are neither good nor evil. They are neutral, entirely existent in the physical world, and subject to its laws. Believe me, I understand this is the most disappointing explanation possible, but it is the truth."

"But who gave this power to you if not God or Satan?" he repeated.

"That, I cannot say."

"Why not?"

"Because I don't wish to betray my friends or bring them trouble. Just be sure of this—no one you know is involved, not even Sergio," I replied.

"I'm certain he isn't involved. If he knew of all this, he'd have done something about it."

"Well, he doesn't, and I expect it to stay that way," I snapped. Regretting my harshness, I softened my tone. "Look, I cannot offer you absolute assurance of anything. But do you honestly think me capable of taking the devil for my master? You know me. How many times did you defend me before that bastard Ignacio, just to turn around and say he was right?"

Father Manuel clicked his tongue. "I still think he was wrong about you. At least, I wish to believe he was wrong. I know in my heart you would never have carnal relations with the devil. I only said that because I don't understand."

"I wish I could make you understand. Maybe I'll find a way in time."

"Don't fear either way. I won't denounce you, even if you wouldn't do anything in retaliation. I have no desire to bring you trouble."

"Why did you threaten to go to the authorities before?" I asked.

"Because I was angry and afraid. I'm not afraid anymore. I suppose if you meant to do me harm, you've had no reason to delay. But I would advise you to avoid slipping up before anyone else. They might not be as lenient as I am."

"I'm not concerned about that. I am invulnerable now." I smiled.

"Child," Father Manuel said almost inaudibly, sinking further into his seat. "You'll never be invulnerable while you are surrounded by those you love. As long as you care for anyone who can be harmed, you *are* vulnerable, and you're a danger to us all. So for Christ's sake and mine, keep your secret guarded more closely than you've kept it before me."

Looking back after so many centuries, my life and the lives of others might have turned out much for the better if I'd listened to this: the soundest advice he ever gave me.

"I'll keep my secrets safe. I promise," I murmured, believing at the time I spoke the truth. "But what of the other things we discussed all those weeks ago?"

"What other things?" His head lolled to the side.

"Nothing," I said, thinking better of pressing him any further.

The hour was late, and I needed to be gone before dawn. Father Manuel was drunk and exhausted, leaving me to question how much of this night he'd actually remember in the morning anyhow. Besides, if everything went according to plan, I'd soon have the answers I needed without having to trust in his word alone.

Gently as I could, I lifted him out of the chair and steered him to his bed. Once I'd covered him with a thick quilt and set a pitcher of water on the bedside table, I laid the note I'd planned to tack to his door next to the jug and left.

In the street, I pulled my hair into a thick braid, which I tied into a knot and pinned tightly under a feather cap. When I slipped back outside the walls, Pepito and I shot away from the city before the first streaks of dawn burst across the night sky. Though daybreak approached by the hour, I could not yet feel it in the air. I smiled and let the night's wind caress my face as Pepito and I turned our eyes south—like we would for the next two hundred and some odd leagues.

I couldn't help but grin. Not two days ago, I'd been sitting on my hands awaiting the arrival of a letter, and today I headed almost to the southern coast. It was a new sort of freedom to be riding down a rustic road with such a distant destination in mind, by myself in the quiet of the predawn hours, all the while humming the tune to "Bajo la encina."

Pepito and I rode all day every day, sometimes into the night, for he was a strong young horse and I a fit rider. Often, I got down onto my own two legs and trotted alongside him, finding my physical efficiency much improved since my metamorphosis. I could jog for hours at a brisk pace, giving Pepito plenty of breaks from bearing me. He seemed to enjoy running alongside me, often trotting out ahead and doubling back or lashing me with his tail if I slowed down.

We covered anywhere from eight to twelve leagues each day, stopping only for me to eat and for Pepito to graze and sleep. We stayed close to the rivers when possible and rested in the wilderness, since I was still a woman alone and in no mood to fight off assailants.

I was also keen to avoid any run-ins with the Santa Hermandad, who patrolled the rural roads looking for criminals. I struck an odd figure: a woman dressed in worn men's clothing and carrying a year's worth of coin in her saddlebags. So it was far better to avoid contact with the brothers than it would be to explain myself.

Fortunately, I'd gotten adept at using my technologically enhanced eyes and ears to sense others before they ever sensed me. Pepito and I stayed away from people for the most part, bypassing towns and villages, riding into them only to buy food if the hunting or fishing proved luckless or to draw well water if we had no river access.

If we were obliged to use the roads or enter the towns, my disguise held up well against the fleeting eyes of strangers. Because I avoided speaking and interacting with anyone more than necessary, I had little trouble passing for a teenaged boy teetering on the cusp of manhood. As such, I was infrequently bothered and never outright accosted.

It was easy to grow accustomed to this new feeling of respect and anonymity. For the first time in my life, I did not feel the eyes of strange men as I passed them by, nor did I endure their lustful gazes. They did not follow my footsteps nor question me as to my behavior or my reasons for being where I was. I would miss that most of all, when it evaporated like the dew before the Granadan sun the second I donned a dress.

It took Pepito and me just shy of three weeks to reach Sevilla from Santa Colomba. League after league, we left the northerly emerald coasts with their stretches of undulating grass and golden sand, climbed the verdant Cantabrian Mountains and traversed their rugged alpine passes, and crossed the endless windmill-dotted plains of the Meseta Central, until we arrived in Andalucía. As we trekked farther south, relying ever more on kind strangers to give us directions, I couldn't help but feel a swelling of pride in both myself for having come so far and in my country for possessing such beauty. No wonder Jhasali chose it for her refuge.

When the arid wilderness gave way to orange trees, olive groves, and vineyards, the walls and sprawl of the rapidly expanding city of Sevilla became discernible in the distance. Before we neared the urban areas, I switched to my black dress, my sojourn into the world of manhood over. I grinned as I fluffed the skirts and adjusted the sleeves, having missed their daintiness when I'd been wearing my disguise. Though I was happy to let my hair loose after keeping it tied up under the cap all that time, I still half covered it with a veil to shield me from the eyes of men as well as the blazing sun.

I rode Pepito into the city, intending to head straight for the harbor, where I assumed Sergio would be, though I had no idea how to get there. After talking to several different women on the streets, I made for the Torre del Oro, which marked the place everyone called the wharf. This was not a traditional pier in the sense that it jutted out into the water for ships to pull alongside it. It was more of a platform for the only crane in the city, but it still allowed access to the river. Everyone I talked to assured me I should begin my search there.

Lucky for me, I'd arrived on the east bank, so I didn't need to cross the river to get to my destination. Even so, it still did not prove easy to navigate these winding, unfamiliar streets. I dismounted and led Pepito by the bridle as we cut our way through the crowds, heading toward the tower. Once we drew near to the Torre del Oro, I inquired of many people both there and farther upriver until I found someone who had an inkling of where the *San José* was: back the way I'd come, of course, on the open sands of the Arenal.

Sevilla was not an ocean port, like my own town, but rather a huge waterfront that stretched an impressive length of the Guadalquivir River. Back in those days, the Arenal was a long, wide strip of sand that ran along the eastern bank of this river. The crews beached as many ships on the Arenal as possible, crowding them together and squeezing them perpendicular to the shoreline, sometimes so tightly it was tough to walk between them.

I didn't know whether the *San Bruno* or the *San José* would be pulled up onto the sand or docked alongside the riverbank, nor did I know if Sergio would even be aboard either. I'd just have to walk the port until I found him.

Mounting once more, I steered Pepito back downriver, and we picked our way along until we passed through the Arenal Gate and onto the sand. There, I looked at all the vessels, making my way slowly so as not to miss one. All around me, men hustled down the beach, hauling heavy pallets toward the water's edge, where they loaded them onto barges and smaller vessels that could manage to navigate the river with their cargo onboard. I made Pepito tread carefully; the last thing I needed was for him to break something or bowl someone over.

After a long while of migrating down the beach and eyeing every ship on the shore as well as those in the water, I saw a familiar-looking nao of perhaps a hundred tons dragged up on the sand. Once I decided this might be the *San José*, I dismounted and headed toward where the ship lay tilted on its port side.

As we walked, I scanned the crowd for Sergio, looking not into the faces of the men but at their stature and the texture of their hair. There were not so many men as tall and curly-headed as mine. Yet, no matter where I looked, I did not see him.

Finally, as I rounded the *San José*, I spotted what I sought. Sergio stood between the ship and the shoreline. He had his back to me, and he was engaged in a heated discussion with a grizzled man holding a long mallet and a thin, bent iron.

"Ahoy, sailor!" I cried, beaming.

Sergio stiffened and looked around, seeking me out where I stood next to Pepito. I grinned and raised my right hand to greet him. After a second's hesitation, in which I was sure he attempted to ascertain whether it was really his wife or a mirage brought on by the heat, he abandoned the man and ran toward me. He caught me in his embrace and kissed me, winding his arms around my waist and lifting me off the ground.

Setting me back on my feet, he squeezed me so tight it pressed the breath from my lungs. I didn't care. I'd only spent all last year wishing to be held like this, and I was not inclined to suspend it for a mere thing like air.

"Good Lord, I think I'm getting old. You feel heavier than I remember, but you don't look it." Sergio laughed when he let me go.

I wondered if that would be thanks to the nanos, but before the sensors could answer, Sergio realized just how far we were from home.

"You rode all the way down here by yourself?" he asked.

"Of course not. I met up with a convoy of pilgrims coming back from Santiago de Compostela," I lied.

"But the Feast of Santiago isn't for weeks."

"It was a group of friars who spent Holy Week there and wanted to return before the next rush," I said, hoping he'd not press the issue further.

"Thank God. If some bandit or vagabond had attacked you . . ."

I bit my tongue behind my closed lips. That I had been accosted, under our own roof no less, he would never know.

"What's wrong?" Sergio asked, better able to read my expression than I preferred.

"Nothing. I've just had a long journey, and it's so hot here," I said.

"Of course. Let's get you out of the sun. But first, I have to find Armando."

He kissed my forehead and shot back along the length of the beached vessel, leaving me holding Pepito's bridle. All around, repairmen bustled about with their tools and materials, rushing to get the *San José* seaworthy again.

I didn't have to wait long. In a flash, Sergio reappeared from around the vessel. Armando followed close behind, wearing his finest merchant ship lord's garb, with his beard neatly trimmed and his chestnut hair tied into a wavy ponytail. I smiled and dipped my knees at the sight of him.

As they approached, I noted the both of them had lost weight and looked a good bit worse for the wear since making the crossing. I'd been so excited to see Sergio I hadn't noticed this at first, and I didn't like how prominent his cheekbones had become. I figured I'd better see to it he gained some weight during the weeks we had together.

"I'm sure Sergio is happy to see you, Micaela," Armando said when he reached me.

"I'm glad too, señor," I said. "I couldn't bear the thought of another year without him."

Armando didn't acknowledge this statement, so Sergio chimed in to break the silence.

"I wished Armando to see you before we take our leave. We're staying in an inn over in Triana." He beamed down at me.

"I thought you would stay on the ship," I interjected.

Armando answered. "The *San José* required too many repairs for me to occupy my quarters onboard. More importantly, I needed a change before I'm once again shut up in them. I suppose I'll see you tomorrow evening," he added to Sergio.

"Yes. Thank you," Sergio said.

Armando grasped him by the forearm and gave him a gentle tap on the shoulder before turning toward the old caulker with whom Sergio had been arguing when I first found him.

"You're taking leave today and tomorrow?" I asked when Armando had gone.

"Of course. What else would I do? I didn't think I'd see you for another year, yet here you are on my doorstep." He grinned and pinched my cheek.

Then his smile vanished, and he looked down and all around. "Where is Lobo?"

I hesitated, blindsided by that question, though I shouldn't have been.

"He died," I said.

Sergio's brow knit, and he pursed his lips like he might weep. He had loved that dog.

"How?" he whispered.

I was prepared with my story. Just as I had with everyone else, I told Sergio Lobo had taken ill, and I'd attempted to heal him, but I'd woken up the next morning to find him dead on the hearth. Sergio stuck his tongue in his cheek and swallowed before moving to mount Pepito.

"There's nothing for it now, I suppose." He swung himself into the saddle.

He held his hand out to me and removed his foot from the stirrup so I could mount behind him. I took his hand and allowed him to pull me up. Sitting so far back on Pepito's hindquarters proved awkward, especially since I had to contend with the saddlebags. I wound my arms around Sergio's waist and held tight, enjoying how warm he felt, despite the heat of the late morning.

It was not so easy to get to the inn. In those days, there was only the Bridge of Boats connecting Triana with the other side of the Guadalquivir. Since we were far from this bridge, the most convenient way to get across the river was a barge that could carry both us and the horse to the opposite shore.

Sergio explained while we were being ferried across that he and Armando had not been able to find decent-enough lodgings on the eastern shore, so they'd decided to make the commute from Triana. It annoyed them both, but Armando thought it worth the pain to stay away from some of the rougher spots on the Arenal. He did not wish to sleep amongst thieves, pickpockets, and belligerent common sailors. Armando had never belonged to that crowd, and I supposed Sergio had no business with them anymore either.

Once we found our inn, we rushed Pepito to the nearby barn and turned him over to the stableboy. I didn't even notice the way to Sergio's room, for we bolted down the hallway like we fled the devil himself. When we arrived, he threw my bags to the floor just beyond the threshold, swept me off my feet, and carried me inside.

I laughed upon seeing his room. He was messier when not at home, tossing his shoes and clothes indiscriminately. He moved some things from the bed but put no more effort into cleaning than that.

I undressed while he washed his hands and face, and I took the opportunity to remove the IDOS cuffs and slip them into a saddlebag while he had his head in the basin. When he turned to find me naked beside the bed, he bent and grasped me behind the knees, flipping me backward onto the mattress. He crawled on top of me and went to put his face in the bend of my neck. At this, all my muscles went rigid, my arms curling into my body and my fists drawing up near my face. I pushed him off me and sat up, not having expected that.

He kissed me again while I remained upright. This I accepted, but when he put his hands on my shoulders and made to push me back down again, I shoved him away. It was all I could do to stop myself from screaming at him to get off me.

"Don't you want this?" Sergio asked, confused.

I'd thought I wanted it, but now that it was happening, I couldn't make my damn hands stop shaking.

"Not that way," I said. "I want to be on top. Is that alright?"

He chuckled. "I have no problem lying here and letting you do all the work."

I forced myself to laugh, but my stupid heart raced within my chest. Despite my pounding pulse, I wanted to be with my husband, but I needed it to be my way. Sergio lay on his back and clasped his hands behind his head, grinning like a schoolboy.

Before I knew what I was doing, I grabbed a few of my linen hair ribbons from the floor and tied both his hands to the wooden bedframe. He allowed this, unaware

I fastened him tight. When he realized his hands were truly bound and not just loosely hung, he began to struggle.

"What the devil? I thought you were just playing around," he said.

"If you don't like it, I'll take them off." I kissed his neck and chest.

He moaned and relaxed. "It's fine. I'm always up for something new."

I didn't know why immobilizing Sergio made me feel better, but it did. Somehow, the act of putting him under my control gave me a sense of security. Though I knew if I told him to stop, he'd stop, this felt different—like I wasn't dependent on him taking my no for an answer.

After kissing and licking his upper body one nibble at a time while he gasped and groaned, wiggling his legs because his hands were immobile, I straddled him and grasped the bedposts above where his wrists were tied. I leaned forward enough to allow my chest to be just within his reach. He could only raise his head a few centimeters, and I made him work for access to my breasts as I slid down and took him inside me.

While it still felt good to have his lips sucking my nipples and his cock filling me up, it wasn't the same as it had once been. I'd never had a problem climaxing before; it had always been easy, regardless of Sergio's technique or even his level of sobriety. Yet now, no matter how I rubbed myself against him or how tightly I pressed my skin to his or how much I just willed it, I couldn't get there.

After an eternity of trying, I was covered in sweat and teetering on the verge of weeping in frustration. Sergio complained his hands were going numb. Thus, I untied him so he could finish himself and let the whole thing come to a blessed end.

Once he climaxed, Sergio rolled over and fell asleep in an instant. I was glad of his exhaustion, for it gave me privacy in my grief. I wept without a sound, staring up at the ceiling and stewing in a cocktail of fury and misery brought on by the discovery of this, the latest thing that accursed Rodrigo had stolen from me.

As I listened to my husband's distinctive postcoital snoring, I replayed in my mind all the times I'd slept beside him after experiencing pleasure so intense it almost tested my endurance, leaving me sweating, panting, and sometimes even screaming or laughing as my body flushed with an ecstasy no wine could dream of matching.

Before my marriage, I'd imagined I'd be a good Christian wife who allowed her husband to use her body to satisfy his needs without falling prey to her own carnal urges. Yet, the moment Sergio's hand had slid between my legs after our wedding, it divested me of whatever religious misgivings I'd held, and I'd delighted in him ever since without regard for whether my lust was a sin. His touch had always made me forget decency and propriety, but it couldn't make me forget Rodrigo. It couldn't make me forget that night, and I feared I'd be lucky if I ever experienced such natural and unadulterated pleasure again.

As soon as that thought popped into my head, I decided I would experience it this instant, no matter what it took. This could not be another thing I surrendered to my violators. It would not be. After giving him a short respite, I rolled over and shook Sergio awake, kissing him and sliding my hand around his cock to harden him.

"Again?" he mumbled, not opening his eyes.

"Yes. Right now."

He rolled sleepily on top of me, pressing his hands over mine. I told him to leave my hands free, so he raised his own until they rested on the bed. I reached down and guided him inside me, pushing his face downward so he could caress my breasts.

This time, I gritted my teeth and tensed my muscles, willing my body to cooperate the way it once had of its own accord. I focused on filling my mind with images of our past pleasures, consciously chasing out all thought of Rodrigo. My hips began to grind against Sergio, though I still felt a numbness between them I'd never before suffered.

"Harder," I said, pressing the small of his back and trying to goad him to slam into me until I could feel *something*.

"I don't want to hurt you," Sergio panted as I kept repeating for him to thrust harder.

"I'll tell you if you're hurting me."

Instead of continuing to pound away, he switched methods, angling his body diagonally to mine and using his pelvis to grind between my legs as hard as he could. When even that didn't work, I got back on top of him and scraped myself against him with all my might. This pushed me to completion, though my orgasm felt nothing but hollow and forced, more like a conclusion than a climax. My body did it, but my heart and soul were no longer in it, and it gave me little satisfaction, leaving me almost more disappointed than if I'd been unable to finish.

"Are you alright?" Sergio asked once I'd rolled off him.

"What do you mean?"

"You seem . . . I don't know."

"I'm tired and very hungry. Can you go and get us something from the tavern?" I said, looking for any excuse to be alone.

Sergio let out an exaggerated sigh before shooting me a grin and an eye roll. Pinching the end of my nose, he dressed and walked out the door. Once he was gone, I sat up and stared at the wall, wondering if anything we did in our marital bed would ever be the same again. Even if nothing could be the same, I was going to have to get a lot better at pretending it was.

Next morning, Sergio wanted to make love when we first awoke. Not wishing to hurt his feelings, I let him do as he pleased with me and pretended to enjoy it, though I no longer sought to gain pleasure from it. I only waited for it to end, trying not to upset myself with comparisons of this numb tolerance of his touch to the passion that had once blazed throughout every second of our lovemaking.

After he climaxed, he took me in his arms and held me to his breast. I kissed his chest and belly while he squeezed me tight and ran his fingers through my hair. Now that we weren't having sex, things blessedly proved different; the numbness that clouded my body dissipated like smoke in the breeze. What's more, the nanos had heightened my sense of touch to the point that every millimeter of Sergio's fingers sent a tiny electric shock through my skin, where it traveled up my spine until it made me squirm with enjoyment. When he dragged his nails along the back of my neck, I shuddered and let a giggle escape my lips. Though this was not the primary pleasure I'd sought in my husband's arms, at least for now, I could settle for it.

With the morning wearing on, we got out of bed and started to dress. Sergio squinted his eyes and knit his brow as I slipped on my chemise and pulled my black gown from the floor.

"Is that a new dress?" he asked.

"It's the same one I had on yesterday."

"I had too many other things on my mind to notice. It is new."

"Are you angry?" I said, steeling myself for a fight I feared I could scarce endure.

"No. I like it." He crossed to where I stood, caressing a lock of my hair with one hand while he fingered the dress in the other. "I'm too tired to argue over it anyhow."

I recalled what Sara had said months ago about wearing Sergio down and wondered if the arduousness of his recent journey hadn't done some of that for me.

"What are you smirking at?" he asked.

"Nothing. Lace me up."

Sergio took the day to show me around Sevilla, and I was relieved at the idea of doing something to eliminate any opportunity I might have to obsess about how awful last night had been. The first place I wished to see was the Catedral de Santa María de la Sede, which I'd heard tell of since I was a girl but never thought I'd actually visit. I wasn't disappointed. Though the interior was still under construction, the church dwarfed any other cathedral I'd ever seen. I almost felt ashamed I'd thought the one in Toledo to be so big.

When we first approached the building, Sergio pointed to the steps surrounding the patio, where a large group of men sat loafing about, waiting for something. Several of them perked up upon seeing him, though they lost interest when they realized we meant to walk past them. Sergio told me these men were aspiring sailors waiting to be contracted, and he and Armando had hired many of a similar sort from this very spot when they'd first come to Sevilla. Indeed, they would hire more of them before they embarked once again.

Not much interested in gawking at the waiting lads, I took Sergio by the hand and had him lead me around to La Giralda, the cathedral's bell tower. We tarried long before this soaring structure, formerly the minaret of the mosque that had once stood here. It was so tall it boggled my mind to imagine what the view must be like at the top.

Craning my neck to the very pinnacle, I remembered all the cataclysms this monument had survived: the earthquakes, the wars, the regime changes, and the ever-beating sun. For ages I studied the polished columns and carved horseshoe arches in the windows, the intricate detail laid into every speck of the façade, its sand-colored brick that took on a pinkish hue as it ricocheted the light of the awesome Sevillian sun.

I smiled at the tower touching the sky, feeling an unexpected sense of kinship with it, and I ambled through the crowds in the plaza until I came within a pace of the mighty foundation. Laying my hand on the brick, I noted it already held warmth from the morning sun. By afternoon, it would radiate heat, as it did every single summer day.

"No matter what happens, nothing will knock it down," I whispered.

Sergio had stayed by my side as I walked to the tower's base, and he chuckled upon hearing this. "I nearly fainted the first time I saw this thing. The sun was behind it, so it looked even more imposing than it does now."

"Wow. Tell me you came back here the next morning and saw it in the light."

"I did, but in neither instance did I gawk at it for a solid hour like I thought it'd magically morph into something besides the same old bell tower it's always been." He winked at me.

I grinned at his impatience. "Alright, then. Let's keep going."

We looked at the exterior of every doorway before entering the church. My favorite was the Puerta del Perdón—the portal to the Patio de los Naranjos. Like La Giralda, the horseshoe-shaped entrance was one of the few remaining features of the old mosque. The scent of oranges wafted to my nostrils on the warm breeze as I stared at the elaborate bronze atauriques and the inscriptions that I'd later learn declared Allah the eternal and omnipotent, even in the face of the gate's brand-new relief, which depicted Jesus driving the merchants from the temple.

Sergio came up behind me and put a hand on my shoulder. I reached up to clasp his fingers, and he moved closer until the back of my head almost pressed against his chest.

"Were you able to see any of the construction?" I asked, pointing to the relief.

"No. They finished a few years ago," Sergio replied.

Just as he said this, an ornately robed cleric passed by the open doorway, appearing for half a second before disappearing behind the wall once more. I giggled under my breath.

"What is it?" Sergio asked.

"Nothing. I just wonder if Christ is planning to come back and chase *those* merchants out of *this* temple."

Sergio sputtered as he suppressed a laugh. "Micalita, you irreverent little minx."

"Really? You're going to go pious on me now?"

He let a chuckle hiss between his teeth. "You'll never hear me defend the clergy. I've met pirates who were less greedy. Still, it does feel blasphemous to say that in front of a church."

I raised my brows. "Can't be blasphemy if it's true."

"I guess not. But you've got to be careful in this city. A pirate in a habit will gladly throw a sanbenito over your shoulders to steal everything you own."

"Why are you so worried? You think they've got surveillance bots listening to the whole city?" I laughed.

"What?"

"Spies, I meant."

"That doesn't sound a thing like the word you just said." Sergio turned me to face him. He squinted his eyes and stared down the length of his nose.

He was right, of course. The Sartjyanan word for a surveillance drone is *úk cha' jhelák*—or simply *úk cha'*—as I had said. I didn't know how I could pass it off for the word "spy."

"I . . . uh. I suppressed a sneeze when I said that word," I stammered.

Sergio gave an incredulous laugh. "If you say so."

"Come. Let's go inside."

I took him by the hand and led him into the building, where I proceeded to drag him all over the cathedral's interior. He was none too pleased with this grand tour. We'd spent so much time outside that he'd begun to grow hungry and annoyed, but he'd just have to wait. I kept my eyes focused high above to enjoy the vibrant windows and spectacular ceilings without permitting a flash of any sanbenito that might be hanging on the walls to invade my field of vision.

Having always been partial to stained glass windows, I wanted to look at every pane in the church, as I'd once loved to do in Toledo. Most of the windows modern people know didn't exist at this time, and many were under construction. However, quite a few panes already glowed above and within several chapels. I studied these in turn, enjoying the way the light played with the deep colors and wavy glass, until I came to one that drew my attention. This pane contained a slender female figure adorned with flowing robes and golden plaits. It was none other than Santa Bárbara. I could tell by the three-windowed tower peeking just over her shoulder.

I pointed to her window. "Look at that one, Sergio. Isn't it marvelous?"

"It's nice, I suppose."

"Nice?" I huffed.

He laughed. "I've never understood you with these windows. They're pretty, but—"

"As a girl, I was infatuated with the ones in Toledo. Seems I never grew out of it."

"Father Manuel told me you used to be obsessed with the rosetones there."

"There's just something about them. Maybe it's my own nostalgia for the city itself."

"You know, all the places I've been, and I never got to go to Toledo," Sergio lamented.

"It was too far inland?" I teased. "One day, if you can keep your feet on land long enough, I'll give you a tour."

"You left as a girl. Do you even remember any of it?"

"I remember enough."

Sergio's stomach growled noisily, and he put his hands on his hips. "You'll never get the chance to demonstrate how much you do or don't remember if you starve me to death so you can look at some picture windows."

"Of course. I'm sorry," I said.

In my zeal for the cathedral's majesty, I'd forgotten Sergio had already seen it enough times for its novelty to have worn off. Reluctantly, I let him lead me back to the streets.

He breathed a sigh of relief when we cleared the plaza. "Thank Christ in his mercy I finally got you out of that church! Oh, I need an ale; my head's hurting."

I laughed. I should've known Sergio would get bored if we weren't constantly moving.

While we walked the streets outside the cathedral and searched for a decent place to find lunch, Sergio told me a little of his adventures during his long voyage. He described the blazing blue waters of the Caribbean and the mountains of La Española, visible far out to sea. He also recounted all the troubles the crew had suffered during the crossing.

On the way out, a storm blew them off course, and they'd had to replot their route with dwindling supplies. Even worse, many of the men had died of illness and injury. On the way back, Sergio himself had had to make a dive to do repairs in the middle of the ocean because the crew had no commissioned diver and he was the only one who could stay underwater so long.

The worst travail of all proved to be the endless stretches of terrible boredom that led to conflict and discontent. He said this boredom was often so excruciating that many in the crew almost prayed for a gale or even corsairs to interrupt it.

Sergio and I spent our initial time together exploring the city and discussing his travels as we basked in a haze of contentment. After that first day, he went back to work. Rather than pass his evenings with Armando, however, he spent them showing me the parts of the city that interested him more than the cathedral, like the ship repair yards, the marketplaces, and the bustling streets of Triana.

Armando often met us to dine, and he and Sergio took me to some of their favorite supper spots. With the three of us passing so much time together, it seemed Armando might even be warming to me. Every night, he recounted his own stories of the crossing and the New World. He even laughed at a few of my jokes.

Alas, this budding amiability between the three of us would not long endure, for marital discontent between Sergio and me was as innate as our need for sustenance. As usual, our days of peaceful marital bliss were quite numbered.

## Chapter Fifteen

# THE WAR OF THE BREECHES

The fight that broke Sergio's and my matrimonial armistice erupted around two weeks after my arrival in Sevilla. The night before, I'd endured yet another numb and detached lovemaking session, getting on top and forcing my body to go through the motions of climax just to prove to myself I still could. I was unsure if my attempts at faking the pleasure I'd once enjoyed so genuinely would prove successful, but I felt I had to try if I were to prevent my husband from noticing a shift in my attitude. If he did note any change, he said nothing to me.

While Sergio set about dressing in the morning, I lay on the bed, mulling over the previous night's events and inching closer to a despairing acceptance that there might be no point in trying to make myself enjoy sex anymore. Once he'd dressed, Sergio realized he couldn't find his coin purse. My mind still on last night, I told him to check my saddlebags because I'd put a few things in there when I'd tidied up.

At that point, not only had I already found a spot under the mattress for my cuffs, but I'd also wrapped the scarlet dress and hidden the *av'vysh* tablets, so I thought there was nothing in my luggage for him to find. I was wrong.

He rooted through my half-packed saddlebag, freezing when he dug to the bottom.

"What is it?" I asked, confounded by this strange behavior.

Sergio stood and turned. He was holding a pair of men's riding breeches—a pair much too short for him. I started. I'd forgotten my disguise was in that bag.

"What is this?" he asked.

I proceeded cautiously, unsure of how to broach the subject of my cross-dressing without making him angry. But it was either tell him the truth or leave him to think I was engaged in adultery with a man half his size.

"I rode down here with a convoy of strangers." I fell back on my well-rehearsed story. "So I figured it was best to disguise myself for the journey."

His face remained blank for a second. Then it contorted with fury as it dawned on him what I meant. "So you mean to tell me you went gallivanting across the continent dressed like a common stableboy?"

"I felt it was prudent that everyone think I was a lad. There were only a few sisters in my convoy, and what fool of a woman would trust a horde of clergymen?" I asked.

"I ignored that you rode down here with strangers because I was so pleased to see you. Had I known you did it dressing like a damned bujarrona, I'd not have been so forgiving."

Forgiving? How many weeks had I taken out of my life to ride to the other side of the peninsula just to meet him? A fireball of rage erupted like a pyroclastic flow cascading from my throat to my stomach.

"I wasn't dressing like a female sodomite! You think if I had nothing to fear from men, I'd dress like one? You think if I could walk about as freely as you do, I'd ever be seen in such clothing?" I pointed at the pantaloons.

"You've no right to embarrass me like this!" He shook the breeches in my face.

"How does this embarrass you? You didn't even know about it until just now."

"It's humiliating to find out my wife's been wearing the pants reserved for me. What if Armando saw you dressed like that? Or, God forbid, *anyone* from town? What would Father Manuel say?"

"I won't concern myself with what some men would say about the measures I take to protect myself from other men," I spat.

Sergio took a minute before he spoke in a quivering voice, pausing after each word, as if he could barely keep his anger in check. "Micaela, you will not ever—"

"I will not ever obey your demands without question again," I interrupted. "I was under the impression you wanted a companion, not a slave. If you desire the latter, you'd better go to market next time you're near the Casa de Contratación!"

I knew I should not have said such an awful thing about those poor people whose lot mightn't have been any worse than mine if it hadn't been for Father Manuel, but I was in temper and in no shape to measure my words.

As I'd intended, Sergio took offense to my intimation I would dare make myself his equal. He said nothing, but there was no need, for he cast me a look of deep disdain and terrible fury before he swung his dark-blue cape over his shoulders and stormed out the door, not bothering to grab the accursed coin purse that had started this entire argument.

I didn't follow. To beg for his favor or even reveal a desire for it would put an irreparable fissure in my brand-new armor of authority over myself. I would not cave before his hostility as I had when I'd signed his miserable letter. Thus, I stayed put, fuming, as my husband stomped down the hall and out the door of the inn.

As I expected, Sergio did not return to our room that night; he had decided to punish my insubordination by remaining out. Neither hearing nor seeing Armando or my husband in the inn, I could only guess they'd gone to the lodgings of one of the other officers. They'd brought Pablo and Marcos with them to Sevilla, along with Santiago Salazar—the master of the *San Bruno* now that Armando commanded the *San José*—and several others. They'd suffer no shortage of places to stay.

I remained at the inn the next day, people-watching in the courtyard and sipping wine in my room, sure Sergio would reappear by evening. When he spent yet another night out, I started to get angry. Waking on the third day of his absence and still finding no trace of him did nothing to soothe my temper. By that night, I was furious. I went to bed early and woke in the predawn hours of the fourth day, fuming that this was how he'd decided to spend the minuscule amount of time we had together—and after I rode all the way down here just for him!

I wanted to do something to get back at him, even if it was only in my own mind. Before I knew what I was doing, I clamped on my cuffs and pulled the riding breeches out of my bag. I put them on, bound the linen strips across my breasts, pulled the white shirt over my head, and slipped on my riding boots. As I left the room, I knotted my braid and pinned it tightly inside the feather cap.

I had dressed and departed so reflexively I didn't stop to think of what I'd done until I stood outside on the street. As the front door clicked shut behind me, the weight of what I was doing sank down on my shoulders. The streets were nearly empty, and the inn was too. No one had seen me leave, so I could go back now, put on my dress, and pretend this had never happened.

Yet did I want to do that? Or did I want to simultaneously defy my husband and explore the city with the same shield of anonymity and regard with which I'd explored the countryside? My feet gave me the answer, striding away from the inn almost of their own accord.

Once I had made it some distance, I skipped through the streets and headed to find a boatman to take me to the other side of the river. When I got off the ferry, the first place I went was back to the cathedral and then to the Torre del Oro. It was different wandering to these sites on my own, when I could take all the time I pleased to stare at whatever caught my fancy without enduring Sergio's complaints about my wasting hours that could be better spent drinking.

When it got too hot, I took lunch in an inn pub not too far from the cathedral. I mightn't have been able to take a meal here if I'd shown up as an unaccompanied woman, for the city of Sevilla had ordinances banning us from drinking alone in the taverns so the prostitutes couldn't work outside the brothels, though I did not know how stringently these rules were enforced.

After I ate and took a short siesta in the shade, I wandered down to see the crane and the ships in the harbor. I avoided my husband's, of course, but Sevilla was a massive city with an Arenal full of ships I might look at without going anywhere near Armando's people. I strolled around on the sands while the heat blazed and the sun baked everything it touched, watching the men as they worked and the vendors who tried to sell things to them.

The rows of vegetable carts, fishwives' stalls, and trinket peddlers' stands formed a market everyone referred to as the malbaratillo. I made the mistake of buying an orange from one of the pushcarts, and several more vendors instantly descended upon me. I waved most of them off, but when a pitiful old woman approached me and tried to sell me some questionable-looking mussels, I bought them all from her and gave her a good bit extra, swearing her not to tell anyone.

Not paying heed to the taste, I ate the mussels raw, for spoiled food could no longer hurt me. My nanos would use every last molecule and kill whatever germs occupied it. Knowing them, they might even find a good use for the matter that made up the germs themselves.

As I ate my mussels, I kept walking the harbor, taking in all the different scents. Loading and repair crews bustled about in the spaces between the ships, giving the port an almost anxious sense of urgency and sending innumerable sweaty odors wafting my way. I also noticed, for the first time, the salty scent of the ocean was absent. Rather, my nostrils pulled in great gulps of that fishy smell that always emanates from large rivers.

The parts of the Arenal closest to the city were downright gross, for many people tossed garbage over the wall onto the sands, making mountains of trash that sometimes rose higher than a man's head. The smell of rotting food scraps overpowered me whenever I drew near these muladares, so I tried to stay closer to the waterfront to avoid them.

Yet, when I came across a pair of little children rooting through the trash, I couldn't help but give them the last blancas in my purse, keeping this act as covert as possible. The Arenal was a rough spot to get caught waving around too much money, especially for a short, skinny "lad" like me.

As I walked away from the wall toward the waterfront, I happened upon a fat galleon floating in the channel. I craned my neck toward the top of this behemoth's mainmast. It was probably the largest of its kind that could make it into Sevilla itself. Anything bigger would have had to remain downriver. The mast stood so high that I had to squint my eyes to catch sight of its pinnacle as it baked in the glaring sun. The sails were bound tight to the post, and the heavy anchor chains plunged into the brown water. I assumed this ship must be headed to sea soon, since it was already far out in the river and not tied up near the shore.

Now that I thought about it, I'd not seen any ships that big actually on the sand, so I started wandering around to see if I might find out whether they could haul something that size ashore. They must've been able to. How else could they repair it? I ambled about but failed to find another vessel of similar size, so I stood on the water's edge and watched the barges floating cargoes to meet their corresponding ships all the way down at the mouth of the river.

I was walking the shoreline parallel to one of these barges when a hand clapped me on the back. I wheeled around, prepared to defend against an assault, but I'd forgotten I was still a man. Instead of leering, the face that greeted me wore a jovial smile.

"Afternoon, lad. Which ship you on?" the young man said.

He was taller than me, tan with dark-brown hair, and not very handsome, the kind of lad I'd never have noticed if he had not called attention to himself. He was walking the sands with a group of other common seamen and longshoremen, all of them drunk.

"I, um—"

"What's wrong with your voice?" he asked.

My throat caught. These lads had taken me by surprise, and I'd forgotten to lower my speaking register as I normally did when I donned my disguise.

"Nothing's wrong with it. I've just recovered from an illness," I said.

"Yeah. Infancy," one of his companions interjected, and the others laughed.

"Don't mind them," said the man who'd first spoken to me. "Name's Mario."

"Miguel," I replied.

"Well, Miguel, what say you join us for some fun?"

I wasn't sure I should do such a thing. It was odd these men would just induct me into their group out of nowhere. Still, when else was I going to get the chance to go gallivanting around a huge city with a gaggle of pícaros? The prospect, which would have seemed insane even as recently as this morning, now proved irresistible. Setting aside the little voice in my head that told me I should think it bizarre a group of complete strangers would invite me to accompany them in their after-hours activities for no apparent reason, I said I was always up for some debauchery.

Mario and his band led me away from the river's edge, and I was soon lost in unfamiliar territory, alone with them on streets that the wife of a merchant officer would normally never dare to venture, even with her husband. This part of the Arenal was full of ramshackle houses and dusty, run-down streets intersected by canals of filthy water that could be crossed only on makeshift bridges of questionable structural reliability.

The stench was the first thing I noticed, for this part of the city was nothing but tightly packed residential buildings that left no open space for the sewage gutters to air out. In spots, the odor of urine could've bowled me over, and it was damn near all I could do to keep myself upright and moving forward.

Even though city streets back then weren't exactly what one would call clean, I'd thus far been sheltered from this level of squalor. Refuse lay piled in the back of every alley we passed, and the rats and roaches did not even have the courtesy to pretend to be afraid of us as we made our way through this network of narrow streets and alleyways.

So many people lay sleeping along the edges of the dirt roads there was scarcely any free space. Even so far from the malbaratillo, vagrants tried to sell us cheap junk and contraband, and beggars crossed our paths, asking alms of any man who looked like he had work. Having already given away my last coin, I lamented that I had nothing to offer them.

Not once during the walk to our destination did it escape me that Sergio had lived in a place like this. He hated to discuss his youth, but he'd given me a few details when I'd refused to let it drop that I knew next to nothing about my own husband. Unlike me, he'd actually been dumped on a church doorstep. Equally unlike me, nobody had kept him. He'd been tossed from the foundling home to the street when he was still a boy. I always admired his resolve when I thought of how he'd managed to claw his way out of such a situation when the overwhelming majority never could.

As we walked through the narrow streets, my new companions jabbed me in the ribs with their elbows and clapped me on the back sporadically, and I deduced I was meant to roar with laughter at these aggressive gestures, for some joke had been made that my nausea had not allowed me to hear. I willed my nose not to smell the odors causing that nausea, but as usual, my nanos weren't listening.

Joking and guffawing, the lads led me to the seediest place I'd ever seen. The building stood at the end of the street and had been erected even more sloppily than the rest of the edifices around it; its brick was crumbling in many spots, and the roof barely clung to the few sound areas of the walls.

I realized it must be a brothel. Within, I could hear peals of laughter from many men as well as the falsely high giggles of women faking their mirth. I was grateful we'd arrived at our destination, for I thought at the very least the inside must smell better than these narrow streets.

Was I ever wrong. When the door opened, the odor of sewage evaporated only to be replaced by the overpowering stench of crammed bodies sweating in the radiant heat of the evening and still stewing in the filth of a day's work. Desperate to make the smell more tolerable, I wondered if I could get a mug of ale or sack to shove my nostrils in.

The inside of the structure had a makeshift tavern right in front of the brothel proper. It consisted of a large, empty firepit at the opposite end of the room and several long, rickety tables. There was no door or even a dividing wall between the small drinking area and the cubicles the women used to provide their services. Over the din of laughter coming from the men having their pre- or postcoital drinks, the sounds of sex echoed off the walls.

Every last one of the tables was occupied by groups of working men—not just sailors and dockhands but stable hands, smiths, day laborers, and the like. Each of these groups was tended to by two or three women dressed in bright-colored clothing that accentuated the curve of their hips and revealed their breasts almost to the nipple. Many of them wore yellow headscarves adorned with tinsel.

Somehow, I found myself steered to a table and given a pint so bitter I could not stand to drink it, but at least it smelled strong enough to counter the powerful stench of this place. As I breathed deep the pungent scent of the ale, one of the public women flopped down in my lap, slopping some of my beer onto both her red dress and my white linen shirt.

"Care for a kiss, darling?" She wrapped her arms around my neck.

I stuttered, mouth agape. I didn't know what to say. She giggled again, though I hadn't made any jest.

Mario laughed. "What are you, a sodomite? Everyone wants a taste of Elvira."

"They sure do," Elvira said, to a chorus of cheers from the lads.

"I'm sorry. I just . . . I don't do that type of thing. Not like this," I blurted.

"What sort of man says that?" one of the lads roared.

"Maybe he *is* a she," another piped in.

"Told you," said a third.

I held my breath as terror seized me, but Elvira interrupted.

"Trust me, he's all man." She rose from her seat atop my lap and gave me an odd look. "It's alright, love," she added, turning in the direction of another table.

Before she could move toward it, Mario grabbed her arm and jerked her back. He seized the necklace dangling above her bosom and used it to tug her down. Catching a handful of her hair, he forced her to bend all the way forward and shoved her face into his crotch. Everyone was laughing except for her. She seemed frozen, with her arms at her sides and her eyes glazed over.

"See, boy? This is what a man does with a woman," Mario told me as he held Elvira's face in his lap, and I remembered quite well that Rodrigo had thought the same thing.

Everything that occurred next happened so fast I didn't realize until it was already over. I leapt from my seat and smashed my fist into Mario's face. All the explosive rage I'd been suppressing—my fury at Sergio and Father Manuel and my hatred of Rodrigo, Felipe, and Ignacio—was contained in that one blow.

I crushed Mario's nose flat into his face. The blow spattered blood all over everyone's clothes and into their beers and sent Mario flying backward from his chair. He was out cold before he even hit the floor. I hadn't expected a single punch to do such damage, but I didn't lament it either. I'd simply forgotten my fists were now made of iron rather than clay.

The other lads leapt up, ready to take a swing at me but wary at the same time. They'd not anticipated that a skinny young thing like me could deliver a knockout blow with such apparent ease. I steeled for a fight, realizing too late I'd probably gotten myself into a situation where I'd have to use IDOS.

Just as I prepared to heat the cuffs, a livid female voice cracked like a whip over my shoulder. "What happened here?"

I turned to find an older woman standing behind me. Her curly black hair was streaked with gray, and her eyes were heavily wrinkled.

"That lad there. He attacked our boy for no reason," one of the men said, pointing at me.

"Mario didn't even do anything!" another added.

"I don't care," the woman shouted. "All of you, get out. Take Mario out of here too."

"What for?" all the lads bellowed in unison.

"You all for fighting, and him for roughing up my girls." The woman motioned to Mario's limp form.

"But Sancha!" one of the lads cried.

"No! You can come back when you remember the rules. Now, leave before I send for the padre," she said.

Some of the lads looked ready to argue, but a couple of huge ruffians stepped up behind Sancha, and Mario's boys all thought better of it. They filed toward the door when she pointed at it. I made to exit the brothel behind the last two lads, who were carrying Mario. I had to escape them before they compelled me to fight, but I didn't see how I could.

When I'd almost reached the door, a small hand clasped me around the wrist and yanked me backward. I turned to find Elvira staring up at me. She reached her other hand toward me and, before I could react, grasped my breast under the linen and squeezed it. I struck out at her with my fist, but she ducked the blow like she'd seen the thought of it form in my head. I wondered how long it had taken her to get so good at that.

"I knew it. Come with me, señorita," Elvira whispered.

I was caught. She'd probably realized I was no man when she'd sat on my lap. She took me down the long line of cubicles, through a door at the far end, then out the other side into a storage closet. Back here, a door was propped open to the alleyway to permit whatever scant fresh air might find its way in.

"You shouldn't be here. You shouldn't have done that," Elvira snapped once we reached the threshold.

"I only wanted to help," I squeaked.

"You didn't. You think I can't handle them? If I don't put up with their shit, my children won't eat. Did it never occur to you I deal with those lads and more like them every damn day?"

I was at a loss for words. "I'm sorry. I only wanted . . . I don't know what I wanted. I promise you'll never see my face again."

"I certainly hope not. Go home to your family and stop wandering around here looking for silly adventures to amuse yourself with until you find a husband."

Elvira turned me out the back so I might find my way home without running into Mario's crew again. I thanked her for helping me avoid them, and she slammed the door in my face without another word. I couldn't help but feel stung at her unfairness. There she'd stood, castigating me for being out of the house and fighting with Mario instead of reprimanding him for comporting himself like a brute.

Still, I felt chastened. It was possible I'd overreacted—she clearly didn't need the savior I'd believed myself to be. What's worse, I *had* thought of running around with these lads as a silly adventure, a way to avenge myself on my husband. I'd not intended it to go so far, nor had I intended to deprive Elvira's children of their supper. I would never have come with those boys if I had known they'd lead me here.

A din of shouts emanated from the other side of the brothel—the enraged cries from the men in Mario's group now that they found I was not among them. Time to get out of here before they fanned out searching for me. Mario's body might have been intact, but his pride definitely wasn't, and sometimes a wounded ego is more maddening than a wounded body.

I took off and turned into an alleyway, doubled back through an adjacent one when I reached the other side, and took several random turns before I felt assured that if anyone had been pursuing me, I'd lost them. Deciding I'd had more than enough debauchery for one day, I fled as fast as I could back to the river. I'd be able to locate my inn if I got to the other side.

As it turned out, I was a long distance from anywhere there might be a boatman. I'd let those lads lead me all the way into the roughest part of the Arenal. I could have kicked myself for being so foolish. They probably had intended to get me drunk so they could rob me. Or perhaps they'd seen through my disguise and decided to lure me into a place they could do as they pleased with me. One of them had suggested I was a she rather than a he, after all.

Thank goodness for Elvira. She'd saved me from a fight in which I'd have had to reveal IDOS and maybe even kill someone with it. I should've offered her more gratitude than I did, should've apologized more profusely for being such a reckless idiot.

By the time I found my way to the inn, night had fallen and the city had gone dark. Slipping into the hallway at the first lull in foot traffic, I vowed I would never again do as I'd done today. I snuck down the empty, candlelit corridor until I came to my room, letting myself in and pulling my braid out of my hat as I crept through the door.

I entered the room expecting to find it empty. Instead, Sergio was there, already shirtless for sleeping through the warm night. He curled under the coverlet, using the candlelight to study a stack of papers. Without averting his gaze from the documents, he demanded to know where I'd been so late.

Before I could speak, he glanced up and caught sight of me; his mouth fell open. "You cannot be serious. I had hoped a few days on your own would soften your heart, but apparently not."

"You mean you'd hoped a few days of punishing me with your absence would bend me to your will," I replied.

He leapt from the bed, his teeth and fists clenched. I remained firm where I stood. He could rant and rave all he liked, but I was not backing down.

"What is wrong with you, Micaela? Why all of a sudden are you acting like this? Some quirks I can live with, but there's a line you cannot continue to cross."

"You say you don't want me to be attacked, yet when I take the precautions I find effective at preventing it, you say I'm crossing a line," I said.

"I don't want you to be attacked. You should stay indoors and away from strangers. That's the best precaution," he replied.

"So the man who can't even be kept on the same continent for more than a few months at a time wishes me to be perpetually shut up indoors? Hypocrite! If the thing you expect of me were expected of you, you would lay down and die."

"I don't understand why you insist on wandering around like a vagabond. It's not like you've got anywhere interesting to be anyhow," Sergio spat.

I was incensed at his flagrant dismissal, and I also felt Homeship counted as a mildly interesting place. Deciding this time I would be the one to storm out, I wrenched the door open and made for the hall.

"Don't you dare walk away from me!" Sergio snapped and reached out for me as I strode toward the exit, grabbing my right forearm with his left hand and jerking me back into the room so hard it made me slam to the floor on my knees.

When I hit the floor, the telltale heat rose in my forearm. Sergio yelped and let go, jumping back and gripping his burned hand with the other.

"What was that?" He examined his singed palm and fingertips, which were raw and blistered from even that brief contact with IDOS.

I was speechless. Had I intended to kill him? I had no time to think on it, for he snatched my hand into his own and rolled up my sleeve looking for the source of his injury.

"How did you do that?" he demanded.

"I don't know what you're talking about," I stammered.

The cuff had cooled and was invisible at a distance, but I couldn't let Sergio look too closely. I pulled my hand from his grasp and yanked my sleeve back down, leaping across the room before he had the chance to examine my arm further.

"You burned me!" he shouted.

"No, I did not. Do you hear yourself? You sound mad."

"Does this look mad to you?" He turned his palm and showed off the weeping blisters on his fingertips. I supposed I ought to feel guilty, but I couldn't make myself.

"It doesn't look mad to me, but think about it. How could I have done that? Do you see anything on my arm?" I rolled up my sleeve so he could see from a distance.

The cuff was smooth and the same tone as my skin. As long as I kept him from looking up close or feeling of my arm too carefully, I was certain he'd not be able to see the difference.

He huffed. "I see nothing. But this makes no sense. Why is my hand burned?"

"Maybe you did it to yourself earlier without noticing. Maybe you just now realized it because you grabbed me like a beast," I spat the last word like venom.

"I suppose I must have—I did put a new candle in the stand earlier, but the old one felt cool then."

I seized this opportunity to lay the blame on something explicable. "It must have been hotter than you realized or else cool enough to burn you so slowly you didn't notice. That's the only explanation. Again, if you hadn't been accosting me, it wouldn't have pained you so much."

"I'm sorry. I only meant to make you stay. I didn't intend to pull you back so hard."

He sounded contrite enough, and I had no desire to further any discussion of how he'd burned his hand, so I gave him a curt nod that I hoped conveyed at least a begrudging forgiveness and swept across the room toward him.

"You should let me bandage that." I pointed to his hand.

I had no antiseptic save vinegar, and I'm not going to deny it did give me some spiteful satisfaction to know it hurt like hell when I rinsed Sergio's hand in it, even though he gritted his teeth and didn't make a sound.

Despite that one second of vindictive pleasure, my concern for the manner in which he'd gotten the injury weighed on my mind. I had given him this hurt. *I* had burned him, even unintentionally—or maybe it had been intentional. I didn't know. Did I have the faintest idea what I was capable of anymore?

That incident altered the way I viewed myself in relation to my husband. I now saw myself as a threat to his safety, for I had been angry with him, and in response, I had readied a deadly weapon. I'd seen what this weapon did to the human body once before and had no desire for anything of the sort to happen to Sergio, leastways for me to be the cause of it, no matter how furious he made me. I decided that as soon as I could steal a second alone, I'd remove these cuffs from my body and hide them once more.

"There," I said as I finished wrapping a crude bandage around my husband's hand.

Sergio thanked me but didn't respond further. He began dressing to leave.

"So I am to be punished for speaking my mind, even though I've just helped you?" I asked, resenting every cell in his body.

"I don't wish to punish you," he answered. "I just don't understand you any longer. It's easier this way than to stay and argue until dawn. I don't want to do anything I'll regret."

My heart beat wildly to a rhythm in which I could almost hear the words, "Please don't leave me again." They were right at my lips, on the edge of my tongue. I could taste them, but I bit them back, feeling them disintegrate as I ground them between my teeth. I was no beggar. Thus, I stood in silence, still wearing the clothes that had now become the bane of my marriage, as I watched Sergio dress, gather his cloak, and move for the door. When he put his hand on the latch, I took a step toward him before I could stop myself.

He must have seen it, for he turned back toward me. "What is it?"

"Nothing. Go if you must," I answered.

In a flash, he was gone. I crawled into bed, still in my clothes and shoes, and curled under the covers. Of course, I did not sleep. I lay on my side staring at the empty space where Sergio had reclined before my arrival, fixated on the indentation his head had made in the pillow.

I let my tears flow sideways down the front of my face until the surface of my own pillow was soaked. When I thought I'd finished crying, I swapped the cushions, my wet one for Sergio's dry one. I then caught a whiff of his scent on his pillow, which started my tears afresh.

I was even angrier with myself than with him. I hadn't needed to go out dressed like that today. If I'd been dressed as a woman, I'd have stayed in public places and never gone off with anyone. I would have been fine. The only reason I'd worn the shirt and breeches was to avenge myself on my husband for deriving displeasure from them, and now I lay here alone again, on the fifth day of this ridiculous argument. There were only two or three weeks left until the voyage. I asked myself: Was this fight worth spending them alone?

No. It was not. If I had so little time until I wouldn't see Sergio for another year, possibly ever, I was going to spend it with him, breathing him in, taking him inside me, his soul as much as his body, so I could keep him there to sustain me for another year of loneliness and deprivation. Although admitting this felt like a defeat, pride be damned. I wanted my husband.

I waited until the first shafts of early dawn light began to creep through the tiny gap in the curtains and make their way up the opposite wall. Then I got up and dressed in silence. I washed my tearstained face, pulled my heavy hair into a graceful updo, and laced up my shining ebony dress. Afraid of what could happen if I went armed in Sergio's presence again, I removed IDOS and stuck the cuffs back in their hiding place.

I did not go at once but milled about, taking breakfast at leisure in the inn courtyard. I had no intention of letting Sergio off too easy, so I waited to set out for the ship until the heat of the brilliant morning sun blazed against the black veil and black hair on top of my head to the point that they both must have been scorching to the touch.

I had not exactly been comfortable wandering the harbor along the banks of Arenal the first time I'd come onto it, and I was doubly disquieted now, alone on my own two feet instead of Pepito's high back and wearing a dress instead of a shirt and pantaloons. Many of the young women who came to the shoreline unaccompanied were prostitutes looking to find customers, though, strictly speaking, they weren't allowed to be walking the streets.

I doubted I could be mistaken for a prostitute—modestly dressed and veiled in black as I was—yet I still could not help but imagine what all these strange men must think of me invading their realm with my flowing skirts and thick, coifed tresses. I kept my head high, fixed my eyes forward, and held my back straight, willing every fiber of my being to project a firmness that warned to stay away. I hoped I hadn't made a huge mistake in leaving my weapons behind.

It wasn't long until my paranoia proved more akin to prophecy. As I wandered around, looking out of place and lost, I felt a tug in the middle of my back, and the linen mantilla that had been resting atop my head slid off my hair and dropped down below my shoulders. Incensed someone would dare do that to me, I whipped around to see a group of several young men laughing and jeering.

I wanted to shout at them, but no one in the vicinity acted interested in backing me if I chose to defend my honor. Everyone aside from these men kept their focus intently on their own business. I feared further aggression from them and that showing any emotion would only make them laugh even more. So with all the dignity I could muster, I pulled my veil up, pretended what had happened simply hadn't, and slunk away.

When I felt assured they hadn't followed me, I chastised myself for that split-second decision not to escalate. I'd let them get away with publicly humiliating me because I wished to avoid a scene. Once again, I'd failed to stand up for myself, and, once again, here I stood hating the stupid self I'd failed to stand up for. What was the matter with me that I would defend some strange woman from Mario, but when the same thing happened to me, I would turn around and walk away? Perhaps it wasn't too late to find those men, but they'd already pulled their prank. They'd likely forgotten it the instant I'd turned my back.

Trying to push it out of my mind and think of Sergio instead, I picked up the pace, desiring nothing more than to get off this accursed sand. I finally found the *San José* floating parallel to the shore, and I went straight to the gangplank and boarded as soon as everyone's backs were turned. The second I set foot on deck, a gentle but firm hand grasped my arm.

"Hold on there, señorita. Where do you think you're going?"

I knew that voice. Twirling around, I looked straight into Pablo's chocolate-brown eyes and said, "To find Sergio."

"Oh! Apologies, Toledana. I didn't recognize you from behind," Pablo replied.

I smiled. "No harm done. Is he onboard?"

Pablo didn't answer. Rather, he straightened up and greeted someone behind me. I turned just as the master stepped onto the main deck.

"Good day, Don Armando," I said, though he did not return the greeting. "Where is Sergio?" I pressed.

"I should like to think he's on his own vessel," Armando snapped.

"His own? You made him shipmaster? Why wouldn't he tell me?" I asked.

"I suppose he did not get the opportunity in light of your incessant resistance to his wishes." Armando crossed his arms.

I sensed a retort coming on, but I stifled it and said, "I'm sorry, señor. I didn't intend to upset either of you."

Armando arched a brow but did not speak.

"Please. Where is the *San Bruno*?" I asked.

Armando pointed off to his left. "That way. Six or seven vessels down."

I thanked Armando and took my leave of him as soon as politeness allowed, clutching my veil tight and hating my need for IDOS as much as I wished I had it while I ran the gauntlet otherwise known as the Arenal once more.

When I made it to the *San Bruno*, boarding proved to be a problem. Several new members of her crew stood at the gangplank talking amongst themselves, and when I went to board the ship, these strangers blocked my path. I didn't fault them for this—it was part of their job. Yet, when I told them I was the wife of the new master, they laughed and asked me if I took them for fools who'd believe the word of a well-dressed strumpet posing as the master's wife.

My cheeks warmed with anger. I told them they'd answer to the master if they wouldn't let me onboard, but they laughed again and ordered me gone. I refused. One of them made to remove me from in front of the plank, but I slapped his hand away and shouted for Sergio. My voice was clear and powerful, and wherever he was on the ship, he heard me. His head popped over the railing.

"What are you doing?" he shouted down from the banister.

"She won't leave, señor," one of the men yelled as I opened my mouth to answer.

"Of course she won't. She's my wife. Let her up," he called back.

At this, all of them clambered over one another to get out of my way. I shot them a smug smirk before sauntering up the gangplank and onto my husband's ship. He stood with his hands behind his back and ushered me into his cabin as soon as I set foot on deck.

It was a cozy but spacious stateroom with a writing desk and a chair and a bed built right into the wall—the very same room I'd seen through the door crack when Sergio had snuck me onboard this ship before we'd married.

Sergio closed the door as I sat down on his bed. "I see you've managed to find an actual dress today."

I shot him a warning look. "Did I board two ships and wander all over this horrid sand and endure the unpleasantness of your men for you to speak to me like that?"

"Forgive me—and them, as well. I will deal with them later."

"It's alright. They did nothing wrong."

"Why have you come?"

"Because I didn't wish to spend another day of our short time together in conflict."

"Nor I. I'm glad you came." He sat down beside me. "I would have returned to you tonight if you hadn't. You know that?"

"You should have stayed last night."

"I know I should've."

He took a breath as if to speak again but closed his mouth. I would've liked to hear he was sorry or that he wished he'd returned as soon as he'd left me or that he'd had as miserable a night as I. But from him, this implicit admission of fault was as good as I could hope to get.

"If I'd known you were going to come this morning, I wouldn't have let you wander the sands unaccompanied," he said.

"What did you think I would do when you decided to chastise me by desertion yet again? Sit in the inn collecting dust?"

"It's just, well, this can be a rough place, and you could get yourself hurt. You've really got no business out here all alone."

"My business was to find you, jackass!" I snapped. When his eyes widened, I added, "I didn't mean to say it like that. Really, I didn't come here to start arguing again. But don't you find it even slightly unfair that my options are to sit in the room and rot or be blamed for it when men hound and torment me for doing nothing more than walking out my door?"

"Who's hounding and tormenting you?"

"No one. I just didn't like you intimating if someone had, it would've been my own fault," I said, knowing better than to bring up the veil incident.

"Regardless, you should've sent a messenger. I would've come back."

Tempted as I was to say that was not the point, arguing it further would get me nowhere, so I asked, "Could we please just forget all this and enjoy the time we have left?"

"I'd like that. And Micalita, I've thought all night about it, and I don't want you to be put in danger because I've forbidden you to dress in men's clothing."

I perked up. "So you'll accept it, then?"

"What? Oh no. I've decided I'll send a couple of the lads to escort you home. I think Cristóbal and Gonzalo should do. I've known them both for many years."

"I hardly know them at all."

"I know, but I don't want to pass the entire crossing worrying about you."

"I'm going to pass many months worrying about you! You think I didn't spend the entirety of last year worrying about you?"

"Don't shout at me in front of my men," Sergio hissed. "And I don't see the issue here. It's a way for you to both stay safe and not gallivant across the peninsula dressed like a—"

"I don't care," I snapped, trying to keep my voice down. "I made it here on my own, and I'll go back on my own. I won't be babysat by a pair of men who cannot defend me half as well as I can defend myself."

"What does that mean?" Sergio said.

I stopped short, fumbling for an answer. "I only meant, um, my disguise is a much better defense than escorts. No one will bother me if they don't know I'm a woman."

"It doesn't matter either way. You're going with the escorts I send you and that's that."

"The hell it is. I won't stand for it. I'll give them the slip as soon as the opportunity arises. I'll tell the Santa Hermandad they kidnapped me."

"Micaela, I will send you home tied up in a sack if I must."

"I'd like to see you try!"

"Why can't you just accept I don't approve of your going alone and be cooperative about it?" Sergio asked.

"Well, I don't approve of you going to the New World again. Maybe I'll leave here and go tell those accursed bureaucrats at the Casa de Contratación to take a harder look at your blood purity documentation."

Sergio laughed. "You wouldn't do that."

He was right, but I couldn't let him call my bluff. "You willing to bet your shiny new master position on it?"

The smile fell right off Sergio's face. "What the devil has gotten into you?"

"Nothing has gotten into me. I don't want things between us to be hostile, honestly. But I am holding my ground this time, no matter what."

Sergio paused before asking, "You've been talking to that damned Sara, haven't you?"

"If I have, it's no business of yours."

He gaped at me for a tick. Then, to my surprise, he abruptly deflated. "I don't want things between us to be hostile either. I don't want you to grow to hate me."

"Then you've got to learn to make some concessions. If we're going to compromise, I cannot be the only one who's doing the compromising."

"I suppose I can learn to live with that." Sergio wrapped an arm around my shoulder and squeezed me tight.

"That is all I ask. Thank you."

I hugged his neck and kissed his cheek, and he returned my affection. We kissed and caressed for a long time. Though we did not make love, the warmth of our gentle embrace evaporated the anger that still lingered between us.

"When did you learn you'd been made master?" I asked, laying my head on his shoulder.

"Only three days ago. I passed the test before we made the first crossing, but there wasn't a position. Now, Santiago has taken ill, and he'll likely never sail again. I hate that I was promoted in that manner, but . . ." He trailed off, and I looked up into his face. He was grinning wider than I'd ever seen.

"You should show me around for old times' sake," I said.

Sergio gave me a full tour of the *San Bruno* that day, a far grander affair than my first venture aboard the vessel. There was no sneaking around, no lying about impending punishments to keep my voice hushed, no friends looking out for the officers. On this ship, my husband was the officer, and everyone was looking out for him. The apprentices even waited on me, bringing me lemon water and leading me to the shade when the sun got too hot.

"When I return from this voyage, I'm going to move us into town," Sergio said whilst we ate supper aboard the vessel. "I'll rent out the place we have and buy us a town house on the bay, where we can watch the ships come into the harbor instead of the sheep grazing in the pasture."

"What if I like watching the sheep graze in the fields?" I asked.

"Come now, you've always wanted a house in town. You would be closer to Father Manuel, and I to my work."

It was true; I had wished to be closer to the bustle and energy of the city, but things were different now. The arrabal was much easier to slip out of unseen. At the same time, it would be nice to be rid of our current house—the place I could never again call home.

"You know. If things keep going this well, instead of getting a house in town, we might all be moving down here in another two or three years," Sergio said as one of his apprentices entered and poured us more wine.

"Armando would give up the wool trade?" I asked between bites of buñuelo.

"Of course not. Gabriel would stay up north and run that side, and we would move down here to run this one. I even walked around and looked at some of the places on La Calle Larga."

"Who would move?"

"You and I and Armando and Sara," he replied.

I nodded without speaking. I didn't know what I'd say to Jhasali if we did wind up moving to Sevilla. I feared how she'd react upon learning I might not be around anymore. Would she accept my moving away after she'd given me her gift? What might she do if she didn't?

"What's wrong?" Sergio asked after I'd stared into space for some time.

"Nothing. I'm just so happy for you is all," I said.

I had no desire to displease him any more than I already had. I could sort out whatever details needed sorting when the day came.

He took my hand. "Be happy for both of us. My success is just as much yours as mine."

Squeezing his hand, I smiled and forgot why I'd ever been angry with him in my life.

\*\*\*

To my delight, we discovered next morning that Sergio's departure date was to be delayed because of some issue with the final paperwork, and it would be nearly September before his ships departed. Still, those extra weeks of peace passed quicker than the preceding days of conflict—too quick for my liking.

Sergio came back to the inn and stayed with me from there on out, and I went to work with him for a few hours every day, watching him direct the final preparations. He supervised the loading of the few supplies with which they would sail down to the ocean and ensured the barges were packed with the proper cargo: textiles, wine, iron bars, olives, almonds, and other assorted goods that would prove rare and valuable in the New World. He was a firm commander, but fair and reasonable as well. No anger nor frustration ever tainted the collected authority in his tone, and the workers he directed obeyed without question.

He was kinder to me, too, perhaps having made the same choice I had about keeping the peace until his departure. Every morning, he brought me to the sands with him, and when I tired of being out in the heat, he either had one of his apprentices take me back across the river for the siesta or accompanied me himself. Though I'd made it clear I had no intention of being escorted back to Santa Colomba, I permitted Sergio that small act of chivalry while we were together.

Even with the delay, all too soon we found ourselves back in our room at the inn, packing our bags for the long journeys ahead, his to the west, mine to the north. When we took breakfast on the last day of his stay, Sergio asked me how I planned to travel back. I told him I'd stay in Sevilla until I found some pilgrims headed north.

If I could not find any of those, there would be lots of people headed that way after the harvest ended. Many migrant workers came from north to south (though not quite *this* south) for the annual reaping, and I told him I could head up the plateau and join them when I ran into them. Though he was displeased at the idea, he also seemed to have accepted there was nothing he could do about it without causing himself as many problems as he caused me.

That afternoon, Sergio and I returned to the Arenal to meet up with Armando as well as Santiago's younger brother, Álvaro, who served as the pilot for the *San Bruno*. We engaged in the requisite pleasantries: Álvaro telling us of his brother's ailing health, and us wishing him a speedy recovery and a happy retirement.

As we talked, I happened to glance down the port. A lad with a battered face caught my eye as he helped roll barrels from a small frigate toward the city walls. I studied this face to be sure it belonged to Mario. I shouldn't have been surprised to see him. After all, we were not all that far from where he and his mates had found me when I'd been wandering on my own. I watched as he approached, rolling the heavy barrel closer and closer to where we all stood.

"Isn't that right, Micaela?" Sergio squeezed my hand, raising his brows when I blankly met his gaze, as if this were not the first time he'd asked me whatever it was he'd just asked.

"I'm sorry, what?" I said.

"Eduardo is much bigger now than he was when we last saw him? Is he not?" Sergio motioned to Armando and himself.

Thank goodness. Just small talk. "Oh, yes. Much bigger. I'm sorry; I got lost in thought."

Sergio squeezed my hand once more and turned back to the men.

I glanced in Mario's direction to find he had now gotten close to us. I examined his face while his eyes were focused on his barrel. He sported two black eyes and a broken nose, both partially healed by now. Served him right. He should be thankful he'd gotten no worse. Aside from his bashed-in nose, he'd escaped his encounter with me unscathed.

I laughed to think how it must irk him that a "sodomite" had gotten the better of him. Then again, he was out here working just as he had been before he'd met me. As he approached, I decided his pride hadn't been wounded to my liking, so I called from across the way.

"Christ, lad! Who got hold of you?" I shot him a disdainful smirk as I glittered in my black dress, lazily dusting off the fold of my skirt with the back of my hand.

The look of rage that twisted Mario's battered face made me think he might move to accost me. He opened his mouth to retort before looking from my face to Sergio's and seeming to think better of it. I hoped he recognized me as I stood here amongst this group of merchant officers and held the hand of my husband. With my eyes, I dared him to reply. He did not. He cast his gaze back to the road and continued pushing his barrel.

"What was that?" Sergio whispered.

He pulled me aside whilst Armando continued to speak to Álvaro as if nothing had happened. My husband glared down the length of his nose, squinting at me.

"It's nothing. That man was just harassing me the other day when you weren't nearby. Thought I'd get him back," I murmured.

"What reason would he have to bother you?"

"None. I'd never even seen him before. Does he need a reason?"

I hadn't whispered that last question, and Sergio didn't press me further, lest we have a discussion right here in front of the master and the pilot.

"Do you want the lads and me to rough him up before we leave?" Sergio muttered.

"No need. From the look of him, I'm not the only sailor's wife he's been messing with."

Sergio turned back to Armando, making nothing more of it. I feared I might have made a mistake in suggesting Mario had bothered me. Sergio was good at putting up an apathetic front, but he could get jealous, same as any other man. I hoped he would not do anything foolish to Mario before he left. The last thing either of us needed was for him to earn himself a hanging over some nonsense I'd already handled myself.

That night, we spent our final hours together aboard the ship because I told Sergio I wished to experience sleeping on it at least one time. Once the loaders had finished and everyone had left except the night's watch, Sergio rolled me over in bed and began to undress me. By this point, I'd settled into the idea that sex without a true climax was to be my new normal, and I'd made it my habit to let my husband use me for his own pleasure rather than reject him for reasons he'd never understand.

We kissed for a long while, sliding our hands over one another's naked skin as the river current rocked us back and forth. I tried to enjoy the pleasure of Sergio's touch, the sensations of his fingers and tongue running all over my body, and the other parts of the act besides the penetration itself.

As I focused on the feel of his fingers weaving into the hair on the back of my head, Sergio abruptly stood, grasped me by the thighs, and pulled me to the edge of the bed.

"What are you doing?" I said.

"Giving you a parting gift." He dropped to his knees and put his head between my legs.

I started to tell him not to, afraid to discover this too could offer me no joy, but as he gently kissed the insides of my thighs, I began to relax. When he increased the speed and pressure of his caresses, I found my body responding to them in a way it hadn't to anything else. At long last, I discovered one thing Rodrigo hadn't tainted.

Soon, my legs spread wider of their own volition, my hips undulating as Sergio alternated between sucking me with his lips and licking me with his tongue. I grasped two big handfuls of his hair and pressed his head more firmly between my hips while he put his mouth to good use. He took this as a positive sign and increased the intensity. At this, I screamed with delight.

"Micaela, for Christ's sake! The night's watch is onboard," Sergio hissed, slamming a pillow over my face to quiet my shouting.

I held the pillow in place with my left hand and continued to tug on his curls with my right, doing my best to keep from making any sound that would cause him to stop what he was doing. When he ran his tongue in a circular motion, he pushed me over the edge and gave me the first real climax I'd experienced since my attack. As I began to orgasm, he slid into me, intensifying my pleasure to the point I screamed out loud again. He didn't make a fuss this time.

Sergio climaxed right as the final ripples of pleasure passed through my body. I'd had such a powerful release I couldn't speak. I just lay flat on my back, trying to calm my breathing.

"I wanted to give you something to last you the year." He lay down beside me, grinning.

"Mmmm," I moaned, still unable to string words together.

"You alright? You liked it?" He chuckled.

"Yes," I whispered.

"Good." He sighed, seeming more satisfied than he had after our last few encounters.

I was more than alright. I'd finally been able to indulge in the delight I'd once enjoyed so purely, and it ignited a spark of hope that what had become my new normal did not have to remain so. Maybe all I needed was the right kind of pleasuring.

I snuggled up to Sergio, placing my head in the dent between his shoulder and chest. "You've got to do that more often."

He did not respond. Instead, he sat up and gathered me into his arms, laying his head on top of mine and using his chin to press my face even tighter to his chest. Soon, his hushed tears made tiny plunking sounds as they fell from his cheek to my hair while he rocked me back and forth in his tight embrace. He eventually soaked the top of my head; still, I said nothing. He didn't weep often, but I'd learned long ago not to make a fuss of it when he did.

# Chapter Sixteen

# THE WITCH IS BORN

Pepito and I left Sevilla as soon as Sergio set sail, for I could not bear to spend another night alone at the inn. The first leg of the ride home went off without so much as a bout of bad weather. August had nearly ended, and the sun still burned away any chance of Pepe and me being rained on.

Since I'd never had an opportunity to see my own country at my leisure, I decided we would take a more scenic route, going out of our way to pass through cities like Córdoba and Ciudad Real that we had not come near on the more direct route from Santa Colomba. Often, we spent the night in city inns so I might explore the streets during the day, strolling through the markets and observing the architecture. I bought a few trinkets I shouldn't have, but I didn't fret too much over them, for Sergio had given me some extra coin to get home.

Though I had still not worked up the courage to wear the red dress, I did wear my black one, no longer fearing to be seen as a woman. After I'd gotten over the initial shock of it, the episode in the Sevillian brothel had given me a strong shot of overconfidence. What's more, the incident with my veil had rendered me defiant, and Sergio's attitude toward my traveling unaccompanied made me wonder if all the men in the country hadn't colluded together to make themselves both the assailants and the protectors of women so as to keep us obedient. Going about my travels in feminine costume gave me a tiny thrill of rebellion against them all.

Pepito and I followed a longer route and stopped frequently, so it took us several weeks to arrive in the city I'd planned to visit since I'd set foot on the road to Sevilla, the city in which I'd spent the earliest years of my childhood: Toledo. I couldn't help but smile as we took our first step onto the Puente de San Martín. It was still early, and I squinted my eyes in the bright eastern sun as it rose to beat back the autumn chill. I heaved a great sigh of contentment to see my city upon the hill, adorning the rocky crest like a crown adorns the head of a queen.

Though Father Manuel and I had never had any real occasion to cross this bridge, he'd brought me to it and the Puente de Alcántara many times when I was a young girl, just so I could see them. San Martín spanned longer than any other bridge I'd ever encountered, and on the instances I'd walked it as a child, Father Manuel had allowed me to run up and down its length and lean over the stone railing to throw pebbles into the Tajo far below.

Now, I looked up at the high city walls—as strong this day as they had been the day I was thrust beyond them into the cold and damp north—and I grinned at them like they were old friends. I breathed deep the smell of the Tajo and the pungent scent of horse sweat. Even the dusty roads looked paved with pure gold. I realized as I entered the city how much I'd missed it, how much I'd adored the narrow, winding streets and the shops and homes all crowded into this horseshoe riverbend. This was the same Toledo I'd left behind: the Toledo of my childhood.

I found lodging just within the wall. Next morning, I left Pepito in his stall and made my way to the cathedral for the first time in over ten years. Before arriving in Toledo, I'd feared how I might respond to being on the same streets that Ignacio and I had walked on the day of the auto de fe. Yet, when I laid eyes on the rose window above the Puerta del Reloj, a rush of nostalgia took hold of me, blinding me to the present as I remembered all those times I'd wandered to this place as a girl just to stare at this wheel of melted sand. I bought myself an apple from a fruit cart in the square so I could stand in front of the entrance and eat it while I looked up at the intricate stonework around the stained glass and the door, same as I had as a child. For just a little while, I felt pure and simple happiness, despite what awaited me within.

I'd staunchly refused to enter this place since the fall of 1513. Every pane of stained glass in my favorite windows held a positive memory, but the floor level was a different matter. In the cloisters and central courtyard hung dozens—maybe hundreds—of sanbenitos. Most of them, the ones for the penitents who had not been relaxed, were yellow with a red cross emblazoned upon them. Yet many were black with painted red devils and flames, like the ones I'd seen in the quemadero.

Those particular sanbenitos had been the final garments their owners had ever worn.

Before the incident in the vega, I'd not had much interest in these garments. After the auto de fe, I'd discovered that, hidden within these decorated façades and carved walls, the stain of my parents' humiliation hung like a dark cloud over both their memories and their progeny. Now, those aging rags were the one clue that could help me discover their fates.

I stood outside the cathedral long after I'd finished my fruit, trying to savor the ability to half believe my mother and father had escaped with their lives. When I read the inscriptions under their sanbenitos, I would know for sure. I was tempted to turn around and walk away; blissful ignorance seemed better than confirmation of the worst. But I had to know. Breathing deep, I entered the cathedral, the nostalgic happiness I'd felt at the sight of the window vanishing along with the light of the morning sun once I passed the threshold.

Walking through the cloisters, I looked over the sackcloth garments one by one, scanning the names and dates and crimes until I came to a couple of aging, threadbare ones at the end of a row. There they were: the yellow sanbenitos my parents had worn almost twenty years ago. The inscriptions told me all I needed. My mother's read, "Josefa de Toledo. Punished on the 30th of November in the Year 1508 of Our Lord for dissemination of heretical teachings and leading the faithful astray. Sentenced to one hundred lashes, confiscation of goods, and five years' exile."

I didn't wish to sob and draw attention to myself, so I took a break before I read my father's. I held my breath to stop it from coming in gasps. When I had gained enough composure, I read the inscription. His said his Christian name as well, Miguel de Toledo, and the same crimes as my mother's, and it specified that he had received a sentence of one hundred lashes, confiscation of goods, and perpetual prison. My eyes drifted downward. Underneath this inscription, someone had tacked on an addendum stating this sentence had been commuted to service in His Catholic Majesty's galleys.

At these words, I lost my composure. I had to put my hand against the wall to keep myself on my feet, and before I could stifle them, my sobs came so loud they echoed off the stone walls of the cloisters. Father Manuel had been truthful that my parents had not been executed, but my father might as well have been.

I almost regretted my choice to seek out these awful garments. Was this why I'd come—to learn my father had perished at the oar? I had been thankful to see my parents' sanbenitos were yellow and not black, but now I knew it made no difference. The hardiest of men did not survive galley slavery for long.

And what the devil had happened to my mother when they took him away from her? I guessed they'd torn her out of his arms and dumped her at the most convenient border. I hoped someone had helped her avoid starvation, and I wondered if she'd even made it to the Barbary Coast or if she'd just become a slave or public woman somewhere in another Spanish kingdom.

"Is something wrong?" a voice said somewhere behind me.

I leapt up from my knees so fast it didn't dawn on me I'd sunk to the floor until after I was already standing once more. My veil had slipped to my shoulders, and I reflexively pulled it back over my hair.

The man who'd spoken to me seemed a student, maybe preparing for the priesthood or the monastic life—he was quite young, wore only a long dark-brown tunic, and carried a load of books under one arm.

"Do you know anything about these two?" I pointed to the timeworn sanbenitos.

"No." He looked at the inscriptions under the garments. "But I think I know who might. Wait here."

I slid back down to the floor, wrapped my arms around my knees, and wept right there underneath my parents' sanbenitos. Nobody approached me, though many people passed.

The young man returned perhaps half an hour later, tailed by an ancient parish priest. He was fat, shrunken and bent, a head shorter than me, and bald except for a thin wisp of hair encircling the lower third of his skull almost like a natural tonsure. The student pointed at me, then hurried away, still carrying his books. Staring at his back as he rushed off, I wondered if this kind young man might someday soon become another Ignacio.

When the squat old priest limped over, I scrambled off the floor and put to him the same question I'd asked the student.

"Yes. I remember them," he said.

"How did you know them?" I asked.

"I was their confessor many years ago," he replied.

"What can you tell me of them?"

"Why do you ask?"

"What would it take for me to learn what I want to know without having to answer that?"

The old man lecherously eyed me up and down. "I have a private place we can go."

"Father! Would you make an adulteress of me?" I placed my hand over my heart, flashing my wedding ring.

He pointed at my coin purse and nodded. "That, then."

I passed him the bag, lamenting that Sergio had brought it to me from Flanders, but I couldn't dump the coins in the old man's hand. Luckily, the money inside wasn't all I carried.

The priest slipped the purse into his cassock and began to speak. "The pair of them appeared out of nowhere one day in the winter of 1498 or the spring of 1499. I don't recall. Nobody knew them or where they'd come from. They had a significant sum of money, though they were as tight-lipped about that as they were about everything else. They bought an inn over near the old Judería and ran it for a few years without any issues."

"Did you ever find out where they'd come from?" I said.

"There were many rumors swirling around the two of them, but I never discovered if any were true."

"What rumors?"

"Well, the man was a Moor; he spoke Castellano with a thick Arabic accent. But the woman was not of his ilk. I suspected she might have been an Old Christian. Her accent was flawless, she had blue eyes and golden hair, and her airs were much more refined than what one would expect from those infidels. Then again, she spoke Arabic, and she had a Muslim name. Many people said she was an Old Christian he had kidnapped for a slave before the fall of Granada. Some people said he'd bewitched her to convert to Islam and stolen her from her father. Others said she'd been betrothed to an Old Christian man and fled with her Moorish lover to escape the marriage. Some said the pair of them were involved in the revolt of the Alpujarras, but that didn't make sense. They arrived in Toledo too early."

"What were their Arabic names?" I asked.

"The man's Muslim name was Omar, and the woman's Aixa, if I remember correctly. After I baptized them, I never knew them as anything other than Miguel and Josefa."

"What about their surnames?"

"Those I don't recall. I only know they took the city name at their baptism."

"How did they cross the Inquisition?"

He hesitated to think. "It happened not long after the mass conversions. If my memory serves, they were detained in the summer of 1503. I don't know who denounced them, only that after they were arrested, dozens of people started saying they'd done all sorts of awful things like holding clandestine meetings to convert Old Christians to Islam, burning the scriptures, and disseminating Qurans. I even heard they'd profaned a Host, but surely if that had been true, they'd have been put to death."

"You thought they were innocent?"

"I believed so at first. I thought they'd been accused because their inn did so well—made many people jealous. But then they were found to have in their possession certain unfortunate writings, and I heard they both confessed to their crimes," he said.

"Funny how torture tends to provoke that," I replied.

"I suppose if they'd been innocent, they'd have preferred death to bearing false witness. No matter, there were many others who testified to their misdeeds."

"Witnesses can be bought and papers planted," I said.

"If the Inquisition had thought that the case, they'd have absolved them."

I had a hard time believing the Inquisition would absolve anyone with a nice, profitable inn to confiscate. Regardless, what chance had a couple like my parents stood against a host of Old Christian witnesses?

I crossed my arms and stared at the sanbenitos. "What became of their daughter?"

"Josefa was getting big with child when they took her. I suppose it would've gone to a foundling hospital after she gave birth. Unfortunate." The old man shrugged, then paused before adding, "Wait. How did you know she had a daughter?"

"I . . . um . . ." I stammered before finding my words. "I thought I paid so I didn't have to answer questions."

"I suppose you did," the priest said.

"Did she ever return? Aixa—Josefa, I mean—from her exile?" I asked, wishing to move the conversation along quickly.

"In 1518 or '19, if my memory serves, though she never contacted me. I only discovered she'd returned after she'd already left again. I never found out any more about it. Her goods had all been confiscated, so I suppose there wasn't much motive for her to remain in the city."

I could bear no more. On the verge of losing my composure again, I asked if I might have some time alone, and the old priest left me. I bowed my head and held my knuckles to my brow. The weight of this discovery pressed so heavy on my soul that for a few moments I felt nothing—not sadness nor grief nor anger—just nothing. My mother had come looking for me, and I was already gone. That was all.

I leaned against the wall and pressed my head to what had been my mother's sanbenito, caressing the rough cloth with my hands and my nose and my brow. I breathed deep and took in its scent. This piece of old sackcloth smelled of moths and rot and dust. I wondered what scents it might've carried when it had first been hung here, how my mother's flesh and breath and hair might've smelled. This was the first time since infancy I'd touched a piece of her clothing. I turned to the one marked for my father and did the same thing.

These tattered rags were all I had left of my parents, and I was certain they were all I was ever to have of my father now. Part of me wished to throw the sanbenitos in the fire to burn away the memory of what had been done to my family and the shame we would endure for generations to come, but the other part wanted to take them home with me. To whom else could these final pieces of my parents belong?

I heard the rustling of clerical robes behind me and realized the elderly priest had returned.

"Child?" he whispered.

Not giving him the opportunity to say more, I asked, "Can't you take them down?"

"It is against the law," he said.

"Isn't it our duty to disobey unjust laws?"

"Tread carefully, my dear. There is no law too severe for heretics, and it isn't a layman's place to question the teachings of the Church."

"They'd probably not agree with you." I waved at the rows of sanbenitos.

"Child, you are coming dangerously close to heresy. I'd suggest you remind yourself what awaits all heretics and blasphemers by attending the auto de fe."

"What? What auto de fe?"

"There is to be a celebration Sunday. How can you not know? The town crier has been through already," he said.

"I'm not local, I'm from—somewhere else."

I stared at the wall and fumed while the heat of my tears burned my cheeks. I bit my tongue to keep it from spitting poisonous heresy. I tried to make it bleed, but I could not.

"Do you wish to go to confession, my dear?" the old priest asked. "It might help to unburden your soul."

I turned to him, evidently unable to keep my rage from tainting my expression, for the old priest backed up a pace or two when my eyes met his. I'd worn IDOS since the start of my journey home, and the cuffs heated involuntarily again. I worried they might burn my sleeves despite Jhasali's treatments to make the fabric flame retardant, but this old man was in no danger. I knew well the identity of my real enemy.

"No, Father," I snapped. "I don't have anything to confess. It's you who should be begging my pardon, not the other way around."

With that, I turned on my heel and marched back out into the streets.

I didn't know what to do. Another auto on Sunday? That was only two days away. I supposed I ought to get out of the city while I still had the chance. I wandered the streets for a long while, somehow winding up in front of the Puerta del Perdón once I stopped. My feet took me there of their own accord.

I remained on the edge of the square and stared up at the massive cathedral. It loomed over my head with its colossal doors and its intricate façades. Just this morning, I'd stood at my favorite window reliving the happiest times of my girlhood. Now, I looked upon the church with burning hate.

I wished I could take IDOS and fire a round into each pane in the whole building, raining colored shards of that stained glass all over these streets and these people before heading to Zocodover and incinerating the scaffolding that was to hold the parade of prey as they sat through the droning sermon to learn their fates. Shaking with fury, I turned away from the cathedral to avoid doing something stupid.

As I faced the plaza once more, I recalled all the times I'd come out to these same streets as a young child to witness the holiday processions, with the Corpus Christi parade being a particular favorite of mine. I remembered the colorful banners and wreaths hung from every window for weeks on end, the feverish happiness in the crowds as they pressed together to view the procession squeezing through the narrow passages, the magical fluttering of the flower petals tumbling like snowflakes from all the balconies. At my final Corpus festival in Toledo, I'd held Antonia's hand while she led me to the front of the crowd to wave at Father Manuel as he marched in the parade. I could never forget the smile he gave me in return.

How innocent I'd been, how naïve. My memory of it all was tainted now. Never again could I see a Corpus procession walk these streets without recalling the other procession that passed the same route. If I saw a banner with an image of the Virgin hanging out someone's window or winding its way through the avenues, never again could I see any other María than María González. But should I? Is the happiness of some worth the sacrifice imposed on others?

Tears had soaked through the cloth of my collar by the time I somehow wandered into the Plaza de Zocodover. Viewing the scaffolding brought on a powerful cocktail of revulsion and rage, though IDOS couldn't get any hotter than it already was. The cuffs had not cooled since I left the church.

I needed a place to sit and think, so I made my way toward a decent-looking tavern at the opposite end of the square. As I walked there, a man grabbed me by the shoulder, spun me around, and jovially asked if I was excited for the spectacle on Sunday.

"Yes! It's a fine sport, isn't it?" I shrieked, spit flying from my mouth.

The man let me go and turned away after giving me a stern look. I didn't care. He'd been lucky I hadn't caved his face in like I'd done Mario's. If there'd not been so many witnesses, I might have.

I wandered into the inn just off the square and entered the adjacent tavern. There, I caught one of the serving women and pulled her aside, asking her if there really was to be an auto de fe on Sunday.

"What did you think the scaffolding was for? I assumed that's why you're here. Sorry. There's no vacancy." She bustled away before I could reply.

I went back outside, having lost whatever remained of my appetite for the Toledo of my childhood.

*Today is Friday, so that means I have all night tonight and all day tomorrow to get as far away from this city as possible*, I thought, wishing for nothing more than to avoid being anywhere near another auto.

I'd meant to ask that dumpy priest if he had any inkling of where Josefa might be now, but when he'd mentioned the impending reconciliation, I'd forgotten myself in my fury. Yet I had hoped I might give it another go in a day or two, before I was gone for good.

Just then, I had a different thought—a stupid yet brilliant thought I took with me back into the inn, where I waited for the same serving woman to bustle past me once more. I tapped her on the shoulder.

She whipped around and snapped, "If you aren't going to order, don't bother me again!"

"I'm sorry. I just had one more question. What are the names of the city's inquisitors?"

"I forget the name of the older one. But the younger one I know. Everyone knows Don Ignacio."

I nearly gasped in horror at the revelation that my hunch had been right, but I stifled myself and asked, "Why does everyone know him?"

"He is a bulwark of the Church. He has made himself a reputation for his fervent belief and unwavering piety," she exclaimed in a half-frightened tone, as if she now regretted saying Ignacio was known to everyone.

Thanking the woman, I ordered a wine both as a courtesy to her and so that I might think in peace. Then I let her go her way in what I hoped was a reassuring manner. I needed no more information from her; I'd made my choice.

Sitting down at a table, I sipped my wine and took some deep breaths to calm myself. My cuffs had not cooled, and try as I might, I couldn't make them. I put my elbows on the table and kept my wrists off any surface, placing one hand over my mouth and gripping my forearm with the other.

My tears started to flow once more, cooler now, sliding gently down my cheeks and over my hand. I tried to hide them, but more came every time I wiped away the current ones, like a swarm of bees that swells in number whenever one of their fellows is smashed. I had to mourn my impending loss, for if I were to go through with the thing I planned to do, I'd forever eliminate any opportunity to find whatever extended family I might have in other cities, as well as any possibility of locating my mother.

Of course, I could still change my mind. I could go back and apologize to the priest and ask him the questions I'd planned to put to him earlier. I could spend the day of the auto de fe outside the city walls, fishing the partially dried-up Tajo or roaming the farms and villages, and return after the proceedings had concluded. But to what end? To pass a pile of burnt bones whose owners I might've spared? After I pondered the prospect, I decided I could live without whatever family I might find—I'd always been without them—but I could not pass up a chance to prevent dozens more children from being fitted for my shoes.

"You want another wine, love? Or something stronger?" the serving woman asked.

I shook my head. Stronger would do me no good. At least I liked the taste of the wine.

"Are you alright?" she added.

I wiped my eyes with my sleeve. My cuffs had cooled, and my tears had slowed, but I assuredly looked a mess.

"I'm fine. Just . . . man troubles." I sniffled.

Pursing her lips, she said, "I understand." She then patted my shoulder and rushed off.

Not long after, I paid my bill and left, intending to make the most of the short time I had before the auto. I abandoned my inn that night and made my way quietly outside the city, picking out a path north until I came to an inn by the side of the road in a small village well beyond the walls of Toledo. Waiting until morning to purchase a room under the name Teresa Rivera, I then spent the day preparing my approach.

I would leave Pepito at the village inn stable and my things in my room and walk back to town on my own two feet. I paid for a week at the inn and added a good bit extra to avoid being disturbed for any reason. I also ate all the *av'vysh* tablets so no one would find them if they broke into my room. Fearing it might be foolish but having no other option, I left my remaining money and my ring in the room, hiding them behind a loose brick in the wall.

I snuck off before dawn on Sunday, slipping out a window so as not to arouse suspicion and wrapping a dark-brown cloak I had bought in Toledo over my scarlet dress, which I deemed a most appropriate color for what I had planned. Heading straight for the vega at the bottom of the hill upon which the city stood, I did not enter Toledo nor attend the ceremony in Zocodover. I was well aware what awaited me there, and I wanted none of it.

I was also certain that if Ignacio was to be involved with this auto, there'd be a burning, even if there was no cause for one. Plenty of autos were nonfatal, after all, but Ignacio was not the kind of man for a nonfatal auto de fe. I knew him well enough to be sure that if he hadn't had any capital victims, he would've forced his prisoners to confess to capital crimes just to cook up an excuse to kindle the sacred fires. I would also not have put it past him to prevent his victims from yielding to their final exhortations so he could avoid being compelled to strangle them before burning them.

Sure enough, when I made it to the quemadero, the very same burning place Ignacio had dragged me to as a child, I found a row of eight long stakes driven into the scaffolding that had been constructed for this illustrious occasion. I bowed my head and thought of the terror those poor souls must be feeling as their final hours on Earth were paraded before them in an endless exhibition of ceremonial agony.

I waited half the day, perched on a hill far from the quemadero so as not to be seen until necessary. The sun soared all the way across the sky and tracked to the west before I got the first hints we might be receiving the procession soon. A few individuals who'd left the ceremony early to get a better view began to filter into the areas of the vega designated for spectators. I might not attract too much attention if I made my way down to join them. Though I didn't much want to watch the procession as it migrated to the quemadero, I situated myself there anyhow, along with the unsavory characters who wished for a front row seat.

Even unto the heat death of the universe, I'll never understand the type of person who'd arrive early to attain an ideal vantage point to watch his fellow man roasted alive or garroted and burned to ash before his very eyes. I felt a scorching revulsion for the crowd around me, but my disgust mixed with a sense of smug self-satisfaction that, today at least, they were going to get a very different show than they'd bargained for.

I thought a great deal on my mother and father as I stood amongst this ever-growing vile swarm. I was thankful to know for certain they'd not been marched out here to face their doom for daring to let the name of Allah pass their lips after they'd been baptismally raped during the forced conversions.

Yet I also wondered if they hadn't wished to be martyrs. If that had been the fate they'd desired, they would not have had a difficult time getting it from these people. Perhaps they'd been falsely accused and all evidence fabricated. Perhaps they'd gotten on the wrong side of the wrong person. I was never to know now.

The crowd grew to a few hundred people, and their collective exaltations roused me from my thoughts. I looked on as the procession made its ghastly approach to this consecrated ground. My eye found Ignacio as he marched at the front of the line alongside the first victim's escorts. The good friar pled with that defeated man to save his soul from the fires of the world to come, even if he could not save his body from the fires of this world—the flames to which, out of pure concern for his victim's eternal soul, Ignacio himself so quickly ushered him.

The poor man appeared deaf to these entreaties, as terror and fatigue had rendered him insensible. Nevertheless, Ignacio shamelessly led his pack of hounds in their most crucial of duties, even while the guards wrestled the condemned to his feet when he stumbled and dragged him the final paces to the stake.

Ignacio had not changed one dot. As little as I knew of the auto procedure back then, I was still aware of just how unusual it was for an inquisitor himself to walk to the burning place next to his own victims. Inquisitors liked to stay away from the quemadero to make themselves appear blameless, preferring to relax their victims to the state, who carried out the actual executions at their behest. Ignacio, as he had ten years prior, cared less about the optics and more about being close enough to feel the heat of the flames.

The mere sight of him forced from the depths of my soul such a caustic hatred it brought tears to my eyes. My heart was molten lead, my lungs a blast furnace, my innards ready to vomit liquid fire. I could hardly force my trembling feet to remain in their spot rather than rush to the scaffolding to take blessed vengeance. My feet and I would have to hold on a little while longer, until the opportune moment.

The procession came to the edge of the platform, and a city official took his place to read the sentences once more. I made my way toward the scaffolding, and when I got close enough for the guards surrounding it to see me, I staggered and swayed as if edging toward a swoon. Reeling like a drunk all the way up to the stage, I made a show of fanning myself with my hand and saying I might faint.

One of the guards in front of the platform took the bait and reached out his hand. I almost felt sorry for what I was about to do, since he was trying to be kind to me—almost sorry, but not quite. When I took his hand with my right, I flung my left toward his head with the speed of a striking viper. Reaching under his helmet, I grasped a handful of his hair and yanked his head down toward the ground before he had time to realize what occurred. Then I jumped onto his shoulders and used his back as a springboard to vault myself onto the stage. I leapt to my feet and threw my brown cloak away to reveal my scarlet dress, rushing to make good use of the few seconds I had before the stunned guards got to me.

"Stop talking!" I shouted, pointing at the official, who was so shocked at my behavior he obeyed at once. "I have something I wish to say to the condemned." I paused to steady my voice. "Wretches, look upon your salvation, for today, I commute your sentence."

With that, I ran to the middle of the platform, where I smashed a jar of oil over my head and another at my feet. A third I laid aside in case I needed it to keep the flames going. Everyone shouted at me to get down. Ignoring them, I whipped around, my dress and braids flying. Before they could approach, I sparked my cuff and lit the oil at my feet.

The flames erupted before my eyes and ran up my body like a swarm of ants. I'd anointed myself in oil even before my arrival, so the flames were bright and blue and voracious. They rose higher than my head in a matter of seconds, pushing the men back off the platform. The crowd gasped as I was engulfed. Feeling a terrible heat, I cried out in fear that I'd made a fatal mistake. I looked down at my feet to ensure they were not burning. My leather shoes were shriveling, but my skin merely absorbed the heat of the flames as a sheet of metal might.

I grew hideously hot in a matter of seconds. Yet I suffered no injury and felt no pain. The nanos did their job without needing my input. I watched as the blaze blossomed all over my skin, trying to consume my limbs only to realize it was to be starved of flesh. I stretched out my right hand and observed the flames swirling in tendrils around my fingers. Each cord of fire wrapped my hand in a friendly embrace.

I raised my arms as if in crucifixion, hoping the realization I was incombustible would be enough to induce the crowd to panic, but I was wrong. The fools all stood there staring at me, mouths agape like a gaggle of madhouse patients. Maybe they believed it to be an illusion, that I was not really on fire but in a ring of flames or behind them.

I twirled around and danced a step or two to demonstrate the fire moved with me. Still, no one budged. Escalating, I ran at the official frozen in his place on the scaffold and frightened him so badly he threw his book at me and leapt right off the stage. I laughed aloud. It appeared, for some reason, he found the idea of being set ablaze unappealing.

I stepped on something and looked down to find the book he'd launched at my head had bounced off me and fallen at my feet. I didn't know what was in it. Probably just a list of names and crimes and a reminder that the Church had pled with the "state" for "mercy." Giving not one fig, I stood on it and let it fry. Any book worth burning people over is worth burning in my book.

Then, it hit me like a bolt of lightning: I was really doing it, really immolating myself in front of all these people. Dear God! How in hell was I going to get out of here if the crowd refused to panic? I'd anticipated they'd all flee back toward the city gates, leaving the condemned free to bolt wherever they chose and myself to leap off the cliff into the river. But none of us would ever escape if this multitude kept standing around and gawking. I had to make more of a show of myself.

Walking to each stake in turn, I lit the base kindling with my own flaming hand until I had a real hoguera raging on the scaffolding. This done, I returned to the center, pressed my back against a burning stake, and slid down it. Nestling cross-legged amid the kindling, I rested my arms directly on the blazing logs as if relaxing upon a throne of fire with a crown of living flame adorning my head.

As I sat on my throne, the roar of the flames engulfed my ears, and a gleaming orange wall blinded my eyes to the faces before me. I couldn't help but let my mind wander to poor María González. Hers had not been a seat of living flame that danced beneath her, filling her nostrils with a burnt offering of arboreal incense, but a cage of agony and death. I wondered if any thoughts had flashed through her mind as she'd screamed. Had her eyes been able to perceive this blazing curtain before they melted away?

Perhaps she'd never had a chance to see the orange curtain. After all, she'd been afraid and pleading, not defiant, so our mutual enemies might've throttled her and spared her the flames. I hadn't seen who had received the mercy of the garrote and who had not.

Of course, if María had been shown that mercy, it would mean, in the end, she'd prostrated herself before the very men who spilled her blood. If she'd refused to humiliate herself, she'd have been burnt alive. I didn't know which idea was worse.

I tried to think of other things while the stakes continued to burn. It took so long for the thick, hard wood to reduce I grew almost bored, the novelty of being on fire and unburnt wearing off once I was certain that even this would not induce the chaos crucial to my success. Even now, the crowd still watched, mesmerized as everything around me burned to cinders while not a hair on my head suffered a singe.

I was going to have to do much more than put on a show to get this throng to panic. Damn them all! The condemned would have no chance to make a run for it if this herd refused to stampede. Getting to my feet, I took the last jar of oil from the edge of the platform, stuffed it in my pocket, and sauntered off the smoldering scaffold.

Striding up to Ignacio and his Dominicans, I got my first detailed glimpse of the man I'd loathed for the last decade. He was older now, and the lines of age were beginning to show on his countenance. But these lines were all he had attained from advancing in years, for it was clear he'd gained no more wisdom than he'd had when I first knew him. Indeed, if anything, age had made him harder, and a quick ascension within the ranks of the Inquisition had allowed him to gorge his lust for misery and humiliation with little real limit.

I moved in closer, and Ignacio and the two forwardmost Dominicans backed away not more than a pace, apparently trying to shrink from me as much as possible without looking like the cowards they were. When I got within a few centimeters of them, I struck out like a cobra, seizing Ignacio's right hand with my left and compelling him to grasp my wrist, which I'd heated to blazing. I wished him to feel what it was like to be immobilized and forced to burn.

At first, his pride got the better of him, and he stood still, putting on a brave face. After a few seconds, he cried out and tried to pull away from my scalding grasp. I let him feel the strength of my will as well as my body, obliging him to prove himself at once a weakling and a coward. He was as powerless to free himself from the grip of a tiny woman as he was unable to bear the pain he inflicted on others.

I should have killed him then and there. All I had to do was raise a hand to his face, will his head to be rent from its perch on his accursed neck, and it would have been so. Yet, as I stood upon the brink of falling to that temptation, Ignacio finally spoke.

"Stop! Please, let me go!" he screamed, still struggling to tear himself from my grasp.

At this, I looked into his eyes. In their terror and agony, I caught my first and only glimpse of the little boy who'd sat on the steps of Father Manuel's church and read to the younger children, the frightened child who'd wished for a miracle that would allow his father to trade places with his mother in the grave.

I then imagined a different Ignacio, one whose father hadn't terrified and humiliated him before packing him off to be inducted into the Orders of Hate. What might that Ignacio have looked like? What might have become of his city and his country and his planet if there weren't ten thousand more like him in every kingdom the world over? There, struggling with my foe in the dirt, I envisioned what our sad little planet might have been if humans didn't ruin one another in childhood, and my fury melted into grief for that lost world.

Despite myself, I doubted Ignacio had been wholly ruined, and I made the greatest blunder of my life: I stayed my hand. I released him and allowed him to back away. He slid behind his guard, cradling his burned fingers.

As soon as Ignacio got clear of me, a sword came crashing down on my neck. It was a true stroke; the gleaming Toledo steel would have severed my head if I'd been made entirely of meat. Seeing as I was not, the blade bounced off as if I'd been wearing a chainmail coif.

I glanced around and noted that many soldiers had arquebuses and crossbows trained on me. I remained unsure what would happen if they decided to shoot. Yet none of them did. The soldiers and the crowd still stood rooted to their places, stunned and perhaps wondering what good a bullet might do against one as impenetrable and incombustible as I. If I was to get away from here, I needed to take advantage of this amazed and fearful irresolution before it wore off.

"Am I correct in assuming your hapless victims are of the heretical variety?" I asked Ignacio, maintaining a steady tone whilst I moved once again toward him and his men.

"Why would you assume anything else?" Ignacio hissed through his gritted teeth.

"Let me tell you something, then." I leaned forward so I could make eye contact with him over the broad shoulder of one of his cronies. "I am the heretic of heretics. The apostate of apostates. And I claim all their crimes and accept their sentences upon myself. As you can see, I've already suffered the penalty." I pointed back to the smoking stakes.

Ignacio uttered an inane snarl of fury but made no comment.

I looked to the closest sanbenito-clad victim. "Are you a heretic?"

The man shook his head without speaking or making eye contact.

I raised an eyebrow. "I need you to answer."

"No!" he said.

"Then why don't you leave here and not come back?" I replied, hoping that if this crowd was all that scared of me, I might start giving orders.

The man to whom I gave them stayed put, seeming almost not to have heard me.

Ignacio burst into speech. "He must be burned. His immortal soul—"

"I don't care if he's Satan's spawn. I forbid you to touch him or anyone else," I snapped. Turning to the prisoner, I added, "What are you waiting for? Go!"

The man needed no more command than that and dashed off like a doe freshly escaped from the jaws of a lion, the brown dust stains on his sanbenito swaying from side to side as he sprinted. The throng stayed so focused on me no one so much as lifted a finger to stop him.

I forced myself to maintain a collected demeanor, but I could see the crowd's state of frozen shock was wearing off. The guards and spectators still had some trepidation as to what might happen to them if they touched me, but something had snapped when I'd commanded the first of the human sacrifices to flee.

"Do you want to try burning me again?" I asked Ignacio, thinking of no better way to stall for time than to taunt him, but I got no answer.

Looking around, I realized with a jolt of terror that he was nowhere to be seen. That could only mean one thing: he'd gotten himself out of harm's way to let his men deal with me. I didn't want to shoot them. Doing so might risk setting off a full-blown firefight, but I didn't know what else to do. One of them struck out at me, not with a weapon but with a pair of irons.

Stifling a cry, I leapt back and prepared to fire IDOS. If I killed one of them, it could shock the others into submission once more, but it was equally likely to set them all upon me at once. I looked wildly around, forgetting not to show fear, but the guards on all sides appeared intent on boxing me in. The spell was broken at last.

In that instant, however, I recalled nobody could catch me if nobody could touch me. I ripped my last jar of oil from the pocket of my dress and smashed it over my head. Sparking my cuff, I was aflame once more.

Squishing my molten boots, I hurled myself toward the closest of the Dominicans and grabbed the man in a lover's embrace, pressing my body to him and wrapping my arms around his neck before he could escape. He started screaming in agony and wrestling against my grasp with all his might. The smell of his burning skin sickened me, and he lifted me off my feet in his efforts to fling me away, but I had to hold on.

I kept the shrieking Dominican in a death grip until the crack of an arquebus resonated behind me. One of the guards fired at me at the same time a donkey next to him reared in fright and bumped him. He missed me and hit a bystander in the leg.

That single stray bullet was the catalyst the crowd needed: a corporeal threat and not a supernatural one. The people around me screamed and bolted in all directions, and their panic spread with pandemic speed to the rest of the crowd. As I had been trying to induce it to from the outset, the situation descended into chaos.

I let go of the Dominican and left him to sink to the ground, where he lay sobbing and writhing in the dirt. Standing over that poor man, I felt wretched as a slug as I listened to his pathetic howling, yet I had no time for guilt now. He was burned, but he'd live. Let him get a taste of the medicine he'd been doling out.

Everyone who'd been anywhere near me when I'd burned him got the message. No one touched me or made to approach me. I took that opportunity and ran toward the river, flaming through the fields and wailing like a phantom. I swung my arms madly at anyone who came near me and sent drops of burning oil flying all around. The civilians fled back toward the city, screeching and colliding with one another as they parted like the waters of the Red Sea to avoid bumping into me.

Arquebus fire echoed through the vega, and one or two balls whizzed past my ears. The guards would have a difficult time firing at me without hitting any more bystanders, but I feared that in their zeal to capture or kill me, they would stop caring about who got caught in the crossfire.

I turned back for one second to see if the condemned had fled as well, and I caught no flash of sanbenito among all the howling and sprinting audience. I didn't know whether to take that as a good or bad sign. Regardless of the dearth of sanbenitos, I found a terrible sight: the terrified crowd had trampled the Dominican I'd burned. I stifled a gasp and squeezed my jaw shut, reminding myself to focus on flight if I didn't wish to join him in death.

When I turned my face away from the lifeless cleric, I discovered several of the guards had swung around the panicked crowd to block my path to the river, and these men now hurled themselves toward me. By now, my oil had fizzled out, leaving me no more untouchable than anyone else.

The soldiers were still far enough away that I managed to escape by doubling back and heading toward the walls, mixing in with the crowd where it bottlenecked at the gate. I slipped into the mob easily enough, for the people along the edges recognized me and scrambled to get away, opening an avenue for me to claw my way deeper into the multitude. The pack of humanity pressed in on all sides, crushing into one another so tight they covered me with their bodies, hiding my scarlet dress and camouflaging me among them.

Just behind me, the guards reached the throng and tried to push into it, screaming for people to get out of their way. This only caused everyone to squeeze in tighter, shriek louder, and shove harder to get through the gate. Within seconds, the tide of bodies swelled around me and swept me back inside the walls with it.

It took me a long while to liberate myself from the mob, and by the time I did, they'd pulled me halfway up the hill and deep into Toledo. Damn me! How could I have let myself get dragged back inside the city? Disoriented, I had no idea where I was or how far I'd have to run to get to the nearest gate; I knew only to get out of the open.

Dashing through the narrow streets, I ducked into the first alley I saw. This alley turned out to be another narrow street, for it had no rear and led straight to the opposite side of the two long rows of shops and homes it sat between. I ran to the end of the row, crossed, and slipped into a true alley, frantically looking for a place to hide and hoping beyond hope there might be some clothes I could change into on a line somewhere, anywhere.

I was on the verge of real panic now, and my alarm made it difficult to think straight. I had to rest a minute, just to get my bearings and ponder what to do. I didn't see anyone around. All the guards and civilians still stampeded through the main streets in absolute disarray, but the alley itself was empty, so I crept along toward the back to take a reprieve.

My first mistake was failing to turn around and face the outside of the alley once I'd gotten to the back of it. My second was placing my hands on my knees and crouching to get a breath, forgetting all the world around me. As soon as I'd begun to calm myself, a huge, hot hand clapped over my mouth, and another grabbed my right wrist.

There was a sharp intake of breath, and after it, a deep male voice shouted, "I'v—"

He didn't get to finish the first word. I raised my left wrist to the side of his head and fired, drenching my back and hair in his blood as his head shattered to pieces before his hands let loose their grip and his body slumped to the ground.

"No. No. No," I whispered. Before I'd set out on this mission, I'd limited myself to a body count of zero, but I'd killed this one reflexively, my hand doing it without my brain's input.

I glanced up to find a second guard raising a crossbow. Reluctant as I was to do it, I had no choice. I extended my arm and fired once more, hitting my enemy in the side as he aimed his weapon. Other than a shocked gasp, he made no sound. Instead, he leapt around and ran, spilling intestine and spraying blood in every direction.

I was amazed he could stand in that condition, for he had a hole the size of a grown man's head underneath his ribcage, and he was trailing his own innards as he fled. His adrenaline-fueled strength only lasted so long; he made it halfway out of the alley before he collapsed to the ground and lay still.

I stood with my hands over my mouth and nose, shaking my head and repeating the words "oh no" under my breath. Nothing the training chamber had thrown at me had prepared me for this horrid display of slimy blood and torn guts and stinking shit all over the ground.

I had to get out of here! Leaping over the body, I fled blindly from the alley and into a narrow, overshadowed street on the next block, where I hid behind a stack of old crates.

There, I wiped my gory hands on my torn, sooty, bloodstained skirts and thought I'd never be able to get so much as five paces away from here in such a distinct and distinctly ruined dress. I had to get out of these clothes and into a masculine costume before someone else discovered me. More importantly, I still had to get out of the open.

I pushed on the first door I could reach. No good. Going down the line of doors, I tried each one until I came to the second or third to last. As I laid my palm on the wood, a voice materialized somewhere behind me.

"Come with me," it said in the small tone of a child.

I'd already stretched out my arm to fire, but finding no one facing me, I looked down to see a boy of ten or eleven staring up at me.

"Come." He took my hand.

I did not know what else to do. The city swarmed with soldiers, so I squeezed the boy's hand and let him guide me through whatever unfamiliar barrio I'd stumbled into. He led me two blocks down the narrow street and steered me into an alley so fast I barely had time to wonder who he was or what he wanted. He took me to the back of this alley, where we waited, hidden behind some clotheslines covered—to my terrible luck—in linens and not pants, until a company on horseback passed by.

A minute or two later, the boy grabbed my hand and led me back out onto the street, sneaking me into another alley behind two long rows of town houses. He led me through to the other side of this passage. Then we crossed the street and passed into yet another similar alley on the other side. I was now completely disoriented, but the boy knew his way around.

We were sure to be caught. What good was jumping from alley to alley if we had nowhere to go? Even as this thought occurred to me, the boy opened a door inside the alleyway we currently occupied and beckoned for me to pass through.

I slid into the building and turned to find a surprised old man standing in the middle of a room full of tables and tools, which I recognized as the workspace of a cobbler's shop once my eyes adjusted to the dimness. He shielded a cowering boy of no more than three or four. I put my bloodstained finger to my lips to beg for silence, sure the look of me was enough to frighten boys much older than this one.

The elder child, who'd never shown the slightest hint of fear, shoved his way in behind me and shut the door, chasing the last of the sunlight from the shuttered room.

"Look what I found!" he called proudly and strode around me.

"You're her, aren't you? The one who ruined the execution?" the old man asked.

"Yucé!" a female voice cried before I finished wondering how on earth word of my exploits had spread so fast.

A ruffled woman of perhaps thirty flew into the room and fell to her knees in front of the older boy, whose name was apparently Yucé. She grasped the child by the shoulders, squeezing him to her breast and scolding him for following her to the auto when she'd forbidden him from leaving the house today. Clearly, she'd borne witness to my performance. They likely both had.

When her eyes fell on me, I begged, "Please don't turn me in. I only wanted to help."

The old man scoffed. "Turn you in? Absolutely not. My son was to be sent to the flames this day, and because of you, we have him hidden away upstairs."

My lip quivered, and I put my hand over my mouth to stifle my relief.

"Angel of the Almighty," the woman said, letting go of her son and rising to stand beside the old man, whom I now assumed was her father-in-law. "What do you need?"

"Clothes. I need men's clothes and a safe place to hide until it gets dark."

I had some trepidation about trusting these strangers, but it was not like I had a choice. The woman motioned for me to follow, leading me out of the rear workspace, through the rest of the family's darkened shop, and up a narrow, steep staircase in the back.

"Saúl? We're coming up," she called when we neared the top.

Once we finished the ascent, we entered one large, dimly lit room with a few chairs, a table on the left, and a row of three beds on the right with a partition separating one bed from the other two. Behind one of these beds stood a shirtless man, sobbing and shredding his devil-and-flame-painted sanbenito with a kitchen knife. His mouth fell open at the sight of me.

"Our guest needs to borrow the other set of your father's clothes," the woman said.

Saúl was frozen, his eyes wide as saucers, his feet rooted to the spot they'd been planted before I'd arrived. He was not the man I'd sent running from the procession, but I could tell from the black-and-red cloth in his hands that he'd been a part of it.

The woman who appeared to be Saúl's wife walked over to him and took his arm.

"You need to go into the attic. As soon as we can, we'll be getting you out of the city—and you, as well, if you need our help," she added, looking toward me.

When I told her emphatically that I did indeed need their help, the woman nodded, and such intense relief washed over me I feared I might melt into a puddle on the floor. She put a shirt into her husband's hand, shooed him up a wooden ladder in the back of the room, and threw the pieces of his sanbenito into the empty fireplace.

She then got me a basin to wash the blood from my hair, shoulders, and hands, and she gave me a shirt and a pair of pantaloons from among her father-in-law's things. They were a bit big for me, but I tightened my belt and made do.

"Your husband doesn't have his own things?" I asked, for he was shorter than his father, closer to my height.

The woman shook her head. "Saúl has been in prison for three years. They took everything we owned after they arrested him. If this weren't his father's house, they'd have seized it too. And now that we've spent my father-in-law's savings to feed the children, we haven't a penny left."

I did not know how to respond to this, so I told her she mustn't try to burn my dress and assured her I'd take it with me so she wouldn't be caught with it. But she replied that she would hide it where it'd never be found, for being caught with it during our impending escape would be much worse. She also reminded me she already knew burning it wouldn't work. I'd forgotten she'd seen me interrupt the ceremony.

"Why did you go to the auto?" I blurted. "Why would you want to see that?"

"I didn't want to see it. But the last time I laid eyes on Saúl before this day was the morning he left to get supplies for the shop. The ecclesiastical guard dragged him away, and he never returned from shopping. I went to the auto because I thought he might be in it, and when they read his sentence, I followed them to the quemadero because I wished my husband to know there was at least one person in that crowd on his side. Should I have let him die alone because I couldn't bear to watch it?"

At this, I burst into tears of exhaustion and rage and pure sorrow for this woman and all her family had suffered. She walked to one of the beds and moved a few pillows to make a place for me to sit down, and I plopped onto the straw mattress with the pillows behind me. She stood at the foot of the bed, letting me weep a while.

Once I started to calm, the woman said, "We need to get you to the hiding place until the fervor dies down."

When she turned away from me, I cried, "Wait, I don't even know your name."

"María," she replied as she wrapped the tattered remains of my dress in a brown sack.

I must have inadvertently cast her a look of disbelief.

She smiled, cocked her head, and said, "Míriam. What about you?"

"Call me Aixa." It felt wrong not to trust her with my given name when she'd trusted me with hers, but if Saúl was recaptured, I didn't need the name Micaela passing his lips.

Míriam led me to the wooden ladder at the rear of the room. In the attic, there was a desk with an empty coin box on top, some crates with stored supplies like leathers and soles, and a chair I guessed Saúl's father probably sat in when he tired of his grandsons' roughhousing.

At the far end of the attic, a false wall opened into a tiny secret chamber, empty except for a couple of benches against the interior walls. The entry was invisible unless open. These people had obviously known the day they'd need such a room would come; it already had come at least once. Míriam motioned for me to enter this hidden chamber. Without a word, I took my seat on the bench opposite Saúl, biting my lip as she closed the door.

## Chapter Seventeen

# FLIGHT OF THE WITCH

When Míriam shut us in, cutting off the waning daylight from outside, Saúl and I barely dared to breathe, much less speak. Even my heart pumping away behind my sternum felt loud enough to be detected from outside the wood-paneled trick wall. Hours passed in silence. Poor Saúl was so worn out he slumped into the corner and fell asleep.

In this absolute darkness, it would've been impossible to ascertain the passage of time except for the ringing of the church bells in the distance, a sound that became more distinct as the commotion from the auto died down. I might not have been able to pick up the ringing before my implantation, for it was far away and blocked by both wooden and brick walls, but now I could hear it over Saúl's muted snoring. Though I could only expect it on the canonical hours, I was thankful I had some measure of the time, for each hour that ticked by was another hour we'd evaded detection.

So far, we'd been left in peace, though the Inquisition had records of Saúl's name and sentence, and it would not take them long to discover he was missing. They likely already had, but it seemed they were too busy with the other escapees, for the evening wore on, and no one came knocking.

Sitting there in the dark, with the hours passing at a glacial pace and my heart freezing every time I imagined I heard the clip-clop of horses' hooves, I found it impossible to stop myself from thinking about all the opportunities for capture that stood between myself and freedom. No doubt, I'd be wanted for a double homicide now. The bodies of those two men in the alley would not have lain undiscovered for long. What if the guards had found my room at the inn and were rooting through my possessions? What might they be doing to Pepito?

Of course, such thoughts were ridiculous. The inn was leagues away, and I'd bought my stay under a false name and left outfitted in a dark cloak that covered the scarlet dress. Pepito was safe in the stables, and the worst he could expect were I never to return was being sold off to a different owner. My inn would never be found; all the possibilities for arrest lay between this attic door and the city wall.

In all this empty time, I couldn't avoid thinking of the soldiers I'd slain earlier. I put my face in my hands and wept as I recalled leaping over their shredded carcasses in the alley. That was three dead men in my wake now, if I counted the one I had injured and the crowd had stomped to death, which I did, for it really was my fault. I'd not intended to kill him, only to hurt him enough to trigger a panic. The knowledge I'd taken life this day made me feel dirty, foul, contaminated, and every other synonym for "unclean" I could conjure.

I tried to disperse this feeling by remembering that the life of the innocent man across from me took precedence over the lives of the men kindling the flames around his stake. If I hadn't done as I did, Saúl would now be ashes, Míriam a widow, and her sons orphans. Worst of all, that brave boy who'd saved my hide would've watched his father burned alive.

Even that proved cold comfort. The life of the soldier burning innocents and pointing his weapon in my face was one thing, but the lives of his family and his dependents were quite another. I wondered if the guards' wives would get on without their husbands and how many years their little ones would pass not understanding why Papá never came home this night.

I did not regret having saved Saúl. Yet I wondered, as I sat there listening to his subdued snoring, what I might have done differently in that alleyway for the sake of the widows and orphans I'd made today.

Perhaps the thing I really mourned was the loss of my innocence. Up until this fateful afternoon, I'd never taken a life. Now, I saw the stain of the blood on my hands almost as if they were still slick and shining with it. Regardless of the guilty status of that blood, regardless of its owner's intent to do me harm, I felt a terrible sense of shame for having shed it.

To comfort myself, I ran my fingers through my hair, which hung loose around my shoulders because the ribbons that once held my braids had disintegrated in the fire. Twirling my locks, I thought I must be gaining some conscious control over my nanos. The bottom thirty or so centimeters of my hair had burned off, but the rest of it remained intact. It fell only to my shoulders now, not to my waist, meaning the bots must have understood me when I'd commanded them to protect it during that first IDOS training session. The burning away of my old hair from these fresh-formed threads of steel meant the last of my fully biological material was now gone.

I supposed I understood how the ship of Theseus must have felt when the last of its original planks was replaced. But no matter how many planks it lost and regained, the ship still belonged to Theseus—or it would've if he'd lived to see all its boards supplanted. As I ran my fingers through my unburned hair, I thought my body must now be more my own than it ever had been. Who besides me could command their own hair and flesh?

A thunderous snore from Saúl refocused my thoughts. He still slept like the dead; this was probably the most peace he'd gotten in three years. Just as I wondered if his wife might return to pass some of the night with him, the door opened, and the flame of a candle lit up the dark room. Saúl awoke, leapt up with a gasp, and slammed his face against the opposite wall as he turned to flee. Míriam coaxed him down beside her on the bench and wrapped her arm around his shoulder.

"It's alright," she told him, reaching across the aisle to hand me the candle.

"What's happening?" I said.

"Nothing. It's after midnight. Things have calmed down, so I deemed it a good time to let you both out to stretch your legs and eat something."

She brought us out into the attic, where she'd laid a basket of bread and cheese on a blanket on the floor. Saúl did not act all that interested in it, but the sight of it reminded me just how starving I was. I'd not eaten since this morning, and I guessed the only reason my nanos were not already harrying me for sustenance was that I'd been in a state of near-constant terror since I'd fled the quemadero. I ran to the blanket and shoved my hand in the basket, devouring everything in sight. It was all I could do to remember to leave some for Saúl.

"Have you got any meat?" I asked, before remembering it was impolite to make such demands. "I'm sorry. Please don't think me greedy. I have a condition that makes me starve much easier than a normal person."

"How awful," Míriam said.

"It has its perks," I replied, thinking of the number of times I would have been dead today if not for the nanos.

"Don't think yourself greedy. After today, you're welcome to whatever you like. We haven't any beef or mutton, but do you eat salted pork?"

"Of course," I answered between bites.

"Good. Since Saúl was arrested, I've been keeping a supply of it around in case anyone came inquiring."

"Why would anyone inquire about that?" I asked.

Míriam raised her eyebrows.

"Right," I said. "Sorry."

Míriam told me to think nothing of it and went to get the pork. When she returned, she apologized and said she feared it might be spoiled. I told her spoiled food would not hurt me—only no food. It was not spoiled, however, at least not badly, and it tasted like it had been cut from a fatted piglet after an entire day of nothing to eat.

As I gorged myself, Saúl barely touched anything. Míriam coaxed him to eat some bread and drink a sip of wine, but other than that, he refused. She rose and left the room again, and still he did not speak. He didn't do anything more than pick pieces of bread off one of the loaves and drop them on the blanket. Not a word had passed his lips the entire time I'd known him—not to me or his sons or even his own wife.

"What's the matter with you? Why won't you talk? Did they cut out your tongue or something?" I blurted.

I cringed as soon as those words escaped my lips. I shouldn't have even conceived of them, much less said them aloud, but once again, my mouth thought faster than my brain. Saúl looked stunned, as if my tactless remark shocked him more than seeing me douse myself in oil and light myself on fire.

I winced. "I'm sorry. Sometimes I say stupid things. I don't mean them."

"I suppose three years of not being allowed to speak has taken its toll," he whispered.

It was the first time I'd heard his voice, but the words were so awful I almost wished he'd stayed silent.

"They did not let you speak?" I asked, incredulous.

"Only on occasion."

"I suppose it's become somewhat of a habit?"

He nodded, silent once more.

"You should speak!" I exclaimed. "You're not in their power anymore. You never shall be again. Don't let them hound you everywhere you go for the rest of your life."

I wondered if I were even speaking of Saúl anymore. Before he replied, Míriam returned with a plate of sweet cakes. He did not set upon them as I had the pork nor devour them like a ravenous wolf. He ate them slowly and deliberately, savoring every bite.

"He loved these before he went to prison," Míriam said.

"I still love them. Thank you." Saúl leaned over and kissed Míriam on the cheek, and she gave him a beaming smile—the sort of smile I'd not yet seen on the face of anyone in this house.

Míriam told us it would be wise to spend the remainder of the night in the attic hideaway, since there was no way to know who might come knocking in the wee hours. I agreed and allowed myself to be shut back behind the trick wall once more. Of course, I had no plans of staying there. Once Saúl had drifted back to sleep, I let myself out and snuck down the ladder.

Míriam sat at the table with her eyes shut, her elbows on the slab, and her hands on the back of her neck. The boys and their grandfather all slept quietly in one of the beds.

"You should get some sleep," I whispered.

She gasped and jumped before realizing it was me. "You should not be down here. What if someone comes?"

"If they come in the middle of the night, they'll be here for one thing, and you know it."

"They can interrogate me all they like; it won't make me betray my husband."

"And if they make you disappear like they did him?"

"I don't know." Míriam laid her temple on her knuckles.

"Go sleep. I'm heavily armed, though I don't look it. If they come, I won't let them in."

"You are a strange woman, Aixa."

"So I've gathered. I've learned to live with it, somehow," I said with a chuckle.

She rose from the table. "Come get me before dawn. I received messages earlier. We're to be taken from the city tomorrow—before anyone comes looking for us."

"We're leaving in broad daylight?" I asked.

"I'm told it will be less suspicious because of the curfew. I don't see how we'll manage it, but I won't question them. My father-in-law has been planning every detail of our escape since the day Saúl was arrested. He was in terror they might return for the rest of us."

"I'm so sorry," I replied, before bidding her goodnight, afraid to respond further lest I say anything as idiotic as I'd said to Saúl.

Descending the stairs to the ground floor, I shuddered at the idea of living in a state of perpetual agony for three years, seeing your life's savings drained, your valuables confiscated, and wondering every time you closed your eyes if this was the night you'd be snatched from your bed because your spouse finally yielded to torture and named you.

I'd seen the dreadful marks on Saúl's arms from the interrogations he'd endured—ugly striped scars from biting cords and deep, unnatural dents from hastily set broken bones. I wondered if the last time he had spoken, he'd been signing his own death warrant, but he must have held up when it came to denouncing his family. I pushed these thoughts from my mind. If I dwelt on them, I'd lose myself to fury. Instead, I simply resolved that tonight, if anyone came for any member of this household, I'd slay them on sight and not give one fig about my body count.

I sat on a stool just inside the shop door, listening all night as the sounds of companies passing on the main streets and the shouts of soldiers floated in from a distance. Sometimes, my technologically enhanced hearing could prove a curse. The shouts and the metallic ringing of horseshoes were some blocks away, but they resounded so clearly in my ears that I almost rose from my seat several times during the night.

When dawn approached, I went upstairs to the second floor. I felt uncomfortable going back to the beds with everyone sleeping, but Míriam had told me to wake her. I slipped over to her bed only to find it empty. Lurching around, I scanned the room. How could they have come and dragged her out the window?

I smacked my forehead. Of course, no one had dragged her out the window. I'd have heard that like the clang of a gong, and the rest of her family certainly wouldn't be sleeping undisturbed.

I went up the ladder to the attic and opened the false wall to find Saúl asleep against the far corner of the tiny room and Míriam lying curled on the bench with her head in his lap. Waking her seemed almost a crime when I knew this to be the first night she'd slept next to her husband in three years, but she'd made me promise. I gently knocked on the trick wall and roused her, waking Saúl in the process. He did not attempt to bolt this time.

"Don't you need a light?" Míriam asked.

I hadn't remembered the predawn gloom still enveloped us. The night vision of my new eyes sometimes led me to forget when it was dark.

"I'm fine," I said.

Míriam rose. "Both of you stay here. I'll be back for you."

It must have been an hour before she returned for anything other than to slip us some food. When she opened the door again, morning light streamed in through the threshold, though it was blocked not only by her body but by the body of a strange man.

Míriam inclined her head to the man. "This is Haim. He's going to get us out of here."

I stood from the bench to size him up. He was taller than Saúl, and portly, too, though not so much that I would have called him a glutton. His beard was graying but well-kempt, and he wore a simple brown shirt and tan breeches.

"How are we going to get out?" I demanded.

He looked taken aback at my tone, but he answered curtly that we were all getting out the same way he got in. He led us downstairs, and I noticed on the way that Míriam had also changed into men's clothes. Haim handed us both caps into which we might tuck our braids. Míriam and Saúl gave a tearful but quick farewell to the old man and the two boys. I wondered why they were not coming too, but I had no time to ask, for Haim threw the door open to the back alleyway, checked with someone outside, and motioned for us to follow.

As we made to leave, Saúl froze at the threshold, suddenly shaking from head to toe. Míriam took his hand and tugged, but he refused to budge. Haim stood in the doorway and shook his fists in the air. Saúl still balked, like a horse that couldn't find the courage to cross a ford.

"Come, Saúl, we have to go," Míriam said.

Haim growled for us to hurry up. Saúl still did not move. Guessing what he needed to hear, I slapped him on the shoulder just hard enough to get his attention.

"Brother, if it looks like capture is inevitable, I'll kill you quick. How's that?"

"Yes. Absolutely," he exclaimed.

"Saúl!" Míriam hissed.

"I am sorry, Míriam, but I am not going back to that place. Death is far preferable. I will not fall back into the clutches of that man—"

"You mean Ignacio?" I snapped.

"You know him?" Saúl said.

"We've had the misfortune of crossing paths. I should have killed him yesterday."

"Yes, you should have," Saúl replied. "Why did you not?"

"I thought I could accomplish my goal without spilling blood. I was wrong, and if I ever get another chance at him, I won't make the same mistake," I said.

"Let's go. Now. Damn you all!" Haim spat through gritted teeth.

Míriam nodded to her husband and walked straight out the door. Saúl followed, and I went last, turning to the old man and the boys and giving them a final word of thanks before I stepped beyond the threshold.

I expected us to head out of the alley in the direction of the street, but to my surprise, we found a mule-drawn baker's cart—complete with bread, cakes, and pastries—parked near the town house's rear door. Several men and women stood at the end of the long passage, both to keep a lookout and to block the cart from view. They kept their backs to us and pretended to talk amongst themselves to avoid looking too suspicious.

"In, now. We've already tarried too long," Haim pulled an unseen lever underneath the cart, which popped loose a false floor that slid forward to reveal a hidden compartment underneath all the baked goods. "There's only room for two. Someone will have to walk."

"I'll walk; let the women get inside," Saúl said, sounding unsure but seemingly trying to make up for his earlier moment of failing courage.

I stepped between him and the alley exit. "Absolutely not. They're looking for you—they're looking for me, too," I added before he could state the obvious, "but the difference is that you both have neighbors, friends, enemies, acquaintances, and any number of strangers who know your faces. I haven't set foot in this city in my adult life, and no one has seen me like this." I motioned to my men's outfit. "Of the three of us, I am the least likely to be recognized."

I was also far and away the *most* likely to survive in the probable event of our discovery, and if we were all going to die, I wished to be in a position to fight to the last breath, not hiding in the false bottom of a baker's cart. Of course, I didn't mention that last bit.

Saúl agreed. He and Míriam stepped over the wooden rails along the sides of the cart and slid into the hollowed space under the bread. Haim pushed the floor and all the baked goods back into place to shut them in.

He turned to me. "Before we go, you must know my Christian name is Bartolomé. Call me that, and that only."

When I concurred, he led the mule to the end of the narrow street, and the group that had been standing watch bought some cakes from him for show. Then, we walked the wider road, stopping at each block to ply our wares just as Haim would any other day. A few people asked who I was, and he said he'd given me a one-day trial run to see if I could serve as his assistant.

I tried to do my work in as surly and incompetent a manner as possible, so no one would think twice about his not taking me on. I feared there might be checkpoints along our way, but if there were, Haim deftly avoided them, and we passed through the city as though we had no business other than to feed the hungry customers on our usual route.

We came to a main avenue. There, we quit making planned stops and began walking as though headed to set up at the market for the day. The streets teemed with His Majesty's men, and I pulled my cap down low over my face, but I needn't have bothered. None of Míriam's neighbors had recognized me in this state, and none of the soldiers looked twice at me now. Working our way through the streets, still stopping on the occasions we were hailed, we headed uphill toward a small plaza and a neighborhood closer to the cathedral.

We made our way past the high walls of a grand house I thought must have a lovely garden in its courtyard, for the tops of trees peeked out from above the walls. As we passed the courtyard gate, it burst open, and someone called to us from within the wall.

"Ho! Baker. Bring that cart inside."

"No. If you want to purchase, you'll have to come out here," Haim replied.

"My master demands to see your wares. Will you force him to come out into the street like a common beggar?" the servant bellowed.

Haim lowered his head and made for the gate. My jaw dropped and my eyes widened before I forced my face back into what I hoped was an expression of annoyed indifference.

The grouchy servant ushered us through the entrance and into the empty courtyard. The thick wooden door slammed behind us, blocking us in on all sides. The hair on my arms kept trying to stand on end, and I had trouble keeping my breathing steady. Were we going to be forced to enter some nobleman's house?

I tried to remain calm and keep in mind this was probably just some blue-blooded brat who'd found himself dissatisfied with his servants' baking this morning. I breathed deep as we walked through the courtyard and around a playing fountain until we came to the side of the house farthest from the main entryway, parking next to a large carriage already fitted with two sorrel draft horses. I would have been fascinated with their long manes and coifed tails if not for my dread of their owner.

"You have them?" the man who'd demanded our entry whispered to Haim.

"She's one. The others are in the bottom," Haim said.

"You let her walk? You shouldn't have done that," the other man hissed.

"I know, but what was I to do, leave her? David was only prepared to take Isaac and the boys." Haim leaned into the back of the cart and rummaged for pastries. "And, Carlos, pull the lever only halfway this time."

The other man reached under the cart and made what I assumed was his version of pulling the lever halfway, though it resulted in the floor coming completely unlatched and popping forward rather violently. Haim caught it before it slid all the way off, but not before a few loaves and cakes fell to the ground. Haim shot Carlos an angry look as he bent to gather them.

Haim put the pastries back onto the pile while Míriam and Saúl scrambled out of the cart. Then he put some loaves of bread in a basket and handed it to Carlos before saying, "This is where I leave you all."

Saúl embraced Haim, and Míriam offered him a few words of gratitude. Haim nodded to them without speaking and turned the cart to the gate, where he and Carlos waited until as few people as possible were nearby. When a servant boy sitting in a tall tree with a view over the wall signaled that the streets were as empty as anyone could hope, Carlos showed Haim out quickly so as not to make a display of the fact that I was no longer with him.

While we all waited, a tall, dark-headed, impeccably dressed young man came out.

"You must get in right away. I'm ready to depart, and we mustn't give an opportunity to too many prying eyes," he said with the inflection of a born nobleman.

He pulled a metal bar from under the carriage's seat and prized open another false bottom—this time, a trapdoor leading to a space beneath the floorboards. The entry was small, though the interior was much larger than the one in the mule-drawn baker's cart. I slid in first, and Míriam followed.

"What about the rest of your family?" I asked as she lay down on my right side.

"Haim's friend David is getting them out, and they'll meet us at an undisclosed location. Even I don't know where. I just couldn't leave Saúl to be taken out alone after all he's suffered," she said while her husband lay down to her right and Carlos closed the floor above.

"Quiet! Do floorboards speak?" Carlos hissed.

"They do when they contain a horde of heretics," I replied.

The coachman uttered an unamused huff, but even in our current predicament, Míriam let an almost imperceptible giggle escape her lips.

We were not laughing for long. If the hours spent in the attic hideaway passed sluggishly, the ride in the carriage was an eternity. I could hear the sounds of the streets passing all around as well as the movements of the nobleman whenever he shifted his weight on the leather bench above our heads. I tried to tell where we were by the noises coming from outside, but it was all a blur of horses' feet, cart wheels, braying mules, and muddled voices.

I held my breath, along with Míriam and Saúl, as the men guarding whichever gate we'd stopped at questioned Carlos and the young aristocrat. They demanded their papers. They demanded to know where they were going. Carlos answered these questions without the slightest hint of trepidation in his voice. Still, the guards kept up their inquiries and even went so far as to open the carriage door.

At that, the gentleman roared that they were overstepping their bounds and that he had every right to leave this city any damned time he pleased to visit whatever manor house he damn well pleased. The soldiers closed the door and apologized, though they told him he must understand given the severity of the circumstances. He replied he did understand but his patience was limited. That was that. They ushered us through the gate with a quick "good day" and an implied "good riddance."

When it seemed we had gotten well away from the city, I dared whisper to Saúl, asking as gently as I could if Ignacio had been the one who'd put those marks on his arms.

"Yes," he murmured. "And I was one of the lucky ones. I managed to snatch a few conversations with other prisoners. Evidently, Ignacio is infamous amongst inmates and officials alike because of all his accidents."

I was unaware of what he meant, so Saúl had to explain that, in the tribunal's vernacular, "accident" was a euphemism for death or permanent crippling from torture. I could have struck my head on the ceiling for my foolishness in not killing that sorry excuse for a man. How could I have ever believed Ignacio was not wholly ruined?

Not only had he relaxed dozens that everyone knew of, but he also had an unknown toll of others whose names might never be recorded, whose families might never be notified, whose lives had been erased because Ignacio was incapable of restraining himself. What justification could I offer poor Saúl for having failed to relieve his tormentor of his head when I'd had the opportunity? Unable to concoct anything close to a passable excuse, I lay back and stared at a crack between the floorboards above.

Eventually, the orange light of evening began seeping through this crack. It had all but faded to darkness when the ride, which had become increasingly bumpy as the hours wore on, came to an end. Someone pulled the floor open from the outside, and we exited the carriage to find ourselves in a wild meadow far away from Toledo.

I was startled to see we faced three men wearing dark-brown hooded robes and sitting atop black draft mules. One of them dismounted, lowered his hood, and greeted Míriam as if he knew her. The nobleman came up and stood beside me as I watched Míriam and Saúl whispering to this cloaked man.

"Is it true what they say of you?" the gentleman asked.

"I don't know. What do they say?"

"You do know. It's been little more than twenty-four hours and the whole city is already calling you the Witch of Toledo."

I had to laugh; it wasn't an elegant title, but at least now I had one.

"Why would anyone assume I'm a witch?" I said.

He pursed his lips and raised his eyebrows. "Are you in jest?"

"No. I mean why do we always jump to a negative conclusion? Why didn't anyone who saw me yesterday remember that a prophet was once told, 'When you walk through fire, you will not be burned, and the flames will not scorch you'?"

"I am not sure that's applicable here, but I'm no priest. I don't pretend to be an expert in such things." He paused to take a breath. "If you're no witch, then what are you?"

I shrugged. "I haven't the words to explain it. I don't know how to make anyone understand. Believe me; I have tried and failed already."

He gave me a confused look, so I attempted to pacify him.

"Sometimes, you must accept a thing you cannot explain is simply a thing you cannot explain. The fact that you don't have the answer to a question means you should seek one, not concoct one just to feel wiser."

He didn't answer. I looked at Míriam and Saúl as they spoke to the three men, who'd handed them hooded robes like their own.

"Are you a converso too?" I asked the gentleman.

"No," he replied.

"Morisco?"

"No, but you aren't wrong to ask. Most of the people in our network are conversos; few are Old Christian, though we're desperately needed. The authorities wouldn't have let me leave the city so easily if I were anything but an aristocrat and an Old Christian."

"That was easy?" I said.

"Of course it was. I'm one of the few in Toledo who can get the live ones out without too much trouble."

"Live ones?"

"Apologies. It is our term for the ones like you. The ones being actively pursued."

"Why would you take live ones?" I pulled my cap off and let my braid fall out.

"For the same reason you'd burn yourself at the stake. I don't appreciate our faith being dragged through the mud in the manner of the Inquisition."

"If there were more Christians like you, I might still share *your* faith," I said.

That statement wasn't entirely accurate. I'd rejected his faith because I'd seen little evidence of its validity, not for the behavior of its adherents, though such behavior didn't help. Still, sometimes it's easiest to say the thing people find easiest to hear.

"What faith do you claim, then?" the gentleman asked.

"No faith can claim me."

His jaw dropped. "I refuse to believe a godless heathen would put herself at mortal risk to save innocents."

"Well, I refuse to believe an Old Christian would put himself at mortal risk to save Judaizers," I snapped, more hostilely than I intended.

He seemed to take no offense. "I suppose we'll both have to rethink our beliefs, in that case. I will keep my faith and save those I can."

I was sorely tempted to remind him that were it not for his faith, there'd have been nothing to rescue these people from in the first place, but this man had just saved my life, so I kept my comments to myself. Instead, I asked if he made runs like this often.

"No. Doing it this way too often would get us caught. Usually, people are arrested and never have a chance to flee, or they manage to escape without involving me. I'm only called if there is a dire need, but you, my dear, have given us a multitude of dire needs all at once."

I perked up at these words. "How many escaped?"

"I am uncertain," said the gentleman. "But the rumor mill is saying six have either fled the quemadero or been put into hiding within Toledo. Hopefully, they'll all manage to evade recapture."

"Christ! Oh my God!" I grabbed him by the elbows, jumping up and down.

He clapped his hand over my mouth. "Shush. Have you forgotten your predicament?"

I slipped to the ground, stunned to find myself sobbing. He crouched down beside me and asked what on earth could be the matter with what he'd said.

"I assumed at best I'd managed to save one or two. I never dreamed I got three-quarters of the procession." I wiped my tears with my dusty hand.

"You know, you shouldn't be all that shocked. For some unfathomable reason, when you provided the opportunity, the condemned didn't need much extra motivation to flee."

I laughed and threw him a tearful smile, deciding I liked him greatly, for that sounded like something I would have said, were I in his shoes.

He helped me to my feet. As he took my hand, I recalled that he was the first of these people to voluntarily touch me. Even Míriam and Saúl had not done that. Only Yucé had. They probably all feared that if they did, they might find a hand made of stone or flesh cold as brass.

"So you don't care I'm an aberration?" I asked the gentleman.

"Of course not. I wouldn't care if you told me right now you are a bona fide witch, which I am still not certain you aren't. It isn't the power you have but what you did with it that matters. The world needs more people of your quality. In times like these, indifference to evil is the same as approval; inaction the same as malevolent conduct. I would encourage you, wherever you may be headed, to continue to do as you've done here."

I squeezed his hands. He looked down at me and then up at the horizon, which remained striped with the last fading streaks of orange from the setting sun.

He furrowed his brow. "You must get changed. They need to get you to the hiding place so you can rendezvous with the others. You have a long ride ahead of you this night."

I smiled and shook my head. "Thank you, but no. Here is where I part ways with all of you. I don't plan to escape in the manner you've selected for me. I'm going home."

"Are you certain? A woman alone out here—"

"I managed to foil Church and Crown and throw the entire city of Toledo into chaos all by my lonesome. I think I can make it where I'm going. I only need directions."

The nobleman let out a resigned sigh.

"Where are we in relation to the city?" I asked.

"More than four leagues west of it," he replied.

Shit. That would mean I had five or six leagues to walk before I made it back to the inn. "I'll take one of those robes, if you're offering."

The gentleman bade Carlos fetch me a garment, and I slipped it over my head. It was too long for me, clearly made for a man, but I wanted a hood for my face. I went over to Míriam and tapped her on the shoulder.

She turned from Saúl. "Are you ready to go?"

"I cannot accompany you."

"I feared as much, but thank you. Thank you for giving me back my family. I thought yesterday was the last time I'd ever see Saúl's face, but you've made us whole again," she said.

Once more, the tears welled up in my eyes. I tried to bite my thumb to stop them, but I suffered no pain. I reached out and took Míriam's hands. I did not want to frighten her, only to show her that I was warm and alive and very much still a person. When I did this, she kissed me on both cheeks and embraced me. Then Saúl thanked me for sparing him the flames by enduring them myself. I told him no thanks were needed, for his family had saved me just as assuredly as I'd saved him. I suppose nobody owes anybody anything in cases like these. If you're good to people, then they'll be good to you, and the circle of kindness will always come round.

"I hope one day very soon you are so long gone from this city that its residents shall have the privilege of seeing you burned in effigy," I said to Saúl, and this comment elicited a real laugh from him and the men behind him.

Míriam shook her head and smiled, before taking my hand and pressing it between hers. Without another word, she ushered Saúl toward the frightening-looking men on the huge black mules. The men had brought two extra draft mules with them, and Saúl helped Míriam climb onto one of their backs before mounting in front of her. A cloaked rider looked at me and motioned to the unridden mule, but I shook my head. At that, he turned and followed the others as they headed west.

"Take care, heathen." The gentleman smiled as he entered the carriage, while Carlos mounted at the front and took the reins.

"Take care . . . heretic," I replied, and we both chuckled before I shut the door.

Carlos lashed the shining horses and sped off, leaving me alone. I took off at a brisk run northward. I wanted to be as far from the city as possible before I made the track back east. The nanos did not make me run much faster than I could before, but they gave me the same stamina I'd noted on the way from Santa Colomba—a stamina I'd never have believed possible if not for the fact that for every league I thought would be my last at this pace, I ran another and another without tiring.

I tried to evade the road regardless of how rough the terrain became. The utter darkness made it much easier to avoid running into people—whom I could see, though they could not see me. Despite my efforts, about halfway between the wild meadow and my inn, I was forced to cross a road as I turned east.

When I approached the highway, I caught a whiff of horseflesh and hid in the scrub atop a hill as a large rabble of brothers trotted past on the road below. I had no idea if the Santa Hermandad would still tie me up and shoot me like a common bandit if I revealed I was a woman. Much as I wanted to avoid testing whether I could be pierced with an arrow or crossbow bolt, I was even less keen to find out what the brothers would do if it turned out I couldn't be. Thus, I waited until the sound of hooves had faded before continuing on my clandestine route.

I made it to the inn within hours of starting my run. The first thing I did was check on Pepito, who was happily munching away on some of the oats I'd bought him before I left. I'd given the stable hand a handsome tip to care for him in my absence. After I ensured he was safe, I shed the cloak and walked to the front door, only to find it locked.

At this, I realized I'd have to stay outside until morning, though that couldn't be far-off by now. I hid in an alleyway between the bakery and the blacksmith's shop and waited, watching the front of the building.

Sure enough, the innkeeper came and unbarred the door as the first streaks of dawn began to lighten the sky. I slipped inside once he exited the inn and headed around to the stables. When I got to my room, I found it untouched, thanks to another well-placed tip to the proprietor. I threw myself on the unfortunate straw mat they tried to pass off as a bed and rested the whole day, thinking it better to leave the inn under the cover of darkness.

That evening, I put on my own men's clothes, and Pepito and I slipped out of town in the wee hours. When we'd cleared the farmland outside the village, we practically flew down the open road into the depths of the night.

## Chapter Eighteen

# THE WITCH'S PACT

P epe and I stayed well off the roads for the ride home. At first, I dared move only at night, but once we'd traveled more than a dozen leagues north of Madrid, I felt safe to move during the day. Still, it took a long while for me to become convinced we'd not been pursued.

The going was slower than I liked, for my lack of *av'vysh* obliged me to hunt for sufficient food to sustain me in its absence. All those nights of solitary stalking and leagues of open road left me with plenty of time to dwell on what might be happening in my birth city. Too late, I realized others might come to harm because of my actions, and innocent bystanders could be arrested or interrogated in what was sure to be a full-scale witch hunt. Alas, the time to act on that realization had vanished the instant I'd relaxed myself to my own authority.

Moreover, the thought of my mother coming back to find me already gone was so unpleasant it took my mind a few days to start wandering in that direction. Once it did, however, it barely wandered anywhere else. Before I'd burned myself, I hadn't stopped to consider the true cost of my actions. I had known I would never be able to return to Toledo and search for my relatives if I interrupted the auto de fe, but I'd known it in a far-off, abstract way—the same way I knew, in some distant part of the world, my country had a colony toward which my husband sailed.

Now, I trekked north as empty-handed as I'd trekked south, and the full weight of what I'd done finally fell on me. My mother had come looking for me. I hadn't been there for her to find, nor could I ever return, not to ask about possible extended family, not to see if she had told anyone where she currently lived, not for anything.

I rode for several days in a state of deep mourning, anger, and confusion. I regretted I hadn't taken more care to think through the consequences of my actions. I'd decided to set myself on fire in an instant and spent the time between the choice and the act planning my performance and escape, giving barely any consideration to what would come after.

At the same time, had I not done as I did, poor Yucé would now be where I was more than ten years ago: orphaned and broken, his head full of images of torture and burning that would take months, maybe years, to subside. I'd spared him what I could not spare myself, and that did give me a little comfort in my sorrow.

As I continued to ride north along some of the same terrain Father Manuel and I had traversed so long ago, my anger at myself began to redirect toward him. Although the ancient priest in the cathedral had been clear my parents had no relatives in Toledo with whom he might've left me, that in no way resolved the question of Father Manuel's motivations for fleeing the city.

In light of my newfound certitude that my mother had indeed been spared the stake, I wondered all the more if he'd sought a pretext to transfer out of Toledo because he was aware she'd soon come back. Ignacio's behavior would've provided a convenient-enough excuse. I obsessed for many of the following days over why Father Manuel had dragged me to Santa Colomba, if he'd even let anyone in Toledo know where he was being transferred, and if he'd ever made any effort to find my mother. All these questions I planned to put to him as soon as I made it home—no matter how much he still feared me.

A day or two before my arrival in Green Spain, I stopped to wash off the yellow dust of the south in a marvelous, frigid stream that flowed forth from the rain and snow of the Cantabrian Mountains. After I'd bathed and drunk my fill, I stood to climb onto the bank.

About halfway to the shore, I lost my footing on the slick stone bottom. I cried out as my legs flew out from under me and I pitched forward onto my hands and knees, scraping them along the sharp rocks beneath the water's surface. Sure I'd flayed my palms and shins, I flopped down in the riverbed to assess the damage. Yet I was stunned to find myself unhurt. In a flash, I recalled why I suffered neither pain nor injury, and the realization boomed like a thunderclap inside my head.

Jhasali! Of course! I could still find my mother for the same reason I'd been able to burn myself alive. If Jhasali could radically alter her appearance on a whim, that meant I could too. If I better learned to control my nanos, I could return to Toledo as a blonde-headed, blue-eyed man if I wished. I might even be able to get Jhasali to use the surveillance bots for me.

Naturally, all this was predicated on my learning to work the technology. Right now, I still couldn't even get my nanos to let me get drunk, nor had I been able to convince them to restart my menstrual cycle so that I might someday bear a child, though I'd often consciously willed it or outright commanded it inside my own head. No matter. I hadn't truly been motivated before now.

I scrambled out of the stream and threw my pants and shirt back on, not bothering to don my shoes in my haste. They could go in the saddlebag; I didn't need them anyway. When Pepito came to my whistle, I took off at a run toward the north, and he trotted behind me, sometimes having to break into a slow canter to keep up as I all but flew toward the mountain range—the final barrier that stood between me and the means to find my mother.

***

When we arrived in the dead of night, I discovered someone had broken through the window and looted my house. I'd half expected it; robbery had always been an issue for the single men who left their homes unattended when they set off for the sailing season. The thieves had probably guessed Sergio and I kept more of value in the house because it was still occupied in his absence.

They'd trashed the place when they'd been disappointed, only making off with the bedclothes and the pewter dishes and a few other assorted items. Those, I could replace. All my valuable things—Sergio's and my extra clothing, his box of papers, every piece of jewelry I owned save my wedding ring, and a pair of silver cups we'd gotten as a marriage gift—remained safe in Homeship. The thieves had a few scruples, at least, for my little altar remained untouched. I gave it a cursory dusting before turning my attention elsewhere.

As I mended the broken window shutter and cleaned my wrecked house, I tried not to allow myself to recall what had passed within these walls the last time the place had looked like this. Even if I hadn't returned to this messy welcome, this house could never be what it had once been. I'd felt no happiness upon seeing its gray stone exterior with its red tile roof and its empty animal stall on the ground floor, and I felt no warmth within it now. It was walls, a door, a roof, and a few windows, a place to keep my head sheltered from the rain and my body warm in the winter. That was all. I wondered if those feelings would change when Sergio returned, but I doubted I'd have a place to call home again until he bought me that town house he'd promised.

After I finished cleaning, I sat down on my empty bed in my empty house and recalled the two men I'd shot in that Toledo alley. In all the time I'd been racing toward Santa Colomba, I never once forgot that I'd ridden out an innocent wife, wishing for no more than to see her husband, and I'd returned a thrice-guilty murderess. I wondered if those soldiers' wives felt the same sense of isolation I did when they stared at the place where their husbands' heads had lain. No. Certainly, they felt worse, for in the end, I had the hope my husband would return in time, and I had no children to hamper my remarriage if he didn't.

I decided the weapons that had allowed me to kill my victims must be locked away for good. Weeks before my departure for Sevilla, I'd pried up a couple of floorboards under the bed to make myself a spot to store the cuffs whenever I was not wearing them. As I recalled the two men who'd fallen prey to IDOS, I opted to put it in that safe place and only wear it to ride to and from Homeship. For that, I had no choice.

Next day, I went to confront Father Manuel. I did not intend to scold or argue with him—only to probe him. I'd spent many hours on the way up from Toledo concocting a detailed list of questions I planned to ask him as well as my own responses to a range of possible answers. I'd rehearsed the dialogue over and over along the way, to the point Pepito must've thought me mad.

Several of the children to whom I'd always given alms waylaid me once I made it to the plaza in front of the church, greeting me gleefully and asking why I'd been away so long. Glad I'd remembered to bring extra money, I kept enough coin to buy some groceries for later and distributed the rest of it among the children, telling them of my journey to Sevilla.

After I spun a long tale of huge ships and wide rivers and Moorish towers so tall they boggled the mind, I sent the children on their way and headed for the parish house. I entered to find Father Manuel seated at his writing desk, reading by a couple of candles meant to supplement the swirling sunlight pouring through the open window.

Upon seeing me, he leapt from his desk, shaking a finger. "Micaela! I cannot believe—"

"I passed through Toledo on the way home," I said, silencing him at once. "And I went to the place where the sanbenitos are hung. Ten years my parents' barrio was a hundred paces from ours, and you never took me there."

"You wanted me to take you there and show you the proof your mother and father were humiliated and paraded through the streets? Should I have shoved their sanbenitos before your eyes as well?"

"I wanted you to show me who they were. I wanted you to tell me where to search for them so I wouldn't return to Toledo only to find my mother had come looking for me after you'd already spirited me out of there," I snapped.

"What else could I do but take you away? You were in a dreadful state finding out what happened, and Ignacio was spreading around the barrio that your parents wore the sanbenito."

"So you saw an opportunity to get me out of the city before I could be taken away from you?"

"Of course not. I thought the diocese would move me across the province, not across the kingdom. I'd never intentionally keep a babe from its natural mother."

"Not even a penanced and formerly exiled mother?"

He smacked the desk. "No."

"That's not what you told Father Enrique."

"I don't remember that conversation."

"You told him years ago you thought infidels ought to have their children confiscated if they refused to raise them properly."

"I might've said something to that effect, but that doesn't mean *I* would do such a thing."

I snorted. "I see. You'll just support the dirty work as long as someone else is doing it?"

"I . . . well, you cannot deny it benefited you not to have been raised by a pack of infidels," he spat.

"It didn't benefit me; it benefited you. You didn't want to save me from heresy. You only wished to be at liberty to raise me as your concubine!"

"Micaela!" he shouted.

"If you wanted a whore, you didn't have to steal me from my mother. There were plenty of unclaimed orphans lying around."

Of course, I knew whatever reason Father Manuel had taken me, it hadn't been to make a concubine of me. Ignacio probably started that rumor himself because that's what *he* had meant to do with me after he'd taken me home from the burning. Yet, when Father Manuel once again defended his actions by claiming I ought to be grateful to have been raised a proper Christian, all the things I'd thought about saying on the way up from Toledo fell out of my head.

Now, I wanted nothing more than to say the cruelest thing I could think of, and repeating that baseless old rumor that followed us no matter where we went seemed the ideal choice. Damage done, I stormed out before Father Manuel could respond and fled all the way back to my house without so much as a pause to speak to Catalina at the city gate.

I stood in the kitchen, glowering at the pots hanging in the fireplace. I'd spent the ride up from Toledo planning every detail of the calm, rational conversation I was going to have with Father Manuel, and yet I'd shouted and stormed off like a child. I was too angry to go back and continue the discussion, so I sat at the table with my head in my hands, wondering how else I might make my life a bigger mess than it was already.

After perhaps an hour, a forceful knock sounded at the door. Father Manuel called through the other side, keeping up his relentless pounding until I opened.

"I didn't steal you. And if I'd ever intended you to be my concubine, you'd certainly have known it." He swept past me, slamming his walking stick on the floor with all his might.

"You lecture me about what I should and shouldn't have done with you, yet you've no appreciation for the position I was in—let me finish!" he snapped when I opened my mouth. "I wasn't meant to have you. I snuck you out of the Inquisitorial prison in the dead of night. If I'd gone round asking too many questions, they might've taken you away from me. As for your mother, I didn't hide you from her. She never returned, not even a year after her exile ended. She could've been dead for all I knew. Was I to sit on my hands while the whole neighborhood gossiped with Ignacio about your disposition toward heresy and your contaminated lineage until they set the Inquisition after you?"

"None of that excuses your refusal to tell me the whole story *before* Ignacio outed you. Would you have let me carry on in ignorance forever if he hadn't?" I demanded.

"I don't know. I thought you weren't ready for the truth, and I am not sure what could've changed my mind. It was a mistake. I won't pretend I never made any. But I swear, I didn't do it to keep you from your mother. Please, believe me."

He sank to a seat at the kitchen table, gasping for breath. I clung to every bit of anger in me to avert feeling pity for him. I didn't know what to think, whether he had truly done nothing more than make the best of a situation he'd had no control over or if he was trying to avoid losing the last familial tether he had left in his old age.

"How can I be sure what to believe? Especially with you always reminding me how thankful I ought to be that the state ripped me from my mother's bosom," I whispered.

"I never said that. I only meant that sometimes the Lord works good out of misfortune, even if we won't fully understand how in this life."

I rapped the table with my fingernails. "It makes sense you'd wish me to believe that, given everything I've suffered so needlessly, thanks to you."

"I didn't make the Inquisition come after your parents, Micaela."

I'd been referencing his failure to protect me from Ignacio and Rodrigo, but I didn't clarify. "Even so, no good came of my family's misfortune. My father is gone, and I might never find my mother. What good can amend that? Even if some good results from evil, it doesn't negate the evil, nor does it compensate the loss the evil caused. Such thinking only provides an excuse, a justification for allowing preventable evil to happen."

"But again, look at the greater good. It's true you were separated from your parents, and unfortunate as that is, the loss is offset because it offered you the chance to be spared a life of heresy and an afterlife of eternal damnation, if only you'll take that opportunity."

"Thanks be to Christ I lost my entire family so I could be spared an imaginary punishment doled out in a fictional world to come!" I cried.

"That is enough!" Father Manuel slammed his hand on the table. "Does your heresy know no bounds? It seems even my tutelage wasn't sufficient to stop you auctioning your soul to the highest bidder."

"What of your ironclad belief I'd never do such a thing? When last we spoke—"

"I recall full well what we discussed, and I was drunk that night; I didn't know what I was saying."

"Yes you did."

He shot me a furious glare but didn't reply, so I went on.

"Try to see things from my perspective. I know you never met your father. Now, imagine you never met your mother either—never heard her voice, never knew her scent, never felt her embrace—and the reason was a certain group of people who believed in a certain god. Would you be keen to worship such people's god? Would you be glad to be raised in the faith of your persecutors?"

He contemplated for a while, as if this thought had never hit him. "I suppose not. I guess I can see why you'd be tempted to run off to the devil."

"I didn't run off to the devil!" I shouted.

"And I didn't steal you!" he shouted right back.

"Alright, we're approaching an impasse. What if we made a pact?"

"I thought you'd already made one of those."

I huffed but didn't dignify that jab. "Our pact will be that I will give you the benefit of the doubt that you didn't deliberately keep me from my parents—"

"I didn't!"

"—and you will give me the benefit of the doubt that I didn't get my powers by lying with Satan or through any other form of dark magic."

"I cannot believe that on your say-so alone," he muttered.

I shrugged. "You said yourself you wish it to be true. If you believe what I say, then it shall be true, at least to you."

"I do wish to believe it. But how can I?"

"You've never taken issue with lending credence to the incredible before now."

"Yes I have. You know as well as I that I never accepted the validity of witchcraft. It was you who made a believer of me."

"Well, I wish I hadn't."

"I wish that too."

We sat long in silence. I fetched Father Manuel a cup of wine, which he accepted. I poured myself a cup as well, staring at the fireplace and pondering the offer I'd made him. I wasn't sure why I'd promised to give him the benefit of the doubt. Perhaps it was because I wanted some of that benefit for myself. Or maybe I'd done it because I still deeply wished his assertion he never intended to steal me was true, though I remained unsure if I'd ever be able to verify it. Lucky I'd promised him the benefit of the doubt, not unwavering confidence.

"I suppose if I want you to trust my word on its merit alone, I'll have to do the same for you," Father Manuel muttered, drawing my gaze from the fireplace. "I won't accuse you of devilry again, and I'll try to believe such accusations are baseless."

"Thank you. And I shan't ask you again if you hid me purposefully from my family, but I do have a few other things I wish to discuss about my visit to Toledo," I replied.

"Such as?"

"What was my name?"

It was a strange initial question to put to him, but it was the first thing that came to mind. I'd asked it so many times as a child and never believed Father Manuel when he said he didn't know the answer. I hoped he'd be honest with me now.

To my disappointment, he repeated, "I don't know."

"Are you certain? If she were indeed guilty of Mohammedanism, surely my mother wouldn't have given me a Christian name."

"If she ever gave you any other name, she never trusted me with it."

"Though she trusted you with my life?"

"That was different. She had no choice," Father Manuel replied.

"How did you find out what her eventual punishment was if you never asked anyone about her or me?"

"You know I went to her auto de fe in 1508. I learned her fate when they read her sentence. Once they got to your father, I knew you'd be an orphan," he added darkly.

"And you never asked anyone about me? Honestly?"

"I was afraid to. If I had trusted the wrong person even once, then the ruse I'd found you on the church doorstep would've collapsed. I suppose someone in the Inquisition's circle must've known it was me who'd taken you, but perhaps they didn't care. Or perhaps they were trying to cover for having allowed it to happen."

"How did Ignacio find out about me?"

"He became an Inquisitorial notary in 1510. He must've stumbled across records of a girl born in the cells and my ministrations to the prisoners, then added things up from there."

"What about when we moved up here? Did you not tell anyone where we'd gone?"

"Of course I did. How did you think I wrote to all my friends in Toledo?"

I put my hand to my brow. I couldn't understand why my mother would have left without finding out where I'd been taken. Maybe she'd also been afraid to ask too many questions. Or maybe she'd never run into any of the people Father Manuel had informed of our whereabouts. Toledo was a densely populated city, after all. But what if she'd never come back for me to begin with? Could it be she'd returned to the city for some other reason and never spared a passing thought for the child she'd left behind?

"Why did she not discover where I'd gone when she came back?" I wondered aloud.

"She didn't ask for my name," Father Manuel replied. "She believed she was going to burn, so we barely exchanged words. She pressed you into my arms, told me what to call you, and swore me not to abandon you. The guard opened the cell door as soon as I'd slipped you under my cloak. It all happened so fast I was still unsure how I wound up with a babe in my arms when I got back to the street."

I bowed my head, laying my face in my hands. After Father Manuel had taken me, my poor mother had languished for years in the Inquisitorial dungeon waiting for her auto de fe, just as Saúl had, and she'd spent it all believing she was to burn as a heretic. How she'd managed to survive such an ordeal, I couldn't guess. Possibly, like Míriam, she had wished to see her husband a final time.

Father Manuel spoke again when I didn't respond. "Listen, however your parents managed to run afoul of the tribunal, once they had, there was no way any authority would've allowed you to be raised by infidels. If it hadn't been me, it would've been an Old Christian family or a home for orphan girls."

"Why keep me, then?" I asked. "Rather than send me to one of those places?"

"I promised your mother I'd never abandon you."

"Oh, piss on your promises. Why did you really keep me?"

He sighed. "In truth, out of loneliness, I suppose."

"So you did wish to have me all to yourself."

"No. Maybe. I don't know. I was so young when I was set on the path to the priesthood, and when my mother died, I had no one. I very much regretted that I could take no wife and father no children. I know it's quite common for priests to do such things anyway, but I didn't wish to break the prohibitions—"

"You broke them with Leonor," I interjected.

He ran a finger over his brow. "God forgive me, I did. I did not realize you knew that."

"I'm not a fool."

"No. Of all the things anyone in this world could accuse you of being, a fool isn't one of them." He chuckled.

"Were there others?" I asked. When he didn't reply, I added, "Come on. All the petty sins I've confessed to you over the years, and you cannot be honest with me even once?"

"Yes. There were others."

"Antonia?"

"No, not her."

"What about—"

"Micaela, stop it." He rubbed his closed eyelids. "I guess I'm just another hypocrite."

"Everybody's a hypocrite."

We sat quietly for a while. In the distance, the church bells rang to mark the hour of Vespers, but Father Manuel didn't move from his spot at the table.

"I'm so sorry," he finally whispered. "I'm sorry I never trusted you with the truth about your own life when I had the chance. If I had, you might put more faith in my word now. I have nothing else to offer you."

"I can't promise you forgiveness, not now. But I'll try to believe you meant me no harm."

"I don't ask your forgiveness for my actual handling of the situation. I ask you to tell me what you'd have done differently, were our roles reversed."

I hadn't expected that question, but when I considered it, I had a hard time concocting something to change besides the errors for which he'd already apologized. I wouldn't have abandoned a newborn babe to a foundling home. I wouldn't have left it to its fate in a squalid prison cell. I'd certainly never have let a little girl become the parish's pariah after everyone discovered the truth about her heretical heritage. Even so, Father Manuel might've put more effort into reuniting me with my real family—perhaps it was not too late for that.

"There is something you can do for me, if you're willing," I said.

"Of course. Whatever you need, if it's within my power, I'll do it."

"Help me find my mother. Write to anyone you can think of who might know what happened to her. Just . . ." I hesitated. "Don't mention my name or the fact that I'm still living in town with you."

"Why on earth not?"

"Don't ask that question. I cannot answer it."

"Alright. I'll get started straightaway, but try not to get your hopes up. Many of the people I knew in Toledo have passed by now."

"Why have they passed?"

"It's what happens when you grow old, child. People start leaving you."

As I stared at Father Manuel, he looked smaller than he ever had, as if I was realizing how old he truly was for the first time. I thought back to my intentions with Jhasali's surveillance drones and hoped the day I found my mother might come soon enough that I could sort all this out before time finished its ugly work on him. Then all three of us might be able to leave this awful mess in the past where it belonged.

\*\*\*

"I need you to help me with something," I said when I arrived at Homeship before dawn the next morning and found Jhasali outside enjoying the October chill.

"Well, hello to you too." She laughed. "Now you don't even greet me properly? You were all atwitter with your human rules when we first met: I can't open your door without knocking. I can't surveil you. I can't kill members of your species whenever it pleases me. I have to hold a necklace in my hand and say some words to a picture—"

I chuckled. "What about all the rules you laid out for this place? I can't bring any other humans near Homeship. I can't mess with the control or comms systems. I can't go into the training chamber alone. I have to stay out of the way of the drones. I have to look behind me a thousand times every time I ride out here to make sure nobody followed me."

"Alright, I catch your meaning. What is it you want help with?"

"I want you to teach me how to better command my nanos. They work when I'm using them in tandem with the other devices, like IDOS, but when it's just me alone trying to get them to cooperate, they won't listen to me except in the most random of circumstances."

"We can certainly work to improve that. But why the sudden interest?"

"My mother is alive. I'm certain of it. If I can change my appearance, I might be able to find her."

"Why do you need to change your appearance to search for your genetic progenitor?"

"I, uh . . ." In my frenzy to begin working toward my goal, I'd forgotten that question would crop up. "It would be much easier for me to ride across the country searching for clues and talking to people if I could actually *be* a man rather than just dress like one."

"Oh. That shouldn't be a problem. You ought to be able to alter your genitalia and a couple of other meaningless dimorphisms without any external aid."

"You can do it at will?"

Jhasali rolled her eyes. "Do you even need to ask? Though, technically, I don't have to."

"Because your people eliminated their sex characteristics so long ago?"

"Exactly. We're neither male nor female because our kind has multiple biological sexes and none at all. We can alter the default physical traits with which we were born as we see fit."

"I guess it makes sense, then, that there are no gendered words or gender-based pronouns in your people's language. And I suppose, since you all evolved away from sexual intercourse, you have no need for different genitalia."

"Been using our sensors, have we? They seem to be working."

"Better than my nanos."

Jhasali furrowed her brow. "The sensors are more intuitive when it comes to simple data location. You ask a question, and they provide whatever information from their datastores answers it. Your nanos must be taught how to distinguish command from thought and subconscious desire from conscious will. Since you integrated with them as an adult, I might've guessed it would not come as naturally for your bots as it does for everyone else's. They may be confusing your unconscious wants with your conscious commands. If the two conflict, they could be obeying the former when they should be obeying the latter."

"That may be the case. Even IDOS malfunctions sometimes. It works when I command it, but it also heats up when I don't mean it to, especially if I'm angry."

"That is definitely not supposed to happen," Jhasali replied.

"That's why I need help learning to control the implants. I also thought you might assist me in my search by using your surveillance network."

"If you wish to use the surveillance bots, you'll have to learn to forge the link."

"Why?"

"Because I'm not going to do everything for you. I will help you learn to utilize the technology, and I will allow you the use of it, within reason, but the actual search is something you should conduct yourself."

"I suppose you're right," I admitted.

Though my lip quivered and my knees grew weak at the idea of the mental violation I'd have to endure to bond to a drone, I took a deep breath and declared I was prepared to do whatever it took to find my mother.

Jhasali nodded. "Good. We can start straightaway."

# Chapter Nineteen

# MICAELANGELA

To prepare me for my first attempt at bonding, Jhasali bade me ask the sensors about the master-drone union and how it worked. The implants told me every node on the network—including ships, drones, and even people—carried a unique identifier, a distinct signature that the node could reveal or conceal. Living nodes concealed their identifiers by default, as did bonded drones, while unbonded devices projected theirs so potential masters could use them to distinguish the target drone from all others. The master forged the link by seeking out the identifier, focusing on it with all her might, and willing its corresponding drone to connect to her brain. Most unclaimed drones were open to accepting a connection request unless programmed otherwise.

This exclusive nexus was a security feature invented to protect the brain-to-computer interface between living beings and bondable drones designed to belong to one owner at a time. As long as their link was not broken, master and drone were one, and the device was loyal to no one else. There were also many drones that would only link up with certain verified masters, so even if their connections were cut, they would not accept another commander under any circumstance. This was especially important for armed drones so they could not be turned upon their masters.

Many special concessions were also afforded to bonded drones because their masters were always in constant real-time communion with them. For instance, Jhasali could command drones inside the security perimeter even when she was outside it, as her fellowship with her personal devices was never broken, though the logical perimeter confined every other signal. Distance commands to unbonded drones were not possible if a virtual boundary existed between the device and its commander, but only a minute number of specialized physical barriers could successfully interrupt the connection between master and bonded device.

The master-drone nexus was meant to be no different than being attached to IDOS or any other wearable device, only instead of being physically linked, the user was mentally linked. Ideally, I could communicate my will to a drone using this connection, and my will would be done. However, my command of IDOS had already proven less than ideal, and I feared that exerting my will over a device not physically attached to me would be even more difficult.

For our initial lesson, Jhasali took me outside to the woodlands within the ship's security perimeter. There, she disconnected from one of the small drones with thin pincer arms, among the basest models she owned, so she could coach me through asserting myself as its master.

"I must warn you," she began. "I do not remember a time when I had to learn how to link with drones. I've been able to do it since I was a hatchling, for our sensors can work with external devices long before our nanos fully mature. Thus, my ability to teach you how the first time ought to feel may prove limited."

I didn't reply. My stomach was in knots and my hands trembled. I wondered if the drone that was to invade my mind could hear my racing heart.

"Now, I've cleared the air of any stray identifiers that might be tangible to you once you start searching for signatures. So the only one you should feel is the one from your practice drone." She pointed to the machine as it floated next to her, all its lights off, all its limbs folded.

"How should it feel?" I asked.

"It's not easy to put into words. Each identifier has its own pulsation that your sensors pick up on and parse. It feels almost like a vibrating inside your brain, but not in a literal sense."

"I don't catch your meaning."

"It's like when you earthlings say you can feel thunder. Even if you can't hear it, you sense it in the air. Though you cannot explain it, you know it when it's there. I fear that's not helpful, but I know of nothing else to do but tell you to quiet your mind and instruct your sensors to seek your target identifier."

Quieting my mind proved a daunting task. I could stop my thoughts from racing for a few seconds—not long enough to feel any vibrations. I wondered if the sensors had already linked up without my knowing it, hoping it might be that easy.

"How will I know when I'm connected?" I asked.

"That will be unmistakable. There is a distinct signal your sensors send to your brain when the process is complete. It feels like someone tugging a string tied inside your head."

"That sounds awful!"

"It doesn't hurt. It's to let you know the connection is forged. If you haven't felt the tug, you aren't linked."

"Then I'm not linked," I said.

"Keep trying."

Try as I might, attempt after attempt, I did nothing but stare at the drone without success. Jhasali kept repeating my sensors were programmed for this, and they should allow me to feel unique identifiers at will. Yet I felt nothing. Concentrating with all my might brought only defeat, and quieting my mind did no good. There was only nothing.

After an hour or two of failure, I got too frustrated to quiet my mind anymore. So Jhasali and I gave it up for another day and decided to work with the nanos instead. We went back into the ship and stood before a drone as it reflected a hologram of myself back to me, like a high-tech mirror.

"We can start with something easy. See if you can command the bots to redden your lips," Jhasali said.

"Like rouge?"

"If that's what you wish to call it. Now focus. Command your lips to turn red."

"Lips, turn red," I ordered.

Jhasali held up a hand. "Not that way. Speech is obsolete. No one's verbally commanded devices in eons. You must direct them in your mind."

"I talk to Homeship. Why can't I talk to my nanos?"

"You can speak to them, but you must be in mental command of your internal and bonded devices. The ship is different. It obeys telepathic and spoken directives from anyone on the network up to their privilege level, but if you have no cerebral control over your personal devices, they're not going to obey your words any more than they obey your thoughts."

"Oh, alright. I'll try it your way."

My attempts to redden my lips were no more fruitful than my attempts to bond to the practice drone. No matter how hard I focused nor how intensely I desired it, my lips stayed their natural shade. I didn't understand it. The only reason I had any hair left was that the nanos had obeyed my command to protect it, but now I couldn't get them to do the exact same thing with my lips, nor could I ascertain what I'd done right in that instance that I was doing wrong in this one.

At Jhasali's suggestion, I tried thinking a few different word combinations in both Sartjyanan and Castellano, to no avail. Disappointed and frustrated, I gave up on all of it and rode to my house late in the night, weighed down under the realization it might well be months or even years before I became proficient enough to begin the search for my mother.

*** 

My impromptu ride across the whole of Iberia had made me the absolute talk of Santa Colomba. For the first few days after my return, the words "La Toledana is back from Sevilla" were just about the only phrase on anyone's lips. Everyone was fascinated to see my newly cropped hair, and I endured quite a bit of teasing when I told them I'd had to cut it after tangling it in a tree branch while galloping through the woods.

People I'd never even met were now stopping me in the streets, begging to hear of my travels. Isabel sat wide-eyed and spellbound as I told her, Catalina, Susana, Andrés, their children, and a crowd of neighbors about the wonders of the massive Sevillian cathedral, the frenzied bustle of the Arenal, the breadth of the Guadalquivir, the height of the crane, and the brawn of the ships that crossed the Atlantic.

Not everyone was pleased with my stories, however. Gabriel and Gracia couldn't believe I'd done as I did and said no number of letters assuring them I'd made it safely gave me the right to abandon my husband's home, even if it was to visit him. Gracia was particularly upset that I'd missed her father's requiem because I'd been gallivanting around Sevilla when he'd passed. His illness and death had been painful and drawn out, and I did lament I'd not been present to ease his passing for my friend.

If Gabriel and Gracia were irate, Sara was livid. When we first reunited, she could scarcely say anything but the phrase "how could you." Once she managed to string a sentence together, she demanded to know what I'd have done if something terrible had happened.

"But nothing terrible did happen," I said.

"Well, it could have!" she spat, before she leaned in and whispered, "I would have thought you'd have learned your lesson from being raped the first time."

"What lesson should that have been?" I took a step away from her.

"I don't know. That you must exercise more caution, I guess. I shouldn't have said it like that, alright, but I'm so furious I could slap you! All this after you promised you wouldn't leave."

"What I actually said was that I wouldn't do something foolish," I snapped.

"I suppose I can't believe a thing you say if it's all omissions and half-truths."

I balled my fists, wanting to scream in her face she had no more right to tell me whether I could visit my husband than she had to tell me how I should feel about being raped, but I didn't. Throughout our friendship, I'd always been aware of my true place beneath her. Although our mutual care for one another normally allowed us to forget such things, I now measured every word I said, fearing each syllable of this conversation had the potential to blow back on Sergio.

"I'm sorry," I muttered. "But I couldn't wait an extra year to see my husband."

"I understand that, but you cannot expect me to forget you lied to my face."

I wanted to remind her I hadn't technically lied, but I thought better of it. For her part, Sara said it was best if I called on her some other time, and I found myself back on the street before I realized she was throwing me out of the town house. She'd never done that before.

I might've been angrier about it if I hadn't had other things on my mind. By that point, I'd come to see almost every earthly aspect of my life as nothing but a distraction from my mission of achieving control over Jhasali's technology.

At this, I showed little improvement. I managed to rouge my lips after a lesson or two, but it didn't go as I'd hoped. Staring at my hologram reflection, I placed all my concentration on the task at hand and willed with every nano of my being for my lips to turn red. It took tremendous focus, but a dark ruby stain finally spread from the center of my bottom lip over my cupid's bow and all the way to the corners of my mouth.

I smiled with my newly scarlet lips. "I did it!"

"Good," Jhasali called from the other room.

I happened to glance from my lips to my eyes, but instead of staring into my own ebony irises, I found I gazed at two orbs of emerald.

"What? Oh no. Shit!" I cried. "How did this happen?"

"What happened?" Jhasali entered with a couple of drones tailing her.

"This. How can this be?" I pointed to my green eyes.

"Relax. It's not the end of the world if you give a few inadvertent commands."

"I can't give this inadvertent command. I can't return to town like this."

"Why ever not?"

"You know why. My people cannot alter their features. It's impossible they won't notice." I pressed my eyelids with my fingers, begging the eyes underneath to return to their normal hue.

"I thought the whole point of these lessons was to make you able to change your appearance," Jhasali said.

"Not like this. It has to be intentional—and reversible. I need to be able to do it at will."

"Then change them back." Jhasali waved her hand.

"If it were so easy, I wouldn't have spent multiple lessons trying to change my lip color!"

"Mica, if you panic, you'll only make it more difficult. Just concentrate."

Jhasali sat me down on the floor so she could coach me. I managed to fix my eye color, but not without first enduring an entire day of terror and frustration.

After becoming aware there was a possibility I'd make radical alterations to my looks without being able to undo them at will, I decided to focus on making invisible changes in order to improve my ability to give commands. I chose to concentrate most on convincing the nanos to let me get drunk and restart my menstrual cycle. After so long of sporadically attempting these commands and failing, I knew it wouldn't come easy. Yet I imagined if I had Jhasali's help, I might have more success. Then I could use those successes to begin making and unmaking visible alterations to my body.

I also chose to focus harder on the drones, though these devices proved no less infuriating. With practice, I did manage to learn to seek out the unique identifier—the tingling sensation deep within the recesses of my brain that I could not define except to say I knew what it was when I felt it. This turned out to be a minuscule accomplishment. No matter how I concentrated, begged, or demanded, I couldn't get even a flicker of reaction from the drone to which the identifier belonged.

Sometimes, after hours of failure, I grew so frustrated I pounded the trees or even the drone itself. Jhasali grew frustrated as well, though her own irritation was channeled into cold remoteness rather than bursts of sobbing and shouting. Indeed, the angrier I became, the more apathetic she acted, which served no other purpose than to enrage me further.

"You are not helping me!" I shouted one afternoon after she told me once again I was overthinking and making things more difficult. "You don't know how to teach me. You never had to learn any of this the way I do."

"That's why I know of no other mechanism to help you than trial and error. Now try again." She pointed at my practice drone.

I stalked closer to the device, resenting myself for failing and it for ignoring me and Jhasali for having no sympathy for my plight. I tried several more times to connect, directing my mind, willing the bot to acknowledge me in any way whatsoever. Still nothing.

"Why won't you work?" I groaned, though I expected Jhasali to admonish me for speaking to the drone like it was a living being.

Sure enough, she chimed right in. "Don't talk to it. It isn't alive. We've already discussed how if you're not connected, it won't respond to your verbal commands any more than it responds to your mental ones."

"I know that! This is impossible."

"It is only impossible because you believe it to be. Try again." She crossed her arms.

I huffed at her before turning back to my drone. Suddenly, Jhasali told me to stop.

"What is it?" I asked.

"I've got an idea. If you can't connect to the drone, there might be a way it can connect to you. I'll master it again, and then I may be able to direct it to automatically link with you upon my disconnect."

"What good will that do if you must forge the nexus for me every single time?"

"I won't. I'll only forge it this once—assuming I can. If you see how it feels to be linked, it might help you independently connect next time."

I was unsure if this would work, but it had to be better than what we were doing now.

"Go ahead and tell your sensors to project your identifier," Jhasali instructed.

Though my implants were programmed to reveal my identifier only to the drones I commanded, even I could give so simple a directive as telling them to expose it temporarily.

"I'm ready, I hope," I said.

"Try not to think about anything. Your mind must be open if this is going to work." Jhasali turned from me to the drone, which still floated motionless in the air near us.

The second her eyes fell on it, it leapt to greet her like an old friend. I hated myself for not being able to reproduce this effect, but I made every effort I could to shut out all that and think of nothing but the tree roots at which I stared.

As soon as my mind blanked, I lost my vision and awareness. Next I knew, I stood in the exact spot the drone had been a second ago. I couldn't piece together how I'd moved to that spot without realizing it, and I wondered where on earth the drone had gone. I couldn't fathom why I no longer felt the ground beneath my feet. Now that I thought of it, I no longer felt anything.

"Oh no!" Jhasali cried.

I turned my gaze to where she was looking and realized that she and I both stared at my unconscious body. I tried to scream, but no sound came out. I tried to flail my arms and realized I had only spindly appendages. I decided to move toward my body, and the hum of a minuscule engine buzzed inside my nonexistent ears as it propelled me forward.

Jhasali put herself between me and me and reached for the front of the drone that was now my body. She grabbed hold of me and held me firmly, flipping me upside down. I sensed she fumbled with the bottom of my new body, but I couldn't tell what she was doing. Without warning, I lost consciousness once more.

Once again, next I knew, I opened my eyes in a different spot. This time, I lay on the ground, staring up at the trees. I moved my hand and felt I had one. Just to make sure, I held it to my face and stared at it, watching the fingers curl and uncurl at my command.

"Are you alright?" Jhasali knelt beside me, holding the motionless drone in her arms. Its humming had stopped.

"I think so." I rose to a half-seated position. "What happened?"

"When the drone connected to you, you put your entire consciousness into it. You should not do that. You should command it as an extension of yourself, not possess it bodily. You leave your own body vulnerable in that state. If your whole essence is within a drone, even involuntary bodily functions like your heartbeat or breathing could cease. Except under certain circumstances, the brain activity that controls these functions must remain operative and *inside* the living body. The nanos can only do so much without some conscious will."

"How did you make me go back inside my body?" I asked.

"All these drones have a manual switch for emergencies. It doesn't do anything besides cut the power, but sometimes that is necessary."

She turned the device over and showed me a small hatch she'd unlocked with a touchpad on top of the lid. Inside the compartment was a smaller touchpad labeled Manual Override in Sartjyanan writing.

"I don't think we should try that again. You must learn to split your consciousness and make the link yourself," Jhasali said.

I lay back down on the soft forest peat and moaned. Bonding, splitting consciousness, possessing alternative bodies—it was all too much.

Jhasali looked down at me. "If you're too tired, we can cease for now."

"Yes. Please," I replied.

She led me back into Homeship and sat me down in the galley. One of the drones came to attend me, and I allowed it to strip me of my outer layers, clean the leaves from my hair, and bring me food. I commanded none of this, of course, and I watched Jhasali for any indication she directed the device to wait on me.

As always, she gave not the slightest hint she even thought of the drone. My sensors had told me it was independent enough to figure out how to fulfill her desires without her input yet as much a part of her as her own limbs. They were all one great web, Jhasali and her devices, a tangle of mechanical bodies and minds all interwoven into a single biological will: hers.

Yet, on some level, I couldn't accept this plain fact. I had never maintained a nexus with any drone, so I still couldn't understand intuitively how they could think all on their own, how they could operate without being constantly commanded and directed. Their synthetic intelligence felt like a great big lie.

"You know," Jhasali disrupted my musings as a drone refilled her *av'vysh*, "I'm sure that was an unexpected and likely unpleasant experience for you, but I would deem it a success."

I took a bite of fish. "How so?"

Jhasali sipped her drink before speaking. "You left your living form, and that was not supposed to happen. But you did link up with the drone, and you *did* manipulate its body. You felt what it's like to command it."

My heart leapt. I had commanded it! "Is that what it's supposed to feel like?"

"No. Your mind should never lose awareness of your body like that. Ideally, you will get to the point where you are like me and able to see through the eyes of the drones as well as your own eyes, to hear through their ears as well as your own, to speak using their voices and allow their thoughts into your head."

I scoffed. "I can't imagine being able to do all that."

"You cannot imagine it because you have not yet experienced it. I hope, in time, you'll be able to learn what to do, but I fear your lack of confidence is hampering you more than your lack of ability. I was trying to help you understand how the connection is supposed to feel by making it for you, but I believe that was a mistake. The drone took too much of your mental capacity into itself when it bonded to you rather than you bonding to it. That is the reverse of how it's intended to work."

"Is there any chance I could become trapped in it?" I asked.

She shook her head. "I don't think so. I cannot be entirely sure, but as long as your partially organic body is living, if you put too much of your mind into the drone, that should be remedied by shutting it down or, worst case, destroying it if the override isn't accessible."

"Do you have to direct all the drones all the time?" I asked, fearing that once I did forge the nexus, commanding the device would suck up my whole life.

"No. They operate with constrained independence. That is to say, they can think, learn, and remember, which means they can carry out their orders without direct intervention from the bonded master. But it's up to the master to ensure the parameters of all orders are clear, especially if they are variable. This requires little effort for those of us who are integrated, so we need not mind our drones all the time as long as we remain connected to them."

"What happens if no one is connected to a bondable drone?"

"It reverts to a state of limited capability. Such restriction on the devices' autonomy is a safety feature to protect the living. If I as the master am disconnected from my personal drone, it will erase its memory of me and cease to fully function until another master seizes it, not because it cannot function without a biological master but because it's programmed not to."

"Does that not mean another user could steal them from you?" I asked.

"It is possible to compel a master to give commands to their bonded drones if you have physical possession of the master. Drones will often comply with certain coerced commands to protect their owners from harm. But it isn't easy to force or trick a drone into accepting a new master against the will of the old one. They can refuse a new owner if their current one is forcibly disconnected from them."

"How could they know you're being forcibly disconnected if they aren't conscious?"

"They aren't sentient, but their analytical skills are beyond parallel, and they can learn faster than any living being. They're attuned to the needs and feelings of their owners and wouldn't allow a usurper to connect with them if their master did not willingly sever the nexus."

"How do they know it's you?"

"Your bonded drones become familiar with your unique brain waves once they integrate into your personal network."

I knit my brow. "Won't the manual override allow someone to steal a device from you?"

"No. The override turns off the power and nothing else. It does not break the bond."

"Why did it put me back in my body, then?"

"Because your drone lost power. If your consciousness resides inside a device that loses power, it must make a jump to another physical host. We call the moving of the mind between devices 'snapping.' Since most of us split our consciousnesses between many devices as well as our physical bodies, losing one doesn't mean anything. We lose nothing except that device's sensory input and cognitive output. But because you just have the drone and your physical form, the loss of one means you can only snap to the other."

"Can you snap to Homeship?"

"Of course. All I have to do is prioritize its perception over my own."

"But if your consciousness is the only one that resides in the ship, if you're its only bonded master, why can I use it?" I asked; after all, I could now call the ascension platforms and turn on the water sources and do all the simple things I couldn't do before.

"Ships are different than bonded drones. You don't have to be fused to one to be able to perform some of its operations, but you must be listed as a secondary user. Think of me as the ship's captain. I am the only one with an actual bond to the device, meaning I have total control of all its functions. I can even go so far as to run the vessel by myself if I must. Assuming I have a crew, I list out a chain of command, so if I'm killed or otherwise incapacitated, the ship recognizes another captain. However, I also give the cruiser a manifest of all the rest of the crew and passengers so they can perform necessary functions for their privilege level."

I took a sip of *av'vysh*. "What are my privileges?"

"You've been listed as a base passenger since your implantation. I hope one day to list you as an officer."

"What can I do?"

"All the things you've been doing. You can access your room, the training chamber, and the common areas. You can command the ship's basic functions, such as waste systems and food distribution. You can utilize the internal communications system. But I don't believe you can—let me check—no, you cannot command the communal drones on this vessel unless you're ranked as a crew member."

"Communal drones?"

"Yes. Some of the unarmed drones that don't have access to sensitive information can be commanded without a nexus, meaning you don't have to be their master. If you're on their network and have the right privilege level, you can just tell them what to do," she explained.

"By speaking to them?"

"If you must, but that isn't necessary. You can project commands to them through your implants, like you would with a bonded device. The only difference is that you don't have to master them first. They're programmed to take orders from anyone with the right access."

"This is all so confusing," I replied.

"You know, you can ask your sensors to explain it."

"Discussing things with you helps me sort them out in a way I can't with my sensors."

"It isn't supposed to be like that. The implants are meant to be indistinguishable from the rest of your mind. I wonder if you've had more issues integrating with them than we thought."

I snorted. "Feels like my whole damned body is one big issue."

"It would indeed appear your internal devices are functioning adequately but not optimally. Don't worry. We'll figure it out."

"When? After I'm dead and gone?"

"What do you mean, dead and gone?"

"You know, I'll get old and die eventually."

Jhasali laughed. "I suppose you weren't listening when I said my people can outlive your species' civilizations."

I took a breath to come to grips with this new revelation. "So I'm to remain unchanged like you?"

"You knew that before I transformed you. I assumed you'd made your peace with it."

"How could I make my peace with something I didn't know?" I demanded.

"Of course you knew it. If I don't age because of these things, why would you?"

I had no answer. It had never occurred to me these little devils would make me so much like Jhasali, though at present I realized it should have.

"Change me back, then," I said.

"Mica, I told you before I gave you the nanos there would be no turning back. If you lose them now, you'll die."

"Override their programming. You said you could. Make them let me grow old like everyone else."

"I said you can override their programming to reproduce. I did not say you can override it to die. That is a safety feature. If you could tell the bots to kill you or allow your demise at your fancy, then you might do such a thing for no good reason. The end of one's life is something to be thought out and worked for, not achieved on a whim."

"So if I'm not killed by violence or mishap, I must die by my own hand?"

"Naturally. How else do any of us ever die?" Jhasali snapped.

"And if I cannot end my own life?"

"Then, assuming no calamity befalls you, you shall live on to the collapse of your solar system, and should you leave it, perhaps unto the heat death of the universe."

The tears welled up in my eyes as images flashed through my head, awful scenes of watching Sergio's black hair go gray and his bright eyes dim, of seeing the lines of age cut into Gracia's yet unmarred countenance, of standing by as even Eduardo grew swiftly into manhood and then died before my very eyes as I stayed fixed for eternity.

"I don't understand why my sensors didn't inform me of this!" I cried.

"Did you ask?"

"Well, no, I . . ." In truth, I'd never thought to ask. I'd operated under the assumption I would age and die, and the sensors never divested me of that notion.

"The implants wouldn't have answered a question you never asked. They're passive devices. You can't expect them to magically know which information to prioritize," Jhasali said.

"You should've warned me yourself. I wished to be invulnerable, not immortal."

"There is no such thing as immortality. As long as your consciousness is housed in a host and subject to the physical laws, death is inevitable. You are now free to choose the time and the manner, but you will assuredly die. One day, the last of the suns will explode, and the universe will burn out, and then you too shall go with it, as will we all."

"And how am I supposed to explain all this to Sergio? How can I sit by and watch him shrivel into an aged husk whilst I've delayed the inevitable indefinitely?"

"Again, I assumed you'd already worked this out."

We sat long in silence before I spoke again. "You should make him as you've made me."

"No." Jhasali's tone was calm but unmistakably resolute.

"Why not?"

"I transformed you because I know and love you, and you were in urgent need. I don't know or love Sergio, nor do I wish to."

"Is it not enough that I wish it for him?"

"No."

Knowing it would do me no good to press her further, I rose and left the ship without another word. I wandered the woods on foot for a long while, deep in thought. It was not as though I found the idea of an indefinite lifespan all that unappealing. In truth, if I'd had no complications, I'd have been thrilled to find death no longer had dominion over me. But I had many complications, the biggest of which was named Sergio. He might notice when I passed ten and fifteen and twenty years without aging a day.

More than that, I had spent the entirety of our marriage in fear he'd leave me a widow. Now, this fear had gone from being a possibility to an absolute certainty. Sergio's lifespan had become to mine what Lobo's would have been to his. No matter what Jhasali said, I could never make my peace with that.

***

In the weeks after my return from Toledo, I got so caught up in the drone lessons and the impending search for my mother that I flitted off to Homeship whenever the mood struck me, regardless of who might be watching. I sometimes spent days on end there without giving anyone so much as a cursory explanation of my whereabouts. Naturally, it did not take long for people to start talking.

One cool autumn morning, I came to call at Armando's family tower house after Gabriel sent a messenger to get me. Rosa showed me into the parlor, where Gabriel and Gracia sat quietly, seeming to have been in the middle of some grave conversation. Gracia gave Eduardo to Rosa and bade her leave the room.

"Come in," Gabriel said, his tone so serious it gave me the urge to laugh out of nerves.

I sank down on the chair opposite the sofa on which they both perched. Gracia sat with her hands clasped together and folded on the blue damask of her dress.

Gabriel leaned forward with his elbows on his knees and his chin on the knuckles of his left hand.

"What is this?" I asked.

"Micaela, you're often nowhere to be found of late. And we feared—"

"Gabriel!" Gracia interjected. "Not like that. Micaela, we know you've been lonely, what with Sergio gone on such a long journey. We were concerned you might be bored since returning from Sevilla . . ." She trailed off.

It dawned on me why we were here, and I needed to quell any rumor of my adultery lest it bring up a much more dangerous set of questions. Alas, I had no explanation for my frequent comings and goings and sometimes dayslong absences that did not involve a wild tale none would understand or believe. I thought fast.

"Are you accusing me of something?" I asked.

"Should we be?" Gabriel replied.

"No, you should not," I snapped, more angrily than I'd intended.

"No one is accusing you of anything." Gracia gave Gabriel the side-eye. "We just don't understand where you've been going. People are talking."

That hot, familiar sensation of anger rose in my chest, but it mixed with a strong feeling of foolishness. I should have known people would talk.

"Alright, here is the truth," I muttered without a clue as to what would come next. "I have a patroness."

The lie flowed forth with ease. It was ludicrous, of course, but it might work if I stuck to it. I certainly had no alternative.

Gracia barely suppressed her surprise. "You paint?"

"Yes," I replied, having nothing better to say.

"Why haven't we seen any of your works?" Gabriel crossed his arms.

"I was ashamed of them. I believed I wasn't all that talented. That's why I always kept all my painting things hidden," I answered.

He raised an eyebrow. "Then how did you find a patroness?"

"I met her a few summers ago. We got to talking about artworks, and she asked to see some of mine, so I showed her." I tried to avoid giving too much detail.

"Where does she live, this patroness?" Gabriel asked.

"On the other side of Santander, closer to Bilbao, but still in La Montaña. That's her main residence, but she has another house much closer to Santa Colomba. That's where I go—when she's staying there."

"What's her name?"

"I don't wish to divulge that. She's an eccentric and prefers her privacy."

"Where did she get the funds to sponsor you?" he demanded.

"Her late husband was a rich lord. She has plenty of gold to do as she pleases," I replied, surprised at how easily the lies now rolled off my tongue.

"May we see some of your work?" Gracia was trying to steer the conversation in a lighter direction than this rapidly intensifying interrogation.

"I would, but"—I paused, my thoughts racing to catch up to my needs—"all my works are at her house."

Gabriel squinted, and a fine crease appeared between his brows.

"I'll bring some home with me next time I go see her," I added.

Gabriel shot me a suspicious look, but since he had no proof anything I said was untrue, he relented, at least for the present. "I don't think Sergio would like you riding out all alone to see this patroness. I promised him I would look after you, and—"

"Don Gabriel, with all due respect, I don't need looking after. I rode all the way to Sevilla without issue."

"Regardless, I'd feel better if you had an escort to your patroness's house." He rolled his eyes at the word "patroness."

Gracia didn't see this and chimed in with her agreement that I shouldn't travel alone. I swore I wouldn't ride unaccompanied again, promising to send for one of my patroness's servants to escort me when I went to her manor. I then excused myself as politely as I could and fled back to my house.

What in the name of Christ had I been thinking? I was no painter. I had not so much as read a book about painting. I had to get back to Jhasali and figure out a way to fake some artwork that could make my lies passable. I was also going to have to resume my old habit of absconding in the dead of night if I wanted to avoid any more run-ins with Gabriel.

Next time I made it out to Homeship, I recounted the exchange to Jhasali. By the time I finished, I was in a real panic.

"I don't know what to do. I don't paint. Why did I say I paint? It was Gracia's fault. She put the words in my mouth, and I didn't contradict them!"

I was shouting, my hair flying and my arms flailing, but I didn't care. I was in a serious predicament, and Jhasali was failing to understand the gravity of it.

She laughed. "Micalita, this is not a problem at all."

"How is it not a problem?" I yelled. "I can't even hold a paintbrush. Why didn't I just say I'm an adulteress and get it over with?"

"Perhaps because you are not an adulteress?"

"As if anyone will believe that," I snapped.

"You're not listening. If you say you make paintings, then we will make paintings."

"How? Are you going to paint them for me?"

"Of course not. Come." She slid out of her chair and beckoned me to follow.

She led me down to one of the communal living quarters and stood me in front of the big clear wall in the middle of the room. The early morning light vanished from the ship, and the screen lit up with a beautiful scene I'd seen a thousand times before: a sunset over the ocean.

This had to be the most realistic realist work I'd laid eyes on. The orange half-circle sun sank into the water, and the ripples of its light danced in the golden waves and on the coral clouds. The shimmering ocean was interspersed with whitecaps, and a few stars peeked out near the top of the frame.

I should have known this picture would take no more effort for Jhasali to produce than desiring it. Nevertheless, I was shocked to see a still of this very sunset, a sunset I remembered well, having seen the same one many times in high summer, when the sun crawled far enough to the north that it set over the sliver of ocean visible off the western edge of the ridge below Homeship's deck.

"How did you do this?" I whispered.

She shrugged. "It's just a picture. It's a still shot from the drones' memories. I can upload everything I see to their storage banks, as well. You can too, you know."

The scene changed from that of the sunset to that of a slender raven-haired woman in an embroidered black dress, standing alone in a wooded clearing and looking down at a cluster of tiny flowers blooming out of a bald spot in the snow. I gasped; she was me.

I remembered the day this image was captured. It was some months after I'd taken the nanos, and I'd found this clearing after I'd gone into the woods with Jhasali to enjoy the break in the winter weather and forget my sorrows. She'd had drones with us, of course, but I'd become so accustomed to them I hadn't thought anything of it. I'd ignored them in favor of picking a few of those delicate early-spring flowers before the frost got them.

Approaching the glass wall, I looked up at myself as I gazed at the blossoms, immobile and unchanging. I'd never seen myself in this manner. Obviously, I'd seen my reflection in plates and pools and windowpanes—even the drones' hologram projections. But since I had little money and no status, I'd never in my life beheld myself in the form of a portrait.

I looked at the woman in the picture. Instead of looking back at me the way she did when she was my reflection, she cast her eyes downward. The movement of her hair, her dress, her hands, her eyelids had all been frozen in real time, as if the essence of her life itself, of my life, had been solidified into place. I put my hand on the glass, right at the hem of my dress, the same dress I wore now.

Just a picture? Jhasali had said that as if it meant nothing, for she could capture thousands of these images in a mere second. She could never comprehend what these "meaningless" pictures meant to me.

Her voice came bounding out of the silence, snapping me out of my stupor. "If I take that and print it on a canvas, will it suffice as proof of your patronage? Will it pass as an artwork?"

"I think so," I whispered.

She laughed, and I realized I remained open-mouthed before the glass. I clenched my jaw shut and yanked my hand away from the screen, but I couldn't avert my gaze from the picture. How could I make Jhasali understand what it was like for me to see myself as I existed? For the first time, I had the privilege of looking on my own image, and I gaped at that young woman clad all in black and casting her eyes down to the flowers at her feet. She was beautiful.

I waited while Jhasali gathered supplies and then set the drones to work by afternoon. She'd already made some paints and dyes out of different elements of the forest for the manufacture of her own earthly clothing, so she recommissioned these for the prints. The drones also made a makeshift easel by having two of the eight-armed devices position themselves on the top and bottom of the canvas to stretch it tight. Jhasali did not concern herself with the printing; she said the drones would figure it out on their own.

I wished to watch, so I entered the chamber where they were painting to discover how they would manage it. I came round to the other side of the stretched canvas to find a drone imprinting my image onto it. It worked in a bizarre manner, taking its arms, which were now all tipped with tiny needles, and dipping them into variously colored ink pots. It then took this ink and injected it into the surface of the canvas, dyeing the individual threads. It worked so fast it painted half the picture in the time I stood there watching it.

"Fascinating enough?" Jhasali's quiet voice said behind me. "My people have not printed anything on physical media in thousands of your Earth years, so the drones had to improvise."

"Seems they've had no trouble," I replied, staring at my face on the canvas.

I could see the lines in my lips, the glistening of my eyes, the outline of each individual eyelash. The drone had even gotten the texture of my hair right: the way it so often rebelled and broke free of whatever ribbon bound it, despite its heaviness.

I came up behind the drone and put my face near the canvas. As I did, the device began emitting a horrible buzzing sound.

"Step back, please," it said in a monotone voice.

Jhasali laughed and took my hand. "You have angered it. Come. I wish to show you the others anyhow."

"What others?" I asked, thinking there'd hardly been time to produce more of these, but my question was answered as soon as we stepped into the adjacent room.

Two more paintings stood leaned against the wall, already completed and stretched in makeshift wooden frames. The image of the marine sunset I'd seen before was embossed on one of the canvases, but the other gave me such a start I actually cried out. When I cast my gaze on it, I stared into the deep, dark eyes of my husband.

He was "painted" from the shoulders up, and the portrait looked so lifelike I was tempted to speak to it. It was all correct: his loose and wild curls, his black irises—so dark a shade they were hardly distinguishable from his pupils—his thick lashes and brows, his shaven cheeks, his tapered jawline. The drone had even managed to capture the way his solemn expression was often countered by that hint of a smile that always played at his lips, just out of reach.

"Where did you get his image? You have never met Sergio. You've certainly never brought the drones into his presence," I said.

"I don't need to meet him. You think the surveillance bots never got a look at him?"

I whipped around. "Are you back to spying on me?"

"Of course not, but the bots saw him around town same as everyone else. I observed the city many times before you and I met. As often as you two used to walk the streets together, it wasn't hard to guess who your husband was after you told me what a husband is."

A sharp pang pricked my heart. I had once walked the streets of Santa Colomba with Sergio every day when he was ashore, but those days felt like a lifetime ago.

I wiped a stray tear from my cheek. "So you're keeping clear of my home but watching me in the street?"

"I'm not following you specifically. Yet, if a bot does a flyover and you happen to be outside, how do you expect it to not see you along with everyone else?"

When I gave her a dubious look, she cried, "If you want to root through every image the damned surveillance network has recorded these last Earth years, be my guest. I periodically survey all the towns and villages surrounding my ship for security, but I'm not singling you out."

"I believe you, but this image is so lifelike, it's so . . ."

"I shouldn't have printed that one. I thought you'd like it, but clearly, I was wrong."

"I do like it. It just makes me miss him." I covered my mouth with my hand.

Jhasali wrapped her arms around my shoulders and reminded me he'd be home soon. I hoped she was right, for if she wasn't, this painting would be all I'd ever see of him again.

Later that night, I arrived at my house with the paintings rolled up in my saddlebags. I decided to frame the picture of Sergio and find a space to hang it. I built a fire and lit every candle I owned to chase away the darkness. Though I did not need these lights, I liked the dancing glow they cast around the room, giving it a warmer, happier feeling than that of my cold, almost-colorless night vision.

Workspace lit, I set about reconstructing the wooden frame from Homeship and fitting the picture inside it. I then hung it on the wall opposite the bed and sat down to view my handiwork. Seeing Sergio there, his visage so convincing, only served to make me miss him more. Deciding to employ the traditional sailor's solution to this problem, I pulled a wineskin from the kitchen. I filled my cup to the brim, thinking if I could drink enough, I'd be able to put myself into a dreamless stupor.

Yet no matter how I willed it, I still could not make the nanos stop cleaning my blood. I went through the entire wineskin and achieved nothing more than having to use the privy every five minutes. I finally gave it up and hurled the empty vessel in the smoldering fire before I stomped off to bed, frustrated and still sober as a priest—actually, a lot soberer than many priests.

Next day, I took the paintings to Gracia and Gabriel, wishing to put any gossip of my infidelity to rest as soon as possible.

"I wanted to show you something." I pulled the painting of the sunset out of its leather tube, stretching it on the table.

Gracia gasped when she saw it. "It's incredible. But why aren't there any brush-strokes?"

"I use my own technique, dabbing the canvas with a tiny brush, so there are no visible strokes." I pulled the portrait of myself from the container and laid it out.

"Micaela!" Gracia exclaimed. "How did you paint such a stunning self-portrait?"

"I paint all my works from committed memory," I replied.

Gabriel, however, was not so easily convinced. "There's no way you painted this."

"Who would have painted it for me?" I asked.

"I don't know. Someone with a better eye than da Vinci."

I suppressed my anger that he thought whatever lover I'd taken was an artist passing off his work as mine to ease suspicion. "I'll paint one of you and your family, Don Gabriel."

"Good. Then we can watch you do it," he snapped.

"I only work in solitude, but don't worry," I said, aware I was getting myself right back into the same situation I'd just managed to escape. "There will be no doubt who created it."

# Chapter Twenty

# THE NEW COVENANT

During all the business with my drone lessons and false artistic virtuosity, Father Manuel and I initiated our epistolary investigations. He wrote to a few contacts in Toledo, and I began to visit the rectory once more, both to see if replies had arrived and to socialize with the old man. No matter how foolish his past actions might've been, I couldn't bring myself to abandon him.

One particular afternoon, I went for a social call. As soon as I set foot in the rectory, Father Manuel scowled at me without uttering a word.

"What?" I asked.

"One of my Toledo contacts sent me a reply containing the most interesting news."

"Of my mother?"

"No. He said he knows nothing of her, but he was more concerned with other events. The authorities are conducting a manhunt in the areas surrounding Toledo. A hunt for a powerful and dangerous sorceress who can burn at the stake without so much as singeing a hair of her head, who can be struck with a heavy blade and suffer not a scratch, who can douse herself in boiling oil and run flaming through the streets. A woman who calls herself the heretic of heretics. You wouldn't happen to know anything of her, would you?"

I pursed my lips. "Do you plan to turn me over?"

"Do you think if I planned that, I'd be telling you about the search for you? I'm sure you guessed you couldn't pull such a stunt without repercussions."

"I did not exactly think it through at the time."

"You don't say," he snapped. "I might've hoped all the witch lunacy in Navarra would've made an impression on you."

"What was I to do? Let innocent people burn?"

"Yes! You would burn yourself for a horde of marranos. How many real inno-cents might be burning now for your stupidity?"

"Don't you dare disparage them after all your ilk have done to those poor people," I shouted as an image of Saúl's mangled arms flashed before my eyes.

"You act like my disapproval of your actions is as good as lighting the stake."

"Is not tacit acceptance as good as participation? And I am no better than 'those marranos.' I'm just another heretic, so maybe you *should* turn me in."

"I already swore I'd do no such thing. Though, if I could ensure it would have no impact on you, I'd denounce your foreign friend Juana, if that's even her real name."

I remained still to catch my breath, as one does when recovering from a too-close-for-comfort lightning strike. The flash and thunder of his words had come and gone, but they still rang in my ears.

"What makes you think any of this has to do with Juana?" I asked.

"I'm no fool, Micaela. I've had plenty of time to think on it, and with this incident in Toledo, I'm certain all this is her fault. I know she wasn't Gracia's midwife. Gabriel told me weeks before Eduardo's birth they were going to be using Clara García as a midwife. And you think I didn't notice Juana's accent or her strange manner of dress? I didn't ask you about her because I feared you had called some enchantress to try to save Gracia. I'd hoped it was a one-time mistake you'd only made out of desperation, but clearly I was wrong."

Now, I felt serious alarm. If he thought Jhasali was an enchantress running around transfiguring women into Achillean monsters, he might very well denounce her to the alguacil or the Inquisition. What might she do if a torch-bearing rabble *did* come after her? Would she wreck the whole kingdom or even decide all human-ity needed exterminating?

"Father," I breathed. "You are dealing with forces you don't comprehend, and you cannot involve the Crown or the Church in any of it. Juana is benevolent and intelligent, but if you provoke her, you could put the entire kingdom, nay, the entire world at risk. If you value your life and the lives of your flock, you will keep your silence absolute."

A concussive quiet followed my words, the kind of quiet that is, in its own way, more stunning than any shock of sound. It left a void that was soon filled with the soft, yet vibrant, hum of the outside world floating through the window. The last of the fall bees buzzed, and the breeze rustled the leaves of the shrubs. The waves babbled and hissed as the tide came into the estuary. Thunder rumbled over the ocean, perhaps leagues upon leagues offshore. My ears picked up the whirring of the storm as it kicked sea spray in its unseen fury.

Father Manuel finally murmured, "I cannot allow this woman to run wild, sowing seeds of scandal and sorcery. If something is done about her, your soul might yet be saved."

"You can't burn her; she is like me. What is the threat of your Christian fires to us?" I held my hand in the flames of the candles burning beside him to make my point quite clear.

When he didn't respond, I pressed my position. "You know that if you bring the authorities here, you bring calamity with them. If they fear Juana's power is spreading, they'll raze this port to the ground. How many of your flock's lives is my soul worth to you?"

"I value the lives of my flock. But what of their salvation?"

"How is Juana a danger to anyone's salvation? Gracia's seems just fine, though my 'foreign friend' saved her from childbed fever."

"That was a miracle!" he cried.

"No, it was Juana. If you would call her a sorceress for healing the sick, perhaps you're no different than the Pharisees. They didn't like Christ's ministrations very much either."

"She couldn't have done that. It was impossible without divine intervention."

"She did do it—no divine intervention necessary. She filled a vaporizer drone attachment with tranquilizer to sedate everyone in the house. Then she used several rounds of antimicrobials and a container of synthetic blood to eliminate the infection and rehydrate Gracia."

Father Manuel looked at me as if I'd gone mad, and I realized I'd switched to Sartjyanan at some point during my explanation. Damned sensors. I knit my brow and backed up.

"I'm sorry. She taught me her language, and some of her words haven't got an equivalent in our tongue. I can explain: Juana put everyone in the house into a state of sleep much like that of a soporific sponge. Next, she used a couple of different medicinal brews, recipes of her native people, to cure Gracia's illness."

"That sounds an awful lot like sorcery."

"I thought you don't believe in sorcery."

"I don't know what I believe anymore." He stroked his chin.

"Well, you needn't believe in magic. Juana's power lies in science, not sorcery. She taught me about her abilities, and she made me understand nothing she does is enchantment."

"So she's an alchemist? She's found some kind of healing elixir?"

"That's not a bad conclusion. In fact, if I had been a bit more learned when I met her, perhaps I might've jumped to that, too. Still, it's not exactly accurate." I paused to think before asking, "Do you recall what color Gracia was when you saw her the night she almost died?"

He thought back and then answered she was green as a summer apple. I told him that was because Juana had replaced the blood the surgeons had taken with an artificial version meant to help her cling to life. I explained that if he had seen Gracia before she'd been treated, he would have understood that nothing, not even a miracle, could have saved her except that synthesized concoction.

Father Manuel put his thumbs on his cheeks and massaged his brow. "Could she perform such healing on a larger scale?"

"Of course," I replied.

"And you have that power as well?"

"It isn't something I possess inside me, but I know the methods."

The cogs behind his eyes began to turn at this unforeseen complication. "Could you obtain this elixir from her by some means and transfer it to the rest of the city? In case we were to have a plague outbreak?"

I laughed. "No. That might fall under the umbrella of provoking her. Besides, there aren't many of your sort I'd be keen to trust with it. They'd probably lock it in a dungeon somewhere and only dispense it to those who could make a large enough offering or impose such heavy restrictions on it as to render it useless."

He was disappointed by this response but also acknowledged I was probably right not to trust the priesthood with such power. Without warning, he leapt from his seat and began pacing back and forth.

"What's wrong?" I asked.

"It's a sin to covet such a gift. Sorcery is always perilous, even if it can be used to save lives. It will preserve the body and damn the soul."

I let out a real guffaw. "I thought we established it's not witchcraft."

"This is no laughing matter." He shook his finger at me. "Your friend is too powerful to not be in league with the devil. Even a philosopher's stone couldn't give her such abilities. She can create lifeblood. She cannot burn. She cannot be pierced. She can pass her infernal talents to others. I could be flirting with damnation just speaking of seeking her help."

"Oh, Father, don't worry. You weren't interested in obtaining Juana's gift when you discovered it could make the body hard as living stone. You only wanted it when you learned it could keep the cemeteries from bursting with the bodies of the dead and the houses from overflowing with the weeping of the dying. I don't think that's worthy of damnation. I think it's the act of a decent person—a truly decent person, not a false one who believes he's righteous because he whips himself and puts innocents to the stake."

Father Manuel stopped pacing at this; his breathing slowed, and he returned to his chair. Taking that as I good sign, I went on.

"It doesn't matter what you want of Juana anyhow, I can't take her medicines from her and pass them out on the street. To attempt it would pose a danger to you and me—especially me," I added, dreading to think what Jhasali would do if she ever discovered we'd had this conversation. "But if you agree to keep her secrets as you already keep mine, she will stay close by, and I can beseech her to use her healing gifts if the need should arise."

"I fear the damnation of my soul if I do," he said.

"I think your Father in Heaven will understand the desire not to see babies turn black as crows and die in their cribs."

He stayed silent, staring at nothing, so I allowed him to ponder what I offered. The candles burned lower, and the faded light of the sun grew dimmer, but he still did not speak. I wondered if his mind would triumph in this crusade for his soul or be crushed under the weight of doctrine and tradition. Perhaps mind and conscience could form an alliance in this regard.

At last, he looked at me. "I fear, if it came down to it, most of my flock would choose to keep their lives at the cost of their souls."

My heart sank. What could I do to keep him from denouncing Jhasali? I could never bring myself to kill him. I might lock him away for safekeeping, but it would not take people long to miss him. I was mulling the idea of getting some sedative from Homeship and keeping him indefinitely in a semiconscious state, claiming he was ill, when he continued.

"However, that is not for me to decide. It's my responsibility to shepherd my flock, not to make their choices for them. If they choose life, I will not deny it to them. Thus, I will receive Juana into our covenant and guard her secrets as well as I've guarded yours. In return, you must promise to use her gifts only if their employment could be deemed righteous—not simply to achieve your own ends, as you did in Toledo."

He stood before I could respond. When I looked up after him, I caught a glimpse of the window behind him and realized it had become too dark too early. The storm had come.

"I'm going to conduct the evening prayers. You of all people should be there," he said.

Assenting, I rose and followed him across the courtyard. Vespers was a subdued affair, heavily interrupted by the towering tempest outside. By the time it was over, the weather had calmed, and the few people who'd attended cleared out quick, wishing to get to their houses during this short break in the rain.

"I should go," I said when Father Manuel and I were the last two inside the church.

"It's dark and the streets are empty. Stay with me tonight."

"Must I sleep in that tiny maid's room cot just because the streets are empty? Considering how many empty streets there were on the journey from Sevilla?"

"Even if things will never be the same for you and me, we can put up the pretense for comfort's sake." He sighed. When I didn't answer, he added, "You can have my bed. I'm going to remain here and pray awhile, but I'll sleep in a chair if I return at all."

I assented. At that, he turned and left me to wander to the rectory alone, pondering what I might've said to thank him for protecting Jhasali's and my secrets, though it flew in the face of everything he'd thought he believed.

Inside the rectory, I glanced over to the table where Father Manuel had placed his worn, aged copy of the Bible. I took it in hand and looked down at what he had been reading. I rolled my eyes. It was all that nonsense of fire and sulfur in Revelation. I shut it up tight, wishing burning it would release us all from the misery of its contents. If only things were so simple.

As I stared at the book, I got the urge to reopen it, remembering a passage I'd seen the night I'd read it cover to cover. Turning to Matthew 25, I took two coins from my purse and laid them on the page to mark two spots: "I was sick, and you visited me" and "I say to you, whenever you did this for one of these, the least of my brothers, you did it for me." I left the book lying open on the table and went to my tiny former bed.

***

I hoped Father Manuel would be the only one to hear of the incident in Toledo, but of course, this was not the case. Letters had already come and gone, and within days of our argument, the town was ablaze with rumors of the Witch of Toledo. I could not walk down the street without overhearing some tall tale about how I'd slain fifty guards and ridden off on a flaming horse of the apocalypse, how I'd received my powers by wedding Satan in the French countryside, or how I'd been the height of two men and escorted by a horde of demons.

I had hoped my countrymen were above such nonsense, but I suspected part of the fervor lay in the simple entertainment value of tall tales. At least with the whole town discussing the Witch of Toledo, everyone forgot to gossip about my allegedly adulterous absences to Homeship.

Jhasali picked up a good bit of their chatter over her surveillance network. So she sat me down in the ship and gave me a long, unpleasant lecture on how clear she'd made her expectations of my behavior and how she didn't appreciate my flagrant disregard for her need for secrecy.

"I didn't intend to trade one owner for another when I took a room in Homeship as well as my husband's house, Jhasali," I spat once I'd tired of her earsplitting monologue.

"I might not be your owner, but I am the master of Homeship and all the drones within it, and you'd do well to remember that," she snapped and kept right on yelling before I could get in another word. "Damn you, Mica, you'd better never ever do anything like that again! And you'd better be glad you got it out of your system down south. If you show such indiscretion here, believe me, you will regret it."

"You're such a hypocrite. Upbraiding me for doing no more than what you did in your own society. If you wanted a fellow Dissenter when you sought me out, by Jove, you got one!" I stepped to her and put my nose a hair's breadth from her own.

"You were lucky to have escaped." She backed up and softened her tone. "I fear you're more like I was than you realize. I didn't understand rebellion always has a price either. If you aren't willing or ready to pay it, you'd best keep your head down and your mouth shut."

"I am ready, whatever may come. But I'm certain I escaped any serious repercussions this time."

"So was I."

That worried me, but I comforted myself by recalling she could never understand just how primitive the technologies of my species were or how limited their ability to hunt me would prove when I'd never given anyone my name nor left any clue as to where I might've fled. I was also certain Ignacio hadn't realized he knew me, for I'd seen no spark of recognition in his eyes. Thus, I took comfort in my anonymity and put my mind at ease.

In the days following that argument, Jhasali cooled off and decided, just this once, she would forgive my indiscretions. With that settled, it appeared annoying tall tales would be the worst consequence of my act of dissidence, though they had permeated every street corner in town by this point.

Even the rich and educated were in on the talk. I discovered this when I visited Sara's town house one evening to find her, Gabriel, and Gracia all engaged in a heated debate about the gossip rolling off the tongues of the townsfolk.

"Hogwash! It's all ridiculous peasant nonsense," Gabriel snapped from the parlor.

"But how many people saw it with their own eyes?" Gracia replied.

"How many people *say* they saw it with their own eyes?" Gabriel corrected her.

"But Gabriel," Sara interrupted, "they say she burned herself before a crowd of people. I've received word from my sister; her husband witnessed the whole thing. He spoke of a young woman in a red dress who could sit within the flame as if it were no more to her than the sun on her hair, who could take the stroke of a blade as if her very flesh were made of chainmail."

My stomach lurched at these words. This was not some tall tale. This was a strikingly accurate description of the facts. At first, I tried to back out of the room to avoid this conversation, but they'd already spotted me.

"What say you, Micaela? Do you believe these ludicrous rumors of flaming witches running through the streets of Toledo?" Gabriel chuckled.

"Of course not, Don Gabriel." I sat down, resigned to my fate. "It's all the ramblings of untutored farmhands with nothing better for entertainment than wild stories."

I hated to contradict Sara and Gracia when they were right and Gabriel wrong, but what could I say? I couldn't exactly exclaim the rumors were all true and I was the fireproof witch in the red dress.

Gabriel cocked his head and smirked, and Gracia seemed content to let the matter lie, but Sara would not back down.

"My brother-in-law said—"

"A brother-in-law who goes to the quemadero for sport?" Gabriel snapped.

I had to give him that one.

"He has some peculiarities, but he would not lie. And he's confirmed this with his own eyes," Sara argued.

"You cannot always believe eyewitnesses, especially the ones with—how did you put it? Peculiarities?" Gabriel said.

"I concede his reveling in the executions is unpleasant, but he isn't mad. Having unfortunate taste in entertainment doesn't make one ungrounded in reality."

"Is that what you call it? Unfortunate taste in entertainment?" I blurted, before remembering my place among the parties here.

Sara looked chastened, however. "I didn't mean to put it so bluntly. I only meant his enjoyment of the burnings doesn't make his eyes blind."

I didn't answer, but Gabriel chimed in. "Say it's true, for argument's sake. What kind of witch saves heretics from the fire?"

"Satan might've wished to spare his own followers," Gracia pointed out.

"So he has to wait longer for their souls to enter the inferno?" Gabriel countered.

Sara swept a lock of hair behind her ear. "She could have been saving her friends."

"Maybe the woman was no witch. Maybe she was guiltless. God preserves the innocent from execution, right?" Gracia asked.

"I don't think that applies to a free woman who burned herself voluntarily." Gabriel laughed and patted Gracia's hand.

Sara frowned. "Did it ever occur to you that the condemned might've been guiltless? What if the woman were indeed there to save the innocent?"

"Are you saying the Holy Office was about to burn every single one of them in error?" Gabriel arched an eyebrow.

"I'm saying the reasons they burn them *are* the errors. They don't burn them erroneously but unjustly," Sara replied.

I feared she should not be making such implications about the validity of heresy laws while the servants were in the house, but she did not seem concerned.

"Then what would that make the Witch of Toledo?" Gracia took a sip of wine.

"I think she must be an angel or a saint sent to pull the innocent from the fire," Sara said.

Gabriel huffed. "Why would God rescue this batch of heretics and not others? Furthermore, what sort of angel do you know that's ever set itself alight?"

"The Psalms say the Lord makes the winds his messengers and the flames his ministers," Sara answered.

I didn't like the condescending way Gabriel had spoken to her, so I searched my sensors' internal database to see if I could find something I'd read in Father Manuel's Bible to back her up. I found Hebrews 1:7.

"Hebrews says, 'He makes his angels spirits, and his ministers a flame of fire.'"

"I think all that's meant more metaphorically," Gabriel mused.

Sara scoffed. "It's not metaphorical if it actually happens."

Gabriel turned to her, and his face hardened. "The whole thing is still a load of peasant rubbish anyhow."

Gracia's hand slid up to the silver-and-emerald cross around her neck. "If it is true, if it was a divine apparition, that must mean the Holy Office is no longer burning only heretics."

I found it challenging not to laugh at the notion their activities had ever been limited to true heretics instead of rich minorities with a heap of property to confiscate, but I didn't say so.

Sara rolled her eyes. "Were you under the impression they ever burned someone who actually merited it?"

"If they're only running around using the name of Christ to slaughter the innocent, then God wouldn't allow it," Gracia said.

"I don't know why he does, but I suppose his ways are not our ways," Sara replied.

"That's not good enough," I snapped. "Either God has no ability to stop the Church's evil, or he approves of the Church burning people and tossing their families into the street."

Sara squinted. "Don't conflate the Holy Office with the Church. They're not the same."

"They *are* the same. All the Inquisitions of Europe enforce the Church's theology, and if the Church did not sanction their work, they would cease to do it." Images of that gruesome work filled my head, and I added, "They all ought to be executed for war crimes."

"Even Father Manuel?" Sara asked.

"I meant the inquisitors," I answered.

"So you admit they're not the same!"

"I admit nothing of the sort. I only meant the guilt of the members of the Holy Office is a given. The rest of the clergy executes a different function for the same malevolent institution. They certainly all answer to the same papacy." I crossed my arms.

"Malevolent? So you just want to burn it all then, is that what you're saying?" Gabriel's eyebrows slid almost to his hairline.

"I suppose not. I'm not so vengeful as to want every last ecclesiastic treated the same way they've treated me."

"What do you mean?" Gabriel asked.

I paused. I'd gotten swept away in my tirade and said more than I'd intended. Everyone in this household still believed my parents had died of illness after dumping me on a church doorstep. If they discovered the truth, I'd be humiliated before them and everyone else in Santa Colomba.

"What I mean by 'me' is"—I bit my thumbnail—"I'm including myself in the collective. We're their collective victims. If one is oppressed, we are all oppressed. If one is unjustly punished, we are all unjustly punished. We shouldn't be willing to forget that because, at present, the target is someone else. Today, it's the conversos, but what happens when they're gone?"

Gabriel and Gracia concurred when I said this, but Sara looked at me doubtfully, as if she sensed I held something back.

I felt like a hypocrite for uttering those words whilst keeping secret my family's sufferings at the hands of the Inquisition, but I was afraid of what my companions might think of me if they knew the truth. I had yet to reject the notion that I somehow carried the stain of my parents' heresy, for it took me longer to let go of the attitudes behind the faith than it took me to let go of the faith itself. Even as I sat in that parlor and lambasted my former creed to its foundations, I saw myself as a secret pariah who might be cast out anytime. I feared, not unjustly I might add, that everyone else might come to see me in the same light if they learned the truth.

Thankfully, nobody questioned me further on my slip of the tongue. After I said my last piece, we all decided we had let ourselves get carried away with hypotheticals, and we changed the subject to something less contentious.

For several days after our discussion, I pondered Sara's harsh words toward the Holy Office. She'd outed herself as a heretic by uttering them, for criticizing the Inquisition was a crime of heresy in itself. Yet she'd taken it much further, insinuating that the ecclesiastical authorities had no right to punish heresy. It wasn't as though I disagreed with her, but I was surprised to find she agreed with me. Over and over, I asked myself, "Could she be like me?"

At the same time, she'd worked hard to distinguish the Inquisition from the Church that spawned it, which left me doubting my suspicions. I burst to ask her if she too had abandoned the faith of her youth, but I feared to as well. She and I had just gotten back on cordial terms after I'd absconded to Sevilla. Wrongly accusing her of apostasy might well be the end of our friendship, so I decided not to take the risk.

I had other things on my mind anyhow, as I planned to spend the next few weeks "painting" Gracia's family portrait. After All Saints' Day, I had her, Gabriel, and Eduardo dress in their best clothing and pose themselves in the parlor. I closed the doors to eliminate the question of whether the four of us were alone.

Gracia sat on the sofa with Eduardo in her lap and Gabriel standing behind her, placing his left hand on her right shoulder and his right hand on the handle of an ornate rapier. Cliché as it was, they'd posed themselves that way. I was only the method of record.

The pose was dignified enough, though I would have chosen a different outfit for Gracia if I could've dressed her myself. She wore a severe black dress and a chemise with a collar that rose to her chin. The black did not do her complexion any favors. While it contrasted well with her auburn hair, it rendered her skin so pale she looked dead, which, unfortunately, was the style at the time. She'd enhanced the whitening effect with almond powder or ceruse. I wished she'd chosen one of her more delicate and feminine dresses, like her pine-green, gold-embroidered gown that showed more skin and was less restrictive around the chest and belly.

I had the three of them sit for a long time while I stared at them, memorizing as many details as I could. Though my memory was nearly perfect now that it was complemented by my sensors, I nevertheless wished to get as many specifics burned into my brain as possible. I studied the slashed sleeves of Gabriel's doublet, the embroidery of Gracia's silk gown, the creamy color of Eduardo's simple robe, the part of Gabriel's blonde hair and the sheen the sun cast on it as the light came through the window.

As I analyzed, Gabriel grew impatient and argued that it was ridiculous for them to stand there for nothing because I should be painting, not staring. Gracia told him if they wanted a portrait of mine so badly, they'd better let the artist do her work. Once they started talking, however, they set Eduardo to fussing and squirming.

I gave it up, hoping I had enough recollection for a good image. Being not such a terrible sketch artist, I drew a quick outline, wrote down the colors, and hoped Jhasali could piece it all together when she uploaded the image into the drone.

Naturally, I knew better than to come back the next day with a portrait. It took actual artists weeks and months to produce the sort of picture Gabriel and Gracia expected me to create. They would've thought it a miracle if I returned with a painting so soon, but I had another motive for taking my time. As long as I was "painting" with my "patroness" at her estate, I could come and go to Homeship as I liked.

Going home to the ship a few days after I'd drawn my sketch, I asked Jhasali to set me up to make more paintings. She agreed but stopped short of consenting to upload the images herself.

"If you want more pictures, I'll be happy to have my devices print them. But you must master your drone, upload the true image, and share it with the ship's network. I'll do no mishmashing of sketches and description and recollections from my own memory," she said.

I was at a loss, for I'd stared so long at Gabriel and Gracia in preparation to draw and describe, not connect and upload. Even after many lessons, I'd never bonded with the drone on my own. I'd only connected with it on the sole occasion Jhasali had done so for me.

Disinterested in these excuses, my tutor brought my drone to me and disconnected from it. It cut its lights and hovered by my side, impotent without a commander to give it orders. My frustration mounted just looking at the thing.

Jhasali left the room. I wasn't sure if she had abandoned me because she knew the pressure of her presence only added to the difficulty of my task or if she had simply decided there was nothing more she could do to help me and didn't want to waste her time.

I stood alone, listening to the drone humming. I resented it for not making things easier for me, but I also felt like an idiot for being resentful of it because, after all, it was just an object, one that was meant to obey me. I looked away from it and thought of the image in my mind, the one of Gracia and her little family. I hoped if I concentrated on this image and tried to direct it toward the drone, I might link up with it more easily than if I fixated on making the connection. So I focused my attention on this memory of my friend's perfect young family.

Soon, however, my mind began to wander. I didn't wish to think of Gracia and her "perfect" family. Instead, I saw a vision of Sara—not Sara as she was at present but Sara as she should have been, as she surely had been in days gone by before the fever came and stole away her youth and her children and any hope she might've had of a happy life.

I tried to recall how her laugh had sounded, but it had been so long since I'd last heard it after the Masses of my girlhood. I wondered if laughter might've etched lines on her pretty face if only she'd done more of it; if it would've made her green eyes sparkle and her gentle smile more luminous. A deep sadness descended over me as I imagined what Sara's face might have looked like in the throes of laughter, her head tilted back, mouth open a tad but not too wide.

I'd forgotten the drone was present until I felt a tug in my mind. An unfamiliar pulling deep inside the recesses of my consciousness that let me know I was no longer alone inside my own head. I'd done it! I'd forged the nexus.

*Are you there?* I thought to the drone.

I heard no words in response. Rather, I sensed on an instinctual level that this device was listening to me, waiting for me to command it. It is impossible to describe how it feels to commune with a thing without language, without words or gestures. All I can say is it's akin to moving your limbs. Do you think "move, fingers" before you make a fist, or do you will it to happen and know it shall? The operation of the drones is like that. I must admit I am limited in my ability to describe this fellowship, for I must use words, and within the internal, mental union of artificial servant and living master, there are none.

I decided I wished to see a portrait of Sara laughing more than I wished to see Gracia sitting stiff-backed and holding Eduardo in a position she'd never adopt in life. I wanted life in my portraits, not the false reality of artistic pretense. I gave the drone the image of Sara I pictured in my mind, of her deep-green eyes shimmering, her smile wide and carefree. That was the image I wanted to see.

I made sure to upload my memory of Gracia's family, as well, in case I lost the link. Then I accompanied the drone around the ship until we found Jhasali.

"I'm ready," I said.

Not two hours later, I stared at a life-size canvas painted with an image of Sara so realistic I might have mistaken it for the actual person. She sat, relaxed and comfortable, in a cushioned chair, her shoulders tilted slightly to the side. She turned her face full on to the observer, her cocoa-brown hair shimmering in the light, her forest-green eyes matching the color of the dress that covered her shoulders. Her mouth opened in a pretty, elegant laugh that showed a sliver of her teeth.

Jhasali tilted her head in admiration. "It's a lovely image."

I was sure she commented on the quality of my memory and my communication of it, not the loveliness of the subject. It was a lovely image, but only because Sara was lovely. I wondered how I might present this painting to her but knew in an instant she could never see it. Why would she wish to be reminded of what she had once been and could never be again?

## Chapter Twenty-One
# THE OTHER VISITORS

As the weeks of Advent came and went, the wild tales of my witchly escapades lost their entertainment value and were soon replaced by stories of a more standard and salacious variety. Rumors swirled of townswomen's scandalous behavior, and the usual uncorroborated gossip of who was wearing cuckold's horns supplanted the incredible anecdotes of the Witch of Toledo. Normalcy returned, as it always does, even after the fiercest of storms.

Once the rumors from Toledo died off, I almost missed them. I wondered if anyone might someday write an epic romance about my irreverent exploits. Of course, as the so-called Witch of Toledo—a scarlet woman who'd reached into the fire and plucked a half dozen heretics from the hand of justice—I was sure to feature as the villain. I assumed if my story were ever told in literary form, they'd find some brave, holy knight with a heart of gold, veins full of pure blood, and a magical sword capable of piercing my dragon scales to send me back to the devil from whence I came. I laughed at the thought. Somehow, I *must* relearn to sleep at night despite my terrible wickedness.

Throughout the Christmas season, I remained so devoted to keeping up the ruse of my artistry to cover for my increasingly frequent visits to Homeship that I hadn't much time to focus on what I had done in Toledo anyhow. I gave Gabriel and Gracia their family portrait a few weeks after Epiphany, and my masterful work of art put to rest the last remnants of skepticism that I was the one painting the pictures. I had been the only one to see the three of them posed in that manner. With the intricate detail laid into the portrait, there could be no question I had painted it. Combined with the fact that Father Manuel had confirmed to Gabriel that he'd indeed met my mysterious patroness, this picture further solidified my ploy that I was painting other portraits at her house, which gave me unfettered freedom to visit Homeship at my leisure.

The portrait of Sara I kept in my room within Homeship, where I'd accumulated quite a collection of things. I kept a pair of Sergio's trousers and a shirt of his there so I could sleep with some of his clothes as I always did during his absences. I'd also bought some dishes and cookware for Homeship when I'd replaced the things that had been stolen from my house during the burglary. Now, I even kept many of my books and an extra nightgown on the vessel. Every time I rode for Homeship, I took something else there with me.

To my delight, as I brought more items to make Homeship feel like an actual home, I also began to have more intermittent success with the drone and my nanos. Although I'd passed the Christmas season depressingly sober, I'd managed to convince the bots to start my menstrual cycle once more—though it was more efficient and less intrusive than it had been in the past.

There were no days of bleeding and pain. Rather, my bots now eliminated only what they considered to be unnecessary, preserving my blood and sparing me discomfort. They also took care of everything all at once, warning me about it beforehand. Instead of having a period that lasted days on end without my ever knowing for certain when it would start or stop, I would suddenly realize the bots planned to expel what they deemed must be passed, and it would all come out of me a minute or two later. At present, they told me when it was about to happen, but I hoped one day soon I would be able to tell them when and where they were to do it. Right now, I was just thankful to be barren no longer.

As far as my practice drone was concerned, Jhasali and I had had a long conversation about possible reasons why I'd failed at mastering my device except on the single occasion I'd uploaded my images. When she realized I viewed the connection as an invasion of the mind, she said it was a wonder I'd been able to link up at all. She told me if I thought of the bond as a mental violation, then my mind was always going to be in a mode to defend itself.

I needed to accept the drone's connection just as much as it accepted mine, and if I did not give consent, my mind would always remain closed to the interface. She was right, of course. The sole reason I'd succeeded that single time was that I'd been thinking of Sara and my desire to see the image of her I'd created in my imagination.

I came to understand that the master-drone union was never meant to be a violation. I'd only been thinking of it on those terms because it was so unfamiliar, so beyond anything anyone from my planet had ever imagined. I'd been afraid of it because I did not know it. I comprehended how it functioned, but I had never truly comprehended its meaning and its significance.

From that conversation forward, I tried to change my attitude toward the link. My drone was not a cerebral violator I'd have to endure to find my mother. It was a loyal servant and dear friend that only needed to access my mind to ascertain my bidding. Once I adopted this mindset, I found the device more receptive to my advances because I was more open to its reciprocation.

Even so, my ability to achieve and maintain the bond remained far from perfect. Sometimes, I could link up so easily and maintain the connection so strongly it felt I'd been doing so my whole life. Other times, I experienced the same difficulty initiating the link that I had in my early lessons. Still other times, I could make a connection, but it would break once I began to think about other things. All I could do was continue to practice, improving my abilities until I could one day apply them to other drones on the network, including the surveillance bots, to launch my search.

Speaking of my search, a few of Father Manuel's contacts in Toledo had written back to him intermittently throughout the Christmas season. He knew I was well past the point of taking his word for anything, so he would put the sealed letters into my hand whenever they arrived on his desk.

Most of them stated one way or another that they had no idea what woman he was talking about. One of them contained nothing but a curt reply asking why Father Manuel thought an old man would remember something that happened to a pair of strangers almost twenty years ago. Another demanded to know why he inquired about the whereabouts of some heretic who'd gotten no worse than she'd deserved.

Only a single letter was more promising than these. It came from a former parishioner of Father Manuel: an alguacil's assistant who knew half the city. This acquaintance said he'd heard long ago the heretic in question had gone to Aragón, but he didn't know any more about it. Father Manuel had written back, asking this contact to see if he mightn't find more information, but we never received a reply.

Though Aragón was a large swath of territory, I was not disheartened, for I was prepared for the long game now. My initial frenzy to find my mother as fast as possible had cooled into a more rational, focused determination that I would find her soon but not this instant. If I started the search prematurely, I would endanger its success. I could not act on impulse as I had in Sevilla and Toledo. That would lead only to disaster.

As the weeks marched on, I made sure to behave myself, not wishing to make any more waves that might interfere with my ability to begin my quest. I went to Homeship as often as I could get away with so I might practice under Jhasali's tutelage in preparation for the day I'd take the form of a man and ride back to Toledo to speak to this alguacil's deputy and see if he might be more helpful face-to-face.

From there, I planned to head to Zaragoza—or wherever he sent me—armed with the ability to alter my appearance at will and a swarm of tiny spherical bots that could surveil the peninsula and beyond. Focused on the journey ahead, I continued practicing linking to my drone, training inside the chamber in case I needed to defend myself on the road, and working on whipping my nanos into submission.

Yet, despite all my desire and preparation, week after week, month after month, the bots inside my body proved more resistant to my commands than any other device. I did manage to gain some capacity to alter my appearance. It started with the ability to rouge my lips and give myself a line of freckles across my nose and cheeks. Then it matured to the point I could elongate my nose and strengthen my jaw to make myself more masculine. These changes I could do and undo at will without making any additional unintentional alterations.

However, I remained unable to make more drastic modifications. For instance, I'd been attempting to alter my height, even by a centimeter, and I'd failed utterly. As always, I had no idea why my bots obeyed some of my orders and not others, but while my command of them was so inconsistent, I feared to attempt the kinds of changes that would give me true freedom of movement and a bulletproof disguise, especially not with Sergio's return date drawing nearer. He might notice if he came home to a wife who'd grown a half meter taller and sprouted a beard—or a cock.

After several months of struggling, I began to worry. I'd prepared for a long game, but not an endless game, and it occurred to me my mother was no longer a young woman. I was the only one of us who had eternity to delay our reunion.

Thus, sometime after Easter, I decided to ask Jhasali again why I had such trouble consistently commanding my internal devices.

"You cannot expect things to move that quickly, Micalita," she answered. "The nanos' connection with their owners is meant to develop as the juveniles grow, and the integration can take many years to get to the point where the bots obey every command on demand."

"So what, they've got to grow up?" I said.

"I suppose if that's how you wish to look at it. You'll grow up together, mature in your comprehension of each other. The bots are still learning your system, how to understand your directives, how to distinguish what you're thinking in your mind from what you're telling them to do. Not to mention you're still learning how to give them proper instructions."

"I don't understand why they'll permit my monthly bleeding but not let me enjoy a damn drink. Why they'll let me change some things about my appearance but not others."

"Again, this is a new process. You are a new species. You may have to live with some imperfections, especially in the beginning."

I sighed. "Isn't there anything I can do to speed things along?"

"I doubt it. The nanos' inexperience combined with your own lack of skill at controlling them means there's not much you can do other than wait and keep practicing."

"But I don't have time to wait. If my mother is still living, she won't be forever."

"The only thing I can tell you to do is either delay your search as many years as it takes to hone your skills or set out as soon as you can and make do with the abilities you have."

I smoothed my hair. "Why don't we use the surveillance network to start now? Since it's taking me so long to gain proficiency, you could send the bots to do the searching in my stead."

"The surveillance drones can only observe. In this case, they cannot ask questions or conduct interviews. I believe much of this inquiry's direction will be predicated on information you glean from individuals who know more than we do, isn't that right?"

"Yes, but can't the bots just do a grid search or something?"

"No. I'm using them to keep the areas surrounding my perimeter under observation. I cannot spare you enough bots to send them sweeping all the regions of Spain and North Africa until you find this needle in the haystack. I think you may have an inflated idea about the capabilities of such a minuscule network."

"What do you mean?" I asked.

"If this planet belonged to my people, it would be so full of probes not even the sweeping away of an anthill would go unnoticed. I only have fifty, and I can spare you no more than ten, so they're not going to be as much help as you think. They can aid you in learning the geography of towns and cities. They can help you hear conversations that might be useful and let you view things you might not otherwise see. But they cannot replace you as the investigator."

"I just thought—"

She held up a hand. "That is another example of your inexperience. If you'd asked your sensors, they would've told you the limits of my capabilities under the current circumstances. You must have patience and continue practicing with both your internal and external devices. Otherwise, you'll never eliminate the bad habits contributing to your difficulties."

I didn't reply. I was aware I should have asked my sensors to better explain Jhasali's network, but I'd once again made the mistake of assuming they knew my informational desires when I'd failed to make them explicit.

"I know all this isn't what you wish to hear," Jhasali said when I remained quiet.

I rubbed the spot between my eyes. "No. It isn't."

I wandered the woods in silent disappointment for a long while after receiving this news. Every damned time I had a breakthrough, something happened that pushed my search further off, and now it was looking more and more like I'd have to wait until the start of the next sailing season before I'd be able to launch my quest. If Sergio arrived on schedule, there'd be nothing I could do but linger in town until he left again. Though I continually repeated Saúl's and Míriam's names in my head, trying to remind myself why I'd done as I did, I still sometimes lamented ever setting foot in that quemadero. Unfortunately, as I would soon discover, I was about to have yet another reason to lament it.

***

The mild May evening I learned we were to receive additional visitors besides the one from outer space, I was cooking alone in the rectory, waiting for Father Manuel to return from lunching with some friends near the harbor. I knew he would not have much of an appetite, but I'd already bought the lamb from the market, and I was starving, as usual. I figured if he didn't wish to eat, I'd have the lot for myself.

When he arrived, however, Father Manuel was in a worse mood than I might have expected of a man who'd just come from a spring afternoon spent lounging near the shore. I offered him some food, but he refused. I poured him a mug of wine, but he set that aside also.

"I've received word we're to have a visitation," he said.

"A what?" I took a seat at the table and tucked into my lunch.

"A visitation from the district tribunal."

I threw up my hands, still unsure what he was talking about.

"The inquisitors, Micaela, one of them is coming here," Father Manuel snapped.

My stomach dropped. Ignacio? Here? If that were the case, I'd be recognized for sure. I'd shoved my face a hair's breadth from his in Toledo.

"His name is Don Luis," Father Manuel continued. "And he'll be here with his crew in less than a week. Apparently, since they found no incombustible heretics in Toledo last year, the tribunals have begun making rounds across the kingdom because of your little stunt."

"Luis? Why is he different?"

"Different than what?"

"Oh, um, than, I don't know." I still hadn't told Father Manuel that Ignacio was the one who'd been in charge of the Toledo auto de fe. "The one in Toledo had a different name is all."

"It's a different jurisdiction." He tilted his chin down and wrinkled his forehead.

"So the same ones from Toledo won't be the ones coming here?"

"No."

"Christ! Thank God." I let my head fall back in relief.

"That doesn't mean everything is fine. You could still be denounced."

"By whom? You? You're the only one in town who knows the rumors aren't just bullshit, and you're the only man in the world who knows I am the Witch of Toledo."

"You never know. There could be familiars we aren't aware of or people who have personal issues with you. It's still the scandal of the decade that you went to Sevilla, after all. Worse, I fear there might be a slew of denunciations. Everyone tends to use these visitations to air their grievances."

"They do?" I pulled a hunk of lamb off the bone.

"You wouldn't remember. The last time this parish had one, I was not even its priest. I heard the tribunal did a string of them when it was first founded in Logroño, but that was a couple years before we came here. Oh, I'm dreading it. I don't wish to see my parishioners carted off because the Garcías are having a feud with the Ortegas."

"They are?"

"It's just an example." He rolled his eyes. "And if you'd kept your damned fireproof head down, we'd likely never have seen a visitor. Why, Micaela? Why?"

His tone rendered me defiant. "You're the one who's always told me to do the honorable and righteous thing. I guess that only applied when it didn't inconvenience anyone. When the righteous thing becomes difficult, am I meant to put my head down? Or did 'what's right' only apply to my virginity? Have I no honor other than what's between my legs?"

"Don't be vulgar!"

"Tell me, then. What did you mean when you said, 'Do what's right'?"

"I certainly did not mean for you to take my words as a command to rescue a bunch of unrepentant Judaizers from the hands of justice." He pointed a finger at me.

I slammed my fist on the table. "Father! How can you tell me I was wrong to save a bunch of Judaizers when you're simultaneously harboring an apostate atheist?"

It was the first time I used the A-words to Father Manuel, but I was an A-word. I knew he knew it, though perhaps he didn't know he knew it until I said it. Yet I didn't stop there.

"I suppose if you're going to talk like that, you better write to this Don Luis and tell him you have a heretic for him to burn."

He coughed. "You already know I won't do that."

"Why not? By your very own logic, I'm worthy of the fire. So bring it to me. Maybe they'll find a way to make it hot enough to melt me down like an old suit of armor."

I went as far as telling him I'd play his scrivener. Fetching his writing utensils, I sat down and commanded him to start dictating the letter denouncing me.

"Tell me. List what I've done to be worthy of death." I dipped the quill in the inkwell and held it over the parchment.

"I don't know," he muttered.

"I can't hear you."

"Nothing! Alright? Nothing. You're not worthy of death."

"Why am I the exception? Surely, one cannot be a bigger heretic than me."

"Why must you torment me with your constant contrarianism?" he asked.

"Because if you'd met that poor, beaten-down man and his resigned wife and his wrecked family with his children who didn't even know any better, you'd be ready to harry and torment everyone in the country too. How can you have taken me from my mother's arms in some wretched ecclesiastical jail and *still* defend what they're doing?"

"I don't know. All this makes my head hurt." He rubbed his temples.

I softened my tone and dropped the issue. "Regardless of whether I should have done as I did, it is done now. So, what are we going to do about these visitors?"

"Don't worry about that. Just, for once, try to keep a low profile."

"Should I make myself scarce for a few days?"

"No. Attendance at their Mass is mandatory. It'll be more conspicuous if you aren't present." He rose from the table.

Walking to the old trunk where we always stacked used dishes before washing them, he pulled the lid open, rummaging to the bottom. When he rose, he held a few ancient, moth-eaten sanbenitos that had been collecting dust within. I gasped.

He sighed and offered an explanation. "These were from before our time here. I took them down because the people were agitating, but I suppose I'll have to put them back up for the next couple of weeks."

I laughed. "You are a walking contradiction. You scold me for saving heretics, yet you hide me from the tribunal and tuck these old things away in your junk trunk?"

"I suppose I support the punishment of heresy until I see it with my own eyes."

"Seems your eyes handled the autos alright," I mumbled.

"Micaela, I never went to an auto de fe unless I had no other choice. I wanted to help my parishioners in their darkest hours, not watch them burn. You ought to know that much, at least."

"Fine, I'm sorry. I just wish all this heresy nonsense would stop. I'd roast myself in a traveling exhibition if it would put an end to it. Ha! If they tired of failing to incinerate me, they could always burn me in effigy and be through with it."

Father Manuel tossed the sanbenitos on the table. "You can dispense with the ridiculous jokes. Don't forget, I have been harboring you for over a year. If the right people find that out, I might wind up serving as your effigy."

I sighed deeply. "You're right. I'll keep my head down when the inquisitors are here and not do anything stupid."

"You mean anything *else* stupid."

I stared at the floor and did not reply.

I managed to show up to Mass the following Sunday and was pleasantly surprised by an announcement Father Manuel made once he ascended the chancel.

"I'm sure some of you are already aware of this, but we are to receive a visitation from the Inquisition within a few days," he stated.

There was an audible gasp from several of the women, followed by a collective grumbling, and a few people even started to boo and hiss.

"Now, now. I know many of you who remember the last one are probably displeased with this news. However, there is nothing we can do to prevent it. Thus, I'm encouraging you all, for the sake of your neighbors and your families, if you don't wish to see any more sanbenitos on these walls, keep your silence with the visitors. Do not denounce one another. Do not denounce yourselves. Do not speak to the inquisitor at all if you can avoid it."

I couldn't help but smile. Father Manuel might be misguided, but he was plucky when it counted, and I had to respect that. I winked at him from my place next to Isabel and Susana, but he pretended he hadn't seen.

Isabel leaned over and whispered, "Do you think they'll arrest us for not speaking?"

"Not if we all refuse to speak. If no one denounces anyone, they won't have enough evidence to make arrests." I feared my tone might betray my concern that

Father Manuel's announcement mightn't be enough to keep everyone silent. I hoped it would be, if not for my sake, then for everyone else's.

After a few days of collective unease in which I was sure each person in the entire city took private stock of everything they'd ever said to anyone they'd ever known, the visitors arrived. The first thing this fellow, Don Luis, did was usurp Father Manuel's lectern, read the Edict of Faith, and swear us all to maintain allegiance to the Inquisition and to tell all we knew of our neighbors' transgressions. Otherwise, the investigation would uncover everyone's secrets, which would be much worse for us all.

I sized up Luis as he read through a list of all the heresies one might denounce if one encountered them. I fit into quite a few of the boxes. Blasphemy? Check. Unorthodox ideation? Check. Criticizing the tribunal? Double check. Judaizing? Not technically, but one would have to list me in the "other" category when it came to apostasy. Sorcery? Definitely not, but how could I make anyone believe that? It was all I could do not to roll my eyes and laugh. This Luis character almost made a joke of the exercise.

He was old, not as old as Father Manuel, but still above fifty. He was tall, too, so tall, in fact, that his attainment of years had rendered him awkward as an older man. I was sure his size had made him intimidating in his youth, but now that he'd aged and gone soft and gotten himself a portly belly, he was so top-heavy it seemed he might tip over if the wind blew the right direction. I wondered if Sergio might become that awkward when he reached a similar age. He was just as tall as Luis, maybe a hair taller.

I reminded myself Luis might look silly, but the power of his pen was not a thing to be trifled with. Judging by his girth and his soft, uncalloused hands, he'd done well for himself in the pursuit of his career, and that could mean only one thing: he had a trail of victims in his wake—victims whose confiscated property had allowed him to gain that girth and those uncalloused hands.

At this recollection, I found my humorous contempt replaced by another familiar emotion: barely controlled wrath. I'd taken to wearing IDOS again, at least while the inquisitor and his retinue remained in town, and though it did not heat up at this sudden flare of temper, I became aware of its presence on my forearms. Yet I had promised; I'd sworn up and down I would not do anything *else* stupid. Not only had I said so to Father Manuel, but this city was all but Jhasali's seigneurial territory by now. If she discovered I'd done something as outrageous as I had in Toledo in her own backyard, I might inadvertently bring her silver birds down upon all my friends and neighbors. I took a deep breath and mentally checked out for the rest of the service. That was all I could do to restrain myself.

The day after the reading of the Edict of Faith, the investigation began in earnest, but I had no way of knowing whether anyone told the visitors anything. They slept in Inés's inn at night and holed up in the courthouse during the day, and I almost never saw their faces again the entire time the Inquisitorial retinue remained in Santa Colomba.

For the duration of the investigation, I stayed in Sara's home. She was worried because of the things she'd said when we'd had our debate about the Witch of Toledo. I tried to reassure her that Gabriel, Gracia, and I would never betray her. Not only that, but we'd run our mouths with some damned heretical ideation too. She told me she was not concerned with them but with the servants. We'd been alone when we'd spoken so frankly, but one can never know for sure. The walls have ears everywhere.

The first day or two of the investigation passed without anything remarkable occurring, though the longer these guests remained with us, the more intrigued I became with them. On the one hand, I was tempted to go and speak to this Don Luis on my own, for he could put me in little real danger here—not armed with IDOS, on my own turf, and so close to Homeship. I wanted to see what this new visitor was like.

On the other hand, I couldn't do anything rash when it might be the death of Father Manuel or one of my friends. I had to act like I knew better, even if, on some level, I didn't. No matter the temptation, never would I indulge the foolish desire to incite another fiasco like my auto de fe. That had been to save the innocent. Confronting Don Luis now would serve no other purpose than to satisfy my own impulses.

Soon, however, the choice was removed from me altogether. While I was walking from the rectory to Sara's town house, which took me on a street near the courthouse, a stranger grasped me by the wrist. He startled me, and both my cuffs heated automatically, though I yanked my arm out of his hand before he could be burned.

I bent my fist down and aimed IDOS at his head for a split second before I remembered myself and dropped my arm, realizing I stood face-to-face with one of Luis's men. Behind him stood several others and Don Luis himself.

"There's no need for that," the inquisitor told the guard who'd grabbed me. He then turned to me. "That's an odd way to react to being startled."

"Maybe I'm an odd person," I said, not in control of my tongue because of my nerves.

Luis laughed. "You're funny."

"What do you want?" I demanded.

His smile vanished, and I recalled to whom I spoke.

"I'm sorry, señoría." I bowed my head. "I meant to say how can I help you."

"That's more like it. Now, you are Micaela, wife of Sergio Marín and former ward of the parish priest, are you not?"

When I affirmed I was, he said, "I was going to send one of my men to fetch you, but since we've already run into one another here, I would like to speak to you. Come."

My heart raced. I didn't want to go with him, but I couldn't refuse. He walked ahead of me, and his men walked behind. They had not clapped me in irons, but what could I do besides fall in line? I wasn't concerned for myself; I was armed and durable as ever. Yet I dared not think what might become of anyone who had anything to do with me if I were forced to slay these men to protect my own wretched hide. I'm not sure I've ever felt as foolish as I did walking into the courthouse in the middle of that row of men, thinking all the while of the imbecilic things I'd done to draw them here.

I remembered the ancient priest in the cathedral in Toledo. I hadn't told him my name, but I had asked about my parents and their child. Could it be possible they'd discovered my identity based solely on that? They had records of my parents' sentences, but those would be with the Toledo tribunal. How much I could reasonably expect Luis and his associates to be aware of, I did not know, but I feared I followed them if not to my doom, then to the doom of many others.

We entered the courthouse and made our way down the hallways, passing deeper into the building. Preparing to heat my cuffs lest Luis tried to take me to a dungeon or torture chamber, I was stunned when his men opened the door to a rather comfortable-looking office with a large desk and a cozy sitting area with a few chairs arranged around a low table.

Two men already sat in these chairs. One I'd seen before; he'd been behind Luis at the lectern when the inquisitor had read the Edict of Faith. I did not know the other one. Luis sat down between these men and motioned for me to take the seat across from him.

"This is my secretary, Francisco." Luis gestured toward the short, pale, thin-faced man of maybe thirty-five or forty.

This man nodded at me but said nothing. He looked suited to no other sort of work than this, for he had a delicate constitution, with narrow shoulders and a large forehead.

Luis pointed to the other man, a young and handsome blonde called Hernando, who served as the notary. I almost hoped they didn't force me to fight so I might not have to kill this one. He smiled at me and said hello, and I found myself grinning like a schoolgirl.

*What in God's name is wrong with me?* I thought, trying to focus on my predicament.

"Would you like something to drink?" Luis asked.

He didn't wait for me to answer before having one of his guards bring me a large pewter mug full of ale. The man tried to hand it to me, but I wouldn't take it, so he set it on the table in front of me. After this, Luis told everyone to leave us except the notary and the secretary.

"This isn't what I expected," I said when they closed the door.

"What did you expect?" Luis took a sip from his own cup.

"I don't know, dungeons, interrogation, torture."

Luis chuckled. "I find, at this stage, people respond better to this sort of environment than the other. Besides, we aren't nearly far enough into the process for any of that."

"What process?"

"There's no process yet; I only have a couple of questions. Drink and try to relax."

I refused the cup. I didn't fear that whatever he'd laced the ale with could harm me, but neither did I know how the nanos might choose to expel it from my system. I didn't want to drink it and immediately regurgitate it all over the room.

Seeming almost to read my mind, Luis grabbed my mug, took a deep gulp from it, and put it back in front of me. "It's not poisoned."

Surprised, I blurted, "You've got to know why people don't trust you."

He raised an eyebrow and leaned across the table. "I understand why, but it is my duty to God and country to root out all forms of heresy. Anyone who cannot be counted among the heretics' number should be happy to help."

I did not appreciate the insinuated threat, so I made one in kind. Leaning back in my chair, I pushed up my sleeves and crossed my arms in front of me, displaying the business ends of IDOS. Though none of them had a clue I brandished a lethal weapon, it comforted me to know their secret peril, for although I was armed and difficult to kill, I still felt vulnerable in this room full of strange men.

Yet an odder feeling washed over me, as well. It was as if the assurance I was caught and the inevitability of the impending confrontation eliminated my terror of its coming. Now, at least, I knew what I must do.

Luis nodded to Hernando, who dipped his quill in the ink and put it to the parchment, preparing to take down everything we said. Though I didn't heat my cuffs yet, I prepared to slay them as quickly as I could. Luis would be first, for he was the greatest threat. I wished I had three arms, for then I could kill all three of them at once, but someone had to die last, which meant someone would scream for help.

Luis leaned sideways onto a cushion under his right arm and asked me his first question: "Have you ever heard Father Manuel Romero state he believes simple fornication is no sin?"

"No," I answered, stunned. "He would never spout such heresy."

"But he did live with a local widow, one Leonor Rivera?"

"Leonor did stay with us, but it wasn't anything like what you're insinuating."

"That's not consistent with other information I've gathered."

"Well, who lived in the house with them, your other source or me?"

Luis gave me a stern look, but I kept my voice steady and my gaze dead in his eye. If this inquisitor saw himself not as a hunter of witches but as a herder of wayward clergy, I didn't need Father Manuel to lie for me. He needed me to lie for him.

"Whatever information you've gathered, it's nothing but gossip. You know how rumors run wild. Who's spouting this nonsense?" I demanded.

"I ask the questions here. You give the answers."

"I'm sorry, señoría. Father Manuel needed a housekeeper because I was still a young girl when we came here from Toledo, but she was never anything more than a housekeeper."

Luis raised his eyebrows. "Toledo?"

I cursed my damn loose tongue, trying to remember I must tighten it here. "Yes. Why?"

"No reason, but your guardian failed to mention he got you in Toledo." Luis looked down at a piece of paper on the low table.

He'd answered my question that time, and I got the distinct impression this was no accident. I thought Luis must be more dangerous than Ignacio had ever been, for his casual demeanor was so disarming it made me forget his occupation or the reasons we were here. I'd said more than I'd meant to already, and he'd done nothing worse than offer me stale ale.

"Have you ever returned to your home city?" Luis asked.

"Not since I left as a child."

"Not even when you traveled the length of the kingdom last year?"

My stomach tightened. "How did you know about that?"

Luis's face hardened. "Who in this town doesn't? Now, answer."

"I never went back to Toledo. I had no reason. My late parents were my sole tie to that place. I wanted to see my husband before he set sail again, so I rode to Sevilla and came home."

"Relax. I believe you."

At that, I realized my body was tense, arms folded over my chest and both fists clenched. Not wanting to appear defiant, I dropped my arms and put my hands in my lap.

"I'm not interested in punishing you for loyalty to your husband. I only want the truth," Luis added.

"Why would I say anything other than the truth?"

"You'd be surprised at the things people believe they can hide from Father God and Mother Church." He smirked.

I didn't reply, listening instead to Hernando's quill as he scribbled away at the paper and the scratching of Francisco's pen as he took his own notes. The secretary cast me dubious glances while he wrote but said nothing. I'd gotten tunnel vision for Luis and almost forgotten the other two were here. We sat in silence until Francisco informed Luis he had finished with his commentary and asked if he had any more questions.

When Luis said he was through, Hernando put his quill down and stood to get me a cup of water, as I'd never touched the ale. Once he handed it to me, he sat down beside me again and went back to looking at his work. I sipped while Luis arranged his papers.

After what felt like an eternity, the inquisitor spoke again. "Do you have anything else you feel you need to tell me?"

I shook my head without a word.

"Then you have my leave to go. Thank you for speaking with me," he stated, as if I'd had the option.

I got up and made for the door, but then I decided to push my luck and see where I stood when it came to all the questions Luis ought to have asked me and did not.

Turning back around, I looked him dead in the eye and said, "Have you found the Witch of Toledo?"

He leaned back in his chair, looking incredulous. "We were never going to find her. And you'd best be careful not to let your curiosity about such things blossom into heresy."

I smiled. "Don't worry, señoría. I promise I shall always view heretical ideations in the manner they deserve."

"I certainly hope so." He waved me out the door.

I gave him a final bow and vanished into the hallway. So that had been Don Luis. Under different circumstances, I'd have thought him a not-so-unpleasant human being, but these were not different circumstances. Recalling the scars Saúl bore on his arms, I wondered how many people now bore those scars because of Luis and what he might say for himself if I ever got the opportunity to ask him about it.

I stopped in the street outside, on the point of turning around and reentering the courthouse. I imagined what I'd do: I would tell the guards there was something I had been afraid to confess to Luis before, but it wore on my conscience. I'd go back into the office and, when the guards left us, I'd simultaneously slay Hernando and Francisco while forbidding Luis to scream.

Then, I would have my way with him. I'd ask him whatever I wanted. I'd demand of him a reckoning for what his cohorts had done to me and others. I'd make him pay for the crimes of the institution for which he worked, for he bore as much of the blame as any of them, no matter how politely he spoke.

Of course, I was aware this scenario was pure fantasy. How long could I hold Don Luis hostage before his men found out? If I did murder him and somehow got away, no doubt there would be a much more intense investigation than we'd suffered already. No doubt, too, the triple homicide of an inquisitor and his sub-ordinates fell under the umbrella of what Father Manuel would label "something else stupid." Loathing myself for what I saw as an act of complicity in allowing Don Luis to finish his visitations and return to his caged prey in Logroño, I did the smart thing (though maybe not the right thing) and went back to Sara's.

A few more days passed, and neither she nor I nor anyone else we knew was arrested. Indeed, it appeared that aside from Luis hearing of my trip to Sevilla and Father Manuel's illicit relationship with Leonor, the wall of silence had not cracked. I supposed Luis and his men had hoped to operate in secrecy, but people always talk. We knew no one had disappeared. Thus, we deduced no one had been detained.

I went to the rectory to celebrate this feat on the day Luis and his entourage were to be on their way. Good riddance. Father Manuel was sitting at the table writing a reply to one of our Toledo contacts, and I plopped down opposite him.

"I suppose if you've not been charged with heresy by now, Don Luis must have believed me instead of whoever told him about you and Leonor," I said.

"I have a good idea of who it was. The inquisitor would have reason to be skeptical, especially sans corroboration," he replied, not looking up.

"Who was it?"

Father Manuel raised his gaze and scowled at me.

"Oh, fine. Don't tell me after I lied through my teeth for you," I huffed.

"I'll be forever grateful for that, but you still need to let me handle my own business."

"Fair enough. But did you actually say what they accused you of saying? That fornication is no sin if neither lover is married?"

"I don't know. It's possible. I say all sorts of absurd things when I've been drinking."

"Well, goodness. You're as dirty a heretic as me." I giggled.

He rolled his eyes. "I'd like to think I'm not *quite* as much of a heretic as you."

I laughed aloud, and he smiled, laying the quill aside and shaking his head.

"Heretic or no, at least you managed to keep your promise not to do anything stupid."

I opened my mouth to reply when a sudden knock sounded at the door. Luis's voice spoke from beyond to someone else outside. Father Manuel ripped the letter off the table, shoved it into my hand, and bade me sneak out the back. Doing no such thing, I went into the bedroom and knelt on the other side of the threshold. Father Manuel opened the rectory door and ushered someone in. The heavy footfalls told me that someone was Don Luis. I rolled up my sleeve and brought the heat to my cuff.

"To what do I owe the pleasure?" Father Manuel said from the other side of the door.

"I think you know." Luis's tone was harsher than it had been when we'd spoken before.

There was a pause in which I guessed Father Manuel made some silent negative response to Luis's statement.

"I haven't been able to coax more than one or two of your parishioners to tell me so much as 'Good morning.' You wouldn't know anything about that?" Luis asked.

"That's unfortunate, but—"

"Did you or did you not tell your congregation to keep silent when we questioned them?"

Drawing a deep breath, I caught a whiff of smoke and looked down to find IDOS singeing a hole into the part of the doorframe my arm was pressed against. I pulled my wrist away from the wood, but I did not cool the cuff. From the other side of the door, I heard Father Manuel admit he had told his congregants to stay quiet. I shut my eyes.

"Do you think I enjoy wasting my time?" Luis spat. "I don't appreciate riding muddy roads through this windy, sodden countryside only to be shut out at every town I visit. Why would you say such a thing?"

"I prefer to keep any disputes my flock might have with one another in-house. I'd rather not involve outside entities that don't understand this city or its citizens." Father Manuel's voice was steady and assured, but I feared that might provoke Luis all the more.

I got from my knees to a squatting position on my feet. All my previous confusion and mixed emotions toward Father Manuel evaporated for the time being. Just then, he was not the man who'd possibly kept me from my mother nor the man who defended her persecutors. He was the man who'd carried me on his shoulders through the streets of Toledo, the man who'd held me after I awoke from my nightmares of the quemadero, the man who'd led me around our neighborhood on the church cart mule when I was but a toddler, holding me tight because my legs were too short to reach the stirrups. For that man, I would slay Luis.

All I needed to hear was the inquisitor open the rectory door or utter the words "Come with me," and I'd strike out like an asp that's trodden on as it's buried in the sand. I'd get off one shot, a shot I could take without allowing myself to be seen, and I would whisk Father Manuel out the back and into the wilderness.

I didn't know where I'd stash him. I didn't know how I'd deal with the consequences of murdering an inquisitor making his rounds. I didn't know how I'd mitigate Jhasali's wrath for bringing the fallout so close to Homeship. I had only one thing on my mind. Whatever I must do, Father Manuel was not under any circumstance going anywhere with this man.

Luis, however, respected Father Manuel's fortitude. "I understand your position, but when I come on these trips, I expect to be aided and abetted by the local clergy, not undermined and deceived at every turn."

"No one has deceived you because there is nothing to find. You should be thanking me. I might have saved you the trouble of investigating a load of baseless accusations fabricated to settle old scores," Father Manuel retorted.

I smiled. Father Manuel had some serious cojones to speak to Luis like that. I heard the scraping of bench legs against the floor and figured the inquisitor must've sat down at the table.

"Well, at the very least you should have let the people speak for themselves," Luis said.

"I am their priest, not their master. If they wished to speak, they would have."

Luis sighed and went silent for a moment. When he spoke again, his tone had softened. "I suppose you're right. Can I be frank?"

"Of course."

"I'm half glad these visits aren't turning up much of anything. I'd rather not travel the countryside like a common circus performer, but when I get the word from down south . . ."

"I understand," Father Manuel affirmed.

"Honestly, I wouldn't be the one doing these visits if my colleagues hadn't wasted so much time looking for witches under every rock in Navarra."

"You disagree?"

"Of course. This entire Witch of Toledo thing is ridiculous. The Toledo authorities devised it to cover for their own incompetence. *They* lost control of *their* crowd, and the majority of *their* condemned escaped. Witchcraft—humph. I shouldn't have to deal with witch hysteria when I could be focusing on real heresy like all this Alumbrado nonsense."

Father Manuel stayed quiet, but Luis was on a roll. "I mean, a woman in a red dress burns herself and then disappears, never to be seen again? Please. I only want to see this business concluded so I can get home before the harvest and start putting on my winter weight."

He laughed, and the distinct sound of him slapping his own rotund belly echoed through the house. Father Manuel gave a nervous chuckle, but I deflated. Whatever this man might be, he wouldn't be sitting at Father Manuel's table making jokes if he planned to arrest him. I cooled IDOS, sat down on the floor, and leaned my back against the wall.

My heart thumped violently. I'd been so focused on the conversation I'd forgotten it was still beating away inside my chest. I concentrated on slowing it down while Father Manuel made a few more minutes' worth of small talk with Don Luis before he saw the inquisitor out the door. When we were alone once more, I leapt from the bedroom and ran to him.

"You were amazing!" I cried.

Father Manuel did not respond. He sat at the table, leaning over the rough wood and pressing his fist into his chest.

"My heart," he murmured through his coughs.

"Oh no!" I grabbed the wineskin, filled a cup to the brim, and forced it into his hands. "Drink. Drink all that. It'll calm you."

He took some tentative sips and tried to smell the berry-red wine. After a few minutes of gasping and hacking, he was able to catch his breath.

"I'm lucky that man didn't arrest me," he wheezed.

"He's lucky he didn't try," I replied.

Father Manuel buried his face in his hands and started sobbing.

"I'm so sorry," I whispered. "This is all my fault."

Wrapping my arms around his shoulders as he wept, I thought of how frightened he must have felt, how hard it must have been for him to keep his head with his heart problems, and how even when I did the right thing, it still always turned out to be wrong.

"Can I tell you a story?" I asked, and he assented.

Slowly, I recounted every detail of the auto de fe, how I'd planned my performance and my escape route beforehand, how I'd not been able to induce the crowd to panic, how I'd managed to burn the Dominican and throw the situation to chaos—though I left out the part about Ignacio being present. Then, I spoke of Saúl and Míriam, how their boy had saved me when I'd been swept back into the city and how they had hidden me and fed me and made room for me in the carriage they'd planned to serve as their own escape. I told him about that noble gentleman who'd never given me his name and how he'd risked everything to rescue total strangers.

When I was finished, Father Manuel had stopped crying, but he looked at me with an expression I couldn't decipher.

After sitting long in silence, he spoke. "I am very glad, child, that you were listening when I told you to do the righteous thing."

Nodding, I laid my head on his shoulder and said nothing more.

# Chapter Twenty-Two
## BITTER MEDICINE

The visitors departed at the start of June, leaving me free to head to Homeship again. I told Jhasali as little as I could of their sojourn in town. The last thing I needed was for her to start interrogating me about what an Inquisition was and if it might come inquiring into the woods after her. It wasn't as though I wouldn't have set her like a dog on the lot of them if I could have, but if I somehow convinced her the inquisitors posed a threat to her, I couldn't be sure she'd limit her self-defense to them alone.

Her surveillance bots had picked up on some of the conversations during the investigation, but I was able to explain that while these men might pose a danger to humans, they wouldn't come wandering into the wilderness looking for giant spaceships. She paid the issue no more heed after that. I expected her to be flabbergasted by the notion of a policing unit devoted to prosecuting crimes against imagined entities. However, by this point, she'd become desensitized to the preposterousness of it all, and she lost interest as soon as she heard the words "This has nothing to do with you." Maybe she was more human than I thought.

I had little time to worry about the visitors after their departure, as the day now drew near for Sergio to return. I felt a strange ambiguity at this prospect. Though I'd missed him dearly since I'd left Sevilla, his arrival also meant I'd have to delay my search for my mother until next year. Down south, Sergio had explained that he and Armando did not plan to sail again once they returned to Santa Colomba, for they'd need to recover from two back-to-back crossings. They'd be in town until the spring of next year.

As happy as I was at the idea of having my husband home for so long, it also felt like I'd never be able to begin my journey—not that I was prepared for it. My command over my drone and nanos still needed much work, but I hoped to practice enough during Sergio's stay that by the time he set sail again, I could leave right away.

In preparation for my husband's return, I brought from Homeship all the valuables I knew he'd miss. Then I began to ride Pepito into town every morning to watch the ships coming in and out of the harbor, though I had yet to spot the sails of either the *San José* or the *San Bruno* on the horizon.

After each disappointing morning, Pepito and I trudged home so I might attend to my household chores before I spent the evening sitting by the fire and castigating myself with worry that those sails might never appear on the horizon again. So the days passed one after the next, and neither ship nor letter arrived.

One evening during this endless wait, I sat at the table practicing giving directives to my bonded drone over a distance. In recent weeks, the nexus between myself and the drone had grown stronger. Though I remained unable to utilize its senses in my own head, I could now intermittently maintain the link over some distance. Sometimes, I could even command the drone in Homeship without being there. Though I could not see through its eyes, there were instances where I could give it simple instructions, such as telling it to float down the hallway, and I'd know it had obeyed the same way I didn't need to look down to know my feet obeyed my command to walk.

Jhasali had promised to no longer interact with my drone, even when my link failed, so as not to interfere with my connection to it. Whenever it did fail, I could only reforge the nexus by riding to Homeship. Under normal circumstances, the identifiers should be detectable without physical proximity, but because Jhasali's drones resided in Homeship's security perimeter, the only distance communication possible was from bonded master to bonded device, meaning I could not reforge the link to the drone unless we were both outside or both within the perimeter.

Often, the reforged bond broke again when I rode back to town; it almost always broke when I chose to sleep; and it sometimes broke for no reason at all. On this particular evening, however, my union with the drone had managed to remain intact for several days, though I'd slept a few hours and had been thinking much more on Sergio than the device. I'd sporadically checked in with it since my last visit to Homeship and was pleasantly surprised each time to find I'd maintained the connection despite all my distractions.

I was attempting, without success, to see Homeship through my second set of eyes when my original set of ears picked up a stirring outside the door. I leapt from the kitchen table to flee upstairs for IDOS. Then a familiar voice called my name. Forgetting about my drone, I unbarred the door to let Sergio in, noting gratefully he was not as thin as I recalled him being in Sevilla.

I flung myself into his arms and opened my mouth to tell him how much I'd missed him, how I'd worried about him day and night, how I'd hoped with all my heart for his safe return. Before I could articulate any of this, he grabbed my face and kissed me.

Seizing a handful of my hair, he tilted my head back. "Fuck now. Talk later."

He gripped me by the hips and lifted me from the floor, wrapping my legs around his waist. He was not the only one who'd endured ten long months of abstinence, so I allowed him to carry me upstairs to the bed. There, he fell backward with me on top, tearing my nightgown off and sliding his hands over my breasts. We made love several times before either of us spoke, barely stopping to rest between sessions. When we climaxed for the final time, we panted as if we'd run a marathon.

Once we were through, Sergio gathered me to his chest, uttering only the words "I'm so tired" before drifting off.

Alone with my thoughts, I listened to him snoring and pondered what we'd just done. I'd hoped the passage of another year would heal some of the old wounds that had been fresher when Sergio and I had made love in Sevilla, and, in some respects, it had. I no longer found myself stiffening at certain touches or panicking at specific positions, but our lovemaking still felt tainted—permanently, I feared.

Unlike in Sevilla, I'd been able to achieve a real orgasm while I was on top instead of struggling until I forced myself to a hollow, unsatisfying climax. With Sergio on top, I no longer had to suppress the urge to fight back, but I still went numb, unable to find the pleasure that position had once given me.

How I yearned to feel the intimacy I'd once felt when Sergio slid his hips between my knees and I wrapped my arms and legs around him, using my thighs to press him as deep inside me as possible, running my hands over his back and into his hair, squeezing his chest so tight to mine it pained my breasts. Now, no matter how I tried to enjoy those sensations, I always felt the same amount of numbness.

Sergio had noted my sudden affinity for being on top last year, but I was able to pass it off as my tastes changing as I got older, and he'd grown used to it without much fuss. I wished to tell him the real reason for my alteration in preferences, but no matter how much time had passed, I could never work up the courage to consider it.

I feared he might accuse me of adultery or at least impugning his honor by failing to fight my rapists to the death. Just as likely, however, was the possibility my honesty would result in him seeing me as even weaker and more helpless than he thought me already. I suffered such anguish that I could trust him with the darkest secrets of my body but could not trust him with the darkest secrets of my heart.

I sat up next to Sergio and watched him sleeping. He lay on his back, his face relaxed and his hand pressed into the coverlet. I ran my fingers over his smooth cheek, sweeping his eyelid with my thumb and brushing through the long lashes. He turned from his back to his side and nestled his face into my hip, though he continued to snore away.

I moved Sergio's curls from in front of his forehead and thumbed the skin of his brow, thinking of Jhasali. When I had asked her to make my husband like me, she'd refused so resolutely. Yet she'd been equally resolute when she'd declined to make me as I now was.

Perhaps if she met him, she'd see that he and I had already been separated so much in life that we deserved to be together eternally. She might even come to like him and wish to have him as a second companion. A sudden explosion of jealousy detonated in my chest at this notion, but I reminded myself that Jhasali's people didn't mate, so her relationship with Sergio would be no more sexual than her relationship with me. I determined that if she refused to bring him to the ship, she'd have to bring herself to him. Somehow, the pair of them were going to meet.

Smiling, I fantasized about the family I'd rebuild from the ashes of my childhood tragedies. I hoped my impending quest would be so smooth and its fruition so swiftly achieved that by end of season next year, my husband would return from his voyage to find he had a mother-in-law. Such a development might not please him, but he'd have to learn to live with it.

I couldn't wait for the months to pass until March or April, when Sergio would make for the sea and I for the south. It was a strange feeling. I'd never looked upon the sailing season with anything but dread, but if I found my mother, I'd never endure it alone again.

Not only would I have her, but when I gained enough control over the nanos to have full command of my organs, I could fill her arms with as many grandchildren as I liked, regardless of whatever issue ailed Sergio. If Jhasali would offer him the gift she'd already given me, one day he might learn to heal his own body from within.

Trying not to get too far ahead of myself, I put my mind to rest and settled back into the mattress. There, I allowed Sergio's warmth to engulf me, and I absorbed the smell of his skin: scents of salty spray and varnished wood and barreled wine. His embrace cocooned me as my body had just cocooned him. If I focused on his breathing rather than my racing thoughts, it proved easier to fall asleep. I shut my eyes once to darkness and chirping crickets and opened them next to the calls of songbirds and a shaft of dusty light stabbing through the shutters of the eastern window.

Sergio was not at my side when I awoke. I turned toward the door and saw he stood at the foot of the bed, wearing his white nightshirt and a pair of linen pants. He stared at the painting of himself I'd hung on the wall across from the fireplace. I slid out of bed, naked as a babe, and rooted around for my nightgown amongst all the clothes on the floor.

"What do you think?" I tossed aside his cape, locating my gown underneath.

"What did you think I would think?" He sank to the bed. "I hate it."

I slid the gown over my head and sat on the bed beside him. "Why would you hate it? Isn't it precise enough?"

"That's the problem. It is too precise. It's too . . . too real."

"Is that not the point of a portrait? To be real?"

"Why would you commission this?"

"Why wouldn't I? And I didn't commission it. I made it."

"Ah. I heard the gossip about your painting skills before I got both feet off the gangplank. I didn't believe it."

I arched a brow. "Why not?"

"I've never seen you paint. I've never even heard you speak of it, much less that you've had some patroness all this time."

"Perhaps that's just what happens when you're away for months and months at a time: you miss things."

"Regardless, why the devil would you paint me?"

"Because I wished to look at you, and you were not here."

"You didn't ask my permission. You didn't ask me if *I* wanted it," he cried.

I was stunned. I'd suspected he might balk at the portrait at first, but I'd also thought he'd be shocked at how good it was and even flattered I'd made an image of him. But this undisguised anger I had not anticipated.

"I wasn't under the impression I needed your permission to paint what I want to look at," I said, unsure whether to be angry or laugh at him.

"What if I don't want to look at myself?"

He stood and reached for the painting. Grasping it on both sides of the frame, he lifted it off the wall and placed it in the empty fireplace.

"No!" I leapt off the bed.

It hadn't cost me any effort to make this picture, and indeed all I needed to do was go home and have the drones make me another. Yet this painting was all I'd had of my husband in this house for so long, and I'd grown attached to it.

"Sergio, don't. You've no right. This picture is of my making," I snapped as he grabbed a few logs and some kindling out of the rack beside the hearth.

"But it's my likeness!" He was shouting now. "I don't want it in my house. I don't want to look at it every time I lie in my bed. I just don't want it."

I planted myself between him and the fireplace. He held the fuel and the kindling bundled in his arms, ready to set the blaze.

"Don't do this. Please!" I bellowed.

He tried to swerve around me, but I maneuvered into his path again.

"No, Sergio. No! This is all I've had of you in this house for the last two years. What will I have when you go out again?"

"Go out? I just returned."

"No you haven't. You've returned in body, but your soul is still on the sea. You'll never stop sailing. How am I to live if I can't even look at you?"

"How am I to live if I have to look at that?" He motioned to the picture.

I gazed at his likeness in the fireplace, then into the eyes of the real thing. He was handsomer in the picture because his expression, while intense, was serene and unmarred by emotion. He smiled slightly in the painting, eyes dark and deep but vacant, like the recesses of a well long bereft of water. The real-life Sergio's brows were furrowed, his teeth clenched, and his jaw set. I couldn't understand how he could be so disturbed by a mere portrait.

We remained at an impasse for a long while, until Sergio said, "Fine. Keep it, but put it away when I'm here so I'm not compelled to look at it."

"No. Burn it," I blurted. "I hadn't expected it to make you this unhappy. If I had known, I wouldn't have made it. Or at least I wouldn't have left it up when you returned."

I stepped aside so he could get to the fireplace. He tossed the kindling in first and the logs on top. Soon, a crackling fire blazed forth, giving off an odd whooshing sound as the canvas caught and emitting the pungent odor of dye as the paint was consumed. First the chest and shoulders went to the flames, then the jaw and the bottom lip. Finally, the dark eyes and the loose curls over the brow. It only took a few minutes, and we stood before the fireplace, watching in silence as the memory-turned-painting burned to cinder, still stretched within its swiftly charring frame.

"Why?" I asked as the last vestiges of the canvas sank into the pyre.

"I don't know. I couldn't bear to look at it. That's all," he whispered.

"I'm sorry."

"Don't be. You didn't know." He put a finger under my chin and tilted my face up to look at his. "And you're quite good, fantastic even. If you'd painted anything else, I would've been impressed—just not my image."

"Why not?" I repeated, but he held up his hand.

"You should keep painting, but not me. Never again."

I knew better than to ask why for a third time. Instead, I agreed I would not render his image on so much as a napkin and spoke no more of my artistry.

Sergio built up the fire and undressed me. I wasn't so sure I wished to make love in that instant, but when he slid to the foot of the bed and put his head between my legs, I decided I wanted to after all.

Once we finished, we lay on top of the quilt with our fingers intertwined and our heads pressed together, listening to the dying fire. I was thankful the flames were beginning to burn out. The air had become warm in here as the morning wore on.

I glanced toward the embers. "Sergio, did you ever kill anyone?"

The question came out of the blue, the words forming of their own accord. No matter what I'd done over the past few months, I'd not been able to push the remorse for killing the guards in Toledo from the back of my mind. As I lay in Sergio's arms and pondered possible reasons why he had been so desperate to destroy the painting, it dawned on me that guilt could be one of them. Perhaps he carried his own shame and regret for having shed blood.

"That's a strange question to ask now," he said.

"Won't you answer it?"

"Of course I've killed before. You know I did back when I used to sail down south. Don't you remember when I told you about my ship being boarded on the way to Italy? Did you think we asked the corsairs nicely to leave us be?" He laughed, but there was no scorn in it.

"Did you ever feel guilt for it?"

"Not once. Killed the one who gave me this." He raised his arm to reveal the huge scar he'd received courtesy of a pirate blade: a long, jagged stripe that ran up his left side from his hip to just under his armpit.

"But you felt no remorse? You never thought of his family? His dependents?"

"What was I supposed to do, remember he had a mother while I let him gut me like a pig? Or let him auction me off in some Barbary port city so he might feed his children? They all had loved ones, Micalita. If you waste time worrying about such nonsense, you won't survive your first brush with combat." He paused, weighing his words. "You don't understand. When someone does this sort of thing to you, you kill him and forget it. You don't think of his family or his humanity."

I had to act as though I took him at his word because I'd not experienced such things. But I had experienced them, and it hadn't gone that way for me. I did think of my victims' families often. I did consider their humanity. Though I'd only been protecting myself, I felt crippling remorse—not as much for the men I'd killed as for their widows who might never get on, their children who'd never know why their fathers hadn't returned.

Sergio couldn't comprehend the fear of such a loss, for if he lost me, he'd surely grieve, but he wouldn't be left destitute and forsaken. He wouldn't lose his livelihood along with me. Perhaps that was why he acted none too concerned about the ones the incessant conflicts left behind: he couldn't empathize with our plight as wives.

"I can't understand how you can look a man in the eye, take his life, and feel nothing," I muttered.

A confounded look passed over his face. "Are you trying to make me feel something?"

"No. I'm not trying to make you feel anything. I just wished to know how you did feel."

"Why is this all of a sudden so interesting to you? I don't want to rack my mind with thoughts of those men's wives and children. What good would it do to drive myself mad with the memory of the light leaving their eyes?" he snapped.

At that, I understood. It wasn't that Sergio felt nothing. It was that he chose to ignore it. Maybe he was naturally my superior when it came to such flat denial of his own emotions—or maybe he'd simply had more practice at it. Whatever the case, this conversation wouldn't help me, and I had no wish to extricate him from his self-imposed obliviousness. I kissed him and apologized for speaking of such things when we were meant to be lovemaking, deciding that, for this, he could offer me no aid.

***

A few days after the fleet's arrival, Armando summoned the pair of us to the family's tower house. He and Sergio talked business in the study for a long while, leaving me to fend for myself in the sitting room. Once they'd finished, one of the servant girls, Elena, came to me and said Don Armando wished to speak with me.

Apprehensive, I followed Elena upstairs, wondering what he might want—Armando had never before asked to talk to me about anything. She led me to a balcony where Armando sat near the railing, watching the street below and sipping a cup of brandy. When he looked up, I bowed my head, and he waved for me to come to him.

"I wanted to talk to you about something," he said once I reached his seat.

He motioned to the chair opposite his and commanded me to sit. When I obeyed, he looked into my eyes in a manner that made me uncomfortable, like his own eyes searched for something and knew where to find it. His gaze was so intense I dropped my own to my lap.

"You would consider yourself a friend of my wife, wouldn't you?" he asked.

I stared at my knees. "I suppose, señor, if calling myself her friend isn't too presumptuous."

"It is not. I am not pleased with how things have gone with her in my absence. I'd hoped my nephew's birth might assuage her spirit, but she's even more miserable than when I left."

Upon hearing this, I glanced up. Armando's hazel eyes locked onto mine, holding them almost against their will. I did not speak, unsure where he was going with this.

"Has she said anything to you? Indicated anything I might give her to make her happy?"

I didn't know how to respond. To speak my true feelings might anger Armando, which could prove disastrous for Sergio.

"I don't know. I'm sorry." I dared not add more.

"Speak your mind, Micaela. If you have something to say, then say it," he snapped.

I took a deep breath and exhaled into my closed mouth before letting the air hiss out between my lips. Not only did I wish to avoid damaging my husband, but I also didn't want to betray Sara. Armando had never shown the slightest interest in making her happy before, but I could guess why he was so keen on it now. I wondered if he knew of Sara's vow never to bear him another child.

"I may be out of line." I tried to measure my words. "And if I am, please punish me and not Sergio. But Sara needs you, señor, to fix whatever it is you did to her in the past. She never told me what it was, but she's still angry with you. She almost hates you."

"I am more than aware of that," Armando spat. "I'm asking if you know of something I might do to address the hostility between us—a specific act or gift or anything."

I pondered for so long I feared it might make Armando angry before I thought of something: her sister in Flanders. Sara's power over her husband was immense compared to my own, but it did not seem to extend to her ability to convince him to allow her the use of one of his vessels to visit Beatriz. He'd always found some excuse: he was too busy, the crossing too dangerous, the journey too expensive.

Of course, with his influence in the guilds and the town council, no one else had dared risk his displeasure by ferrying his wife out of the country on one of their own vessels, no matter how much she'd offered as a bribe. The two of them had fought over it so often she hadn't bothered to broach the subject in years. I decided to give it a go, wondering how much a final chance at a legitimate heir might be worth to Armando.

"Sara is so lonely without her family. She misses her sisters, and she has spoken to me many times of her favorite in Antwerp. Take her to see Beatriz as soon as you can, or at least give her a ship and a crew to take her."

I looked back down at my clasped hands and waited for the shouting to start. I was sure I'd been too free with my words, but I couldn't abandon Sara when I had an opportunity to help her get what I believed she desired.

Instead of shouting, Armando barely whispered. "Things have been, well, complicated since our last child passed."

"I'm sorry for your loss—all your losses. But you and Sara must stop blaming one another for things that were never in your control to begin with." I uttered these words before I remembered who I was talking to. I was quick to offer my apologies.

Armando waved his hand in dismissal. "That was something I needed to hear. I think the intuition of youth can rival the wisdom of age, and we should not be so quick to discount it."

He was silent a long time before saying, "Thank you. I give you my leave to go if you do not wish to be here."

I thanked him and stood.

He took a sip from his cup, looking up at me. "Sergio loves you very much, you know."

"I know, señor," I replied before taking leave of him.

The knots untwisted inside my gut as soon as I escaped Armando's presence. I hoped I'd done right by Sara, but I couldn't be sure until I saw her again. Wishing to leave this place with all haste, I asked Elena to take me to my husband. She led me downstairs and across the courtyard to the stables, where she pointed toward a stall before bustling off.

The stable was unoccupied save the horses and Sergio, who hummed softly in a stall toward the rear. There, I found him brushing Pepito's coat and feeding him pieces of carrot from a pouch on his hip. Every now and again, Pepito snuck his head around to the pouch and gave Sergio a gentle nip. Whenever he did, Sergio chuckled and reached for another cut. He even teased Pepito a couple of times by eating the slice himself.

I liked to find Sergio in these situations, where no one was around to impress and he could enjoy some simple pleasure. I was sure he knew I stood at the threshold. Pepito had perked up and snorted as soon as he'd caught sight of me. But Sergio pretended not to notice and kept on humming as he lifted Pepito's feet and picked his shoes clean, then brushed his tail until he'd removed the tangles, all while Pepito strained to get his head back around to the carrots.

After Sergio started a braid in Pepito's forelock, he glanced my way and gave me a grin. "You're not going to come in? And get out of the weather?"

I looked up and realized I'd been watching them so long I'd not noted the storm blowing in from the ocean. The clouds had darkened the surrounding courtyard, and the first few drops of rain teetered on the very edge of the precipice. I could feel the thunder, though I couldn't hear it.

I swung the stall gate open and entered, shutting it behind me. It was dark in here now that the clouds had come. This sudden storm had turned the air cold as well. I approached Pepito and wrapped my arms around his warm head, smelling the strong but not unpleasant scent of his fresh-brushed forelock. Sergio bent down, planting a kiss on my temple.

"I thought we might head home, but I suppose that's out for a while," he said.

A sudden clap of thunder and the sound of pouring rain punctuated his words, as if the storm itself agreed with his assessment of the riding conditions. I grunted at him, my mind still halfway on my conversation with Armando.

"What's wrong? What did Armando want?" Sergio asked.

"Nothing. I mean, he wanted to ask me if there might be something he could do for Sara because she's so despondent."

"I assumed as much, although I have no idea what she's got to complain about now. She has plenty of money and her own house and a prominent husband—"

"As if she wants him," I interjected.

"I don't know what you want me to say, Micalita. She just needs to buck up."

"Would you appreciate being told to buck up if you'd been through what she has?"

"Armando has lost as many children as she, yet you don't see him in constant misery."

I threw my hands up. "That's because we don't ever see him. Who besides you catches more than a passing glimpse of him before he leaves for the sea or some larger city? He should stay home and be with his wife."

"Are we still talking about Armando?" Sergio chuckled.

I didn't answer. We were definitely not still talking about Armando, for Sara wanted him gone as much as I wanted Sergio near. It would do no good to reopen that old wound, so I stayed silent, enveloping myself in Sergio's warm arms as we listened to the rain and waited for the storm to clear enough for us to make for the arrabal before dark.

*** 

About a week after Armando's and my conversation, I accompanied Sergio to the estate, where Armando had ridden with his household. While Sergio went to find the master, I caught Sara in the dining room. She was smiling as I hadn't seen her smile in many years.

Unlike her usual smile, which was contrived and always stopped right at the mouth, this one went all the way up to her eyes and made lines around the corners of her lids. It made her look older and younger at the same time, for the lines of age were more pronounced, but all the years of suffering on her face were blunted by the delight in her expression.

"What's happened that's made you so happy?" I asked, the image of her in Homeship flashing before my eyes.

"Armando has made arrangements for us to go to Antwerp to see my sister," she said. "And Micaela, I know you're the one who suggested he do this for me."

She embraced me tightly. She was warm and soft, and she smelled of rose water. I breathed her in and wound my arms around her waist. She clasped the back of my head and looked up at me.

"Thank you." She kissed me on one cheek and then the other.

I hugged her and pursed my lips, wondering if I ought to warn her of Armando's probable motivations for doing her such a favor, but I feared it might be patronizing. She knew her husband well enough to never expect altruism from him.

Armando would soon confirm my fears that he had no real interest in repairing his relationship with Sara. Later that day, as I walked through the estate house looking for Sergio, I caught my husband's voice coming from the study and realized he was talking to the master behind closed doors.

Reaching up to knock, I stopped short at the anger in Sergio's tone. I pricked my ears, leaning closer to the heavy wood of the study door to ensure I caught every word over the bustling servants downstairs. I didn't want to eavesdrop, but I wanted to miss out on this conversation even less.

"What do you mean Micaela made you see reason?" Sergio snapped.

"I mean she helped me see how I can make things right. I thought Sara was beyond letting me near her again, but when I told her I'd take her to see Beatriz, she was so pleased," Armando said.

I rolled my eyes. She hadn't seen Beatriz in years. Of course she'd be pleased. Armando shouldn't have needed my help to figure that out.

"But we were already separated for the whole crossing. Now you're leaving again?" Sergio replied.

"I must. These last few months have made me rethink some things."

"What things?"

"Nothing drastic. It's just, I'm forty-three now, and I wonder if I can take another long voyage. If I keep sailing, it'll be the death of me."

"What are you saying? That when you return from Antwerp, you're done?"

Armando sighed. "Sergio, you knew this day would come."

"Yes, but not now. It was always some other time, some other—I don't know."

"I'm sorry, but I don't want to kill myself at sea. Not when Sara and I are still young enough that we might try one more time for a child."

"I understand. It's only that I didn't expect this to happen so soon." Sergio cleared his throat. "But that doesn't matter."

"Yes, it does. Of course it does," Armando whispered.

"No, it doesn't. Because I've got to accept it either way."

"But you don't. You could stay, leave the sailing to someone else."

"I can't do that."

"Why not?"

"I haven't got enough money to retire comfortably yet."

"You have plenty. I haven't given you enough share in the business?" Armando asked.

I almost gasped aloud. Share in the business?

"I was under the impression I'd earned it," Sergio said coolly.

"Of course. I'm sorry."

"Armando, don't you condescend to me—"

"I mean it," Armando interrupted. "I'd never entrust this part of the business to anyone but you. You are the only man other than Gabriel I can trust, and he isn't suited for sailing. He's too delicate. Everything you have you've earned. If it weren't so, you wouldn't have it."

I could hardly see through when I put my eye to the crack at the doorframe, but I could just make out Sergio's nod of assent.

"Why not let me give you this one thing? As a token of affection, I could help you retire," Armando said.

My heart leapt at these words, even though I anticipated my husband's answer.

"No," Sergio replied. "I want to have enough to settle on my own. It wouldn't really be mine if you bought it. You know I won't accept charity."

A wave of rage broke over my heart, and I fell back from the door. Not only did Sergio seem more upset about being parted from Armando than he'd ever been about being parted from me, and not only was he turning down the chance to stay by my side, but he had been lying to me about our finances whilst leaving me to fend for myself with almost nothing more than what I needed to survive. All these years, he'd been sitting on a pile of gold and acting as though we were on the brink of debtors' prison! How could he deceive me like this?

Sergio's voice floated through my racing thoughts, carrying words that said he wanted to be alone. The stamping of heavy boots followed these words as he and the master approached the door. I leapt to my feet and hurled myself down the hall and around the corner before they got to the handle, slipping through the doorway to the servants' staircase.

"Sergio, you are dead. Oh, I will never let you hear the end of this," I whispered as I descended.

I exited the stairwell into the kitchen, fuming to the point I could practically feel the steam whistling from my ears. Rosa jumped halfway out of her skin when I burst through the threshold, and she dropped the basket of bread she'd been carrying.

"So sorry." I knelt to help her clean up.

She did not reply, but she looked at me like I'd lit the loaves on fire and flung them at her. I put them all back in the basket as fast as I could and got the hell out of there.

I rode to our house without Sergio, where I waited for his return, sitting at the kitchen table and seething all the while. It took him hours to show up. When he entered, he glared at me, cowing me for a split second. He was angry with me for separating him from Armando. No. He had it backward. He was supposed to be angry with Armando for separating him from *me*!

"So you got what you wanted, did you?" he said darkly.

"Of all the things I wanted in this life, my husband lying to my face wasn't one of them," I snapped.

His scowl deepened. "I lied about what?"

"You know good and well what. How much money have you been sitting on all these years you've forced me to live on so little?"

His eyebrows shot up, but he quickly smoothed his expression. "Micaela, I did not lie to you about that. I simply didn't inform you of it. I'm under no obligation to discuss our financial situation with you."

I was glad I'd made a habit of keeping IDOS buried beneath the floorboards, for otherwise, I might've been tempted to use it. Instead, I clenched my fists and bared my teeth.

"All these years you've gone off sailing and never left me enough to buy more than necessities." I leapt to my feet and stepped to my husband. "I could've had a servant. I could've had help."

"You certainly had enough to buy fancy horses and pretty dresses," he retorted.

"No thanks to you."

"I always leave you plenty to run this house. What do you need besides food and fuel? When I was much younger than you, I lived without even that."

"So that means it's good enough for the rest of us?" I shouted, trying to make my voice quit shaking.

"You've no right to be angry about this. It isn't like I've been gambling or keeping up some other woman. I am putting money away for *our* future. Can't you understand that?"

"I do understand that! What I don't understand is why in blazes you would hide it from me all this time. Did you think I would never find out about it on my own?"

"Speaking of," he said smoothly, which enraged me further. "How did you find out?"

"I heard you and Armando talking," I spat, too angry to be ashamed for spying on him.

"You were listening to us?"

I shook my finger in his face. "If you're going to sneak around and lie through your teeth, you'd best be prepared to be eavesdropped on every now and again. Not that you seem to care what I think. The only one whose opinion you ever gave a good goddamn about is Armando."

"Micaela," he said in a warning tone.

"What? Apparently he's also the only one from whom you've ever had a qualm about being separated. Maybe the two of you should divorce Sara and me and marry each other!"

"How dare you!" he shrieked, now as enraged as I'd wished. "How dare you? You—"

"No. How dare *you*! You'd rather lie to me about everything than treat me like you ought to. How about you learn what it's like to sleep in that bed all alone for a change?"

Before Sergio could see the tears that threatened to rip my eyelids off their hinges, I shoved him aside with all my might and flung myself out the door. He didn't follow me, though I'd expected nothing less.

Regardless, I was too livid to fight further. I'd go to Jhasali, if she'd have me, considering I'd ignored her recent calls so I could be with my husband.

*What a mistake*, I thought as I saddled Pepito.

We fled to the ship at a pace unsuitable for this humid summer afternoon, and Pepito was soon covered in a thin layer of sweat that ran through his hair before dripping off and forming a trail of tiny droplets on the ground. When we got to Homeship, I loosed him near the stream and marched into the vessel.

Still furious, I could barely speak a word to Jhasali. She did not demand an explanation but asked if I'd take a walk with her in the forest. I assented, and we passed through the ship and outside once more.

"You wish to tell me about it?" Jhasali asked once we'd planted ourselves on a high cliff overlooking a deep gulley down below.

I sighed and ran my nails up the back of my neck. Taking some time to calm myself, I told her all that had passed between Sergio and me: the money and how he'd hidden it, his burning his own image, his anger with me for convincing Armando to take Sara away for a few weeks, and his placement of his master and comrade over me when it came to his affection.

When I finished, she said, "Why don't you leave him and move in here?"

I didn't have much of an answer to that question. If she'd asked it three years ago, I would have had an easy out. How could I leave my husband when I had nowhere to go, little means to support myself, and no real hope of obtaining an annulment? Now, my circumstances were different; I could move into Homeship anytime I pleased. Thus, my answer was more complex, but I didn't know if I could make her understand.

"I wish things were that simple," I said. "I wish I despised my husband, because then I could abandon him without pain or regret. But I don't hate him; I love him. He has his flaws, but he's also a tender man at heart, though he often cannot bring himself to show it. I wish he and I could find a way to make our marriage work in a manner that suits us both. I grow tired of this constant conflict. I suppose if it gets bad enough, I'll have to come here whether I like it or not."

"I could kill him if you want. Rid you of the trouble of his company," Jhasali said flatly.

"I pray you're joking. If you did such a thing, I'd never forgive you or trust you again."

"Fine, then. I won't harm a hair on his head. But what are you going to do?"

"I want to find a way to merge our dual worlds and live a single life again. If you won't make him as you've made me, let me bring him to you. You could show him Homeship, teach him what you've taught me. It might make him see things differently."

"Absolutely, positively, unequivocally not."

"So that's a firm no?" I laughed.

Jhasali shot me a glare the devil himself couldn't rival.

"Why?" I asked.

"You know exactly why," she snapped. "I will not say it again. You're all I need. Anything more will make things too complicated. Not only that, but I trust the knowledge and accomplishments of my people to no one save you."

"Will you at least consent to returning to my house and meeting him?"

She sighed and put her hand to her brow. "Alright. If it'll put this issue to rest, I will do this one thing, but don't expect more."

She got to her feet and tramped back up the trail toward the ship. I didn't follow her—not immediately, anyway. I sat on the cliff, watching the sunset and the moonrise, savoring this one small victory and hoping beyond all possibility it might not be the last.

I stayed the night in Homeship, for I'd told Sergio he was going to learn what it was like to sleep alone in our bed, and I wouldn't make myself a liar. I wanted him to get a healthy taste of the medicine he'd been forcing down my throat all these years. Maybe it'd soften him up a bit.

Jhasali rested in my bed with me, wrapping her arms around me and holding my head to her breast as Sergio often did. I felt her cool flesh as it engulfed me like the waves of the Atlantic. She was colder than any human I'd ever touched, and I noted, as I lay in her arms, I could neither feel nor hear her heartbeat. Perhaps that organ was too protected within the recesses of her hybridized body to be detectable to outsiders. If my heart were now equally inaudible within its new metallic enclosure, I wondered if Sergio might ever note he could no longer hear it.

As soon as we rose the next day, I took my leave of Jhasali, and she promised me she would come to call the following Monday evening at six sharp. I told her I'd have a veritable feast laid out for her, but she informed me I needn't bother, for she knew how inconvenient it was for humans to prepare food. I replied the inconvenience was no issue and I intended to make her first introduction to Sergio perfect.

I went to the estate house once I returned to town, figuring Sergio would be there grumbling to Armando as he always did after we fought. The house, however, was unoccupied except for Gracia, Eduardo, and the women servants.

When she laid eyes on me, Gracia's jaw dropped. "I cannot believe you, Micaela! Of all the insane, irresponsible, inconsiderate things."

"I don't understand. You know I sometimes stay at the home of my patroness," I said.

"Yes, but you've never stormed out and disappeared before. The men have spent all this time looking for you. I've been up all night worrying about Gabriel. Don't you ever think of anyone but yourself?"

That question stung, especially since if not for me, she wouldn't even be here to pose it. I bit back that retort and apologized for worrying everyone. I asked when the men planned to return. Gracia said she didn't know, but I'd better wait for them in my own home, for she was too angry to endure my presence. Offering my apologies once more, I made my way back to my husband's house.

I wondered if I should go looking for the men myself, but I had no idea where they might have gone and no way of communicating to them that I sought them, so I stayed put, kicking myself for upsetting everyone. I hadn't anticipated Sergio would come after me, and I certainly hadn't thought he'd involve Armando's entire household in our little spat.

My husband finally stumbled into the house long after dark, and he heaved a deep sigh to find me sitting in the kitchen. I expected him to be fuming. Far from it, he crossed the room in two strides, clutched my waist, and squeezed my head to his breast. His heart thumped wildly, and I did not resist his embrace, though his grip was too tight for my liking.

"Micalita. Mother of God! How could you do such a thing? What's the matter with you?" he cried.

"Has everyone utterly forgotten I rode to Sevilla and back not ten months ago?" I demanded, pushing him off me and crossing my arms over my chest.

"With a convoy. You didn't wander off on your own into the wilderness. Where in Christ's name have you been?"

"I stayed with my patroness, Juana."

"Juana, again. Seems you're always with this patroness no one knows and no one save Father Manuel has ever seen."

"I suppose, then, it's a very good thing she's agreed to call on us in a few days," I snapped, savoring the look of shock that flitted across his face.

"What?"

"You heard me. I figured we could use some of that gold you've been hiding to make her an acceptable reception."

He ignored my jab and returned the subject to my flight the previous evening. "Regardless, it's unacceptable for you to storm out of here and go missing all night. If I have to lock you up and sell every horse in the damned city to keep you from doing it again, I will."

"You promised you wouldn't sell Pepito!"

"Well, you promised to honor and obey me all the days of our lives."

I gritted my teeth, fighting the impulse to retort that if he kept this up, the days of his life might not last as long as he anticipated. I kept my cool, remembering I loved him, and remembering, too, my goal of presenting him to Jhasali.

"I did promise that." Loath as I was to admit, it was true, though my intent to keep such a vow had flown the coop alongside my belief in the god to whom I'd made it. "I'm sorry. I didn't mean to make you spend all night searching for me. I only left because I was so angry."

My admission of wrongdoing soothed Sergio, though he still looked at me with an expression of displeasure and concern. I felt remorse for upsetting him, but not that much remorse, for Jhasali was to come on Monday! I smiled at the thought, and his countenance softened in response.

"I would be angrier with you, but I'm just so thankful you're back," he said.

I took his hand, finding it cold to the touch. "Come. Let me make you something to eat. You look famished."

# Chapter Twenty-Three

# A VISIT FROM THE VISITOR

The days leading up to Jhasali's arrival were a whirlwind of giddy anticipation. Sara caught wind that my patroness was to call, and she insisted on receiving Jhasali in the estate house instead of Sergio's and mine. Reluctant though I was, I acquiesced.

Jhasali was none too pleased with this development when I told her about it over the communicator. I feared she might decide to cancel her visit rather than put herself amid a group of humans. Her voice radiated annoyance, but to my surprise, she still intended to keep her promise.

Everyone in Armando's household was eager to satisfy their curiosity as to my enigma of a patroness who had descended from her invisible tower only once to meet Father Manuel. Sara and Gracia theorized about what she might be like when they thought I wasn't listening. Sergio pummeled me with a barrage of questions about Jhasali's lineage and repeated several times that neither he nor Armando had ever heard of this supposed noblewoman, though I eventually quieted him by demanding he name the widow of every deceased aristocrat of every rank from the Galician coast to the French border.

Rosa, Ximena, and Carlota also peppered me with inquiries about my peculiar and reclusive patroness. I answered everything I dared, sharing in their anticipation and caught up in the impossible hope that if this meeting went well, Jhasali might wind up with two human companions instead of one.

I spent a great deal of the days leading up to the party preparing everyone for Jhasali's social ineptitudes. My warning that she traveled with no retinue gave them the greatest shock of all. They thought it beyond bizarre a woman of her wealth would ride about without servants—Gracia in particular was downright scandalized—but I passed it off as just another of her endless eccentricities.

Jhasali had been preparing herself, as well. When she and Father Manuel had met, I'd told him she grew up in Bilbao, and I thought it best to stick with that story for consistency's sake. Over the years, the surveillance bots had trawled the northern coast, including the País Vasco. They'd collected and uploaded all the data they'd gathered during their observations. From these observations, Jhasali downloaded the language, the layout of Bilbao, and enough of the customs to answer whatever questions might crop up. Our lies had never come under the kind of scrutiny they would this night.

When Jhasali arrived at the estate house, unaccompanied and unannounced, Rosa let her in while everyone crowded around the door, eager to meet the circus sideshow who'd been sheltering me while I painted all these years. There was a collective sigh of disappointment once everyone saw she'd come attired in a black silk dress and was not visibly out of place.

After the introductions were made, Armando invited her into the parlor to await dinner.

"Tomás tells me you didn't leave a horse in the stables," Armando said when we'd all been seated and served drinks. "Did you come all this way without a mount?"

"I flew here," Jhasali teased while the room laughed.

"You can't have flown here, Juana. Only witches fly." I giggled to pass off my warning as a joke.

"Of course, I didn't really fly here. I let my mare run free. She comes to my whistle like Pepito does," she explained.

"So you're the one who bought my wife a horse and taught her to rove around alone like a man." Sergio chuckled, though it bore no hint of mirth.

"Yes, I suppose that's my fault. But if I hadn't taught her to ride by herself, she would never have visited you in Sevilla last year." Jhasali gave Sergio a smile he didn't return.

Instead, my husband cast me a look of deep displeasure. I had never informed Jhasali I'd lied to him about traveling with a convoy, so she'd shot this lie down without knowing it. Though I was certain I would pay for this later, Sergio decided to keep that impending conflict private for now.

Sergio and Armando drilled Jhasali about her late husband's rank and his pedigree and where his money had come from, trying to disguise their interrogation as polite interest. She gave the scripted answers I'd written for her, and even I had to admire the way my lies rolled off her tongue, smooth as silk, opaque as velvet.

Gabriel eventually directed the conversation to Jhasali's support of my painting. She and I explained once again that we'd met by happenstance while she'd been exploring Santa Colomba. She told everyone she liked to travel the countryside disguised as a peasant so she could see every town and village, each one a world in itself. With the help of the surveillance bots, she knew all the cities nearby: Santander, Comillas, San Vicente, and the like.

She talked at length about Bilbao, impressing Sergio and Armando, who'd been there many times. Armando spoke fluent Euskera, and when she conversed perfectly with him in that tongue, even he seemed satisfied that she was who she said she was.

"What made you decide to sponsor Micaela's work?" Gracia asked Jhasali.

"The quality, of course. You've seen her paintings. Why wouldn't I want such artworks all to myself?"

"They really are incredible. The one she did of Gabriel and Gracia was superb," Sara chimed in. "Mica, you ought to be at the royal court, not stuck here."

Sergio cast her a filthy look, thinking she wouldn't see, but she smirked back at him, and he dropped his gaze to his wine goblet.

"Though it is an odd choice to paint strictly from memory," Gabriel added.

"I like doing it that way. It allows me to paint in solitude, as I prefer," I replied.

"Still, I'd love to see you actually paint one day, lest we all disbelieve you're the one doing it." Armando gave the same mirthless chuckle Sergio had.

"Armando." Sara rolled her eyes.

Jhasali laughed. "What could Micaela do to make another person paint what only her eyes have seen? Open a window in her mind and fling her memories at a real artist?"

Most everyone got a good laugh at that, though Jhasali's jest didn't land well with either my husband or his master. Just then, Rosa came to the rescue when she entered to announce dinner—an excellent meal of roast partridge, cabrito, and veal. The cabrito was so succulent that, for a while, we were all silent, absorbed in the savory saltiness of the meat, so tender it fell off the bone at the slightest touch.

"This cabrito is phenomenal," Jhasali said as we all sucked the bones.

Gabriel nodded. "Rosa and Elena are excellent cooks."

"You should try Elena's venison," Armando added.

"If it's half as good as Micaela's, I'm sure I'd love it." Jhasali took one last bite.

Sergio turned to me. "When have you ever made venison?"

"She has many times after we shot a deer," Jhasali answered.

"Jha—Juana, it's not polite to talk of such things at the table," I blurted, trying to keep her from slipping up again.

"You've taken Micaela hunting?" Sergio demanded.

"Did you all know Juana plays vihuela? She's quite good," I interrupted before Jhasali could tell the room that I ran around with her in the woods dressed in my husband's old trousers.

I was growing angry with her. She and I had discussed at length what was and was not acceptable to tell people, yet she was ignoring it like she knew no better.

At my announcement that Jhasali played vihuela, everyone at the table exclaimed, and Gabriel sent a page to fetch two of his instruments. We retired to the parlor again, where she accompanied him as he led us through many of the songs she'd learned from spying on the musicians in town. I breathed a sigh of relief that it appeared we were to play music the rest of the night—the more singing we did, the less talk there'd be.

"Micaela tells me you have a beautiful singing voice, Sergio, though I notice you haven't joined us," Jhasali said once she and Gabriel paused for a drink.

Sergio shot me an angry glare from where he sat on the hearth with his back to the fire.

"He does sing well," I replied, not breaking his gaze.

"You should sing for me." Jhasali lifted the vihuela and held her fingers at the ready.

My heart leapt. Though she'd caught him off guard, he'd drunk twice as much as anyone else tonight, and I hoped that might make him more open to fulfilling my fantasy of them playing music together.

Despite all the wine in him, Sergio resisted. At first, he shook his head without a word.

Sara pressed him. "Come on, Sergio. Armando has told me you've got a lovely voice too. I don't understand why you won't let anyone hear it."

Sergio looked in dismay to Armando, who sat in a chair to his right, before turning to Sara and saying, "I don't know. I don't like that sort of attention."

"Just do it," Jhasali interjected. "Your wife has the cojones to ride into the wilderness all alone, but yours aren't even big enough for you to sing in front of your friends?"

"I hardly see what either of those things has to do with the other," Sergio snapped, scowling across the room at Jhasali.

She smirked back. "I wouldn't expect *you* to understand. After all, it takes cojones to do many things. Sing in front of others, protect your household, get your wife pregnant."

Sergio's mouth fell open, and everyone else went quiet while their eyes floated from Jhasali to him. I held my breath.

Armando cut in before either Sergio or I could respond. "Don't you dare speak to him like that under my roof."

"I think you just didn't understand what you were saying. Right, Juana?" I asked.

Jhasali put the vihuela on the floor beside her chair. "I understood perfectly. I wouldn't have said it if I didn't think it apt."

I glowered at her. "What is the matter with you? What's he done for you to insult him like that?"

Sergio had allowed Armando to defend him, but when I did it, it proved too much.

"You wouldn't dare talk like that if you were a man," he hissed before Jhasali could answer me. "Because if you were, I wouldn't be debasing myself by drawing my sword on you."

Jhasali laughed in his face. "I doubt you'd be able to put your hands on me regardless."

My stomach dropped as I recalled the bandits in the woods. She'd sworn she'd never hurt a hair on Sergio's head, but that assurance rang hollow at the moment. Without a doubt, Jhasali's invisible retinue lurked just beyond the threshold of this house. Not that she'd need them wearing IDOS. What had I been thinking bringing her here? There was still time to salvage the situation if I could get her to stop talking.

"Juana, no one here has been anything but gracious to you. Apologize right now," I said.

Jhasali snickered. "I see no reason to apologize for speaking the truth as I see it. From where I sit, you wear your husband's pants better than he does."

Gracia gasped and Gabriel gave an inarticulate yell as Armando and Sergio leapt to their feet. If my husband still had reservations about drawing his sword on a woman, he seemed close to forgetting them.

"Juana, shut up!" I screamed.

"No." Sergio pointed his finger in my face. "You shut up."

"You can't tell her to shut up!" Jhasali jumped to her own feet.

I rose as well, ready to step between Sergio and Jhasali if she turned violent, still clinging to the hope that she wouldn't if he kept himself in check. I couldn't keep up with how fast things were devolving, nor could I understand why she was so determined to worsen them.

Sergio rounded on Jhasali. "You don't get to dictate what I can and cannot tell my own wife. You've done more than enough meddling already, and it ends now! I won't have some cheap whore usurping my authority over my own household."

"Usurping you?" She laughed again, though this time she uttered that awful, unnatural cackle she'd given before she'd learned to imitate a human laugh.

"Juana, stop it!" I cried. "You cannot speak to them like this."

"I didn't realize I was obligated to care if I give offense to these organic primitives that stand between me and my creation," she said in Sartjyanan, which gave a great shock to everyone in the room. Sartjyanan doesn't sound like any terrestrial language, and they could all tell it was not Euskera.

Their shocked expressions deepened when I replied in kind. "You promised to be on your best behavior and try to get my friends to like you!"

I knew I sounded like a child, but I was so angry—she could have averted all of this.

"I have no intention of allowing this impudent ape to silence you like you are a slave. You're his superior in every conceivable way. I've made it so. You should tell him to go jump in that well outside," Jhasali spat.

"You don't own me either. I'm your comrade, not your house pet. I will tell him no such thing, nor will you," I retorted, still in Sartjyanan.

"So," Sergio's voice barked in Castellano. "You've taught my wife some heathen tongue so she can hold conversations with you that the rest of us cannot understand. You insult us in a language we don't speak!"

I turned to face him. "No, Sergio, she wasn't insulting—"

"Fine, I'll insult you in a language you do speak. You're an insolent dog who dares to command its rightful master. You have no right to make any demand of Micaela when she is now under my protection."

"Jhasali! Don't say anything more," I screamed in Sartjyanan.

I did not understand how many times I had to tell her that in our world, he had every right to command me, whether he should have or not.

"Micaela, I cannot believe you've accepted such an odious bitch for a patroness," Armando cried.

Gracia and Gabriel agreed, and Sergio seemed to relish Armando putting me in my place.

"You should've followed my lead," I said to Jhasali in Castellano. "I understand how things work here better than you."

"Fine. Then I'm sure you can handle them now." Without another word, she swept out the door.

I slammed myself into my chair and put my head in my hands. Everyone glared at me in outrage. Though my fingers covered my eyes, I felt their infuriated gazes.

Armando collapsed into his seat. "This is who you've been spending all this time with, Micaela? What is wrong with you?"

"If you keep the company of such a woman, she'll make a devil worshipper of you," Gabriel added.

"She will. You don't want to be like that, do you?" Gracia said.

None of them was anywhere near through, and soon their rebukes of Jhasali and chastisements of me for associating with her created such a cacophony I couldn't decipher individual words. I looked to Sergio to defend me, but he was shaking with rage, unable to form any speech. If he could have, it would not have been in my defense.

"I'm as surprised as all of you. I didn't expect such behavior from her. She has never been like this before," I muttered as soon as I could get a word in.

"You . . ." Sergio growled, and I stiffened. "You brought her here to insult us all in the master's house. How could you be so stupid?"

I winced at his words. I had been stupid to think bringing Jhasali around him could possibly go well, but I remained defenseless as he castigated me in front of the whole household. More and more servants kept filing in to watch my husband stand on the hearth and shout at me. Out of everyone, only Sara seemed to understand that this was the exact opposite of how I'd wanted this night to go. She stayed quiet, but her look of pity humiliated me more than everyone else's wrath.

"And hear this, Micaela." Sergio's use of my name snapped me out of my thoughts. "I won't let this woman turn you into any more of a rebellious harpy than you've already become. You will not now, nor will you ever, see her again."

"Sergio!" I exclaimed.

"Silence!" His roar drove me down. "You will agree to this. You will swear it."

My breath caught in my throat. As angry as I was with Jhasali, I couldn't fathom never seeing her again. Yet how could I defy my husband in front of all these witnesses who expected me to obey him? Out of options, I nodded while looking down at my hands.

"I need an actual answer," he said.

"Alright. I won't see her again."

"I warn you, if you do . . ." He didn't finish that sentence. He didn't need to.

Unsatisfied, Armando protested. "Sergio, that is not at all proportionate to this outrage. I've a mind to see you punish her more severely than that—"

"That's enough, Armando," Sara said coolly. "Sergio, sit down."

Gabriel and Gracia cast wide-eyed stares at Sara. Sergio obeyed her command to sit, and, to my astonishment, Armando actually shut his mouth.

"It's obvious this isn't how Micaela intended things to turn out," Sara continued.

I hung my head and shook it without looking at anyone.

Sara leaned over and tilted my face up. "It's alright. I know you didn't mean it. No one is going to punish you, but I do agree it's best you not see this woman again. You may go."

I stood and hurled myself out of the estate house as huge, hot tears spilled from my eyes and cascaded down my cheeks. Every salty drop tasted of shame, rage, guilt, and an overwhelming sense of the injustice with which both Sergio and Jhasali had treated me. I collapsed on the stoop of my house and curled up in the doorway, convulsing with sobs, unable to get ahold of myself enough to push the door open. I just sat there with my forehead on my knees and my arms wrapped around my head, crying uncontrollably.

***

I awoke all alone in the morning. I'd somehow found my way to my bed with no memory of how I got there. As the haze of sleep cleared from my eyes, I remembered my fury at both my "patroness" and my husband. I crawled out of bed and dressed, intent on riding Pepito into the woods to be alone, but when I went to his stall, he wasn't there.

I walked to the estate pastures and whistled, but he didn't come. After a long while of walking and calling, I decided Sergio must have taken him into town to sell him in vengeance for the previous night. I returned to the house and cried most of the day, too proud to run to town and beg Sergio to keep my horse and too angry to contact Jhasali.

When I pulled myself together that afternoon, I walked to the estate house to apologize for Jhasali's behavior. Since Armando wasn't interested in speaking to me and Sergio still hadn't returned from wherever he'd gone with my horse, Sara and I were left to discuss things alone.

"Why did you defend me last night when Juana acted like that in your own house?" I asked once we'd gone out to the garden.

"You think she said anything I disagree with? Somebody needs to put Armando and Sergio in their place every now and then," Sara replied.

I snorted. "Seems you're the woman for that job, not Juana."

"Well, someone besides me. Honestly, Juana was not so bad. I envy her widowhood, to be frank, and the way she handled herself with the men threatening her like that . . . But I still don't think you should see her anymore, regardless of whether Sergio knows of it."

"Why not?"

"I don't know. There's something about her that's so off. She walks into the room, and the hair on the back of my neck stands up."

My own neck hair rose on end. "Does anyone else feel that way?"

"Armando told me not to be ridiculous. He said she's just a standard puta, but I'm not so sure. I cannot explain it. Maybe I am being ridiculous."

I squirmed and tried not to let my expression give me away. Sergio had only been interested in Jhasali's besmirching of his honor, and his eyes had been blind to what Sara's had seen without recognizing they'd seen it.

"She's not a puta," I said aloud.

"Is she a witch?"

"No!"

"Micaela, the lies you tell your husband aren't any of my concern, but I thought I've made it clear you're not to lie to me."

"I'm not lying. She isn't a witch. She's just odd; that's all."

Sara gave me a look of deep skepticism, but I changed the subject before she could take things any further.

"Speaking of husbands, I still don't get how you put yours in line like that."

"Do you still want to save your marriage?" Sara arched an eyebrow.

"Of course I do."

"Then stop asking me that question."

There was such conviction and finality in her tone that I kept my mouth shut. Whatever it was she did to make her husband so compliant, that was not how I wished to conduct things with my own. I wanted neither a master nor a servant; I wanted a partner.

When Sergio came home that night, I discovered, to my immense relief, he'd returned on Pepito. In my days as a novice wife, I'd have rushed out the door and thanked my husband for not selling my horse. To do so at present would have been to acknowledge that he still held such power, and if I planned to remedy that, the first thing I had to do was to behave as if he had no authority over me. I would not thank him. I would not even admit I'd been in fear that he had sold Pepito. If I was going to make a partner out of him, I had to play my cards just right. So I kept my cool when he came in, and he too maintained a stony silence.

I served us a late supper of bread, cheese, and vegetables from my garden. Sergio sat at the table without a word, picking at the meal more than eating it. He rarely refused food, and I was on the verge of asking if he was ill when I remembered Armando would soon set sail without him.

"I'm sorry," I said.

"About time you apologized," he snapped.

"I'm not apologizing!"

"You aren't?"

"I've nothing to apologize for, and you can spare me the tongue-lashing," I added as he opened his mouth to respond. "I'm simply sorry Armando is leaving and you are so unhappy. I'm sorry you don't enjoy time with me half as much as you enjoy it with him."

"I do enjoy time with you. It's just not the same. I cannot do with you many of the things he and I do."

"What can't I do? I can ride. I can swim. I could even sail if you'd teach me. I suppose you'll have to settle for me for the next few weeks anyhow."

"You don't understand." He sighed.

"What if the only reason I don't understand is because you've never bothered to tell me? Over the past few years, I've discovered I'm capable of comprehending quite a lot."

"What does that mean?"

"*You* wouldn't understand."

He threw up his hands. "Fine. Be like that. With the way things have been going between us lately, I suppose I shouldn't expect any different."

I stayed silent; I wasn't about to let him force remorse on me. We didn't resolve much that night or the rest of the days between Sara and Armando's departure. Sergio stayed gone as much as he could, and when he was home, we scarcely spoke. We might've said ten words to one another in the whole period between our last argument and the embarkation.

The day the master and the mistress sailed, Sergio took Pepito and rode off to sulk alone, leaving me without transport once more. It irked me when he took my mount, for he could have borrowed any one of Armando's horses, and he knew I'd bought Pepito for myself. Still, it gave me no end of pleasure to know his hijacking of my horse would do nothing to accomplish the goal for which he did it: keeping me away from Jhasali.

I'd been too angry with her in recent days to consider speaking to her. Now, my initial wrath had cooled from a boil to a simmer, readying me to confront her about her behavior at the estate house.

I made a passing attempt to call her using my drone as a proxy to transmit my speech. Ideally, the drone could give voice to the thoughts I wished to articulate, as my own mouth could, but I hadn't yet mastered that skill any more than I'd mastered seeing through the drone's eyes. In my fury about the argument, I'd broken the bond anyhow. Thus, I pulled the communicator from its place next to IDOS.

"We need to talk," I said. "But you must come to me. Meet me at the coast."

"I'll be right there," Jhasali replied.

I walked a half league or so in the pleasant July warmth until I came to one of our meeting spots on the forest cliffs overlooking the sea. She awaited me already, seated on a flat transport drone and dangling her feet above the ground.

"What the devil is wrong with you? Why did you start that massive argument with Sergio?" I demanded.

"I didn't like the way he spoke to you. He has no right," Jhasali said.

"First off, I can handle him. It isn't your business to put yourself between me and my husband. Second, he hadn't said a damned thing to me until you insulted him. You started one hundred percent of that utterly avoidable nonsense. Why did you do it?"

"I thought if you could see him for what he is, you would—"

"You mean you thought you could persuade me to move into Homeship by making us fight," I interjected. "Hear this: living in Homeship is my decision. I won't be manipulated by you any more than I'll be commanded by him. I am the master of myself. Do you understand?"

"Yes, of course. You're right. I shouldn't have done as I did."

"I think you did some serious damage, but that doesn't mean we've lost hope of you two getting along."

"Us getting along?" she snapped. "You talk like the decision of his being allowed into our circle is already made."

"I just meant—"

"I know what you meant, and it isn't going to happen."

"Why not? You're the one who insulted him. Nothing that passed that night would've happened if not for you."

"That doesn't matter. I did as I did to test him as much as anything else, and he failed spectacularly. If he can't even handle a stranger slighting him, how's he going to react to Homeship? How's he going to accept me as captain of that vessel and everything in it? If I appear as a female, he won't do as I say. But if I appear as a male, he'll think the pair of us are copulating. You know better than I how he'll react to that; from what you've told me, I cannot imagine it would be pleasant."

Though I hated to admit it, she was right on that front. "That might be true, but if you'd put him to a different test, he could've done better. You humiliated him in front of his wife and his master. How did you think he'd react? If you'd been a man, he'd have dueled with you."

"Regardless, I hope this matter is settled once and for all. He will never be allowed near Homeship, nor will he be told what I really am."

I put my hands on my hips. "This matter is not settled. You are Homeship's captain, but that doesn't render my opinion irrelevant. I'm more your equal than any living thing on this planet. You said so yourself, and that means you ought to start listening to me."

"I know. I've begun to think of you in this manner, but your primordial scum of a mate is not like you. He can never become as you have."

"He's not primordial scum, and neither are the rest of them. The only difference between them and me is you chose me. You could have given your gift to any one of them and they would have become just like me."

Jhasali scoffed. "Not Sergio. He's too abrasive."

"You don't understand him." I paused, realizing as those words escaped my lips that neither did I. "He's forbidden me from seeing you, you know."

At this she burst into a fit of hysterical laughter. She doubled over at the knees and gripped her sides, guffawing in a wild, uncontrolled manner, though I didn't think what I'd said was all that funny.

"Oh! Imagine that brute commanding you," she exclaimed. "Let him command other brutes like himself whose eyes will never comprehend the heavens nor see them without the veil of your planet's atmosphere."

"He isn't going to command me any longer. I love him more than anything, but I'm going to tell him that if he won't start showing me some damned respect, the next time I go to see my 'patroness' will be the last time I see him."

"You mean it?"

"If you're still willing to have me."

I bristled at the fact I'd have to give up my friends for the crime of being unwilling to submit to my husband. On the flip side, living in Homeship would make preparing and conducting my search for my mother infinitely easier, if I could make peace with having no home and no family to offer her once I'd found her—assuming I found her.

"Of course I'll have you," Jhasali cried. "You should move in straightaway. I've already listed you as a crew member on the ship's manifest—"

"You did what?"

"Yes. I suppose it slipped my mind. Next time you're inside the perimeter, you can try commanding the communal devices."

"I don't know when I'll get to come to Homeship again with Sergio moping around."

"You know, I can still kill the son of a bitch if you've changed your mind on that." Jhasali giggled like Christmas had come early.

"No. How many times do I have to say it?"

"You wish to kill him yourself?"

"No!" I yelled. "No more talk of killing him. I don't like it. You scared the devil out of me the other night."

Jhasali rolled her eyes. "I'd never have harmed him against your will. I promised you."

"It won't ever be my will to hurt him. All I wish is for the smallest of dynamics to change in our marriage. I don't see why he protests. It'll be barely more than an inconvenience to him, and it means everything to me."

"You know you'll never change him."

"I don't want to. I don't wish to alter a thing about his personality. I only wish to alter the terms in which he thinks of me. If he held me in the same regard as he holds men, I'd want nothing more. I just don't know how to make him do that."

"Couldn't you take the form of a man for him once you master your nanos?"

It was my turn to laugh hysterically. "Absolutely not! You don't understand what would happen if everyone found out I could do such a thing. They'd call me a witch and a degenerate."

"None of this makes a shred of sense."

"Do you ever think maybe you're the one with the problem for expecting it to?"

"No," she said flatly.

"Regardless, I'm going to have to lie low with you for a while. There's nothing Sergio can do to prevent us from meeting when he isn't around, but if I spend the night with you again before the sailing season starts, it could put me in a real bind."

"You think he would try to harm you?"

"Never, but I don't want to create a mess of unnecessary problems for myself."

"I still don't know why you tolerate him." Jhasali sighed.

I hadn't had a choice until recently, but even now that I did, I didn't know how to explain to her that we loved one another, and—in all honesty—I was the one who had changed. Before I'd met Jhasali, I'd been content with my marriage. Not happy, perhaps, but content in the manner that children are content with their upbringings. They don't know any better; thus, they are happy with what they receive. The problem only arises when they are exposed to finer things beyond their own environments, or when they finally learn to call dysfunction and discord by their proper names.

I wished I could tell Jhasali of the day Sergio had brought me Lobo when he'd realized I was lonely, the tender way he always held me when I needed comfort, or the time he'd cared for me on my sick bed, abandoning all his obligations to bathe my face and help me drink as I lay in that feverish haze between sleeping and waking. I had no words to explain that his flaws were not the measure of his soul nor to make her see that for the roses, we must water the thorns. How could a creature such as her comprehend the way humans love one another? It is inexplicable even to ourselves.

## Chapter Twenty-Four

# THE BREAKTHROUGH

Upon arriving at our house, I found Sergio wasn't there, though he returned not long after I did. I asked him where he'd been as he appeared at the top of the stairs.

His face hardened. "You believe you have the right to demand my whereabouts when you refuse to offer me the slightest hint as to yours?"

"I was not demanding, merely curious. But if you don't want to tell me where you've been, then fine. I don't care."

"Where did you go today? I came home a while ago, and you weren't here."

"I walked in the woods alone and went nowhere else," I snapped. At least that was half-true. "And tomorrow, I wish to go into town to see Father Manuel. So you'd better leave Pepito here for me."

Sergio undressed and went to bed without another word. I spent the night in my chair, watching the fire die and deciding not to sleep. When the birds began to chirp and the first silver light crept over the eastern hilltops, I stole out to get Pepito before Sergio could.

I rode away from town just before dawn, planning to wait for a less ungodly hour to visit Father Manuel. Getting off the road, I loafed in the pastures, watching as the sunrise cast a bright yellow glow over the green fields where the sheep shook the morning dew off their growing wool and pickily browsed through the lush grass.

Sheep were one of my favorite things about summer, and I always missed them when the herders migrated them south for the winter. I loved the constant bleating, the cheerful tinkling of bells, and the beating of tiny lamb hooves as they romped around the meadows. It gave me a laugh whenever one of the lambs tripped on its own long legs and toppled over, only to bounce back up and keep running.

Now, the lambs were half-grown, and the ewes ignored them. They also ignored me, Pepito, and the herd of fallow deer foraging near the edge of the woods. I observed the deer for as long as they stayed within eyeshot, allowing their serene grazing to fill my soul with peace.

Being here reminded me of Lobo, for when he'd been alive, I would never have been able to watch a herd of deer for so long without him whining and wiggling until he wore me down and made me let go of his fur so he could give chase. In my mind's eye, I saw him flying across the field, tail swirling in a great circle, a loud, cracking bark emanating from his throat. Of course, he'd never gotten anywhere close to catching a deer, but he loved to send them flying, scattering them in all directions and then running in circles, unsure of which to pursue.

I laughed at the memories of him romping through these very fields, infuriating the shepherds, chasing sheep and deer and anything with legs, though the largest thing he'd ever caught was a rabbit. He'd been a real friend, and I still missed him. Smiling and tearing up all at once, I looked to find the deer had spooked at something and were fleeing back into the forest. Perhaps Lobo had been here in spirit.

I left the fields after a couple of hours and went to the rectory to find it empty, so I assumed Father Manuel must be in the church. I walked toward the entrance, pulling my scarf over my hair as I made for the threshold. Father Manuel stood just beyond the doorway, still in his vestments. When he saw me, such an intense glare emanated from his gray eyes that I stopped in the entryway, trying to recall why he might be angry with me. Maybe he'd heard how things had gone with "Juana."

I stepped into the church and opened my mouth to ask what was wrong. Then, I looked past Father Manuel to the unlocked side chapel behind him. Sergio knelt inside, feet crossed over one another and tucked underneath his thighs, brow pressed into his folded hands, elbows resting on the altar platform.

At that, I understood. Father Manuel must have thought I'd come here to argue with my husband. When I made my way toward the chapel, he stepped into the aisle to block me, but I whispered I only wanted to check on Sergio, not fight with him. He allowed me to get by, squeezing me softly on the shoulder as I passed.

I was thankful for his gentleness. Even now, I always felt a sense of bereavement every time I entered this place and remembered there was nothing for me here anymore. A void had opened in my heart, and nothing could fill it; a wound had been inflicted on my very soul that no unguent could mend.

I don't intend to say I missed the belief itself. Indeed, my lack of faith had brought me a sense of peace that passed all my previous understanding. The fires of Hell were no more, and all the talk of damnation and holy wrath in every church in all the world could stir no fear in me. The connection to my fellows in humanity, the sense of collective belief and shared identity—that was what I missed. As far as I knew, Jhasali and I were the only two in my whole little world who thought as we did, and the shift in my consciousness had opened a vast gulf between myself and those I loved.

In my heart, I understood it was too late to bridge this gulf. The truth had outed, as it so seldom did in those days, and it might've driven a wedge between myself and my friends, but it had also set me free. It had opened my eyes to the dazzling light of a trillion suns, and even if I wished to turn away now, even if I preferred the darkness, there was no going back. Once the illusion is shattered, no amount of desire or sorrow can repair it. The shards of the mirage are delicate as glass, ephemeral as grains of sand blown in the wind. They are caught up, swept away, and gone.

When I entered the chapel, I knelt beside Sergio and stared at his miserable face as he prayed, moving his lips ever so slightly without making a sound. He seemed to have been weeping. My heart softened as he cast me a fleeting glance before turning away.

I wondered what might be troubling him. I hadn't expected he'd feel shame about his treatment of me, but perhaps I was wrong. Maybe all his remoteness and deception and ungentle conduct were weighing on him at last. As this thought passed through my mind, I realized it gave me no satisfaction. It saddened me to think he might torment himself in this manner when all I desired was for us to start things afresh.

If Sergio could prove himself willing to mend certain faults, I'd forgive and forget anything he'd done in the past. Who besides me had the right to offer pardon? Father Manuel, who had been no more sinned against than any random stranger on the street? Some far-off god that no more existed than the devils and witches I'd once feared? No. The right to forgive lay only with me, and I needed neither confession nor penance. I wanted to grant my pardon freely.

I reached out and twirled my fingers around Sergio's curls, keeping my touch light, for deep caresses did not belong here. He turned to me and took my hand, bringing it to his lips and allowing me to slide the backs of my fingers across his damp cheek.

"What's troubling you so?" I asked him.

"Habitual sin should trouble the consciences of all men," a voice said behind my back; Father Manuel had knelt just to my rear.

"I'm sorry, Father, but you must know by now there is a fundamental difference between what you and I would consider sin. I don't think any of us are habitual sinners." I tried to say this as gently as possible, but I couldn't stay silent with my husband so distraught.

Sergio lifted his head, and a confused expression passed over his visage. "You don't know everything, so how can you say I am no sinner?"

"I say you are not because whatever wrong you may have done, as your wife I'm more likely than anyone else to be the one against whom your sin was committed—meaning I'm the only one with the right to offer pardon. Whatever it is, I don't need to know. I forgive you."

"That might not hold true if you knew what it was. I can't be redeemed."

"Perhaps there's nothing to redeem. Many of the acts the Church calls sin are not so."

I forgot Father Manuel sat behind me. His indignant huff was so intense I felt a puff of air hit my left ear. I pursed my lips. I had no desire to offend him, but I also had to say my piece.

I laid my hand on Sergio's shoulder. "What if redemption isn't necessary because the whole idea is flawed? Maybe absolution cannot exist because what's done is done, and that's all there is. But do you need absolution, my love? Or even salvation? Perhaps there's nothing to be saved from. Have you seen such a thing as Hell, or have you only heard tell of it from those who wish to govern your thoughts?"

Sergio's eyes widened and flitted to his confessor before returning to me.

"Micaela, I cannot abide your heresy at the altar of the Almighty," Father Manuel spat.

I turned to him, but he sat high on his knees while I sat on my hip, so instead of catching his gaze, I found myself staring at his waist and the black cloth of his chasuble, which covered the white alb underneath. I took a sharp breath as I was reeled back to the memory of the black-and-white robes Ignacio had worn when he'd dragged me to the auto de fe all those years ago.

That recollection rendered me livid. What right did any man of any cloth the world over have to decide what constituted sin, considering what so many of their sort had done and the rest had failed to stop? None of them were innocent of the crimes of their brothers! Though I hate to admit it now, for a split second, I wanted to strike the man in that alb and chasuble.

I shook myself out of this fit of blind temper by remembering that Father Manuel alone could not stop the crimes of the Church. He *had* gotten rid of Ignacio after he'd discovered the monstrous thing he'd done to me. Despite his misgivings, he'd also kept all my secrets and offered a tolerance of my "sorcery" that far exceeded the virtue of our time. However, I decided this goodly disposition must be the result of some inner force of character, for it existed in spite of his profession, not because of it.

"Father," I whispered, "I don't wish to upset you, but I must speak my mind. I don't understand why it's always my burden to mollify those around me, and why I get so little in return. I cannot be expected to please everyone at the expense of myself all the damn time."

Sergio began to sob afresh as I said this. I lifted the veil off my head, letting my hair fall loose down my back, and handed it to him so he could mop his face. Father Manuel gave no response, so I continued speaking.

"Maybe my husband doesn't need to hear any more about habitual sin or damnation or penance or anything like that. I know I've had my fill. Perhaps what he needs is to feel worthy of something better than crawling on all fours like a dog begging for crumbs of clemency from a merciless god who will never be pleased nor satisfied, no matter the horrors done in his name."

"Did your foreign friend put that idea in your head?" Father Manuel snapped.

"My foreign friend doesn't know enough about the faith to formulate such an idea. I concocted it all on my own, if you can believe that."

"Can I talk to you outside?"

Christ. I'd done it now. Father Manuel and I left Sergio at the altar, passed through the nave, and exited the main door, stepping beyond the threshold onto the patio.

I spoke first. "Father, I didn't intend to anger you, but sometimes I cannot keep silent."

"I fear it'll be the death of you, love. But I've become so accustomed to your heresy I hardly notice it any longer. I just don't wish to hear it in the house of the one whose ears it most offends."

I laughed. "It's good you've become desensitized, but if you don't want to hear my heresy in your domain, I'll save it for another location."

"It's the domain of the Lord, Micaela, not mine."

"Regardless, I'll speak my mind to you elsewhere. You know I must. Who else can I talk to? Who else knows my secrets? I wish Sergio and I could confide in each other the way we both have in you."

"I cannot tell you what he's confessed."

"I know. I wasn't asking. We all have our secrets, and I don't want to know his. Truly," I added when he looked at me dubiously. "It's not my business what Sergio's done. Even if he went so far as to find himself some New World trollop while he was away, nothing can change it now. I suppose if I'm going to keep so many secrets from him, I cannot expect him to be forthcoming with me in everything."

Father Manuel inclined his head. "That seems a fair assessment."

I looked back at the church, thinking of the pain that coming here always caused me. "You know, sometimes I feel I shouldn't return to this place. It doesn't belong to me anymore."

"Of course you should return. Whatever belief you espouse now, your pretense is necessary for all our survival."

"If more people dispensed with the deception, it might become unnecessary. If others like me broke our silence, we might discover minds like ours are more numerous than we'd believed. We might find we are legion."

"Or you might bring the authorities knocking on our doors. The last visitation from our friends in the Inquisition was close enough." Father Manuel's eyes bored into mine.

I held his gaze. "I don't care. Let them do as they will."

"Don't be ridiculous. We've had this discussion before. I will not have it again. Who of all those you love can they not harm? Who, save you, has no reason to fear them?"

"I know. I'll do what I must to protect you all."

"If that were true, you wouldn't have done as you did in Toledo."

"In Toledo, I had the opportunity to save innocent lives, and I took it."

"I know, and I thank Christ you were able to help them. I just wish you could've done it in a manner that attracted less attention."

"Well, I couldn't have." I sighed.

"You could've at least deceived the crowds. You could've called yourself the Queen of Heaven, not the heretic of heretics, and they might be venerating you instead of hunting you."

I shrugged. "It's easy to think of such things in hindsight, but everything happened so fast. I only had time to act, not to contemplate. How long will you keep throwing Toledo in my face?"

"Until we have nothing to fear."

I didn't know what to say. The only way we'd ever have nothing to fear would be if I mastered Homeship and conquered the whole empire. My anonymity was our sole shield now.

"Can I ask you something?" I wished to change the subject before he could chastise me further.

He nodded without answering. I knew what I was to say might anger him, but we were no longer inside the church. I hadn't made any promises about heresy out here.

"What happens if this life is all we're to receive, and we've ruined it with burnings and holy wars and persecutions? Have you ever feared there is only this?"

He furrowed his brow. "I've considered it before, but I couldn't bear the terror it whipped up in my soul, nor the uncertainty I feared would be ceaseless if I continued in that thinking. I felt it better not to question such things."

I pictured the sanbenitos all over the walls of the cathedral in Toledo. I remembered the autos de fe, the one I'd witnessed and the one I'd interrupted.

"Is it really better not to question? If so, who is it better for?" I asked.

"Micaela, you're not going to 'catch' me nor convert me to your sacrilege."

"I'm not trying to. I don't want you to abandon your faith. I only wish your fellows would stop setting people on fire over it!" I snapped, before I inhaled deeply and added, "Did it ever occur to you I am legitimately asking your opinion?"

"Don't think I've never doubted. I've spent many a sleepless night wrestling with the will of God. Yet when will humanity be ready for the sort of world you want, a world without faith?"

"Juana comes from a world without faith, though now that I consider it, her world is one that worships a sort of deity, a living one. Her people left blind faith behind but not blind devotion, and they've all paid the price, especially the ones who dissented."

"I'm not sure I understand. How could she come from a world without faith?"

"If I tried to make you understand, she'd be furious. When she and I last spoke—"

"I was under the impression your husband has forbidden you from seeing that woman." Father Manuel scowled.

I guffawed. "I'm forbidden from many of the things I do."

Father Manuel rolled his eyes before reverting to our original point. "My child, you wish to find a spark to set the world on fire, but it's already ablaze with enough dangerous ideological controversies that don't take things nearly as far as you have taken them. It's too soon for you to expect of people what you do."

"I am a patient woman. It won't be too soon forever."

"Are you to live forever?"

I shrugged, not knowing how to respond to such deep irony.

He dropped his voice. "What is she? Your foreign friend, I mean."

"I'm sorry. I already told you I'm not permitted to discuss it."

"Apparently Juana the Mad is the only person on Earth capable of prohibiting you from anything anymore."

"Juana isn't mad," I huffed. "She's the only one who comprehends enough about our circumstances to deserve to command me. You and Sergio don't get to claim that right by virtue of sex any longer. You must earn it."

"How?"

"I don't know."

"I believe I've already earned it by virtue of my more advanced age and my greater experience," he said firmly.

"I'll accept that. For now."

"Then this is my command to you. Go inside and get your husband. Take him home and comfort him. He needs you to be normal right now, for once."

I turned from Father Manuel, lifting my skirt off the ground and stepping back into the church. Sergio was now lying prostrate before the chapel altar. I'd have thought he'd fainted if he hadn't been breathing so heavily.

Kneeling beside him, I laid a hand on the back of his neck. We remained silent for a long while. When he clasped my hand, I pulled him up to his knees. He stared at the stone floor and asked me if I meant it when I said I forgave him for what he had done, though I didn't even know what it was.

"Sergio, I forgive you for the things I do know you've done. Ostensibly, it's easier to pardon what has never offended me because it was out of my sight."

"Why?" He still glared at the floor. "Why do you forgive me?"

"Because I want to. It's a burden on me to hold an account of all your transgressions, especially when I want nothing more than to make amends and look to the future."

He wiped his eyes. "I don't deserve you."

"Who can decide what someone deserves? I won't hear any more talk of anyone deserving anything. It's never done anybody a shred of good, and it never will. Now, let's go. This place is not where you need to be at present, and I want to get home."

Once we made it to our house, I took Sergio straight to the bed and lay down with him, situating myself in a half-seated position so he could lay his head on my chest in the same manner I always laid my head on his. He allowed me to pull him to myself, placing his head just below my breasts and wrapping his arms around my waist. He was so quiet I might've thought he'd fallen asleep, but his body was still too brutally tense to find slumber.

"What if my sin is the reason we have no children?" Sergio whispered. "What if your forgiveness is not enough?"

I held my breath. We had thus far avoided a serious conversation on our failure to produce offspring, but I was thankful for this because I'd always been sure if we ever discussed it, Sergio would blame me for our dearth of heirs. I recalled what Jhasali had so flippantly said about his infertility as well as all the innumerable nights I'd squandered on my knees pleading for a child. I guessed he'd wasted as much time on that futile prayer as I.

Uncertain of what I could say to reassure him, I simply spoke my heart. "I think things just happen the way they happen, and there is nothing productive or positive about assigning meaning to them. Our barrenness is what it is. There is no 'why.'"

Sergio squeezed me tight but stayed quiet, so I interwove my fingers within the spiraling locks of his hair. Taking my nails and gently grazing his scalp, I separated the bigger curls into smaller ones. He sighed and relaxed. I took hold of a curl near the back of his head and turned it over in my hand, noting it was flecked with several strands of gray. I then remembered how much older he was than me.

Our ages were not a topic I preferred to think about, for I would soon be twenty-three, but he was already thirty-four. Now I feared this gap in our years in a way I previously hadn't. I'd never seen any hint of silver in all this black mane nor recognized that we'd married well after he was past the peak of his youthful vigor, for men of his occupation passed it early. I'd been so young and in love on our wedding day it had not occurred to me he'd leave me a widow.

Recalling the minuscule stowaways I had allowed into my body, I remembered my husband would die hundreds, perhaps thousands of years before I did. I'd already wept too often for this reason, but that recollection started the tears afresh. I didn't wish to see these curls change from pitch-black to blue-gray while I sat by and could do nothing.

A bud of resentment for Jhasali blossomed inside my breast, for, after all, it was she who'd placed me in this position and refused to give me recourse; she who held the key to stopping this march of graying strands in its tracks and offering me a companion of my own kind to commune with me in a way she never would and understand me in a way she never could.

Sergio looked up when he noticed I was crying. "I don't wish to be the reason you weep."

"If that were the case, you'd treat me better," I blurted before recalling I'd decided to forgive him not an hour ago. Forgive him I could do, but I could not allow things to continue as they had, bygones or no.

"I know you're still angry about my handling of our finances."

"I'm angry you lied to me, yet again, and also that you didn't respect me enough to think me worthy of being involved in the funding of my own household, especially since you're so often absent from it. Other women's husbands turn over all their wages to them when they leave for so long, yet you cannot even give me a number as to yours."

"I didn't know you wanted to be involved." He lifted his head off my ribcage and lay on his side, propping himself on his elbow. "I never intended to deceive you. I just . . . when I heard the Crown was selling hidalguía, I had this daydream I would come home to you one day a real hidalgo with a legacy for the both of us in my hand, and I might surprise you with it after all these years of toil. I see now that was foolish."

I am not sure I've ever felt like more of a wicked bitch than I did when he said those words. My husband had wished to make me a hidalga and bestow the status upon me as a gift, and I'd ruined it for him. I'd been so caught up in the notion he didn't trust me when he was only trying to be sentimental in his own way. I lamented that I had not put better faith in his intentions, but I still did not wish to be kept in the dark, nor did I regret having seen the light.

I forced my voice to remain steady. "I'm sorry I ruined your plans. Such an intention was thoughtful, and I appreciate it. But I want your whole trust now—not a fraction of it, not some diluted version of it, not at some other time. Can't you understand that?"

Sergio rolled out of bed and strode across the room. At first, I thought he would storm out. However, he opened his trunk and retrieved his private lockbox, the key to which he'd always kept to himself. He unlocked it and rummaged through before removing a stack of papers. Sitting on the bed, he took my wrist, turning my hand up and stuffing the papers into it.

"Most of our money isn't in coin. It's tied up in partial ownership of the *San Bruno* and the *San José*, among other ventures. These papers will tell you all you need to know. I want you to keep them. Store them where you will. Make copies if you like. And take this as well." He put the key to the lockbox in my other hand.

"I don't need it," I said, causing him to give me a confused look. "I mean, I won't use it. However you want to manage our money, I'll defer to you. You're the one who's going to have to retire, not me. All I wanted was for you to treat me as a partner."

I put the papers back in the lockbox and handed him the key, which he placed on our bedside table instead of stuffing it in his coin purse. I shot him a weak smile and wrapped my hand around the back of his head, bringing it down so I could kiss his brow, his cheeks, his soft lips. This was what I'd wanted. This was enough.

Things were different between Sergio and me from that moment. He began to sit me down every morning and explain our finances—what parts of the business Armando had entrusted to him, how he managed his share of the resources and the men, how he'd divvied up our own accounts and invested his earnings with other traders.

As for me, I told him I had lied to him and snuck off to see Jhasali even though he'd forbidden me from doing so. He didn't ask how I got to her without Pepito, nor did I volunteer the information. I also did not agree to a cessation of contact, but he didn't attempt to force me to. However, I did promise when I went to call on her, I would be forthcoming with my whereabouts. I'd have come clean to him about everything if I hadn't feared he'd put me in the madhouse for my delusions or that Jhasali would kill him rather than allow him to walk about knowing what she was and where her ship was located.

I hoped our shift in dynamic could make Sergio more receptive to trying again with Jhasali. She'd offended him deeply, and he her, but both their tempers would cool with time. Once that happened, I might bring them together without it being an absolute disaster.

I was optimistic that if I introduced the pair of them alone, I might one day be able to coax Jhasali into agreeing to take Sergio into our fold. With her help, I could explain things to him as they'd been explained to me, teach him as I'd been taught. Then we could be true comrades in eternity, and there would be no more secrets between us.

Of course, this dream would be no more realized than that of the alchemist for gold or the conquistador for the Fount of Youth. For a few weeks, I continued to engage in my tenuously tolerated relationship with Jhasali. I visited Homeship only on those days when it might not interfere with my time with Sergio. He and I developed a system where I did not exactly lie about my whereabouts, but I did not exactly rub his nose in them either. Out of consideration for his reputation, I also didn't make a show of his relinquishment of control. I resumed my habit of slipping off to Homeship unseen, maintaining the illusion of his authority over his household.

We got along quite well, in fact, when he didn't attempt to impede my comings and goings and I didn't attempt to force him to accept them. I simply did as I would regardless of his opinion, and he did not change his opinion regardless of my doings. We chose to coexist in this silent stalemate, which might not have been the healthiest thing on the planet, but it cut down on our marital strife. Not to mention what a huge step it was for Sergio to allow me to do as I wished without making a fuss.

He demonstrated how much effort he was willing to put into repairing our relationship one evening during the last days of August, when we paid a visit to Father Manuel. I made us a fabulous meal of roast pork leg, white bread, bean stew, and fine Canary sack we'd been saving since Sergio had picked it up on the way home from the New World. After we ate, I whipped out some quesada I'd brought as a surprise, and we unstopped a decanter of Liébana orujo that Armando had given Sergio.

I downed a cup of the brandy and attempted, unsuccessfully yet again, to get the nanos to allow me to feel the same warm happiness I'd felt before I'd given them their permanent home. Even now, after all my small victories over them, I still failed to assert myself as their true and indisputable master.

Why was my hold over them so tenuous? I'd managed to make them restart my menstrual cycle, so a little thing like getting drunk should've been easy. After another cup, I gave up and figured since I hated the taste of the brandy and couldn't get any satisfaction from its effects, I might as well let the men drink.

Sergio had begun to show the first hints of a tipsy grin and I was on the point of slicing myself a second helping of quesada when a sudden knock sounded at Father Manuel's door.

*Damn*, I thought.

This late, it was likely someone coming to fetch Father Manuel to administer the viaticum or deal with some other emergency, and if that was the case, we would not see him again tonight. He'd had one too many already, and I wasn't sure he was sober enough to go with whoever waited outside.

However, when I opened the door, I found not worried parishioners come to speak to him about their dying abuela's last rites, but two strange men sporting poorly concealed daggers. From their stances and their intense glares, I figured them for Santa Hermandad, but what would the brothers want with us? I opened my mouth to tell them to go away, but Father Manuel appeared beside me before I could say a word.

He slid his body between me and the strangers. "What can I do for you, gentlemen?"

"Are you Father Manuel Romero?" one of them asked.

He affirmed he was indeed the man they sought and ushered them in, much to my displeasure. I endured an intense unease in their presence, and I guessed from Father Manuel's tense tone and stiff movements that he did too. Sergio, who remained oblivious to these men's probable reasons for seeking us out, seemed unperturbed, even going so far as to offer them a drop of orujo and a slice of my quesada. They sat down at Father Manuel's table and motioned for him to do the same, as if he needed an invitation to take a seat in his own house.

I wondered if making it my habit to leave IDOS hidden under the floorboards at my house had been a mistake. I'd never been one to enjoy the carrying of arms, so it had been a relief to leave the cuffs somewhere where they could do no harm. Yet now, in the presence of these armed strangers, I felt naked without them, like I'd been stripped of the only amulet I'd ever worn that had any real power.

I kept my cool and got fresh cups and plates for these strangers. I then poured them brandy and cut them two small slices of quesada. They spoke a few polite words of introduction but did not seem too keen to talk openly in front of me. Indeed, they didn't acknowledge me at all except to cast odd glances in my direction while speaking to Father Manuel. I didn't recognize either of them, but I got a strange feeling they knew me.

When I handed the shorter of the two his orujo, he said he and his companion wished to speak of men's business. I turned to go, but Sergio objected.

"Sit down, Micaela." He patted the empty seat to his left and turned to the strange men. "Anything you have to say to us, you can say to her."

My mouth tried to form a grin, but I stifled it. Sitting down beside him, I squeezed his hand under the table.

"We came to discuss things of some importance," the taller man argued.

At these words, Sergio's expression hardened with fury. Just as his lip curled into a snarl, Father Manuel diffused the situation by inviting the men to talk in his bedchamber and sweeping them from the dining table.

"What was that about?" Sergio glared at the closed bedroom door.

"I have no clue." I slid his brandy closer to him.

He picked it up and sipped it, still staring at the door. I tried to prick my enhanced ears to catch any hint of conversation, but the three of them kept their voices low. I allowed my eyes to wander to Sergio, who had returned his gaze to the brandy, though he acted no less annoyed. I laid my hand over the top of his as he wrapped it around the base of his cup.

I said nothing, feeling nothing needed to be said to tell him it had not been lost on me, this effort he was making to amend the wrongs in our relationship, even if he couldn't amend such wrongs anywhere else. Acknowledging it outright might embarrass him, so I stayed quiet, still listening, still unable to pick up more than a few snatches of whispered discussion.

Father Manuel and the men did not remain long in his room, and soon he ushered them back into the main living area and sat down at the table. He invited them to do the same, but they refused, saying they'd better return to their inn.

"I'll show you out." Sergio rose from the table, motioning for Father Manuel to remain.

I had to stifle the urge to beg him not to go with them. I still feared they'd come to do us harm, but at the same time, he could handle himself. As soon as he stepped out and shut the door behind the three of them, I turned to Father Manuel.

"They were here asking about 'the incident,' weren't they?" I whispered.

"What do you think? We know the tribunal found out you were absent during the Witch of Toledo sightings, and though Don Luis didn't deem that enough evidence to pursue a case, those two somehow received word of it in Toledo. Don't worry. I told them they had bad information because you arrived here by the end of August last year."

"Thanks for throwing them off the scent."

"Of course."

I clicked my tongue. "You know, if you're ever in real trouble, I don't wish you to protect me. Don't let anyone hurt you. If you must, denounce me and save yourself."

"What sort of man do you take me for, thinking I'd denounce you to save my own skin?"

"I don't care about that. I want you to do it. I can protect myself much easier than I can protect you."

"No. I won't help them do the devil's work. If the Lord anointed you and your foreign friend to save the innocent, I won't be the one to interfere."

"I saved the innocent because it pleased me, and it would also please me if you didn't allow yourself to be interrogated or, God forbid, tortured over me. Promise you won't."

He nodded halfheartedly, and I was not sure if that counted as a promise, but I didn't want to push him. My husband returned an instant later, obliging me to drop the matter.

Sergio and I took the orujo and rode home in the wee hours of the morning. Father Manuel had pressed us to stay, but I wished to sleep in my own bed and not on my former mattress in the maid's room. That tiny cot was barely large enough for me, and tall as Sergio was, he wouldn't even fit in the adjacent one Leonor had occupied.

When we arrived at our house, I sat down at the table and popped the brandy cork, thinking to give it another go. I downed three cups in quick succession, desiring with all my might for the nanos to filter out the alcohol slowly enough to let me feel its effects. Sergio saw me do this, and he sat down across from me, staring at me with a stunned expression.

"You shouldn't drink like that," he said.

"You do."

"I'm not a woman."

"You want to catch up?" I slid the decanter over to him.

He smirked and pounded four in a row. I laughed at his nerve. He had no idea that at this, he could never outdo me. It was just my luck that, again, the brandy's only effects were its unpleasant aftertaste and the predictable urge to urinate almost as soon as I'd drunk it.

Sergio, however, was debaucherous within the hour. He'd had another drink or three after his original four, against all my protestations and on top of the sack and brandy he'd had at Father Manuel's house, so he soon became so inebriated I could scarcely understand him.

He took huge swallows of brandy one after the other until he polished off the entirety, and then he ranted about everything from the overburdensome taxes we were obliged to pay to the price of meat to the state of political affairs. He had the filthiest mouth, too, and he left me in hysterics trying to figure out how he could stuff the words "hijo de mil putas" into a single sentence so many times. I'd never heard him swear like this, but then again, he'd never been this drunk in my presence either.

Eventually, the silliness and cursing gave way to more personal, if slurred, discussion.

"You know the first, uh, the first time I knew I wanted to tire with you?" He leaned over the table and laid his head on his elbow.

"You mean marry me?" I asked.

"Yeah. That. It was the day you jumped off the boat. I thought the . . . I mean, you. You were the funnest, the bravest girl I ever met."

"I don't understand. You expected me to give up that side of myself when we married? The qualities that make a fine lover should make a fine wife."

"I didn't want you to. It's just, there's all these inspections when you get married. What could I do? Let you run off and launch clothes like a peasant?"

"Launch? *Wash* clothes?" I laughed.

"Yeah! I would have liked it for you to stay the way of before. You know, almost like a man in a dress. But what would people think?"

"What's it matter what they think? And a woman doesn't have to grow a set of cojones to be brave or fun. I'm not a man, dress or no dress."

"I'm not a man either," he muttered, almost inaudibly.

"What are you talking about? Of course you're a man."

"No, I'm not. Not really." He leaned so far to the side he looked as if he might pitch to the floor.

I repositioned him so if he did fall, he'd be deposited onto the kitchen table. "Cariño, what are you trying to tell me? Is this because of what Juana said about our failure to conceive?"

I never got an answer. Before the final words escaped my lips, Sergio slumped forward onto the table and passed out. I took off his shoes, covered him with a quilt, and let him sleep where he sat. I then curled by the kitchen fireside and reread *Amadís* into the night, worrying if I left him alone, he might throw up on himself and have to lie in it. When he partially woke a few hours later, I helped him stagger into bed to finish sleeping it off.

Next morning, he stumbled into the kitchen, cradling his head in his hands, to find me making us a light breakfast. Even if he couldn't stomach the egg, he could have a slice of bread and a bit of cheese. He sat down and pantomimed a graphic vomiting motion, complete with sound effects. Laughing, I told him he did it to himself. He asked me how in hell I was not as sick as him, since he'd seen me drinking too, to which I replied I'd mixed my brandy with water.

"You drink like a girl." He chuckled.

I winked at him. "I am a girl. Until last night, I thought that's what you liked about me."

"Wait. What did I say?"

"About what?"

"About anything."

"You said quite a bit. You rambled about the things you normally ramble about when you're sober. Then you called me a man in a dress. What did you think you said?"

He sighed. "I just feared I'd made a fool of myself is all."

"You made a complete fool of yourself, but I don't care. You were funny." I set a plate in front of him, though he wasn't keen on eating, and tucked into my own breakfast.

*** 

I never forgot the events of that night. They gave me a strange new sensation of being bonded to my husband in a way I'd never been. In the days and weeks following, we didn't fight as severely or as frequently as we had; we spent more time enjoying one another's company; and we spoke of more meaningful topics, like his eventual retirement from seafaring and all the things we'd do once we'd obtained hidalguía. Sergio even suggested we build a raft so he might teach me to sail.

I could feel us growing into a new level of maturity in our dealings with each other, one that made us more akin to amorous bosom friends than to husband and wife. This sense of companionship led me to think more seriously of attempting to reconcile Sergio to Jhasali.

Of course, I hadn't yet dared to suggest a second meeting. If I came home late, he still grew sullen, for he knew where I'd been, and if I so much as mentioned the name of Sergio to Jhasali, she somehow found a way to bring the conversation around to all the violent manners in which the ancient rulers of her species had executed petty criminals. Still, she no longer directly threatened his life, and he no longer attempted to prevent my seeing her. Those were steps in the right direction.

One crisp September morning, I drummed up enough gumption to nudge Jhasali toward the idea of resolving her and Sergio's differences. When I arrived at Homeship, I entered its tubular hallway and greeted my bonded drone as it floated to meet me. We both made for the observation deck, and I was intent on compelling her to hear me out. Before I could mount the ascension platform, however, my ears caught a string of odd sounds emanating from the galley.

There, Jhasali was curled on a seat with her head in her hands, clawing at her own hair and gnashing her teeth. Her body was filled with tension, every muscle rigid, every limb contorted.

"What on Earth is the matter?" I asked.

"The matter is not on Earth. I've lost communication with Homeship's jump hoop."

"The superluminal wave generator?"

The SWG was an enormous apparatus meant to accordion the spacetime continuum in front of its corresponding vessel to haul the ship through the incomprehensible distances of the universe at even more incomprehensible speeds. I knew she kept such a device hidden in a large comet belt outside our solar system, as it could not approach a planet too closely. Until today, I'd not given the issue much thought.

"Yes," she snapped. "I had it set to ping me once per Earth week, but it did not do so yesterday, and all my attempts to communicate with it have failed."

"I'm sure it's alright. It probably just took a hit from a big asteroid or something."

"You don't understand. If I don't have that jump hoop, I cannot leave. Ever."

"I thought you didn't wish to leave."

"Good Lord! Of course I wish to leave. Have you gone mad? I don't know what I must do to make you comprehend there is no circumstance under which I will allow myself to be marooned here permanently. I can hardly bear it temporarily."

"What will you do?" I asked.

"There's no way around it. I must take one of the pods and go find the hoop."

"Are you insane? You'll be completely exposed!"

"No I won't. All the transport pods are large enough to generate serviceable security perimeters. If I don't fire their weapons, they'll leave no trace. You know that."

"Why can you not send the drones and stay here?" I cried.

"Because the hoop is my only means of escape, and I don't have the equipment to build another. This is too important to leave to drones. I must see things with my own eyes."

"What if it's a trap? What if your enemies know you're here, and they're trying to lure you off the planet?"

Jhasali huffed. "If they knew I was here, they would not go through some ridiculous, convoluted attempt to smoke me out. They'd just come and capture me."

"But what if they—"

"Listen. I'm not saying there's no chance this is some sort of trap. I'm saying it's more likely the hoop has undergone a malfunction. So I'm going to find it and see what's happened. Depending on the circumstances, I might leave my maintenance drones to do the repair work and come back here myself."

"How long will you be gone?"

She shrugged. "The pod is much slower than Homeship. It can only reach a fraction of light speed. So I'll be out at least an Earth month. Probably a lot longer."

"A month!"

"Yes, a month, depending on how long it takes me to locate the hoop. And while I'm outside your planet's atmosphere, you cannot use your bonded drone to communicate with me. I'm going to seal the pod's perimeter against all signals from devices not linked to me, so I won't receive your transmissions anyway, but someone else might intercept them."

"But all the signals are encrypted," I protested.

"That's irrelevant. If a transmission is present, it could be sufficient to draw unwanted attention. It's bad enough I'm going beyond the atmosphere without us sending signals back and forth that will bounce around space forever. If you need to contact me, come to Homeship and speak to it, but you must keep your linked device inside the perimeter, and you must never try to send me a transmission using it or your communicator. That tiny thing doesn't have the range."

"When do you depart?"

"Are you serious? Immediately. I was on the point of calling you when you showed up here."

In the recesses of my mind, a thousand images flashed by at the same time: Jhasali being dragged off to face whatever justice her own planet might deem fit; her ship, empty and disused, rotting in the wilderness; her drones, unattended and without directive, wandering the security perimeter until they rusted or switched off. Of course, I was aware the ship would not rot nor the drones rust, but my imagination still operated on those terms.

Jhasali patted my back. "My darling, try not to worry. I've been fastidious in my precautions, and I don't plan to break that habit now. I'll return as soon as I can. I'll also leave you on Homeship's manifest."

"What?"

"You will still be listed as a member of the crew. The ship will accept you without my presence, though it'll stay bonded to me as its captain. I'm entrusting you with a great deal of responsibility. I hope you'll not make me regret it."

"I won't."

"Since you'll remain a crew member, the communal drones will obey you as they have the last few times you've visited. I also want you to link up with a passenger pod so you can have something with decent weapons. Your bonded drone is defenseless."

"I am to defend Homeship?" I asked.

"Of course not. You're to defend yourself. It is unlikely any of my race will show up on the planet if I'm away, but if they do, and they discover you, they will not leave you in peace."

"What am I supposed to do?"

She motioned wordlessly to one of the defensive pods sitting just inside the visual camouflage and then popped the hatch, opening the clear roof so we could enter the two-person craft. Though I'd done this before in the training chamber, this was my first attempt to master a passenger drone in real life. Breathing deep and trying not to let my nerves get the better of me, I ascended into the cockpit.

"I haven't got time for lessons. I've already disconnected from the device, so I need you to find the unique identifier and connect now," Jhasali said once we'd taken our seats in the otherwise empty compartment.

The abruptness of her departure and the pressure of her demand proved too much. Though I'd grown more adept at forging and maintaining a nexus with my practice drone, I was no more able to link up with the pod than I'd been during my earliest bonding lessons.

I could feel the pod's identifier—that indescribable, unique vibration inside the recesses of my mind—but I could not initiate a connection. I tried several times, but I never felt the tug on my sensors that let me know the pod had accepted me as its one true commander. It appeared my mastery of my own device did not translate into the ability to master others.

"Forget it. There's no time," Jhasali snapped after perhaps an hour of failure. "I thought we'd have decades, centuries, to worry about this."

"How will I protect myself, then?"

"It's highly improbable you'll have to. If you wish, just to be safe, you could come with me into space."

"No. I cannot leave my husband for a month."

Sergio provided a convenient excuse, but truth be told, the idea of being yanked from the familiar protection of my atmosphere terrified me more than being on Earth without Jhasali.

She laid her chin on her fist. "Alright, here's what we'll do: I'll set up an alert so if any member of my species bothers you, I'll know it. I'll also command Homeship to defend you from them if need be. If you won't come with me, that's our only option."

"That'll do. It has to. I'm not going with you."

"Fine. I cannot deal with any of this now. I am ready to launch."

Jhasali lifted off not twenty minutes later in one of the escape pods meant for the transport of the cruiser's passengers in case of its permanent destruction. This pod had room for the slew of drones and supplies she needed for the journey, but it was still much tinier and less conspicuous than Homeship itself.

Though Jhasali made no outward sign of sadness at our farewell, she did have enough tenderness to assure me I should not waste too much time worrying for nothing. It was a futile gesture; I was going to worry regardless.

# Chapter Twenty-Five

# IGNITION

During the days following Jhasali's departure, I tried to see the positive side of the situation. I did relish having Sergio to myself, and he seemed to have grown more accepting of Armando's absence. We spent our time with Susana and her family, calling on Gracia and Gabriel, and visiting Father Manuel. Sometimes, Sergio went to play cards at the tavern with Marcos and Pablo, but we also passed many hours with just each other. After years of voyage upon voyage, we finally had the chance to make up for the time we'd lost.

One morning, perhaps a week after Jhasali left, Sergio and I went to the market close to the harbor. I always felt a pleasant jolt of nostalgia when we took this particular outing together. These streets, with their booths of fish and vegetables and bread, were where I'd first glimpsed Sergio's teasing hint of a smile and been drawn into his deep black eyes.

I held his hand as we walked through the carts and stalls set up in the plaza for whatever portion of the day the rain decided to hold off. We needed no words to express our comfort with one another, requiring nothing but a look to communicate our basest emotions.

Watching Sergio while he took his time selecting the bread and fish he wished me to cook for dinner, I noticed his dark-blue cloak was frayed at the bottom. I decided I'd come back here later and have Teresa make him a fashionable cape for the coming winter: something simple, so he'd wear it, but stylish too, with a fur trimming and a silk inner lining.

When he looked up, Sergio cast me a mischievous grin. My smile widened as his eyes met mine. At the same instant, I caught movement behind him. My gaze flitted past him, coming to rest on the face of a man whose countenance appeared somewhat familiar, though I couldn't place it. Not wanting to stare, I made to look away, but before I did, our eyes locked for a split second. The man's expression changed. Where had I seen him before?

My stomach tightened; I recalled exactly where I'd seen that face. This was one of the men who'd shown up at Father Manuel's door seeking information on the Witch of Toledo. Now, he stood at the edge of the plaza in the company of several soldiers.

My heart raced. If he'd come all this way back, he could only be here for one thing. I backed up a few paces, careful not to betray panic. Trying to keep calm, I told myself he must've returned for some other reason. Maybe he liked my quesada. That hope dissipated as the man grabbed the arm of one of his lads and pointed to me. I supposed now that we'd spotted each other, he thought it better to make a scene of arresting me than let me escape.

I had no IDOS, no sword, not even a knife to protect myself or Sergio. A pounding terror for him overwhelmed me. When these men came for me, he would defend me, and then what? He was sturdy and strong, but he was not made of the same stuff as I. He was tender flesh and spillable blood and breakable bone.

Breathing deep, I took him by the hand, making him look back down at me. Trying to keep my voice steady, I told him we needed to go now. He chuckled, confused as to my sudden change of mood.

"Why?" he asked.

"Now. We need to go now," I said, too late. Several guards rushed in our direction.

"Get as far from me as possible. Go home. I'll meet you there," I barked at Sergio before fleeing into the crowd.

If I could draw the men away fast enough, maybe I could dispatch them before they got the chance to arrest us. There were only three or four of them, and they were lightly armed. If I could grab one of their knives by the blade, I might wrest it from his hand.

As I'd anticipated, the soldiers ignored Sergio and followed me when I ran through the crowd. The men pushed and shoved, trying to catch up to me as I thrust people out of my way. I'd had a good head start, so I burst from the packed market and into the open street before my pursuers did. I ran toward the stables as fast as my long dress would allow, whistling for Pepito to let himself out of his paddock.

Seconds later, the men erupted from the crowd behind me. They were wearing breeches and leather jerkins, which rendered them faster than me now that they had gotten free. They caught up easily. One of the men snatched at my braided hair, so I plowed my fist into his face, sending a jet of blood spurting from his nose and eyes. He reeled and fell flat on his back. I grabbed the hilt of a dagger on his belt, yanking it from its sheath.

Thundering up from behind me, Pepito reared to his full height and slammed his hooves down on the fallen soldier's shoulders, crushing him into the ground. The bones crunched and blood gushed all over the street as Pepe gave a savage roar that sounded more akin to a lion than a horse.

At that instant, one of the other men raised a crossbow and fired at Pepito. Without thinking, I stepped in front of him and took the bolt myself. It hit the dead center of my chest, just below the collarbone, and the pain exploded like I'd been struck with a club. With the breath knocked from my lungs, I bent forward and nearly fell to my knees. My mouth gaped wide, but I couldn't get air. Yet the bolt had not pierced me. After a few desperate gasps, I managed to drag in a ragged breath. I then rose to my full height, eyes welling with tears.

The soldiers froze with astonishment, and several in the crowd near us gasped as they looked down to find the bolt that had hit me lying limply on the cobblestone. The pain in my chest still astounded me, but I squeezed my mouth into a tight line and forced my eyes to stare ahead, unblinking.

The weapon I'd depended on to protect me in Toledo—my assailants' stunned immobility—worked beautifully. They'd shot me at point-blank range, yet I stood, not only alive but unhurt, save a hole in my chemise.

I sucked in a deep breath and bade Pepito kneel so I could mount him with no saddle. When I climbed onto his back, he stood, and I scanned the crowd for Sergio. I couldn't see him anywhere, so I assumed he must have actually done as I'd asked and gone home. Afraid to delay any longer, I gave the soldiers a stiff nod as they stood there like confounded statues.

Turning Pepito on his heels, I galloped off as I had done so many times in the baldíos: no saddle, no bridle, nothing to keep my seat but Pepito's mane and my own strong legs. I spurred him onward so fast we made it to the arrabal in half the time it normally took. All the while, I furiously planned our escape. Sergio wouldn't understand, but he'd just have to see we had to go without his comprehending everything.

I ran Pepito to the door of my house and leapt off straight in front of the entrance. Flinging myself inside, I yanked IDOS out of its hiding place under the floorboards. Hell with secrecy. What good was Jhasali not being discovered if she returned to find us all dead? I slammed the cuffs onto my wrists and threw a few essentials in a knapsack: some money and food, Sergio's favorite dagger, and enough warm clothes to get him through rain and chilly nights.

Over and over, I screamed his name, and all I got in return was silence. I feared he was angry with me and refusing to answer my calls, but I searched the house and found nothing. Thus, I figured he must have been delayed. He had no reason to go anywhere else. He wouldn't go anywhere else.

Still calling for my husband, I tore off my blue dress and put on the linen shirt and breeches I'd tailored for myself. I threw the shirt on in such a hurry I popped a seam near the collar, but I didn't have time to care. Stuffing my braid into my cap, I ran down to the stall, where I tossed the extra saddle on Pepito, tied the knapsack to its rear, and spurred him toward the vega.

I knew better than to stay at the house and wait until the soldiers showed up to arrest me. Finding myself a good climbing tree in the groves at the edge of the pasture, I mounted a branch from which I could observe the house until Sergio arrived. He never came, though other men appeared soon after I'd taken my perch. They bashed in our front door and searched the place, but there was nothing to find—at least nothing extraterrestrial. I wore my cuffs already, and I'd stuffed the communicator in my sack before I left.

The men remained inside the house for hours, hoping I'd return without realizing they were there. I stayed put in case they waylaid Sergio on his arrival, but he did not appear. By the time the soldiers gave up and left, the sun had climbed so high it had to be long past noon. I began to panic, suspecting my husband had already been arrested in town.

I didn't know what to do. If they had Sergio, I had no idea how I might rescue him or even discover where they were holding him. I waited a long time, encumbered by indecision, uncertain if my suspicions were correct and wanting to ensure beyond any doubt Sergio was not coming back. When he had still failed to arrive by late afternoon, I fetched Pepito and headed back toward town.

Before we got two paces through the arrabal, Susana caught us, putting herself in Pepito's path and crying, "Micaela, what the devil is happening? Everyone is saying you were shot! Why are there soldiers knocking down your door? Why did they drag Sergio to the tower?"

"What?" I shouted.

"They took him this morning. The whole town is crawling with men looking for you. They questioned me and the children for an hour."

"Shit. I'm so sorry, but I've got to get Sergio." I tried to veer around her, but she stepped in front of me again.

"This doesn't make sense. There are rumors; people are saying you were shot but unharmed. They're saying you're a witch."

"Don't put stock in such things. I wasn't shot. It's all nothing but a bunch of false accusations." I swerved around her and goaded Pepito to a gallop.

Of course, I couldn't prance through the city gate, so I stayed well off the road and found a spot in the vega to turn out Pepito. I removed his bridle but left the saddle on, cinching the stirrups all the way up and looping the straps so they couldn't fall. I told him to stay close to the wall—I'd call for him when I needed. I feared he might not understand my words, but he'd never failed to catch my intent. Kissing his hairy brow underneath his forelock, I turned toward Santa Colomba proper.

I managed to sneak through my preferred gap in the wall without being spotted. This gap was not so far from the church, and in my male clothes with my braid in a cap, I was able to slip undetected through the blocks between me and the rectory. I had to get to Father Manuel before the soldiers did, for I was now certain the Toledo tribunal knew exactly who I was, which meant Ignacio did, too.

I let myself into the rectory, petrified I'd find the place ransacked and Father Manuel captured, all because I'd hesitated like an irresolute idiot. When I looked around, however, I saw no signs of struggle. Everything sat where I'd last left it: books stacked on the shelves, dishes hidden away, fireplace empty. Even the papers sprawled on the desk lay undisturbed. I sighed and sank to my knees in relief, holding the supper table for support.

I hoped the townsfolk might've warned Father Manuel of the danger and tucked him away. To make sure, I snuck across the courtyard and went to the church, slipping in through the rear door. No one was inside save Pedro, one of the street children to whom I'd often given alms in the past.

Now nearly a teenager, the boy had improved his station over the years. He'd found work in the harbor and, with Father Manuel's help, a place to stay outside the western wall. He stood with his back to me, lighting a candle and unaware of my presence. I didn't wish to alarm him, so I cleared my throat to announce I stood behind him, and I removed my cap to reveal my face, letting my braid swing free.

When he turned toward me, he started. "Señora! What are you—"

"Where is Father Manuel?"

"I don't know, but I suppose we can expect him back soon."

"When you see him, give him a message from me. Tell him we've got some unwelcome guests from Toledo, and he needs to find a place to lie low right now. Hang Vespers. Hang morning Mass. Hang all of that. He mustn't show his face again until I clean up this mess."

I told Pedro as much as I dared. I wished to impress upon him the gravity of the situation without going into too much detail, hoping if he understood the direness of the circumstances, he wouldn't fail to inform my guardian of his peril. After that, it'd be up to Father Manuel's flock to shelter him, but I didn't doubt they would. He was a rare breed of parish priest who managed to keep his hands off both his congregants' bodies and their money. If they'd learned anything from some of the priests they'd endured in the past, they knew what they had in him.

Pedro promised he would deliver my message as soon as possible. Loath as I was to do it, I thanked him and slipped out of the church. There were still a few more hours to go before sunset. If I were to attempt a rescue, I thought I'd best do it under cover of darkness, when I would have the advantage of night vision. I crept back to the rectory, hoping Father Manuel would return before I left so I might deliver my message myself.

As I sat at the table, I began to work out a plan to rescue Sergio, thanking my lucky stars he was being held in the tower. Many years ago, the city had converted an old watchtower on the corner of the southern and western walls into an above-ground dungeon to house offenders and alleviate overcrowding in the real jail. This tower would be much easier to assail than the prison, for it had direct access beyond the wall.

I'd been a fool to think Sergio would make it home. The soldiers had likely arrested him on the spot rather than risk us both escaping. No matter; they wanted me. If they had me, they wouldn't have any reason to hold him. Thus, I could offer to trade myself for him, and I'd sort them all out once he was safely away. What could they do to me, anyhow?

I was now certain I couldn't be killed with a handheld weapon. They didn't know to melt me in a blast furnace or fire a cannon at me. They'd probably try to put me on the potro or something. Ha! Good luck with that. More importantly, they did not know I was armed. As long as I could make them let Sergio go, escaping on my own would be easy.

Popping my head out the doorway after dusk, I pricked my ears and listened to catch hints of Vespers as they floated in on the twilight breeze. Thankfully, the distinct tenor of Father Manuel's voice drifted through the open church windows. I couldn't catch all the words he said, but I knew the pitch and rhythm of his liturgical tone as well as I knew that of his regular speech.

I was displeased he'd not heeded my warning, but perhaps Pedro hadn't been able to communicate with him yet. I wished I might stay in the rectory to speak to him after the evening prayers, but I dared not. I couldn't waste even a second of darkness, so I wrote him a note detailing as much as I deemed safe and hoped that would suffice if Pedro were unable to give him my message.

This done, I slipped back out the gap in the wall and returned to the vega for Pepito. I gave him the bridle I'd hidden in a nearby tree, and I clasped the reins to the saddle pommel so they'd not fall and trip him up. I then had him follow me as we snuck around to the south side of town, where the tower was situated.

I had never been inside the tower. The closest I'd come was the threshold of the front door the one time I'd gone with Armando to bribe Sergio out of the drunkards' cells after he'd let his mates convince him to stay out all night. From previous conversations with Sergio, I'd learned the tower had several makeshift holding cells on the second through the fourth floors, though they were not well-constructed or even organized in much of a sensical manner. There were two staircases, as well. The stone exterior one had been built into the original design back when the tower had functioned as a guard post. The wooden interior one was a recent addition, built to make it easier to get prisoners in and out of the cellblocks.

I had Pepito wait for me in the pastures once more, far from the road and the southern gate, and I snuck to the exterior of the city wall, sliding along in the shadows until I came to the single barred door that led to the tower's outer staircase. Oddly, no guards were posted at this door. I presumed they were inside the cellblocks or perhaps out searching the countryside.

I used IDOS to break the lock. Though I attempted to keep quiet, the resounding clang of projectile striking metal might as well have been a cannon blast. Gritting my teeth, I listened to the interior from my place at the bottom of the stairwell, but there was no indication anyone had heard the commotion.

I made my way up the outer staircase to the cellblocks with no idea how I might find Sergio. As I ascended, noises from the cells above told me someone was on the fourth floor. I followed the sounds of voices up the stairs, but only when I neared the top did the speech become apparent. The echo on the stone walls had jumbled the distinction of words.

Male voices—two of them for sure, possibly three—argued amongst themselves. None of these voices was Sergio's, though I now suspected one of them belonged to someone else I knew. Once I came to the top of the stairs, around the corner from the cellblock door, I established that the owner of the familiar voice was indeed the most loathsome of all the men I'd met: Fray Ignacio.

I froze, daring not enter the block yet. I crouched in place at the top of the staircase, fixed as stone, and listened as Ignacio spoke with a feigned amiability and compassion that only a seasoned interrogator could've mastered.

"I know you must wish to unburden your conscience. Think of your eternal soul. It's not too late to save that, my friend. You can still be reconciled if you tell the truth. I might even see my way into allowing this unfortunate incident to count for your penance—right, Francisco?"

"I'm not sure. We're already incurring so many irregularities at present," the one I assumed to be Francisco replied in a voice I recognized but couldn't place, though I did not need to place it to be aware its owner was terrified.

Ignacio snickered. "Pfft. Irregularities. Christ save us! That might just be worse than eternal damnation."

"I am not in jest," Francisco whined. "You're breaking *all* the regulations. There's no physician present, no notary either; we aren't trying to obtain a confession but information on another suspect's whereabouts; there's no formal charges laid; and, for the love of God, man, you've bled our prisoner half to death. Oh, Christ! Señor, please don't die. Oh, oh, don't die. We'll be in so much trouble if you die!"

Ignacio burst into laughter. "You're pathetic. Are you a child caught sneaking into the family larder? If this one manages to live, he won't do it because *you* might get a sternly worded letter from a herd of senile bureaucrats halfway to the other side of the peninsula."

Though I didn't know the identity of the prisoner they spoke of, I guessed it might be Sergio. My heart thumped wildly as I wondered what they might have done to him, but I couldn't know for sure unless he spoke or they said his name or gave some other indication it was, indeed, my husband they'd bled half to death.

Thus, I sat tight and called my practice drone. Though I'd failed to master the passenger pod, my link with my own drone remained airtight. I hated to betray Jhasali by calling it out of the perimeter, but my need was pressing. I tried to focus on both communicating with my device and hearing Ignacio's words as he carried on.

"I know this is not exactly standard protocol, but we are tools of the Almighty. Nothing is a crime when performed in the service of God. Besides, when I return to Toledo with that thing, everyone will forget what we did to capture her."

"This man won't," Francisco said.

"I hope not. Get him back up, Diego."

"Yes, señoría," a third voice replied.

This voice I recognized as belonging to the town jailer. I'd met him on a few occasions when he'd come to the pub at Inés's inn. He was gruff and always stunk of brandy, but I'd never thought him one to participate in whatever dreadful act Ignacio must have committed.

"Stop!" Francisco bellowed. "I cannot allow you to kill him. You likely already have."

"If he's willing to die to keep a whore of Satan from facing the Lord's justice, he's getting what he deserves," Ignacio said.

"No! I forbid it. This is my jurisdiction!"

Suddenly, I recalled where I'd heard that voice. This was the Francisco from the visitation: Don Luis's secretary and right-hand man.

Ignacio gave a condescending chuckle. "We are all under the jurisdiction of the Almighty. God is merciful, and he understands the commission of a lesser sin to prevent the commission of a greater one. This sorceress cannot be allowed to escape, whatever is necessary. I assure you I'll go to confession as soon as I return to Toledo, but right now, it's his turn."

"You want me to confess?" a fourth voice asked.

My breath caught in my throat. It was Sergio. He struggled to force the words out, like his lungs were unable to attain enough capacity for him to speak at normal volume.

"Fine. I'll confess," he whispered.

I tried to make my accursed legs work the way they were supposed to, but I couldn't move. My limbs had become another drone I'd failed to master. No matter how much I desired it, I couldn't get them to function.

"Go on," Ignacio said in a tone of barely suppressed triumph.

Sergio took a labored breath and gave his confession. "I'm often too quick to anger. I don't always treat my wife the way I should. I drink a great deal too much. Once, I got so drunk I pissed on a church. I eat meat on fasting days, and I don't give a damn. I know I've sinned, but I'll never ask forgiveness from the likes of you again."

"Get him up!" Ignacio shrieked in rage.

"Leave him there!" Francisco shouted.

"No. If you stand in the way of my pursuit of this she-devil, you stand in the way of God himself, and you're no better than the fireproof witch or the curs harboring her."

Francisco caved, saying he did not wish to impede the will of God. At that, Sergio gave a sharp cry that loosed me from my catatonia and filled me with a fury so intense I forgot all danger and all strategy. I screeched and flung myself through the open door into the cellblock.

Pure horror greeted me. Sergio, stripped nearly naked, lay flat on his back on the floor, surrounded by a huge pool of blood. He was coated in a shining scarlet layer of it, smeared across his face, chest, belly, and arms. He had his hands and head partially lifted off the planks, as if he were attempting to rise but couldn't. The bits of skin I could see beneath the blood were white as milk. Even Ignacio's black-and-white robes were dappled with glistening bloodstains.

The other three men stood in a group around Sergio. When I'd shrieked at the top of my lungs, they'd all jolted in my direction. I moved to strike out with IDOS, but I was unsure of my aim. In terror I might carve my husband's innards out of his body as I had my last adversary, I lunged at the men, lowering my head and charging like a bull. I had to put myself between him and them before I could fire.

Ignacio grabbed Francisco and flung both his collaborator and himself out of my way. As soon as I reached Sergio, a metallic clang rang out behind me. I whipped my head around to find Ignacio and Francisco had slipped outside and shut the cell door, locking me inside with Diego and Sergio.

"See? I told you she'd come for him," Ignacio shouted to Francisco. "God has vindicated me. He's sent the infidel witch right into my grasp."

I raised my wrist to the good friar, but before I could fire, a heavy blow crashed down on my head, sending my feet flying out from under me. I hadn't been prepared for it, and though it did not pain or injure me, the force of it knocked me to the floor. Diego fell to his knees and got on top of me before I could rise. He reeked of sweat and alcohol, and he pinned my arms above my head, trying to clamp irons onto my wrists. My husband's pooled blood soaked through the back of my shirt and into my hair while I struggled against the jailer.

Though he could do nothing, Sergio still cried, "Please, don't hurt her. Leave her alone."

The more he begged, the more Ignacio laughed.

I kicked and squirmed until I made eye contact with my enemy. "Listen, Ignacio! You want me, not him. You have me now, so let him go."

Ignacio leered at me as I lay helpless in the confines of his makeshift trap. "My dear, since I cannot give you the fate you deserve, I think it only fitting he should suffer it in your place. Assuming he makes it back to Toledo alive, of course."

Upon hearing these words, I struggled even harder, but Diego held my shoulders to the floor and used his thighs to pin my legs together, immobilizing my torso. I still hadn't allowed him to get sufficient hold of my forearms to clap me in irons.

Ignacio called delightedly over my screams. "You will not escape me again. You'll be a guest in my dungeons until I devise a method of destroying you that will not be foiled by your witchcraft. Perhaps I shall just leave you on the pillory until you die of exposure."

"Listen to me. You can kill me. There are ways. If you'll only let Sergio go, I'll come quietly. I'll tell you how to destroy me."

"I don't need you to come quietly. You'll come in chains. I told Manuel you should have been packed off as a girl, but you turned out to be a cleverer witch than even I anticipated."

I felt an overwhelming compulsion to try to kick and scream my way out of Diego's grasp, but he was much larger than me and already had the upper hand, so I went still and allowed him to grab my wrists. I readied IDOS, and the great heat rose in my arms. Diego cried out and released me, shaking his burned hands and wailing in agony. Without a second's hesitation, I aimed at his brow, willing the cuff to fire its tiny cannon.

I shouldn't have been surprised at the cascade of slick blood that burst from his skull and gushed all over my face, but I was. It drenched me. It blinded my eyes, then ran into my open mouth and tasted of liquid metal. Distracted by all the blood and bone and brain, I didn't expect to find myself pinned yet again until the jailer's immense weight toppled, heavy with death, onto my body.

With only my head still mobile, I looked up at Ignacio, whose stunned countenance needed no explanation. He'd thought my power was limited to the hardness of my body. I threw him as evil a smile as I could muster and tried to shove the decapitated jailer off me.

I managed to free my left arm. Francisco was closer, so I took aim at him. Before I could fire, Ignacio realized my intent. He leapt to Francisco and tackled him to the floor, and the shot meant for his head exploded on the wall behind him. Ignacio wrenched Francisco to his feet and hurled them both back down the stairs in a marvelous whirring of long capes. No matter. I could deal with them later. I writhed and shoved until I dragged myself out from under Diego.

"I'm fine! I'm not hurt," I cried to Sergio, who moaned where he lay. "It's alright."

The blood still flowed from his body like wine from an uncorked barrel. It was definitely not alright. I couldn't figure out the source of all the bleeding. I checked his body for an open wound, but his chest and belly were uninjured. His arms and face had no visible cuts either. Then I grasped him around the arms and tried to pull him off the floor, only to find his back was shredded from one end to the other.

I was so horrified I gasped and let go of his arms. Realizing my error, I tried to catch him as he fell, but it was too late, and he plunged to the hard floor before I could prevent it. He cried out again, but I did not have time to feel guilty. Though it hadn't been long since Ignacio had fled back downstairs, the voices and footfalls of his men already echoed from below as they ascended to the cellblock.

I whispered in Sergio's ear that he had to use his legs, but I knew he'd never be fast enough. I looked around for any weapon that might be more effective than IDOS against a whole company. There was nothing in the room other than a blood-caked whip and a small barrel of pitch. I snatched up the barrel and looked inside. It still had plenty left.

Bounding to the threshold, I blasted the cell door open and smashed the barrel at the top of the interior stairwell, spreading the thick black fluid all over the floor before running back to Sergio and recommencing my frantic efforts to get him up. I asked him if he thought he could walk, but he didn't answer.

Instead, he told me he loved me; he said it over and over. "I'm sorry. I'm so sorry. Please, no matter what, never forget I did love you."

He was scaring me now. He'd said he loved me a thousand times, but I'd never heard him speak like this, as if he thought himself about to die. I looked down at his body again. His skin pumped out huge beads of sweat. These tracked through the coating of blood and left long snail trails that looked like tiny white rivers running through crimson banks. For all his caterwauling about the immortal soul, Ignacio hadn't had a speck of hesitance about spilling Sergio's all over this place.

While I tried futilely to get him to his feet, Sergio stopped talking and went still, his breathing rapid and shallow. Before I could rouse him, six or seven men burst up the staircase, weapons at the ready, hard faces set on me.

"Get back, all of you. I'll kill you if you come closer!" I shouted.

When several men stepped through the doorway into the pitch, I sparked on them and set the floor at their feet ablaze. The ones standing on top of the pitch howled when they started roasting in the flames that erupted as high as the ceiling. The front line fell back on the rear as the company broke ranks and toppled over one another to get away from the inferno. The flaming tar filled the block with thick, rank smoke in a matter of seconds.

Fire. I hate fire. Why was the only weapon available to me always fire? If I didn't get Sergio out of there quick, he was going to suffocate on the fumes before he even got the chance to burn to death. He still lay on his back in the cell, unaware flames now engulfed the far side of the room.

I lifted him into a half-seated position and shoved my shoulders underneath his armpits, wrapping my arms tight around his torso. I heard a sizzling noise and realized my cuffs were burning him. He regained consciousness at this, screaming as my hot wrists seared his back, but I couldn't let him slip to the floor again. He'd have to endure it if we were to escape, but God help me! I could barely endure it either. His torn flesh squished in my hands, and the hideous odors of blood and cauterizing wounds engulfed me. Overcome with a wave of nausea, I heaved up from my knees anyway and tried with all my might to push us both to our feet, but I couldn't move his dead weight.

"Sergio, stand up!" I cried over the shrieks of the men battling the blaze. They'd gathered their courage and were trying to push through the fire, but the flames held them back, for now. "Cariño, please, you must help me. If you don't stand, we're both dead."

Something in my speech roused him. I don't know if it was the desperation in my voice or the realization I was in danger as well, but he was able to gather the strength for one last burst of effort. He took hold of the bars on the side of the cell and hoisted his weight off me, dragging himself to his feet. I managed to scramble to my own feet in time to catch him as he collapsed onto my shoulders, but he summoned every modicum of vigor he had left to aid me as I steered him toward the outer staircase. I half carried, half dragged him to the top and shoved him into the stairwell, simultaneously whistling out a long, narrow window for Pepito.

I looked down to find two armed men already ascending from below, so I raised the arm not holding Sergio and shot them both dead. Their bodies flew back down the stairs with such force they didn't even touch the floor again until they landed at the bottom of the flight. Without another thought for them, I helped Sergio descend, letting him use my shoulders as well as the wall to hold himself steady and guiding him down. I directed his feet as we trod over the dead men and turned the corner to the next set of steps.

We had made it onto the final flight when his foot lost traction, sliding in the blood running down his legs. I tried to break his fall, but he didn't loosen his grip in time and dragged me down with him. We tumbled over one another to the bottom of the stairs, hitting the ground floor with a heavy thud. He struggled to catch his breath, seeming to have reached a threshold of pain beyond bearing, for he lay on the last stone steps, eyes unfocused, body slumped in an awkward, twisted position.

I left him where he lay and ran to the barred door, which I shoved open. I cried for Pepito, blessedly hearing his galloping hooves slamming into the ground as he hurtled toward me. Grabbing him by the bridle, I led him to the door. He'd come just in time, for the sound of deep voices shouting beyond the wall told me the men had given up on the staircases and were now circling the building from the outside.

Pepito knelt to allow Sergio to mount, but before he had the chance, two or three riders and several men on foot appeared outside the door, boxing us in whilst brandishing arquebuses and crossbows.

"Don't shoot! He wants her alive," one of them cried.

I fired IDOS, blowing a round clean through the chest of my closest adversary. The others backed off a pace but did not flee. They knew they had me. I closed my eyes and went still, for my drone had come down from the mountain when it'd heard my call. Now, I sent it charging from the trees straight at our attackers.

I'd dared not use it until the opportune moment, for it was unarmed and no larger than a cat, but it was so bizarre to everyone on Earth I guessed these men and their horses would spook at the mere sight of it. Sure enough, when I launched the drone at the company—lights blazing, pincer arms flailing—they scattered. The riders yelled as their horses shrieked and bolted in terror, leaving the fleeing foot soldiers in their dust.

Trying to heave Sergio's limp body onto the horse, I leaned his head against Pepito's thick neck, but I couldn't lift the rest of him. His upper body kept slipping to the stones.

"Sergio, hold onto the mane," I commanded.

He gripped the thick hair on Pepito's neck, holding his own torso up while I grabbed an ankle and swung the rest of him into the saddle. Pepito stood just as more men rushed through an inside door to the exterior staircase.

"Go!" I seized the cantle and held on tight, dragging myself onto Pepito's back as he burst into the night.

He whisked us straight from the roads to the comparative safety of the open fields. I leaned low over Sergio and wound my fingers around Pepito's long mane to keep my husband steady in the saddle, though he groaned in protest as I pressed myself over his wounded back.

The men's terror of the tiny, helpless drone would not long endure, and we needed a place to go. Not our house. I could not imagine any scenario in which Ignacio hadn't already placed men there to await us. There was nothing for it. We'd have to go to Homeship. I had no medicine and no other place that offered even a smattering of the safety the cruiser provided. The whole world could assail us and not succeed if we were entombed within its metal walls.

With Jhasali still gone, I could at least get Sergio inside and tended to before incurring her wrath. Perhaps I could even have him in and out before she ever returned, not that the drones still stationed in the perimeter would keep that secret for me. But it had to be done, wrath or no wrath. When I screamed for Pepe to take us home, he turned in the direction of the ship. I ordered my drone to end its chase of the company and meet us there.

By the time we made it to the security perimeter, Sergio had fainted. All secrecy abandoned, I would have thrown open the doors even if he'd been perfectly lucid. Lucky for him, he was out cold, for it would have terrified him when the escape pod I'd failed to master before Jhasali's departure switched on as we passed through the barrier. I didn't have time to bother with any damned transport drones, so I ignored it.

Sliding off Pepito, I took his leather lead to walk him up the ship's ramp so that he could carry Sergio directly to the cruiser's medical unit. Pepito had no real fear of the ship from the outside, having come often within steps of its doors, but he whinnied in protest as I bid him to pass through the threshold and into the tubular hallway. He did not buck or kick, aware of the condition of his remaining rider, but he bobbed his head and dug his feet in outside the doorway, where he refused to move without several minutes of coaxing and pleading from me. Only when he sensed my panic had reached fever pitch did he allow me to lead him through the door.

The communal drones had awoken, by the sound of their low humming, but they did not attempt to impede my entry as I led Pepito to the medical ward, where I bade him turn to the side so he could be close to the floating table on which I intended to place Sergio. I tried to drag my husband off Pepito's back to lay him on its surface, but I struggled to budge his dead weight.

When a pair of communal drones attempted to come to my aid, I gave in to base instinct and chased them away from Sergio's limp form. Yet, try as I might, I couldn't lift him off Pepito alone. After a long while of tugging and shifting his body, I commanded the devices to help me get him onto the cold slab.

They were gentler than I'd anticipated, and once they'd positioned Sergio on the table, I pulled Pepito's tack off and told the drones to guide my horse back outside. He was accustomed to them and let them herd him toward the exit without a fuss. When he gave me his bare broadside, I noticed his buckskin coat was stained with wide crimson stripes that ran from his withers to his belly: Sergio's blood.

I shuddered and looked back to my husband, who remained unconscious. His breathing came in short, shallow gasps.

*What to do?* I asked in my head as I removed IDOS, scrubbed my filthy hands, and stripped him naked.

Almost the instant I thought this, my drone floated to a cold-storage cabinet and pulled out a large bladder of blue liquid from one of the top shelves—the very same liquid that Jhasali had once injected into Gracia.

My artificial servant guided me with its invisible hand. It told me to order the damselflies to position a tube in Sergio's arm so the blue liquid could flow into him, just as it had Gracia. As communal devices, the damselflies could be commanded by Homeship's crew with no need for a bond, and they obeyed me without question, though I was forced to voice all my commands because I'd yet to master the art of giving telepathic directives to unbonded devices.

Soon, the very same stuff that had filled Gracia's every capillary and tinged her skin with that awful green hue began to tinge Sergio's complexion as well. But this liquid was the final barrier between him and death, so tonight I deemed it the most beautiful color in the world.

As more damselflies and medical drones surrounded Sergio's unconscious form, I recalled how violated I'd felt when I'd learned Jhasali had allowed them to have their way with me while I slept. I had no choice but to let them inject Sergio with their medicines, or I would've had to fumble through that ugly work myself. Yet, when a large drone with a pair of soft sponges approached alongside a beakless damselfly attached to the end of a long hose, I didn't let them near. Instead, I took a sponge from the drone, soaked it in the water and ointments from the hose, and dabbed his wounds with my own hands.

I didn't know how to tend such awful injuries, so I depended on my linked drone to guide my movements as I'd so often guided its own. Here, for the first time, I truly understood what it was like to be a bonded master. We were one, it and I. Its thoughts were my thoughts and mine its. Its body was my body, and its mind occupied my skull as fully as my own consciousness. I no longer needed to concern myself with maintaining the connection. This drone was mine, as though it had always been mine and always would be, same as my own hands and feet.

The medical drones continued to bring me fresh pots of ointments and new sponges while I washed Sergio's wounds. He needed to be cleansed and no longer bleeding before he could enter the medicinal pool. Though the drones probably would have taken less time to tend him themselves, I knew he wouldn't want them to touch him any more than I'd wanted them to touch me when I'd been wounded. As much as possible, I wanted to give Sergio the choice Jhasali had unintentionally denied me and I had unintentionally denied Gracia.

Once we got Sergio's bleeding stopped, I ordered the table to carry him down the hallway to the pool. When the slab moved, he moaned and grabbed my arm, tugging on my wrist as if to fight me off. It was the first time he'd made a peep since he'd passed out. I laid my hand on the back of his head, telling him I was there to help him. He let go and relaxed—too late to avoid tearing his back open again near the spot where he'd lifted his arm. I groaned at the sight of the blue fluid seeping from him. I'd just managed to stem that azure tide.

After I'd stopped the bleeding yet again, I took him to the pool. I commanded it to fill, and it began to well up from the bottom. Though I knew Homeship would figure out what was needed of the pool once we entered the water, I still spoke aloud to it, informing it that it was about to receive a fully organic lifeform, not a biomechanical one, and that under no circumstance was it permitted to let this lifeform die.

I got a sudden urge to turn to my linked device. To my surprise, it held between its pincers a large beaker of the silvery goo Jhasali had injected me with when she'd converted me: nanobots. Looking at the drone, I opened my mouth to form words of protest before recalling that was pointless. The machine could hear me in my mind, and it was there to do my bidding anyhow. When I silently asked what it planned to do with the bots, it informed me I could release them into the water, allowing them to apply a graft that would help Sergio's own system heal his injuries.

With the pool filled almost to the brim, the jets released clouds of rusty brown liquid to sterilize the water. The stuff turned the pool a ruddy, muddy color that didn't exactly look inviting. I removed my clothing and backed down the stairs, bringing the stretcher underneath the water. Once Sergio floated on his back, I bade the table leave us.

He'd been so silent after his sole protest at the movement of the stretcher that I expected him to remain so when we entered the pool. However, the warm water roused him as it got into his ears and the strong chemical scent of the sterilizing agents, so unlike anything he'd ever smelled, filled his nostrils. He didn't act as though the water pained him. Rather, he moved his arms like he knew he was floating, and his eyes popped open.

"Where am I?" he asked.

I pushed his hair from his brow. "Doesn't matter. You've been hurt, but you'll soon be alright. Just sleep."

He was so exhausted he didn't offer a single word of argument. Trusting me to keep his head above water, he closed his eyes and drifted back off. Another pang of guilt pierced me as I took note of his implicit confidence and felt thoroughly undeserving of it. I held him in my arms, moving his limbs and manipulating his body as it floated in the pool. I'd never seen him so compliant, and it stung my very soul.

As I stroked his hair, my drone called to me from inside my head, and I turned to find it still holding the container of nanos with its pincers. I took the beaker in my right hand, continuing to support Sergio's head with my left, and turned it over into the pool. The nanos fell out in one great ball of viscous goop and smacked the water with a plunking splash.

As the bots started to spread out in a cloud underneath Sergio, I wet my fingers and used them to bathe his face, which I now noticed had taken a battering of its own—I presumed from his resisting arrest. His lip was split, and one of his eyes was black and swollen. I brushed my thumb under his injured eye, and the wince he gave in response told me he was still somewhat aware of his surroundings, so I bade my drone keep out of sight.

Before it floated away, it handed me something else to put in the water: a rubbery black ball about the size of a melon. The nanos formed a cloud around this ball as soon as it broke the pool's surface, taking pieces off the whole and carrying them under Sergio from all sides. They looked like a great swarm of microscopic gnats floating beneath him, interspersed with strips of dark, almost-opaque parchment moving toward him. My primordial impulses screamed to get him out of this water and away from them, but I knew better. They were using that rubbery substance to create a barrier over his wounds so he could heal underneath.

It took the bots forever to install this barrier. They didn't need much assistance from me, so I sat down on one of the benches on the side wall of the pool and cradled Sergio's head in my hands. Every once in a while, he'd wince or groan, so I tried to soothe him by running my fingers through his waterlogged hair. I wondered if I ought to cover it to keep it from contaminating the liquid, but my linked drone informed me I needn't worry. The nanos could dispose of any stray strands that got in their way.

A fresh wave of guilt broke over me as I held Sergio in the warm water and recalled once more my own responsibility for this mess. I was thankful I no longer believed in the god of my youth because how could I ever confess any of this? Father Manuel could not devise an act of contrition severe enough to atone for it.

With a lurch of the stomach, I remembered Father Manuel. In the confusion and fear, I'd focused on Sergio and forgotten Ignacio had come all the way up here knowing my identity. Since his attempt to trap me using Sergio had failed, he'd be looking for other bait. Thank goodness I'd had the wherewithal to tell Pedro to send Father Manuel running for shelter.

I moaned at the thought of him cowering in someone's attic as I had in Toledo. I wished I could return to town to find him and bring him back here, but I couldn't abandon Sergio. Sitting in silence while the bots continued to work, the immense weight of this terrible choice between Father Manuel's safety and my husband's life pressed on me so heavily I felt crushed. Overwhelmed with remorse, I doubled over until my brow pressed against Sergio's, unable to stop imagining what Ignacio must be doing to our neighbors and friends.

When the bots finished applying the graft, they crowded back into their beaker, which I'd left sitting on the bench underneath the water, and I set them on the side of the pool. I got Sergio rinsed off and had the communal drones return him to the stretcher, padding the metal surface with a cushion of thick towels so he'd be comfortable.

I was relieved to see his back looked considerably better. It appeared cauterized, but of course, he hadn't been burned. Rather, his wounds were now covered with a black film glued on in overlapping strips. I wondered if I ought to put a bandage over this film, and my implants told me it was best for the graft to be lightly covered but there was no need for thick dressing.

I wrapped Sergio's torso in a few strips of cloth, dressed him in the pair of linen trousers I'd brought to sleep with long ago, and took him to my room. There, I lay him prostrate on the left side of my bed, with his head turned toward the mattress's edge, half his face buried in the pillows, and the covers pulled up to his waist.

The terrible loss of blood had sucked the natural color from him, and the blanching made the green tinge in his skin all the starker, but the blue liquid was clearly working. His breathing was not as labored as it had been. His ashen skin was also drawn taught with fluid, no longer shriveled from dehydration. When I fully covered his bandaged back with the quilts, the sight of him didn't make my stomach turn.

I sat down in the chair next to the bed to ponder what I might do about Father Manuel. I had warned him of his danger both through Pedro and in writing, but I couldn't be sure he'd gotten those warnings. At the same time, I could never leave Sergio here alone and unconscious because Jhasali might return whilst I was absent. She could also have Homeship expel us at any moment, and I feared the only reason she hadn't yet was because she knew I'd resist and might injure myself in the process.

Without me standing guard, Jhasali's bonded devices might attack Sergio. I hoped even she would take pity on him lying drugged and wounded in my bed. To my mind, it would be unthinkable to harm someone in his state, but then again, she didn't think of him or any other human as I did. I could never forget what she'd done to those poor, unsuspecting bandits, nor could I trust her linked devices with my husband's life.

Even as I considered all this, Sergio stirred, and I rolled the blankets down to see if he'd torn himself again. To my immense relief, the dressings stayed clean and white, though he'd moved his arm underneath the pillow and turned his head to the other side. He was so peaceful that when I returned the blankets to his neck, he looked to be sleeping, shirtless and freshly bathed, his damp curls leaving water marks on the pillows.

I crossed my arms over my chest and realized I was still naked, so I went to fetch some clothes—a simple nightshirt that came to my knees. When I returned to the bed, I curled on the other side of the mattress and nestled my body next to Sergio's. Listening once again to his shallow breathing, I felt I couldn't bear his suffering for one more minute.

I remembered how, after my attack, I had lain in this exact bed in the exact position he lay in now because I was so badly bruised I couldn't stand to turn onto my back. Even if I had to do that all over again to spare him this, it would be worth it.

The tears I'd been trying to hold at bay flowed freely in the undisturbed silence. I could think of nothing but how much my stupidity and arrogance had cost everyone I loved on this awful night. How terribly I'd made them suffer because of my vindictiveness and my foolish, reckless abandon. How many widows and orphans I'd made in my quest to rescue my husband—some of them my very own townsfolk. Had I met Diego's family? I didn't recall, but I must have. How could I look his wife in the eye now? How could I look any of them in the eye again?

"What have I done?" I asked my sleeping husband.

I caressed Sergio's damp hair and kissed his pale cheek. His skin had warmed a bit, but it was still so cold.

"I'm sorry," I whispered over and over. "I'm so, so sorry."

It was all I could manage to say.

# Chapter Twenty-Six

# A TREACHEROUS SANCTUARY

I must have drifted off during my silent fit of sobbing, for I awoke to hot light streaming through the window. My fingers clutched something freezing cold. With a horrid start, I realized it was Sergio's hand, and for one awful moment I believed he had died sometime in the night. I actually begged him not to be dead before I noted he was still breathing gently under the coverlet. His fingers just held the chill of the cold room.

My bonded drone had stood watch over us all night, positioning itself behind the sofa to keep my order that it stay out of sight. Our softly humming guardian angel emitted the only sound in the room besides Sergio's tranquil breathing. Though the drone would have awoken me if something had gone wrong during my slumber, I still cursed myself for falling asleep.

The shame and remorse for what had occurred the previous night filled me once more. Most unwillingly, I recalled the time I'd jumped the railing of Sergio's ship because I'd thought he might be whipped for having me aboard. That night had always brought a smile to my face when I'd remembered it in the past. Now, the very thought taunted me.

A damselfly interrupted my recollections when it came to inject Sergio with a huge vial of thick white liquid. I waved it away after it finished this task and rose to sit in the chair at the bedside. Sergio seemed to sense my presence, for he turned his head toward me and gave a weak moan. The tears welled up again, but I forced them back. I couldn't do this now.

Sinking to my knees beside the bed, I laid my head next to his on the pillow. I stared hard at his closed lids, wishing they would open and knowing they would not. They didn't even flutter. I took his large, rough hand in mine, noting how pale and green it still was.

"You're so strong, my love," I whispered. "Not many could survive this."

He squeezed my hand. I lay there feeling his warmth, listening to his soft breathing—still feeble but much deeper and slower than yesterday. My muscles relaxed at the sound of it. I could go back to sleep if I let myself. Closing my eyes, I stayed on my knees, right hand in Sergio's left hand, head pressed to his on the pillow, the fingers of my left hand tangled in his hair.

My mind started to wander again, dwelling on what the future might be like for us after this incident. I feared Sergio could be ruined, for even if he lived, he'd never be the same again. He might be so scarred it left him crippled. I didn't think his proud heart could bear being nursed in his bed for the rest of his days, all thanks to some zealous friar with an overabundance of conviction and a dearth of supervision.

I wanted nothing more than to go back to Santa Colomba, hunt Ignacio down, and do as I should have done in Toledo. Yet, even as I recalled the passionate defense the inquisitor had given to justify his illicit use of torture, I could think only two words: my fault.

Once again trying to keep this thought out of my head, I got back in bed with Sergio. He needed me now more than he ever had. He would need me for a long time yet, and if I had to choose reprisal against my enemy or caring for my husband, I would not even consider the former, for I loved Sergio more than I hated Ignacio.

Darkness had fallen when I became aware of myself again, waking once more without having realized I'd fallen asleep. Within seconds, I deduced that Sergio had roused me this time. He stirred fitfully, trying to wake. I rose from the bed and sat down in the chair next to him. I wanted to be prepared if he tried to get up or rolled too close to the edge.

Sure enough, he fidgeted a bit longer before putting his hands underneath his chest and pushing himself off the mattress. At this, he cried out and collapsed on his belly.

"Be still. Are you alright?" I asked.

"I have to piss. Now," he said.

"Shit!" I shouted. I'd forgotten about that. "Not yet. Just wait."

I leapt from the chair to fetch my chamber pot. Running it back to the bed, I helped Sergio position himself on his side, with his hip on the edge and his right elbow propping up his weight while he slung his left arm over my shoulder so he could get his cock into the pot on my knee. The stream began to flow, making him moan with relief. I chastised myself for letting something like this slip my mind. When he finished, he gingerly lay back down on his side, facing the edge of the bed, and I propped some pillows behind him.

"I'm so thirsty," he groaned.

That I had anticipated, recalling the torturous thirst I'd awoken to after Rodrigo's assault. I had a pitcher ready. Pouring him a glass of water, I pressed it to his lips and helped him hold his head off the pillow. He downed cup after cup, draining the pitcher.

Once he got his fill, he rested his head on the pillow again. "I'm so sorry."

"What in the world for?" I asked.

"All of this. It's not supposed to be like this."

It took me a while to realize what he meant. It must have been terribly humiliating for him to have me helping him drink and piss.

Before I could respond, Sergio reached out for me. He coaxed me down beside him on the bed and kissed me. I guessed what he intended, and if it would make him feel better, I wanted to do it, just in a manner gentle enough not to hurt him. Squeezing me tight, he kept kissing me as I lay on my side facing him. He reached inside my shirt to fondle my breasts, and I soon moaned and wiggled my hips in anticipation. But the thing he needed to do to ready himself never happened. We tried for a long while, but he couldn't get hard.

Finally, I told him it might be best to give it up, and he laid his head on the pillows, dejected. I tried to console him by telling him he wouldn't have enjoyed it if he was miserable and hurting the whole time, but he didn't reply. Instead, he squeezed his eyes shut and let out a soft groan. He made the same sound every time he exhaled.

I asked if he was in pain. He didn't answer, but a fine line appeared between his brows.

"Sergio, if you're suffering, maybe I can help you," I said.

"Have you got a sponge?" he asked, meaning a soporific sponge.

"No, I haven't got one of those, but—"

"I suppose I'd better buck up then, no?"

I sighed, rolled my eyes, and told him I'd be right back. As I rose and made for the door, I ordered my drone to get me whatever veterinary anesthetics it knew to be safe for a nonhybridized member of my species.

After I'd waited a few minutes outside my room, my drone arrived, accompanied by a needle-beaked damselfly already loaded with a vial of pain medicine. I told them we couldn't inject him now that he was awake, and I needed something he could take by mouth. I also reminded the devices that no matter what, they all must keep out of his sight. My drone hovered off, taking the damselfly with it.

It returned alone a while later, bearing a cup of wine spiked with anesthetic. It informed me this medicine would be more effective delivered intravenously, but it should retain some potency if ingested. Without responding, I took the cup and left the drone to its own devices.

"Drink this," I said when I returned to Sergio's bedside.

"That won't work. You have to make yourself sick with wine for it to kill pain."

"I laced it with opium," I lied.

"I thought you said you didn't have a sponge. Where did you get opium?"

"Juana has a taste for it."

He huffed. "Of course she does."

"You might want to show some gratitude since you're in her house."

"Are you serious?"

"I am. We cannot exactly go home with that bastard Ignacio sniffing around, can we?"

He rolled his eyes, but he must've known I was right, for he offered no argument other than remarking that Juana was the last person he wanted to see him in this state. I told him he needn't worry, since she was traveling. He dropped the subject of Juana after that and asked how long he'd been unconscious, to which I replied a little more than twenty-four hours. Then he asked what happened in the tower.

"You don't remember?" I said.

He shook his head in reply.

I brushed a curl behind his ear. "I'm not sure, but I think you were beaten pretty badly."

"No, I remember that part. I meant, how the devil did you get me out of there?"

"Some things are better left unsaid, Sergio."

"My God," he breathed. "What did they do to you?"

"Nothing like that! I just . . . I may have set the place on fire and killed a few of them."

"That's good. How did you manage that?"

"I'll explain when you're feeling better."

He assented and sank deeper into the pillow as I plumped it underneath his head.

I lifted the wine cup to his lips. While he drank a deep draught, I asked him what happened before I arrived, but he shook his head in silent refusal to discuss it. I'd expected that much. When I pressed him gently, he snapped that he thought he'd already proven he couldn't be forced to say what he didn't wish to say, so I dropped the matter.

Within minutes, he had to piss again, and I helped him lean over the bed the same way I had before. While I was assisting him in pulling his linen pants back on, he kept furrowing his brow and pursing his lips. He said nothing, but I guessed what he thought.

"Do you remember that time, maybe a year after we married, when I caught a fever and was sick for days? How I threw up on myself again and again and sweated all over everything else?" I asked.

He stuck his tongue out and grimaced.

"And what did you do? You held my hair back for me. You wiped vomit off my face. You changed my clothes and my bedding every time I needed it, and you helped me drink when I was too weak to lift my own head. Did you not?"

"I did," he replied.

"So why don't you feel you can expect the same from me as you've already given?"

"It's not that. I never wanted you to see me like this; that's all."

"Well, I suppose if we're planning to spend the rest of our days together, I was going to see you like this one way or another."

He nodded, and I had him drink the rest of the pain medicine. A pleased and serene look was already migrating across his face, like the warm glow of crackling firelight had somehow entered his body. He yawned without the grin leaving his visage.

Suddenly, a thought popped into my head. It might be easier, now that he felt less pain, to do what he'd wished to do before. I rolled him from his side to his back, making sure to prop him up on the soft pillows I'd piled behind him. He sensed what I intended, and he helped me position his body halfway upright, so I might straddle him without putting my weight on his torso.

Sliding my hand below his waist, I found him flaccid still, so I took his sleeping trousers down and put my lips around his cock, sucking the tip. I felt a shock of dread and dismay upon initiating this act, but it slowly subsided. I'd not pleasured my husband in this manner since before he'd left for the New World, since before Rodrigo, but I found the use of it to heal rather than to harm made me feel safer and—perhaps paradoxically—more powerful. I could use this act to take Sergio's mind off his suffering; I could use it to prepare him to give me pleasure. Couching it in those terms, I found that in healing him, I also healed myself.

In my heart sprang a renewed hope that, in time, I might erase the stain Rodrigo had left on this act above all the others he'd ruined for me. Maybe one day, I'd be able to give Sergio my favors and think only of his pleasure and my own without even considering Rodrigo. When that day came, some of the things my violator stole from me, I might steal back.

As I kept kissing him down there, Sergio reclined his head and moaned. Soon, his body responded in a manner it hadn't been able to before. When he was erect, I straddled him and slipped him inside me. I was already wet from his previous caresses, and a giggle of relief escaped my throat as I brought myself all the way down to his pelvis. Pulling off my nightshirt, I squeezed my naked breasts against the soft linens wrapped around his chest, though I kept my weight on my knees to avoid putting too much pressure on his back.

He ran his fingers through my hair, bringing my head down so he could kiss my lips, my eyelids, the spot between my eyebrows. Smiling, he gently pressed the tip of my nose with his finger. I chuckled and kissed the spot where his own nose met his cheek. I then bent to kiss his neck and shoulders.

Sergio squeezed my body to his, pressed my cheek to his own, and thanked me for helping him, which only served to prick my soul. He would never have needed my help if it weren't for the help I'd given to strangers. Perhaps he could know some other time why he'd been made to suffer so; maybe he would even find it had been worth the pain.

When we were ready to finish, I moved carefully up and down, fearing any lack of tenderness on my part might worsen his injuries, but we were so stressed and exhausted that even that restricted motion was enough to bring us to climax. I rolled off Sergio when we were done and helped him return to resting on his side. Before lying down and facing him, I made sure his bandages were still clean and white. Assured we'd not done any damage, I folded my arms and tucked them into the pocket between our chests so as not to touch his back. He wrapped his arms around my shoulders and squeezed me to himself, letting out a contented sigh.

Sergio then asked me if I still wished to know what had happened in the tower, and I affirmed I did. This time, comforted by the anesthetics, and maybe a little afterglow, he told me the story.

"They arrested me in the market square when you disappeared. I fought them. That's how I got this," he whispered, before motioning to his bruised face. "But there were too many, and they dragged me off to the tower. They held me on the bottom floor at first, and Ignacio sat close by. He had a few men, and they kept coming in and out saying they couldn't find the witch. I didn't know they meant you until one of them said your name. That's when I understood why they'd arrested me, because no one had said anything to me about charges.

"Ignacio kept getting angrier as the day went on, and I worried he might interrogate me, but I didn't think he'd take it so far. He and the others came in sometime in the late morning or early afternoon and started asking me questions about you. I told them to go to Hell. They said the only one going there would be me if I continued to protect you. So I said, in that case, they could eat shit.

"They asked who I thought I was talking to when I said that, but they didn't do anything more than threaten me. Then they left and were gone some time, but when they came back, they had the jailer with them. I heard them arguing in the hall, and I'm pretty certain money changed hands because they kept talking about Diego's payment for torturing me. I was sure they were putting on a show of it to scare me.

"They took me upstairs, where they had a bench and rope waiting. They showed it to me like it was supposed to frighten me, and they told me if I didn't give them your location, I'd regret it. I said even if I knew where you were, they could still go fuck their mothers. Ignacio said they didn't have time for this, but the other one, the whiny one—"

"Francisco?" I asked.

"Yeah, him. He kept saying they didn't have authorization and what they were doing was illegal, but Ignacio didn't care. He and the jailer tied me to that bench and shoved a rag into my mouth, but I got a good breath because I knew what they were going to do. Diego kept pouring water down my throat, but I didn't try to breathe. I just swallowed and held my breath. I don't think they knew I can hold it so long."

I understood what Sergio meant. He was a practiced diver. Aside from going down to make ship repairs, he also liked to harvest mollusks off the seabed. I'd never seen him do it, but both Marcos and Pablo had told me he could stay under longer than anyone they'd ever known. I couldn't imagine a more ineffective form of torture they could use on him, and I told him so.

"I said the same thing," he replied. "When they pulled the rag out, I laughed at them, and I told them I've nearly sunk to the crushing depths and almost suffocated in the driving rain. I said they were going to have to come up with something besides drowning if they wanted to scare me."

"Oh, Sergio."

"Well, what sort of man would I be if I let them worry me into submission?"

"A smart one," I answered. "I'm sorry, go on. I didn't mean to interrupt."

He took a breath. "They didn't want to get it through their heads that a bit of water wouldn't work on me. They kept pouring it, and I kept laughing when they tried to get me to talk. I guess they'd had enough after a while because Ignacio said something about a potro. Diego asked what kind of town they thought this was to have a fancy torture chamber in every little lockup. That sort of thing costs money, I suppose. He said the only things they had on hand were scourges, so Ignacio told him to get the worst of them.

"They tied me to the bars, and the jailer started whipping me, but Francisco kept telling him not to cut me. He repeated many times that Diego shouldn't break the skin. I laughed again because that meant he couldn't strike hard enough to hurt, leastways not to me. But then, I don't know what happened. Something changed.

"Diego cut me once, I think by accident, and soon after, they stopped scolding him. He kept on cutting me. Then Ignacio took the whip from him and beat me himself. Next thing I knew, I was bleeding down to my ankles and barely feeling the pain anymore because it got so hot in there." Sergio's voice cracked for the first time, and his lip became unsteady.

I squeezed his arm. "Don't say anything more if you can't bear it."

He sighed deeply. "I just—I realized at some point, after they kept beating me and wouldn't . . . wouldn't stop, they'd probably end up killing me. That ball-less one, Francisco, he sat on the bench and sobbed like a woman. Ignacio quit asking about you or anything else. He just kept hitting me over and over. I knew he liked it, and I decided if he was going to murder me, I wouldn't give him the satisfaction of getting any information out of me first.

"When I felt I might faint, the jailer said if they lashed me much more, I wouldn't survive. So they cut me down and started acting like my buddies. Ignacio even told me he'd get a physician to save my life if only I'd save my soul first. The last thing I remember is him letting me lie there face down in my own blood, and I figured at least I'd managed not to die a coward's death. If he'd done that to me, I couldn't imagine what he planned to do to you."

"I shit in the milk," I whispered.

If they'd started questioning Sergio while I'd been waiting at our house, that meant the interrogation had lasted five or six hours. I felt nauseous. How could I not have foreseen this? I'd thought they would simply hold him! I should have gone to the tower as soon as Susana told me where he was. I should have gone straight there. If I had, I might have spared him all this.

"You shouldn't have let them torture you. You should have said whatever they wanted you to say," I murmured.

"I guess it probably wasn't the smartest thing to laugh at them, but I was so furious. Plus, I truly didn't know where you were, so what would've been the point of concocting something to make them stop? So they could find out I'd lied and then condemn me for false witness?"

"No. Of course not. This is Ignacio's fault, not yours." I began sobbing. "It's mine too."

Sergio asked me how it could be my fault. I didn't know what to say. How could I tell him these men were here because the rumors of my self-immolation might be exaggerated, but the basic story they told was true?

I was so desperate to come clean to him I actually opened my mouth to confess. Then I shut it. To disclose one thing would lead to another and another, until I'd spilled my entire load of secrets and left him certain I was a witch and Jhasali the devil.

Even if I couldn't recount the story of how I'd relaxed myself, I also couldn't let lie that he'd been open with me about what Ignacio had done to him. I might return his candidness in kind. I could tell him we hadn't both been left on a church doorstep, but we had both been marked by the same man. I took a breath, preparing to recount my first auto de fe with Ignacio, my true origins, and the impending search for my mother. Before I could, however, Sergio pressed me tighter to himself and drifted off to sleep.

That moment was the closest I had ever come to telling another human being what Ignacio and the Inquisition had done to me, and it passed me by with little more than a fleeting glance. So miserable was I, so desperate to escape the sinking feeling in my chest at the loss of this one chance to bare my soul to Sergio, it didn't take me long to join him in slumber.

We didn't wake again until late morning. My hair was soaking wet and plastered to my face; I'd been weeping as I'd slept. At some point during the night, Sergio had rolled over onto his back and taken my head to his breast. I woke him, shaking his forearm gently until his eyes opened a slit.

"You should not be lying on your back," I said.

"It feels alright." He turned onto his side.

"Let me see." I slid my hair off my cheek and motioned for him to sit up.

I helped him right himself and unwound the few linens from his body, casting them aside. When I turned my gaze to his back, I gasped before I could stop myself.

"What's wrong?" he asked.

"Nothing."

It was the opposite of wrong. The strips of black parchment the nanos had used to seal off Sergio's wounds had begun to merge with his flesh and heal him. In fact, the shallowest wounds had all but closed. In their place grew soft new skin only slightly marred by some dimpled scarring—nothing that would impede his movement. All the deeper cuts still covered his back, but the black stuff had shaped itself to fill the wounds, akin to putting the dirt back in a new hole. Fresh skin had already formed around the edges. Tender as I could, I touched one of the wounds on his shoulder. The graft felt almost like a natural scab but softer, more flexible. Sergio inclined his head at my touch, but he didn't make a sound.

"It's healing much faster than I expected," I said.

Sergio shrugged but didn't reply.

I wrapped him in fresh bandages, as much to prevent him from somehow getting a look at the graft as to cover his wounds, and I helped him get into a linen shirt. Tossing some soft pillows on the back of one of the chairs, I told him he could get out of bed if he wished. When he assented, I took his arm to help him hobble to the chair. He eased himself onto the cushions, groaning as he discovered he was sorer than he'd thought.

He asked if there was any food in this house, so I told him I'd return in a bit. Once in the hallway, I pressed my back against the cold wall and slid down to the floor, pinching the bridge of my nose while I waited for my drone to bring something for Sergio to eat.

My next order of business could be nothing other than getting him off this ship as soon as possible. Once I found a safe alternative where he might continue recuperating, I could return to find Father Manuel. The longer we stayed, the more dangerous the situation became for both of them. The longer we stayed, too, the likelier Sergio would be to start wishing to wander around the place. I'd never convince him I was no sorceress if he got a good look at Homeship.

Then again, what was the reason I should not trust him? Nothing made him so different from me. I'd come to understand the nature of this place because I'd grown to love and trust Jhasali. Who in all this tiny world should Sergio love and trust more than me? I had been wrong to think he'd listen to Jhasali about the nature of her technology, but he would listen to me, and we'd never have a better chance to speak of it alone than we did now.

If Jhasali's bonded drones hadn't yet expelled us, I had no reason to think they would. Perhaps Homeship had not betrayed me. Maybe, since I was a member of its crew, it had decided I had the right to bring aboard whomever I wished—and show them whatever I wished.

By the time my linked drone appeared with a plate of bread and stew, I had decided to consider showing Sergio some of the ship.

"Why am I green?" he asked when I entered with his food.

He stared at the backs of his hands, which retained the tint of the artificial blood, same as Gracia's once had. His skin was darker than hers, so the effect was not quite as shocking, but it was still more than noticeable. I weighed how much I ought to tell him.

"You lost a lot of blood that night," I began.

"Believe me, I'm aware." Sergio winced as he reached to take the stew from my hand.

"Juana is an accomplished healer. She has medicines that can deal with injuries as serious as yours were. That's why I brought you here."

"What kind of medicine?"

"The one that turned you green was meant to replace your blood. Remember when you came home a few years ago and Gracia was green? We had to do the same thing to her after she'd given birth. Your color will fade, as hers did."

"That sounds an awful lot like witchcraft." He sipped the hot stew.

I sighed. "Medicine isn't witchcraft."

"I know that. I'm not an idiot. But a potion that can replace blood. What the devil does that sound like to you?"

"It sounds like magic, but can you believe me when I tell you it isn't? It took her a while to explain it to me, too, but Juana showed me the truth. She practices no sorcery."

Sergio gave me a skeptical glare but returned to his meal without further comment. He'd taken that well enough, which gave me hope he might be able to tolerate stranger things. Still unsure just how bad an idea it was, I decided to continue biding my time, mulling over whether he could see Homeship and how much I should show him.

Alas, time was a limited resource around here. Sergio was healing faster than I'd expected. Not only could he get back and forth from the bed to the chair on his own by afternoon, but he was in a voracious mood, wolfing down everything I gave him like he'd starved for a year. I should have known the graft would mold itself to him so quick, for when I'd been injured, Jhasali's medicines had healed me in a matter of days.

Even so, as badly as he'd been wounded, I'd expected him to need weeks to recover. Yet, by the following morning, I woke to find him wandering around my room. He tried the locked doors and opened the curtains to examine the glass wall.

"Come look at this, Micaela." He held the curtains back with one hand and tapped the glass with the other. "Have you noticed this? It's so thick and smooth. It's like it isn't even glass. It's like some kind of barrier made of clear stone."

"How are you feeling?"

"Fine," he said distractedly.

"You aren't hurting?"

"Yes, but it's not unbearable. Forget that. Look at this. It's not like anything I've ever seen. And have you noted there's no fireplace in here? How do they get through the winter? What are these holes in the ceiling?"

I came up behind him as he stood with his brows knit and his nose nearly pressed against the pane. "Sergio, you trust me, do you not?"

He turned to me. "Of course."

"Completely?"

"Completely. Why?"

"Because, if I showed you something you did not understand, and I explained it to you, would you believe me?"

"What is this about?"

I didn't answer, nor did I think any more on what I was about to do. I just took him by the hand and led him into the hallway. Once we'd exited my very human chambers—the only place on the ship that stood a chance of passing for normal in his eyes—he gasped.

"What is this place?" He stared up at the ceiling.

"This is Juana's house."

"How is the ceiling glowing like that? How are the walls so smooth?"

"The house is made of forged metal."

"That's impossible."

"I think your eyes can see it's not. Come on, I'll show you around. Don't be afraid."

"I am not afraid!" Sergio snapped.

I wrinkled my nose and clicked my tongue. I should've known better than to suggest he could be afraid of anything.

Trying to amend my error, I said, "Well, I was afraid when I first saw what I'm about to show you."

I took him first to the elevating platform that allowed passengers to ascend and descend from one floor to another. I expected him to make a fuss of it, but he didn't comment. I rolled my eyes, sure he was being so stoic to show me up for daring to think he might feel fear of this place. Regardless, I explained a system of pulleys levitated the platform from below. From aboard, it wasn't visible that the slab floated freely. He could learn how it really functioned later.

Once we'd descended, I led him to the medical ward and showed him the pool where I'd tended him, demonstrating how it could fill from the bottom and explaining how I'd put healing potions in the water. I asked him if he remembered, but he did not.

I then took him to the observation deck and bade him look at the mountains and the sea. He banged his fist on the window, unable to get over the hardness and thickness of the glass, the perfection with which it allowed for unimpeded viewing and kept at bay anything that might be hurtling through the air. I told him it was bulletproof—a cannonball could not break it.

I was careful not to show Sergio too much too fast. I needed to lay the foundations of understanding, as Jhasali had with me, before allowing him to meet the drones or see much more of Homeship than he already had. I also needed to explain the celestial bodies before informing him Jhasali's home was a planet beyond our sun.

Though we had a long way to go, I was unsure what I'd been afraid of. He was tranquil as I led him around the parts of Homeship I deemed fit for him to see, making no comments and letting me lay things out uninterrupted. I could tell he was waiting until I finished to question me. I laughed to myself. If Sergio were not so stubborn and confrontational, Jhasali would have likely preferred him as a companion over me. His manner of learning was easier on the teacher than my incessant stream of comments and questions.

"Do you have anything to ask?" I said once we'd returned to my room.

"Just one question. All this seems normal to you?"

"Of course it does. It'll seem normal to you, too, in time."

He raised his eyebrows. "So you see no issue with any of it whatsoever?"

"No. What issue is there to see?"

"But you said you were afraid of it."

"I got used to it the more I learned about it."

Sergio didn't answer. Instead, he threw me a bizarre look, almost like the expression one might use when placating a sick child.

"I'm not a fool, if that's what you're thinking. I put Juana to many tests before taking up with her," I said. Then, I added, "It's best we go."

"Why?"

"Because she might be angry if she returns to find you here. You offended her greatly last time you two met."

"*I* offended *her*?"

"Yes, Sergio. You did. But I want you to consider reconciling with her so you can start spending some time here with me."

"That is never going to happen!" he shouted.

*It may yet*, I thought, though I refrained from saying it aloud.

I unpacked Sergio's warm clothes from my knapsack so we could depart. He donned the boots and breeches but refused the doublet, preferring to drape his cloak over the lightweight linen shirt he already wore. I passed him his dagger, and he tucked it into his pants. When I slipped from my sleeping clothes into my own breeches and men's shirt, Sergio shot me a filthy look but made no fuss otherwise.

Once we were ready, I left the sack on the bed and led Sergio toward the bottom level, trying to concoct a way to walk him off the ship without him looking at the drones sitting in the yard. When we arrived at the door to the passage that led outside, I bade it slide up into the frame. As it did, a pair of feet emerged on the other side.

The thrill of my horror and panic struck so acutely I watched the revelation in slow motion. The door rose at a crawl, revealing each infinitesimal detail of the feet, the knees, the waist, and the chest, until it finished its dread but inevitable climb to unveil the face of Jhasali.

Her countenance was cold and stony, her expression unfathomable, but I could tell by her stance and by the way she pressed her fists to her sides that she was furious. Homeship had informed on me, after all. I threw myself between Jhasali and Sergio, using my arms to try to pin him behind me. His pride could not handle being protected from a woman by a woman, but this was no time for chivalry.

"Please. Let me explain," I said in Castellano, keeping my tone low and trying not to provoke her.

"How dare you? How dare you?" she repeated in Sartjyanan through her clenched teeth.

She seemed incapable of saying anything else, and my terror heightened at the idea of her fury rendering her speechless.

Without warning, Sergio swung around me before I could stop him, stepping toward Jhasali. He obviously didn't wish to do her harm. In fact, he only opened his mouth to speak, but she backhanded his face so hard he hurled across the room as if he weighed no more than a toddler. His skull smacked the wall with a terrible crunch.

"Stop it!" I flew at Jhasali. I grabbed her arms and wrestled her for an instant before she overpowered me and flung me to the floor.

"What is wrong with you?" she demanded in her native tongue.

I tried to go to Sergio, who lay limp on the floor across the room. His mouth gaped, and he blinked at the ceiling.

Jhasali stepped between us. "Do you take pride in disobeying my direct orders? Do you write down a list of my rules so you can be sure to break each one without missing any?"

"Please let me explain," I shouted back in Sartjyanan.

"I hadn't even found my jump hoop yet when the ship informed me of your treachery. I'm going to have to go out there again because of you. What explanation could you possibly offer to justify this?"

"If you'll listen, I'll give you one!"

She sat on a flat drone that floated over to receive her, crossing her arms and legs and looking down at me like I was a condemned criminal awaiting sentence.

I stood to face her. Forcing myself to remain collected, I told her what Ignacio had done to my husband in his attempt to capture me. I was sure to put particular emphasis on the facts that I'd had to bring Sergio to Homeship to save his life and I'd had no alternative. She was silent a long time after I finished.

When she did speak, it was barely more than a hiss. "The only reason he isn't dead right now is Homeship has confirmed you aren't lying."

I didn't dare breathe nor withdraw my gaze from hers. I would try to stop her if she moved to harm Sergio, but if she were intent on it, I wouldn't be able to do much for him. She, however, was uninterested in him. She stared at me with disquieting intensity, as if everything else in the room ceased to exist. She remained silent, waiting for me to finish explaining myself.

After another pause, I dared to speak to her. "I swear, Jhasali. I was getting ready to remove him from the ship when you arrived. He only saw a small portion of it. I didn't know how else to get him out, so I showed him only what I thought would make it benign in his eyes."

"Hostia!" Sergio shrieked, causing both Jhasali and me to whip around.

He stood at the end of the hall, at the very threshold to the outside. Just beyond, a drone blocked his path, brandishing a gun that hung from its undercarriage.

"No. Don't! Let him go. I'll take care of him," I cried.

Jhasali called off the drone and allowed Sergio to flee. He stumbled down the gangplank before barreling off into the woods.

"You'd better catch him quick," she said. "And I expect, should he become a problem, you will do what you must to defend your Homeship."

She headed into the interior of the vessel without another word. Taking that as a dismissal as much as a warning, I tore out the door and away from the ship before she changed her mind, slamming IDOS onto my wrists as I hurtled into the forest.

I whistled for Pepito, who had thankfully not strayed too far. The copious amount of blood I'd left drying on his withers had caked up and flaked off, leaving his coat shining, though his mane and tail were tangled with twigs. Saddling him as soon as my drone brought me his tack, I took off to find Sergio.

My husband's sense of direction was superb, but he had not the faintest idea which way town lay in relation to our location, so I was unsure which direction I should set out in. Knowing Sergio, he'd be more comfortable trying to get his bearings on the coast, so I headed north and trekked down the ridge toward the ocean, wishing I had Lobo's nose or, better yet, Lobo himself.

Even without my poor dog, the sounds of crashing branches and stomping footfalls soon told me I approached my leopard-footed quarry. The minute I spotted Sergio, I dismounted and jogged toward him, begging him to wait. He ignored me.

"Sergio! Please come back," I screamed as he stamped through the woods.

Pepito clambered through the trees behind us, confused as to why I'd dismounted.

Sergio kept on fleeing. "No! I see things as they are now. She's a sorceress, and she's cast a spell on you to make you believe she's harmless."

I chased him down the slope. "Wait, please. You don't understand."

When I closed the gap between us, I grabbed the back of his cloak. He spun around and yanked the cloth from my grasp, shoving me to the ground in the process.

"Then why don't you sit there and tell how much of an imbecile I am?" he shrieked.

"Don't you dare push me." I stood to my feet. "In all the time we've been together, you have never once put your hands on me. You'd best not start now."

"Why? What will happen to me if I do?"

"Nothing good."

My temper had flared, and my pulse pushed against the cuffs on my wrists. The heat had not yet risen, but I feared to permit my restraint to fail me while I was so armed.

"It's never been my wish to harm you, nor will it ever be. But let me go." Sergio continued down the ridge.

I took several deep breaths before I followed. "Now, you listen! Juana isn't inevitably a witch just because you don't understand her."

"Well, what is that unholy creature she commanded to hold me inside her metal castle?"

"It isn't a demon."

"Then what is it?"

My speech failed me. I had never truly comprehended what the drones were until I'd been implanted with the sensors.

"It's a machine," I managed to say. "A machine that thinks."

"You are mad," Sergio yelled as he tromped through the woods.

"I am not. If you'd come back to the metal castle, we could show you how it works. I could teach you about the ocean of space and the ships that sail it."

"I'm never going back there. I won't let that demoness turn me into a raving lunatic, too."

"Obviously, we cannot return right this second. But in a day or two, Juana's temper will cool. Even now, she poses no real threat to us." I was not sure this statement was all that accurate, but I wished to calm the situation.

"You don't know that. You can never know that. Her unnatural strength is threatening enough." He stopped and put his hand to his bruised face. "You chose to throw in your lot with this evil—"

"How can she be all that evil when I saved your life with her inventions?" I interjected.

"By your own admission, my life was only ever in danger because you chose to ally yourself with this thing, whatever it is."

"Is your suffering the fault of the lifeless objects she possesses or of the people who assign malice to them because they don't comprehend them?"

Without offering a retort, he turned away from me again.

"Where are you going?" I demanded.

"Home."

"We have no home. Ignacio's probably sequestrated it by now."

He slowed his pace as if that fact had slipped his mind. "Even so, I'm going back to town to see if I can salvage any of our money. I need to get to a clearing so I can read the stars when it gets dark."

"I know the way home, but you cannot go there. They surely have a post waiting for us."

"I don't care. I've got to find Gabriel; I've got to somehow warn Armando to stay out of the country."

"No. You can't go home." I slid down the slope and planted myself in his path.

He sneered. "I can and I will. I may have little power to command you anymore, but that doesn't mean you get to turn the tables. You can either come with me or get out of my way."

Knowing I couldn't keep my husband here without having a drone physically restrain him, I relented. "This is a terrible idea, but I'll go with you. I must find Father Manuel, anyhow."

My finally acquiescing to his will placated Sergio for the present. He strode to where Pepito stood, taking him by the bridle. The only thing that overrode my trepidation at returning to town was my desire to protect Sergio from suffering another incident like the one he had already, as well as my augmenting desperation to ensure Father Manuel hadn't met a similar fate. Thus, I picked my way down the mountain beside my husband and my horse.

We had to lead Pepito a long way before we could mount, for the slope was too steep for him to carry us both. Once we got to flatter terrain, Sergio mounted and beckoned me to take my seat behind him. I pulled myself onto Pepito and wrapped my arms around my husband, squeezing my body to his. He squirmed away and inhaled sharply. I let go; I'd forgotten not to press on his back.

"Town is west," I said.

When I leaned away from him and took hold of his hips instead of his waist, he turned Pepito left and spurred him toward Santa Colomba.

# Chapter Twenty-Seven

# THE REVELATION

We were careful to keep our cover and stay off the roads. By the time we managed to make it out of the baldíos, the sun had swung right over our heads and tracked off to the horizon. We didn't get back to town until after nightfall, and we made straight for the estate house once we arrived. Sneaking into the stables, we crouched in a stall.

"We have to think of a way to get in the big house," Sergio whispered.

"Why can't we just go in?"

"I'm sure they know by now Gabriel is my master's brother, so they might be watching the place to see if he'll harbor us. Stay here. If I don't return in half an hour, leave without me and find someplace safe to hide."

"I'm not going anywhere!" I hissed.

"Quiet, Micaela."

"I will not be quie—"

Sergio clapped his hand over my mouth and shushed me frantically. I'd been so focused on him I'd not heard the barn door unlatch. Now, someone was inside with us. Sergio drew his dagger and crouched behind the stall door. Loath as I was to deploy my weapons in front of him again, I brought the heat to my forearms anyhow.

"Who's in here?" a voice called. It was Tomás.

"Tomás?" Sergio peeked out of the stall. "Is anyone with you?"

"No," he replied.

Sergio and I exited the stall to find Tomás standing in the stable corridor with a cleaver in his hand.

"What in Christ's name happened to you?" Tomás eyed Sergio's bruised face and his green complexion.

Sergio gave me the side-eye. "I'm not even sure myself. Why have you got that?" He motioned to the cleaver.

"I saw two men enter the barn. I thought they might be bandits who'd heard the master and mistress were taken."

"What?" Sergio and I cried in unison.

"They arrested them a couple days ago. Rosa had to hide in the woods with Eduardo, or they might have taken him too. They didn't even tell us about any charges, but the rumors have been spreading that it has to do with *her*." Tomás pointed to me.

"We must get them back. Let's go inside. I want to speak with the others," Sergio said.

Tomás led us into the house, where several of the servants huddled in the parlor. Rosa held Eduardo, who was whimpering and repeating the words "Where is Mamá." They all breathed sighs of relief to see Sergio but glared at me as though I were the Antichrist incarnate.

"The house hasn't been sequestrated, then?" Sergio asked.

"I overheard someone saying they might send for an assessor, but we haven't learned anything since. We didn't know what to do." Rosa's voice cracked as if she'd been crying, and she bounced Eduardo on her lap. "How could they take my lady? I nursed her from my own breast! How could they do this?"

"I'm glad they didn't take all of us," Tomás snapped.

"So no one denounced either of them?" Sergio's eyes bored into Tomás's.

"What reason would any of us have to do such a thing?" Rosa cried from the sofa, rocking Eduardo back and forth.

Several of the others voiced their assent, saying Gracia was a wonderful mistress and Gabriel never did any of them wrong.

"I believe you all, but I had to ask," Sergio said.

"Don Sergio, please, you have to bring them back." Rosa sobbed, and all the other servants agreed he must do something.

Sergio remained unfazed by this sudden burden on his shoulders. Then again, he had no reason to be surprised. Everyone already called him Armando's second brother, and the master's obvious favoritism of him had always put him in an unspoken but well-understood tertiary role beneath Armando and Gabriel. With them gone, he was all the leadership the household had.

Sergio told everyone to stay downstairs except for me and Tomás. He took us upstairs to the master's bedroom, where he bade Tomás open the vault. Tomás pushed a large armoire to the side to reveal a blank wall. He then knelt and fiddled around at the base. Finding what he sought, he pushed on a portion of the wall that had thus far looked ordinary. This section gave way when he pressed on it, which made the wall pop out just enough for him to grab onto it, pull it to the side, and expose a hollowed-out chamber within. When Sergio gestured toward this secret closet, Tomás entered and retrieved a few bags of money.

"Consider this your wages," Sergio said once we'd descended the stairs and distributed the money. "Plus payment for your silence."

"What are we to do if they seize the house?" Tomás asked.

"Nothing. What can any of us do? They'll probably pocket everything regardless of who gets charged with what," Sergio spat bitterly.

"What do you mean?" I demanded, unready to accept the likelihood Ignacio's people would swoop in and steal everything my husband had worked for all his life.

Sergio didn't answer. Instead, he took me by the hand and led me into the study alone. "I'm going to pull Armando's emergency fund. If we offer enough, the inquisitors might be willing to forget this whole thing. I know something of these people from living down south. All they ever want is money. That, we have."

"What's to stop them from arresting everyone and sequestrating the estate?" I said.

"First of all, they cannot sequestrate money they cannot find. Second, they only have perhaps two dozen men, three dozen at the most. If I go to port and stir up Armando's boys, they're going to have a much bigger problem than inventorying the estate. The only reason they don't already have a riot on their hands is they've managed to keep all this quiet and the servants frightened enough not to resist."

"Why don't we just go get your boys now?"

Sergio shook his head. "It'd be foolish to do it that way if we can avoid it. Sure, we'd overpower them now, but we'll get Gabriel and Gracia, and then what? If we use violence, there'll be consequences for us later. But if they don't take my terms, there'll be consequences for them tonight. It'll be to everyone's advantage if they take what I offer and leave quietly."

"That would be a great strategy, except Ignacio doesn't want money. He wants me."

"Everyone wants money, Micaela."

"No. You don't know what kind of man he is."

"You think I don't know exactly the kind of man he is after what he did to me?"

"You don't know him like I know him!"

"How in the name of Christ do you know him?" Sergio demanded.

"From Toledo. It's a long story. I'll have to tell you later. The point is, he's got a grudge against me, and no amount of money is going to make him go away. If I trade myself for Gabriel and Gracia, he's more likely to take that deal than yours."

"Are you mad? You're going to let him cart you down south? They think you're a witch. Don't you understand what that means?"

"I know what it means. And I have no intention of going to Toledo."

"We're not doing that. That is the most insane plan I've ever heard."

"But Serg—"

"Look, regardless of whatever grudge he has against you, I've never met a man in my life who wouldn't take a bribe. I'm sure I can reason with him."

"Why don't you take off your shirt and show me how well you reasoned with him last time?" I snapped.

Sergio set his jaw and raised his eyebrows. I hadn't meant to say that. I didn't want to humiliate him, but he wasn't hearing a thing I said.

I took his hand in mine. "I'm sorry."

"It's fine. But this is what's going to happen. You are to wait in the vega. I'll get Marcos and Pablo and explain the situation. I'll tell them if they don't see me again after three hours, they're to bring every man we employ to the tower and get me and the master and mistress in whatever manner they deem necessary."

"And they'll do that for you?"

"They'll do it for the man who's paid their bills the last decade."

I had to concede that. Armando had been wise to keep a permanent crew for his ships. Long years at the command of the same master usually breed much loyalty.

"It's a good plan, but it's still got a flaw. Under no circumstance am I going to cower in the vega," I said.

"You'll do as I s—"

"If you finish that sentence, I am walking out of here right now."

Sergio ground his teeth as if he had to clamp down on the very words to keep them from slithering out, but he didn't utter the last crucial one.

Instead, he said, "Tomás and I will tie you up and bury you in the wine cellar if that's what it takes to keep you safe."

"You'll do no such thing. I understand your intentions are benevolent, but I will not be left behind. This entire situation is because of me, and I intend to be part of the solution. You are not my head. Do you understand? It's my choice, and I'm going with you."

"Will you at least concede it's a bad idea for that damned Ignacio to see you?"

"That I will concede, but allow me this. I'll talk to Marcos and Pablo. You go with your promises of money and try to end this peacefully. When it doesn't work, I'll have them ready."

Sergio agreed Marcos and Pablo would listen to me. However, I had no intention of finding them, for Sergio was only right on a single point: stirring up a riot was sure to have consequences for many people not involved in this mess. Enough innocent bystanders had paid for my mistakes already.

I'd told Sergio I wished to exchange myself for Gracia and Gabriel in a futile attempt to get him to allow me to go alone to the tower, but I had no plans to make such an exchange. Rather, I intended to sneak into the tower and hide until I could catch Ignacio unawares. This time, there would be no negotiation, no trade of myself for anyone else's life. I would assassinate the inquisitor on sight, capture Francisco, and force him to call off his men. If I were captured myself, I hoped I could call Jhasali using my connection to my drone. I knew she'd be livid, but I was also certain she'd never allow her only friend to be carted off to some dungeon down south.

Sergio and I returned to the parlor, where he told the servants they'd done well, but they must leave the estate and not return until summoned. Eduardo was to go with Rosa, and Tomás was not to let them out of his sight. At these words, Rosa began to cry again. Sergio told her to buck up and everything would work itself out, but she glared up at me with her bloodshot eyes and hissed this was all my fault. Several others chimed in with agreement. They called me a sorceress and demanded Sergio turn me in so Gabriel and Gracia might be allowed to return.

"I am not a witch!" I cried. "And I had no idea they'd arrest the master and mistress."

I couldn't help but engage them. I'd had about enough of everyone calling me a sorceress, and their laying of blame on my shoulders just exacerbated the weight of the blame I'd already taken on myself.

"She is a witch. She was shot in the street and completely unharmed. Everyone saw it," Elena said.

"She calls demons from the wilderness to defend her," Ximena added.

Tomás shouted over them. "Sergio, look at yourself. She's turned you into a monster."

"That is enough. I am not a monster, and she cannot help the asinine rumors about her. You all need to stop it," Sergio snapped.

I didn't want to stop it. "But they—"

Sergio took me by the hands, pressing his thumbs into my palms. I expected him to be angry, but the look on his face exuded exhaustion more than fury.

"Please," he whispered. "We need these people on our side."

I folded my fingers over his thumbs and didn't argue further. Several of the servants attempted to insult me again, but he shut them right up by saying the next person who called me a witch would not be asked to return to the estate once this unpleasant business concluded. He then ensured Rosa told him where she'd be keeping Eduardo before sending them on their way.

"We need to leave too," I said once they'd gone. "They might or might not be disloyal, but that doesn't mean Ignacio hasn't got a man checking on the house."

"I know, but wait a minute." Sergio headed back upstairs.

When he returned, he had a sack of money in each hand, saying he hoped these would be enough to let the Inquisition officials know he was serious about making the release of our friends worth their while. He'd also strapped a sword around his hips, pushing the belt low enough that it didn't cross over his back. The idea of him engaging in combat while he was still wounded concerned me. However, I was more than aware of how the conversation might go if I mentioned it: probably about as well as when he'd admonished me to stay behind.

Sergio had kept one of Armando's horses for himself when he'd sent the servants off, and he saddled up quickly. We rode to Marcos and Pablo's to find they weren't home, so Sergio told me to slip through the gap in the wall and check their normal haunts in town until I found them. Meanwhile, he would take the sample money to the tower and explain the rest would be delivered to Ignacio upon Gabriel and Gracia's release.

We rode toward town through the vega, avoiding the roads, and we made it close to the city wall before we were ambushed. The soldiers had learned from their last encounter with me. They delayed revealing their presence until they had sandwiched us between themselves and the wall, all but eliminating my ability to react in time. Then they descended on us at once, charging at us on horseback and trying to drive us into the wall or through the gate.

Pepito saw our pursuers first. Leaping into a gallop, he fled sideways along the wall, sprinting so fast it seemed his feet never touched the ground. Sergio called out to the men, trying to explain he wished to talk to Ignacio, but when one of the riders shot an arrow at him, he spun around and followed me. Pepito hurtled along the wall as our pursuers closed in. Just before they reached us, he burst through the gap between horsemen and stone and then flew away from town in the direction of the ship, with Sergio's mount hot on his heels.

For one pathetic moment of absurd hope, it looked like we might outrun them. Then a ball from an arquebus whizzed past my knee, zooming between Sergio and me. Infantrymen awaited us ahead! They aimed low, intent on killing the horses and taking their riders alive.

More than a dozen horsemen closed ranks behind us, driving us toward a line of marksmen who'd stepped out from a grove of trees in the vega. Out of options, I twisted in my seat and fired my cuff at the riders. I blew the nearest clear out of his saddle into the horse behind him. I shot another in an instant, hoping if I demonstrated how rapidly I could fire, it might deter them.

"What the devil?" Sergio cried as I fired a third round ahead, killing an arque-busier.

I'd hoped to break the infantry line, but they held their ground, no longer shocked enough by my "magic" to be frightened off.

"Nevermind! Explain later," I shouted through gritted teeth as I scanned our surroundings for any avenue of escape.

Sergio turned his horse to the side, hoping to flee through the gap between our pursuers and the line of infantry. As soon as he gave them the animal's broadside, they shot it out from under him. The horse reared, and I turned just in time to see Sergio thrown to the ground behind his mount, whose body came crashing down on top of his own before he could scream.

I leapt from Pepito and threw myself to the ground. Shrieking and clawing at the dirt, I tried to drag myself to Sergio between the heavy hooves of all the horses that now surrounded us. The immense weight of a chain-link net collapsed onto me. Several men drew it taught, sealing me within as I screamed and struggled, my only weapon pinned uselessly against my body. I squirmed, trying to get my arm in a position to fire, but it was impossible to move. Someone slipped his hands between the net's metal cables, clamping thick irons around my wrists to bind my arms behind my back.

"That should hold her." The man spat on me and kicked me.

Someone called from behind, saying they needed bonds for the other one. My heart leapt. If they wanted to bind Sergio, he had to be alive. I shrieked for him, but he didn't answer. Not far-off, Pepito screamed and whinnied as a pair of men tried to subdue him.

Many of the men laughed as I tore in vain at the net, cursing them all the while. They chained my ankles and tied a rope to my tiny prison, securing the other end to the saddle of a massive cream-colored horse that had belonged to one of the riders I'd killed. A couple of men lifted Sergio's limp form and threw him over the back of this horse. They'd divested him of his money, his cloak, and his weapons. His back was bleeding again.

I began attempting to burn the irons off my wrists as soon as the company headed toward the city, but try as I might, the chains were too thick and too heavy to melt. I feared if I fired a round to break them, I'd amputate my own arm. So I tried to communicate with my drone to relay a message to Jhasali. No matter how much

I willed myself to connect, though, I couldn't make it happen. It felt as if something physically blocked the signal from my mind.

I wondered if Jhasali had finally had enough of my defiance and sealed the ship against me. She could have powered down my drone using the manual override and taken me off Homeship's manifest. But she couldn't remotely disable IDOS, and the heat burned in vain against the irons, so scalding I feared it might scorch even me if it remained insulated inside the thick metal. I twisted against the net, unable to straighten my knees or turn my head.

The soldiers dragged us down the road, Pepito bucking as they drove him along. He put up an impressive fight, rearing and stomping so hard he sent vibrations through the ground and turning his head to bite the toes of the man who'd mounted him. I had to admire his nerve, but like me, he was trussed up and tugged back to town whether he liked it or not.

The men took us exactly where I feared they would: straight to the tower. When we arrived, they yanked my still-unconscious husband from his mount. They carried him and dragged me into the entry chamber on the first floor, where several dozen guards now stood in the stone corridor. Reinforcements had arrived during the days we'd passed in hiding.

An outraged, almost-frantic male voice resounded through the chamber, and it took me only a second to place it as the voice of Don Luis. He stood in the center of the room, shouting at the top of his lungs. Though I lay on my stomach, weighed down by the netting, I was still able to get my head off the floor to stare at him as he screamed at Ignacio and Francisco, spit flying from his mouth, his arms flailing. He looked as mad as he sounded.

Luis's scribe, Hernando, stood behind him, open-mouthed and unblinking, like he'd never seen the inquisitor in such a state. Francisco teetered on the verge of tears, but Ignacio stood beside his accomplice, glaring at Luis with that same hard gaze he'd cast at me when he'd forced me to witness my first burning.

"Look! See?" Ignacio shouted when he laid eyes on me. "They've captured the witch."

"Yes, because I'm a halfway-competent commander. I did in five hours what you've not been able to do in the last week. Oh, is that really necessary?" Luis motioned to the iron net wrapped around me.

Ignacio, Francisco, and a couple of the soldiers all shouted, "Yes!"

"You didn't send me enough men to capture her," Ignacio argued. "What's one alguacil and a few soldiers supposed to do against a monster like her?"

Luis laughed. "She looks like a real monster to me."

"She is. You're just not listening," Ignacio replied.

"Why would I listen to you? The only reason I allowed you to come up here in the first place is that I thought it might quiet some of these ludicrous rumors when you found nothing. I certainly didn't expect you to kidnap some poor farm girl and terrorize half the countryside."

"But the girl. Look at the girl," Ignacio said.

"I will hear no more of this. How can you put stock in ridiculous stories peddled by common folk? You'd let the mob tell you who to burn."

Ignacio gesticulated toward Sergio. "No. That one, her husband. I swear I whipped him half to death not four days ago. And look at him now. How could she heal him so fast?"

"So you confess to having unlawfully put him to the torment?" Luis snapped.

"That is irrelevant. Come here!"

They went to where Sergio lay groaning as he began to revive and realize he was shackled at the wrists and ankles. Ignacio rolled him onto his stomach and pulled up the back of his shirt while Sergio screamed for him to take his filthy hands off him.

"There. See?" Ignacio removed the bandages and pointed at the black graft that was still in the process of molding itself to Sergio's deepest wounds. "What is this?"

In their roughness, the soldiers had torn Sergio's flesh away from the graft in several spots. Ignacio ran his thumb over the purple liquid—a mix of artificial and human blood—that oozed from the reopened wounds. Sergio gnashed his teeth in protest.

"She's obviously applied some magical unguent or cast a spell on him. What else could turn him so green?" Ignacio asked.

Luis gave a deep sigh. "Perhaps she's used some herbal recipe these montañeses concocted eons ago. Do you even hear yourself?"

"No! He was at death's door when she set the block on fire and spirited him away using her sorcery. The men were raving about a devil she set upon them. Francisco, isn't that right?"

Francisco nodded vehemently but did not reply.

Hernando squeaked from the corner, "Señoría, if I may—"

"You may not," Luis snapped.

"But Don Luis! If this woman is the real witch, that means the other one is innocent," Hernando cried.

"I'll be the judge of who is guilty and who is innocent, boy," Luis spat before turning to me and asking, "Girl, are you a witch?"

"No," I growled through my clenched teeth.

"If you are not a witch, then how is it your husband's wounds have healed so quickly?" Luis's tone was sarcastic.

"How is it he was illegally given those wounds in the first place?" I retorted.

Luis turned to Ignacio. "She has a point."

"Listen, you've got the wrong people," Sergio shouted. "The real witch lives on the mountain in a huge castle made of metal. She's enchanted it to appear as a sinkhole from a distance. That's what I came to tell you. Micaela isn't the one you want. It's Juana you're after."

"Sergio, shut up! You don't understand what you're doing," I shrieked.

"It is strikingly convenient the 'real witch' is some random woman in some nameless location instead of your very own wife. Would you not say?" Ignacio scoffed.

"It's the truth," Sergio said.

"Why did you fail to tell us before?"

"I didn't know then."

"How do you know now?" Ignacio asked.

"Because I've seen the place. I can lead you all there," Sergio replied.

"Sergio, please. Ignacio, listen to me. You confused him when you tortured him. He doesn't know what he's saying," I shouted.

"Quiet, witch!" Ignacio bellowed. "It's beyond me how this fool thinks bearing false witness will divert my attention from you."

"So then you admit you perpetrated this spectacle of irregularities because of your bias against the girl?" Luis snapped.

Ignacio opened his mouth, but Luis interjected before he could utter a word.

"Both of you are finished! Everything you have done over the last week has been in flagrant disregard for one protocol after another."

"That's right!" I yelled.

They all turned and looked at me as if I'd lost my mind, but I just shrugged from my place on the floor. After blinking a time or two, Luis continued as though I'd said nothing.

"Hernando, take this down. My first mistake was not dismissing *you* the instant I discovered you'd written to this abominable excuse for an official of the Holy Office." Luis flailed his arms at Francisco.

Hernando pressed his parchment to the wall and scribbled furiously as Luis continued to scream.

"My second mistake was extending you any professional courtesy whatsoever. I never should have allowed you to investigate in *my* jurisdiction." He shook his finger at Ignacio before turning back to Francisco. "And my third mistake was thinking a sniveling weasel like you could control this situation."

I held my breath, unwilling to believe we might get out of this entire mess on some bureaucratic technicality.

"You can consider yourself dismissed," Luis shouted at Francisco. He then snarled at Ignacio. "If I had any authority over you, I'd have you carted off in chains. As it stands, our superiors will be hearing of this."

Ignacio stomped in indignation. "Hypocrite! You'd condemn me for an accident that was necessary to capture this whore of Satan, while you and your men bend and subvert every regulation against thievery and bribery you can think of."

"At least I never murdered a man of God!" Luis snapped.

"What?" I screamed.

Luis gave me a look of what I assumed was the most compassion a man in his line of work could muster, but the smile that spread across Ignacio's wretched face told me all I needed to know. I laid my brow on the floor and sobbed. How could this have happened? It couldn't be!

Ignacio huffed. "I don't see the issue. The old man kept spouting heresy about how the Holy Office does the work of the devil. I thought I might persuade him to change the subject. How was I to know his heart would give out at the slightest provocation? Besides, this parish can have another priest. Capturing her? That's the catch of a lifetime."

"No, enough!" I glared at Ignacio, willing every molecule in his repugnant body to melt where it sat. Better yet, I willed that one of Jhasali's huge passenger drones would descend from the mountain to tear him limb-from-limb, as I should have done already. "Take me back to Toledo, then. I hope you *do* burn me. I hope you burn me like a traveling circus in every single city in the kingdom so everyone can know who and what I am."

Luis looked aghast, but these words had a profound effect on Ignacio. It took him a long while to recover his faculties enough to respond. When he did, it was clear he'd lost his head.

"I'll cart you and all your accomplices back to Toledo and burn every one of you if it's the last thing I do. If none of my methods can destroy you, witch, I'll sink you to the bottom of the sea. Then your accursed mouth will be shut up!" Ignacio ran at me. Reaching me before anyone could react, he kicked and stomped me as I lay helpless on the floor.

"Calm yourself, man." Luis grabbed Ignacio by the shoulders and shook him.

Ignacio shoved Luis away. "Get your hands off me, you old fool. No one understands the true nature of this sorceress save me."

"The poor girl is clearly mad. Are you going to let yourself be sucked into the hallucinations of some hysterical housewife?"

"She's not deluded. You weren't there when she came for her damned husband. She shot several of the men and set some sort of flying monster on the rest."

Luis rolled his eyes. "Assuming even half that ridiculous tale is true, so the girl can use a bow. That doesn't make her a witch."

"She shot them with her own flesh!" Ignacio cried, demanding the soldiers who'd been present back him up.

They kept quiet, cowed by the furious look Luis cast them when Ignacio insisted they contradict him.

"You must see," Ignacio added when he got no aid.

"All I see is a foreign official taking full advantage of my good graces in my own jurisdiction to persecute some misguided girl. Get out. Get out of my district now."

Ignacio shouted he was not leaving without me, since my crimes had been committed in his jurisdiction. Luis ignored him and, turning to his men, told them to unchain me.

"You cannot unbind her. If you do that, she'll kill us all!" Ignacio shrieked. He was right on that account. "I can prove it. Go get some oil and set her ablaze right here."

"No!" I screamed. I couldn't let him prove me a witch when we were so close to escape.

"There. See? She doesn't want to be set on fire because it will prove she cannot burn," Ignacio said.

"Or she doesn't want to be set on fire because she doesn't *want* to burn," Luis snapped.

"Shoot her!" Ignacio yelled to the men.

Luis smacked his forehead. "Is there something in the water in this town that's made you all go mad?"

Disobeying Luis's protests, one of the arquebusiers who stood closest to me took aim and fired, striking me square between the shoulder blades. The ball hurt like the stroke of a rod, knocking the wind from me and causing me to sob with pain when I caught my breath, but it did not pierce me.

Just as I feared, Luis made an about-face. He leaned against the wall, mouth agape, running his hands through his gray hair. The quiet was absolute. The scratching of Hernando's quill ceased. None of the soldiers dared to breathe. Sergio, who had been screaming inanely and flopping against his bonds like a beached dolphin, gaped at me wide-eyed.

After a long stretch of total silence, Luis spoke. "You did not miss?"

"Of course he didn't miss." Ignacio beckoned for Luis to come to where I lay.

They bade the soldiers pull the net off me. Ignacio grabbed my braid and jerked me to my knees. Then he borrowed a knife from one of the men and sliced the back of my shirt from the bottom seam to the collar. Though my hands were still bound behind me, the pieces of the shirt fell forward and hung off my body, exposing my whole back to this room full of strangers—right in front of my husband, who could do nothing to prevent it.

If Luis still found Ignacio's treatment of me distressing, he no longer did anything to stop him. I squeezed my mouth and eyes shut, but my breath still came in sobs. Humiliated, incensed tears cascaded down my cheeks as the two inquisitors examined my back for signs of injury.

"Shoot her again. I didn't see it well enough the first time," Luis ordered.

Another soldier stepped up and shot me once more, this time with a crossbow instead of an arquebus. Yet again, the bolt ricocheted off my back and bounced to the wall, then the floor, paining me and leaving me winded but otherwise unharmed.

Luis squeezed the bridge of his nose. "Take her back to Toledo. I don't even want her in my sight. What if I try to put her to death and fail? It'll cause a panic ten times worse than anything we've seen in Navarra."

"Yes. Now you're seeing things as they are," Ignacio said.

Luis glared at him. "I have a condition. Who knows what my associates will do if they discover such a witch was under our very noses? So you have got to promise me you will try her and execute her in utter secrecy. No public penance. No auto de fe. If you can keep all this quiet, I won't allow anyone to find out what you did to that poor old man."

Ignacio grasped Luis's hand. "You've got a deal."

"I'll try her three accomplices here, but you can have her right now," Luis told Ignacio. Looking to his men, he added, "Someone go get the other two."

"No! Please. They don't know anything. I've hidden all of this from everyone," I said.

"If they have nothing to hide, they have nothing to fear," Luis replied coldly.

"Are you joking?" I squeaked.

Ignacio went back over to where Sergio lay, still immobilized but swearing afresh. "I pray you'll let me take this one to Toledo as well. He might have information that proves useful in her trial. And I'll be damned if I cannot break his spirit."

When Ignacio said this, Sergio spat on his foot. He aimed a kick at Sergio's face, but Sergio turned, and Ignacio caught him on the side of the head instead, making his ear bleed the same purple blood as his back. I screamed for them to leave him alone.

Luis held up a hand. "You will not take him. You clearly have a bias against him too. I'm loath to send her with you, but it seems I've got no choice. Regardless, I prefer to try the citizens of my district myself. I'm sure you don't believe it, but I'll be more than adequate at obtaining from him whatever information you need."

A tsunami of panic broke over me at these words. I struggled against my bonds, but I still could not manage to break free.

"Please, please let them go. Do what you will with me, but let them go," I begged.

"Gag her," Luis ordered. "I don't want her using her forked tongue to tempt any more of my men. I'll send an escort with you to Toledo to ensure she cannot escape."

At this point, the soldiers brought a disheveled and sobbing Gracia and an impassive Gabriel into the room. Luis told his men to take my accomplices to the cart, and one of the men forced a gag between my teeth as well as Sergio's. Gracia pleaded to be allowed to go home and raise her son, but the soldiers ignored her. They began to drag my three companions to the door, while I tried in vain to move my arms or force words through my gag.

Without warning, an apparent earthquake rocked the tower's foundations. The men lurched, some of them falling to the floor. Shouts of terror erupted outside as the earsplitting cracks of rapid-fire weapons filled the air. Arquebus fire resounded seconds later, and the telltale hum of a transport drone's engines vibrated the atmosphere so furiously I could damn near feel it in my eardrums.

Sergio writhed and kicked, trying to free himself from his bonds. Gracia cried out for help, and though she screamed at no one in particular, Hernando ran to her. Francisco cowered in the back of the room, but Luis wrenched the tower door open, and he, Ignacio, and most of the soldiers ran outside.

Still trussed up like a wild boar, I had to roll and shimmy out the door. While I dragged myself toward salvation, two pairs of feet stepped over me and fled the tower. I didn't see nor care to see who it had been—probably Francisco and one of his cronies seeking a more secure hiding place.

Finally, I wriggled onto my knees and bellowed Jhasali's name through my gag. When I did, a two-passenger drone swung into view, hovering above my head. The soldiers screamed and fired their weapons at it, but the arquebus rounds might as well have been cotton balls.

I called to Jhasali that she had to cut my bonds, and the drone extended two of its repair arms out of its hull. I turned my back and allowed it to use a tiny rotating saw to snap the chain that bound my arms behind me. Then it cut the irons from my wrists and ankles. Yanking my gag off, I stood and tied the two halves of my shirt in a knot that sat on my lower back.

The drone lowered itself almost to the ground, and I looked through the windshield, expecting to find an enraged Jhasali, but the pod was vacant. Perhaps she was controlling it remotely. Suddenly, I experienced an involuntary viewpoint shift: I stared at myself from the pod's perspective. Tears ran down my cheeks. I was covered in dirt, my clothes torn, my hair disheveled. Then, something clicked. I realized I had been so preoccupied with my terror, humiliation, and fury that I hadn't noted whatever communication the device had attempted.

I wondered how this had happened and knew in an instant I'd bonded to this drone the very first time I'd tried, the day Jhasali had left to find the jump hoop. Back then, I'd been so distraught I'd failed to note the pod's acceptance of my connection or to communicate a directive to it, so it had remained in sleep mode. It received its inaugural directive from me a few minutes ago, when I'd wished for a big drone to descend from the mountain.

Jhasali had not sent this craft at all. In her haste to depart for her superluminal wave generator, she must've forgotten to try to forge a new nexus with this pod, just another of her dozens of devices. Now, this was my drone. I had called it to myself—I, its bonded master. I returned myself to my own viewpoint and saw my bonded servant floating serenely in front of me, a dragon awaiting orders. I gritted my teeth and let out a livid screech, which I magnified through the drone's outer speakers.

At this, some of the soldiers fled in the direction of the church. I put my vision into the drone's eyes and pursued until a company of half a dozen men made it through the door into the nave. I sank my second body nearly to the street so I could see into their sanctuary. Unsure what I wished to do, I hesitated, feeling it almost abominable to accost them there.

However, at the precise instant I peered through the open door, I saw the darkened silhouette of a woman. Startled at the arrival of a company of soldiers, she leapt to her feet in front of the main altar. She alarmed one of the younger men, and before anyone could stop him, he raised a crossbow and shot her dead.

"Oh!" I shouted with my own voice.

If this was how they planned to behave, I had no intention of letting them seek sanctuary before Father Manuel's very altar. I bade my new ally strike. It flew away from the church and fired a round it prepared by whipping up a ball of bright blue light between its two biggest arms. The drone hurled this bolt of azure lightning at the church, collapsing the edifice with an explosion so massive it rocked the foundations of every building near the plaza, killing the soldiers inside.

Fearing the men nearby might realize I commanded this Leviathan, I called the drone to myself. I used the tailguns to herd the soldiers who had not been inside the church back toward the main regiment in front of the tower, slowing the device so it could pursue them. The primary company fired upon the drone as it approached behind their comrades, determined to bring it down despite their weapons having already proven useless.

I was preparing to respond to their fire with one of those bolts of blue lightning when someone called my name. Sergio! He must have wriggled free of his gag. I ran inside the tower, bringing the drone to heel outside the open door and telling it to kill no one else without my express bidding but to keep them all away from me.

The chamber was empty save Francisco, Sergio, and Gabriel. I ran to Francisco's hiding place in the corner and demanded the keys to Sergio's cuffs. He cowered and squeezed his hands over his ears like a child.

I jerked his head up and slapped him. "Keys! Give me the keys."

"I don't know. Check the hooks along the wall."

Leaping over him, I charged at the hooks only to find them devoid of keys. Shit! I did not have time for this. I ran back to Sergio, helped him sit up, and pulled his arms as far away from his body as I could. Then, I told him to hold his wrists apart and be very still. Taking my own wrist and pressing it to the chain, I fired a hard round into it and severed the links right in the middle. I did the same thing with his ankles. We'd have to worry about getting the actual irons off later, but with the chains severed, at least he could move.

As soon as I cut the bonds from Sergio's limbs, he did exactly as I feared he might. He leapt to his feet and set upon Francisco, snatching him up bodily and slamming him against the stone wall. Francisco couldn't even cry out because Sergio had both his hands around his neck. He raised his left fist and struck the man in the face.

"Stop it, Sergio!" I cried.

Ignoring me, he continued to pummel Francisco, strangling him with one hand and battering his head with the other. I tried to pull him off; he didn't budge. I screamed that I needed to learn the location of Father Manuel's body before he killed this piece of shit, to no avail. I tried smacking his bloodied back—nothing. So I brought the heat up in my cuff and pressed it to his upper right arm. Focused on his target, he didn't immediately realize his skin was singeing. When he turned his head to me and gasped, I pulled my wrist away.

He let Francisco slip to the ground. "I knew you burned me in Sevilla. I knew it, and I let you convince me I'd done it to myself!"

"I'll explain everything later. Right now, you've got to get Gabriel and Gracia out of here. Where the devil is she?"

"That boy took her, the scribe."

"Hernando?"

"Yes. He told her he'd take her somewhere safe."

"You must find out where they went." I led him away from Francisco, who crumpled into a ball on the floor.

We crossed the chamber to where Gabriel remained stunned and immobile, almost in a trance. I took a small knife from my belt and cut the cords that bound his wrists.

"You should be able to get out the back," I said to Sergio, hoping they'd not blocked off access to the rear exit and feeling no small amount of fury when I recalled the threshold might still be smeared with his blood. "I'll hold them off. Find Gracia and go to the tower house. I'll meet you there."

"But how can you?"

"Just go!" I ordered.

Without another word, Sergio lifted Gabriel to his feet and led him toward the rear exit.

# Chapter Twenty-Eight
# SOUL CONTAGIONS

I grabbed Francisco by the hair, forced him to his feet, and dragged him out the door. The drone hovered in front of the tower, flashing its exterior lights and pointing its five huge guns on its five separate tails, which it had extended from its stern and aimed at the street. The eight arms stretching from the front and five tailguns curling over the back made the device look like a massive floating scorpion.

The company had regrouped and formed a rudimentary line whilst I'd been inside. Though the drone had offered no more violence after I'd entered the tower, the guards kept up their vain efforts to destroy it. A few men haphazardly fired at will, while others volleyed in a manner similar to a battlefield countermarch, with some loading as others shot at the drone.

Though Ignacio was nowhere to be found, Luis had stayed with his men and even taken up a weapon. He was no military man; while all his troops stood and pressed their gunstocks to the ground as they loaded, he sat on his knees with the barrel of his weapon between his thighs, struggling with the ramrod. Still, he must have had some hunting or sport-shooting experience, for despite being unpracticed, he knew what to do. When he saw me exit the tower with Francisco, he screamed to the men who raised their arquebuses and crossbows at the drone.

"Don't fire at that! Fire at her!" He pointed at me.

The drone floated above me now, and its shield expanded over me as soon as it heard these words. I released Francisco and descended the single stair from the tower threshold. Holding my right hand in front of me to ensure there could be no mistake that I was the one in control now, I locked eyes with Luis and walked straight into the volley. Both bolt and bullet bounced off the shield around me, so ineffective they barely caused a ripple in the clear, lavender light that demarked my area of protection.

I opened my mouth to speak, but the second round of the volley cut me off. A surge of rage coursed through me, so I had the drone give them a sampling of its own volley. Its tailguns erupted, firing round after round into the street behind the company. For an instant, I wondered why it was not slaughtering them, but then I remembered I'd directed it not to kill unless I expressly ordered it. Just then, I was sorely tempted to give such an order.

Why should I restrain myself toward them when they'd shown me no such courtesy? Why couldn't I hound them halfway across the peninsula and kidnap them or torture and murder their loved ones?

I stood before the soldiers, shrouded in my shield, and watched the projectiles from the drone's guns rip up the street, sending huge chunks of cobblestone flying into the air and raining back down on the men, who'd all abandoned their attempts to reload. Instead, they curled on their knees with their arms shielding their heads, some praying, some shrieking in terror, and some simply waiting for the end. For a split second, I prepared to tilt the guns downward at them. Then, I realized the reason I should not: I didn't want to.

I remembered the day in the training chamber when Jhasali had compelled me to shoot my fake prisoner. She'd made me look him in the eye and fire right into his face while he begged for mercy. That had been the virtual me, and I would not allow her or these men to make it the real me. I'd already spent so much time wondering what had become of the wives and children of the men I'd slain out of necessity. I'd not spend eternity wondering the same thing about the families of the men I'd slain out of wrath.

On the other hand, though I had decided to offer these men my mercy, I would temper it with conditions. Just as I had offered my forgiveness to Sergio on the condition he change his ways, I would offer my compassion to this regiment on the condition of their surrender and a radical change in their attitude. I would take no vow of pacifism, for in the end, my renouncement of violence could prove deadlier than my use of it. I had chosen to do grander things than simply saving myself and my friends. I'd done that already, and if it were my only goal, I could mount the drone now and fly off into the darkness. But I did not desire that; I desired something better.

I allowed the drone to keep tearing up the street behind the company while they continued to shield their heads for dear life. I wanted there to be no question I'd had the opportunity to massacre them a thousand times over and had chosen to spare them instead.

When I ended the barrage, using a hand gesture and a verbal command so the regiment could see my power over the drone, they wrenched their weapons from the rubble and attempted to find their loading equipment among the broken stones.

"Please stop." I whispered the words, but the drone magnified them for me.

Every man on the battlefield dropped his jaw and gazed up at me as though I'd sprouted a peacock head next to my own.

"You think I have any wish to slaughter my own countrymen? I don't. I want you to go home and be husbands to your wives, fathers to your children. I don't blame you for following orders. I blame the man who gave them to you." I shot Luis a malicious glare.

My voice sounded wobbling and unsure, so I took a deep breath. "I have allowed you to live because I wish you to understand you are fit for better things than being slaves of body and thought, taking ever more brutal orders from men who've no more right to rule any of us than a slug crawling in the mud. You are free men with free minds, and you have a right—nay—a responsibility to exercise them rather than to blindly lay them at the feet of authority."

Without hesitating, I exited my shield's protection and strode to the man I guessed to be the leader of the regiment. I took the gun from his fist and cast it to the ground. Grasping his hand, I pulled him from his knees to his feet. Then I made a wide gesture to the rest of them.

"You are not beholden to that invader from the Church who no more cares for his fellow man than he does a rat, but you are not beholden to me either. If you continue to resist, I shall slay you to the last. If you choose to leave now, I will offer no reprisal. Yet I ask you to stand with me against Ignacio. Stand with me against his abettors who permitted him to set you like dogs on your own people. Do not the thing you've been told. Do the thing you know to be right."

The men threw down their weapons and got to their feet. The vast majority took a last look at the drone, turned tail, and fled. Only a few decided to stay. No matter—I had other business to attend to.

I dragged Francisco from beneath the cart he'd crawled under during my assault. Shoving him to his knees, I demanded one of the remaining soldiers relight his match and pass me his freshly loaded arquebus. Though I still had no intention of slaying the others if they didn't oppose me, some things could not be forgiven.

I brandished the arquebus. "So did you drown Father Manuel or whip him to death?"

Luis leapt toward us, but a couple of his own men prevented him from approaching.

"Please, it was not my fault," Francisco cried. "Ignacio! I warned him not to do it, but he said we had to make the old man talk. I told him he ought to have some reservations about laying his hands on a man of the cloth."

"But if he'd been a merchant or a sailor, it would have been just fine?"

"It was not fine then, either. I sent for Don Luis the moment Ignacio started to disregard protocol. Please, I swear I called Don Luis here to help."

"So am I correct in understanding that when your boss didn't believe the person who denounced me, you called the mad dog up from Toledo to do your dirty work, and when the mad dog got off his leash, you called your boss to come and catch him?"

Francisco sputtered like a broken mill wheel but didn't offer anything that resembled speech. He kept staring at the drone as it loomed behind me, hovering over my head.

My impatience amplified. "Don't look at that. Look me in the eye, and . . ." I paused for effect. "Tell the truth."

"It was an accident! I tell you, we only showed that priest how we use the water. We weren't actually going to do it. We didn't even touch him. He fell and started convulsing, and then he just died. It wasn't my fault. I told Ignacio not to threaten him with the water when he knew we mustn't use it."

"Water *torture*, you mean," I corrected him, irked by his refusal to admit what exactly they'd been doing. "And you're telling me the sole reason you didn't manage to torment a frail old man was because you frightened him to death before you got the chance?"

Francisco fell back to stuttering and mumbled something about it being the old man's own fault. Wrong answer. I backhanded him across the cheek with all my might. Blood poured from his mouth, and he spat out a few pieces of molar.

I understood why he'd not been able to maintain control over the mad dog. Men of Ignacio's disposition are difficult to confront or contradict. Ignacio's hate was strong and Francisco's will weak, and the former's force of personality had overridden the latter's protestations. None of that excused Francisco's utter dereliction of the basest of his duties.

"You didn't need to wait until your superior arrived," I snapped. "If you were all that concerned about Ignacio's behavior, then why didn't you *do something*? You were in your jurisdiction with your men. Because of your spinelessness, Father Manuel is dead!"

"Please, have mercy," Francisco begged.

"Did my husband ask the same thing of you while you filleted him like a fish, or was he too proud? I suppose it doesn't matter if Father Manuel did, does it?"

"I swear to Christ, we only intended to frighten him."

I fired the arquebus into the ground not a hair's breadth from Francisco's ear and then said that was only supposed to frighten him, but he didn't hear me. As soon as I squeezed the trigger, he fainted. I rolled my eyes and thought I might have seen Luis do the same.

I turned to the inquisitor on the verge of speaking when I caught movement out of the corner of my eye. Two of the soldiers who'd run away earlier had returned, dragging someone who struggled and cursed them both. I burst into laughter when I realized it was Ignacio. Apparently, these men had listened to my speech.

"Wherever did you find him?" I exclaimed once they'd shoved him to his knees next to Francisco's limp form.

"Hiding in the courthouse," one of the men answered.

I didn't reply. I'd forgotten everyone else in the world except Ignacio.

"Why?" I breathed so that only he could hear.

"Because I predicted something like this would happen. You don't think I anticipated the danger you infidels pose to the natural order?" Ignacio spat.

"The natural order! If not for you, I'd never have met the woman who gave me command of that thing." I motioned to the drone. "If you'd left me in peace when I was a girl, none of this would've happened."

"How could I let you be? I had to protect the real believers."

"From what? Me wrenching the innocent from the flames of your fires?"

"From that!" He pointed down the street toward the column of smoke that still rose from the burning rubble of the church.

I shrugged. "You started a war. Did you expect no casualties?"

"I am but a foot soldier in the holiest of wars. For my service, I shall be a martyr, like all the other persecuted believers who preceded me." He made the Sign of the Cross.

"You think I'm going to kill you? No. I'm going to force you to watch me disassemble everything you've propped up with your violence. Then I'll ensure you get proper retribution for your crimes. There are many whose blood demands justice."

"The only justice you'll ever dispense is that of the Whore of Babylon with her seven-headed beast."

"You can call me a whore all you like. It won't change a jot about the predicament in which you currently find yourself." I chuckled.

"If it's my only consolation, at least I seized that unrepentant heretic who should have dashed your infant head on the rocks and helped him find his place in Hell!"

I saw red. My hold over myself was already quite tenuous, and his words erased what little self-possession remained to me. I plowed my fist into his face so hard it sent his head flying backward. I only meant to hit him once, but the feeling of his skull cracking against my knuckles and the scent of the blood pouring from his nose goaded me on. I soon found myself striking him over and over. I tackled him to the ground, straddling his chest and pinning his arms with my thighs. Everyone around us looked on, but they did not dare move to stop me.

I don't remember much about the next few minutes except they weren't my proudest. Even now, centuries later, they are almost a complete blank from the moment Ignacio opened his filthy mouth to the moment I shut it up for good. I mostly recall flashes of pounding his face. At first, he attempted to resist, but after a few blows, he went still. Next I knew, I was on my feet, looking down at my boots as they stomped on a bloody, crushed mess of fractured skull and pulverized brain. It took me a second to realize this was all that remained of his head.

I hadn't intended to kill him—at least not that way, like a raging bull who'd cast down his torero. I'd planned to make it more official, to hold a legitimate public trial in an actual court and execute him for the murder of Father Manuel and the attempted murder of Sergio, among all his other crimes. I'd wanted his living victims to see him punished for what he'd done to them and their families. I'd wanted all the Saúls and Míriams of Toledo to have the privilege of speaking against him. So much for that.

As I stared down at the remains of my adversary, a wave of nausea broke over me. Pieces of his skull and brain had been fractured from the whole and now lay oozing into the dirt, and his face was battered beyond recognition. I almost couldn't believe that, not a second ago, I had been the cause of this.

For an instant, I feared that in his passion for misery and cruelty, Ignacio had passed to me whatever contagion infected his own soul. Never had I reveled in any act of violence. Yet on this night, for the first time, I'd taken pleasure in killing a man and felt no shame afterward. In my rage and my grief, had I allowed my enemy to make of me the thing he was himself?

All the men gaped at me. My lip quivered, yet I held my tears at bay. I tried to find words to express what I felt, but I could not. It was not sorrow or shame or pity. It was something else, something undefinable.

I stuttered, "I shouldn't have. I shouldn't—"

"I suppose it's true what a man sows, he also reaps," Luis muttered.

"Couldn't the same be said about you?" I asked without looking up from Ignacio's lifeless form. Luis went silent.

Gazing upon my latest handiwork, I felt furious with myself for giving Ignacio what he'd wanted. He had wished to be a martyr, and now he was. I hadn't meant to allow myself to be manipulated into stooping to the level of my persecutors. But damn me; I'd done exactly that.

At the same time, my knee-jerk regret over killing the inquisitor was morphing into a realization that I owed no apology for being the only one on the planet willing to impose any real penalty upon him for his crimes. None of the men who surrounded me had done a thing besides obey his orders without a single word of protest. Among all these sheep, I was the she-wolf who'd opposed him, and now, he'd never torture or murder again.

Wiping Ignacio's blood off my hands onto my already-filthy shirt, I shook off my residual anger before I turned to his accomplice.

"Can I call you Luis?" I said.

At this, several of his men stepped between him and me. I opened my mouth, but to my great displeasure, one of them cut across me.

"Doña, you promised not to harm anyone else." The man glanced at Ignacio's body.

"What I actually said was I didn't wish to slaughter my countrymen. My guardian's murderer does not fall into that category. Would you let a man live after he'd killed a member of your family?" I asked the soldier.

"No," he admitted.

"Then don't tell me I should do as you would not even do yourself." I gestured to Luis. "I only wish to speak with him."

The man looked first at me and then at the drone. He and his comrades moved out of my way, giving Luis a piteous look that said "You're on your own."

I smiled at the inquisitor. "Don't be afraid, caballero. We don't have any personal problems, do we? Besides, I'm sure you're so pious that if I were to kill you, you'd be knocking down San Pedro's door. Right?"

He didn't reply, so I went on. "Considering your line of work, it appears you need to hire people with a stronger constitution." I tilted my head toward Francisco, who still lay unconscious on the ground. "Or is he fine as long as the person being 'just frightened' is someone besides himself?"

"If you expect me to die begging like a whipped cur, you'll be sorely disappointed!" Luis shouted.

"I'd be much more disappointed if you did beg, but I don't intend to kill you."

Admittedly, I'd just said something similar to Ignacio, but this one was different. This one I could work with; all he needed was a little retraining.

I dropped my eyes to the bloody corpse at my feet. "Why is it you let him come here? Why did you let him do this to us?"

Luis was fearful, but if I did not know better, I'd have thought him repentant too. He told me that somehow Ignacio had come to suspect me of being the

Witch of Toledo from his investigations in his own jurisdiction. Privately, I cursed myself for going to the cathedral and asking about my family, for Ignacio must've discovered my parents' old confessor.

Luis said Ignacio had written to him several weeks after his visitations across the district had concluded, demanding he arrest and send forth the ward of a certain parish priest called Manuel Romero. Luis had ignored the letter, but he'd mentioned it in passing to the man who'd served for so long as his delegate.

He hadn't realized Francisco had responded to Ignacio, nor had he known when Ignacio had sent men in secret to search for me. He'd only found out about all this two or three weeks ago, when Ignacio had shown up in person, insisting he be allowed to arrest me himself. Luis swore he had refused and told Ignacio to return to his own district, though whether I believed this, I was unsure. Luis was a more prudent man than Ignacio, but he was also motivated to shift as much blame as possible off himself.

"I didn't want to allow that man to investigate in my jurisdiction," Luis continued. "But he kept insisting, and then he had his men spread rumors that I knew where the Witch of Toledo was hiding and refused to arrest her. I feared if I expelled him from my jurisdiction, he'd stir up a panic. I thought if I permitted him to conduct a supervised investigation for a few days, he'd find nothing and go home."

I put my fist to my chin. "What I don't understand is why you sent your little fool to accompany him in your stead."

"Perhaps I put too much faith in my subordinates," he replied.

"That, or you were too focused on your winter weight."

A look of surprise passed over Luis's face. I was certain he remembered exactly where I'd heard him say that, and I wondered if he realized now the peril he'd been in then and counted himself lucky to have spared the parish priest who'd silenced his congregants. If he did, he did not acknowledge it, choosing instead to continue with his explanation.

"I gave the pair of them clear instructions to do nothing but investigate. I never dreamed Ignacio would do as he did, nor that Francisco would allow it."

"Speaking of what they did, where is Father Manuel's body?" I asked.

"The third floor of the tower. But listen, I just arrived a few hours ago. He's been there a day or two. I don't believe you should—"

"Thank you. I'll be deciding what I do with his body, no matter what state it's in," I snapped, hearing in my speech a note of tears welling dangerously close to the surface.

They'd killed Father Manuel all that time ago and left him to rot? I stayed silent, afraid saying more might betray how close I was to weeping, and turned to go into the tower. Before I could take one step, the sound of artillery fire resonated from the harbor and a cannonball made a direct hit on the drone still hovering above me.

"No!" I cried, but I needn't have bothered.

The ball bounced off the drone's shields and fell with a deep thud into the rubble of the shredded street. The drone, however, did not take the assault lightly. It sent a blaze of retaliatory fire toward the ship that had shot at it, blowing a massive hole in the hull and setting the deck ablaze. The shouts of men echoed from the harbor as they tried to either fight the fire or leap from the sinking wreckage into the sea.

"What did you do that for?" I shrieked aloud to the drone.

*Primary directive: protect the master*, it replied in my head.

*Not like that*, I answered, but I worried it wouldn't understand. I was not sure how I could explain to it that our foes were also my countrymen and I wished to have a care for how we treated them, even as we defended ourselves against them.

I turned and sprinted to the waterfront, the drone hovering overhead and the men tailing just behind.

"We have to fix this! You have to undo it," I spat when we arrived at the blazing harbor. "This is not your directive, understand? This will never be your directive. Now, put the fire out."

The drone rose high above us and flew over the harbor, sending the men on the ships and the docks scurrying in all directions. When it arrived over unobstructed water, the drone tilted itself downward and revved its front and rear engines. The front it used to keep itself immobile, and the back it used to create a mighty wind that blew torrents of water out of the estuary and onto the deck of the burning ship, raining sheet upon sheet down on the vessel it had set alight as well as a few smaller ones to which the fire had spread.

Soon, a great wall of sea spray had formed behind the fire, pouring down from above, growing ever higher as the drone continued to sink toward the surface while it blasted its engines. Everyone stopped battling the flames to watch. The display was spectacular, this twenty-meter-tall black curtain of rain rising from the estuary, illuminated only by the drone's lights and the blazing glow of the flames it was now extinguishing.

To my not-so-distant rear, some of the soldiers argued amongst themselves, and I tilted my head so I might pick up what they said above the din of falling water.

"I tell you, it's a culebre she's tamed and trained," one said.

"No. Can't you see? It's a giant cannon she's enchanted to fly," replied another.

I turned and motioned to the second man. "He is closer to right, but there is no enchantment involved. This thing is just a very advanced machine."

"How is that possible?" they asked.

As usual, I had no words. How was I supposed to explain I had befriended an extraterrestrial refugee seeking asylum in the mountains, and she had converted me into a living, breathing computer whose every cell was fused with elemental metals from deep space and whose mind had been added to a network that allowed her to telepathically control these artificially intelligent beings now at her command?

I bit my lip as I recalled that every single word I would need to explain how this machine was capable of thought had no equivalent in any language on Earth. These men would not understand tonight. I'd have to create my own damned university to make them comprehend.

I drew in a deep breath. "I will need a more conducive environment to explain how it works. All I can say now is that this thing is a device just like a grain mill or a clock or a printing press, only it can think and learn as we can. It is not living or conscious, nor is it inanimate or insensate."

"Where did you get it?" Luis chimed in.

"As if I would tell you that," I snapped.

His question made me uncomfortable not only because he had no right to pose it or any other, considering what he had permitted to occur under his very nose, but also because it made me recall the person from whom I had gotten the drone. Jhasali lurked not so far off, sitting on a cache of weapons that could destroy mine in a second.

I hoped I might get the chance to beg her forgiveness before she discovered my latest act of defiance. In my naïvety, I believed since I'd already revealed her devices to so many humans, I might convince her to help me with my fledgling plans to initiate a new era of peace and parity. She had failed to right the wrongs of her world, but maybe she still had the instinct. Perhaps she'd be willing to serve as a partner in my efforts to right my own people's wrongs.

Even if Jhasali wouldn't help me herself, she might allow me the freedom to do as I would with her weapons. I had taken over this entire town with a tiny drone in less than half an hour. What might I do if she allowed me the use of Homeship? There would never be another María González ever again!

Still, I needed to be the one to inform her of our new circumstances. If she found out on her own, she would become furious before she could hear an explanation. My new drone would not betray that I had called it, for it was now loyal to me and not her, but I couldn't prevent her from walking past a window and realizing it was gone, nor could I keep one of the other drones from alerting her to its absence. If that happened . . .

I heard Luis's voice from far off, saying something about how it was imperative the men not be deceived into believing this strange entity was anything other than a demon beast. I bit my tongue and ordered the drone, which had at this point finished dousing the harbor, to lower itself to my level and face me. The men scattered, fleeing a short distance before turning to see what it might do.

The device sank so low its hull nearly touched the ground, the airflow from its exhaust vents sending the tiny stones on the dock rolling away from its undercarriage. Leaning forward, I embraced myself with all eight of my new arms and pressed my brow against my hull. I could feel the rapid shuddering of my engine against my skull. The sensation of having my bones gently vibrated was rather pleasant. I closed my eyes and studied the men using the drone's vision. They were calming as I demonstrated the docility this frightening creature could exhibit if I so chose.

After a short while, I lifted my head and faced the men. "You think this is a deception? Come then, those of you who will, and touch my 'demon beast.'"

Most of the soldiers stayed right where they stood, but a couple crept toward the drone until they'd come within a pace of where it hovered. Neither of them moved. They did not even blink as they stared at its shining dark-gray surface. The crowd at the dock held its collective breath. Finally, one of the men stretched out his hand and placed it on my hull.

He let out a nervous chuckle. "It's metal."

"I told you it's not alive. And it's perfectly docile if you don't force it to defend me. Come, all of you." I beckoned the rest of them.

Several more approached the drone now that the first of them had touched it and lived—including Luis. He advanced slowly, not daring to get within arm's length, even though several of the men were now pulling on the drone's limbs and gazing at its undercarriage and through the glass into its cockpit. Luis seemed to think it might behave differently toward him, and he had reason to believe so: neither he nor I had forgotten his ultimate culpability for Ignacio's sins. Yet he underestimated the nature of my own spirit. He didn't understand I was much more willing to pardon ignorance than malice.

I reached toward him, motioning for him to touch the drone. He stepped forward and closed his eyes. Unclenching his fist, he raised his hand without opening his lids until his fingers brushed the cool, smooth surface.

"Now do you believe me?" I asked.

"It feels like a giant suit of armor," he said, more to himself than me.

He opened his eyes, and I could see the wheels turning in his head as he stood with his hand on the drone, but he couldn't let go of the idea of devilry. He told me he did not believe me and insisted this had to be some sort of trick. I sighed, trying not to become frustrated. After all, I had been as he was.

I breathed deep. "Does that look like flesh and blood to you? If you'd believe your own damned eyes instead of clinging to your presumptions, we'd all be better off."

Luis shook his head, so I told him I remembered that he hadn't accepted I was a witch until Ignacio had offered him proof, and I was prepared to do the same to prove I was not one. I didn't expect him to take my word for it, but I needed a few days to figure out how I might go about things.

I recalled Jhasali had made a believer of me when she'd shown me Homeship, but she'd been a much more adept teacher than I judged myself to be. Now that I considered it, I wondered if I had ever truly believed these things were unmagical until I'd taken them into my body and downloaded all the words and information pertaining to them.

Of course, I couldn't give nanos to the entirety of the human species. Not only was I in enough trouble with Jhasali as it stood, but I was not so foolish as to know no better on my own. If I were to implant these people in their current state of mind, they'd just go crusading with extraterrestrial weapons instead of earthly ones. Yet it was going to be so much harder to explain everything the old-fashioned way. All this was so complicated it'd be easier for them to believe my drone was a beast from the abyss than to learn what it actually was.

Luis derailed my train of thought. "I do believe my eyes. They tell me if you're not a sorceress, you must be a genuine succubus." He fiddled with the crucifix around his neck.

"I am so sick of everyone accusing me of devilry." Reaching up to break the chain of his necklace, I shook the crucifix in his face. "And this! You don't get to shove this down one more throat. Not one more!"

I threw the necklace away. Luis protested, but I interrupted before he could chase after it. "I'm going to let you get it later, but for yourself only. Do you understand? No one else."

I was unsure if he did understand. Yet I wanted him—all of them—to see that my demon beasts and I would burn the world as it existed. I had burned myself to save strangers; I had burned the tower to save my husband; now, I would burn the planet to save my species. Mine would not be a literal fire to save the soul by searing the flesh but a figurative fire to save the collective soul of my people from its own ruthless violence and its own apocalyptic hate. I would usher in an age of peace that would be matched by no other, and when I was through with it, this planet would be unrecognizable to those who now occupied it.

I knew when I made my intentions known, I'd be telling these men I meant to do exactly as they'd feared, but I wished them to understand my plans were not to be dreaded but welcomed. How could my brothers be degraded by their sisters' elevation? What would the Christian lose if all humanity had the freedom to choose their own gods—or none at all? Who wouldn't benefit from the suppression of endless bloodshed?

In hindsight, of course, I realize I was deluded, my understanding of the world and its people incomplete and immature. Even if I hadn't had to worry about Jhasali, I could never have erased my species' impulse toward violence, nor could I have brought about peace through force. Yet, at the time, I wished with all my heart for nothing more than to douse the fires of persecution once and for all, and I honestly believed I could.

I waited while the soldiers continued to examine the drone. They'd become almost jovial, grabbing at its sensory organs and even dragging their daggers along its sides to prove to each other the blades couldn't scratch it. The drone endured their analyses with saintly patience. After all, we both knew they couldn't hurt it.

I switched perspectives once more, watching out of the drone's eyes. As I scanned the crowd of men that surrounded us, one in particular caught my attention, a tall one with a head of curly hair. Sergio stood alone on the rise above the shoreline, his arms crossed, his mouth agape, and his gaze not on the device or the soldiers but on me.

"Shit," I whispered.

I should've known he'd never sit on his hands in the tower house. I had hoped to explain the situation before he saw me commanding the same sort of flying beast that had held him hostage in Jhasali's vessel, but that ship was well beyond the horizon now. Running my hands over my hair, I headed away from the docks to join my husband.

The drone didn't let me. Out of nowhere, it revved its engines and spread its arms around me, terrifying the soldiers as it wrapped me in its powerful embrace while I struggled and protested. It whisked me into its cockpit. The men all ran. Before I could react, the pair of us hurled away from the harbor and along the coast, speeding over the ocean.

*What the devil are you doing?* I thought.

*Fulfilling primary objective*, it replied.

As soon as I'd gathered my wits enough to wonder what that was supposed to mean, a huge explosion detonated over the top of my head. The drone dove down first and then took me up away from the sea, soaring toward the rocky outcroppings that dotted the coastline.

I needed no further explanation. Jhasali had come to undo the mistake she'd made in creating her hybrid. A quick backward glance confirmed this suspicion, and I told the drone to wheel around and return fire without making contact. I didn't wish to harm her, only to show her I'd fight back. If I could escape her for long enough, it'd give her time to cool off and come to her senses.

When I shot at her, however, she became all the more enraged. Pushing a row of fat, oval tubes from both sides of her drone's hull, she slowed almost to a stop, turned her broadside to me, and sat there for a split second. Her pod vibrated violently, and I feared I'd damaged it—perhaps I'd fired closer than I'd thought. Though my own drone warned me we must go, I forbade it to move. I should have let it flee, but I remained to watch, prepared to help Jhasali should she need it.

In an instant, a concussive discharge burst from her drone and slammed into mine, sending it reeling backward, tumbling over and over itself as I fell from the ceiling to the floor to the ceiling to the floor again. Only when we came to a midair stop did I understand this blast had been to disable the shields protecting my craft.

With the shields down, Jhasali loosed an almighty volley, blowing apart my device, which, as a last act of protection, ejected me from its vicinity before exploding. I hurled toward the rocky outcroppings far below, hitting the ground hard enough to hurt even my hybridized body. I cried out as I rolled down the slanting stones, coming to a stop only when I hit the water.

When I managed to climb out of the sea, Jhasali's drone—one of the multipassenger transports—roared down, hovering a few centimeters above the seawater in front of me as I knelt on a rock. She popped the top and stood from her seat.

"How could you betray me like this?" she thundered, the drone magnifying her voice. She looked half-mad, her hair flying about her, her face contorted with fury.

"I know I shouldn't have. But I had no choice. They were going to drag me back to Toledo. They killed Father Manuel!" I shouted.

"What of me? Do you care so little for me that you would be this indifferent to the danger in which you've placed me?"

"Of course I care for you, and I haven't placed you in danger. These men won't harm us. They were starting to listen to me."

"The danger is not from them! If you truly loved me, you wouldn't have done as you did for any reason."

I shook my fist at her. "Kill me then and be done with it."

She stood in the cockpit, shaking her head for what felt like an eternity. Finally, she let out a scream of rage. "Damn me! I cannot."

I got to my feet, thankful for the temporary reprieve but unsure how certain my salvation was. I took a tentative step forward and held my hands up in supplication. "I'm sorry. I didn't mean to take the drone. It just came."

"I have to go. I cannot delay."

"What do you mean?"

"Large munitions have been deployed, and multiple passenger pods were jettisoned from the perimeter—yours without any perimeter of its own. There are too many signatures around this planet. If they're detected, they'll be traced." She threw herself into the captain's seat.

"You cannot go," I screamed.

"No, Micaela. You have brought this on yourself. I must get off Earth before someone finds me."

Before I could utter one more word, she sealed the pod and took off, leaving me alone on the freezing, soaking sea rocks.

# Chapter Twenty-Nine

# THE ASCENSION

I knew nothing except I must somehow get to Homeship before Jhasali abandoned the planet. With my pod destroyed, I had no means of transportation other than my own pitiful feet. I wished I could call my small drone, but it was clear by now that Jhasali had disabled it manually.

I took off in the direction of town, unaffected by the cold or the seawater that soaked me to the bone. I whistled for Pepito, more out of habit than anything else. To my shock, when I came closer to the edge of the city, he appeared. Either he'd let himself out of whatever stall he'd been locked in, or else our captors had turned him loose when the drone had begun its attack.

It took us a few hours to get up the steep pitch-dark trails to Homeship. When we arrived, I found Jhasali stark naked and transformed into the four-armed, tentacled demon I'd seen in the training chamber. She sprinted around the yard, her gaze darting this way and that as she silently directed the final preparations for takeoff.

"Why did you change?" I said, shuddering at the sight of her.

"Because I detested that awful body, and if I'm not staying here, I'm not obliged to remain caged in it like an animal," she snapped.

"But you mustn't go!"

She wheeled around. "This is your fault. If you didn't wish me to leave, you should not have removed my device from the security perimeter or deployed its weapons."

I tried to catch her arm as she turned her back on me. "No! You can't leave."

"Micaela, stay or go. I am departing right now either way." She jerked away.

"No! Don't go. If you abandon me now, I have nothing."

"You should have thought of that before you stole my drone."

"I didn't steal it. I was fused to it from before. I'm sorry."

She rounded on me again. "That's all anything ever is with you, isn't it? Sorry! You're sorry you stole my pod. You were sorry when you brought your miserable mate into our home. You were sorry when you burned yourself."

"I *am* sorry."

"It's too late for that. Make your choice now; I have just changed the security perimeter from stationary to flight mode."

"Don't." I reached for her arm once more, seizing her wrist this time and trying to tug her back from the ship's gangplank.

She made to shove me away, but something strange was happening. As soon as she said she'd put the perimeter in flight mode, the armed drones extended their weapons for battle.

Jhasali seemed to know something I did not, for she looked up and said, "Oh no."

At that, some invisible force wrenched her from my grasp and caught her up in the air. One of her drones rocketed to where she flew upward. She took hold of its arms with all four of her hands and pulled herself toward it, as if she were trying to help it win some awful game of tug-of-war in which her body served as the rope.

While this midair struggle transpired, all the armed drones started firing at some invisible enemy in the sky, causing Pepito to bolt into the wilderness. This enemy returned fire, using a concussive blast to disable the transport devices' shields before it began picking them off one by one. Homeship's external lights blazed into the night, and I noted with great apprehension it appeared to be preparing to take off. Would it leave without us? Or did Jhasali plan to pilot it remotely so it could provide a buffer against this new adversary?

With a massive lurch, the drone holding Jhasali jerked her to the side and tossed her to the ground, freeing her from whatever force had hold of her. It then turned its guns on the forest canopy and fired alongside its compatriots, but the fire it received in return came from the side. Our assailants—whoever they were—were on the ground now. Many unfamiliar drones burst through the trees, attempting to get past the barrage of fire from our own devices.

I remained stuck in shock, squatting at the base of a big tree farther away from the ship. Covering my ears to block out the noise, I screamed so loud I could hear nothing but my own voice, though I could still see Jhasali shrieking and turning on her heels. She waved at me with all her arms. Was she calling my name?

With the blast of a volcanic eruption, Homeship fired, sending a shockwave through the forest, setting a huge portion of the canopy ablaze, and raining down fiery hunks of whatever its target had been. These chunks set the tree trunks alight, and an inferno ignited all around us. Something fired back at Homeship, taking a huge piece out of its roof and damaging the hull badly enough that the rear gun must've been disabled. Whatever hovered above us was capable of penetrating Homeship's armor, but I could not make out anything through the blazing canopy except for a colossal white glow emanating through the cloud cover.

When I looked down again, Jhasali was running straight for me, waving her arms frantically toward the vessel she'd used to pursue me earlier. I realized she meant for us to make our escape in this pod, so I leapt to my feet and dashed toward it. The enemy devices did not let either of us reach it.

Catching Jhasali up in their viselike grip, several drones hauled her, kicking and flailing, to a cylindrical container that floated nearby. It was long and gray on the outside, and it opened by a slit right down the middle, just like a trunk. The inside contained a set of long, curved red bars that resembled a bleeding ribcage. The adversary drones forced Jhasali into the middle of this ribcage as our friendly drones attempted to fight their way to her. I careened toward the container to save her, terrified something awful would happen once she was shut inside.

Before I could get to it, the cage closed around her and the lid slammed down, sealing her within. The battle stopped. Fearing further opposition could bring harm to their captive master, the few drones left on our side ceased all attempts to resist their foes. This allowed the opposing drones to flip Jhasali's container vertically and send it shooting toward the sky.

I watched the tube fall upward as though the world had been turned upside down just for Jhasali. The reverse gravity yanked her out of sight behind the clouds in a matter of seconds. I fell on all fours, trapped in the grip of terrestrial gravity and without a clue as to where our enemies were taking her. Desperate, I began trying to bond with the large pod myself, but a buzzing engine thundered up behind me before I got the chance to see if its identifier was available.

The enemy drones surrounded me and lifted me in their arms, thrusting me toward a container just like the one that took Jhasali. IDOS still functioned, so I fired round after round at them, punching and kicking between shots. Jhasali's remaining drones took up the fight again, this time to free me, but our resistance didn't stop these foreign drones from shoving me into the ribs of the cylinder and sealing me inside. The ribs altered their shape to form a tight cage around me, pinning my arms to my sides and holding my head and body immobile.

Even considering all that had happened to me before, this moment was still one of the worst of my life. I was suffocating in a high-tech sarcophagus, buried alive in a tomb in the clouds. My tears ran down my face, but I couldn't even raise my hand to wipe them away. No matter how rapidly I breathed, the air felt bereft of oxygen. The walls of my prison closed tighter and tighter, crushing me with their cushioned restraints. I could not bear this slow asphyxiation—every second was an eternity.

Immobilized and deprived of sensory information, I could do nothing but wallow in my futile panic, all the while imagining what sorts of awful torments and terrors awaited me. I'd never done anything to offend these beings—except I was a hybrid who'd stolen their technology and taken it into herself. Worse still, I was Jhasali's hybrid, elevated to her status as a biomechanical being by associating with her even though she was a fugitive and an outlaw. I hoped at least our new captors wouldn't think Sergio or the others had anything to do with this.

Sergio! Last I saw, he was standing in the open before a horde of Luis's soldiers. I'd thought I would be able to keep him safe while I finished establishing my new authority. Now, in my absence, Luis and his men would retake possession of Santa Colomba. I could only hope Sergio would have the wherewithal to flee when I did not return. Surely he would. He and Armando were already prepared to flee something. Why else would they have all that secret money stashed in holes in the wall?

My heart thumped savagely as I sat in the dark, unable to move, unable to see or hear, unable to stop pondering what awaited me upon the opening of that lid or what might already be happening to my friends on Earth. I knew further panic would only make it worse, so I lay still and tried to master my own breathing.

When I'd managed to calm down, I discovered I could feel the vibrations within the shell that surrounded me. If I listened hard, I could make out certain sounds as they floated in through the coffin's ventilation system. The feeling of being dragged ever upward had ceased, and I now heard faint, far-off noises of humming drones and maybe the whir of a vast engine.

Holding my breath to quiet its noise, I tried to ascertain my location. My own container no longer moved, for certain, but had it come to a stop on something that was moving? I couldn't tell if the vibrating and whirring meant I'd been deposited on a massive ship or if I was letting my imagination get the better of me. I didn't have any way of knowing if enough time had even passed for my casket prison to reach a starship. I might've been in here for an hour or two. Although, for all I knew, it could've been days.

Without warning, my container lurched sideways. The vents brought to my ears the distant but unmistakable noises of battle. From far away, the sound of plasma cannons rent the air with the crackling of their projectiles and the roar of their firing mechanisms. Many people shouted in Sartjyanan, but the words were indistinct, drowned in the booming gunfire that shook the very walls of my prison.

I struggled with all my might, trying to break the ribs that bound me. Writhing against the cage, which followed my movements and remolded itself every time I changed position, I managed to wriggle my arms free to the elbow. I pushed as hard as I could against the coffin lid, but it did not budge. I continued squirming, trying to free my arms entirely or, better yet, my legs, but all my efforts proved fruitless.

The quaking and thundering continued unabated for a long time, interrupted now and again by the shouts of living beings as they participated in whatever skirmish had erupted outside my prison. I couldn't imagine what might be happening. Hopefully, Jhasali had somehow escaped this horrid ribbed casket and now battled with our captors. I was certain she was still furious with me. Would she take me with her or leave me behind if she managed to flee?

While I strained to listen for the sound of her voice, the echoes of gunfire ended as abruptly as they'd begun, and the quaking and shouting stopped. I lay still an even longer time in the silence than I had in the noise of battle, trying to ask my sensors what could be going on, but they knew as little as I did. The only information I could gather would have to come through my ears, but the apparent end of the battle had left a sound vacuum that was not readily filled. I knew nothing and could do nothing but sit tight.

I waited for what seemed an eternity, pricking my ears until they caught the sound of voices. Unlike during the battle, these voices were calm and collected. They were also moving ever closer to me. None of them belonged to Jhasali, but the nearest voice called her name several times. I held my breath, afraid to respond to whoever now stood outside my tiny prison.

"I'm not sure what's in here," the voice said. "Could be nothing. You go back to the upper level and keep searching. This container hasn't been put into an external lock yet, so it shouldn't take long to open. I'll join you after."

Upon hearing this, I stiffened and brought the heat up in my cuffs. When the lid of my coffin popped open, I was ready. I fired at the blue Sartjyanan staring down at me, missing it by a hair because the sudden inundation of white light blinded me. I took aim once more and screamed Jhasali's name at the top of my lungs, but before I could get another shot off, a drone clamped some sort of neutralizer on each of my arms. It then yanked me all the way out of the container and tossed me at its master's feet.

The blue being cocked its head, eyeing me quizzically. "*You* are looking for Jhasali too?"

"I am," I stammered in Sartjyanan. "Who are you? What do you—"

The creature didn't answer. Instead, it wound a clawed hand around my upper arm and jerked me off the floor, steering me down the hallway.

This new Sartjyanan had told its companion to keep searching the ship, which led me to believe neither of them belonged here. Yet the stranger guided both me and its drones as if it knew where to go, keeping a firm grasp on my arm as it dragged me along. We got onto a flat drone repurposed as a makeshift elevation platform and ascended many floors through the empty shaft. Nearer the top of the vessel, we walked through a darker corridor until we came to a large chamber at the end of the hall. This room's door had been blasted open, and it housed a number of freestanding vaults obviously made to serve as containers for the ribbed coffins.

Another Sartjyanan who looked just like my captor—only it was pastel green instead of faded blue—already stood in the room, staring at the long gray cases.

"This thing was in the container below, not Jhasali," my captor said.

"No matter. I think I've got the commander," the green one replied.

My captor tugged my arm and yanked me forward, asking its comrade, "Jhasali's in one of these?"

"I believe so."

My heart pounded wildly as I wondered what these people would do to us once they extricated Jhasali from the container, but I dared not ask them their business with her.

The green being went to each of the huge sarcophagi in turn, looking at a small screen on every device until it came to the one in the dead center. There, it stopped and tapped on the shell with its claws.

"Jhasali?" Its voice broke the eerie silence that had descended upon the ship after the firefight, and a muffled response came from inside the container.

"Jhasali's in there?" I gasped, unable to contain myself any longer.

When I started to struggle, my captor shook me and told me to be still. I did not comply, though this made precious little difference. I wasn't nearly strong enough to loosen its grip.

"Don't worry. We'll get you out," the green one said to the gray vault.

The ship was not at all inclined to obey its apparent hijackers, but it seemed to have little mechanism with which to expel them—not when they had already broken inside and defeated its crew and drones. That did not mean it gave them an easy time of it. It took the green being and its accompanying devices a long while of intense drilling, cutting, and prying to work the vault's shell apart. When it broke in half, the coffin had to be popped open and the ribs forcibly separated before Jhasali could uncurl her arms and fall onto the floor.

At this, I cried out and fought even harder against my indifferent captor, who still held me in that vise of a grip. The green one grasped Jhasali by the hand to help her to her feet. When her eyes fell upon its face, her jaw dropped and she gasped, though she quickly stifled this reflexive reaction. Instead, she laid a hand on her companion's shoulder, squeezing it tight.

"Jhasali!" I squealed, still trying to push my captor off.

She turned her gaze to me. "Micaela? Zaki, let go!"

My captor released me without argument, and I flung myself at Jhasali. She knelt to receive me, entwining my body in her four arms. The two shorter, soft-fingered ones wrapped around my torso, while the longer arms used their clawed hands to cautiously caress my head, the fingers tangling themselves in my hair. She stood up, lifting me with her. I wrapped my arms around her neck, letting my own fingers find their way into her mass of tentacles, and I wound my legs around her waist. In the purity of my relief, I no longer cared she looked like a monster.

"Where is Aenwi?" Jhasali asked.

"We thought it best if Aenwi stayed in a safe place until we found you. No sense in bringing your twin into the open to be used as bait if we were captured," the green one said, staring at me. "What's wrong with it? Why is it leaking from the eyes like that?"

"Vi is crying. What have they done to vir?" Jhasali demanded, using the Sartjyanan pronoun for sentient life rather than the one for unintelligent lifeforms, like her companion had used when referring to me.

"How should we know what they did to it? I found it below. I believed it to be you until I opened the shell," the blue one replied.

Jhasali lifted my head off her shoulder, brushing the hair out of my face. "Are you alright? I was so angry before, but now I'm just glad you're not hurt."

The blue one interrupted before I could respond. "What happened, Jhasali? Why is it this random creature from that forsaken hunk of rock can understand our language and wear our weapons?"

Jhasali squeezed me all the tighter. "I implanted vir."

"I feared something unfortunate would happen if you and Aenwi separated, but I didn't think it'd be this," sighed the green one with an air of resignation.

I positioned my head to the side so I could see them. The green one seemed to have taken the news in stride, but the blue one looked livid. Its face was expressionless, but the slithering mass of tentacles adorning its head writhed and rose to form a lion's mane of twisting serpents.

Jhasali continued. "You must understand. I was alone and trapped, and things just . . . they just happened."

"This is an outrage!" the blue one cried.

"No," Jhasali spat. "Mica is a brand-new species. And vi is mine."

The blue one snapped its jaw shut but did not look any more pleased.

"Micaela, this is U'aosni." Jhasali pointed to the green one. "And this is Zakishti." She motioned to the blue.

I was not sure if I was supposed to embrace them or bow or if they had some other, far more sophisticated form of introductory custom. As it stood, I simply gave each of them a cursory glance and continued to hold tight to Jhasali, trying to recover from my terror.

"This is unacceptable," Zakishti repeated.

U'aosni waved a dismissive hand. "Don't be hyperbolic. Knowing the Tanmorayans, they'll be fascinated by the whole thing."

"What do you mean?" Jhasali asked.

"The Tanmorayans have offered us refuge," U'aosni replied.

Jhasali did not immediately respond. When she did, her tone was somber. "You believe they can be trusted?"

"They have not proven otherwise thus far," Zakishti answered.

"How did you receive this offer?" Jhasali wound one of her tentacles around my wrist.

"Our ship was captured by a patrol vessel from the Tanmorayan Coalition when we stumbled across their borders by mistake. Once they realized who we were, they informed us their government would like to take us in," U'aosni said.

Jhasali remained skeptical. "And there's nothing in it for them?"

U'aosni twisted a tentacle around a claw. "The situation is complicated. We'll have more time to discuss it once we get you settled in."

"How do you know they won't turn us over to the Adoruch as soon as they have us?"

"Why would they help their enemy? They already did have U'aosni and me. They allowed us and the rest of our crew to leave when we said we needed to find you. They even armed us with the vessel we used to defeat your captors," Zakishti said.

Jhasali huffed. "If they wanted to offer me shelter, why wouldn't they find me themselves?"

"Don't be silly," Zakishti answered. "You know they cannot engage in battle with any official vessel. If they'd done what we just did, the Adoruch would call that an act of war. As it stands, I wouldn't think it counts as a Tanmorayan act of war for Sartjyanan agitators to fight Sartjyanan scouts to recover the agitator in chief."

"You couldn't have communicated any of this to me before?" Jhasali asked.

"We tried. None of our transmissions were received. You concealed yourself too well, Jhasali," U'aosni said.

She nodded. "That's right. I forgot that I was so concerned about communications tracing, I defaulted my entire network to reject all transmissions from outside devices. I never thought I might actually need to be located. How did you find me?"

"The Adoruch's scouts found you. Apparently, they detected signatures from one of your devices. We intercepted communications saying they believed they'd discovered your location, so we followed them to this solar system," Zakishti replied.

Jhasali gasped and shouted, "After I was so careful! How could this happen? I kept everything so locked down!"

U'aosni's tentacles curled themselves into several knots, but vis voice was calm. "We believe they detected your jump hoop's signature. It looks like the perimeter glitched and self-repaired at some point, but that was enough to allow indicators of its presence to leak. From what we know, once these scouts eventually traced the source of those indicators, they set a trap for you by destroying the hoop to lure you into the open."

"I knew the hoop's perimeter had malfunctioned some time ago, but it repaired itself so fast I thought there was no way it left a signature," Jhasali whispered.

"Wait a minute." I wiggled free of Jhasali's grasp, leaping to my own two feet. "That means it *was* a trap. And you fell for it, but you blamed me for deploying my own weapon!"

"Why do you allow that thing to speak to you in that manner?" Zakishti said.

I spun around and snapped to both the strangers, "You stay out of this. You don't know anything of it."

The pair of them puffed up their tentacles and bared sharp fangs. Though they could kill me if it pleased them, I was too incensed to be afraid.

Jhasali held up her hands. "Enough, all of you. Clearly, I should have left Earth as soon as the hoop's perimeter glitched. What I don't understand is why these scouts didn't just capture me while I was vulnerable and away from my host planet."

"They likely never detected you in space, not if you kept your transport's perimeter as tight as you kept your ship's. But they were close enough to your host planet that they almost immediately detected the signatures you produced when you deployed your weapons inside its atmosphere. Everyone in the vicinity noticed those," U'aosni said, and Jhasali shot me a filthy look.

Zakishti chimed in. "You must realize they wanted your homeship and all the information it contains. The easiest way to find it was for you to reveal its location. You incited their attack when you changed the primary security perimeter's modes. They already had some clue as to the ship's whereabouts, so the instant of visibility during the protocol switch was enough for them to pinpoint its exact position. Leastways, that's what we've gleaned from the captain."

Jhasali's tentacles bent forward. "You've seized the captain?"

"Of course. Why do you think this ship has not expelled us? The first thing we did when we boarded was kill as much of the crew as it took to subdue the rest and shove the captain in a specimen container to interrogate vir. Good thing, too. Vi seems to be of some importance. That could prove useful," Zakishti said.

"We haven't much time," U'aosni interrupted. "We must get your vessel and leave. Our convoy is waiting for us outside the solar system."

Had I heard that correctly? They'd said "our" convoy awaited "us."

I glared up at Jhasali. "What do they mean 'we' are meeting a convoy?"

"It means *I* at least am returning to some semblance of a civilized society," she replied.

"Vi must come with us too. You know that," U'aosni said.

At these words, panic on a scale I'd never known seized me. Jhasali must've realized this, for before I grasped what was happening, she swept me from the room and bade me wait for her at the other end of the hall. She returned to the chamber but couldn't shut the broken door, so I could hear the others arguing with her even from a distance.

"I don't wish to force vir to leave vis own world. Micaela's is a single-planetary species whose members don't even understand that their central star doesn't revolve around them. Our environment may be more of a shock than vi can handle," Jhasali murmured.

"Then why did you give away our implants?" Zakishti demanded.

"When I landed on that planet, I was all alone, and I reached a point where I couldn't bear the isolation. I felt I might do something foolish, like send a transmission. I didn't plan to transform Mica, but certain things occurred, and it happened almost on its own."

"That's because you always act. You don't think!"

"U'aosni . . ." Jhasali's voice carried a tone of warning.

"I'm sorry, Commander, but I must speak my mind while we're still alone. Our new circumstances are vastly different than they were during the rebellion. In some ways, our situation is more precarious than it's ever been."

"Your new little specimen only complicates things further. No one knows we've located you yet. They're still searching the rest of the vessel. We could kill it and destroy the body—"

"That's enough, Zaki. You will not touch Micaela," Jhasali snapped.

"Zaki, what is the matter with you? You can't just eliminate an integrated biomechanical intelligence because you find vir inconvenient."

"That thing is more than an inconvenience. It's a disgrace. Never before in the history of our civilization has anyone dared to hybridize a member of another species," Zakishti hissed.

"If I remember correctly, the whole point of the revolution was to change the course of our civilization's history," Jhasali huffed.

"Well, it didn't work, did it?" Zakishti snapped.

"No matter. Regardless of how Micaela came into being, now that vi is as we are, the same laws that apply to us should apply to vir. Thus, vi cannot be eliminated without cause," U'aosni said.

"If that's the case, vi should be allowed to decide whether vi wishes to remain on vis home world," Jhasali insisted.

"So the Adoruch's people can capture vir if they conduct a sweep of the planet? There's no way the scouts didn't share this location with the wider network before we got to them."

Jhasali heaved a deep sigh. "You're right."

The three of them whispered for a few more minutes, but I needed to hear no more. I knew I wouldn't be left behind. Initially, I'd felt terror at the suggestion I might leave Earth, but now that it was more than a suggestion, now that the possibility of my return to my planet had been all but eliminated, a strange numbness descended over me.

There was no dirt on this floor, so I stared at the walls instead, noting this ship, like Homeship, was adorned with deep cracks and sparkling crystals. I gazed at these decorations, imagining I'd shrunk to the size of a gnat and crawled inside to live within this artificial geode. The shining crystals would be my shelter, the infinite cracks my new world, and I could explore this deep and winding canyon of gemstones forever.

Jhasali emerged from the room as I glared at the wall decorations, and I asked her flatly if she planned to allow me to be kidnapped. She did not answer. Instead, she had a drone remove the IDOS neutralizers from my wrists. Then she beckoned me into the main passageway leading back to the ascension platform. U'aosni joined us, though Zakishti was nowhere to be found. When Jhasali bade me follow, I fell in line behind the pair of them. U'aosni led the way, and Jhasali strode ahead of me.

Now that I walked on my own two feet instead of being manhandled by Zakishti, I felt clumsier than usual—like I'd developed the world's worst sea legs. Though this ship did not sway like a sailing vessel, my body ricocheted from wall to wall, my every step propelling me like a catapult. Reeling like a drunk, I tried to keep my feet, but I still somehow bounced around with the slightest movement.

"Jhasali!" I cried as I tumbled to the floor.

When she caught sight of me, she came back to where I'd fallen. Taking my hand, she gently but firmly lifted me in front of her and held me steady. "Apologies. I should've known you wouldn't grow accustomed to this low artificial gravity in an instant."

She kept on following her companion, holding me before her with both hands on my shoulders as we continued through the corridors. It seemed she was unwilling to let an insignificant thing like a lack of sufficient gravity slow us down. After winding our way to the exit, we departed the captive ship into the captor ship. This one couldn't have been a starker contrast to the Sartjyanan vessel.

The craft teemed with life. The walls were covered in ivy of every imaginable hue. It crawled from floor to ceiling and hung in long tendrils from above. The vines were all vividly bioluminescent, their glow so bright it lit the hallways and the vast chamber in which the captive Sartjyanan vessel sat. Tiny flying animals—real creatures and not devices—mixed in with the bustling drones, which swerved to avoid crashing into the slower winged things. If I listened, I could hear the pulsing vibrations of organic life, the sounds of beating hearts and wings overpowering the steady hum of the mechanical devices.

Jhasali was as shocked as I. When we entered the strange vessel, she started so violently she nearly let me fall to the floor. Before I could exclaim, she seized several of U'aosni's tentacles in her own, and the pair of them gazed at one another with such intensity I could almost hear the thoughts they shared in their silence. Without breaking the link between their cranial appendages, U'aosni and Jhasali took me to a huge door, and we passed into a hallway wide enough for transports.

I wanted to ask them what they discussed, but I dared not. There were other Sartjyanans here besides the two I'd already met, great tentacled creatures of every conceivable color, covered in iridescent tattoos of every conceivable design. When Jhasali passed them, they all greeted her as an old friend, giving her accolades and stating how pleased they were to see she'd been rescued.

Yet, when their eyes fell on me, their speech died, and then they asked all manner of questions, the worst of which was where she'd found her new pet. I wanted to scream that I was perfectly intelligent and could understand every word they said, but there were so many of them and they were so fascinated with me that I remained silent as Jhasali ushered me into a transport, leaving U'aosni standing on the platform with a horde of curious gawkers.

The pod whisked us through the ship so fast I couldn't observe any more of our new host vessel, for everything became a blur. I pulled my knees up to my chest and stared at Jhasali.

"Where are we going?" I finally asked.

"You'll see."

I didn't bother to push her. I simply waited out the twisting trek through this living, breathing vessel, the pod ascending ever inward and upward, until it came to a stop.

Jhasali stood and took my hand. "I wish you to close your eyes, and do not open them until I command."

I did as she asked, and I allowed her to guide me out of the pod, down a final hallway, up one last ascension platform, and into a room I could not see. She whispered some words to persons unknown, bidding them to leave us alone.

Once the room grew still, she squeezed my hand. "Open."

I complied, though I had no clue what I was about to see. When I opened my lids, a gasp of shock escaped my lips. The room in which we now stood was nothing more than a field of glass so clear it looked as if it were not there, yet it appeared so strong I could scarcely imagine the force it would take to shatter it. An impact from a meteor mightn't have been sufficient.

The clear field stretched in a firmament over our heads, a translucent dome from one end of the floor to the other. Even a good portion of the floor itself was transparent, allowing me to see that we hung suspended over Earth, caught up in the irresistible embrace of orbit and watching the vast blue sphere turning underneath our feet.

"Look that way." Jhasali motioned to the sun, which was reddened and darkened by some unseen force meant to shield our eyes from its blazing fire. She then gestured to the eternal field of stars behind it. "I know being removed from your home planet right now is less than ideal, but how can you consider remaining on Earth when this is what I offer you?"

I turned to stare at her eyes, those infinite pools of liquid lead reflecting the sweeping starfield outside the window. "What about Sergio? What about Sara? What about my mother? I cannot leave when I've not yet found her." I knew full well none of that mattered now.

Jhasali didn't respond, so I turned from her to the pane that faced the moon. The cratered silver disk orbited nearby. It was so bright it obscured my vision of the stars, so I looked away to view the inky blackness of the vast ocean that was to be my home, each twinkling grain of glitter scattered across its dark waters both an island in itself and a speck of sand inextricably entangled within the web of the universe.

Jhasali was only trying to soften the blow of my kidnapping by bringing me here, but it was working; my terror of this infinite void now mingled with my awe at the depth of its darkness and the brilliance of its light. If I'd had no husband, no friends, and no mother, I might've agreed to set sail for the eternal horizon then and there.

"Can't I be allowed to search for my mother? Can't I be allowed to live out my natural lifespan on my natural planet?" I whispered.

Jhasali shook her head. "This solar system exists outside the realms of the Adoruch and the Tanmorayan Coalition alike. There's no law, nothing to protect you here. Everyone will soon know of my occupation of this planet. If we don't leave now, others won't be long in coming."

"I can't just give up."

"You must, at present anyway. My hope is that if we go now, perhaps we can sort things out, and you might be allowed to return once it's safer."

"How long will that be?"

"There's no way of knowing."

"I suppose my opinion on the matter of my own abduction is irrelevant anyhow," I spat.

Jhasali remained silent, but I needed no affirmation. My marriage, my mother, my home, my past, and my future had all vanished, washed away in the tide of dark matter that now inundated me, on the verge of sweeping me out with it. I tried to feel anything even remotely proportionate to the new circumstances that had materialized around me, but I could not. I felt only that same overwhelming numbness. My heart was more desolate than the void about to swallow me alive.

"I need to arrange my affairs before I go. I must say goodbye," I muttered. Goodbye. The word felt torn out of me by invisible forceps.

"I'm not sure that's wise."

"It's the least you can do, all things considered."

Jhasali shrugged. "I suppose so. I must retrieve Homeship anyhow. If it's severely damaged, it may need repairs before it can be moved into this vessel. In that case, we'll return to your planet instead of performing the work remotely."

"And if it's not that badly damaged?"

Jhasali didn't answer.

I turned my gaze toward Earth and sank to my knees, leaning against the window and staring out at the only home I'd ever known. Weeping, I traced the outline of the delicate blue marble. My mind became filled with flashes of memories: making music by Jhasali's campfire, leaping over the ship's railing with Sergio, galloping through the forest on Pepito.

Even as I wept for my lost home, I could not dismiss the nagging fear of the people who populated my new one. Jhasali had used the phrase "jealously guarded" to describe her society's view of what should be done with its vast achievements. Yet she had flouted this regulation by making me. Zakishti already saw me as a problem to be eradicated. Would more of the Sartjyanans agree once they discovered my biomechanical nature? If so, would Jhasali be able to stop them from harming me? Would she even try?

I pondered whether I should once again bring up the possibility of Sergio accompanying us, but that was pure fantasy. In the unlikely event Jhasali agreed to it, he never would. The only way I could get him to allow himself to be hurled into a void he'd never even conceived of would be to abduct him just as Jhasali was abducting me.

I could never bring myself to do that to him, especially if I couldn't trust Jhasali. She was allowing her old friends to kidnap me, after all—and she liked me. I couldn't imagine what she might allow them to do to Sergio, considering her opinion of him. Thus, there could be only one answer: when I exited the protection of my planet's atmosphere for the last time, I'd be going alone.

# Chapter Thirty
# THE PALE BLUE DOT

As it turned out, Homeship was indeed too damaged to be called to us. Moreover, the Tanmorayan star cruiser's tractor beam was too weak to overcome Earth's gravitational pull for something the size of Homeship, meaning Jhasali's craft needed enough repairs to render it able to fly on its own and dock with our host vessel. I was glad of this news, for it meant I would have a chance to put my house in order before we embarked.

Zakishti and U'aosni were quick to argue that we should remain onboard the host vessel while the drones did the repairs, but Jhasali stood firm in her decision that I be allowed to return to my planet to settle my affairs. She had a ferry pod set us in the harbor next to the burned ships. She didn't bother to camouflage this transport—even in broad daylight. Now that we had the protection of an orbiting battle cruiser full of her allies, the chances of any more scouting vessels assailing us were low. Thus, her sole motive for secrecy was gone.

"You've got until Homeship is in the air again. That's it," Jhasali said when I exited the ferry drone. As soon as my feet hit the dirt, she sped off.

A larger escort vessel had accompanied our ferry from the borrowed Tanmorayan cruiser. This heavily armed craft now hovered over the bay to keep an eye out. I feared its presence would cause a panic, but there weren't any people in the streets to panic anyhow. Perhaps the authorities had imposed restrictions. Or maybe everyone had been in the streets cleaning up the mess from last night's battle, and they'd fled when they saw the approach of the ferry and its gargantuan guardian.

I took one last glance at the vessel that now defended me but would soon abduct me, then turned my eyes toward town. Walking away from the water, I only made it a pace or two off the docks before I stepped on something hard. A metallic sound rang out as I put my weight on it. It was the crucifix I had tossed away from Luis, still abandoned out here in the harbor. I picked it up, recalling how Jhasali had thought my own crucifix so absurd when we'd first spoken while sitting on a rock in the woods with dappled sunlight peeking through the green canopy.

At first, I thought to fling the golden cross into the sea and let it sink to the bottom of the ocean where it belonged, but then I had another idea. Though I wanted nothing to do with it, if Father Manuel had a say, he'd wish to be buried with a crucifix, even this crucifix, if it was the only one on hand. I turned it over in my fingers, taking the arms of the cross and the tiny Christ figure and bending them back into place from where my step had warped them. Then I stuffed the thing into my pouch.

I would place it around Father Manuel's neck and melt it in the reactor upon his cremation, for that was what I planned to do with him rather than leaving him to rot where he lay. Building him a funeral pyre would be the final sin I committed against him. I had neither time nor desire to give him a Christian burial, and I would not permit him to be buried by his own murderers.

I entered the empty plaza mayor, making for the tower house so I could speak to Sergio. Though I'd resolved to say goodbye, in the darkest depths of my soul I still held out hope I mightn't be parted from my husband. I wished to discuss his accompanying me in terms of embarking on a voyage in the metal castle, just to ascertain how open he might be to the possibility. If he agreed, I'd refuse to ascend without him. Surely Jhasali wouldn't deny me a consolation prize, seeing as she was robbing me of everything else.

I'd nearly made it across the plaza when Sergio's voice rang in my ears out of nowhere. Before I could turn around, he set upon me, grabbing me by the shoulders and shaking me.

"You witch! You succubus! You've been in league with the devil himself this whole time," he screamed as he threw me to the ground.

"Sergio, stop it," I shouted, but he was beyond reason.

When I tried to rise, he shoved me back down, barking, "I should have known something was wrong when your rebelliousness got out of control."

Resisting his attempts to keep me down, I leapt to my feet. I backed up a few paces as I pondered how I could calm him enough to hear me.

"How dare you show your face here after what you've done!" he raged.

"What I've done? You mean saving all your lives?"

"You rode that demon. You commanded it to attack us!"

I rolled my eyes. "For the love of Christ. That wasn't a demon. I tried to tell you before. Will you listen to me for once in your pathetic life?"

"What if I don't? You going to do to me what you did to Ignacio?"

"So you're on his side now?"

"No! He got no more than he deserved. But still, I trusted you. I slept with you. I defended you before the Inquisition." Trembling, he looked down at his still-green hands. "What have you done to me? You did make me a monster."

"No, I didn't. I haven't hurt you."

He burst into tears. "You hurt everyone! You've brought us all ruin and disaster. Poor Gracia didn't do anything to deserve such a death."

My stomach jolted. That couldn't be right. "Gracia isn't dead. Hernando took her from the tower. You said so yourself that he took her someplace safe."

"He took her to the church!" Sergio sobbed.

The breath evaporated from my lungs. Gracia couldn't have been inside when I'd demolished the church. She couldn't have. The only people in there were the guards seeking sanctuary and—my God. The woman! The woman that idiot soldier had shot. That had been Gracia?

"Oh no. Oh no, no, no!" I cried.

"Did you steal her soul as well as her life?" Sergio spat.

"I didn't touch her. I destroyed the church because the men inside shot her. I didn't wish to give them sanctuary if they only planned to use it to slaughter civilian women."

"Nobody shot her. You murdered her."

"I did not. I followed them there, and a woman was at the altar. One of the men spooked and put a bolt through her. I didn't know it was Gracia."

"You expect me to believe you when everything that has ever come out of your damned mouth is a lie?"

I threw up my hands. "I'm not lying. You think I'd kill Gracia? You think even by accident I'd ever do such a thing?"

"How should I know what the bride of Satan is capable of? You'd never have been able to control that beast, you'd never be able to withstand the crossbow and the arquebus if everything they've been saying about you was not true."

"You don't understand."

"Ignacio was right to come after you. I just wish I hadn't kept my silence to protect you."

"Please, I'm begging you to listen. You know I would never hurt any of you."

"Like you wouldn't hurt Father Manuel? Like you wouldn't hurt me? Like you wouldn't hurt everyone and everything that comes near you?"

Sergio swayed as he wept, squeezing his palms against his temples, and he seemed about to sink to his knees. Stepping toward him, I put out a hand to steady him. At this, his eyes grew wide as saucers. He backed away and ripped his sword from its scabbard.

I shook my head. "Sergio, give me that."

He swung the blade at my belly, still sobbing even as he advanced. I backed up pace by pace while he kept swinging. Though I wore IDOS, he was not himself, nor was he an actual threat to me. So I kept backing away as he kept coming, slashing and thrusting his blade the whole time.

My rear hit stone—I'd backed right up to a building wall. Upon pinning me to the brick, Sergio swung the sword again, and if I hadn't ducked, it would have struck me in the throat. I'd had enough. To end the barrage, I grabbed his sword by the blade. I then yanked it from his grasp and tossed it aside. Raising my wrist, I fired IDOS off to my right, aiming for the top of Santa Colomba's column of justice and blowing the statue clean off the pillar. At this, Sergio froze.

"If I were really a demoness, I'd have no qualms about slaying you here and now, but I don't want to harm you, and I didn't kill Gracia!" I shouted.

"Liar! If I could, I would kill you where you coil, serpent."

At these words, the familiar caldera of rage reached a boil under my diaphragm. The weight of everything for which I'd promised to forgive my husband collapsed onto my shoulders at once. All the times he'd wielded his anger and his legal authority and even my own love for him as weapons against me. All the times I'd cowed before his temper or caved to his demands. Not this time!

I was so outraged it took me several minutes to render myself capable of speech. When I managed to form words, they hissed through my clenched teeth.

"You stupid, stubborn, bastard son of a whore! I've stuck by you through voyage after voyage. I protected you from my patroness, though she wanted to destroy you. And this is what I get in return?"

What a fool I'd been to think anything could ever be different between Sergio and me. I was on the verge of slapping him, but I did not wish to give more credence to his belief in my demonic nature.

"You know, Sergio, I was half tempted to beg my patroness to let you come with us, but I now see you were never worth the trouble. Go and spend eternity where you belong."

Before he could offer a retort, I swung my body around so fast my hair flew over my shoulders, slapping my chest and neck, and I stomped off.

I staggered like a drunk through the empty streets, weeping with anger and grief. Somehow, I found my way to the smoking ruins of the church in which I'd grown up, the church Father Manuel had loved this last decade, the church that, in my wrath and my sorrow, I had destroyed.

I sat on a fallen pillar in what was left of the nave to ponder what I might do. Putting my face in my hands, I tried to calm down, but I couldn't stop shaking. I was furious with myself for having been so merciful to the soldiers. If I'd known Gracia was the woman they'd slain, I mightn't have been so lenient with the rest of them. Sobbing more deeply now, I looked around for Gracia's body in the wreckage of the church, but she was not among the soldiers, who still lay right where they had been killed. Gabriel and Sergio must have taken her.

A loud snort sounded behind me, and I whipped around to find Pepito standing with his muzzle not a meter from my face. He still wore his saddle and bridle, so I divested him of those before wrapping my arms around his long hairy head and burying my face in his forelock. There, I breathed in my last whiffs of his earthy scent.

"My darling. I wish I could take you with me," I whispered.

Jhasali could have compelled the others to allow it, but how could I do that to my Pepito? It would be unspeakably selfish of me to drag him away from his planet's grass and trees and rivers to die one day in a giant metal bubble a million light-years from home.

As I stood in the amber autumn sun and the smoldering wreckage, with my forehead pressed to Pepito's, the familiar high-pitched whirring of one of Jhasali's tiny, spherical surveillance drones buzzed in my ears. A few minutes later, she came like an apparition, her bare feet making no sound on the ground as she walked, though they were tipped with sharp talons.

Pepito did not spook; he barely even acknowledged her presence. I wasn't sure whether this was because he recognized her scent somehow or if he'd become so accustomed to the bizarre and unearthly he no longer bothered to fear it.

"We have to go. Homeship is ready," she said.

"I don't want to go," I breathed.

"You must, and I'm sorry about that. All this is my fault." She looked at the rubble and then Pepito. "I was so concerned with creating a suitable companion for myself that I lost sight of your well-being. Now, I've taken this choice away from you. It was not my intent."

"None of that matters now."

In truth, it hadn't mattered in years. The choice as to whether I remained on Earth was made the second I accepted my nanos. I just hadn't known it then.

"I suppose it does not. Now let's go." Jhasali turned away.

"We must take Pepito someplace safe and get Father Manuel."

"Hurry, then! Everyone is ready to depart," she snapped.

I abandoned the debris and headed back toward the tower house, with both Pepito and Jhasali in tow. When I looked over the bay, I saw Homeship. It sat next to our escort, hovering over the water off the coast, wounded and limping but still flyable. Its owner caught up and took her place beside me, and I wondered what the townspeople thought of her as they peeked out their shuttered windows to watch her pass.

I led Pepito by the forelock to the wall of Armando's tower house. There, I opened the unlocked gate and ushered him inside the courtyard while Jhasali stood to her full height and attempted to peer inside the windows. The curtains were drawn, though I thought I might've seen them flutter behind the glass. No matter.

Even if Sergio emerged now and begged me to take him wherever I went in the wide universe, he and I were done.

I kissed Pepito's brow a final time and left him standing in the courtyard. When I turned from him, I did not look back, for I didn't wish the consternated expression on his face to be the last memory I had of him. Rather, I walked straight from the tower house to the tower prison, leading Jhasali by the hand.

The door was barred against us, but it was no match for our drones. One of them broke it off the hinges and had us inside in a minute. When we entered, several men stood in the foyer with their weapons trained on us. Seeing Jhasali, they threw down their arms and dropped to their knees without resistance. I didn't blame them. The mere look of her was enough to frighten the cojones off the bravest man.

When we ascended, we discovered the soldiers had been able to contain the fire damage to the fourth story. The third level had many blackened, burned-out holes in its ceiling, but its floor remained intact. I was unsure in which room they'd hidden Father Manuel, but it was not difficult to follow my nose. The stench augmented with each step we took down the hallway. Jhasali balked when we'd gotten about halfway through the passage.

"That smell. What is that awful smell?" She sputtered and retched as if she'd never before been exposed to the like of it.

I bowed my head and did not reply, unable to bring myself to say "Father Manuel."

Jhasali stood still a second and then moved on as though nothing had happened. I inferred she must have told her nasal passages to filter out the unwanted odor, for she no longer made a fuss of it. I decided I didn't want to smell it anymore either. An instant later, I discovered I no longer did, as if that was much favor to me.

We found Father Manuel laid out on a low bench in a rear cell with a solid oak door that had its tiny window shut from the outside. Ignacio had stuffed him in here to prevent his murder being discovered until after my capture. I went to him and slipped down, leaning my shoulder against the wall and lying half-prone on the floor. I wrapped my arms around him and pressed my brow against the top of his head, running my fingers through his thin, wispy hair.

His body was bloated, but it was no longer rigid with death, and I was able to move his fingers and his arms without struggle. What did I care that he was cold and putrid and rotting out in the open because his killers had abandoned him in a storage room like a sack of bad flour? I still had to touch him. I wouldn't be able to accept the truth if I didn't.

I asked Jhasali if I might have some time to collect myself, and she told me to make it quick before slipping out of the room. As soon as she'd been gone long enough that I believed her to be out of earshot, I began to weep. A long, low moan squeezed out of me, interrupted only by fresh sobs or the intake of a ragged breath. The face before me belonged to Father Manuel, but the face that occupied my thoughts belonged to Gracia. I'd saved her life three years ago just to draw death to her doorstep last night. And for what?

The burning I'd wished to stop would go on and on, an unquenchable flame, an inferno without end. Ignacio had reached up from the grave to take his vengeance, and Gracia had died for nothing. Father Manuel had died for nothing. It was all for nothing.

My tears soon saturated the collar of my decimated shirt, which grew chill on my neck and chest. Still, I did not raise my head, not even when I heard the door open and Jhasali return. I hoped she would note my current state and give me more time, but a heavy, warm hand fell gently on my right shoulder. I reached back with my right hand and grasped the fingers, only to discover they were human. At this, I jolted up to find I faced not Jhasali but Luis.

"I'm sorry. Truly, I am," he whispered.

"Get out!" I shouted. "You should have been sorry before this happened."

"I don't know what to say. I judged my actions right at the time."

"None of your ilk gets to talk to me about what's right."

"No. I suppose not," he conceded.

"How did you even know I was here?"

"I heard you from below. I was praying in private. I wouldn't have bothered you, but I wished to ask about that thing floating over the bay."

"What if I tell you nothing? Are you going to drown me? Rack me? Burn me? Don't think I've forgotten that if I hadn't had my devices to defend me, you'd have handed me over to that mad dog Ignacio and you'd be carting my husband and my friends to your own dungeons right now."

"I only want to know how we might make it go away."

"Why don't you pray about it and see how well that works?" I snapped. The nerve he had to come to me and inquire about anything after letting Ignacio leave Father Manuel here to rot.

Luis looked down at my guardian's lifeless form. "I wouldn't have let Ignacio get away with this, you know. I would have seen him punished, one way or another."

"You mean you would've broken your promise to keep silent for him once you were sure he'd murdered me in secret."

"If that's what it took. Everything he did was a bridge too far, and he knew better."

"Why would he bother to know better if there were no consequences if he didn't? But I'm sure you intended to have him punished. Right after you let his latest victim putrefy up here another day or two."

"I only arrived last night. I haven't been able to handle everything yet," Luis said, though he did not press the issue further.

Instead, he crossed the cell to the long, narrow window on the other side. I watched him, hoping he might accost me and offer me an excuse to harm him, but he gave me a wide berth as he made his way over to the tall slit and looked out. The window faced north, so I was sure he could see Homeship and the guardian vessel that awaited Jhasali's and my return.

"Christ save us; now there are two. Why are they here? How can we make them go away?" he said again.

"If you don't go away, I know how to make you."

"You won't—"

I fired a hard round at the stone next to his skull. The projectile exploded with a tiny boom and a shower of rock splinters. Luis brought his hands to his head and dropped to the floor.

"Don't you dare presume to know what I will and won't do," I hissed.

"I'm sorry! Please. If you make it go away, I'll call my men, and we can bury the old man right now."

"I'm perfectly capable of ensuring he gets a proper burial without your help. You and your men have done quite enough."

"Not me. It wasn't me."

"Your men, your permission, your jurisdiction."

Luis stood and dusted off his knees. "Why not kill me, then? Why not kill us all?"

I shrugged. "Because that's not who I am. I won't let your sort turn me into yet another Ignacio."

"Holy God! Mother of Christ!" Luis collapsed to the floor, fixing his eyes on a point behind me.

I turned to find Jhasali had entered the cell. She raised her cuff to Luis, probably because she thought him accosting me. Leaping from my place on the floor, I put myself between her and him. I held out my right hand to stop her from firing.

"No. That's enough," I said in Castellano before falling back to the floor and leaning against the wall.

Jhasali lowered her weapon and pondered Luis while he babbled about the name of Christ being able to repel Satan. I shut my eyes and rolled them behind my closed lids. Opening them a slit to glance at the inquisitor, I noticed his hands scrabbled at a spot below his neck. I realized he searched for the crucifix I'd pulled off him, and I recalled I'd stuffed it in my pouch after stepping on it. I still wished to give it to Father Manuel for his burial shroud, but what good was it to either of us now? Enough blood had been shed over it already.

Then I got an idea. Standing back up, I walked over to Jhasali. I pulled the crucifix from my pouch, offering it to her.

"Not this again. We haven't got time for this nonsense," she complained in Sartjyanan.

"It's not mine. It's his." I motioned to Luis.

Jhasali did exactly as I hoped beyond hope she might. She took the necklace from me, sneered at it irritably, then strode straight to Luis and bent to hand it to him.

"Take it if you want it," she said in Castellano. "For whatever good it'll do you."

Luis sucked his breath in great, heaving gasps, but he did not dare refuse to do as he was told. He acted confused as to why she would touch this thing. Just as I'd believed three years ago, he did not think a demon capable of handling it. He took it from her and laid it aside, not removing his startled gaze from her face the entire time.

Jhasali turned indifferently from Luis. Bending her long torso almost to the floor, she gathered Father Manuel in her lower set of arms and cradled his body like a babe. Without a backward glance, she ducked through the door, her tail curling around the doorframe before following her from the cell so its cluster of sensory organs could continue to watch the inquisitor until she'd made it into the hall.

Waiting to follow her, I looked down on Luis. "I want you to recall that on this day, not only did I spare your life multiple times, but I saved it as well, for I did not have to intervene just now. I ask nothing in repayment except that you remember this when you return to Logroño."

Luis gave a wide-eyed nod, and I cast him a last glance as I made to follow Jhasali. He, however, was not through with me.

"What the *devil* is that thing?" he shouted from the floor.

"Whatever you believe it to be. Explaining it won't make a difference." I trudged to the threshold.

"I don't understand."

I stopped in the doorway and put my hand on the frame before twisting my neck around to face him. "Did you ever really want to?"

Luis might not be through with me, but I was through with him. Before he made any reply, I stepped through the threshold, swept into the hall, and was gone.

I knew I took a risk in allowing Luis to live, and I considered slaying him before I walked out that door. I'm not sure he realized how close he came, that last second in my presence, to death. It concerned me that he appeared not to have altered his perspective one jot, even in light of everything that had happened before his very eyes.

Yet he also seemed a reasonable man in comparison to the two stooges he'd sent before him, and he might just be the only man in this mess who wished to get to the real truth of what had happened. The last question he'd asked me had not been how a demon had managed to touch a crucifix but what Jhasali was. That, at least, was a step in the right direction.

Church and Crown would come no matter what, and when they did, I wished there to be someone alive who—though he might not have been unequivocally on our side—had seen that I had been the one in command of the seven-headed beast. There would be no need for witch hunts or arrests or torture because Luis could serve as my ready-made credible witness. I didn't wish to trust him with such responsibility, for he was still as deluded and dogmatic as ever, but I had no other option. It was either depend upon him, unreliable as he was, or leave my town with no one. A powerful man who owed me a life debt was certainly better than no one.

When I caught up to Jhasali, she and I walked toward the harbor, Father Manuel still in her arms. Once we got into the open, our ferry descended upon us. It lowered the gangplank, and Jhasali climbed it without so much as a backward glance, but I hesitated. Like a condemned criminal mounting the scaffold, I knew I had already witnessed my last sunrise—just from a hundred leagues above my planet's surface.

Once I ascended that ramp, there'd be no turning back. My friendships would be ended and my search for my mother cut short. My marriage was over regardless, but that proved cold comfort now.

My basest instincts screamed for me to flee this place, run to the woods, and find a cave to hide in until Jhasali and her friends left. But I could do no such thing. That ship and those creatures on it expected me whether I wished to accompany them or not. All that was left was the journey to my waiting chariot, a journey I'd take one way or another. I could be dragged by a drone as I struggled and pled, or I could walk on my own two feet with my head held high.

As I stood upon the brink of the ascent into the void, my right hand on the railing and my left hand pressed over my pounding heart, I discovered I could not move. My legs had carried me to the very edge, but now that I'd reached it, I felt as though I'd disconnected from my own feet and left my toes digging hopelessly into the last bit of earth they'd ever feel, unwilling to let go, unable to hold on.

I laid my chin on my chest, looking with my peripheral vision at the city and the country and the planet I was about to leave behind. Breathing deep my final gasp of terrestrial atmosphere, I ascended to my waiting transport.

Jhasali still held Father Manuel, though she now sat in the captain's chair, his body laid across her lap and his head cradled with her lower, softer pair of arms. I sat down beside her, taking my rightful place as her first officer, her new twin. I decided no matter what these other companions said or did, she belonged to me. I deserved her as much as any of these others, and I didn't give a single fig about how much longer they'd been with her than I had.

When we arrived onboard the Tanmorayan star cruiser, I said not a word to any Sartjyanan, though dozens had appeared in the corridor to gawk at me. I marched past them, ignoring them as though they were unworthy of my attention. The only words I uttered were to inquire of Jhasali where I might cremate Father Manuel. Following her direction, we headed for the interior of the cruiser, where Homeship had already docked within its underbelly. I barely noted the low gravity now. I needed no more weight than that of all my mistakes.

Once Jhasali and I reached the battered hull of the ship that had sheltered us for so long, she patted the threshold affectionately with one of the hands not supporting Father Manuel's body. After an instant, she swung her tentacles behind her shoulders like a sheet of hair and stepped inside. We headed for Homeship's reactor, located in the craft's dead center.

There, Jhasali laid Father Manuel's body on a small pallet that her drones had prepared for the purpose. I noted she'd told them to bring flowers—the strange and beautiful blossoms that were born of our living host ship and flourished within its walls. They were so fresh their pungent scents perfumed the air around us.

I wanted to thank Jhasali for remembering how I'd wished to put flowers in Lobo's grave, but I couldn't find any words that might express what I felt as I stood on the edge of both being flung out of my planet's orbit and flinging Father Manuel's body into the fire. I dropped to my knees beside him, wishing I might give something, anything, to send with him into eternity. Yet I had nothing but the clothes on my back.

Then I remembered I'd seen half these creatures walking around with no clothing at all. Jhasali hadn't bothered to put on anything since she'd changed bodies. I needed none of that nonsense here, for these creatures didn't think my body a sin any more than they did their own. So I removed my shredded shirt and my dusty pantaloons, folding them and laying them across Father Manuel's breast. I took off my shoes and pressed them between his feet. This done, I stood stark naked before the host of alien beings that had followed us into our sanctuary.

Though I was not embarrassed of my nudity, I did ask Jhasali if I might mourn without an audience. She shooed them all away and shut the door. I sank back down, wishing I had something better to give than a dirty, torn shirt and a pair of discarded pantaloons. Still, at least Father Manuel would have something to go with him into eternity, something of mine. By giving him these clothes, I would also rid myself of my last earthly possessions.

"How can I put him in?" I asked.

"Are you sure you wish to do this? If you put him in, he will be incinerated, and you can never bury him in a hole in the ground," Jhasali said.

"It's better this way. He's been defiled enough already."

Even as I said this, the distant roar of an engine penetrated the fog of my thoughts. Though it was no more than a faint whir inside these walls, it was still a sure sign I was about to lose whatever earthly possessions remained to me anyhow, regardless of what or whom I put in this reactor.

Jhasali sat on the floor next to me, staring at the unremarkable metal wall. We could see not a spark of the fiery furnace within. She said nothing, nor did I. We just stayed there for a long while, me weeping with her sitting at my side.

Finally, I asked her to open the door. When she did, instead of glimpsing the blaze of the reactor, I saw nothing but a long metal arm extending from a dark tunnel. This arm grasped the pallet that held Father Manuel's body and slid him into the shadowy passage from whence it came. The door shut with a hiss and a thud. I was certain its closure marked the last I'd ever see not just of him but of my friends, my husband, and my planet.

I was unsure why I burned Father Manuel when I knew full well he'd have preferred a Christian burial. Maybe I attempted to adopt the customs of my new people. Or perhaps I exacted some small vengeance against him for errors he'd assured me were unintentional but for which I couldn't forgive him all the same.

I stood and wiped my eyes, grieving yet undefeated, naked yet unashamed, among strangers yet not alone. I raised my right hand above my head, and Jhasali took it with her soft left hand. Leading her to the doorway, I allowed her to pass in front of me as we stepped through the threshold to greet the anticipant crowd of her people beyond.

Everyone wished to get a glimpse of me, but Jhasali defended me against their prying gazes. I understood then how she could have once been at their helm in a rebellion. She dominated them utterly, cowing them all with a gesture of her hand, and they allowed us to pass.

I don't remember how we got to the star cruiser's command bridge—its main observation deck—only that somehow we did. I crawled into a massive floating chair and curled up in it, wrapping my arms around my legs and burying my face in my knees so I could weep. Jhasali conversed with her comrades for a long time, but I heard nothing, saw nothing, felt nothing. Though my body no longer dwelt on Earth, my thoughts still did. They swirled around my broken marriage, poor Gracia and Father Manuel, the mother I'd never meet, and the fact that I'd never ever see Sara again. She'd been so good to me all these years, and I never even got to say goodbye.

I was jerked from these thoughts when Jhasali's strong arms wrapped around me, lifting me from the seat where I lay motionless.

She set me on my feet and led me toward the window. "I know you wish to rest. But you shouldn't leave your solar system without seeing it."

I offered no resistance, though I was tired, numb, and not eager to see anything other than the inside of my own eyelids.

When we got to the glass, she pointed outside. "There's your planet."

Looking up, I gasped, astonished and interested despite my pain. We'd already moved so far away from Earth that it was scarcely visible anymore, every detail of its marble surface blurred by a fuzzy blue-white glow.

One day in the not-so-distant future, I would learn my fellow humans had followed my footsteps into the void and had even sent mechanical devices to perform their space exploration in their steads, as their interstellar counterparts had done long before them. When they turned their eyes backward to observe that faint and forlorn fleck, they composed a perfect description of our infinitesimal planet and of the last view I would get of it for many of its years to come. Earth is nothing but a pale blue dot floating vulnerable and alone in the celestial blackness of that endless, radiant night.

# ACKNOWLEDGEMENTS

T here are so many people without whom this book would never have made it to publication; I cannot even begin to express my gratitude.

First and foremost, I would like to thank my developmental editors, Beth and Cora, for reading my early drafts during their messiest stages. Thanks to both of you for catching plot holes, giving me character advice, and generally helping me bring this story to life. An additional thanks to Beth for guiding me through so many marketing and promotion tasks. I would've been lost without you.

I would also like to extend my gratitude to my copyeditor Kimberly Laurel of The Trusty Bookmark. Thank you so much for helping me polish the late-stage drafts and get the final manuscript over the finish line.

Many thanks also to the wonderful staff and curators at the Alcázar de Toledo, the Museo Marítimo del Cantábrico, the Museo de la Naturaleza de Cantabria, the Torre de Pero Niño, the Torre de Estrada, the Torre del Oro, the Catedral Primada de Toledo, and the Catedral de Santa María de la Sede de Sevilla. I want to extend my deepest gratitude to everyone who answered my questions and helped me understand and contextualize so much information. You all do incredible work preserving such beautiful and fascinating history. I can only hope I've done it even a fraction of the justice it deserves.

I'd also like to offer a special shoutout to my mom. Thank you for your support and encouragement—and for accompanying me on that marathon of a first research trip. Sorry I almost killed you on the Picos de Europa. Next time, we'll go hiking on the beaches and in the vineyards.

Finally, and above all, I want to thank my husband Mustafa. Thank you for pushing me when I wanted to give up, helping me stay focused on the end game, keeping me company on research trips, and reading more drafts of the same book than you ever thought you would in your life. Without you, this novel would be sitting on an external hard drive, half-done and collecting digital dust. Thank you for making sure that didn't happen.

# ABOUT THE AUTHOR

E lanor Landrie was born and raised in Chattanooga, Tennessee but currently lives in Jacksonville, Florida. She earned her MA in Creative Writing from the University of Tennessee at Chattanooga and has been a writer, blogger, and editor for over ten years.

She became an avid fan of science fiction and fantasy as a young child reading in the cow pasture on her family's farm, but she learned to love historical fiction during her college days.

In her free time, she likes to paddleboard, grow her own food, learn languages, hang out with her dogs, and take day trips to St. Augustine—the United States' very own little piece of Spain.